Praise for *Thirteen*

"Morgan's bare-knuckle procedural plot makes room for provocative takes on race, gender, and religion. [Rating] A–"   —*Entertainment Weekly*

"*Thirteen* is almost unbearably good. . . . Harrowing truths, gritty romance, complex politics, synapse-swift action, technological advances just vanishing over the event horizon: they're all there. They're all achingly good."

—*The Seattle Times*

"This stellar stand-alone from Morgan . . . raises tantalizing questions about the nature of humanity."   —*Publishers Weekly* (starred review)

"Sharp, edgy, visceral."   —*Magazine of Fantasy & Science Fiction*

"Similarities in tone and substance to the genre bending works of Philip K. Dick and William Gibson are surely not accidental, although Morgan is no imitator. He's too good for that."   —*Booklist* (starred review)

"Impossible to put down."   —*Philadelphia Weekly Press*

"Morgan is a very talented writer, giving the reader several very well-developed and sympathetic characters, a gripping narrative, and a future well worth looking at."   —SFReader.com

"*Thirteen* is [Morgan's] most interesting [novel], especially in terms of conceptualization, extrapolation and subtext. Anyway, if you liked Morgan's Kovacs novels, you certainly won't go wrong with this one."   —SFSite.com

"A seething techno-thriller filled with political machinations, murder, cannibalism, conspiracies, mafia families, space travel, raw sex and enough blood-and-guts violence to make Quentin Tarantino blush. *Thirteen* is a ten."

—*Cape Cod Times*

"Morgan's bravado and ideas make for a significant (and entertaining) book in the genre."   —SFWorld.com

BY RICHARD K. MORGAN

Takeshi Kovacs Novels:

Altered Carbon

Broken Angels

Woken Furies

Market Forces

Thirteen

The Steel Remains

Thirteen

Thirteen

RICHARD K. MORGAN

DEL REY **BALLANTINE BOOKS NEW YORK**

2008 Del Rey Books Trade Paperback Edition

Published in the United States by Del Rey Books, an imprint of The Random House Publishing Group, a division of Random House, Inc., New York.

DEL REY is a registered trademark and the Del Rey colophon is a trademark of Random House, Inc.

Originally published in hardcover in the United States by Del Rey Books, an imprint of The Random House Publishing Group, a division of Random House, Inc., in 2007. Originally published in Great Britain as Black Man by Gollancz, an imprint of the Orion Publishing Group, London.

Library of Congress Cataloguing-in-Publication Data

Morgan, Richard K.
Thirteen / Richard K. Morgan
p. cm.
ISBN 978-0-345-48089-7 (alk. paper)
I. Title II. Title: 13.
PR6113.O748T48 2007
823'.92—dc22   2007010617

Printed in the United States of America

www.delreybooks.com

9 8 7 6 5 4 3

Book design by Mary A. Wirth

This book is dedicated to the memory of my mother

MARGARET ANN MORGAN

who taught me to hate bigotry, cruelty, and injustice with
an unrelenting rage, and to despise the hypocrisy that looks away or
makes comfortable excuses when those same vices
crop up closer to home than we'd like.

I miss you.

It seems feasible that over the coming century human nature will be scientifically remodelled. If so, it will be done haphazardly, as an up-shot of struggles in the murky realm where big business, organised crime and the hidden parts of government vie for control.

—John Gray, *Straw Dogs*

Human, to the discontinuous mind, is an absolutist concept. There can be no half measures. And from this flows much evil.

—Richard Dawkins, *A Devil's Chaplain*

ACKNOWLEDGMENTS

This has been a tough one, and I owe a great deal of thanks in a great many places. I have begged, borrowed, and stolen from just about everywhere to get *Thirteen* written.

It being a novel of science fiction, let's start with the science:

The original idea for variant thirteen was inspired by the theorizing of Richard Wrangham on the subject of diminishing human aggression, as described by Matt Ridley in his excellent book *Nature Via Nurture*. I have taken vast fictional liberties with these ideas, and variant thirteen as it emerges in this book is in no way intended to represent either Mr. Wrangham's or Mr. Ridley's thoughts on the subject. These gentlemen simply provided me with a springboard—the rather ugly splash that follows is of my making alone.

The concept of artificial chromosome platforms is also borrowed, in this case from Gregory Stock's fascinating and slightly scary book *Redesigning Humans*, which, along with *Nature Via Nurture* and Steven Pinker's brilliant *The Blank Slate* and *How the Mind Works*, served as the bulk inspiration for most of the future genetic science I've dreamed up here. Once again, any mangling or misuse of the material I found in these outstanding works must be laid solely at my door.

Yaroshanko intuitive function, though my own invention, owes a large debt of inspiration to very real research done on social networks, as described in Mark Buchanan's book *Small World*. And I'm personally indebted to Hannu Rajaniemi at the University of Edinburgh for taking the time to (try to) explain quantum game theory and its potential applications to me, thus giving me the basis for the New Math and its subtle but far-reaching social impact. Thanks also must go to Simon Spanton, star editor, for patiently helping me wrangle the technical logistics of Mars–Earth cryocapping.

In the political sphere, I was heavily influenced by two very perceptive and rather depressing books about the United States, *The Right Nation* by John Micklethwait and Adrian Woolridge and *What's the Matter with America* by Thomas Frank, as well as the brilliant and slightly less depressing *Stiffed* by Susan Faludi. While these books all fed into the concept of the Secession and the gender themes arising in *Thirteen*, the Confederated Republic itself (aka Jesusland) was inspired by the now famous Jesusland map meme, created (according to Wikipedia) by one G. Webb on the message board yakyak.org. Way to go, G.! Special personal thanks must also go to Alan Beatts of Borderlands books in San Francisco for listening to my meanderings over whiskey and shwarma, and lending me a little informed American opinion with which to polish up what I had.

For insights into a possible future (and widely misunderstood past) Islam, I'm also indebted to Tariq Ali for *The Clash of Fundamentalisms*, Karen Armstrong for *Islam: A Short History*, and the very courageous Irshad Manji for *The Trouble with Islam Today*. Here also, I have done my fair share of mangling, and the outcomes in *Thirteen* do not necessarily bear any relation to anything these authors might endorse.

And finally, I owe a massive debt of gratitude to all those who waited with such immense patience, and still told me to take all the time I needed:

Simon Spanton—again!—and Jo Fletcher at Gollancz, Chris Schluep and Betsy Mitchell at Del Rey, my agent Carolyn Whitaker, and last but not least all those well-wishers who e-mailed me during 2006 with messages of condolence, reassurance, and support. This book would not exist without you.

Thirteen

Gleaming steel, gleaming steel . . .

Larsen blinks and shifts slightly on the automated gurney as it tracks under a linear succession of lighting panels and lateral roof struts. Recognition smears in with vision, blurry and slow; she's in the dorsal corridor. Overhead, light angles off each metal beam, sliding from glint to full-blown burst and back as she passes below. She supposes it's the repeated glare that's woken her. That, or her knee, which is aching ferociously, even through the accustomed groggy swim of the decanting drugs. One hand rests on her chest, pressing into the thin fabric of the cryocap leotard. Cool air on her skin tells her she's otherwise naked. An eerie sense of déjà vu steals over her with the knowledge. She coughs a little, tiny remnants of tank gel in the bottom of her pumped-out lungs. She shifts again, mumbles something to herself.

. . . *not again . . . ?*

"Again, yes. The cormorant's legacy, yes, again."

That's odd. She didn't expect another voice, least of all one talking in riddles. Decanting's usually a wholly mechanized process, the datahead's programmed to wake them before arrival, and unless something's gone wrong . . .

So you're the big expert on cryocapping now, are you?

She isn't—her entire previous experience comes down to three test decantings and the one real deal at journey's end on the voyage out, whence, she supposes, the déjà vu. But still . . .

. . . *more than three . . .*

. . . *it is* not *more, it is* not . . .

The vehemence in the retort has a ragged edge on it that she doesn't like. If she'd heard it in another person's voice, a test subject's voice, say, she'd be thinking sedatives, maybe even a call to security. In her own thoughts, it's suddenly, intimately chilling, like the realization that there's someone in the house with you, someone you didn't invite in. Like the thought out of nowhere that you might not be wholly sane.

This is the drugs, Ellie. Let go, ride it out.

Gleaming stee—

The autogurney bumps slightly as it takes a right turn. For some reason, it sets off a violent jolt in her pulse, a reaction that, drugged, she labels almost idly as panic. A tremor of impending doom trickles through her like cold water. They're going to crash, they're going to hit something, or something's going to hit them, something massive and ancient beyond human comprehension tumbling endlessly end-over-end through the empty night outside the ship. Space travel isn't safe, she was insane to ever think it was, to sign up for the contract and think she could get away with it, there and home again in one piece as if it were no more than a suborbital across the Pacific, you just *couldn't*—

Let go, Ellie. It's the drugs.

Then she realizes where she is. The autosurgeon's folded arachnoid arms wheel past in one quadrant of her vision as the gurney slots into position on the examination rack. A qualified relief seeps into her. Something's wrong, but she's in the right place. *Horkan's Pride* is equipped with the finest automated medical systems COLIN knows how to build, she's read it in a *Colony News* digest, the whole shipboard AI suite was overhauled a couple of weeks before she left. *And look, there's a limit to what can go wrong with a cryocapped body, right, Ellie?* Organic functions slow to a chilled crawl, and so does anything hostile that you might be carrying.

But the panic, the sense of inescapable nemesis, won't let her go. She feels it dull and insistent, like a dog worrying at an anesthetized limb.

She rolls her head sideways on the gurney, and sees him.

More familiarity, sharper now, jolting through her like current.

Once, on a trip to Europe, she went to the Museo della Sindone in Turin and saw the tortured image printed on cloth that they keep there. She stood in dimness on the other side of the bulletproof glass, surrounded by the reverent murmurs of the faithful. Never a believer of any sort herself, Larsen was still oddly moved by the harsh and hollow lines of the face staring back at her out of the sealed vacuum chamber. It seemed a testament to human suffering that completely short-circuited its divine pretensions, that rendered the devotions paid it beside the point. You looked at that face and you were struck by the sheer stubborn survivability of organic life, the heritage of built-in, bitten-down defiance that the long march of evolution had gifted you with.

It could be the same man. Here, now.

He's propped against a tall corner cabinet, staring at her, rope-sinewed arms folded across a cage-gaunt chest whose ribs she can see even through the T-shirt he wears, long straight hair hanging either side of narrow features drawn even thinner with pain and want. His mouth is a clamped line, etched in between the sharp chin and blade-boned nose. Hollows cling under the bones in his cheeks.

Her heart surges sluggishly in her chest as she meets his eyes.

"Is it—" With the words, an awful understanding is welling up inside her now, a monstrous recognition that her conscious mind is still sprinting hard ahead to evade. "Is it my knee? My leg?"

Out of somewhere, abruptly, she finds strength, she props herself up on her elbows, she forces herself to look.

Sight collides with recollection.

The scream shrills up out of her, rips momentarily through the cobwebby drapery of the drugs in her system. She can't know how weak it sounds in the cold dimensions of the surgery, inside her it seems to splinter in her ears, and the knowledge that comes with it is a blackening of vision that threatens to suck her away. She is not, she knows, screaming at what she can see;

Not at the neatly bandaged stump where her right thigh ends twenty centimeters below her hip; not that.

Not at the stabbed-home comprehension that the ache in her knee is a phantom pain in a limb she no longer owns; not that.

She's screaming at memory.

The memory of the gurney ride along the quiet corridor, the soft bump and turn into the surgery, and then, veiled in the drug haze, the rising whine of the saw blade, the grating slip in tone as it bites, and the small, suckling sizzle of the cauterizing laser that comes after. The memory of the last time, and the sickening, down-plunging understanding that it's all about to happen again.

"No," she husks. "Please."

A long-fingered hand presses warmly down on her forehead. The Turin shroud countenance looms above her.

"Shshshsh . . . the cormorant knows why . . ."

Past the face, she sees movement. Knows it from memory for what it is. The stealthy, unflexing spider-leg motions of the autosurgeon as it wakes.

Gleaming steel . . .

part I

DOWN IN FLAMES

*Above all, the hard lessons of
this century have taught us
that there must be consistent
oversight and effective constraint, and that the policing
systems thus required must
operate with unimpeachable
levels of integrity and support.*

**—Jacobsen Report,
August 2091**

CHAPTER 1

He finally found Gray in a MarsPrep camp just over the Bolivian border and into Peru, hiding behind some cheap facial surgery and the name Rodriguez. It wasn't a bad cover in itself, and it probably would have stood standard scrutiny. Security checks in the prep camps were notoriously lax; the truth was that they didn't much care who you'd been before you signed up. But there were still a few obvious signs you could look for if you knew how, and Carl, with a methodical intensity that was starting to resemble desperation, had been looking for weeks. He knew that Gray was up on the altiplano somewhere, because the trail led there from Bogotá, and because where else, ultimately, was a variant thirteen going to run. He knew this, and he knew it was just a matter of time before the traces showed up and someone called it in. But he also knew, with induction programs everywhere skimping and speeding up to meet increasing demand, that time was on the other man's side. Something had to give, and soon, or Gray was going to be gone and Carl wasn't going to get his bounty.

So when the break came, the tiny morsel of data finally fed back from the web of contacts he'd been plying all those weeks, it was hard not to jump. Hard not to dump his painstakingly constructed cover, fire up his Agency credit and badge, and hire the fastest set of all-terrain wheels available in Copacabana. Hard not to tear across the border at Agency speed, raising road dust and rumors all the way to the camp, where Gray, of course, if he had any kind of local support, would be long gone.

Carl didn't jump.

Instead, he called in a couple of local favors and managed to blag a ride across the border with a military liaison unit—some superannuated patrol carrier with a Colony corporation's logo sun-bleached to fading on the armored sides. The troops were Peruvian regulars, drafted in from dirt-poor families in the coastal provinces and then seconded to corporate security duties. They'd be pulling down little more than standard conscript pay for that, but the interior of the carrier was relatively plush by military standards and it seemed to have air-con. And anyway, they were tough and young, a sort of young you didn't see so much in the Western world anymore, innocently pleased with their hard-drilled physical competence and cheap khaki prestige. They all had wide grins for him, and bad teeth, and none was older than twenty. Carl figured the good cheer for ignorance. It was a safe bet these kids didn't know the subcontract rate their high command was extracting from its corporate clients for their services.

Sealed inside the jolting, sweat-smelling belly of the vehicle, brooding on his chances against Gray, Carl would really have preferred to stay silent altogether. He didn't like to talk, never had. Felt in fact that it was a much-overrated pastime. But there was a limit to how taciturn you could be when you were getting a free ride. So he mustered some lightweight chat about next week's Argentina–Brazil play-off and threw as little of it into the conversational mix as he thought he could get away with. Some comments about Patricia Mocatta, and the advisability of female captains for teams that were still predominantly male. Player name checks. Tactical comparisons. It all seemed to go down fine.

"*¿Eres Marciano?*" one of them asked him, finally, inevitably.

He shook his head. In fact, he had been a Martian once, but it was a long, complicated story he didn't feel like telling.

"*Soy contable,*" he told them, because that was sometimes what he felt like. "*Contable de biotecnologia.*"

They all grinned. He wasn't sure if it was because they didn't think he looked like a biotech accountant, or because they just didn't believe him. Either way they didn't push the point. They were used to men with stories that didn't match their faces.

"*Habla bien el español,*" someone complimented him.

His Spanish was good, though for the last two weeks it was Quechua he'd been speaking mostly, Mars-accented but still tight up against the Peruvian original that had spawned it. It was what the bulk of the altiplano dwellers used, and they in turn made up most of the grunt labor force in the prep camps, just as they still did on Mars. Notwithstanding which fact, the language of enforcement up here was still Spanish. Aside from a smattering of web-gleaned Amanglic, these guys from the coast spoke nothing else. Not an ideal state of affairs from the corporate point of view, but the Lima government had been adamant when the COLIN contracts were signed. Handing over control to the gringo corporations was one thing, had oligarchy-endorsed historical precedent on its side in fact. But allowing the altiplano dwellers to shake themselves culturally loose from the grip of coastal rule, well, that would be simply unacceptable. There was just too much bad history in the balance. The original Incas six hundred years ago and their stubborn thirty-year refusal to behave as a conquered people should, the bloody reprise by Túpac Amaru in 1780, the Sendero Luminoso Maoists a bare century back, and more recently still the upheavals of the *familias andinas*. The lessons had been learned, the word went out. Never again. Spanish-speaking uniforms and bureaucrats drove home the point.

The patrol carrier pulled up with a jerk, and the rear door hinged weightily outward. Harsh, high-altitude sunlight spilled in, and with it came the sound and smell of the camp. Now he heard Quechua, the familiar un-Spanish cadences of it, shouted back and forth above the noise of machinery in motion. An imported robot voice trampled it down, blared *vehicle reversing, vehicle reversing* in Amanglic. There was music from somewhere, *huayno* vocals remixed to a bloodbeat dance rhythm. Pervasive under the scent of engine oil and plastics, the dark meat odor of someone grilling *antecuchos* over a charcoal fire. Carl thought he could make out the sound of rotors lifting somewhere in the distance.

The soldiers boiled out, dragging packs and weapons after. Carl let them go, stepped down last and looked around, using their boisterous crowding as cover. The carrier had stopped on an evercrete apron opposite a couple of dusty, parked coaches with destination boards for Cuzco and Arequipa. There was a girdered shell of a terminal building, and behind it Garrod Horkan 9 camp stretched away up the hill, all single-story prefab shacks and sterile rectilinear street plan. Corporate flags fluttered whitely on poles every few blocks, an entwined G and H ringed by stars. Through the unglassed windows of the terminal, Carl spotted figures wearing coveralls with the same logo emblazoned front and back.

Fucking company towns.

He dumped his pack in a locker block inside the terminal, asked directions of a coveralled cleaner, and stepped back out into the sun on the upward-sloping street. Down the hill, Lake Titicaca glimmered painfully bright and blue. He slipped on the Cebe smart lenses, settled his battered leather Peruvian Stetson on his head, and started up the slope, tracking the music. The masking was more local cover than necessity—his skin was dark and leathered enough not to worry about the sun, but the lenses and hat would also partially obscure his features. Black faces weren't that common in the altiplano camps, and unlikely though it was, Gray might have someone watching the terminal. The less Carl stood out, the better.

A couple of blocks up the street, he found what he was looking for. A prefab twice the size of the units around it, leaking the bloodbeat and *huayno* remix through shuttered windows and a double door wedged back. The walls were stickered with peeling publicity for local bands, and the open door space was bracketed by two loopview panels showing some Lima ad agency's idea of Caribbean nightlife. White sand beach and palm trees by night, party lights strung. Bikini-clad *criolla* girls gripped beer bottles knowingly and pumped their hips to an unheard rhythm alongside similarly European-looking consorts. Outside of the band—jet-muscled and cavorting gaily in the background, well away from the women—no one had skin any darker than a glass of blended Scotch and water.

Carl shook his head bemusedly and went inside.

The bloodbeat was louder once he got in, but not unbearable. The roof tented at second-story height, nothing but space between the plastic rafters, and the music got sucked up there. At a corner table, three men and a woman were playing a card game that required calls, apparently without any trouble tracking one another's voices. Conversation at other tables was a constant murmur you could hear. Sunlight fell in through the doorway and shutters. It made hard bars and blocks on the floor but didn't reach far, and if you looked there directly then looked away, the rest of the room seemed dimly lit by comparison.

At the far end of the room, a boomerang-angled bar made from riveted tin sections held up half a dozen drinkers. It was set far enough back from the windows that the beer coolers on the wall behind glowed softly in the gloom. There was a door set in the wall and propped open on an equally dimly lit kitchen space, apparently empty and not in use. The only visible staff took the form of a dumpy *indigena* waitress slouching about between the tables, collecting bottles and glasses on a tray. Carl watched her intently for a moment, then followed her as she headed back toward the bar.

He caught up with her just as she put down her tray on the bartop.

"Bottle of Red Stripe," he said, in Quechua. "No glass."

She ducked under the hinged access section without comment and opened a cooler cabinet on the floor. Hooked out the bottle and straightened up, gripping it not unlike the *criollas* in the ad panels outside. Then she cracked it deftly open with a rust-spotted key that hung off her belt, and set it on the bar.

"Five soles."

The only currency he had on him was Bolivian. He dug out a COLIN wafer and held it up between two fingers. "Swipe okay?"

She gave him a long-suffering look and went to get the machine. He checked the time display in the upper left corner of the Cebe lenses, then took them off. They'd cycled for low light anyway, but he wanted clear eye contact for what was coming. He dumped his hat on the bartop and propped himself next to it, facing the room. Did his best to look like someone who didn't want anything, like someone fitting in.

In theory, he should have checked in with the GH site manager on arrival. It was procedure, written into the Charter. Extensive previous experience, some of it sticky with his own blood, had taught him not to bother. There was a whole shifting topography of dislike out there for what Carl Marsalis was, and it touched on pretty much every level of human wiring. At the high cognitive end, you had sophisticated dinner-party politics that condemned his professional existence as amoral. At a more emotive level there was the generalized social revulsion that comes with the label *turncoat*. And lower still, riding the arid terminology of the Jacobsen Report but swooping into the hormonal murk of instinct, you could find a rarely admitted but nonetheless giddy terror that he was, despite everything, still *one of them*.

And worse than all of this, in the eyes of the Colony corporations, Carl was bad press walking. Bad press and a guaranteed hole in finances. By the time someone like Gray was ready for shipping out, Garrod Horkan could expect to have plowed several tens of thousands of dollars into him in varied training and mesh biotech. Not the sort of investment you want bleeding out into the altiplano dust under the headline INSUFFICIENT SECURITY AT COLIN CAMP!

Four years previously, he'd announced himself to the site manager at a camp south of La Paz, and his target had mysteriously vanished while Carl was still filling out forms in the administration building. There was a bowl of soup still steaming on the kitchen table when he walked into the prefab, a spoon still in the soup. The back door was open, and so was an emptied trunk at the foot of the bed in the next room. The man never surfaced again, and Carl had to conclude, to himself and to the Agency, that he was now, in all probability, on Mars. No one at COLIN was going to confirm that one way or the other, so he didn't bother asking.

Six months after that, Carl announced himself late one evening to another site manager, declined to fill in the forms until later, and was set upon by five men with baseball bats as he exited the admin office. Fortunately, they weren't professionals, and in the dark they got in one another's way. But by the time he'd wrested one of the bats free for himself and driven his attackers off, the whole camp was awake. The street was lit up with flashlights and the news was spreading at speed; there was a new black face, an outsider, down at the admin building, causing trouble. Carl didn't even bother braving the streets and streets of stares to check on the camp address he had for his target. He already knew what he'd find.

That left the fallout from the fight, which was equally predictable. Despite numerous passersby and even one or two blatant spectators, there were suddenly no useful witnesses. The man Carl had managed to hurt badly enough that he couldn't run away remained steadfastly silent about his reasons for the assault.

The site manager refused to let Carl question him alone, and cut short even the supervised interrogation on medical grounds. *The prisoner has rights*, she iterated slowly, as if Carl weren't very bright. *You've already hurt him badly.*

Carl, still oozing blood from a split cheek and guessing at least one of his fingers was broken, just looked at her.

These days, he notified the site managers after the event.

"Looking for an old friend," he told the waitress when she got back with the machine. He gave her the COLIN wafer and waited until she'd swiped it. "Name of Rodriguez. It's very important that I find him."

Her fingers hovered over the punch pad. She shrugged.

"Rodriguez is a common name."

Carl took out one of the hardcopy downloads from the Bogotá clinic and slid it across the bartop at her. It was a vanity shot, system-generated to show clients what they'd look like when the swelling went down. In real time, that soon after surgery that cheap, Gray's new face probably wouldn't have looked amiss on a Jesusland lynching victim, but the man smiling up out of the clinic print looked uninjured and pleasantly unremarkable. Broad cheekbones, wide mouth, an off-the-rack Amerind makeover. Carl, eternally paranoid about these things, had Matthew go back into the clinic dataflow that night just to make sure they weren't trying to fob him off with an image from stock. Matthew grumbled, but he did it, in the end probably just to prove he could. There was no doubt. Gray looked like this now.

The waitress glanced incuriously down at the print for a moment, then punched up an amount on the wafer that certainly wasn't five soles. She nodded up the bar to where a bulky fair-haired male leaned at the other end, staring into a shot glass as if he hated it.

"Ask him."

Carl's hand whipped out, mesh-swift. He'd dosed up that morning. He hooked her index finger before it could hit the transaction key. He twisted slightly, just enough to take the slack out of the knuckle joints. He felt the finger bones lock tight.

"I'm asking you," he said mildly.

"And I'm telling you." If she was afraid, it didn't show. "I know this face. He's in here drinking with Rubio over there, two, maybe three times a week. That's all I know. Now, you going to give me my finger back, or do I have to draw some attention to you? Maybe notify camp security?"

"No. What you have to do is introduce me to Rubio."

"Well." She gave him a withering look. "You only needed to ask."

He let go of her and waited while she completed the transaction. She handed back the wafer, beckoned, and walked casually along her side of the bar until she was facing the blond and his shot glass. He tipped a glance at her, then sideways at Carl as he joined them, then back to her. Spoke English.

"Hey Gaby."

"Hey Rubio. See this guy here?" She'd switched to English, too, heavily accented but fluent. "He's looking for Rodriguez. Says he's a friend."

"That so?" Rubio shifted his weight a little to look directly at Carl. "You a friend of Rodriguez?"

"Yeah, we—"

And the knife came out.

Later, when he had time, Carl worked out the trick. The weapon had a cling-pad on the hilt, and the blond guy had probably pressed it up against the bar within easy reach as soon as he saw the waitress talking to the stranger. Carl's careless approach—a friend of Rodriguez, yeah *right*—just closed the circuit. These two were Gray's friends. They knew he'd have no others.

So Rubio grabbed the knife loose and stabbed Carl in the same blunt rush. The blade winked once in the low light as it came clear of the bartop shadow, ripped low through Carl's jacket, and slugged to a halt in the weblar beneath. Gene-tweaked spiderweb mail, expensive stuff. But there was too much rage and hate behind the thrust to stop easily, and it was likely a monofil edge. Carl felt the tip get through and slice into him.

Because it wasn't really unexpected, he was already moving, and the weblar gave him the luxury of not having to cover. He hit Rubio with a *tanindo* move— palm heel, twice, short, stabbing strikes, broke the man's nose, crushed his temple, sent him sprawling away from the bar to the floor. The knife tugged loose again—nasty, grainy intimacy of metal in flesh—and he grunted as it came out. Rubio twitched and rolled on the floor, possibly already on his way to dead. Carl kicked him in the head to make sure.

Everything stopped.

People stared.

Beneath the weblar, he felt blood trickle down his belly from the wound the knife had left.

Behind him, Gaby was gone through the kitchen doorway. Also pretty much expected: his source had said she and Gray were close. Carl scrambled over the bar—savage flash of pain from the newly acquired wound—and went after her.

Through the kitchen—cramped, grimy space, gas ranges with blackened pans left to sit and a door to the outside still swinging wide with Gaby's passage. Carl caught a couple of pan handles as he shimmied the narrow clearance, left clatter and clang in his wake. He burst through the door and out into an alley at the back of the building. Sudden sunlight blasted his vision. He squinted left. Right, and caught the waitress sprinting flat out up the hill. Looked like about a thirty-meter lead.

Good enough.

He took off running.

With the combat, the mesh had kicked in for real. It flushed him now, warm as the sun, and the pain in his side dropped to memory and a detached knowledge that he was bleeding. His field of vision sharpened on the woman running from him, peripherals smearing out with the brightness in the air. When she broke left, out of line-of-sight, he'd closed the gap by about a third. He reached the turn and hooked around, into another back alley, this one barely the width of his shoulders. Unpainted prefab walls with small, high-set windows, stacked sheets of construction plastic and alloy frames leaning at narrow angles, discarded drink cans on the dirt floor. His feet tangled momentarily in a loose wrap of polythene from one of the frames. Up ahead, Gaby had already ducked right. He didn't think she'd looked back.

He reached the new corner and stopped dead, fighting down the urge to poke his head out. The right turn Gaby had taken was a main thoroughfare, paved in evercrete and loosely thronged with people. He squatted, dug out his Cebe lenses, and peeked around the corner at knee height. With the relief of not having to squint in the harsh light, he picked out Gaby's fleeing form amid the crowd almost at once. She was glancing back over her shoulder, but it was clear she hadn't seen him. There was no panic-stricken bolt, only a deep-drawn breath, and then she started to jog rapidly along the street. Carl watched her go for a few seconds, let the gap open up to a good fifty meters or more, then slid out into the street and followed, bent-kneed to keep his head low. It earned him a few strange looks, but no one spoke to him and more importantly, no one made any comment out loud.

He had, he reckoned with meshed clarity, about ten minutes. That was how long it would take news of the fight in the bar to reach someone in authority, and that someone to put a chopper into the air above the rectilinear streets of Garrod Horkan 9. If he hadn't found Gray by then — game over.

Three blocks up, Gaby crossed the street abruptly and let herself into a single-story prefab. Carl saw her dig the matte-gray rectangle of a keycard out of her jeans and swipe it in the lock. The door opened, and she disappeared inside. Too far off to make out a number or name panel, but the place had hanging baskets of yellow-flowered cactus out front. Carl loped up to the near end of the 'fab, slipped into the alley between the building and its neighbor, and circled to the back. He found a bathroom window left open, levered it up, and heaved himself over the sill. Vague pain from the stab wound, sliced muscle moving against itself in a way it shouldn't. He narrowly missed stepping into the toilet bowl, hopped sideways instead and crouched by the door, grimacing.

Voices came through the finger-thin wall, bassy with resonance but otherwise clear. Soundproofing on 'fab shells was pretty good these days, but if you wanted the same for interior partitioning, it cost. Not the sort of thing GH were going to provide at base; you'd have to buy the upgrade, and whoever lived here, Gaby or Gray, obviously hadn't. Carl heard the woman's accented English again, and then another voice he knew from filed audio playback.

"You stupid fucking bitch, *why'd you come here?*"

"I, you," Her voice stumbled with hurt. "To warn you."

"Yeah, and he'll be *right fucking behind you!*"

A flat crack, open hand across her face. Carl caught the sudden jump of her breath through the wall, nothing more. She was tough, or used to this, or both. He eased down the door handle, cracked the door, and peered through. A big form jerked across his sliver of vision. An upthrown arm, gesturing, there and gone too fast to see if there was a weapon in the hand or not. Carl reached under his jacket for the Haag pistol. Something weighty went over with a thump in the next room.

"He's probably tracking you *right now*, probably let you go so he could do it. You empty-headed *cunt*, you've —"

Now.

Carl threw the door open and found himself facing the two of them across a tiny living room laid with brightly colored rugs. Gray was half turned away, looming over a flinching Gaby, who had backed up and knocked over a tall potted plant by the front door. The reddened handprint was still visible on her face where he'd slapped her. More plants around the room, cheap painted ceramics and Pachamama icons on shelves, a small statue of some saint or other on a shelf, and a Spanish prayer in a frame on one wall. They were in Gaby's house.

He pitched his voice hard and calm.

"That's it, Frank. Game over."

Gray turned slowly, deliberately and, fuck, yes, he had a weapon, a big black cannon of a handgun that seemed welded in the fist at the end of his right hand. A tiny part of Carl, a subroutine immune to the mesh and the betamyeline flooding the rest of his system, identified it as the murder weapon, the '61 Smith caseless. Better than forty years old, but they said you could lockvoid that gun in orbit, swing around, pick it back up, and it'd still kill things like it just came out of the factory. For the first time in quite a while, he was grateful for the chilly bulk of the Haag in his own hand.

It didn't help when Gray smiled at him.

"Hello there, UN man."

Carl nodded. "Put the gun down, Frank. It's over."

Gray frowned as if seriously considering it. "Who sent you? Jesusland?"

"Brussels. Put the gun *down*, Frank."

But the other man didn't move at all. He could have been a holoshot on pause. Even the frown stayed on his face. Maybe deepened a little, as if Gray was trying to work out how the hell it had all come to this. "I know you, don't I," he said suddenly. "Marceau, right? The lottery guy?"

Keep him talking.

"Close. It's Marsalis. I like the new face."

"Do you?" The Smith still hung loose in his grip, arm at his side. Carl wondered if Gray was meshed yet. It'd make a difference to his speed if he was, but that wasn't the real problem. The real problem was the difference it'd make to Gray's attitude. "Try to fit in, you know. *Deru kui wa utareru.*"

"I don't think so."

"No?" And the slow, alarming smile Carl had hoped he wouldn't see.

"You were never going to get hammered down, Frank. None of us does, that's our problem. And that's an appalling Japanese accent. Want my advice, you'd be better off delivering your folk wisdom in English."

"I don't." The smile became a grin. He was going, sliding into the crack. "Want your advice, that is."

"Why don't you put the gun down, Frank?"

"You want a fucking list?"

"Frank." Carl stayed absolutely still. "Look at my hand. That's a Haag pistol. Even if you get me, I don't have to do more than scratch you on the way down. It is *over*. Why don't you try to salvage something?"

"Like you have, you mean?" Gray shook his head. "I'm nobody's puppy, UN man."

"Oh grow up, Frank." The sudden snap of the anger in his own voice was a surprise. "We're all somebody's puppy. You want to get dead, go right fucking ahead and make me do it. They pay me just the same."

Gray tautened visibly. "Yeah, I'll bet they fucking do."

Carl got a grip on his own feelings. He made a slow, damping motion with his free hand. "Look—"

"Look, nothing." A mirthless grin. "I know my score. Three Euro-cops, couple of Jesusland state troopers. You think I don't know what that means?"

"It's Brussels, man. They got jurisdiction. You don't have to die. They'll put you away, but—"

"Yeah, they'll put me away. You ever spend time in the tract?"

"No. But it can't be a lot worse than Mars, and you were going there anyway."

Gray shook his head. "Wrong. On Mars, I'll be free."

"That's not what it's like, Frank."

Gaby ran at him, screaming.

There wasn't a lot of space to cross, and she'd come more than halfway, hands up, fingers splayed like talons, when he shot her. The Haag gun made a deep cough, and the slug caught her somewhere high in the right shoulder. It spun her completely around and knocked her into Gray, who was already raising the Smith. He got off a single shot, a sprung-sounding boom in the tiny room, and the wall blew apart at Carl's left ear. Deafened, stung in the face and side of the head with impact fragments, Carl threw himself clumsily sideways and put four slugs into the other man. Gray staggered backward like a boxer taking heavy blows, hit the far wall, and thumped down into a sitting position on the floor. The Smith was still in his hand. He stared up at Carl for a moment, and Carl, moving cautiously closer, shot him twice again in the chest. Then he watched carefully, gun still leveled, until the life dimmed out of Gray's eyes.

Biotech account—closed.

On the floor, Gaby tried to prop herself up and slipped on some of her own blood. The wound in her shoulder was leaking copiously down her arm and onto the gaily colored rug under her. Haag shells were designed to stay in the body— the wall behind Gray was pristine—but they made a lot of mess going in. She looked up at him, making a tiny panicked grunting in the back of her throat over and over.

He shook his head.

"I'll go and get some help," he said, in Quechua.

He stepped past her to the front door and opened it.

Then, in the flood of light from outside, he swiveled quietly and shot her once more, through the back of the head.

CHAPTER 2

They arrested him, of course.

Drawn by the gunfire, a squad of body-armored camp security came scuttling up the street, clinging to the cover of building edges and stopped vehicles like so many man-size beetles. Sunlight gleamed on their dull blue chest carapaces and the tops of their helmets, glinted off the barrels of the short, blunt assault rifles they carried. They were as silent as beetles, too—in all probability, their GH-stamped riot gear and weaponry came with an induction mike and coms link package. He imagined it from their point of view. Hushed, shocked voices on the wire. Goggle-eyed vision.

They found Carl seated cross-legged on the steps up to the prefab's front door, hands offered outward, palms up. It was a *tanindo* meditation stance, one he'd learned from Sutherland, but he was anything but meditative. The effects of the mesh were ebbing now, and the pain from his injured side was beginning to creep back. He breathed through it and kept his body immobile. Watched intently as the security squad crept up the street toward him. He'd set out the Haag pistol and his Agency license in the street a good four or five meters away from where he sat, and as soon as the first armored form nosed up to him, assault rifle slanting down from the shoulder, he lifted his hands slowly into the air above his head. The boy in the riot gear was breathing harshly; under the helmet and goggles his young face was taut with stress.

"I am a genetic licensing agent," Carl recited loudly in Spanish. "Retained under contract by UNGLA. That's my authorization, lying there in the street with my gun. I am unarmed."

The rest of the squad moved up, weapons similarly leveled. They were all in their teens. A slightly older squad leader arrived and took stock, but his sweat-dewed face didn't look any more confident. Carl sat still and repeated himself. He needed to get through to them before they looked inside the 'fab. He needed to establish some authority, even if it wasn't his. Inside the high-tech riot gear, these were conscripts just like the ones he'd ridden into town with. Most of them would have left school at fourteen, some even earlier. The European Court might mean next to nothing to them, and their attitude toward the UN was likely to be ambivalent at best, but the Agency license was an impressive-looking piece of plastic and hologear. With luck, it would weigh in the balance when they found the bodies.

The squad leader lowered his rifle, knelt beside the license, and picked it up. He tipped the holoshot back and forth, comparing it with Carl's face. He stood up and prodded the Haag gun doubtfully with the toe of his boot.

"We heard shots," he said.

"Yes, that's correct. I attempted to arrest two suspects in an UNGLA live case and they attacked me. They're both dead."

Looks shuttled back and forth among the young, helmeted faces. The captain nodded at two of his squad, a boy and a girl, and they slid to the sides of the pre-fab door. The girl called a warning into the house.

"There's no one alive in there," Carl told them. "Really."

The two squad members took the door in approved fashion, swung inside and banged about from room to room, shouting their redundant warnings to surrender. The rest of them waited, weapons still leveled on Carl. Finally, the female member of the entry team came out with her assault rifle slung, crossed to the captain, and muttered in his ear. Carl saw how the squad leader's face darkened with anger as he listened. When the girl had finished her report, he nodded and took off his sun lenses. Carl sighed and met the customary stare. The same old mix, fear and disgust. And this young man was already unfastening a blue plastic binding loop from his belt. He pointed at Carl like something dirty.

"You, get up," he said coldly. "Get your fucking hands behind your back."

By the time they cut him loose again, his fingers were numb and his shoulders ached in their sockets from trying to press his wrists closer together. They'd drawn the loop savagely tight—even clenching his fists as they did it hadn't won him much slack when he relaxed his hands again, and the tension in his arms tended to force his wrists apart so that however he positioned himself, the loop cut into flesh. On top of the stab wound in his side, it wasn't what he needed.

They'd found the injury when they searched him, but they were more concerned with emptying his pockets than treating him for damage. They didn't take off the binding loop. As long as he didn't die in custody, he guessed they didn't much care what shape he was in. At the camp security center, they cut back his clothing; a barely interested medic prodded around the wound, declared it super-ficial, sprayed it with antibac, glued it shut, and taped a dressing to it. No anal-gesics. Then they left him in a lightly piss-scented plastic holding cell while the GH director pretended for two hours that he had more pressing matters to attend to than a double shooting in his camp.

Carl spent the time going over the confrontation with Gray, looking for a way to play it that didn't leave Gaby dead. He measured the angles, the words he'd used, the way the conversation had developed. He came to the same conclusion a dozen times. There was only one sure procedure that would have saved Gaby's life, and that was to shoot Gray dead the moment he stepped out of the bath-room.

Sutherland would have been pissed off, he knew.

No such thing as time travel, he'd rumbled patiently once. *Only live with what you've done, and try in the future to only do what you're happy to live with. That's the whole game, soak, that's all there is.*

Hard on the heels of the memory, Carl's own thoughts came looking for him.

I don't want to do this anymore.

Finally, two members of the security squad, male and unarmored, came and marched him out of the cell without removing the loop, then took him to a small office at the other end of the security station. The camp director sat on one cor-ner of a desk swinging his leg and watched as they cut Carl loose without cere-mony. The solvent squirt left a couple of drops on his skin that scorched. It didn't feel accidental.

"I'm very sorry about this," the director said, in English and without visible re-morse. He was pretty much the type, a tall, midforties white guy in designer ca-suals that approximated light trekking gear. His name, Carl knew from previous research, was Axel Bailey, but he didn't offer it, or his hand.

"So am I."

"Yes, clearly you've been detained unnecessarily. But if you had identified yourself before running around my camp playing at detective, we might have avoided a lot of unpleasantness."

Carl said nothing, just rubbed at his hands and waited for the pain as his hands renewed their acquaintance with blood flow.

Bailey cleared his throat.

"Yes, well, we've confirmed that Rodriguez was in fact who you claim he was. Some kind of slipup in vetting there, it looks like. Anyway, your office wants you to contact them with a preliminary statement on the shooting, but since we won't contest the jurisdiction, of course, there'll be no need for more than that at this stage. However, I would like your assurance that you will file a full report with

COLIN as soon as you get back to London, citing our cooperation. If that's
agreed, you're free to go, and in fact we can assist you with transport out."

Carl nodded. The first traceries of pain branched spikily out through the flesh
of his fingers. "Got it. You want me gone before the press come looking for the
story."

Bailey's mouth compressed to a thin line.

"I'm having you helicoptered directly to Arequipa," he said evenly, "so you can
get a connecting flight home. Think of it as a gesture of goodwill. Your gun and
your license will be returned to you there."

"No." Carl shook his head. Under the UNGLA mandate, he could in theory
have commandeered the helicopter anyway. In theory. "You'll give the gun and
the license back to me yourself, right now."

"I *beg* your—"

"The Haag pistol is UNGLA property. It's illegal for anyone unauthorized to
be in possession of one. Go and get it."

Bailey's leg stopped swinging. He met Carl's gaze for a moment, presumably
saw what was there, and cleared his throat. He nodded at one of the security
guards, visibly reading his name off the lettering on the breast pocket of his uniform.

"Ah, Sanchez. Go and fetch Mr. Marsalis's personal effects."

The security guard turned to leave.

"No." Carl peeled Sanchez a glance and watched him stop with his hand on
the door. He knew he was being childish, but he couldn't seem to stop himself.
He looked back at the director. "I said *you* go and get it for me."

Bailey flushed. He came off the edge of the desk. "Listen to me, Marsalis, you
don't—"

Carl closed one painfully fizzing fist up with the other hand. He grimaced.
The director's voice dried up.

"You go and get it for me," Carl repeated softly.

The moment held, and popped. Still flushing to the roots of his carefully
styled hair, Bailey shouldered past and opened the door.

"You watch him," he snapped at the security guards, and stalked out. Carl saw
a grin slip between the two men. He rubbed at his fist some more, shifted to the
other hand.

"So which of you two humanitarians spotted me with the cuffmelt?"

The grin vanished into hostile watchfulness and a stiff silence that lasted until
Bailey came back with his stuff and the paperwork to match.

"You'll have to witness for these," he said sulkily.

Camp security had bagged everything in a forty-centimeter-wide isolation strip, each item gripped tight in the vacuum-sealed plastic. Carl took the strip, unrolled it on the desk to check that everything was there. He pointed at the storage key.

"This is for a locker down by the bus park," he said. "My pack's in it."

"You can collect it on your way to the helicopter," Bailey said and flicked the release form impatiently at him. "I'll have my men escort you."

Carl took the form and laid it on the desk, tore the activation cover off the holorecorder decal in the corner, and leaned over it.

"Carl Marsalis, SIN s810dr576," he droned, words worn smooth on his tongue with their familiarity "UNGLA authorization code 31 jade. I hereby state that the items on this list are the full complement of property taken from me by GH camp security on June 18, 2107, and now returned to me, date the same."

He thumbed the disk to seal it and slid the form away from him across the surface of the desk. A curious suffocating sensation had settled over him as he recited the witness statement, as if it were he and not his personal effects vacuum-sealed in the transparent plastic.

I don't want to do this anymore.

No, that wasn't it. He looked up and saw the way Bailey and the two security guards were watching him.

I don't want to be this anymore.

So.

Choppered out of camp, tilting across the brilliant blue of the lake and then on through bleak, mountainous beauty as they picked their way down from the altiplano to Arequipa. Helicopters like this had smart systems navigation that ran off a real-time satellite model of local terrain and weather, which meant the thing practically flew itself. Still, the pilot stolidly ignored him for the whole flight. He sat alone in the passenger compartment and stared out of the window at the landscape below, idly mapping it onto his memories from Mars. The similarities were obvious—it wasn't just the thin air COLIN was up here simulating—but in the end, this was still home, with a sky-blue sky up above and the broad sweep of a big-planet horizon out ahead and the slow rolling weight of one full g pulling at your bones.

Accept no substitute. Slogans from the Earth First party political broadcasts blipped through his head. *Don't listen to the corporate hype. Keep your feet on the ground. Fight for a better life* here *and a better world* now.

In the airport at Arequipa, he used his UNGLA credentials to hook a sleeper-class seat aboard the next direct flatline flight to Miami with Delta. He'd have preferred suborbital, but for that you still had to go to Lima, and it probably wasn't worth the extra time and hassle the detour would take. This way at least he could get some rest. There was about an hour to wait, so he bought over-the-counter codeine, took double the advised dosage, and chased it with something generic from a departure-lounge Buenos Aires Beef Co. outlet. He munched his way through the franchise food on the observation deck, not really tasting it, staring out at the snowcapped volcanic cone of El Misti and wondering if there really, truly wasn't something else he could do for a living.

Sure. Go talk to Zooly when you get back, see if she's looking for doormen for the midweek slot.

Sour grin. They started calling his flight. He finished the cold remnants of his pampaburger *olé*, wiped his fingers, and went.

He slept badly on the flight to Miami, ticked with dreams of *Felipe Souza*'s silent passageways and the faint terror that Gaby's ghost was drifting after him in the low-g quiet, face composed and miraculously undistorted by the shot that had killed her, her brains drip-drooling darkly down out of the hole he'd blown in the back of her skull. Variation on a theme, but nothing new—just it was usually another woman who came floating up behind him in the deserted spacecraft, never quite touching him, whispering sibilantly into his ear above the dead-hush whine of silence.

He jolted awake, sweatily, to the pilot's announcement that they were starting their descent into Miami and that the airport was locked down under a security scare, so no connecting flights would be taking off for the foreseeable future. Local accommodation options could be accessed through—

Fuck.

The Virgin suborb shuttle would have put him in the sky over London forty-five minutes after it took off from Miami. He could have been home for last orders at Banners and his own bed under the tree-flanked eaves of the Crouch End flat. Could have drifted awake late the next morning to the sound of birds outside the window and cloud-fractured sunlight filtering through the bright leaves. Some British summer downtime at last—with the wound, the Agency would have no choice—and the whole Atlantic between him and the emotional topography of MarsPrep.

Instead, he carried his suitcase along broad, bright concourses lined with ten-by-two-meter holoscreens that admonished THINK IT'S ALL RED ROCKS AND AIRLOCKS? THINK AGAIN and WE ONLY SEND WINNERS TO MARS. Miami was a transamericas hub, and that meant a hub for every company involved in the Western Nations Colony Initiative. Some color-supplement journalist with access to more mainframe time than she deserved estimated, for a piece of inflight fluff he'd read a couple of years ago, *at present every seventh person passing through Miami International does so on business related, directly or indirectly, to Mars and the COLIN program. That figure is set to rise.* These days it was probably more like one in four.

He rode slideways and escalators up through it all, still feeling vaguely numb from the codeine. On the far side of the terminal complex, he checked into the new MIA Marriott, took a room with a skyline view, and ordered a medical check from the room service options. He charged it all on the Agency jack. As a contractor, he had fairly limited expense credit—working undercover in any case made for mostly wafer and cash transactions, which he then had to claim back as part of his fee—but with a worst-case couple of days left till he could get back to London and officially close the file on Gray, there was still a lot of meat on the account.

Time to use it.

In the room, he stripped off jacket and weblar mail shirt, dumped his soiled clothing in a heap on the floor, and soaked under a hot shower for fifteen minutes. The mesh was gone, back into its spinal lair, and he was a catalog of bruises he could feel through the thinning veils of codeine. The glued wound in his side tugged at him every time he moved.

He dried himself with big fluffy Marriott towels and was putting on the cleanest of his worn canvas trousers when the door chimed. He grabbed a T-shirt, looked down at the wound, and shrugged. Not much point in getting dressed. He dropped the shirt again and went to the door still stripped to the waist.

The in-house doctor was a personable young Latina who'd maybe served her internship in some Republican inner-city hospital, because she barely raised one groomed eyebrow when he showed her the knife wound.

"Been in Miami long?" she asked him.

He smiled, shook his head. "It didn't happen here. I just got in."

"I see." But he didn't get the smile back. She stood behind him and pressed long, cool fingers around the wound, testing the glue. She wasn't particularly gentle about it. "So are you one of our illustrious military advisers?"

He switched to English. "What, with this accent?"

A tiny bend to the lips now as she moved around to face him again. "You're British? I'm sorry, I thought—"

"Forget it. I hate those motherfuckers, too." That he'd killed one in a bar in Caracas last year, he didn't mention. Not yet, anyway. He went back to Spanish. "You got family in Venezuela?"

"Colombia. But it's the same story down there, only for coca, not oil. And for longer. Been going on since my grandparents got out, and it's never going to change." She went to her bag where it sat on the desk and fished out a handheld echo imager. "You wouldn't believe some of the things my cousins tell me."

Carl thought about the uniforms he'd seen on the streets of Bogotá a few weeks ago. A summary beating he'd witnessed.

"No, I would believe you," he said.

She knelt in front of him and touched the wound again, more gently now. Improbably, her fingers seemed warmer. She ran the imager back and forth a couple of times, then got to her feet again. He caught a gust of her scent as she came up. As it happened, their eyes met and she saw that he'd smelled her. There was a brief, flaring moment, and then she retreated to her bag. She dug out dressings and cleared her throat, raised brows and sideways-slanted eyes at what had just happened.

"There's not much I can do for you that hasn't already been done," she said, a little hurriedly. "Whoever glued you up knew what they were doing. It's a good job, should heal quickly enough. Did they spray it?"

"Yeah, they did."

"Do you want anything for the pain?"

"The pain's under control."

"Well, I'll dress it again, if you like, unless you're planning to shower now."

"I've just had a shower."

"Okay, well, in that case I can leave—"

"Would you like to have dinner with me?"

She smiled then, properly.

"I'm married," she said, holding up the hand and the plain gold ring on it. "I don't do that."

"Oh hey, I'm sorry. I didn't notice," he lied.

"No problem." She smiled again, but there was disbelief etched into it, and the tone of her voice said she wasn't fooled. "Are you sure you don't want any painkillers? I'm going to charge you the rate minimum, they'd come as standard with that."

"No, I'm all right," he said.

So she packed up her bag, gave him one more smile, and left him to put his own dressings on.

He went out.

It probably wasn't smart, but sense memory of the unattainable doctor drove him. Her fingers on him, her scent, her voice. The way she'd knelt in front of him.

An autocab took him east from the airport, cruising broad, multi-laned streets.

Most places were still open—LCLS glow from the frontages beckoned, but still seemed oddly distant, like the lights of a seafront town seen from offshore. He guessed it was the codeine, maybe playing off something in the mesh. For a while he was happy to watch it roll past. Then, as the traffic started to thicken, he got out at random where the lights seemed brightest. An avenue named after some Cuban Repossession hero, bronze beachhead-and-bayonet plaque fixed into the brickwork at the corner. Remixed Zequina and Reyes classics splashing out of propped-wide doorways, tanned flesh flexing within or strutting the street around him. It was warm and muggy, and dress ran to billowing scraps of silk over swimwear for the women, linen or tight leather jeans and bared chests for the men. On skin alone, Carl would have blended in well enough—it was one of the few things he liked about Miami—but he'd blown it with his wardrobe. Canvas trousers, the lightest of his trail shoes, and a BRADBURY BUBBLE '97 T-shirt. He looked like a fucking tourist.

In the end, tired of the flickering *he don't belong* glances from the local streetlife, he ducked off the main drag and sank himself in the gloom of a club called Picante. It was seedy and half empty and no closer to his fantasies of how his evening would turn out than the screen ad he'd seen outside the bar in Garrod Horkan 9 was to Caribbean reality. In the back of his mind, there'd been this vague storyboard of images in which he met the Latina doctor—well, a close substitute, anyway—in some classy salsa bar full of dance-lights glittering off cocktail glasses and good teeth. Segue to the easy, low-light surroundings of some other more intimate place, equally upscale, and then the homestretch to her place, wherever that might be. Fresh sheets on a big bed and the cries of an uninhibited woman in the throes of orgasm. Fading out, satiated, in the shadowed, temporary comfort of a strange woman's nighttime home.

Well, you got the shadows, he admitted to himself with a sour grin. Picante ran to a couple of LCLS dance panels not much bigger across than his hotel bathroom, a traditional straight-line bar, and wall lighting that seemed designed in kindness to the handful of fairly obvious prostitutes who hung around the tables, smoking and waiting to be asked to dance. Carl got himself a drink—they didn't have Red Stripe, he settled for something called Torero, then wished he hadn't—and installed himself at the bar near the door. It might have been professional caution or just the odd comfort that being able to see the street outside gave him—the sense that he didn't have to *stay* here if he didn't want to.

But he was still there, nearly an hour later, when she came in and parked herself beside him at the bar. The barman drifted across, wiping a glass.

"Hi. Give me a whiskey cola. Lot of ice. Hey there."

This last, Carl realized, was directed at him. He looked up from the dregs of his latest beer and nodded, trying to calibrate in the dim light. Trying to decide if she was working.

"You don't look like you're having a whole lot of fun there," she said.

"I don't?"

"No. You don't."

She was no *doctora* from the Marriott—her features were sharper and paler, her body curves less generous, and her mestiza hair less groomed. No wedding band, either, just a scatter of cheap and ornate silver rings across both hands. Bodice top made to look like it was sculpted metal, too, clasping her to just below the armpits, midthigh skirt in dark contrast, the inevitable wrenching heels. There was taut coffee-colored flesh on display, thighs below the skirt, shoulders and the slope of pushed-up breasts above the bodice, belly button slice between where the two garments didn't quite meet—but no more than street standard in this heat, didn't have to mean anything either way. Makeup a little on the heavy side, a little caked in the pores on the side of her nose. Yeah, she was working. He stopped trying to kid himself, hung for a moment over his decision like a skydiver in the hatch, then let go.

"I just got in," he said. "Business trip, I'm still kind of wired."

"Yeah?" She tipped her head on one side, crossed her legs in his direction. The skirt slid up her thighs. "You want some help with that?"

Later, elsewhere, and helped out of his tension like it was a tight pair of leather trousers he couldn't take off alone, he lay slumped up against the headboard and watched her move about in the white-blasted cubic environment of the en suite. From the foot of the bed to the open bathroom door wasn't much more than a meter, but it felt as if she'd stepped off into a parallel universe. Her actions seemed to be taking place at a profound distance; even the small bathroom noises, splash and swill of water, click of makeup utilities, were all somehow muffled as if he were staring through a thick-glassed observation panel into some cramped vivarium in an alien-world zoo.

Come see the humans.

See them mate in authentic surroundings.

A grimace twitched through him, too deeply buried to register in the muscles of his face.

See the female's postcoital douching ritual.

Another buried tremor of intent told him to get up off the bed, get dressed, and get the fuck out. There was really nothing else left to do. She'd run his wafer as soon as they'd gotten through the door—swiped it up the crack in the reader with the same clinical competence that she'd later employed to spray-coat his swollen cock and slot it inside her. Then he got some basic pay-per-view tricks — sucking her own fingers as he thrust into her, squeezing her own breasts as she rode him—a couple of well-timed posture changes, and a crescendo of throaty moaning until he blew. Now streetlighting and a tree outside made yellowish swaying shadows across the wall and ceiling of the darkened room, the alkaline smell of recent sex seeped out of the sheets tangled around his waist, and suddenly he felt old and tired and very slightly ill. The wound in his side had started to hurt again, and he thought the dressing might be coming off.

Intention made it to his motor system. He sat up and swung his legs off the side of the bed. In the bathroom universe, the toilet flushed. For some reason, the sound speeded him up, and by the time she came out he'd found his trousers and was stepping into them.

"You going?" she asked dully.

"Yeah, I think it's that time, you know." He hooked his shirt off one arm of the couch and shouldered his way into it. "I'm tired and you, well I guess you got places to be, right?"

Silence. She stood there, looking at him. He heard a tiny clicking sound as she swallowed, then a wet gulp. Abruptly he realized that she was crying in the gloom. He stopped, awkward and halfway into his shirt, peering at her. The gulp became a genuine sob. She turned away from him, hugging herself.

"Listen," he said.

"No, you go." The voice was hard and almost unblurred by the tears, schooled by the trade he supposed. She wasn't milking for effect, unless her method acting ran better to grief than sexual ecstasy. He stood behind her, looked at the untidy ropes of her hair where it had frizzed in the damp heat.

Images of the back of Gaby's head coming apart.

He grimaced, put his hand on her shoulder with a hesitation that should have been broad farce after the cheap intimacy he'd purchased from her twenty minutes ago. She flinched slightly at his touch.

"I'm pregnant," she said.

It ricocheted off the corner of his mind, and for a moment he thought he'd misheard. Then, when she didn't repeat it, he took his hand off her shoulder. She'd fished the Trojan spray can from her bag with the professional dexterity of a blindfolded circus performer, used it on him the same way. There'd been a coolly reassuring comfort to watching her do it, a sense that he—idiot grin—was in good hands. Now the same idiot part of him felt betrayed by this admission of previous error, almost as if she were accusing him of having something to do with it himself.

"Well," he said experimentally. "I mean, can't you. You know."

Her shoulders shook. "This is Florida. Been illegal down here for decades now. You gotta go to the Union or Rimside, and I don't have the parity payments on my medicode for that. I could sell everything I own and still not have enough."

"And there's no one here who—"

"Didn't you hear me. It's fucking *illegal*, man."

A little professional competence, a sense of being on his home ground, asserted itself. "Yeah, legal's got nothing to do with it. Not what I meant. There'll be places you can go."

She turned to face him, palm-heeling the tears off one cheek. The streaks it left gleamed as they caught the streetlight falling into the room. She snorted. "Yeah, places *you* can go, maybe. Places the governor's daughter can go. You think I have that kind of money? Or maybe you think I want to risk a back-alley scrape-bar, come home bleeding to death inside or collapse from enzyme clash because they were too cheap to run the specs right. Where you from, man? It costs a lot of fucking money to get sick around here."

It was on the tip of his tongue to tell her to fuck off. It wasn't his problem, he hadn't signed on for this shit. Instead, he saw Gaby's head come apart again and, as if from a distance, he heard himself saying quietly: "How much do you need?"

Fuck it. He derailed his rising irritation at the girl, at himself, retargeted it north and east. *Let fucking UNGLA pay for something worthwhile for a change. Not like they can't afford it. Let that piece of shit di Palma query it if he fucking dares.*

When he'd calmed her down, stopped her crying, and stemmed her protestations of gratitude before they started to sound hollow, he explained that he'd need a datapoint to download the credit to wafers she could use. That might mean going back to the hotel. At that, she clutched his hand, and he guessed she was terrified that if she let him out of her sight, or at least out of the neighborhood, he'd change his mind. She knew a datapoint that was secure a couple of blocks over, one of her clients from downtown used it now and then. She could show him where it was, right now, she'd get dressed, wouldn't take a moment.

The streets outside were pretty much deserted, the neighborhood was low-end semi-residential, and at this hour people were either inside or downtown. There was alloy shuttering on all the storefronts; bright yellow decals announced the anti-tampering charges lurking in the metal. A couple of bars were still open, showing dim neon signs over corner doorways like weak urban lighthouses. Outside one, a flock of aspiring street thugs propped themselves against walls and perched on parked vehicles, staring dangerously at the few passersby. Carl felt the mesh come gently, suggestively online. He ignored it and avoided gazes instead, put an arm around the girl's shoulder, and picked up the pace a little. He heard the boys talking about him in a densely arcane dialect of Spanglish as they fell behind. It didn't take much imagination to work out what was being said. *Fucking tourists, fucking foreigners, fucking our women.* The age-old plaint. He couldn't really blame them. Then they were lost around a corner and instead music floated down from a window jacked open for the heat, clumpy Cuban jazz that sounded like someone playing the piano with their fists.

The datapoint was a blunt concrete outcrop two meters tall and about the same wide, swelling from the wall of a commercial unit like some kind of architectural tumor. It was fitted with a solid tantalum alloy door. Heavily grilled LCLS panels set into the top of the structure threw down a pale crystalline light. Carl stepped into the radiance and felt, ludicrously, like some kind of stage performer. He punched his general access code into the pad, and the door cycled open. Old memories and scar tissue from Caracas made him usher the girl inside and bang a fist on the rapid-lock button as soon as they were both in. The door cycled again.

The interior was much the same as secure modules he'd used the world over, an iris reader mask on a flexible stalk, a broad screen edged with an integral speaker and set above a wafer dispenser, a double-width chair molded up from the floor, presumably for obese patrons rather than courting couples. The girl, in any case, stayed discreetly on her feet, looked pointedly away from the screen. She really had been here with clients before.

"Hello, sir," said the datapoint chattily. "Would you like to hear the customer options available to—"

"No." Carl fitted the iris reader over his head, blinked a couple of times into the lens cups, and waited for the chime that told him he'd been read. Idly he wondered what would happen if he ever had to do this with a black eye.

"Thank you, sir. You may now access your accounts."

He took the credit in ten limited-load wafers, reasoning that the girl wouldn't want to trust a clandestine clinic with a single upfront payment. As he handed them to her in the cramped space, he realized that he didn't know her name. A couple of seconds after that, the second realization hit home, that he didn't really want to. She took the wafers in silence, looking him up and down in a way that made him think she might try to give him a gratitude blow job there in the cabin. But then she muttered thanks in a voice so low he almost missed it and he wondered if he was, after all, just one more sick-headed fuck with an overactive imagination. He thumped the lock stud again and the door cycled open on a compressed sigh. He followed her out.

"*Okay, boy! Get your motherfucking hands up where I can see them!*"

The yell was off to his left; the shapes that jumped him came from both sides. The mesh leapt alive like joy. He grabbed an arm, locked it, and hurled its owner toward the dying echo of the voice. Curses and stumbling. The other figure tried to grapple with him, there was some technique in there somewhere, but . . . he yanked hard, got a warding arm down, and smashed an elbow into the face behind. He felt the nose break. Pain wrung a high yelp from his attacker. He stepped, hooked with one foot, and pushed. The one with the broken nose went down. There was another one, coming back from the left again. He spun about, fierce grin and crooked hands, saw his target. Blocky, slope-shouldered, fading pro-wrestler type. Carl feinted, then kicked him in the belly as he rushed in. Sobbing grunt and the solid feel of a good connecting strike, but the big man's impetus carried him forward and Carl had to dance sharply aside to avoid being taken down.

Then someone clubbed him in the head from behind.

He heard it coming, felt the motion in the air at his ear, was turning toward the attack, but way too late to get clear. Black exploded through him, speckled with tiny, tiny sparks. He pivoted and went down in the crystalline light around the datapoint. His vision inked out, inked back in. Another blunt figure came and stood over him. Through the waltzing colors that washed up and down behind his eyes, he saw a gun muzzle and stopped struggling.

"Miami Vice, asshole. You stay down or I'll drill a hole right in your fucking head."

They arrested him of course.

CHAPTER 3

6:13 AM.

Low strands of cloud in a rinsed-out, predawn sky. Last night's drizzle still sequined on the black metal carapaces of the rap-rep shuttles, evercrete landing apron damp with it, and spots of rain still in the air. Joey Driscoll came out of the canteen with a tall canister of self-heating coffee in each hand, arms spread wide as if to balance the weight, eyes heavy lidded with end-of-shift drowse. His mouth unzipped in a cavernous yawn.

The siren hit, upward-winding like the threat of a gigantic dentist's drill.

"Oh for fuck's sake . . ."

For a moment he stood in weary disbelief—then the coffee canisters hit the evercrete and he was running resignedly for the tackle room. Above his head, the sirens made it to their first hitched-in breath and started the cranking whine all over again. Big LCLS panels on the hangar lintels lit with flashing amber. Off to the left, under the sirens, he heard the deeper-throated grind of the rapid-response shuttles' turbines kicking in. Maybe a minute and a half tops before they hit pitch. Two more minutes for crew loading and then they'd be lifting, dipping and bopping on the apron like dogs trying to tug loose from a tight leash. Anyone late aboard was going to get their balls cut off.

He made the tackle room door just as Zdena darted out of it, tactical vest still not fully laced on, helmet dangling off the lower edge, XM still long-stocked in her hand from standing in the rack. Widemouthed Slavic grin as she saw him.

"Where's my fucking coffee, Joe?" She had to shout over the sirens.

"Back there on the concrete. You want it, go lick it up." He gestured up in exasperation at the noise. "I mean, *fuck*. Forty minutes to shift change, and we get *this* shit."

"Why they pay us, cowboy."

She snapped the XM's stock down to carbine length and secured it there, shoved the weapon into the long stick-grip sheath on her thigh, and focused on pulling the buckles tight on her tac vest. Joe shouldered past her.

"They pay us?"

Into the riot of the tackle room at alert. A dozen other bodies, yelling, cursing at their superannuated gear, laughing out the tension like dogs barking. Joe grabbed vest, helmet, T-mask off the untidy piles on the counter, didn't bother putting any of it on. Experience had taught him to do that in the belly of the rap-rep as it tilted out over the Pacific. He gripped the upright barrel of an XM in its recess on the rack, struggled briefly with it as the release catch failed to give, finally snapped the assault rifle free and headed back for the door.

Forty fucking minutes, man.

Zdena was already sitting on the lowered tailgate of Blue One, helmet fitted loosely, unmasked, grinning at him as he panted up and hauled himself, ass slithering, aboard. She leaned in to yell above the screech of the turbines. "Hey, cowboy. You ready for rock and roll?"

He could never work out if she was hamming up the Natasha accent or not. They hadn't been working together that long; she'd come in with the new hires at the end of May. He figured—and etiquette said you never *never* asked—she was probably licensed outland labor, at least as legal as he was these days. He doubted she'd hopped the fence the way he had, though. More likely she was across from the Siberian coastal strip or maybe one of those Russian factory rafts farther south, part of that fucking Pacific Rim labor fluidity they were always talking about. Of course, for all he knew, she might even be West Coast born and bred. Out here, mangled English didn't necessarily signify anything. Wasn't like back in the Republic, where they blanket-enforced Amanglic, punished the kids in school for speaking anything else. In the Rim States, English was strictly a trade tongue—you learned it to the extent you needed it, which, depending on the barrio you grew up in, didn't have to be that much.

"You gotta"—still panting from the sprint, no breath to yell—"stop watching all those old movies, Zed. This is gonna be a fucking punt around the deep-water mark. Scaring the shit out of some idiot plankton farmer who's forgotten to upgrade his clear tags for the month. Fucking waste of time."

"I don't think, Joe." Zdena nodded out along the line of shuttles. "Is four boats they got powering up. Lot of firepower for plankton farmer."

"Yeah, yeah. You'll see."

The dust-off went pretty smoothly, for their ship anyway, last month's practice drills paying off, it seemed, despite the groans. Eight troops in, standard deployment strength, all webbed into their crash seats along the inner walls of the shuttle's belly, grinning tension grins. Joe had his tactical vest all hooked up by then, vital signs wired in, though he wondered if anyone bothered to look at that shit anymore now they'd downgraded cockpit command crew from three to two. But at least the automeds would look after him in a firefight, and in the final analysis the vest was somewhere to hang all the spare XM magazines and boarding tools.

Briefing came in over the comset in his ear, drummed from the speakers set in the roof of the shuttle like an echo.

This is a class-two aerial breach incursion, repeat class-two incursion, we expect no combat—

He leaned out and nodded triumphantly down the line at Zdena—*Told you fucking so.*

—but maintain combat alertness nonetheless. Mask and gloves to be worn throughout mission, apply anticontaminant gel as for biohazard operations. Please note, there is no reason to assume a biohazard situation, these are precautions only. We have a downed COLIN spacecraft, repeat a downed COLIN spacecraft inside coastal limits—

Zdena shot him the look right back again.

"Fucking *spaceship?*" someone yelped from the row of seats on the other wall.

—medical teams will stand by until Blue Squad completes a sweep. Be prepared to encounter crash casualties. Squad division in deployment teams as follows, team alpha, Driscoll on point, Hernandez and Zhou to follow. Team beta . . .

He tuned it out, old news. Current rotations put him at the sharp end of deployment for the next three weeks. Now he couldn't make up his mind if he was pissed at that or glad. This was going to be a fucking *trip.* Outside of TV, and a couple of virtual tours of the COLIN museum in Santa Cruz, he'd never seen a real spaceship, but one thing he did know—they didn't land those fucking things on Earth. Not since the nanorack towers went up everywhere, disappearing into the clouds like black-and-steel beanstalks from that stupid fucking story his gran used to tell him when he was a kid. The only spaceships Joe knew about outside of historical footage were the ones that occasionally cropped up at the slow end of the news feeds, docking serenely at the mushroom top flanges of those fairy-tale stalks into the sky, their only impact economic. *Just returned from Habitat 9, the haulage tug Weaver's cargo is expected to make a substantial dent in the precious metals market for this quarter. Measures requested by the Association of African Metal-Producing States to protect Earth-side mining are still before the World Trade Organization, where representatives of the Hab 9 Consortium contend that such restraint of trade is—*

So forth. These days, spaceships stayed in space where they belonged, and everything they carried went up or came down on the 'rack elevators. *Perfect quarantine,* he'd heard some late-night talking head call it once, *and extremely energy-*

efficient into the bargain. A spaceship coming *down* was the scenario from some cheap disaster flick or even cheaper paranoid alien-invasion experia show off the Jesusland channels. For it to happen for real could only mean that something, somewhere had gone superwrong.

Oh dude—this, I've got to fucking see . . .

He was still applying the biosealant gel to his face when the shuttle banked about and the tailgate cracked open. Cold Pacific air came flushing in with the scream of the turbines and the gray dawn light. He unbuckled and shuffled down the line to the cable hoist. His pulse knocked lightly in his temples. Something that was too much fun to be fear coursed in his blood. He wrapped the T-mask across his face, pulled the breathing filter down to his chin, pressed the edges of it all into the biosealant. The wind whipped in off the ocean outside, chilling the newly pasted skin of his cheeks where they were still exposed at either side of the mask. There was an illusory sense of safety behind the curve of impact-resistant one-way glass and its warm amber heads-up projected displays, as if his whole body were sitting back here instead of just bits of his face. They got warned about that shit all the time. Some crudely rendered virtual drill sergeant in the bargain-basement Texan software that was all Filigree Steel Security's training budget ran to. Inexplicably, the badly lip-synched figure had a British accent. *Whole-body awareness, you 'orrible li-uhl man,* the construct was wont to bellow whenever he tripped one of the program's stoppers. *Are your legs on loan? Is your chest a temporary appendage? Whole-body awareness is the only fucking thing that will keep your whole body alive.*

Yeah, yeah. Whatever.

He snapped the cable onto his vest, turned back to the belly of the shuttle and the observation camera fixed in the ceiling. He made the OK sign with finger and thumb. Coughed into the induction mike at his throat.

"Point, ready to deploy."

I hear you, Point. On my mark. Three, two, one . . . drop.

The cable jolted into motion and he fumbled his XM to readiness in both hands, leaning out so he could peer down at what lay below. At first, it was just the endless roll and whitecap slap of the Pacific, outward in all directions. Then he got a fix on the ship. Not what he'd been expecting: it looked like a huge plastic packing case, awash in the water, barely floating. The hull was mostly a scorched black, but he could make out streaks of white with the remains of nano-etched lettering, some kind of corporate insignia that he supposed must have skinned off in the heat of reentry. He dropped closer, saw what looked like an open hatch set in a section that was still above water.

"Uh, Command. Are we sure this thing isn't going to sink?"

Affirmative, Point. COLIN specs say she should stay afloat indefinitely.

"Just, I've got an open hatch here, and with this wind and the waves I figure she's got to be shipping some water."

Repeat, Point. Vessel should float indefinitely. Check the hatch.

His boots hit the hull with a solid clank about a dozen meters off from the hatch and a little downward. Ocean water swirled around his feet, ankle-deep, then sucked back. He sighed and unclipped from the cable.

"Understood, Command. Off descender."

Will maintain.

He crouched a little and worked his way up the shallow slope toward the hatch, peered down into it. Water had sloshed into the opening; he could see it glistening wetly on the rungs of a ladder that led down to a second, inner hatch, which he assumed had to be the end of an air lock. As he watched, a fresh surge washed over the hatch coaming and rinsed down onto the ladder, dripping and splashing to the bottom of the lock. He peered a bit more, then shrugged and clambered down the ladder until he was hanging off the lower rungs just above the inner hatch. The water down there was about three fingers deep, slopping back and forth with the tilt of the vessel in the waves. Just below the surface, the moldings of the hatch looked unnaturally clean, like something seen at the bottom of a rock pool. There was a warning: CAUTION: PRESSURE MUST EQUALIZE BEFORE HATCH WILL OPEN.

Joe figured whatever pressure there was inside the hull must be pretty close to Earth standard then, because someone or something had already unsealed the inner hatch. It was hanging open just enough to let the water drain very slowly through the crack. He grunted.

Weren't for that, fucking air lock'd be a quarter full already from the slop.

He tapped his mike.

"Command? I've got a cracked inner hatch here. Don't know if that's the systems or, uh, human agency."

Noted. Proceed with caution.

He grimaced. He'd been hoping for a withdraw call.

Yeah, or failing that, some fucking backup, Command. This baby's come from space, right, from Mars most likely. No fucking telling what kind of bugs might be loose in there. That's what nanorack quarantine's for, right?

For a moment, he thought about backing up anyway.

But—

You're equipped, he could already hear the patient voice explaining to him. *You're masked and gelled against biothreat, which we don't in any case anticipate. You have no valid reason to query your orders.*

And Zdena's voice: *Why they pay us, cowboy.*

And from the others, jeers.

He shook off a tiny shudder, moved down a couple of rungs, and put a boot through the water to press gingerly on the hatch. It gave, fractionally.

"Great."

Point?

"Nothing," he said sourly. "Just proceeding with extreme fucking caution."

He braced one hand flat on the wall of the air lock, stamped harder on the hatch, impatient now and—

—it caved in under his foot.

Hinged heavily down to the side, dumping the water through into a darkened interior with a long, hollow splash. The sudden drop caught him unawares. He lost his grip on the rung above. Fell, grabbed clumsily with one flailing gloved hand, missed, and clouted the side of his head on the ladder as he tumbled. He went right through the opened inner hatch, had time for one garbled yell—

"Fuuuuuuahhhh—"

—and ended up in a heap on what must have been the sidewall of the corridor below.

Shock of impact, his teeth clipped the edge of his tongue. Sharp bang in his shoulder, gouge in the ribs where one end of the XM jabbed him on the way down. He hissed the pain out through gritted teeth.

For the rest, he seemed to have landed on something soft. He lay still for a moment, checking for damage reports from his tangled limbs.

Total-body awareness, right, Sarge.

He summoned a grin. Didn't think he'd broken anything. Looking up, he figured it for not much more than a three-meter drop.

He blew a hard, chuckled breath of relief into the mask filter. Completed his expletive quietly.

"Fuck."

Point? Command came through, yeah, *finally* fucking concerned now. *Report your status. Are you injured?*

"I'm fine." He propped himself up on one arm, squinted around in the gloom and snapped on the helmet light. "Just took a digger. Nothing to—"

The edge of the beam clipped something that didn't make any sense. His head jerked around, the beam hit full on what he'd seen—

"Ah, *fuck* man, you gotta be—"

And suddenly, with the flood of disbelieving comprehension, he gagged, vomit flooding up and into the mask, burning his nose and throat, as he saw for the first time exactly what the soft thing was that had broken his fall.

CHAPTER 4

Sevgi Ertekin awoke to the curious conviction that it was raining in dirty gray sheets all over the city.

In June?

She blinked. Somewhere outside the open window of the apartment, she heard a siren calling her. Intimate and nostalgic as the sound of the *ezan* she still missed from the old neighborhood, but freighted with an adrenaline significance the prayer call would never match. Rusted professional reflex surfaced in her, then rolled over and sank as memory came aboard. Not her call anymore. In any case, the melancholy caught-breath cry of the cop car, wherever it was, was distant. Noises of commerce from the street market six floors below almost drowned it out. There was shouting, mostly good-humored, and music from stall-mounted sound systems, frenetic neo-arabesque that she was in no mood for currently. The day had started without her.

Against her own better judgment, she turned over to face the window. Glare from the sun hit her in the face and drove her to squinting. The varipolara drapes billowed in the breeze from outside, incandescent with morning light. It appeared she'd forgotten to remote them down to opaque again. An empty bottle of Jameson's was partly hidden where the curtain hem brushed the floor, someone—*someone, yeah, right, Sev, who would that be?*—had rolled it away across the polished wooden boards of the living room when it had nothing left to offer. The same living room where she'd apparently slept fully clothed on the couch. A moment's groggy reflection brought in corroborative memory. She'd sat there after the party broke up, and she'd killed the rest of the bottle. Vague recollection of talking quietly to herself, the smoky warmth of the whiskey as it went down. She'd been thinking all the time, she'd just have one more, she'd just have one more, then she'd get up and—

She hadn't gotten up. She'd passed out.

This is new, Sev. Usually, you make it to a bed.

She made a convulsive effort and heaved herself fully into a sitting position, then wished she hadn't moved quite so rapidly. The contents of her head seemed to shift on some kind of internal stalk. A long wave of nausea rolled through her, and her clothing felt suddenly like restraints. She'd lost her boots at some point—they were keeled over on opposite sides of the room, about as far apart as the dimensions allowed—but shirt and pants remained. She had a vague memory of rolling hilariously about on her back after everyone was gone, trying to tug off the boots and then the socks. In this at least, it seemed she'd succeeded, but obviously the rest had defeated her.

And now the shirt was rucked up and bunched under her arms, and her profiler cups had peeled and worked loose from her breasts as she tossed and turned. One seemed to have ended up in her armpit; the other was gone altogether. Some way below her waist, her pants had somehow twisted about until they were no longer loose; her guts were similarly tight. Her bladder was uncomfortably full, and her head was settling to a steady throb.

And it's raining.

She looked up, and a sudden, raw anger took hold as she traced the low hissing to its real source. In one corner of the room, the ancient JVC entertainment deck was still on. Whatever chip was in had played to its conclusion, and the temperamental default system had failed to return to bluescreen. The monitor showed a snowdance of static instead and the gentle hiss of it filled up the base of hearing, below the sounds of the city outside. Filled up everything like—

Her mouth tightened. She knew what chip she'd been watching. She couldn't remember, but she knew.

It's not fucking *raining, all right.*

She lurched to her feet and stabbed the deck to silence. For a moment then she stood in her apartment as if it weren't her own, as if she'd broken in to steal something. She felt the steady flog of her pulse in her throat and she knew she was going to cry.

She shook her head instead, violently, trading the tears for an intense, sonar-pulsing pain. Stumbled through the bedroom to the en suite, fingers pressing to the ache. There was a plastic bottle of generic headache pills on the shelf there, and beside it a foil of syn. Or more precisely, k37 synadrive—military-issue superfunction capsules, her share of a black-market trickle into NYPD way back when and several times the strength of anything the street liked to call syn. She'd used the caps a handful of times before and found them scarily effective—they stimulated synaptic response and physical coordination, sidelined pretty much everything else, and they did it fast. Sevgi wavered for a moment, realized she had things to do today, even if she couldn't remember right now exactly what they were.

Whole fucking city self-medicates these days anyway, Sev. Get over it.

She pressed a couple of the milissue capsules out of the foil and was about to dry-swallow them when a fragment of peripheral vision caught up with her.

She strode back into the bedroom.

"Hey."

The girl in the bed couldn't have been much more than eighteen or nineteen. Blinking awake, she seemed even younger, but the body beneath the single sheet was too full for the waif-like look. She sat up, and the sheet slipped off improbably thrusting breasts. From the way they moved, it was a subcute muscle web, not implants, that was pulling the trick. Pricey work for someone that young. Sevgi made her for someone's trophy date, the whole fake-bonobo thing, but was too hungover to rack her head for faces from the party. Maybe whoever brought her had gotten too wasted to remember all his accessories when he went home.

"Who told you you could sleep in here?"

The girl blinked again. "You did."

"Oh." Sevgi's anger crumpled. She rode out another wave of nausea and swallowed. "Well, get your stuff together and go home. Party's over."

She headed back to the bathroom, closed the door carefully, and then, as if to emphasize her own last words, hooked over and vomited into the toilet.

When she was sure she could hold them down, she took the k37 slugs with a glass of water and then propped herself under the warm drizzle of the shower while she waited for the effects to kick in. It didn't take long. The tweaked chemistry in the drug made for rapid uptake as well as retained clarity, and the lack of anything else in her stomach sped the process even more. The throbbing in her head began to subside. She got off the tiled wall and groped for the gel, started gingerly on her scalp with it. The soaked and matted mass of her hair collapsed into silky submission, and the foam from the gel ran down her body in clumped suds. It was like shedding five-day-old clothes. She felt new strength and focus stealing through her like a fresh skeleton. When she stepped dripping out of the shower ten minutes later, the pain was wrapped away in chemical gauze and a spiky, clear-sighted brilliance had taken its place.

Which was a mixed blessing. Drying herself in the mirror, she saw the weight that was gathering on her haunches and grimaced. She hadn't been inside a gym in months, and her home-based Cassie Rogers AstroTone—*as used by real MarsTrip personnel!!*—program was settling into oblivion like a deflating circus tent. The incriminating evidence of the neglect was right there. And you couldn't take milissue slugs to make it go away like you could with pain. The ludicrously perfect flanks of the girl in her bed flitted through her mind. The jutting designer chest. She looked at the swell of her own breasts, gathered low on her ribs and tilting away to the sides.

Ah fuck it, you're in your thirties now, Sevgi. Not trying to impress the boys at Bosphorus Bridge anymore, are we. Give it a rest. Anyway, you're due, that always makes it worse.

Her hair was already settling back into its habitually untidy black bell as it dried out. She took a couple of swipes at it with a brush, then gave up in exasperation. In the mirror, her largely Arab ancestry glowered back at her: cheekbones high and wide, face hawk-nosed and full-lipped, set with heavy-lidded amber flake eyes. Ethan had once said there was something tigerish in her face, but Sevgi, sharp from the syn and not yet made up, suspected that today she looked more like a disgruntled crow. The idea dragged a grin to the surface and she made cawing noises at herself in the mirror. Dumped the towel and went to get dressed. Discovered a desire for coffee.

The kitchen, predictably, looked like a war zone. Every available counter was piled with used dishes. Sevgi tracked the party dishes through the debris—dark green remnants like tiny rags where the plates had held stuffed vine leaves, brittle fragments of *sigara börek* pastry, eggplant and tomato in oil gone cold, half a *lahmacun* left upside down so that it looked like a stiffly dried-out washcloth. In the sink, a small turret of stacked pans reared drunkenly out at her like some robot jack-in-the-box. Efes Export bottles were gathered in squat, orderly rows along one wall on the floor. Their slightly sour breath rose up to fill the kitchen space.

Good party.

A few of her departing guests had burbled it at her as she let them out. An abrupt avalanche of memory confirmed it, a tangle of friends throughout the apartment, sprawled on sofas and beanbags, food and drink and gesturing with mouths full, comfortable hilarity. It *had* been a good party.

Yeah—pity you had to murder that bottle of Irish afterward.

Why was that, Sev?

She felt how her face twitched and knew her eyes had gone flat and hard with the feeling as it rolled across her.

You know why.

The syn came on behind the thought, spiky and bright. She had a sudden insight into how easy it would be to kill someone in this state of mind.

The phone spoke, soft and reasonable, like biting into cotton wool.

"I have registered contact Tom Norton on the line. Will you accept the call?"
Recollection of what she had to do that day fell on her like a brick.
She groaned and went to fetch the rest of the painkillers.

The first wrong thing was the car.

Norton usually ran a ludicrous half acre of antique Cadillac soft-top with a front grille like a sneer and a hood you could have sunbathed on. He was grin-proud of the fucking thing, too, which was odd given its history. Built in some Alabama sweatshop before Norton was born, it was a vehicle he'd have been summarily arrested for driving in New York if he hadn't paid almost double the auction price to have the original IC engine ripped out and replaced with the magdrive from a discontinued line of Japanese powerboats. He'd blown yet another month's wages on having it polymered from snout to tail, immortalizing the catalog of scrapes and dents it had collected during its previous life out in Jesusland. Sevgi couldn't get him to see that it was practically a metaphor for the idiocies of the past it came from.

Today, in an abrupt spike of syn insight, she realized it was the kind of car Ethan would have loved to own, and that was why this aberration in Norton's otherwise flawless Manhattan male urbanity drove her time and again to a silent, waspish anger.

Today he wasn't driving it.

Instead, as she let herself out onto the street—still settling a grabbed-at-random tailored summer jacket onto her shoulders—he unfolded from the backseat of a dark blue autodrive teardrop that was recognizably from the COLIN pool. He stood there looking as smooth and self-contained as the vehicle he'd stepped out of, a poem in groomed competence. The filaments of gray in his close-cropped hair glinted in the sun; the tanned future-presidential-candidate Caucasian features that he swore were his own crinkled around pale blue eyes.

He gave her a trademark slanted grin.

"Morning, Sev. Rise and shine."

"Yeah, right."

"What time'd you wind it up in the end?" He'd gone home well before midnight, chemically unimpaired as far as Sevgi could remember.

"Don't recall. Late."

She pushed past him and dumped herself in the car, slid over to let him in beside her. The door hinged down and the teardrop pulled smoothly away, cornered into West 118th, and kept going. Traffic surged around them. They'd cruised four blocks before Sevgi woke up to the direction and the second jarring nail in the day's expected course. She glanced across at Norton.

"What's the matter, you leave something at the office?"

"Not going to the office, Sev."

"Yeah, that's what I thought we agreed to yesterday. So why are we headed east?"

Norton grinned again. "Not going out to Kaku, either. Change of plans. No freefall for you today."

The relief that rolled through her at the news felt like sun on her skin, suddenly warming and way ahead of any accompanying curiosity. She really hadn't been looking forward to the gut-swooping elevator ride up the Kaku nanorack or the creeping around weightless when they got to the top. They had drugs to take the sting out of both experiences at the 'rack facility, but she wasn't at all sure they'd mix well with the syn already coursing through her system. And the thought of starting an investigation in this state—with her abused brain and belly bleating protest at the zero g and the Earth rolling past somewhere sickeningly far below—already had her palms lightly greased with sweat.

"Right. So you want to tell me where we *are* going?"

"Sure. JFK suborb terminal. Got the eleven o'clock shuttle to SFO."

Sevgi sat up. "What happened, *Horkan's Pride* overshoot the docking slot?"

"You could say that." Norton's tone was dry. "Overshot Kaku, overshot Sagan, splashed down about a hundred klicks off the California coast."

"*Splashed down?* They're not supposed to land those things."

"Tell me about it. From what I hear, only the main crew section made it down in one piece. The rest is wreckage along a line from somewhere in Utah to the coast or burned up on reentry. The Rim authorities are having what's left towed back to the Bay Area, where you and I will crack it open and dazzle them all with our lucid analysis of *just what the fuck went wrong*. Those are Nicholson's words, by the way, not mine."

"Yeah, I guessed." Norton spoke four-letter words the way a miser spends wafers—when he was utterly inescapably driven to it or when they belonged to someone else. It seemed to be a linguistic rather than a moral quirk, though, because he evinced no apparent embarrassment or distaste when he quoted other people like this, or when Sevgi swore, which was a lot of the time these days.

"So how come you didn't phone me earlier with this shit?"

"Believe me, I tried. You weren't answering."

"Oh."

"Yeah, so I covered for you with Nicholson, if that's what you were wondering.

Said you were somewhere downtown chasing leads from the Spring Street bust, you were going to meet me at the terminal."

Sevgi nodded to herself. "Thanks, Tom. I owe you one."

She owed him more than one, quite a lot more over the last two years, but neither of them would ever acknowledge it. The debt lay unspoken between them, like complicity, like family. And Nicholson, anyway, they both agreed was an asshole.

"You think any of them are still alive?" Norton wondered.

Sevgi stared out of the window at the traffic, marshaling facts from the file. "*Horkan's Pride* is a five series. They built them to survive crash-landing at the Mars end, and there aren't any oceans there to do it in."

"Yeah, but that's a lot less gravity to worry about on the way down."

An NYPD teardrop cruised up alongside them, panels at opaque except for the driver's window, which was cranked back. A young cop up front had the system at manual and was steering idly with one tanned arm leaning on the sill. She was talking to someone, but Sevgi couldn't make out if it was another occupant of the car or an audio hookup. Under the peak of her summer-weight weblar cap, she looked casually competent and engaged. Memory twinged, and Sevgi found herself wondering about Hulya. She really ought to get back in touch sometime, see what Hulya was doing these days, see if she took the sergeant's exam again, if she was still hauling her tight, man-magnet ass out to Bosphorus Bridge every Saturday night. Sit down somewhere for a good *do-you-remember-when* session, maybe crack a case of Efes.

At the thought of beer and the smell it had left in her kitchen, Sevgi's stomach turned abruptly over. She shunted the nostalgia hastily aside. The NYPD car switched lanes and faded in the traffic. Sevgi took an experimental stab at some engaged competence of her own.

"Cryocap fluid should absorb a lot of the impact shock," she said slowly. "And the fact it came down in one piece at all means it was some kind of controlled reentry, right?"

"Some kind of."

"Did we get any more out of the datahead before this happened?"

Norton shook his head. "Same request for standby at Kaku, same interval broadcast. Nothing new."

"Great. Fucking ghost ship to the last."

Norton lifted hands with fingers draped wide and low, made phantasmal noises to match. Sevgi curled a grin under control.

"It's not fucking funny, Tom. Beats me why the Rim skycops didn't just vapor-

ize it soon as it crossed the divide. It wouldn't be the first time those day-rate morons turned glitched air traffic into confetti when it didn't answer nicely."

"Maybe they were concerned about loss of life," said Norton, with a straight
face.

"Yeah."

"Now, I hope you're not planning to bring that attitude with you, young lady.
The locals probably won't be overfriendly as it is. This is our tin can that fell out
of the sky on them."

She shrugged. "They pay COLIN taxes just like the rest of us. It's their tin can,
too."

"Yeah, but we're the ones supposed to make sure this kind of thing doesn't
happen. That's *why* they pay their taxes."

"Have you talked to anyone at their end yet?"

Norton shook his head. "No one human. I tried to hook whoever caught the
case just before I left. Got the machine. Standard phone interface. It said we'll be
collected at the airport by RimSec. Two of their plainclothes guys, Rovayo and
Coyle."

"You get ID?"

Norton tapped the breast of his jacket. "Hardcopy download. Want to see it?"

"Might as well."

The Rim cops were a balanced sex and eth couple. Under the label DET. A.
ROVAYO, a dark young Afro-Hispanic woman stared out of her photo with jaw set
and mouth thinned, trying rather obviously and without much success to beat a
full-lipped, hazel-eyed beauty. Belying the severity of her expression, her hair
coiled thick and longer than NYPD would have let her get away with. Below her
on the same printout, DET. R. COYLE glowered up, blunt-featured, middle-aged,
Caucasian. His hair was shot with gray and shaved almost militarily short. The
image was head and shoulders only, but it gave the impression of size and impatient force.

Sevgi shrugged.

"We'll see," she said.

They saw.

Coyle and Rovayo met them off the suborb at SFO with perfunctory greetings
and an iris scan. Standard procedure, they were told. Norton shot a warning
glance at Sevgi, who was visibly fuming. This wasn't how visiting cops would
have been treated on arrival in New York. Here, it was hard to tell if they were

being snubbed or not; Coyle, every bit as big and laconic as his holoshot had suggested, showed them brief ID and did the introductory honors. Rovayo took it from there. She leaned in and spread their eyelids with warm, slightly callused fingers, applied the scanner, and then stepped back. It was all done with a detached competence, and among the streams of arriving passengers it had the intimate flavor of a European kiss on the cheek. Norton seemed to enjoy it, anyway. Rovayo ignored his smile, glanced at the green light the machine had given them, and put the scanner away in the shoulder bag she carried. Coyle nodded toward a bank of elevators at the end of the arrivals hall.

"This way," he said economically. "We got the smart chopper."

They rode up in silence, hooked a walkway across the glass-bubbled, white-girder-braced upper levels of the building, then another elevator that spilled them out onto a concrete apron where a sleek red-and-white autocopter sat twitching its rotors. Eastward, the bay glimmered silvery gray in the late-afternoon sun. A ruffling wind took the heat out of the day.

"So you guys are on the case?" Norton tried as they clambered aboard.

Coyle offered him an impassive glance. "Whole fucking force is on this case," he grunted and tugged the hatch closed. "Badge coding 2347. Flight as filed. Let's go."

"Thank you. Please take your seats."

The autocopter had Asia Badawi's voice, low and honey-coated, unmistakable even from the half a dozen syllables uttered. Sevgi vaguely remembered reading, in some mindless magazine-space moment while she waited to see the lawyers, an article about the software contract Badawi had signed with Lockheed. Big PR smiles and clasps all around, outraged fans protest. Yawn, *flick. Would you like to come through now, Ms. Ertekin?* The rotors cranked in earnest, engine murmur rose to a dim, soundproofed crescendo on the other side of the window, and they unstuck from the pad. They settled into seats. The autocopter lifted, tilted, and whirled them out over the bay.

Sevgi made an effort. "You get anything from the skin yet?"

"Scanning crew are going over the hull now." The cabin had facing seats and Coyle was opposite her, but he was staring out of the window as he spoke. "We'll have a full virtual up and running by this evening."

"That's fast work," said Norton, though it wasn't really.

Rovayo looked at him. "They've been busy inside, that kind of took priority."

An eyeblink silence.

Sevgi exchanged a glance with Norton.

"Inside?" she asked, dangerously polite. "You've already cracked the hatches?"

A knowing grin went back and forth between the two Rim cops. Sevgi, fed up with being the least informed person in the room all day, felt her temper start to fray.

"*Horkan's Pride* is COLIN's property," she said thinly. "If you've tampered with—"

"Put your cuffs away, Agent Ertekin," said Coyle. "Time the coastals got out to your *property*, someone aboard had already blown the hatches out. From the inside. Quarantine seal's long gone."

That's not possible. Narrowly, she managed to stop herself from saying it. Instead she asked: "Are the cryocaps breached?"

Coyle eyed her speculatively. "It's really better if you wait and see for yourself."

The autocopter banked about, and Sevgi leaned forward to peer out the window. Below them in the bay, Rim Security's Alcatraz station rose off its island base in pale gray platforms and piers. On the southern shoreline, a floating dry-dock complex was laid out like a schematic, clean lines and spaces, people reduced to dots and vehicles to toys. The bulk of the *Horkan's Pride* crew section showed up clearly in the center dock. Even with the external structures ripped away, even scorched and scarred by the reentry, it leapt out at her like a familiar face in a group photo. She'd seen sister ships in the orbital yards above the Kaku nanorack from time to time, and she'd had archive footage of *Horkan's Pride* itself filed on her laptop ever since the ship stopped talking to COLIN Control. In the frequent chunks of waiting room time at the lawyers' offices, in the sleepless still of the nights she didn't drink, she'd stared at the detail until her eyes ached. *A good detective eats, sleeps, and breathes the details,* Larry Kasabian had once told her. *That's how you catch the bad guys.* The habit stuck. She knew the internal architecture of the vessel so well, she could have walked it from end to end blindfolded. She had the hardware and software specs by heart. The names of the cryocapped crew were as familiar as product brands she habitually shopped for, and biographical detail from each popped into her head unbidden whenever she visualized one of their faces.

It's really better if you wait and see for yourself.

And now, at a guess, they were all dead.

The autocopter settled with machine precision onto a raised platform at one end of the dock complex. The motors wound down, and the hatch cracked open. Coyle did the honors again, levering the hatch back and jumping down first. Sevgi went next.

Badawi's honeyed tones followed her out into the wind. "Watch your step. Please close the hatch behind you."

Coyle led the way down the steps off the platform. There was a reception committee waiting at the bottom. Three RimSec uniforms backing a plainclothes
ranking officer whose face Sevgi recognized from a couple of virtual briefings
she'd attended last year on geneprint forgery. Smooth Asian features that made
him seem younger than she supposed he was, thick gray hair and a rumpled way
with clothes that belied the level scrutiny in the eyes. From that gaze and other
general aspects of demeanor, she'd suspected he was probably enhanced—Rim
officials of any rank usually were these days—but she never had more evidence
than the hunch. In the social sessions after, he'd talked with quiet reservation,
mainly about his family, and his eyes had barely flickered to Sevgi's chest at all,
for which she'd been quietly grateful. Now she scrabbled after a name, and the
syn handed it to her.

"Lieutenant Tsai. How are you?"

"Captain," he said drily. "Promoted back in January. And I'm as well as can be
expected, thank you, given the circumstances. I presume you'd like to view your
vessel immediately. What's left of it."

Sevgi nodded glumly. "That'd be helpful."

"I'm told—" Tsai made gestures at his uniforms, and they sloped off across the
dock. "—that we'll have a working virtual by about seven. Crews are finishing up
with the hull now, but Rovayo probably told you about the hatches."

"That they were blown from the inside, yeah."

"Captain," Norton weighed in. "We're concerned to know what state the crew
of *Horkan's Pride* are in. Specifically, whether the cryosystems were breached or
not."

Tsai stopped in the act of turning to follow the uniforms, and his gaze seemed
suddenly to lengthen, dialing up, out across the dock and then the bay, replaying
something from memory that he'd maybe prefer not to. In Sevgi, the realization
hit home that behind the turf-proud cool of Coyle and Rovayo there was the
same base edginess, and that driving it all was not the jurisdiction envy she'd
assumed.

They're scared, she suddenly knew. *And we're their only solution.*

It was an epiphany Sevgi had had once before, back when she was still a rookie
with the NYPD and dealing with a drugs-and-domestic-abuse case. Talking to the
bruised and still-swelling face of the perpetrator's mother, it hit her with the same
sickening abruptness that this woman was looking at her as some kind of solution
to her problem; that she expected Patrolwoman Ertekin, age twenty-three, to *do*
something about the shitstorm state of her family and her life.

So nice to be needed.

"Breached," Tsai said slowly. "Yes, I think you could say that."

The outer hatches themselves were gone, blown clear by the emergency bolts—by now they'd be somewhere at the bottom of the Pacific. The blackened stub of *Horkan's Pride* had been propped in the dry dock, as close to a usefully even keel as her design would allow. Still, they had to clamber down into Access Four as if it were a well cut into the top of the crew section's hull. A zero-g assist ladder took them to the bottom of the air lock chamber within, and from there they dropped heavily through the inner lock and onto the canted surface of the main dorsal corridor. Maintenance lighting glowed in soft blue LCLS panels along the sides of the passageway, but Tsai's uniforms had set up high-intensity incident lamps by the air lock and farther down. White glare bounced back off the grubby cream-colored walls, and teeth.

Sevgi's gaze caught it as she came down off the last rung of the ladder, and she skidded to a halt at the sight. The ripped-to-the-gums grin of a mutilated human head where it lay only loosely attached to the limbless torso sprawled on the floor.

"You see what I mean?" Tsai climbed down beside her.

Sevgi stood, managing her stomach. Leaving aside the hangover, it had still been awhile. Even her last year with the NYPD had been mercifully short on gore; transferring from Homicide to COLIN liaison hadn't made her any friends on the force, but it had certainly put a brake on the amount of mangled human remains she had to look at. Now she was vaguely aware that without the syn, she would have vomited up what little her stomach contained, all over Tsai's crime scene.

Your *crime scene, you mean.*

This is yours, Sev.

She bent forward a little, peered at the dead man. Took possession.

"Alberto Toledo," said Tsai quietly. "Engineer at the Stanley bubble, atmospheric nanotech. Fifty-six years old. Rotated home."

"Yes, I know." Biog detail bubbled up from the ruined, sneering face, whispering like ghosts. Job specs, résumé, family background. This one had a daughter somewhere. The flesh of both cheeks had been sheared off up to the cheekbone, where stringy fragments of tissue still clung. The jaw was stripped. The eyes—

She swallowed. Still a little queasy. Norton joined her, put a hand on her shoulder.

"You okay, Sev?"

"Yeah, I'm fine." She locked onto facts. *Horkan's Pride* hadn't talked to them for almost the whole seven and a half months of its long fall back to Earth. "Captain, this . . . looks recent."

Tsai shrugged. "Antibacterials in the shipboard atmospheric system, they tell me. But yeah, we're guessing Alberto here was probably one of the last."

"The *last?*"

Sevgi glanced at Norton as he said it, and was pleased to notice that he looked as shaky as she felt. Distantly, she picked out the acidic tang of someone else's vomit in the air of the closed space around her. It was oddly comforting, the knowledge that others before her had seen and reacted in the same way she wanted to. It made it easier to hold on.

"What happened to the limbs?" she managed, almost casually.

"Surgically removed." Tsai gestured up the corridor. "They're still downloading the autosurgeon's log, so we can't be sure that's how it was done, but it's the obvious explanation."

"So how did he end up here?"

The captain nodded. "Yeah, that's a little harder. Could be the impact threw the bodies about some. We found most of the cryocaps hinged open, nutrients all over the floor and walls. Looks like whoever did this wasn't all that tidy, at least toward the end."

"The corridor locks should have engaged when she came down," Norton said shortly. "These ships compartmentalize under emergency conditions. There's no way something could get flung from one end of this hulk to the other like that. No way."

"Well, it's only a theory." Tsai gestured up and down the unobstructed corridor again. "But as you'll see. Not a lot of compartmentalization going on here. You want to look at the cryocap section?"

Sevgi peered along the passageway to where more incident lamps lit the environs of the sleeper racks. She could see figures moving about down there, heard a couple of voices. The brief rattle of a laugh. The sound carried her back, with a force that was almost physical, to her crime scene days with Homicide. Black humor and hardened camaraderie, the quiet thrum of an intensity denied to anyone who didn't work this beat, and the layering on of a detachment that came with custom. *So weird, the shit you can get nostalgic for, girl.* It alarmed her a little, realizing the extent to which, despite her quailing stomach, she did suddenly want to plunge back into that world and its dark procedural workings.

"The other bodies," she said as the syn lit up her head. "They're all mutilated like this one, right?"

Tsai's face was a mask. "Or worse."

"Have you found the limbs?"

"Not as such."

Sevgi nodded. "Just bones, right?"

Oh, Ethan, you should have been around to see this. It really has happened this time, just the way you always used to bullshit me it would.

"That's right." Tsai was looking at her like a teacher with a smart kid.

"You've got to be fucking kidding," said Norton, very quietly.

Sevgi turned to look at him fully. It was reflex denial, shock, not objection. "That's right."

"Someone chopped these people up with the autosurgeon—"

She nodded, still not sure in the bright spin of the syn and the shock of the understanding, how she felt, how she *should* feel.

"Yes. And ate them."

t was like a landscape out of Dalí.

The CSI virtual was a forensics standard Sevgi remembered from her time with the NYPD—pristine Arizona desert as far as the eye could see, blue sky featureless but for a ghost moon that carried the designers' logo like a watermark. Each section of the investigation presented as a separate three-story adobe structure, distributed across the landscape in a preternaturally neat semi-circular arc. The sectional homes were open on the facing side like cutaways in an architectural model, furnished with steps so you could walk up to each level. Labels floated in the air beside each structure, neatly lettered fonts announcing DATA ANOMALY; PATH LABS; RECOVERED SURVEILLANCE; PRIOR RECORD. Much of the display space was still empty, data still to come, but shelved on the exposed floors of the path lab home, the mutilated corpses from *Horkan's Pride* stood on their stumps like vandalized statues in a museum. Even here, not all the organic data was in yet, but the corpses had been scanned into the system early on. Now they posed in catwalk perfection, colored and intimate enough to make your own flesh quail as you stared at theirs. Sevgi had already seen them close up, had focused with irresistible fascination on neatly sectioned bone in the densely packed meat of an arm taken off centimeters from the shoulder, and then wished she hadn't. The syn was wearing off, leaving queasy traces of hangover beneath.

The path lab n-djinn interface, a perfectly beautiful Eurasian female in tailored blue scrubs, narrated the nightmare with machine calm.

"The perpetrator chose limbs because they represented the simplest transfer of the automated medical system's functions from surgery to butchery." An elegant gesture. "Amputation is an established procedure within the autosurgeon's protocols, and it is not life threatening. After each surgical procedure, it was a simple matter to return the subject, still living, to the cryogen units, thus assuring a ready and continuing supply of fresh meat."

"And the automed just let it all fucking *happen*?" Coyle was staring angrily about him, male outrage deprived of targets. "What the fuck is that?"

"That," said Sevgi wearily, "is selective systems intrusion. Someone got into the general protocol level and closed down the ship's djinn. For a good datahawk, it wouldn't be difficult. All these ships have a human override option anyway, and there's a fail-safe suicide protocol wired into the n-djinn. You just have to trick it into believing it's been corrupted, and it shuts itself down. There are a whole series of secondary blocks to prevent that damage from seeping down into the discrete systems, but like we're hearing, he didn't need to worry about that. He wasn't telling the medical systems to do anything they weren't already programmed for."

"He?" Rovayo. Sevgi'd already pegged her as a staunch man's woman, and this looked like confirmation—umbrage taken at potential feminazi chauvinism. "Why's it got to be a *he*?"

Sevgi shrugged. *Because, statistically, that's the way it fucking is,* she didn't say. "Sorry. Figure of speech."

"Yeah, till we get the swab breakdowns back and find out it *was* a man," drawled Norton. He stepped past Rovayo's mutinous look, closer to the white-walled, opened architecture of the path home and its exhibits. The lab 'face gave ground and stood in deferential silence, waiting to be directly questioned. Its higher interactional functions had apparently not been enabled. Norton nodded up at the exposed grin of a female corpse, and it leapt out at them. Visual distance was elusive in the construct: it bowed and swelled like a lens according to user focus. "Thing I don't get is the mess. I can see killing them all—you don't want witnesses left around, with or without arms and legs. But why the blood on the walls? Why mutilate the faces like that?"

"Because he was fucking cracked," Coyle growled. "He probably ate that stuff as well, right?"

"Difficult to say." The lab 'face kicked in again, pointing and pulling in a bubble of data display from one of the other file houses. "Evidence gathered from the kitchen unit suggests meat scraped from the skulls *may* have been cooked and ingested. This does not seem to have been the case with the eyes, which were gouged out and then discarded."

Sevgi barely glanced at the yanked-in focus. It was in any case a little too abstract for easy human digest—sketched molecular traces and a scrawled sidebar summary about microwave effect. Later she'd tramp over to the file house and review it at her own pace. Right now she was still staring up at the ruined face of Helena Larsen. Demodynamics specialist, psychiatric assessor. Divorced, signed up for Mars not long after. COLIN got a lot like this. You split from all you've known, why not. Your life's columnar supports are crumbling all around you, you probably need the cash. Three years, the minimum qualified professional tour of duty, seems suddenly reasonable. On Mars you earn big, and for the short-timers at least there's fuck-all to spend it on. You'll come home wealthy, Helena Larsen. You'll come home with tales of an alien skyline to tell the children you'll some-day have. You'll have the cachet of the trip to trade off and the résumé potential it represents. You'll have moved on. Got to be better than sitting in the ruins of your old life, right? Better than clinging to whatever fragments you—

"Investigator Ertekin?"

She blinked. She'd missed what Coyle was saying to her.

"Sorry, just thinking," she said truthfully. "What, uh—?"

"I asked," said the cop, with the heavy emphasis of repetition, "whether you think it's likely that whoever did this could still be alive?"

The air in the virtuality, already a breezeless sterile cool at odds with the desert landscape, seemed to slip a couple of degrees lower. Norton looked at Sevgi, and she felt the tiny, almost imperceptible nod come up from the roots of intui-tion.

"Someone blew the hatches," Rovayo pointed out.

"That could have been the automated systems." Coyle cast a hopeful glance at the two COLIN reps. "Right?"

"It's a possibility," Sevgi said. "Until we see the damage to the automated sys-tems and the n-djinn, it's hard to know how the ship would behave on its own."

But there was a steady thrum building in the back of her head now, like en-gines under decking, like the rumble of Ethan's voice, reading to her the time she came down bad with the flu, passages out of Pynchon that came and went blur-rily as she faded in and out of focus with the fever. She snapped the memory shut. Leaned into the cold sparkle of the syn, like wetting her face in a fountain. "Look, we'll know if anyone got out alive when—"

"—the swabs come in," Rovayo finished for her. "Right. But in the meantime, what do *you* think? Give us the benefit of your COLIN specialist insight. *Could* someone have made it down in one piece?"

"Outside of the cryocaps, it's not likely," Norton told her. Habitual public statement caution, the COLIN watchword. "And even if they did, that still puts them a hundred kilometers off the coast. That's a long swim."

"Maybe someone came to get them." Rovayo gestured at the empty levels of the RECOVERED SURVEILLANCE adobe. "We got no satellite stream data yet, no overhead incidentals. No way to know what went on before the recovery team got there."

Coyle shook his head. "Doesn't make sense, Alicia. Recovery scrambled as soon as they had the coordinates."

"Who'd they use?" Sevgi asked, trying to sound neutral. NYPD had a long-standing superiority complex when it came to the Rim's subcontract policy on emergency services, an attitude born of, and largely borne out by, New York's disastrous flirtation with similar schemes in the past.

Rovayo glanced at Coyle.

"Filigree Steel, right? Or, wait." She snapped her fingers. "Did they just lose the bid to ExOp?"

"Nah, that was up in Seattle. Down here, it's still the Filstee crew." Coyle looked around at Sevgi and Norton. "They're pretty good, Filigree. Did the job well over spec. Aerial cover inside twenty minutes, drop teams deployed. No way there was time for anyone to get in first. Either this guy's dead inside with the rest of them, or he took the plunge when the hatches came off and just swam off into the sunset."

"Wrong direction then," said Norton drily.

Coyle peeled him a glance. "I was using a metaphor there."

"He does that sometimes," Rovayo said, deadpan.

"I don't think he went into the water," said Sevgi. "You'd have to be suicidal or clinically insane to make that mistake."

Coyle stared at her. "Were you there earlier today, Ms. Ertekin? Did you see the in-flight cuisine? You're trying to tell me this motherfucker might *not* be insane?"

Sevgi grimaced. "This *motherfucker*, as you put it, had spent the last several months completely alone in deep space. Alone, that is, apart from the sporadic company of fellow crewmembers revived long enough to carve edible meat from. At a minimum, he is mentally unbalanced, yes, but—"

Rovayo snorted. "No shit, he's unbalanced. You'd have to be fucking *unhinged* to—"

"No." The force in the single syllable closed the other woman down. Words marched out of Sevgi's mouth, words she remembered Ethan saying, almost verbatim. A cold conviction was growing in her. "You wouldn't have to be insane to do these things. You'd just have to have a goal and be determined to attain it. Let's get this straight, early on. What we've seen aboard *Horkan's Pride* are not the symptoms of insanity; they are only evidence of great force of will. Evidence of planning and execution shorn of any socially imposed limitation. Any mental problems this person was suffering by journey's end are going to be a *result* of that execution, not a cause."

"Speaking of planning," said Coyle. "You going to tell me you guys don't pack these Colony transports with emergency supplies? You know, like *food*? In case someone wakes up unscheduled?"

"Nobody wakes up unscheduled," said Norton.

"Well, excuse the fuck out of me." The big cop looked around elaborately. "I'd say on this trip someone did exactly that. Woke up unscheduled and very fucking hungry."

"Or they stowed away," Rovayo suggested. "Would that work?"

"That'd be next to impossible," said Sevgi. "There's a lot of security written into the launch protocols. You'd have to hack it all in the time between the ship's systems being enabled and the decouple."

Rovayo nodded. "And how long is that?"

"About forty-five minutes. It takes these older ships longer to boot up."

"Look, about this food." Coyle wasn't letting go. "We all know the Colony Initiative don't like to spend any of the cash they tax out of the rest of us on anything resembling people, but are you guys really so fucking tight you won't spring for a box of survival rations? What happens if something goes wrong midflight?"

Norton sighed. "Yeah. Okay. All COLIN vessels have onboard contingency rations. But that's missing the point. On each run, you'll have two qualified spaceflight officers, cryocapped separately from the hu—the passengers."

"The hu what?" Rovayo asked curiously.

Human freight. Sevgi finished Norton's slip of the tongue silently for him. *Yeah, we have some lovely terminology over at COLIN. Contractual Constraint. Soft Losses. Quiet Facts. Profit Drag. Public Perception Management.*

She weighed in. NYPD commandments. *Fuck finer feelings and circumstance, you back your partner up.* Brusquely: "What we're telling you is that there are two systems. The passenger cryocaps are wired to default into frozen. There's no point them being awake in an emergency. They're civilians. What are they going to do, run around screaming *Oh no, we're all going to die?* Onboard air's too expensive for that shit. They've got nothing to contribute in a situation like that. So anything goes wrong, the whole system locks. You can't get it open until the ship docks."

Coyle shook his head. "Yeah, and what if the thing that goes wrong is that it thaws out?"

"How?" Sevgi gave him one of her best *only-an-idiot* looks. "You're talking about deep space. You know how fucking cold it is out there? There isn't enough ambient heat anywhere in the vessel to bring that system up a single degree from emergency frost. The only thing that might is the reactor, and that's programmed to jettison if it fails."

"Yeah, okay," Rovayo doing a little partner support of her own. Sevgi caught herself in sudden sympathy. It was like passing an unexpected mirror. "So what about this other system? The spaceflight guys. They're wired to wake up, right?"

"They *can* wake up." Norton picked up again. "Under certain circumstances. If there's a navigational emergency. The trajectory fails or you get unscheduled activity from the drive datahead maybe. Then the ship brings those two capsules up. Your spaceflight guys fix the problem, or call in the recovery if they can't."

That's spaceflight guy, singular, people. The sour voice in her head would not shut up. *Because—you taxpayers don't need to know this, of course—for about a decade now we've been cutting back on emergency personnel by 50 percent. It's just so fucking expensive, you see, wasting a perfectly good cryocap berth like that, after all this stuff almost never happens, right, and even if it does who needs two pilots to fix it when one can manage. That's just overmanning, right?*

"Right," said Coyle. "And these guys got to eat and drink, right?"

"Yes, of course." Norton gestured. Sevgi let him get on with it. Maybe from the long stay in virtual, her head was starting to hurt. "There's tanked water anyway, for fusion mass, for radiation shielding, for the coolant systems. Even in the backup tanks, there's more than two guys could drink even if they stayed out there for a couple of years. And obviously there's food. But the supplies are calculated on the assumption that these two guys aren't going to be up and about for very long. If it's a simple problem, they fix it and then go back to sleep. If it's not, they'll send an SOS and then go back to sleep until the rescue ship gets there."

"What if the system won't let them refreeze?" Coyle wasn't going to be shaken loose of what was apparently an endemic lack of faith in technology. Maybe, Sevgi thought sourly, he'd grown up in Jesusland and immigrated to the Rim.

Norton hesitated. "Statistically, that's so close to impossible that—"

"Not impossible," said Rovayo lazily. "Because, my memory serves me right, that happened to some poor motherfucker about seven, eight years back. Exactly that. Woke up and couldn't get refrozen, had to sit out the whole voyage."

"Yes, I remember that, too." Norton nodded. "The cryocap spat him out and wouldn't reset, some kind of systems glitch. Guy had to sit out the trajectory until the recovery crew got to him. See, if the transport is close enough to point of origin, emergency systems turn it around and send it back to meet the rescue ship, which cuts the retrieval time right down. If they're closer to the end of the journey, they burn emergency fuel to speed up. However you cut it, you don't need that much food to keep someone alive until they're recovered."

Well, Sevgi parenthesized to herself, *not if you luck out and get a friendly orbital configuration anyway. But we don't like to talk about that, guys. That's what we in the trade like to call a Quiet Fact. Sort of thing even accredited COLIN staff won't necessarily have pointed out to them. Sort of thing you might have to dig a little for.*

But as *Horkan's Pride* fell silently, implacably homeward, Sevgi had done that digging. *Detective Ertekin has a sound analytical approach to casework,* her first-year homicide report had come back one time, *and shows energy and enthusiasm in absorbing fresh background detail. She has a talent for adjusting rapidly to new circumstances.* She did her homework, they were trying to say, and here, nearly a decade later in the heart of COLIN, she did it again. Did her homework and found that the distance between Earth and Mars could vary by up to a factor of six. Mars, it seemed, orbited elliptically, and that plus the different orbital velocities of the two planets meant that they could be anything between about sixty and about four hundred million kilometers apart, depending on when you chose to span the gap. Even oppositions—Mars and Earth catching up to each other, running temporarily neck and neck, so to speak—could vary by a million or more klicks. COLIN transit launches took some account of these variations, but since the cycle worked itself out over several years, you couldn't just wait around and send all your traffic at the short end. That semi-famous unscheduled wake-up guy eight or so years back had gotten lucky, hit somewhere near an opposition with the trajectory down well under the hundred million klicks.

This time around, their homecoming guy hadn't been so lucky. *Horkan's Pride* ate the thick end of the cycle, was coming home across more than three hundred million kilometers of cold, empty space.

And no lunch stops.

"Okay," said Rovayo. "So there's no SOS because the n-djinn is down. But there's got to be provision for a manual backup, right?"

Norton nodded. "Yes. It isn't difficult to do. There are step-by-step instructions nailed up in the coms nest."

"And our guy chose to ignore them."

"So it appears, yes. He ran silent all the way home, and presumably from somewhere close to the Mars end. There's not enough food on board to do that, not even for one person. You want to sit in silence and wait out the whole trajectory, you've got to find something else to eat."

"So the guy *is* fucking cracked." The tinge of *told-you-so* in Rovayo's voice. Bending back to her original assumptions. Okay, so she'd let this be a man, but she wasn't going to believe he could be sane. "Got to be. He didn't need—"

"Yeah, he did," Sevgi said it to the air, detachedly. Time to run this for everybody's benefit. "He did need to run silent. He couldn't call in the rescue ship, and he couldn't get back in the cryocap, assuming that it would have let him, because both those options would have defeated his whole purpose."

A flicker of quiet. She saw Rovayo shoot an exasperated glance at Coyle. The big cop spread his hands.

"The purpose being?"

"To get home free."

"Seems a little extreme," said Rovayo sardonically. "Wouldn't you say?"

"No, it's not extreme." Sevgi could hear herself talking, but the words seemed suddenly heavy, hard to get out. The syn was deserting her, retreating from her speech centers, leaving her with the fading light of the inspiration but no clear way to get it across. She fumbled for clarity. "Look, spaceflight's a closed system. You dock in orbit, that's quarantine control, post-cryocap medical checks, ID download. A week, usually, before they let you down the nanorack elevator and out. Whoever this guy was, he didn't want to go through all that. He couldn't afford to arrive cryocapped with the others, and he certainly couldn't afford to be rescued. Both those options end at the nanorack. He needed to walk away unseen, unregistered. And this was the only way he could do it."

"Yeah, but *why?*" Coyle wanted to know. "Six or seven months of cannibalism, isolation, probable insanity. Risking a splashdown at the end of it all. Plus hotwiring the crycocap, that's got to carry some attendant risk, right? I mean, come on. How badly could you want to get *home free?*"

A wry grin from Norton, but he said nothing. Not for public consumption. Sevgi waved the diplomacy away.

"That's missing the point. It's no secret that there are people on Mars who wish they'd never signed up, who'd like to come home. But they're the grunts, the cheap labor end of the Colony effort. This man was not a grunt. We're talking about someone who's at ease manipulating cryogen and medical datasystems, who's able to operate the onboard emergency landing protocols—"

"Yeah, that's something else I don't get," Rovayo said, frowning. "The whole trip, this guy's taking the passengers in and out of the cryocaps to feed off. Why not just kill one of them and stick himself in the empty freezer in their place."

"Kind of hard to explain when they take you out at the other end," said Coyle drily.

His partner shrugged. "Okay, so you set the cryocap to wake you up a week out from home. Then—"

Norton shook his head. "Can't be done. The cryocaps are individually coded at nanolevel for each passenger, and they've got very rigid program parameters. They'd reject a different body out of hand. You'd need to be a cryogen biotech specialist to get around that, and even then you probably couldn't do it midtransit. That kind of coding gets done while the ship's in dock. They take the whole system down to do it. And you wouldn't be able to recode an early wakeup, either, for much the same reason. The whole point of what happened here is that it was all within the existing parameters of the automated systems. There's programmed provision for bringing a passenger temporarily out of cryogen for medical procedures. There is no provision for swapping passengers around, or letting them wake up early."

"And he was smart enough, or skilled enough to know that," said Sevgi. "Think about that. He knew exactly which systems he could safely subvert, and he did it without tripping a single alarm in the process."

"Yeah, yeah, and he's a mean hand at alternative cuisine," growled Coyle. "Your point is?"

"My point is, anyone with the skills and strengths this man has shown would have gone out on a qualpro tour, which means a three- to five-year gig, no requirement to renew. He could have waited, come home cryocapped and comfortably wealthy." Sevgi looked around at them. "Why didn't he?"

Rovayo shrugged. "Maybe he couldn't do the time. Three years is a long stretch when you're looking at it from the starting line. Ask the new fish up at Folsom or Quentin Two, and that's just jail time here on Earth. Maybe this guy gets off the shuttle at Bradbury, takes one look at all those red rocks, and realizes he made a big mistake, he just can't go through with it."

"That doesn't fit with the force of will he'd need to do this," said Norton soberly.

"No, it doesn't," Sevgi agreed. "And anyway, he could have called in the rescue ships as soon as he was outside the Mars support envelope. He didn't—"

"Support envelope?" Rovayo frowned inquiry at Norton. "What's that?"

Norton nodded. "Works like this. If you launch a COLIN transport from Mars to Earth and something goes wrong, something that requires a rescue, then it's only worth the Mars people coming out up to a certain point. After that point, the transport is so far along the trajectory it would make more sense to send help from the Earth end. Anyone wanting to get home would have to wait at least until the tipover point, otherwise it's all for nothing. Mars rescue brings you back and you're still stuck there, with whatever penalties COLIN chooses to enforce on top. You need the rescue to come from Earth, because that way, whatever else happens to you, you've at least made it home. They're not going to waste the payload cost on sending you back again, just out of spite."

"Just out of curiosity," said Coyle. "What are those penalties you're talking about? What do COLIN do to you if you step out of line on Mars?"

Norton shuttled another glance at Sevgi. She shrugged.

"It works the same as anywhere else," Norton said with trained care. They'd all been drilled in acceptable presentation on this one, too. "There's a suite of sanctions called Contractual Constraint, but it's what you'd expect, the usual stuff. Financial penalties set against your contract, incarceration in some serious cases. If you're a short-timer, your jail time gets added onto the contract length without compensation. So if you're homesick, it doesn't pay to act up."

"Yeah." Rovayo cranked an eyebrow. "And if you do make it back to Earth? Unauthorized, I mean."

Norton hesitated.

Sevgi said it for him. "That's never been done before."

And she wondered vaguely why she was smiling as she spoke. Cold, hard little smile. Ethan stood there in her memory and grinned back at her.

"Oho," said Coyle.

"What, *never*?" Rovayo again. "In thirty years, this has never happened before?"

"Thirty-two years," said Norton. "Over twice that if you count the original bubble crews back before the nanoforming really kicked in. Like Sevgi says, it's a closed system. Very hard to beat."

Coyle shook his head. "I still don't get it. He could have called in a rescue from the Earth end. Okay, he'd maybe do some time, but Jesus fuck, he did the time anyway, out *there*. How much worse could white-collar jail time *be* than that?"

"But he wasn't looking at just a white-collar sentence," said Sevgi softly.

"Look." Coyle wasn't listening to her. He was still looking for somewhere to dump his anger. "What I still don't get is this: why didn't you people send out the rescue ship on spec as soon as the n-djinn went down?"

"Too fucking cheap is why," muttered Rovayo.

"Because there wasn't any point." Sevgi said evenly. "*Horkan's Pride* was coming home anyway. As far as we knew, the crew were unharmed."

"Un-fucking-*harmed*?" Coyle again, disbelieving.

Norton stepped into the breach. "Yeah, I know how that sounds. But you've got to understand how this works. It was only the n-djinn that stopped talking to us. That's happened before on the Mars run, we just don't like to publicize the fact. We've had cases where the djinn goes offline temporarily, then blips back on a few days later. Sometimes they just die. We don't really know why."

He spanned an invisible cube with both hands, chopped downward. Sevgi looked elsewhere, face kept carefully immobile.

"The point is, it doesn't matter that much. The ship will run fine on automated modular systems. Think of the n-djinn as the captain of a ship. If the captain on one of those Pacific factory rafts dies, you don't have to send out a salvage vessel to bring the raft into port, do you?" A self-deprecatory smile at the rhetorical question. "Same thing with *Horkan's Pride*. Losing the n-djinn didn't affect the ship's fail-safe protocols. Mars and Earth traffic control were both still getting the standard green lights from *Horkan's Pride*. Shipboard atmosphere and rotational gravity constant, no hull breaches, cryocap systems all online, trajectory uncompromised, pilot systems active. The baseline machines were all still working, it's just the ship itself that wouldn't talk to us."

Rovayo shook her head. "And the fact that this *hijo de puta* was taking people out of the cryocaps and cutting them up, that didn't register anywhere?"

"No," admitted Norton tiredly. "No, it didn't."

"Without the djinn, there was no way to know what was going on." Sevgi droned on, partly bored, partly trying to bury her own grim conviction that Rovayo had guessed right about COLIN's real motives. Midtrajectory retrieval was still a mind-numbingly expensive call for any flight project manager to make. "The baseline system is exactly what it sounds like. It tells us if something malfunctions. There was no visible malfunction, and since the whole crew was supposed to be in cryocap, that meant—logically—there was no way for them to be harmed. We had no way of knowing any different. And the ship was on course. In a situation like that, you wait. That's how spaceflight works."

Rovayo took the tutorial edge on the last comment without blinking.

"Yeah? Well, if the ship wasn't talking to you, how was it going to dock at the nanorack?"

Norton spread his hands. "Same answer. Autonomic engagement. The docking facility takes over from the pilot systems on approach. We had no reason to think that wouldn't happen."

"Seems to me," said Coyle, "whoever did this knew your systems inside out."

"Yes, they did." *And our miserable cost-cutting souls, too.* Sevgi shook off the thought. Time to get back on track. "They knew our systems, because they'd studied them and they were highly skilled at planning an intrusion into those systems, which means a high degree of raw intelligence and insurgency training. And they were utterly committed to their own survival above and beyond any other concern, which takes an extreme degree of strength and mental discipline. And yet this same person was so terrified of being registered on arrival that they did *this* to avoid it."

Sevgi gestured around the virtuality. Aspects of the crime leapt out at them as the systems read *Focus* in the wake of her sweeping arm. Outraged data, cut-and-splice code wounding marked in siren colors, frozen footage snaps of cryocap fluids spilled across pristine floors, blood spotted on walls, and stripped-skull grins.

She drew a deep breath.

"Now does anyone want to tell me what those pixels paint?"

She wasn't that far ahead of them. Coyle's eyes changed with the understanding, anger finally doused, damped down to something else. Rovayo went very still. Norton—Sevgi twisted to meet his eyes—just looked thoughtful. But no one said anything. Oddly, it was the path 'face that took up the challenge. It thought it had been asked a question.

"The salients you describe," the confected woman said precisely, "are consistent with the perpetrator being a variant thirteen reengineered male."

Sevgi nodded her thanks at the 'face.

"Yes. Aren't they just."

They all stood there while it sank in.

"Great," said Coyle finally. "Just what we need, a fucking twist for a perp."

CHAPTER 6

The humidity loop on string seventeen went down sometime on Friday night, they figured, and once again the backup protectives failed to come online. Saturday came in foggy, so at first no one noticed when the dish covers stayed dialed up to full transparency. But when the California summer sun finally burned through the fog that afternoon and hit the glass, the incubating cultures got it full force. Sirens cut loose back at the wharf. Scott and Ren roared out there at panic speed in the Zodiac, but by the time they got into their wet suits and into the water, they'd lost pretty much everything on the string. They paddled about a bit making sure, disconnected the system, and phoned the detail in to Nocera. Then they powered back to the wharf in glum and dripping silence. Scott didn't need to voice what they both knew. Seventeen was loaded to the roots—it had about a quarter of the month's crop on it. When Ulysses Ward got back from checking the deep trellis range and heard about this, he was going to go ballistic. It was the third time that summer.

"What happens when you buy your software out of fucking Texas," grinned Nocera, feet up on the console while he and Scott sat waiting for some hired-down-the-wires San Diego machine consultancy to trace and fix the fault. "Ward's never going to learn. You want Rim quality, you got to pay Rim prices."

"It's not the software," Scott said, mainly because he knew it wasn't, but also because he was getting tired of Nocera's constant cracks. "It's the seals."

"It fucking is the software. Ward got cheap and cheerful from a bunch of Jesusland hicks probably think altered carbon's what you buy for indoor barbecues. Those guys are running five years behind the stuff coming out of the valley now, minimum."

"There's nothing wrong with the software," Scott snapped. "We had this same shit back in May and that was before the fucking upgrade." *Before you hired on,* he didn't add. And then his own language caught up with him and he colored with the shame. He'd never sworn like that before he started working out here.

"Yeah. Same shit, same shit software." Nocera wasn't going to shut up, he was on a roll. He gestured around the con room. "Ward buys his upgrades the same place he got the original system. Cow Tech, Kansas. Shat fresh out of a longhorn's ass."

"You said Texas a minute ago."

"Texas, Kansas?" Nocera made a dismissive gesture. "In the end, what's the fucking difference? It's all—"

"Leave him alone, Emil. We all got to be born somewhere."

Carmen Ren stood in the doorway of the control room, unlit spliff tucked into the corner of her mouth and hands in her coverall pockets. She'd stomped off as soon as she'd peeled off her wet suit, without a backward word. Scott knew by now not to go after her when she hit that mood. Not till she'd smoked it down a little, leastways.

Nocera sighed weightily. "Look, Carm, it's not like that. I don't get on Osborne here just 'cause he's a fence-hopper. Lot of people would around here, but not me. I figure a man's got to make a living, even if he has to tunnel under a fenceline to do it. But he's not going to sit here and tell me that cheap crap they spin up in Jesusland works as well as Rimtech. Because it just ain't fucking so."

Ren gave Scott a weary smile.

"Ignore him," she said. "With Ward out of sight, there's no telling how much custom-nasty shit Emil here's put up his nose today."

Nocera wagged a cautionary finger at her. "You pick your chemicals, Carm. I'll pick mine."

"This?" Ren removed the spliff from her mouth and held it aloft for general scrutiny. "This is a *cheap* drug, Emil. I won't be the one coming around begging for a sub the week before payday."

"Hey, fuck you."

She put the spliff back in her mouth, crushed the end to life between a callused thumb and forefinger, and drew hard. The ember flared up with a clearly audible splintering crack. She sighed out a cloud of smoke, looked at Nocera through it for a moment.

"Thanks," she said. "I've had better offers this week."

"What, like from altar boy here?"

Scott felt himself flush again, hot on hot. Carmen Ren was the most gorgeous woman he'd ever seen in the flesh, and since they'd been on field maintenance together he'd been seeing a lot of that flesh. She stripped off in the tackle room with an utter lack of self-consciousness that he knew Pastor William would have called prideful and unwomanly. Scott politely turned his back whenever she got naked that way, but he still caught glimpses as she zipped herself into the wet suit or peeled unexpectedly to the waist in the Zodiac when it was hot. Her skin was like pale honey, and the curves of her body were subtle yet unmistakable even in the shapeless Ward BioSupply coveralls they all wore around the wharf. But more than all that, Carmen Ren had long, straight hair that spilled like black water onto her shoulders whenever she unpinned it from the spiderform static clip that kept it up, and a curious, negligent way of tipping her head to one side as she did it. She had liquid dark, ironic eyes that lifted delicately at the corners and cheekbones like ledges on some Himalayan peak, and when she concentrated on something, her whole face took on a porcelain immobility that splintered his heart like the sound of that ember in the spliff.

The last few weeks, Scott had found himself thinking about Ren a lot when he went home at night, and in a way that he knew was sinful. He'd done his best to resist the urges, but it was no good. She floated into his dreams unbidden, in postures and scenarios that made him flush when he recalled them during the waking day. More than once recently he'd woken tight and hard from the dreams, his hands already on himself and the taste of Ren's name in his mouth. Worse still, he had the feeling that when Ren looked at him, she could see right through him to that sweaty core of desire, and despised him for it.

Now she was smoking, looking down on Nocera as if he were something that had just leaked out of the mulch vats.

"You really are being a disagreeable little prick today, aren't you." She turned to Scott. "You want to go get a coffee up on the wharf?"

"Uh, with you, together, you mean?" Scott bounced to his feet as she nodded. "Sure. Yeah. Great."

"Uhm, uh, with, uhm, you?" Nocera sneered, made dying-insect-leg motions with his arms. Cranked up a joke-Jesusland accent from network comedy stock. "Duh, darlin', how kin ah refuse such a *laidy*. Uhm, praise, uhm, th' everlovin' Lord."

Scott felt his fists clench. He'd been in enough scuffles back home to know he wasn't much of a fighter, and to know from looking at Nocera that he *was*. He'd seen the scars when the older man was getting into and out of a wet suit, read it also in his stance and the blank challenge of the unkind eyes. It was like looking at a later edition of Jack Mackenzie's older brother, the one who'd enlisted on his sixteenth birthday and come home a year later, sunburned and full of scalp tales from places none of them had ever heard of.

Still, he'd taken about as much of Nocera's Rim superiority as he—

Ren glided into the gap almost before Scott realized he was turning to face the other man.

"I said a coffee, Scott. Not a broken nose." She nodded at the door. "Come on. Leave this dickhead to play with himself."

"Be a lot more fun than playing with you, Ren." Nocera leaned past Ren's hip, still in his chair, still grinning. "I'm telling you, kid, I know her sort inside out. Been there, eaten the pussy. You *will* have more fun jerking off."

Scott surged forward, fists raised. The new flush slammed through him, itching at the roots of his hair and burning across his cheeks. He saw the grin slide off Nocera's face, replaced with a sudden, speculative interest. The other man's boots swung unhurriedly off the console to the floor. Scott knew then he was going to get a kicking, but *fuck* it—

And suddenly he was pressed up against Ren. Flash scent of her hair, still damp, warmth of skin and soft curves right underneath his eyes, and then she pushed him firmly back toward the door. The look on her face wasn't friendly.

"Get out," she said, firm as the hand on his chest. "Wait for me upstairs."

He went, stumbling a little, shame and relief pulsing through him in about equal quantities. The door closed behind him, shutting down whatever Nocera was sneering to a barely audible murmur. Ren's angry tones trod it down. He wanted to stay and listen but. . . .

He went quietly along the bulb-lit metal corridor, up the clanking metal steps to the topside offices, and out into the late-afternoon sunlight, still breathing tightly. He crossed to the rail on one of the wharf's access gantries and gripped the carbon-fiber weave in both fists as if he could crush it. He stared down at his whitened knuckles.

. . . *fucking Nocera, fucking Rim assholes, fucking* place . . .

But he'd *known,* a small, calm part of himself came and reminded him. He'd *always* known what it was going to be like. He'd known because Uncle Leland, who'd been Rimside before he was born, had told him all about it. Pastor William had told him, too, in bitten-off hellfire-tinged terms. His mother had wept and told him, again and again. His friends had jeered and told him.

Everyone had told him, because everyone knew what they thought of Republicans out on the godless Rim. Hard grind and hatred, it was all they'd offer him. They'd use him up, spit on him while they were doing it, and if the immigration bogeys didn't get him, then debt and the gangmasters would. He'd have no rights there, no one to turn to. He'd be nothing, worse than nothing, one of the silent service underclass that were cheaper than machines and had to be as quiet, as uncomplaining and efficient or else *bang*, your average high-tech high-demand Rim citizen there just went right ahead and junked them for something that'd do the job faster, cheaper, better.

Still, I won't tell you not to go. Leland, the last week before Scott skipped, parked by Scott's side on the split-rail fence, watching sunset smear the sky up over the mountains. He didn't know it, but Scott had already paid the handler in Bozeman the upfront half. He was due on the truck next Tuesday. *I won't tell you not to go, because there's nothing here for you that's better. People hate the Rim, and there's a pot of good reasons for that, but there'll be chances out there you won't get here if you stay your whole God-given life. The money hasn't settled like it has here. It's still moving, it's not all classed up and fossilized. You can track it out there, go where it is. Get lucky, you can maybe carve some off for yourself. And if you stay, get legal, get a family, then your kids can maybe have even more. You know, schooling's free in the Rim. I mean, really free, and real schooling, not the bullcrap we get here.*

They sat for a while, and evening deepened the colors of the sunset. The air started to chill.

Why'd you come back then, Leland? he'd asked finally.

Leland grinned and looked down at his work-worn hands. *You always ask the good ones, Scotty. Why'd I come back? I don't know, maybe I just wasn't strong enough to stay away. I missed this place something grim, you know. We both did, me and your pop. We always talked about coming back, and I think that's what helped us stay away. Then when Daniel had his accident, there was no more talk, no one to talk to, and that missing started to really gnaw at me.*

Scott knew the gnawing well. Sometimes he beat it, for days at a time, especially in the early days, the early shit jobs, when work wore him down and left him no strength or time for anything but itself and sleep. But the longing always came back, and now, now he had time, and money put away, he could feel the same crumbling that must have taken Leland. He said his prayers every night, the way he'd promised Mom he would, went to a Christian church when he could find one, but lately he was confused in the things he thought about praying for.

"You okay now?"

He started. He hadn't heard Ren come up behind him.

"Where I come from," he said tightly, straight off, "you don't talk that way in front of women."

She inclined her head, gave him a gentle smile. "Well, where I come from we don't segregate our speech. But thanks, anyway. It was a nice thought. Especially since Nocera would have walked all over you. He's an asshole, Scott, but that doesn't mean he can't handle himself."

"I know that. I seen his type before."

"Have you?" She examined him closely for a moment. Raised an eyebrow. "Yeah, you have, haven't you. Well then, that was a very brave thing you tried to do."

He felt the bloom of something inside. Felt it wither again as Ren shook her head at him.

"Pretty fucking dumb, but very brave. Shall we go and get that coffee?"

Ward BioSupply had begun life as one of several marine biotech start-ups working off the Kwok commercial wharf complex, but over time it had absorbed a lot of the neighboring competition and now sprawled across the north end of the complex in a patchwork collection of office prefabs, scaffolded sub docks, and newly built warehousing. To find anything that didn't belong to Ulysses Ward, you had to walk one of the narrow linking gantries over to the south side, where a run of eateries with sea views catered to the wharf's workers.

They ducked into a place called Chung's, which was widely reckoned to be the best of the caffeine joints and had a set of displays running club footage from the Singapore bloodbeat scene.

"This is good," Ren said, gesturing at the screens with her coffee mug. "Beats that saccharine shit they pipe in on site."

"Yeah." Gruffly—he was still smarting a little from her calling him dumb. Besides which, he quite liked the on-site music. And he didn't really approve of the massed writhing bodies rubbing up against one another's all-but-nakedness.

She drank, nodded appreciatively at the taste. "Yeah. Be good to be caffeinated, too, come to that. If Ward's going to shout at us, I want to be awake when he does it. I've been up since four this morning."

"Doing what?"

She shrugged. "Ah, you know how it is."

By which he knew she meant she had another job. And was therefore illegal like him, because out here if you were legitimate, you'd get by pretty easily on a single wage. It was the standout difference between the Rim and the Republic.

The hint of solidarity softened his sulk.

"Things'll smooth out when you've been here awhile," he offered in return. "I was working every open-eye hour, three different places, till I hooked this gig. Ward likes to run his mouth when things go wrong, but he's a pretty good boss under that."

She nodded. "I guess things must have been pretty grim where you're from, right?" she said shrewdly. "Where is that? I'm guessing Nebraska? The Dakotas, maybe?"

"Montana."

She raised an eyebrow. "Water war country. Man, that must have been tough growing up."

"They got it worse in other places," he said defensively, though he couldn't have named any offhand. "Just, well, you know. Hard to get paying work, you don't know the right people."

She nodded. *"Plus ça change."*

"Excuse me?"

"Doesn't matter." She watched the screens. "Ward say anything to you about when he'd be back?"

"Not really. Said it might be most of the day. I figure he's got to be aiming on some serious overhaul work. Usually, trip like that, trellis check, he'd be out and back in not much more than a couple of hours." He hesitated. "Carmen, you mind if I ask you a question?"

"Sure." It was said absently; she wasn't really paying attention.

"Where are *you* from?"

Sudden sidelong glance. *Now* he had her attention.

"That's a long story, Scott." She sipped her coffee. "You sure you want to be that bored?"

"I won't be. I like hearing about places I haven't been."

"Makes you think I'm from someplace else?"

But she grinned as she said it, in a way that said he was supposed to join in. He grinned back, flushing only a little.

"Come on, Carmen. You wouldn't be working for Ward if you were Rim born and bred. None of us would." He nodded around at the clientele, dropped his voice a prudent couple of notches. "Everyone in this place is from someplace else. I don't figure you for any different."

She raised an eyebrow. "Detective, huh?"

"I just pay attention," he said.

"Yeah, I guess you do."

"So come on—tell me. Where'd you swing in from?"

There was a long pause. Scott waited. He'd had these moments before with fellow illegals, the weightless gap before trust engaged, before each one shed the load of suspicion and talked together like two free Americans once would have done, back before the internationalist scum and the Chinese—*political* Chinese, he reminded himself, *you're not a racist, Scott*—broke apart the greatest nation on the face of the Earth and cast down the fractured remnants like Moses breaking the tablets.

"Taiwan," she said, and his heart welled up with the knowledge that yes, she *did* trust him. "You heard of Taiwan?"

"Right. I mean, sure." Falling over himself in eagerness. "That's in China, right? It's, like, a Chinese province."

Ren snorted. "They fucking wish. It's an island, and it's off the coast of China, you got that right. But we're an independent state. Written that way into every Pacific Rim trade agreement and nonproliferation pact in the last hundred years. What you call a hothouse economy, same status as the Angeline Freeport, same hyperpowered output and no one wants to fuck with it in case they break it and the whole Rim feels the backwash. That's where I grew up."

"So why'd you leave?"

She gave him a sharp look, for all it had been an innocent question. Scott couldn't see leaving a place that was doing that well for any reason on Earth, not if it was your home, not if you grew up there.

"I mean," he stumbled. "I guess you weren't happy there, right? But, you know, it sounds like the kind of place a person would be happy."

She smiled a little. "Well, it has its upsides. But even in hothouse economies, you got losers as well as winners. I mean, not everyone in the Freeport's a movie star or a nanotech licensee, right?"

"Got that right." He'd worked in the Freeport on and off, would never go back if he didn't have to.

"Okay, so like I said, winners and losers, if you're the loser then—"

"You don't want to talk like that, Carmen." Scott leaned across the table, earnest. "You're not a loser just on account of you gotta go somewhere else to make a better life for yourself. None of us is a loser here, we're just looking for that opportunity to get back on the horse."

For a moment, it got him a blank look. Then the confusion cleared from her porcelain face. "Ah, right. Culture gap. No, I'm not talking about losers the way you people do. I mean losers in the trade-off. Some win, some lose, the wheel goes 'round. That kind of thing."

"You people?" He tried to hide the hurt. "What do you mean, *you people*?"

"You know, guys like you." She gestured impatiently. "Old Americans, heart-landers. From the Republic."

"Oh, okay. But look, Carmen." He allowed himself a superior smile. "We're not the *old* Americans, that's the Union, that sell-out eastern scum, all their UN-loving pals. The Confederated Republic is the *New* America. We're the Phoenix rising, Carm."

"Right."

"I mean, uhm," he stumbled again, looking for language that wouldn't offend. "Look, I know probably you didn't go to a church the same way I always did, guess for you it was some kind of temple or something, but in the end it's the same thing, right?" Pleased with himself for the way he'd eased out from under Pastor William's unremitting hellfire and One True Christ ranting, seen a better light in the succession of more moderate churches he'd had to make do with over the last couple of years. "I mean whatever you call God, if you accept that God as your guiding principle the way the Republic does, then any nation that does that has to succeed, right? Has to rise up in the end, no matter what Satan does to lay snares in our path."

Ren looked at him thoughtfully. "Are you really a, uh, a Christian?"

"Yes, ma'am."

"So you belie—"

Her phone blipped at them. She fished it out and put it to her ear.

"Yeah?" Features tautening, the way he'd seen it that morning when the news about the humidity loop came through. "Got it. Be right there."

She snapped the phone off again.

"Ward," she said. "He's back, and he's pretty fucking pissed off."

Pretty pissed *off* was about right. Scott could hear Ward's bellowing through the metal walls of the con room while they were still at the far end of the corridor. He followed Ren along the narrow space, hurrying to keep up with her curiously long, rapid strides. He would have tried to get ahead of her, to go first in case Nocera was still behaving like an asshole, but there was no room to pass, and anyway . . .

The door sliced back to admit them. Ward's rage boiled out, suddenly on full audio. Scott was used to the sound, but this time he thought there was an edge on the voice he hadn't heard before, something that went well beyond anger.

". . . the *fucking point* of all this *planning* if we're—"

He shut up as he saw them. Ulysses Ward was a big, bearish man, muscular from the constant sub-aqua and surface swimming time the business demanded, balding in a way you didn't see so much of on this side of the fenceline. He flushed when he got angry, as he was now, and he punctuated his speech with aggressive motion of limbs and head. Scott had never seen him actually hit anyone, but he often gave the impression that it wasn't entirely out of the question. Nocera, perhaps wisely, had given him center stage in the con room, and he stood there now, fists clenched.

"We're back," said Ren superfluously.

"So I fucking see." Ward seemed to notice Scott for the first time. "You, get down to the sub dock and take a look at the air scrubbers on *Lastman*. Felt like I was breathing farts and fumes the last hour back, I nearly fucking had to surface it got so bad."

For about half a second, before he spotted the idiocy of it, Scott thought about refusing to leave Ren until Ward had calmed down. He swallowed instead, said: "Might be a compatibility problem, all that software we took out of, uh, *Fell 8* was—"

Ward pinned him with a glare. "And can you fix that for me if it is?"

"Well, no, but—"

"No, that's right. Because I didn't fucking hire you as a software specialist. So why don't you get the fuck down there like I asked you to and take a fucking look at what you can fucking fix for me. All right? Simple enough for you?"

Scott looked at him, knowing he was flushing. Breathed in hard, nodded on clenched teeth and lips pulled tight.

"Good, then why are you still standing here?"

Scott wheeled about and plunged back into the corridor, fury rising through him like heat. *One more month*, he promised himself silently. *One more* fucking *month, and out.* Before today, he'd thought Ward was okay, he'd thought the man was an *American*. Guy lost his temper now and then, but what real man didn't. Point was, he knew where the lines were. But now, talking that way, treating Scott like he was some just-over-the-fence liability who'd fucked up when all the time it was Scott had been warning Ward that if you were going to cannibalize plug-ins from one sub to another, you couldn't just *expect* that the systems would fall in love with each other without you ran a whole slew of up-to-date compatibility patches.

He was on the stairs down to the dock when he became aware that something had changed fractionally in the light in the corridor behind him.

He stopped on the first step, looked back.

Saw a tall figure advancing down the passageway from the other end, darkening the view along the narrow perspectives as it passed under each overhead bulb and got between Scott and the light source. This guy really was tall, and big with it, and advancing with inexorable calm. Someone not used to being stopped, someone who must not have liked the signs all over the topside offices that asked you to buzz and take a seat while you waited, one of our staff will be with you shortly, must instead have decided to just come down anyway and find whatever he was looking for.

Scott lifted an arm and waved.

"Uh, hey," he called.

The figure gave no indication that it had seen or heard him. It moved steadily along the corridor toward the con room door, seemed to be wearing a long coat and had one hand held stiffly down inside the folds of the garment—

And suddenly, out of nowhere, a lever tipped over in Scott's guts. Something was wrong. This was trouble.

He hopped off the step and jogged back up the corridor, toward the newcomer. He didn't call out again; there was no point. He knew from experience how voices boomed and echoed in the metal confines of the corridor—this guy had heard him well enough. And yes, there was definitely something in that coat-shrouded hand, he saw the way the material wrapped stiffly around it. He dropped the jog, kicked into a sprint.

They met at the door. Scott's sprint died, puddled right out of him. What he had to say dried up in his mouth. He gaped.

It was the face. His mind seemed to gibber it. It was the face, *the* face.

Right out of the End Times comics they gave out every fourth Sunday in church, the ones the little kids got nightmares over and the older kids had to earn with red ticks in Pastor William's Book of Deeds. It was the same hollow-cheeked privation and clamped mouth, the long, untidy hair hanging past the hard-angled bones of cheeks and jaw, the same burning eyes—

The Gaze of Judgment. Right out of Volume II Issue 63.

His knees trembled. His mouth worked. He couldn't—

The door hummed—he'd never noticed the noise before now—and slid back. Voices within, still angry.

The coat swirled, the stranger's right arm came free, came up swinging. Something hit Scott in the side of the head and he stumbled, went down in an awkward, twisted-limb sprawl. Lightning switched through his head, left sparks and a wow-and-flutter effect in his ears. The Gaze lit on him briefly, then swung away again, left and into the opened con room. The stranger stepped through.

Yells erupted. Nocera and Ward, almost in unison. "This is private fucking property, asshole, what do you—"

A sudden silence that sang above the numbness in his head where he'd been hit. Then Ward again, raw disbelief.

"*You?* What the *fuck* are you doing in here? What—"

Deep, soft cough—a sound he knew from somewhere.

And the screaming started.

Scott felt the sound wring sweat from his pores, turn his skin shivery-ticklish with horror. Like the time Aaron got his arm trapped in the teeth of Dougie Straker's rock breaker, exactly the same feeling—the sound of agony, of damage so massive it ripped register and recognition out of the voice that made it, left only a flayed shriek of denial that could have belonged to anyone and almost anything.

Carmen!

Scott flailed about. Panic for her got him to his knees, got him to his feet. He felt blood trickling in his hair. He stumbled and almost fell, braced himself on the edge of the door just as it started to slide closed again. The mechanism trembled against his grip a moment, then gave and sank back to full open. Scott shoved himself upright and staggered through.

He had time for one flash-burned glimpse.

Blood, everywhere, the siren color of it shocked onto the consoles and wall, what looked like a couple of fistfuls of offal from the discount end of a butcher's counter drip-sliding down the screens. Nocera was down, face turned awkwardly sideways, eyes open, cheek pressed hard to the ill-swept, dusty floor as if he were listening for rats in the understructure. More blood, a broad, wine-dark puddle of it leaking out around his midriff, tongues of the stuff twisting out through the scattered dust. Over his body, Ren and the stranger wrestled for a squat-barreled weapon—Scott made the match with the soft impact he'd heard, one of the Cressi sharkpunch guns from the cabinet upstairs. Supposed to be locked, he was *always* telling Ward that, but—

Ward lay on his back beyond.

More blood again, the big man thrashing and slithering in it, clutching, Scott saw with numb horror, at a raw red hole where his belly had been. Shredded tissue hung in ropes out of him, was clotted on the floor and smeared on his fingers like some red-stained cake mix he'd stuck his hands into. Ward's mouth was a gaping pink tunnel—you could see right down to the molars and a trembling whitish yellow tongue—and the screams came up out of it in sickening waves. His eyes clawed onto Scott as he stood in the doorway, nailed him there. Wide and pleading, crazy with pain, Scott couldn't know whether his boss knew him or not. He made to throw himself forward into the fray, threw up instead, with punishing, gut-wrenching force. Vomit splattered in Nocera's pooling blood.

Carmen yelled, desperate.

Cough of the sharkpunch.

Another impact, this time in his neck below the ear. He grabbed for something, anything. The floor came up. Blood and vomit, warm and wet in his face as he hit. He tried to get his mouth closed or twisted clear, failed in the attempt. The hot acid stink and taste—his stomach flipped again, weakly. His legs flexed like a crippled insect's. Vision dimming out on a pool of red and flecks of yellow-white. He groped after a prayer, fumbled it, couldn't get his mouth to work, made a handful of scrabbling words in his head—

Our Father . . . deliver me not . . .

And black.

CHAPTER 7

By evening, the news was all bad.

Genetic trace turned up a human occupant aboard *Horkan's Pride* unaccounted for by any of the scattered corpses. It wasn't hard to separate out the trace: it came with the full suite of modifications grouped loosely under the popular umbrella term *variant thirteen.* Or as Coyle had put it, *a fucking twist.*

They had a manhunt on their hands.

Recovered audiovid remained stubbornly the least filled section of the investigation model. There were scant fragments of satellite footage, from platforms busy about other business and nowhere near overhead. A weather monitor geosynched to Hawaii had taken some angled peripheral interest when *Horkan's Pride* dumped itself into the Pacific, and the Rim's military systems had registered the incursion while the ship was still in the upper atmosphere, but abandoned close interest as the COLIN dataheads passed on what they knew. *Horkan's Pride* had jettisoned its reactor as part of the emergency reentry protocols, carried no weapons, and was plotted to land harmlessly in the ocean. One of the milsats watched the ship complete the promised trajectory and then promptly went back to watching troop movements in Nevada.

None of the recovered footage showed any sign of an attempted pickup prior to the arrival of the coastal crews. Nor were there any helpful images of a lonely figure casting itself into the ocean. None of it was conclusive, even enhanced as far as state-of-the-art optics allowed, but neither did any of it provide anything approaching a useful lead.

They had a manhunt on their hands, and nowhere to start.

In the hotel, Sevgi sat and ate with Norton, food she didn't want and conversation she wasn't up to. The restaurant's romantic low-lighting scheme felt like darkness crowding her eyes at the edges. The syn had crashed, definitively.

"How do you feel about this?" Norton asked her as she picked disinterestedly at an octopus salad.

"How do you think?"

It was deflection, something—*yeah, the* only *fucking thing*—she'd learned from the department-paid counseling sessions after Ethan and the rest of the shit came down. The specialist had sat across the room from her, smiling gently and pushing back every question she'd asked him with the same infuriating elicitation techniques. After a while, she started to do the same thing to him. Not helpful, she supposed, but it had brought the sessions to a rapid close, which was what she wanted. *I can't help you if you won't help me,* he'd said at the end, an edge of anger finally awake in his soporific, patient voice. He was missing the point. She didn't want to be helped. She wanted to do damage, gashed red, bleeding, and screaming damage to all and any of the bland facets of social restraint that meshed her about like spiderweb.

"Nicholson's probably going to kick," Norton said quietly. "He'll say you're conflicted."

"Yeah."

"Not enjoying your octopus, then?"

"I'm not hungry."

Norton sighed. "You know we can let this one go if you want, Sev. Tsai's guys don't want us here anyway, and RimSec would just love the chance to flex its secessional muscle. If this guy didn't drown in the Pacific, he's on their land now. Added to which, the fact he's a thirteen pretty much makes it an UNGLA matter. Why don't we just step back and let the UN and the Rim fight it out for jurisdiction."

"No fucking way." Sevgi tossed her chopsticks onto the plate. She sat back. "I didn't join COLIN for an easy ride, Tom. I needed the money is all. And this is as good a way to earn it as busting black-market Marstech or chasing cultists away from the racks. Did you fucking *see* what he did to those bodies? Helena Larsen had a fucking life waiting for her when she got home. This is the first worthwhile thing I've done in over two years. This is *ours.*"

Norton looked at her in silence for a moment. Nodded. "All right. I'll have Tsai upload the CSI files to COLIN New York. That should take the ambiguity out of the situation. What do you want to do about Coyle and Rovayo?"

"Retain them. Joint task force, indispensable local law enforcement support." She found energy for a grin. "Should play well with the Rim media. COLIN fucks up and spills one of their transports into the Pacific, West Coast cops ride to the rescue. It'll open some doors for us."

"And save us some legwork."

"Well, there's that. You know the Bay Area pretty well, right? Got a sister here?"

Norton sipped at his wine. "Sister-in-law. Brother moved over here about fifteen years ago, he's a special asylums coordinator with the Human Cost Foundation. You know, screening, social integration program. But it's probably her you heard me talking about. Megan. We, uh, we get on pretty well."

"You going to see them while we're here?"

"Maybe." Norton frowned into his drink. "How much of this are we going to let the media have?"

Sevgi yawned. "Don't know. See how it goes. If you're talking about the variant thirteen thing, I vote we keep a lid on it."

"*If* I'm talking about the variant thirteen thing? Gee, I don't know, do you think I could be? This is me, Sev. Do you think you could drop the *say-what* casual act for a while?"

She stared off into the gloom of the restaurant. Her eye caught on an underlit motion ad from the fifties—some nanotech dream of change, a ripple of green and blue marches across Martian red to the horizon, a bright new sun rises in synchrony.

"It'll be enough to make him out a stowaway and a criminal," she said carefully. "Say that he murdered members of the crew, keep the details back to screen out all the crank calls we're going to pull down. Bad enough that he's back from Mars. Telling them he's a thirteen as well is just asking for trouble. You saw the way Coyle reacted. Remember Sundersen last year? We don't need another Abomination Among Us panic on our hands."

"You think they'd go that way again? After the spanking they all got from the Press Ethics Commission?"

Sevgi shrugged. "The media likes panic. It boosts viewing."

"Are we going to give race type?"

"If and when Organic Trace get it for us. Why?"

"I'm wondering," Norton said softly, "if he's Chinese."

Sevgi thought about it for a moment. "Yeah. There's that. Don't want a replay of Zhang fever. That shit was fucking awful. Least with Sundersen, no one died."

"Apart from Sundersen."

"You know what I mean. You ever see that lynching footage? They made us watch it in school." Sevgi brushed fingertips to her temples. "I can still see it in here like it was fucking yesterday."

"Bad times."

"Yeah." She pushed her plate away and bridged her arms in the space it left.

"Listen, Tom, maybe we should run silent on this whole thing. For the time being, anyway. Just tell the media everybody died in the crash, including this guy. It's not like there's a plausibility problem with that, after all. Shit, *we* still haven't worked out how he survived."

"On the other hand, if we get a photo ID off the trace—"

"Big if."

"—then broadcasting it'd be our best chance of nailing this guy."

"He can change his face, Tom. Any backstreet salon in the Bay Area'll do it for a couple of hundred bucks. By the time we get a face out to the media, he'll have peeled it and gone underground. Gene trace is the only thing that's going to work here."

"If the gene code is Chinese, and that gets out, then you're up against the same problem."

"But it'll be a specific code we're looking for."

"It was a specific face they were looking for with Zhang. I don't recall it making much difference. Hell, Sevgi," Out of nowhere, Norton burlesqued Nicholson for her. "You know those damn people all look alike anyway."

Sevgi smeared a smile. "I don't think it's like that out here. This isn't Jesus-land."

"You got idiocy everywhere, Sev. The Republic isn't running the only franchise. Look at Nicholson—New York born and bred. Where does he get it from?"

"I don't know. Faith Satellite Channel?"

"Hall-e-*lu*-jah! Praise the *Lord*, Jesus gonna come and *cut* my taxes."

They both smirked a little more, but the laughter wouldn't come. The bodies from the virtual still hung around them in the gloom. Presently, a busboy came and asked if they were done. Sevgi nodded; Norton asked to see the desserts. The busboy gathered the plates and headed off. It dawned slowly on Sevgi that he was peculiarly gaunt for his age, and that his speech had been oddly patterned, as if it hurt him to talk. His features looked northern Chinese, but his skin was very dark. The realization hit her liquidly in the stomach. She stared after the retreating figure.

"Think that's one of your brother's success stories then?" she asked.

"Hmm." Norton followed her gaze. "Oh. Doubt it. Statistically, I mean. Jeff told me they get a couple of thousand new black lab escapees a year, minimum. And he's mostly in management anyway, trying to keep the whole thing together. They got nearly a hundred counselors working, on and off, and they're still swamped."

"Human Cost's a charity, right?"

"Yeah. The Rim gives them a budget, but it's not what you'd call generous." A sudden animation flooded her partner's voice. "And then, you know, it's tough work. Kind of thing that wears you down. Some of the stories he's told me about what comes out of those black labs, I don't think I could do it. I don't really understand how Jeff can. It's weird. When we were younger, it always looked like I was going to be the one with the justice vocation. He was the power-and-influence man, not me. And then"—Norton gestured with his wineglass— "somehow he's out here doing charity work and I end up with the big job at COLIN."

"People change."

"Yeah."

"Maybe it's Megan."

He looked up sharply. "What is?"

"Maybe that was what changed him. When he met Megan."

Norton grunted. A waiter came by with the dessert cart, but nothing appealed. They settled for gene-enhanced coffees, for which the place was apparently famous, and the bill. Sevgi found herself staring at the antique Mars motion ad again.

"You know," she said slowly, because they'd both been skating around it all evening, "the real issue isn't who this guy is. The real issue is who helped him get home."

"Ah. That."

"Trick out the fucking ship's djinn? If he was capped and the capsule thawed him, that should have triggered some kind of alarm all by itself. Before he even woke up, let alone had time to start hacking the systems. And if he wasn't capped, if he did stow away, then the n-djinn wouldn't have allowed the launch in the first place."

"You think Coyle and Rovayo spotted that? I tried to steer past it."

"Yeah. *That's happened before on the Mars run, we just don't like to publicize the fact. Sometimes they just die.* Nice shot."

Norton grinned. "True as far as it goes, Sev."

"Yeah. Maybe a dozen times in sixty-odd years of traffic. And for my money, you're talking hardware-based failures every time."

"You don't think they'll bite?"

"What, the secret flaws of the n-djinn AI?" Sevgi pulled a face. "I don't know, it's got appeal. Machine no match for a human and all that shit. And everyone likes to be let in on a secret. Sell people a conspiracy, their whole fucking brain will freeze up if you're lucky. Baby-eating secret sects, a centuries-old plot to enslave mankind. Black helicopters, flying eggs. Shit like that plays to packed houses. Critical faculties out the lock."

"And meantime—"

"Meantime"—Sevgi leaned across the table, all humor erased from her face—"we both know that someone else on Mars with some serious machine intrusion skills had a hand in this. Our mystery cannibal was capped along with the others, which means heavy-duty identity fraud, and then he was wired to wake up early, which—"

Norton shook his head. "Thing I don't get. Why wake him up so early he's got to eat everybody else to survive? Why not just trigger the cap a couple of weeks out from Earth."

Sevgi rolled another shrug. "My guess? It was a glitch. Whoever took down the n-djinn wasn't so hot with cryocap specifics. Guy wakes up two weeks out from the wrong planet, journey's start, not journey's end. Maybe that shorts out the cryocap so he can't get back in and refreeze, maybe it doesn't but he stays out anyway because he can't afford to arrive still capped and go through quarantine. But however you look at it, glitch or no glitch, he had some heavy-duty help. We're not talking about a jailbreak here, Tom. This guy was *sent*. And that means whoever sent him had a specific purpose in mind."

Norton grimaced. "Well, there's a limited number of reasons you'd hire a variant thirteen."

"Yeah."

They were both quiet for a while. Finally, Sevgi looked up at her partner and offered a thin smile.

"We'd better find this guy fast, Tom."

CHAPTER 8

He caught the last ferry across the bay to Tiburon, hooked an autocab at the other end, and rode out to Mill Valley with the windows cranked down. Warm, green-scented air poured in, brought him a sharp memory of walking under redwood canopies with Megan in Muir Woods. He put it away again with great care, handling the image at the edges like an antique photo he might smudge or a fragment of broken mirror. He watched the soft glow from passing street lamps and the lights in wood-frame homes built back from the roads, shrouded in foliage. It was as distant from *Horkan's Pride* and her cargo of carnage as he was currently from home. You looked at the well-kept, scenic-sculpted roadways, all that quiet and residential greenery, and you didn't want to believe that the man who'd crashed into the ocean that morning with only the corpses he'd mutilated for company could be out there under the same night sky.

Sevgi Ertekin's words drifted back through his mind. The wan intensity on her face as she spoke.

We'd better find this guy fast, Tom.

The cab found the address and coasted gently to a halt under the nearest street lamp. Idling there, it made scarcely more noise than the breeze through the trees, but still he saw downstairs lights spring up in the house, and the front door opened. Jeff stood there framed by the light, waved hesitantly. Must have been waiting at the window. No sign of Megan at his side.

Norton walked up the steep curve of the driveway, suddenly feeling the hours and the distance from New York. Cicadas whirred in the bushes and trees planted on either side, water splashed in the stone bowl fountain at the top. The house stood across the slope in rambling, porch-fronted spaciousness. His brother came down the steps to greet him, clapped him awkwardly on the shoulder.

"You remembered where to find us okay?"

"Took a taxi."

"Uh, yeah. Right."

They went in together.

"Megan not about?" he asked casually.

"No, she's over at Hilary's with the kids."

"Hilary?"

"Oh, right. Haven't seen you since, uh. Hilary, she's our new legal adviser at the foundation. Got twins the same age as Jack. They're having a sleepover." Jeff Norton gestured toward the living room. "Come and sit down. Get you a drink?"

The room was much the same as Norton remembered it—battered cloth-covered armchairs facing a fire-effect screen set in a raw brick facing, Northwest Native art and family photos crowding the walls. Polished wood floors and Middle Eastern rugs. Jeff served them vintage Indonesian arrack from a bar cabinet made of reclaimed driftwood. Low-level glow from the screen flames and the Japanese-style wall sconces lit his profile as he worked. Norton watched him.

"So I guess you saw we made the feeds?"

Jeff nodded, pouring. "Yeah, just been looking at it. COLIN death ship in mystery plunge. That's why you're out this way?"

"Got it in one. It's a genuine class-one nightmare."

"Well, I guess you had to start earning that big salary you pull down sooner or later." A brief, sidelong grin to show it wasn't meant. *Yeah, but somehow, Jeff, it always is, isn't it.* "How are things over at Jefferson Park these days? They treating you well?"

Norton shrugged. "Same as it ever was. Can't complain. Got a new partner, hired out of NYPD Homicide. She's a couple of years younger than me, keeps me on my toes."

"Attractive?"

"Not that it makes any difference, but yeah, she is."

Jeff came across with the two glasses, handed him one. He grinned. "Always makes a difference, little brother. Think you'll nail her?"

"Jeff, for Christ's sake." No real anger; he was too travel-worn and weary for it. "Do you really have to act like such a throwback all the time?"

"What? Girl's attractive, you don't do the math, add up your chances?" Still standing, his brother knocked back a chunk of the arrack, grinned down at him. "Come on, I can see it in your eyes. This one, you want."

Norton pressed thumb and forefinger to his eyelids. "You know what, Jeff, maybe I do, and maybe I don't. But it isn't my primary concern right now. You think we could talk about something that matters for a change?"

He didn't see the way the expression on his brother's face shifted, the way the grin faded out, gave way to a watchful tension. Jeff backed up and dropped into the opposing armchair, thrust his legs out in front of him. When Norton looked at him, he met his gaze and gestured. "Okay, Tom, you got it. Whatever I can do. But it's a long time since I had much pull in New York. I mean, I can maybe make some calls if they're on your back, but—"

"No, it's nothing like that."

"It's not?"

"No, we've pretty much got free rein on this one. Word down from on high, do what you want but clean up the mess."

"And what mess would that be, exactly? Feeds say everyone aboard is dead."

"Yeah. Since when did you trust what you see on the feeds? Truth is, we've got a live one, and he made it off the ship. This is confidential information I'm giving you, Jeff. Can't go any farther than this room, this conversation. Not even Megan."

Jeff spread his hands. Slow smile. "Hey, since when did I ever tell Megan everything? You know me, Tom."

"Yeah, well." He held down the anger, old and accustomed like the kick he got out of the Cadillac when he downshifted without the brake.

"So come on. What's the big secret?"

"Big secret is that this guy is a variant thirteen."

There was a small satisfaction in watching the way Jeff reacted. Eyes widened, mouth dropping to frame a response he didn't have. Norton thought it came off a little phony, but he'd grown used to that aspect of Jeff over the years, the actorly, slightly-larger-than-life way he deployed himself for whatever audience there was. He'd always tried to see it, charitably, as the price of admission into the charmed power circle his brother had inhabited with such aplomb when they were both younger men—but now, now that his brother had apparently become charitable himself without losing any of that mannered polish, Norton was forced to consider that maybe Jeff had always been that way, always playing himself for the cheap seats.

"You deal with this kind of thing on a daily basis, Jeff," he said simply. "I need some advice here."

"Did you call UNGLA?"

"Not yet. Way things are, it's not likely we will."

"You want my advice? Call 'em."

"Come on, Jeff. COLIN wouldn't even sign up to the Accords at Munich. You think they're going to want the UN walking all over their stuff with big international treaty boots?"

Jeff Norton set his drink aside on a tall driftwood table, distant cousin to the cabinet. He rubbed hands over his face. "How much do you know about variant thirteen, Tom?"

Norton shrugged. "What everyone knows."

"What everyone knows is bullshit hype and moral panic for the feeds. What do you *actually* know?"

"Uh, they're sociopaths. Some kind of throwback to when we were all still hunter-gatherers, right?"

"Some kind of, yeah. Truth is, Tom, it's like the bonobos and the hibernoids and every other misbegotten premature poke at reengineering that last century's idiot optimist pioneers saddled us with. Guesswork and bad intentions. Nobody ever built a human variant because they thought they were giving it a better shot at life, liberty, and the pursuit of fucking happiness. They were products, all of them, agenda-targeted. Spaceflight programs wanted the hibernoids, the bonobos were patriarchal authority's wet dream of womanhood—"

"Yours, too, huh?"

Jeff gave him a crooked grin. "Are you ever going to let that go?"

"Would Megan?"

"Megan doesn't know. It's my problem, not hers."

"That's big of you."

"No, it's weak and masculine of me. I know that. Guess I'll just never have your moral fucking rectitude, little brother. But telling Megan isn't going to achieve anything except hurt her and the kids. And I won't do that."

He picked up his glass again and lifted it in Norton's direction.

"So here's to living with your mistakes, little brother. Either that, or fuck you very much."

Norton shrugged and raised his own glass. "Living with your mistakes."

And Megan flitted through his mind, sun-splashed hair and laughter amid the redwood trunks, and later, naked body sun-dappled and straining upward to press against him on the sweat-damp sheets of the motel bed.

"So," he said, to drive out the vision, "if the bonobos were patriarchal authority's wet dream, what does that make variant thirteen?"

"Variant thirteen?" Jeff gave him the crooked grin again. "Variant thirteen gave us back our manhood."

"Oh come on."

"Hey, you weren't there, little brother."

"You're six years older than me, Jeff. You weren't there, either."

"So go read the history books, you don't want to trust what your big brother tells you. I'm talking pre-Secession. Pre-atmosphere on Mars. You got a first world where manhood's going out of style. Advancing wave of the feminized society, the alpha males culling themselves with suicide and supervirility drugs their hearts can't stand, which in the end *is* suicide, just slower and a bit more fucking fun."

"I thought they criminalized that stuff."

Jeff gave him a crooked grin. "Oh yeah, and *that* worked. I mean, *no one* takes drugs once they're illegal, right? Especially not drugs that give you a hard-on like a riot baton and all-night-long instant replay."

"I still don't believe that stuff tipped any kind of balance. That's talk-show genetics, Jeff."

"Suit yourself. The academic jury's still out on the virilicide, you're right about that much. But I don't know a single social biologist who doesn't count alpha-male self-destruct as one of the major influences on the last century's political landscape. Shrinking manhood"—the grin again—"so to speak. And right along with that, you've got a shrinking interest in military prowess as a function of life. Suddenly, no one but dirt-poor idiots from Kansas wants to be a soldier, because hell, that shit can get you killed and there have *got* to be better, and better-paid, ways to live your life. So you got these few dirt-poor idiots fighting tooth and nail for causes"—Jeff's voice morphed momentarily into a gruff Jesusland parody—"*they don't understand real good*, but generally speaking the rest are screaming human rights abuse and let me out of here, where's my ticket through college. And we are losing, little brother, all the way down. Because we're up against enemies who eat, sleep, and breathe hatred for everything we represent, who don't care if they die screaming so long as they take a few of us with them. See, a feminized, open-access society can do a lot of things, Tom, but what it can't do worth a damn is fight wars in other people's countries."

"I didn't ask for a class on the Secession, Jeff. I asked you about variant thirteen."

"Yeah, getting there." Jeff took another chunk off his arrack. "See, once upon a time we all thought we'd send robots to fight those wars. But robots are expensive to build, and down where it counts no one really trusts them. They break down when it gets too hot, or too cold, or too sandy. They fuck up in urban environments, kill the wrong people in large numbers, bring down infrastructure we'd really rather keep intact. They can be subverted, hacked, and shut down with a halfway decent black-market battlefield deck run by some techsmart datahawk we probably trained ourselves on a bighearted arms-around-the-fucking-world scholarship program at MIT. Robots can be stolen, rewired, sent back against us without us knowing it. You remember that memorial stone Dad showed us that time we drove down to New Mexico? That big fucking rock in the middle of Oklahoma?"

"Vaguely." He had a flash on a big, pale granite boulder, sheared on one side and polished on that single surface to a high gray gloss that clashed with the rough matte finish of the rest of the stone. Letters in black he was too young to read. Arid, failing farmland, a couple of stores on a sun-blasted highway straight as a polished steel rail. An old woman behind the counter where they bought candy, hair as gray as the stone outside. Sad, he remembered, she looked sad as they chose and paid. "I was what, five or six?"

"If that. I guess it would have gone right over your head, but I had nightmares for a couple of weeks after that. This Trupex AS-81 straight out of an old toy set I had, but full-size, smashing into the house, flattening Mom and Dad, standing over my bed, pulling me out and ripping my arms and legs out of their sockets. You know those fucking machines sat in that storage depot for *nine weeks* before the *Allahu Akbar* virus kicked in."

"Yeah, I read about it in school. Like I said, Jeff, I'm not here for a history lesson."

"They massacred the whole fucking town, Tom. They tore it apart. There's nothing left there anymore except that fucking rock."

"I know."

"Hardesty, Fort Stewart, Bloomsdale. The marine base at San Diego. All in less than three years. Are you surprised the military went looking for a better option?"

"Variant thirteen."

"Yeah, variant thirteen. Precivilized humans. Everything we used to be, everything we've been walking away from since we planted our first crops and made our first laws and built our first cities. I'm telling you, Tom, if I were you I'd just call in UNGLA and stand well back. You do not want to fuck about with thirteens."

"Now *you* sound like the feeds."

Jeff leaned forward, face earnest. "Tom, thirteen is the only genetic variant Jacobsen thought dangerous enough to abrogate basic human rights on. There's a reason those guys are locked up or exiled to Mars. There's a reason they're not allowed to breed. You're talking about a type of human this planet hasn't seen in better than twenty thousand years. They're paranoid psychotic at base, glued together with from-childhood military conditioning and not much else. Very smart, very tough, and not much interested in anything other than taking what they want regardless of damage or cost."

"I fail to see," said Norton acidly, "how that gives us back our manhood."

"That's because you live in New York."

Norton snorted and drained his arrack.

His brother watched with a thin smile until he was done. "I'm serious, Tom. You think Secession was about Pacific Rim interests and the green agenda? Or maybe a few lynched Asians and a couple of failed adventures in the Middle East?"

"Among other things, yeah, it was."

Jeff shook his head. "That wasn't it, Tom. None of it was. America split up over a vision of what strength is. Male power versus female negotiation. Force versus knowledge, dominance versus tolerance, simple versus complex. Faith and Flag and patriotic Song stacked up against the New Math, which, let's face it, no one outside quantum specialists really understands, Cooperation Theory and the New International Order. And until Project Lawman came along, every factor on the table was pointing toward a future so feminized, it's just downright un-American."

Norton laughed despite himself. "You should be writing speeches, Jeff."

"You forget," his brother said unsmilingly, "I used to. Now, think about the situation the way it was back then, the sinking ship of heartland masculinity, bogged down abroad in complexities it can't understand, failed by its military technology and its own young men. And then you put these new, big, kick-ass motherfuckers into American uniforms, you call them the Lawmen, and suddenly they're *winning*. No one knows exactly where they've come from all of a sudden, there's a lot of deniability going around, but who ever gave a shit about that? What counts is that these guys are American soldiers, they're fighting for us, and for once they're carrying the battle. You just sit there for a moment, Tom, and you think what effect that had, in all those little towns you just flew over to get here."

Jeff lowered the stabbing finger he had leveled on his brother, looked into his glass, and raised his eyebrows, maybe at his own sudden gust of passion.

"That's the way I read it, anyway."

The room seemed to huddle in a little. They sat in the quiet. After a while, Jeff got up and headed for the bar again. "Get you another?"

Norton shook his head. "Got to get back, get up early."

"You're not going to stay the night?"

"Well . . ."

"Jesus, Tom. Do we get along that badly?" Jeff turned from the drink he was pouring, and nailed him with a look. "Come on, there's no fucking way you'll get a ferry back across at this time of night. Are you really going to ride a taxi all the way around the bay just so you don't have to sleep under my roof?"

"Jeff, it's not—"

"Tom, I know I can be an asshole sometimes, I know that. I know there are things about me you don't approve of, things you think Mom and Dad wouldn't approve of, but Christ, you think the old man's been a saint his whole fucking life?"

"I don't know," Norton said quietly. "But if he wasn't, none of us ever caught him."

"You didn't catch *me*. I fucking *told* you about it."

"Yeah, thanks for that."

"Tom, I'm your brother for Christ's sake. Who got you that fucking job at COLIN in the first place?"

Norton shot to his feet. "I won't believe that. Tell Megan and the kids I said hi. Sorry I didn't have time to get them a gift."

"Tom, wait. Wait." Hands out, placating, drink forgotten. "I'm sorry, that was a bitchy crack. All right, look, I didn't get you your job, you were well up the list for it anyway. But I spoke well of you in a lot of ears that summer. And I'd do it again. You're my *brother*, don't you think that means something to me?"

"Megan's your wife. Doesn't that mean something to you?"

"Christ, it's not the same. She's a woman, not, not—" He stopped, gestured helplessly. "It's married life, Tom. That's how it works. You get kids, you get tired, the gloss comes off. You go looking for, for. Something. I don't know, something *fresh*, something to remind you that you're not dead yet. That you're not turning into two harmless little old people in a Costa Rican retirement complex."

"That's how you see Mom and Dad?"

"That's how they *are*, Tom. You should get down there more often, you'd see that. Maybe then you'd start to understand."

"Yeah, right. You fucked one of your bonobo refugee clients because Mom and Dad are old. Makes a lot of sense."

"Tom, you got no fucking idea what you're talking about. You're thirty-seven years old, you've never been married, you don't have a family. I mean—" Jeff seemed to be straining to reach something inside himself. "Look, do you really think Megan would care that much if she knew? I mean, sure, she'd go through the motions, the e-motions, she'd make me move out for a while, there'd be a lot of crying. But in the end, Tom, she'd do what's best for the kids. They're her world now, not me. I couldn't break her heart anymore, even if I wanted to, even if I tried. It's *genetics*, Tom, fucking genetics. I'm secondary to the kids for Megan because that's *just the way she's wired*."

"And you fucked Nuying because that's just the way you're wired, right?"

Jeff puffed out a breath, looked down, spread his hands up from his sides. "Pretty much, yeah. My wiring and hers, Nu I'm talking about. I'm the big alpha male around the foundation, the patriarch and the most expensive suit in sight. For a bonobo, that's a bull's-eye bigger than Larry Lastman's dick."

"So you just obligingly stepped into range, right? Just couldn't bear to disappoint the girl."

Another sigh. This time, Norton heard in it how the fight had gone out of his brother. Jeff dropped back into his seat. Looked up.

"Okay, Tom," he said quietly "Have it your own way. I guess you've probably never fucked a bonobo in your life, either, so you don't know how that feels, all that submission, all that broken-flower femininity in your hands like . . ."

He shook his head.

"Forget it. I'll call you a cab."

"No." Norton felt an odd, sliding sensation in his chest. "I'll stay, Jeff. I'm sorry, I'm just . . . it's been a long day."

"You sure?"

"Sure, I'm sure. Look, I don't want to judge you, Jeff. You're right, none of us is a saint. We've all done things"—*Megan, astride him in the motel, feeds him her breasts with eyes focused somewhere else, as if he's some accustomed household task. Toward the end, she closes her eyes altogether, thrusts herself up and down on his erection and into her climax, grunting* you motherfucker, oh you *fucking* mother-fucker *through gritted teeth. It will make him rock-hard just thinking about it for weeks afterward, though he's close to certain it isn't him she's talking to and when, in the aftermath, he asks her, she claims not to remember saying anything at all*— "things we regret, things we'd take back if we could. You think I'm any different?"

Jeff gave him a searching look.

"You're missing a pretty major point here, Tom." He raised his hands, palms open. There was something almost pleading in his face. "I don't regret Nuying. Or the others, because God knows Nu hasn't been the only one. I just never told you about the others after the way you reacted. Yeah, each time it's emotional complication, Tom, stress I could do without. But I can't make myself feel bad about it, and I can't make myself wish it hadn't happened. Can you understand that? Can you *stand* knowing that about your brother?"

I can't make myself wish it hadn't happened.

Norton put himself carefully back in the other armchair, gingerly, on the edge of the seat. Jeff's words were like staples taken out of his heart, a sudden easing of a pain he hadn't fully known he was carrying. The bright truth about his feelings for Megan welled up in the new spaces. He sat there trying to balance it all out for a moment, then nodded.

"Sure," he said. "I guess I can stand it. I guess I've got to." He shrugged, smiled faintly. "Brothers, right?"

Jeff matched the nod, vigorously. "Right."

"So pour me another drink, big brother. Make up the spare room. What time's Megan getting back?"

CHAPTER 9

They slept in well-worn nanoweave survival bags—*as used by real Mars settlers!*, the fraying label on Scott's insisted—but always inside. *Too many eyes up there*, Ren said somberly as they stood at the hangar door on the evening of the second day and watched the stars begin to glimmer through in the east. *It's better if we don't give them anything unusual to notice.* The abandoned airfield buildings offered shelter from both satellite scan and desert sun; the heat built up inside during the day but long-ago-shattered windows and doorways mostly without doors ensured a cooling through-flow of air. The walls in the rooms they used were peeled of all but fragmentary patches of paint, stripped back to a pale beige plaster beneath, and none of the lights worked. The toilet facilities and showers, oddly enough, did seem to work, though again without the privacy of doors and only cold water. There was no power for the elevator up to the control tower, but the stairs seemed safe enough, and once up there you had long views over the surrounding tangle of ancient concrete runways and the flat open spaces beyond.

Ren spent a lot of her time up there in the tower, watching, he supposed, for signs of unwelcome visitors, and talking in low tones with the stranger, with Him. And that last part worried Scott, for reasons he could not entirely pin down.

He supposed, finally, it was lack of faith. Pastor William had always said it attacked the so-called freethinkers first and worst, and God knew Scott had been away long enough to get contaminated, rubbing up against all the smut and doubt of West Coast life. He felt a vague, uncontrolled spurt of anger at the thought of it, the bright LCLS nights, the nonstop corrosive stimulus-ridden whirl of so-called modern living and no escape anywhere, not even in church, because God knew he'd gone *there* and tried. All that lukewarm, anything-cuddly-goes sermonizing, all the meetinghouse handholding circles and the flaky moist-eyed psychobabble that never went anywhere except to justify whatever weakling failures of moral vision the speakers had allowed themselves to fall into, three fucking years and more of it, clogging the certainty of his own vision, confusing the simple algebra of good and evil he damn fucking well *knew* was right, because that was the way it damn fucking well *felt*.

His head ached.

Had been aching, on and off, since he'd woken in the back of the swaying truck and touched the field dressing wrapped just above his eyes. The doctor Ren took him to that night outside Fresno told him it was a normal symptom for the head injuries he'd sustained; with luck it should fade in a few days.

Head injuries the stranger had given Scott. And how could that be right? At first, he couldn't make sense of it.

He will return—Pastor William's soft tones rolling out over the pulpit like thunder a long way off, thunder you knew was riding in on the wings of a storm coming right your way. They said he'd trained at one of the South Carolina megachurches before he got his ministry, and in the teeth of the gale he blew you could well believe it. *He will return, and how's that going be, you ask yourselves. Well, I'll tell you, friends, I'll tell you,* building now to a roar, *it ain't going be no cluster-hugging happy clapping day like them niggers always singing on about. No, sir, the day of His return ain't gonna be no party, ain't gonna be no picnic and skipping road right up to paradise for you all. When Jesus comes again, He will come in judgment, and that judgment going to be* hard, *hard on man and woman and child, hard on us all, because we are* all *sinners and that sin, that dreadful black sin gotta be paid out once and for all. Look in your hearts, my friends, look in your hearts and find that black sin there and pray you can cut it out of you before judgment because if you don't then the Lord will, and the Lord don't use no anesthetic when He operates on your soul.*

There was a story Scott remembered from the End Times comics, Volume III Issue 137, *The Triumph in Babylon.* Coat wrapped, the Savior stalks the mirrorglass canyons of New York with a long navy Colt on one hip and a billy club in his hand fashioned from the sweat and bloodstained wood of the cross he died on. He kicks in the frosted-glass door of a coffee franchise off Wall Street and beats seven shades of damnation out of the money changers gathered there. Painted, black-stockinged lady brokers twisting prostrate at his feet, red licked lips parted in horror and abandonment, thighs exposed under short, whorish skirts. Fat, big-nosed men in suits braying and panicking, trying to get away from the scything club. Blood and waxed coffee cups flying, screams. The capitalized *crunch* of broken bones.

Judgment!

Scott touched the bandage around his head again, figured maybe he'd gotten off lightly after all.

In the truck, staring at the gaunt, sleeping face, he'd leaned across and whispered to Ren, "Is it really Him?"

She'd given him a strange look. "Who'd you think it is?"

"Him, Jesus. The Lord, come again." He swallowed, wet his lips. "Is this, are we living in the, you know, the End Times?"

No response. She'd just looked at him curiously and told him to rest, he was going to need his strength. Thinking back, he guessed he must probably have sounded delirious with the concussion.

And then the doctor, and other helpers along the way. People Ren seemed to know well. A change of trucks, a house and a soft bed on the outskirts of a town whose name he never saw. Another long, bone-jarring night in an all-terrain vehicle and tipping out at dawn on the airfield's deserted expanse.

And then the waiting.

He tried to make himself useful. He tidied up after Ren and the stranger, put their bags and bedrolls straight every morning—and, oddly, glimpsed in among Ren's gear a Bible and a sheaf of curling hardcopy from Republican ministry download sites, some of which he knew well himself; he closed the bag gently and didn't look again, he wasn't nosy by nature, but it made him frown all the same. He put it out of his mind as much as he could. Instead he put together a table and three dining places out of pieces of junk he found lying around in the control tower block and the hangars. He discovered a wrecked and wingless Cessna in one hangar corner, halfheartedly draped in thick plastic sheeting that he cut up and made into hanging curtains for a couple of the toilet cubicles and the showers. He took care of the food. The supplies the all-terrain driver had left them were mostly pull-tab autoheating, but he did his best to make meals out of what there was, carried them up to the other two in the tower when they showed no sign of coming down to eat. Tried not to stare at the stranger. He took the painkillers the doctor had given him sparingly and he prayed, diligently, every time he ate or slept. In an odd way, he felt better about life than he had in months.

"Won't be much longer now."

He started. When night fell, the quiet in the derelict building seemed to deepen somehow, and Ren's voice jumped him like a gunshot. He looked up and saw her standing in the doorway that led through to the tower stairs. Light from the last red-gold leavings of the sunset outside meshed with the bluish glow of the camping lamps he'd lit, picked up a gleam in her eyes and along the teeth of the zip fastener on the ancient leather jacket she wore.

"What you doing?"

"Praying." Half defiant, because he certainly hadn't noticed her doing it in the last few days.

She nodded. Moved into the room and folded herself down onto her sleeping bag with unconscious grace.

"We need to talk," she said, and he thought she sounded weary. "Why don't you come over here."

He nearly jumped again. "What for?"

"I won't bite you, Scott."

"I, uh, I know that. I can hear you from here, though."

"Maybe you can. But I'd rather we didn't have to shout. Now, come over here."

Tight-lipped, he got up from his own bedroll and walked over to hers. She nodded to her left and he squatted awkwardly beside her, not quite sitting down. Her scent washed over him, faintly unclean with desert sweat—he thought she hadn't showered since early the day before. She looked into his face, and he felt the same old flip in his chest. She nodded upward, toward the ceiling and the tower above.

"You know who that is up there," she murmured. "Don't you."

Exhilaration sloshed in his guts, chased up and met the feeling she'd made under his ribs. He managed a jerky nod of his own. "It is, isn't it."

"Yeah, it is." She sighed. "This is difficult for me, Scott. I grew up in a big family that had some Christians in it, but I wasn't one of them. My religious experience is . . . very different from yours. Where I'm from, we accepted that other beliefs were possible, but we always thought they were just other ways of looking at the same truths we believed in. Less accurate, less enlightened paths. I never thought that maybe *our* truth would be the less enlightened one, that the Christians would be the ones who got it right. That—" She shook her head. "I never considered that."

He felt a warm, protective affection for her surge up inside, like flames. He reached out and took her hand where it lay in her lap, squeezed gently.

"It's okay," he said. "You were true in your beliefs. That's what counts."

"I mean, you have to believe what you see with your own eyes, Scott. Right?" Her eyes held his. "You have to believe what you're told when nothing else makes any sense, right?"

He drew a deep breath. "This makes perfect sense to me, Carmen."

"Yeah, well here's the thing, and I don't know if there's anything in your Bible that covers this, because it certainly isn't what I was taught about the final cycle.

He says"—another upward tilt of her eyes—"that he's come early, that it's not time yet and he has to gather his strength. He has work to do here, but his enemies are out there and they're still strong. And that means we have to protect him until it is time. He's chosen us, Scott. Sorted us from the, uh, the—"

"The chaff?"

"Yeah, the chaff. You saw what he did with Nocera and Ward? They were servants of the darkness, Scott. I see that now. I mean, I never liked Nocera, and Ward, well, I thought he was okay but—"

"Satan has a thousand snares," Scott told her. "A thousand masks to wear."

"Right."

He hesitated, looking at her. "Are you His—" He tasted the word, awkward on his tongue. "His handmaiden?"

"Yes. That's what he's told me. Until one of the, uh, the angels can come to take on the task. Until then, he says he'll speak through me."

He was still holding her hand. He let go, pulled his own hands back as if she were hot to the touch. He tried not to stare at how beautiful she was.

"You are. So worthy of it," he said hoarsely. "You'll be filled with light."

Then her hand was on him, on the buckle of his belt, pulling him to her. She leaned in and brushed her parted lips across his mouth. Pulled back again.

He gaped. Blood hammered in his head. Below the belt buckle, he felt suddenly trapped and swollen.

"What are you doing?" he hissed.

She gestured at the ceiling. "He's up there, Scott. Staying up there, keeping watch for us. It's all right."

"No, it's—" Shaking his head numbly. Trying to explain. "—it's a, a sin, Carmen."

He wanted to move away from her, but in moving he only tipped back over in his awkward crouch and wound up sitting slumped against the wall behind him, still on the bedroll. He hadn't succeeded in opening the distance between them at all. Or maybe—he'd wonder about it afterward—maybe he just hadn't wanted to move away from her after all.

"Carmen," he pleaded. "We can't be sinners. Not now. Not here. It's *wrong*."

But Carmen Ren only hooked a thumb inside the neckline of her shirt, looked down at her own hand, and tugged. The static seam split with a tiny crackle and she ran her thumb downward, opening the shirt on the molded lift of her breasts in their profiler cups. He could see through the clear plastic sheen to where her nipples were pressed flat against the inner surface of each cup. She looked up again and smiled at him.

"How can it be?" she asked simply. "Scott, don't you see? Don't you feel it? This is meant to be. This is a sacrament, a purification for both of us. A gift of his love. Reach inside yourself. *Don't* you feel it?"

And he did.

It had been a very long time.

He was not a virgin, not since the eleventh grade and Janey Wilkins, and Janey hadn't exactly been the only one before he left for the Rim, either, though he tried not to take pride in that because he knew pride in it was wrong. But the girls had always come to him, no way to deny it. Scott took after his mother, was tall and long-legged, and he'd hardened his upper body in his early teens, putting in all the part-time hours he could get stringing fences and doing river security for the big Bitterroot land parcels so later he'd be able to pay his own way through tenth to twelfth grade and not be a burden or have to sign up for a youth stint with the marines if he wanted to finish out his education. And then, for all his muscle and length of limb, he was still soft-spoken and kind, and it seemed from what Janey told him that that didn't hurt too much, either, when a girl was looking.

But in the Rim, something happened to him.

Maybe it was the fact that sex was suddenly everywhere—perfectly toned and tampered-with bodies, impossible to know if they were real flesh or generated v-format interfaces, but there they were, twining around each other on the big LCLS billboards, on storefront display screens, on those high-end pixelated shopping bags the women carried in fistfuls like a harvest of some big, brightly colored oblong fruit held up by the stalks and vines. There was flesh and liquid moaning on every nonfaith channel he had viewing access to, in every ad-tagged piece of mail he opened, on the *trash cans*, for God's sake, and even, once, when he was down in the Freeport, sketched holographically across the sky and booming out of massive speakers along Venice Beach. Maybe it was that, the unending barrage, the overload of it all, or maybe it was just that he was heartsick for what he'd left behind. Whatever it was, by the end of the first year, the gentle confidence he'd enjoyed back home had gone wisping off him like steam off a morning coffee left out on the porch. Had left him lonely and cold.

Carmen Ren burned through his loneliness like a falling star. Months of half-denied fantasy boiled up inside him. Her flesh where he touched it, where she guided his hands, was warm and smooth, and her tongue in his mouth tasted of some dark, unfamiliar spice. She peeled one of the profiler cups for him, dropped the jellied weight of the breast beneath into his hand. It seemed to fit there as if made for him to hold, as if intended that way. Her hands went back to his belt, loosened it and slipped inside. He went rigid as she slid fingers around the shaft of his erection, squeezed hard at her breast in reflex. She moaned into his mouth.

They worked each other out of the clothes piecemeal, stopping to kiss and touch until finally she lay back on the bedroll naked, brushed her own hands down her flanks, and opened her thighs for him. He shifted on elbows and hands, a little awkward with lack of custom, and then gasped as he slipped into her. The evening air was cool and breezy against his skin, and Carmen Ren was heated and wet inside. She smiled, shifted sideways lazily, did something with her muscles. He felt himself gripped along the length of his cock, a slippery, tugging intimacy, and then she pulled him down on top of her, lifted her thighs, and clamped them to his sides—they burned like branding in the cool—and he came, sudden and rushing unstoppable, jolting like there was current through him off some badly insulated cable.

He hung his head, stayed propped on his elbows.

"I'm sorry."

She smiled up at him again, wiggled a little and tensed her muscles around his fading hardness. "Don't be. You know how it makes me feel, seeing you lose control like that?"

"It's just." He could feel himself flushing. "Been a long time, you know."

"Yeah, I guessed that. It doesn't matter, Scott. We've got time. I like you inside me. We'll go again when you're ready." Another twitch of that coiled muscle, and a sudden widening of her eyes. "Oh. In fact."

He didn't know if it was the way she talked, casual as she lay there under him, as if they were sitting in a breakfast diner together, or maybe just the fact that he had her here, the culmination of so many damp, hopeless daydreams when he went home from Ward BioSupply alone. Or maybe it was that word, *handmaiden*, drumming around in his head, still on his lips like the dark spice taste of her. He didn't know, truth be told didn't much care. He knew, because Janey had once told him, that he was uncommonly fast back in the saddle, but even for him this was something else. He felt himself hardening right there inside her, swelling against that thing she did with those muscles, and he knew this time it was going to be all right, was going to be a long, sweet ride.

Afterward, they lay in a tangle of limbs on the bedroll, backs to the peeling wall, partially draped with the sleeping bag and Ren's jacket, gazing at the slice of evening sky just visible through the empty doorway that led outside. Scott thought the stars had never looked so bright and kind as they did tonight, not even back home. They seemed like sentinels, vibrating gently in the soft blue-black, wishing well. He told her that, and she chuckled deep in her chest.

"Postcoital astronomy," she said.

"No," he said, letting her have her joke, but firm despite it. "This is special, Carmen. We're blessed tonight."

She made a small, noncommittal noise and stretched a little.

"You know," she told him, a little later. "It could be for a long time, this hiding. It's going to be tough."

"I don't mind."

"Yeah." She rubbed a hand on the stubble of his cheek, mock roughly. "I imagine you're used to tough, aren't you."

"Will RimSec come after us?"

"I don't know." Her tone was thoughtful. "There are people I've called to tidy up back at the dock. They'll cover our traces, that'll be a start. We have friends, Scott. More friends than you'd imagine."

"And enemies," he said.

"Yeah. Enemies, too."

He twisted his head to look into her face.

"Tell me the truth, Carmen. Is this the End Times? When the world goes down in flames, and the beast rises from the ocean with the names of blasphemy written upon him? Is that who we're up against? The beast?"

She hesitated. "I don't think so. He hasn't talked about that. But I do know this much: somewhere out there, there's a dark man looking for him, and for us. This man is a servant of the darkness, and that's who we have to guard against, Scott. Both of us, whatever happens, we're servants of the light and we have to keep watch. The black man is coming. And when he comes, we have to be ready to fight, if necessary to the death. Are you ready for that?"

"Of course I am. I'll do anything. But . . ."

She shifted, pushing herself up against the wall so she could look him in the eye. "But what?"

Scott looked up at the ceiling. "Can't *He* do anything about this black man?"

"Not yet," she said gently. "At least, that's what he tells me. It isn't time. He has other concerns, Scott, other work to do. It's complicated, I know, I don't pretend to understand it all myself, but I know what's been revealed to me, and all I can do is tell you the same. We have to have faith, Scott, that's what he told me. That's a Christian strength, isn't it? Having faith, not questioning what's revealed?"

"Uh, yeah . . ."

"And, yes, maybe this doesn't make a lot of sense right now, but if we have faith, I think it will. We have a part to play in this, Scott. You have a part. There's a reckoning in the wind, and, uh, a harrowing to come. Those who stand in its way will fall, those who follow in faith will be raised up."

"Then, that means . . ." He squeezed her hand tightly. Blood thudded in him; he felt his groin stir faintly. "He *has* come in judgment. It *is* the time."

And then, abruptly, he remembered the gaunt, hollow-eyed stare of the stranger, remembered how it felt to be fixed by those eyes at close range, and looking up at the ceiling again he no longer felt the warm pulse of longed-for vindication, the affirmation of all he'd struggled to believe and hold true. Instead, out of nowhere, he remembered those eyes, that stripped-to-the-bone face, and all he felt was cold, and afraid.

A *reckoning in the wind.*

CHAPTER 10

Fifty kilometers outside Van Horn, Interstate Highway 10 laid down a lumines-
cent pale strip of gray in the desert night, stretching away toward low, horizon-
hugging mountain ranges whose names the man calling himself Eddie Tanaka
had never bothered to learn. Stars punctured the velvet blue-black above like
knife points, sharp white contrast to the dull red glowing orbs of the autohaul rigs
below as they hammered along through the darkness in both directions, following the highway with insectile machine focus. Rising drone, blastpast rush of
dark noise and wind, drone collapsing back into the distance. Passing the garish
LCLS lights of Tabitha's with a detachment no human driver could have mustered.

Well, maybe a gleech, he allowed sourly. *They don't got much use for this kind
of merchandise.*

He glanced up at the brothel's skyline billboard—the name in vampiric spi-
dery red lettering the original Tabitha would never have agreed to if she hadn't
sold up and moved to the Rim as soon as she had the capital. Behind the spiky-
thin lettering, as if caged in by it, female figures switched back and forth in full
flesh-toned color, pixeled almost—but, legal requirements and all, not quite—up
to human footage perfect.

Gleech wouldn't be out here on the highway anyway. They don't drive.

That you know of.

That Kenan knew of, and he fucking was one, smart guy.

*Smart guy? Yeah, you're some fucking smart guy, Max, out in the parking lot of
Tabitha's with whore's snot on your jacket and not even a blow job to show for it.
All your plans and schemes, your carve-out-a-new-life bullshit, look where you're
standing still. Snot on your clothes and no blow job. That's how fucking smart you
are, smart guy.*

"Smart guy . . ."

He heard his own mutter, final echo off the abrupt, tinny dispute he'd just mounted in his head, knew he was subvocalizing again, knew why. Knew, too, why he hadn't bothered, couldn't *be* bothered to push Chrissie into blowing him.

Never can fucking leave it at just one shot, can you.

He'd dumped the synadrive into his eyes a couple of hours earlier, and the thing was, this was quality product, right out of his own stash, not the stepped-on shit he shifted to the kids in Van Horn and Kent on a Saturday night. So he fucking well *knew* he'd only need that single squirt—and initially that was what he settled for, just the one dropperload dribbled down onto the quivering surface of his left eye, what the kids called pirate dosage. But pirate shots always, fucking *always*, left him feeling weirdly unbalanced, and that was on a good night—which tonight wasn't—and so as the synadrive came on, that feeling of fucked-up symmetry built and fucking *built* until it seemed like the whole right side of his body was just too slow and sleepy to bear, and so he gave in and tipped his head back one more time before he hit the road, and the fluid rolled down his right eyeball like tears.

Was a time, he recalled, *you had the disicipline. Discipline or self-respect, either way something that wouldn't let you do this to yourself.*

He was remembering that time a lot these days, staring into mirrors at rooms he abruptly couldn't believe he belonged in, wondering how he'd wound up here and where it had all leaked away to. That time when syn was a tool like any other, useful and used with a wired confidence that would have been arrogance if it hadn't all felt so fucking clean and right. Back before it all turned to shit and a black pall of smoke across a Wyoming sundown sky.

Was a time . . .

Sure. And there was another fucking time the summers never seemed to end and you'd never paid for it in your life. Remember that? Time passes, Max—get over it. Skip the fucking nostalgia, let's get where we're at.

And here he was. Snot and no blow job, out in the night.

He wiped a hand down his jacket, not bothering to look. The synadrive hooked in visual memory and sparked a link to neuromotor precision, put the gesture right on target, and his fingers came away gummy with the snot. He rubbed them back and forth, grimacing. He didn't need this shit right now, not the way things were. Not like he didn't have enough stress. He told her, he fucking *told* her he had other stuff cooking, stuff that needed managing, not like this pimping shit was his main gig—

Yeah, right, the syn told him crisply. *How many years we been saying that, exactly? Smart guy?*

Different this time. This pays off like it has been, this time next year we're out. Out for good.

And if it doesn't?

If it doesn't, we're already set up to cover. Quit worrying.

Set up to cover, yeah. And go on being a pimp for life. What you going to do about Chrissie then?

What he was going to do then, he reflected somberly, was going to *have* to do about Chrissie then, was probably something violent. Should have seen that one all along—fucking bitch always had been high maintenance, even back in Houston when she was still working street corners. Cotton-candy mane of blond and that manicured fucking Texan drawl, and now the subcute tit work he'd gotten for her, he should have fucking known she'd start with the airs and graces as soon as she settled in at Tabitha's. Acting just like she actually was the bonobo purebred they'd packaged her as. Calling him at all hours, or pushing Tabitha's management so they called instead, bitching about how she wouldn't work on account of some headache or stomach cramp or just plain didn't like some fat fuck who'd paid good money to get between her legs, sitting there on the fucking bed bright-eyed and whining *Eddie this, Eddie that, Eddie the fucking other*, forcing him to wheel out the whole nine yards of bully-threaten-cajole like it was some favorite comic routine she liked to see him do.

So why the fuck didn't you just take Serena or Maggie for that subcute work instead. Either one'd be half the fucking trouble.

In the hyperlucid blast of the syn, he knew why. But he turned on his heel and put the knowledge at his back along with the blink-blink carnal come-on of Tabitha's skyline billboard. The relative gloom of the softly lit parking lot darkened his vision. He blinked hard to adjust.

"Hello, Max."

The voice jolted him as he blinked, kicked him back to the Scorpion memories, to times and places so vivid he opened his eyes and almost expected to find himself back there, back before Wyoming in that other, cleaner time.

But he wasn't.

He was still here, in the deserted parking lot of a second-rate Texas bordello, with a sassy whore's snot drying on his fingers and too much syn for his own good sparking through his brain.

The figure detached itself from the shadows around his car, stood to face him. Soft violet light from the lot's marker lamps threw the form into silhouette, killed facial recognition. But something about the stance chased up the memories the voice had stirred. The syn gave him a name, features to put on the darkened form. He stared, trying to make sense of it.

"You?"

The figure shifted, made a low gesture with one hand.

"But . . ." He shook his head. "You . . . You're on fucking *Mars*, man."

The figure said nothing, waited. Eddie moved closer, arms raised toward a tentative hugging embrace.

"When'd you get back? I mean, man, what are you *doing* back here?"

"Don't you know?"

He made a baffled smile, genuine in its origins. "No, man, I've got no fucking—"

—and the smile collapsed, bleached out with sudden understanding.

For just an instant, the desert quiet and the rushing away of an autohauler on the highway.

He clawed across his belly, under his jacket. Had fingers hooked around the butt of the compact Colt Citizen he kept cling-padded at his belt—

He'd moved too close.

The knowledge dripped through him, and it was a Scorpion knowing from that other time, somehow sad and slow despite the speed at which he could see it all coming apart. The figure snapped forward, bruising grip on his wrist, and pinned his gun arm where it was. He flung up a warding left arm, chopped at the other man's throat, or face, or, *too close, too fucking close in*, and here came the block, he had nothing, could do nothing. A low kick took out his legs from under him, a full-body shove, and he went down. He rolled, desperately, don't let the fucker get on you with his boots, land on your back maybe, the gun, the *fucking gun*—

The cling-clip held. He got a grip of the Colt's butt again, dragged it loose and sprawled backward with a snarl of relief, raising the pistol, the Citizen had no safety, just squeeze hard and—

The figure stood over him, black against the sky. Arm down, pointing—

And something flattened him to the ground again, something with god-like force.

Muffled crack. His ears took it in, but it took him a couple of moments to assign it any importance. The stars were right overhead. He watched them, abruptly fascinated. They seemed a lot closer than you'd expect, hanging low, like they'd taken a sudden interest.

He wheezed, felt something leaking rapidly, like cold water in his chest. He knew what it was. The syn forced a merciless clarity.

He lifted his head and it was the hardest work he'd ever done, as if his skull were made of solid stone. He made out the figure of the other man, arm still pointing down at him like some kind of judgment.

"I figured you'd fight," said the voice. "But it's been a long time for you, hasn't it. Too long. Maybe that's why."

Why what? he wondered muzzily. He coughed, tasted blood in his throat. Wondered also what Chrissie was going to do now, stupid little bitch.

"I think you're done," said the voice.

He tried to nod, but his head just fell back on the gritty surface of the lot, and this time it stayed there. The stars, he noticed, seemed to be dimming, and the sky looked colder than it had before, less velvet-soft and more like the open void it really was.

Dead in a brothel parking lot, for fuck's sake.

He heard the blastpast of another autohauler out on the highway, saw in his mind's eye the cozy red glow of its taillights accelerating away into the darkness.

He ran to catch up.

part II

OFF THE HOOK

*Curtailment of freedom is a
powerful social tool and must
be deployed as such, with
wisdom and restraint. It is
therefore vital to distinguish
between the genuine and
quite complex parameters of
what is socially necessary, and
the simplistic and emotive
demands of a growing popular
hysteria. Failure to make this
distinction is likely to have
unattractive consequences.*

**—Jacobsen Report,
August 2091**

CHAPTER 11

In the end, it went down in the chapel, pretty much as he'd expected it would. Prisons like this didn't offer many places free of surveillance, but Florida's faith-based approach to rehabilitation meant that a man had a Charter-enshrined right to privacy in prayer at any hour outside of the night lockdown. No securicams, no invasive scrutiny. The theory was, presumably, that in the House of the Lord the corrections officers didn't need to be watching you, because God already was. No one seemed to have noticed that the Lord was falling down on the job. In the three months since Carl transferred in from Miami, there'd been at least half a dozen bloody showdowns in the low-light arena of the chapel. Two ended in fatal injury.

Carl wasn't sure if at some level, prison staff were giving sanction to the fights, or if quiet and massive pressure from above kept the matter clean of investigation or review. In the end, it came to the same thing. No one wanted to buck the system, no one wanted to hear about it. Sigma Corporation, by invoking religious status for its operation, effectively sidestepped the bulk of what weak administrative oversight the Confederated Republic was prepared to endorse, and glowing testimonials at the congressional level pissed all over the rest. The bodies were taken away, shrink-wrapped in black.

See, niggah, you gotta put your trust in the Lord, grinned the Guatemalan when he sold him the shank. He nodded at the little oil lamp altar he had on a corner shelf, though it was the black-skinnned Virgen de Guadalupe behind the flickering flame. *Like the governor always sayin' at the assemblies, the Lord got your back. But it don' never hurt to equalize, right.*

The shank itself was a splinter of homegrown practicality that echoed the pragmatism in the Guatemalan's words. Someone had taken the monofil blade off a workshop fretsaw and piece-melted an array of colored plastic beads around the lower half to form a garish, pebbly-surfaced grip. The whole thing was less than twenty centimeters long, and the beads had been carefully selected for a surface that resisted fingerprinting. That left genetic trace, of course, but the Guatemalan was thorough and he'd carefully anointed his customer's hands from a tiny bottle he kept on the same shelf as the Virgen. Brief high-tech reek of engineered molecules cutting through the fart-and-patchouli warmth in the cell as Carl rubbed the fluid in; then the volatile bulk evaporated and left a fading chill on his palms. For a good three or four hours now, any skin cells he shed from either hand would be useless to a gene sniffer. The high- and low-tech mix sent a faint shudder of recollection through him. Going equipped among the nighttime shanties of Caracas. The city center spread out below him like a bowl of stars, the close warmth of barely lit streets up where he prowled. The confidence of well-chosen weaponry and what it would do.

Eventually, of course, the monofil would cut into the plastic enough to loosen the mounting, and with time the blade would drop out. But by then the whole weapon would have been dropped through the grate on some basement ventilation duct. Like a lot of what went on inside the South Florida State Partnership (Sigma Holdings) Correctional Facility, it was strictly a short-term option.

It was also expensive.

Seventeen, the Guatemalan wanted. He liked Carl enough to add explanations. *My boy Danny gotta run big risks down in the shop, puttin' something like this together. Then I gotta hold it for you. Do your hands for you. Find the downtime for handover. Full service like that don't come cheap.* Carl looked back into the man's polished coal features, shrugged, nodded. There was a degree of race solidarity operating in South Florida State, but it didn't do to push it too far. And he had the seventeen. Had, in fact, nearly two dozen of the twenty-mil endorphin capsules that served the prison as a high-denomination contraband currency. Never mind that he'd need them in a couple of weeks to trade against whatever debased form of *griego* Louie the Chem could swing for him this time around. Never mind that he might need endorphins for his own wounds a few hours hence. Short-term focus. Now he needed the shank. Worry about the rest later, if and when he had the leisure.

Short-term focus.

It was a profoundly depressing feature of life in the prison that increasingly he caught himself thinking like his fellow inmates. Adaptive behavior, Sutherland would have tagged it. Like finding himself masturbating to cheap porn, something he'd also done his share of since Florida's penal system had swept him up into its clammy embrace. Best, he'd found, to simply not think about it at all.

So he stepped out of the Guatemalan's cell and went casually back down the B wing thoroughfare, right arm held slightly bent. Under his sleeve, the chill of the monofil strip warmed slowly against his skin. Gray nanocarb scaffolding rose on either side of him, holding up three levels of galleries and the tracks for the big surveillance cams. The wing was roofed in arched transparency, and late-afternoon light sifted down into the quiet of the hall. Most of general population were out on Partnership work projects, paying their debt to society into Sigma's corporate coffers. The few who remained in B wing leaned off the galleries in ones or twos, or stood in small knots across the hall floor. Conversation evaporated as he passed, eyes swiveling to watch him. On the lower right-hand gallery, a grizzled longtimer called Andrews stared down at him and nodded in fractional acknowledgment. Suddenly, despite the sunlight, Carl felt cold.

It wasn't the coming fight. Equipped as he now was, Carl was reasonably sure he could take Dudeck without too much trouble. The Aryans either weren't hooked up outside the prison or just hadn't done their research; all they knew about Carl Marsalis was that he talked funny for a nigger, was up from Miami on some foreign-national retention loophole, and, at forty-one, was old. Possibly they thought he was some kind of terrorist, therefore foreign and a coward who had everything coming to him. Certainly they believed that lean-muscled tat-covered twenty-something Jack Dudeck was going to rip his shit apart, whoever he fucking was. That nigger had to learn some respect.

It wasn't the fight. It was the creeping sense of the trap that came with it.

Three months in this corporate newbuilt shithole, before that five weeks in the Miami High Risk unit. No trial, no bail. Release assessment dates set back time and again, access to lawyers refused. Appeals and diplomatic pressure from UNGLA summarily thrown out, no end in sight. He could feel the time getting away from him like blood loss. There was an ongoing investigation that no one was prepared to talk about but Carl knew it had to do with Caracas and the death of Richard Willbrink. It had to be. Relations between the UN and the Republic had never been great, but there was no way the Florida state legislature would have held out against major diplomacy for the sake of a single low-grade vice bust that already screamed entrapment. No, somewhere in the processing when the fetal murder team took him downtown, his documentation had tripped a high-level wire. Connections had been made, whether in Langley or Washington or some covert operations base farther south, and the national security beast was awake. Ghost agencies were looking for payback, cold covert vengeance for one of their own; they were going to make an example of Carl Marsalis, and while they tried to assemble the necessary legal toys to do it, he was going to stay safely locked down in a Republic prison. And if he shanked Jack Dudeck today as he fully intended to, they might not be able to pin it on him, but it was still going to put him back into Close Management and provide the perfect pretext for another lengthy extension of holding time, maybe even a subsidiary sentence. More than a few times in the last month he'd awoken with a panicky shortness of breath and a dream-like certainty that he would never get out of this place. It was starting to look like premonition.

He locked down the fear, siphoned it carefully into anger and stoked it up. He stopped at the B wing gate and raised his face for the laser. The blue light licked over his features, the machine consulted its real-time records, and the gate cracked open. He paced through. The chapel was left and halfway down a fifty-meter corridor that led to kitchen storage. Surveillance would have him for twenty-five meters along the passage, would see him turn in through the impressively sculpted genoteak double doors, and that was all they would know. Carl felt the mesh shudder online, jerky and grating with Louie's substandard *griego* chlorides.

All right, Jacky boy. Let's fucking do this.

The chapel doors gave smoothly as he pushed them, oozed backward on hydraulic hinges and showed him twin rows of pews, also in genoteak. The furniture sat like islands on the shine of the fused-glass floor. The interior architecture soared modestly in echo of a modern church. Angled spots made the altar rail and lectern gleam. In the space between the rail and the first row of pews, Jack Dudeck stood with another, bulkier Aryan at his side. Both wore their corporate prison blue coveralls peeled neatly to the waist and tied off. Sleeveless generic gray T-shirts showed beneath. A third shaven-headed weight-bench type, similarly dressed, hauled himself up from his slumped position between two pews halfway down on the right. He was chewing gum.

"Hello nigger," said Dudeck loudly.

Marsalis nodded. "Needed help, did you?"

"Don't need me no fucking help to carve a slice off your ass, boy. Marty and Roy here just wanted to make sure we ain't disturbed."

"That's right, *nigger*." The gum chewer squeezed out between the pew ends, eyes screwed up in a grin, voice leaning hard on the insult. Carl tamped down a flaring rage and thought about hooking out those eyes with his thumbnails.

Lock it down, soak.

It was depressing—the same timeslip sense of loss at his reactions. Over the last four months, he could track his own change in attitude toward the antique racial epithets still in wide use across the Republic. *Nigger*. The first couple of times, it was disconcerting and almost quaint, like having your face slapped with a dueling glove. With time, it came to feel more and more like the verbal spittle it was intended to be. That his fellow blacks in general population used it of themselves did nothing to stem the slowly awakening anger. It was a locally evolved defense, and he was not from there. *Fuck* these Republicans and their chimpanzee-level society.

Lock it down.

The gum chewer came ponderously up the aisle toward him. Carl moved to the right-hand bank of pews and waited, nailed the approaching Aryan's gaze as he came level, watched the man's eyes for the move if it was coming. He figured boot to shin and elbow uppercut to chin if he had to, left-side strikes. He didn't want to show Dudeck the shank ahead of time.

But the other man was as good as Dudeck's word. He brushed past with a snort of contempt and stationed himself at the door. Carl moved down the aisle, feeling the mesh now like arousal, like the juddering of bad brakes. It wasn't ideal, but the tidal power of it would do. He stepped out from between the two last pews and faced Dudeck across five meters of fused glass. He lifted his left hand in a casual gesture designed to lead the Aryan's attention away from his right, rejoiced silently as Dudeck's eyes flickered to follow the move.

"So, birdshit. You want to run me your rap now?" Carl burlesqued a Jesusland comedy drawl. "The South will rise again."

"South *already* risen, nigger," blurted the big Aryan next to Dudeck. "Confederated Republic *is* the white man's America."

Carl let his gaze shift briefly to the speaker. "Yeah, that seems to have worked out well for you."

The big Aryan bristled, surged forward. Dudeck lifted a hand and pressed him back without looking away from Carl.

"No call to get all riled up, Lee," he said softly. "This here—"

"Jack!" It was a hissed prison whisper from the door. The lookout, gesturing furiously. "*Jack!* COs coming."

The change was unreal, almost comical. In seconds flat, the two Aryans in front of Carl hit the front pew side by side, shaven heads bent in an attitude of prayer. Back by the door, the lookout moved two rows down and did the same. Carl stifled a snort and found a front seat of his own on the far side of the aisle from Dudeck and Roy. The mesh surged and pounded for release. He kept peripheral awareness of the two men and waited, head down, controlling his breathing. If the correctional officers passed by without stopping, the fight was going to kick off again right where it got paused, only by then Roy would have calmed down and the chances of goading him back up to interference levels would be lost. Carl had planned to fuck with the big Aryan's head just enough to get him in Dudeck's way, and then use the confusion to shank them both. Now—

Footfalls at the back of the chapel.

"Marsalis."

Fuck.

He looked around. Three COs, two from the B wing day crew, Foltz and García, both hefting stunwrap carbines and scanning the pews with seasoned calm. The other guy was a stranger, unarmed, and the phone clip he wore at ear and jaw looked shiny new with lack of use. White male, forties or older. Carl made him for admin-side, and probably senior. There was gray in his hair and the face was lined with middle-aged working weariness, but his eyes lacked the laconic watchfulness of the men who walked the galleries. The fact that Carl didn't know him wasn't in itself of note—South Florida State was a big prison—but the appeal-and-counter game had taken him across to admin close to a dozen times now and he was good with faces. Wherever this guy worked, wasn't somewhere Carl had been or seen.

"Chew doin' here, Marsalis?" Foltz's jaws worked a steady, tight-jaw rhythm on the gum in his mouth. "You ain't no believer."

It didn't require an answer. García and Foltz were old hands; they knew what went down in the chapel. Foltz's eyes tracked across to Dudeck and Lee. He nodded to himself.

"Findin' racial harmony in the Lord, are we, boys?"

Neither of the front-pew Aryans said anything. And back at the door, the third supremacist had the butt of García's carbine almost at his ear.

"That's enough," snapped the new face. "Marsalis, you're required in admin."

A tiny surge of hope. Meetings with Andritzky, the UNGLA rep, were alternate Tuesdays, late morning. For someone to turn up this late in the week unannounced, it had to be progress. *Had* to be. Someone somewhere had found the key log in the Republican logjam of xenophobia and moral illusion. Pressure applied, it would break up the jam and set the whole legal and diplomatic process flowing downstream once more. The trigger line of code that would crack Carl Marsalis out of this fucking prison glitch and send him home.

Yeah, you'd better hope, soak. He let the shank slide out of his sleeve and land gently on the pew beside him. He tucked it back against the upright with his fingers and got up, leaving it there, invisible to anyone, including the Aryans, who didn't have a clear angle of vision on where he'd been sitting. *Seventeen,* he remembered, and felt a faint chill at the thought. He didn't have the finances or the juice to buy again if this didn't work out and they sent him back to B wing to face Dudeck and the supremacist grudge. And mesh or no mesh, without an edged weapon he was probably going to get hurt.

Suddenly the hope in his belly collapsed into sick despair and a pointless, billowing anger.

Reggie Barnes, I hope you fucking die on that respirator.

He walked up the aisle toward the COs. Dudeck turned to watch him go. Carl caught it in peripheral vision, swung his head to meet the Aryan's gaze. He saw the hunger there, the deferred bloodlust, and summoned a stone-faced detachment to meet it. But beneath the mask, he found he was suddenly falling-down weary of the youth and fury in the other man. Of the hatred that seemed to seep not just out of Dudeck and his kind, but right out of the prison walls around him, as if institutions like South Florida State were just glands in the Republican body politic, oozing the hate like some kind of natural secretion, stockpiling it and then pumping it back out into the circulatory system of the nation, corrosive and ripe for any focus it could find.

"Eyes front, Dudeck." Foltz had spotted the sparks. His voice came out rich with irony. "That ain't how you pray, son."

Carl didn't look back to watch Dudeck comply. He didn't need to. Whichever way Dudeck was now looking, it didn't matter. Carl could feel the Aryan's hatred at his back, pushing outward behind him like a vast, soft balloon swelling to fill the space in the house of worship. Faith-based prison charter. Each man to his own personal god, and Dudeck's was white as polypuff packing chips.

Sutherland's voice, deep and amused, like honey ladling down in the back of his head.

Nothing new in the hate, soak. They need it like they need to breathe. Without it, they fall apart. Thirteen's just the latest hook to hang it off.

That supposed to make me feel better?

And Sutherland had shrugged. *Supposed to prepare you, is all. What else were you looking for?*

The hope and despair played seesaw in his guts all the way out of B wing and across the exercise yard to the administration building. Florida heat clutched at him like warm, damp towels. The glare off the nailed-down cloud cover hurt his eyes. He squinted and craned his neck in search of omens. There was no helicopter on the roof of the building, which meant no high-ranking visitors in from Tallahassee or Washington today. Nothing in the gray-roofed sky either, and no sound or sense of anything going on in the parking lot on the other side of the heavy-duty double fence. No journalistic flurry of activity, no uplink vans. A couple of months back, not long after he was transferred up to Florida State, Andritzky had leaked details to the press in an attempt to generate enough public embarrassment for a quick release. The tactic had backfired, with the Republic's media picking up almost exclusively on Carl's UNGLA covert ops status and the death of Gabriella at the Garrod Horkan camp: UN connections, fruitful leverage in any other corner of the globe, here only played directly into a long-standing paranoia that Washington had carefully nurtured since Secession and before. And it didn't help that Carl was the color of the Republic's deepest atavistic fears. Served up through the id-feeding Technicolor TV drip that passed for national news coverage, he was just new dosage in a regime already 150 years screen-ingrained.

Black male, detained, dangerous.

For now, that seemed to be more than enough for Republican purposes. Neither Sigma nor the Florida state legislature had seen fit to leak details of Carl's genetic status so far—for which he was duly grateful: in prison population here it would have been tantamount to a death sentence. There'd be a line out the fucking cell block for him, young men like Dudeck but of every race and creed, all filled with generalized hate and queuing up to test themselves against the monster. He wasn't sure why they were holding back; they must have the data by now. It was no secret what he was, a little digging at Garrod Horkan camp, or into UNGLA general record, or even a trawl back eight years to the *Felipe Souza* coverage would have turned it up. He assumed the Jesusland media had backed off and muzzled themselves in time-honored compliance with governmental authority, but he still couldn't work out why. Possibly they were holding back the knowledge as a weapon of last resort against the UN, or were afraid of the widespread panic it might trigger if it hit the public domain. Or maybe some worm-slow process of interagency protocol was still working itself out, and as soon as it cleared they'd have their vengeance for Willbrink via that long line of shank-equipped angry young men.

If he was still here by then.

Hope. Despair. The wrecking-ball pendulum swing in his belly. They went in through the steel-barred complications of admin block security, where Carl was prodded about, machine-swiped, and patted down by hand. Harsh, directing voices; rough, efficient hands. Foltz bowed out, leaving García and the stranger to lead their charge up two flights of clanging steel stairs, through a heavy door, and into the abrupt thickly carpeted quiet of the prison's offices. Sudden cool, sweat drying on his skin. Textured walls, discreet corporate logos, SIGMA and SFSP in muted tones, the deep blue and bright orange that characterized the inmate uniform bleached out here to pastel shades. The soft, occasional chime from a desk as data interfaces signaled a task complete. Carl felt his senses prickle with the change. A woman moved past him in a skirt, an actual woman, not a holo-porn confection, early fifties maybe, but fleshily handsome and moving for real under the clothing. He could smell her as she passed, scent of woman and some heavy musk fragrance he knew vaguely. Life outside prison came suddenly and touched him at the base of his spine.

"This way." The CO he didn't know gestured. "Conference Four."

His heart dropped sickeningly into his guts. It was Andritzky. Conference Four was a tiny, one-window chamber, no room for more than two or three people around the small oblong table, certainly no room for the assembled worthies of a state legislature or UN delegation. Nothing of consequence was going to go down in Conference Four. He'd have an hour with Andritzky, maybe some updates on the appeal, and then he was going back into general population and watching his back for Dudeck. He was fucked.

Lock. It. Down.

He breathed, drew in the new knowledge, and started to map it. Sutherland's situational Zen. Don't bitch, don't moan, *only see what is and then ready yourself.* Here came the door, here came Andritzky and his attempts at camaraderie and comfort, none of it ever quite masking the obvious personal relief at not being where Carl was. Here came an hour of useless bureaucratic narrative, punctuated with awkward silences and bitten-back rage at UNGLA's total *fucking* impotence in this Jesusland shithole. Here came—

It wasn't Andritzky.

Carl stopped dead in the open doorway. Sutherland's situational Zen spiraled away from him, like a sheaf of papers spilled down a well, like gulls riding the wind. The anger went with it, bleeding out.

"Good afternoon, Mr. Marsalis." The speaker was a white male, tall and smoothly elegant in a gray-blue micropore suit that hung like Shanghai custom as he got up and came around the table, hand extended. "I'm Tom Norton. Thank you, gentlemen, that'll be all for now. I'll buzz you when we're ready to leave."

There was an electric silence. Carl could feel the exchange of glances going on behind his back. García cleared his throat.

"This is a violent-crime inmate, sir. It's not acceptable procedure to leave you alone with him."

"Well, that's curious." Norton's tone was urbane, but abruptly there was an edge in it. "From my records, it seems Mr. Marsalis is being held on a putative Dade County vice charge. And hasn't even been formally arraigned yet."

"It's against procedure," insisted García.

"Sit down please, Mr. Marsalis." Norton was looking past him at García and the other CO. His expression had turned cold. He took a phone from his jacket pocket, thumbed it, put it to his ear. "Hello. Yes, this is Tom Norton, could you put me through to the warden. Thank you."

Brief pause. Carl took the seat. The table held a slim black dataslate, cracked open at a discreet angle. No logo, an ultimate in brand statements. Marstech. Hardcopy lay around, unfamiliar forms. Carl scanned upside-down text—the word *release* leapt out and kicked him in the heart. Norton offered him a small, distracted smile.

"Hello, Warden Parris. Yes, I need your help here. No, nothing serious. I'm just having a little difficulty with one of your men over procedure. Could you. Ah, thank you, that would be ideal." He held out the phone to García. "The warden would like to talk to you."

García took the phone as if it might bite him, held it gingerly to his ear. You couldn't hear what Parris said to him—it was a good phone, and the projection cone was tight. But his face flushed as he listened. His eyes switched from Carl to Norton and back like they were two parts of a puzzle that didn't fit. He tried to say *Yes, but* a couple of times, jarred to a halt on each attempt. Parris, it was clear, wasn't in the mood for debate. When García finally got to speak, it was a clenched *Yes, sir,* and he lowered the phone immediately after. Norton held out a hand for it and García, still flushing, slung it under the other man's reach onto the surface of the table. It made almost no sound on impact, slid a bare five centimeters from where it landed. A *very* good phone, then. García glared at it, perplexed maybe by his failure to skid the thing off the edge of the table onto the floor. Norton picked the little sliver of hardware up and stowed it.

"Thank you."

García stood there for a moment, wordless, staring at Norton. The other CO murmured something to him, put a hand on his arm, was propelling him out when García shook off the grip and stabbed a finger at Carl.

"This man is dangerous," he said tightly. "If you can't see that, then you deserve everything you get."

The other CO ushered him out and closed the door.

Norton gave it a moment, then seated himself adjacent to Carl. Pale blue eyes leveled across the space. The smile was gone.

"So," Norton said. "Are you dangerous, Mr. Marsalis?"

"Who wants to know?"

A shrug. "In point of fact, no one. It was rhetorical. We've accessed your records. You are, let's say, quite sufficiently dangerous for our purposes. But I'm interested to know what your perceptions are on the subject."

Carl stared at him. "Have you ever done time?"

"Happily, no. But even if I had, I doubt it would approximate your experiences here. I'm not a citizen of the Confederated Republic."

Light trace of contempt in the last two words. Carl hazarded a guess.

"You're Canadian?"

The corner of Norton's mouth quirked. "North Atlantic Union. I'm here, Mr. Marsalis, at the behest of the Western Nations Colony Initiative. We would like to offer you a job."

CHAPTER 12

A s soon as he walked through the door, Sevgi knew she was in trouble.

It was there in the looseness as he moved, in the balance of stance as he paused behind the chair, in the way he hooked it out and sat down. It smoked off the body beneath the shapeless blue prison coveralls like music cutting through radio interference. It looked back at her through his eyes as he settled into the chair, and it soaked out through the powerful quiet he'd carried into the room with him. It wasn't Ethan—Marsalis had skin far darker than Ethan's, and there was no real similarity in the features. Ethan had been stockier, too, heavier-muscled.

Ethan had died younger.

It didn't matter. It was there just the same.

Thirteen.

"Mr. Marsalis?"

He nodded. Waited.

"I'm Sevgi Ertekin, COLIN Security. You've already met my partner, Tom Norton. There are a number of things we need to clarify before—"

"I'll do it." His voice was deep and modulated. The English accent tripped her.

"I beg your pardon?"

"Whatever it is you need me to do. I'll do it. At cost. I already told your partner. I'll take the job in return for unconditional immunity to all charges pending against me, immediate release from Republican custody, and any expenses I'm likely to incur while I'm doing your dirty work."

Her eyes narrowed. "That's quite an assumption you're making there, Mr. Marsalis."

"Is it?" He raised an eyebrow. "I'm not known for my flower arranging. But let's see if I'm assuming wrong, shall we? At a guess you want someone tracked down. Someone like me. That's fine, that's what I do. The only part I'm unclear on is if you want me to bring him in alive or not."

"We are not assassins, Mr. Marsalis."

"Speak for yourself."

She felt the old anger flare. "You're proud of that, are you?"

"You're upset by it?"

She looked down at the unfolded dataslate and the text printed there. "In Peru, you shot an unarmed and injured woman in the back of the head. You executed her. Are you proud of that, too?"

Long pause. She picked up his stare and held it. For a moment, she thought he would get up and walk out. Half of her, she realized, hoped he would.

Instead, he switched his gaze abruptly to one of the high-placed windows in the waiting room. A small smile touched his lips. Went away. He cleared his throat.

"Ms. Ertekin, do you know what a Haag gun is?"

"I've read about them." In NYPD communiqués, urging City Hall to issue tighter gun control guidelines before the new threat hit the streets. Scary enough that the initiatives passed almost without dispute. "It's a bioload weapon."

"It's a little more than that, actually." He opened his right hand loosely, tipped his head to look at it as if he could see the gun weighed there in the cup of his palm. "It's a delivery system for an engineered immune deficiency viral complex called Falwell Seven. There are other loads, but they don't get a lot of use. Falwell is virulent, and very unpleasant. There is no cure. Have you ever watched someone die from a collapsed immune system, Ms. Ertekin?"

In fact, she had. Nalan, a cousin from Hakkari, a onetime party girl in the frontier bases where Turkey did its proud European duty and buffered the mess farther east. Something she caught from a UN soldier. Nalan's family, who prided themselves on their righteousness, threw her out. Sevgi's father spat and found a way to bring her to New York, where he had clout in one of the new Midtown research clinics. Relations with family in Turkey, already strained, snapped for good. He never spoke to his brother again. Sevgi, only fourteen at the time, went with him to meet a sallow, big-eyed girl at the airport, older than her by what seemed like a gulf of years but reassuringly unversed in urban teen sophistication. She still remembered the look on Nalan's face when they all went into the Skillman Avenue mosque through the same door.

Murat Ertekin did everything he could. He enrolled Nalan in experimental treatment lists at the hospital, fed her vitamin supplements and tracker antivirals at home. He painted the spare room for her, sun-bright and green like the park. He prayed, five times a day for the first time in years. Finally, he wept.

Nalan died anyway.

Sevgi blinked away the memory; fever-stained sheets and pleading, hollow eyes. "You're saying you did this woman a favor?"

"I'm saying I got her quickly and painlessly where she was going anyway."

"Don't you think that should have been her choice?"

He shrugged. "She made her choice when she tried to jump me."

If she'd doubted what he was at all, she no longer did. It was the same unshakable calm she'd seen in Ethan, and the same psychic bulk. He sat in the chair like something carved out of black stone, watching her. She felt something tiny shift in her chest.

She tapped a key on the dataslate. A new page slid up on the display.

"You were recently involved in prison violence. A fight in the F wing shower block. Four men hospitalized. Three of them by you."

Pause. Silence.

"You want to tell me your side of that?"

He stirred. "I would think the details speak for themselves. Three white men, one black man. It was an Aryan Command punishment beating."

"Which prison staff did nothing to prevent?"

"Surveillance in the showers can be compromised by steamy conditions. Quote unquote." His lip curled fractionally. "Or soap jammed over lenses. Response time can be delayed. By extraneous factors, quote unquote."

"So you felt moved to intervene." She groped around for motivations that would have fit Ethan. "This Reginald Barnes, he was a friend of yours?"

"No. He was a piece-of-shit wirehead snitch. He had it coming. But I didn't know that at the time."

"Was he genetically modified?"

Marsalis smirked. "Not unless there's some project somewhere I haven't heard of for turning out brainless addictive-personality fuckups."

"You felt solidarity because of his color, then?"

The smirk wiped away, became a frown. "I felt I didn't want to see him arse-fucked with a power drill. I think that's probably a color-neutral preference, don't you?"

Sevgi held on to her temper. This wasn't going well. She was gritty with the syn comedown—no synaptic modifiers permitted in Jesusland, they'd taken them off her at the airport—and still fuming from the argument she'd lost with Norton in New York.

I'm serious, Sev. The policy board's all over this thing now. We've got Ortiz and Roth coming down to section two, three times a week—

In the flesh? What an honor.

They're looking for progress reports, Sev. Which means reports of progress, and
right now we don't have any. If we don't do something that looks like fresh action,
Nicholson is going to land on us with both feet. Now, I'll survive that. Will you?

She knew she wouldn't.

October. Back in New York, the trees in Central Park were starting to rust and
stain yellow. Under her window as she got ready for work each day, the market
traders went wrapped against the early-morning chill. The summer had turned,
tilted about like a jetliner in the clear blue sky above the city, sunlight sliding cold
and glinting off its wings. The warmth wasn't gone yet, but it was fading fast.
South Florida felt like clinging.

"How much has Norton told you?"

"Not much. That you have a problem UNGLA won't help you with. He didn't
say why, but I'm guessing it's Munich-related." A sudden, unexpected grin that
dropped about a decade off his seamed features. "You guys really should have
signed up to the Accords like everybody else."

"COLIN approved the draft in principle," said Sevgi, feeling unreasonably defensive.

"Yeah. All about that principle, wasn't it. Principally: you don't tell us what to
do, you globalist bureaucrat scum."

Since he wasn't far wrong, she didn't argue the point. "Is that going to be a
problem?"

"No. I'm freelance. My loyalties are strictly for sale. Like I already said, just tell
me what you want me to do."

She hesitated a moment. The dataslate had an integral resonance scrambler
built to COLIN specs, which made it tighter than anything any lawyer had ever
carried into an interview room at South Florida State. And Marsalis was pretty
clearly desperate for an out. Still, the habit of the past four months was ingrained.

"We have," she said finally, "a renegade thirteen on our hands. He's been loose
since June. Killing."

He grunted. No visible surprise. "Where'd he get out of? Cimarron? Tanana?"

"No. He got out of Mars."

This time she had him. He sat up.

"This is a completely confidential matter, Mr. Marsalis. You need to understand that before we start. The murders are widely distributed, and varied in technique. No official connection has been made among them, and we want it to stay
that way."

"Yeah, I bet you do. How'd he get past the nanorack security?"

"He didn't. He shorted out the docking run and crashed the vessel into the Pacific. By the time we got there, he was gone."

Marsalis pursed his lips in a soundless whistle. "Now, there's an idea."

She let the rest out. Anything to take the smug, competent control off his face. "Before that, he had systematically mutilated the other eleven cryocapped crewmembers in order to feed himself. He amputated their limbs and kept them alive in suspension, then, finally, began to kill them and strip the rest of their bodies for meat."

A nod. "How long was transit?"

"Thirty-three weeks. You don't seem surprised by any of this."

"That's because I'm not. You're stuck out there, you've got to eat something."

"Did you ever think that?"

Something like a shadow passed across his eyes. His voice came out just short of even. "Is that how you found me? Cross-reference?"

"Something like that." She chose not to mention Norton's sudden enthusiasm for the new tactic. "Our profiling n-djinn cited you as the only other thirteen known to have experienced similar circumstances."

Marsalis offered her a thin smile. "I never ate anybody."

"No. But did you think about it?"

He was silent for a while. She was on the point of asking her question again when he got up from the seat and went to stand by the high window. He stared out at the sky.

"It crossed my mind a few times," he said quietly. "I knew the recovery ship was coming, but I had the best part of two months to worry about it. You can't help running the scenarios in your mind. What if they don't make it, what if something crazy happens? What if—"

He stopped. His gaze unhooked from the cloud cover and came back to the room, back to her face.

"Was he out there the whole thirty-three weeks?"

"Most of it. From what we can tell, his cryocap spat him out about two weeks into the trajectory."

"And Mars Control didn't fetch him back?"

"Mars Control didn't know about it." Sevgi gestured. "The n-djinn went down, looks like it was tricked out. The ship fell back on automated systems. Silent running. He woke up right after."

"That's a nice little cluster of coincidence."

"Isn't it."

"But not very convenient from a culinary point of view."

"No. We're assuming the cryocap timing was an error. Whoever spiked the n-djinn probably planned to have the system bring him up a couple of weeks out from Earth. Something in the intrusion program flipped when it should have flopped, and you wake up two weeks out from Mars instead. Our friend arrives starved and pissed off and probably not very sane."

"Do you know who he is?"

Sevgi nodded. She hit the keypad again and pushed the dataslate around so they could both see the screen and the face it held. Marsalis left the window and propped himself in casual angles on the edge of the table. Light gleamed off the side of his skull.

"Allen Merrin. We recovered trace genetic material from *Horkan's Pride*, the vessel he crashed, and ran it through COLIN's thirteen database. This is what they came up with."

It was almost imperceptible, the way he grew focused, the way the casual poise tautened into something else. She watched his eyes sweep the text alongside the pale head-and-shoulders photo. She could have recited it to him from memory.

Merrin, Allen (sin 48523dx3814)

Delivered (c/s) April 26, 2064, Taos, New Mexico (Project Lawman). Uteral host, Bilikisu Sankare, source genetic material, Isaac Hubscher, Isabela Gayoso (sins appended). All genetic code variants property of Elleniss Hall, Inc., patents asserted (Elleniss Hall & US Army Partnership 2029).

Initial conditioning & training Taos, New Mexico, specialist skills development Fort Benning, Georgia (covert ops, counterinsurgency). Deployed: Indonesia 2083, Arabian peninsula 2084–5, Tajikistan 2085–7 & 2089, Argentina, Bolivia 2088, Rim Authority (urban pacification program) 2090–1.

Retired 2092 (under 2nd UNGLA Convention Accords, Jacobsen Protocol). Accepted Mars resettlement 2094 (COLIN citizenship record appended).

"Very Christ-like."

She blinked. "I'm sorry?"

"The face." He tapped the screen with a fingernail. The LCLS glow rippled around the touch. Merrin stared up under the tiny distortions. "Very Faith Satellite Channel. Looks like that *Man Taking Names* anime they did for the Cash memorial."

The smile slipped out before she could stop it. His mouth quirked response. He moved the chair a little, sat down again.

"Saw that, did you? We get the reruns in here all the time. Faith-based rehab, you know."

Quit grinning at him like a fucking news 'face, Sev. Get a grip.

"You don't recognize him, then?"

A curious, tilted look. "Why would I?"

"You were in Iran."

"Wasn't everybody." When she just waited, he sighed. "Yeah, we heard about the Lawmen. Saw them at a distance a few times in Iran, down around Ahvaz. But from what you've got there, it doesn't look like this Merrin ever got up that far north."

"He could have." Sevgi nodded toward the screen. "I'll be honest with you, this is a pretty loose summary. Once you get into the mission records, it's a whole lot less defined. Covert deployments, so-called lost documentation, rumor and hearsay, *subject is understood to have,* that sort of shit. Executive denial and cover-ups around practically every corner. Plus, you've got a whole fucking hero mythology going on around this guy. I've seen data that puts Merrin in combat zones hundreds of kilometers apart on the same day, eyewitness accounts that say he took wounds we can't find any medical records to confirm, some of them wounds he couldn't possibly have survived if the stories are true. Even that South American deployment has too much overlap to be wholly accurate. He was in Tajikistan, no he wasn't, he was still in Bolivia; he was solo-deployed, no, he was leading a Lawman platoon in Kuwait City." Her disgust bubbled over. "I'm telling you, the guy's a fucking ghost."

He smiled, a little sadly she thought.

"We all were, back then," he said. "Ghosts, I mean. We had our own British version of Project Lawman, minus the delusional name, of course. We called it Osprey. The French preferred Department Eight. But none of us ever officially existed. What you've got to remember, Ms. Ertekin, is that back in the eighties the whole thirteen thing was fresh out of the can. Everyone knew the technology was out there, and everybody was busy denying they'd ever have anything to do with it. UNGLA didn't even exist back then, not as an agency in its own right. It was still part of the Human Rights Commission. And no one was very keen on letting anybody else get a close look at their new genetic warriors. The whole Middle East was a testing ground for all sorts of cutting-edge nastiness, and all of it was operating on full deniability. You know how that shit works, right?"

She blinked. "What shit?"

"Deniability. You work for COLIN, right?"

"I've been with COLIN two and a half years," she said stiffly. "Before that I was a New York police detective."

He grinned again, a little more genuine humor in it this time. "Getting the hang of it, though, aren't you. *This is a completely confidential matter, we want it to stay that way.* That's very COLIN."

"It's not a question of that." She tried without much success to get the stiffness out of her voice. "We don't want a panic on our hands."

"How many has he killed so far? Here on the ground, I mean."

"We think it's in the region of twenty. Some of those are unconfirmed, but the circumstantial evidence points to a connection. In seventeen cases, we've recovered genetic trace material that clinches it."

Marsalis grimaced. "Busy little fucker. Is this all in the Rim States?"

"No. The initial deaths were in the San Francisco Bay Area, but later they spread over the whole of continental North America."

"So he's mobile."

"Yes. Mobile and apparently a very competent systems intrusion specialist. He murdered two men at the same location in the Bay Area on the night of June 13th and a man in southeastern Texas less than a week later. There's no trace anywhere in the flight records for that period, and nothing from Rim Border Control, either. We had an n-djinn run face recognition checks on every cross-border flight and surface exit into the Republic for that week and got nothing."

"He could have had his face changed."

"In less than a week? With matching documentation? Rim States fenceline is the toughest frontier anywhere in the world. Anyway the same n-djinn we used for the face recog had instructions to flag anyone with bandaging or other traces of recent surgical procedure to the face. All we got was a bunch of rich brats coming home from West Coast cosmetic therapy, and a couple of over-the-hill erotica stars."

She saw him hold back all but the corner of a grin. It was irritatingly infectious. She concentrated on the dataslate.

"The only options we are seriously entertaining are that either he was able to contact professional frontier busters within days of coming ashore, or he left the Rim for some other, intermediate destination before flying back into the Republic. It would be a tight time frame that way, but still doable. Of course once it goes global like that, there's no way to run a comprehensive face recog. Too many places that refuse to let the n-djinns into their datasystems."

"I take it these are both confirmed kills, Bay Area and then Texas?"

"Yes. Genetic trace material recovered at both locations."

His gaze went back to the dataslate display. "What do Fort Benning have to say about it?"

"That Merrin was never provided with substantial datasystems training. He could run a battlefield deck—anybody in covert ops could. But that's it. We're assuming he upskilled on Mars."

"Yeah. Or someone's doing it for him."

"There is that."

He looked at her. "If he had systems help getting aboard *Horkan's Pride*, and he's still getting it now, then this is bigger than just some thirteen bailing out of Mars because he doesn't like all the red rocks."

"Yes."

"And you're out of leads."

It wasn't a question.

She sat back and spread her hands. "Without access to the UNGLA databases, we're in a hole. We've done everything we know how to do, and it isn't enough. The deaths keep coming, they're steady but unpredictable. There's no crescendo effect—"

"No, there wouldn't be."

"—but he's not stopping. He's not making any mistakes big enough to nail him or give us a working angle. Our inquiries on Mars have hit a wall—he obviously covered his tracks there, or, as you say, someone did it for him."

"And down here?"

She nodded. "Down here, as you've also so eloquently pointed out, we are not on hugely cooperative terms with UNGLA, or the UN in general."

"Well, I guess you can hardly blame them for that." He widened his eyes at her, grinned. It's not like you've been overly cooperative yourselves for the last decade."

"Look, Munich was not—"

The grin faded to a grimace. "I wasn't really talking about the Accords. I was thinking more of the reception we get in the prep camps every time we have to operate in them. You know we're about as welcome down there as evolutionary science in Texas."

She felt herself flush a little. "Individual corporate partners in the Colony effort do not necessarily—"

"Yeah, skip it." A frown. "Still, UNGLA have a mandate requirement in circumstances like this. You report a loose thirteen, they pretty much have to show up."

"We don't really want them to show up, Mr. Marsalis."

"Ah."

"We need access to their datastacks, or failing that someone like you to talk to our profiling n-djinns. But that's all. In the end, this is a COLIN matter, and we'll clean our own house."

Listen to you, Sevgi. Cop to corporate mouthpiece in one easy, well-paid move.

Marsalis watched her for a couple of moments. He shifted slightly in the chair, seemed to be considering something.

"Are you running this gig out of New York?"

"Yes. We've got borrowed space at RimSec's Alcatraz complex, liaison with their detectives. But since this thing went continental, we're back in the New York offices. Why?"

A shrug. "No reason. When I get on the suborb, I like to know where I'm going to be when I get off again."

"Right." She glanced at her watch. "Well, if we're going to make that suborb, we should probably get moving. I imagine my colleague will have finished with the warden by now. There'll be some paperwork."

"Yes." He hesitated a moment. "Listen. There are a couple of people in here I'd like to say good-bye to before we go. People I owe. Can we do that?"

"Sure." Sevgi shrugged carelessly. She was already folding up the dataslate. "No problem. It's a COLIN perk. We can do pretty much anything we want."

The Guatemalan was still in his cell, flat on his back in his bunk and blissed out by the look of him on some of his newly acquired endorphin. A half-smoked New Cuban smoldered between the knuckles of his left hand, and his eyes were lidded almost shut. He looked up, dreamily surprised, when Carl strummed the bars of the half-open door.

"Hey, Eurotrash. Chew doin' here?"

"Leaving," said Carl crisply. "But I need a favor."

The Guatemalan struggled upright on the bunk. He glanced up to the cell's monitor lens, and the cheap interference slinger taped on the wall next to it. No attempt had been made to hide the scrambler, and it had hung there every time Carl had been inside the cell. He didn't like to think what it cost the Guatemalan to have it overlooked on a permanent basis.

"Leavin'?" A stoned smirk. "Don' see no fuckin trowel in your hand."

Carl moved an African-carved wooden stool over to the bunk and seated himself. "Not like that. This is official. Out the front gate. Listen, I need to make a phone call."

"*Phone* call?" Even through the endorphins, the Guatemalan was blearily shocked. "You know what tha's gonna cost you?"

"I can guess. And I don't have it. Look, there are seven more twenty-mil caps taped in plastic up in the U-bend of my cell's shitter. All yours. Think of—"

"That ain't gonna cut it, niggah."

"I *know*. Think of it as a down payment."

"Yeah?" The stoned look was sliding away from the other man. He put the New Cuban in the corner of his mouth and grinned around it. "How's that shit work? You walkin' outta here, how you gonna settle your account? Down payment on *what*? Come to that"—brow creasing—"you walkin' outta here, why you need my little phone service?"

Carl gestured impatiently. "Because I don't trust the people who are walking me out. Listen, once I'm outside, I'm going to have juice—"

"Yeah, sounds like it. Juice with folks that you don't trust."

"I can help you on the outside." Carl leaned in. "This is COLIN business. That mean anything to you?"

The Guatemalan regarded him owlishly for a moment. Then he shook his head and got off the bunk. Carl shifted aside to let him past.

"Sound to me, niggah, like you ridin'. You sure those seven caps still in that shitter bend, not inside you? COLIN getting you out? What the fuck for?"

"They want me to kill someone for them," Carl said evenly.

A snort from behind him. Liquid coursing as the Guatemalan poured himself a glass of juice from the chiller flask he kept on a shelf. "Sure. In the whole Confederated Republic, they can't find one black man do their killin' for them, they got to come flush some high-tone Eurotrash outta South Florida State. You ridin', niggah."

"Will you stop fucking calling me that."

"Oh yeah." The Guatemalan drank deep. He put the glass down and made a gusty, satisfied sound. "I's forgettin'. You only black man in here don' seem to noticed what color skin he got."

Carl stared straight ahead at the cell wall. "You know, where I come from, there are a lot of different ways of being black."

"Well, then you one lucky fucking black man." The Guatemalan moved around to face him. His face was almost kindly, softened with the endorphins and maybe something else. "But see, blood, 'bout now, where you come from ain't where you at. 'Bout now, you in South Florida State. You in the Confederated Republic, niggah. Roun' here, they only got the one way of being black, and sooner or later that's the black you gonna be. Ain't no diversity of product in the Republic, they just got this one box for us, and sooner or later they gonna squeeze you in that box right along with the rest of us."

Carl looked at the wall some more. He took the decision.

"Now, see, that's where you're wrong."

"I'm wrong?" The other man chuckled. "Look around you, blood. How the fuck am I wrong?"

"You're wrong," Carl told him, "because they already got me in a whole other box. It's a box you won't ever see the inside of, and that's why I'm getting out, that's why they need me. They can't get anyone else like me."

The Guatemalan propped himself against the cell wall and gave Carl a quizzical look.

"Yeah? You got moves, trash, I give you that. And what I hear from Louie, you got some fucked-up wirin' inside you. But that don' make you no stone killer. Two hours ago you walk out of here with my boy's best shiv-work up your sleeve, but what I hear is Dudeck still walking around."

"We were interrupted."

"Yeah. By the nice people from COLIN." But there wasn't much mockery in the other man's voice now. He sucked thoughtfully on the cigar. "Shame about Dudeck, that birdshit coulda used some time in the infirmary. You want to tell me what that means, *they can't get anyone else like me?*"

Carl met his eyes. "I'm a thirteen."

It was like peeling a scab. For the last four months, he'd kept it hedged behind his teeth, the secret that would kill him. Now he watched the Guatemalan's face and saw the final confirmation for his paranoia, saw the flicker of fear, faint but there, covered for quickly with a nod.

"O-kay."

"Yeah." He felt an obscure disappointment; somehow he'd hoped this man might be proof against the standard prejudice. Something about the Guatemalan's patient con math realism. But now abruptly he could feel himself through the other man's gaze, sliding into caricature. Could even feel himself go with it, let go, take on the old skin of impassive power and threat. "So. About this phone call. What's it going to take?"

He found Dudeck in the F wing rec hall, playing speed chess against the machine. Three or four others inmates were gathered around: one tat-stamped and certified AC brother, a couple of late-teen wannabe sycophants, and an older white guy who seemed to be there just for the chess. No one from the chapel confrontation—Dudeck would have shrugged loose of them in the wake of the failed gig. Too many undischarged fight chemicals sloshing around, too much blustering talk while they leached back out of the system. Not what you needed at all after a walk-away.

No one paid any attention to the black man as he came up the hall. Dudeck was too deep in the game, and with full audiovid monitoring systems webbed up in the nanocarb vault of the hall, the others were loose and unvigilant. Carl got to within ten paces of the gathering before anybody turned around. Then one of the wannabes must have caught black in motion out of the corner of an eye. He pivoted about. Stepped forward, secure in the knowledge of how the monitoring system worked, puffed up with association and proximity to Dudeck.

"Fuck you want, nigger?"

Carl stepped in and hit him, full force, with one trailing arm and the back of his hand. The impact smashed the boy's mouth and knocked him to the floor. He stayed there, bleeding and staring up at Carl in disbelief.

Carl was still moving.

He closed with the tat-marked spectator, broke down a fumbled defense, and tipped the man into Dudeck, who was still trying to get up from the console. The two men tangled and went down sprawling. The second sycophant hovered, gaped. He wasn't going to do anything. The older guy was already backing off, hands spread low in front of him to denote his detachment.

Dudeck rolled to his feet with practiced speed. A siren cut loose somewhere.

"Got some unfinished business," Carl told him.

"You're fucking cracked, nigger. That's monitored, unprovoked aggre—"

He let the mesh drive him. Dudeck saw him coming, threw together a Thai boxing guard, and kicked out. Carl stamped the kick away, feinted the guard, rode the jab punch response, and then broke Dudeck's nose with a close-in palm heel. The Aryan went over again, explosively, backward. The second serious AC member was staggering upright. Carl punched him in the throat to keep him out of the fight. He went down, choking. Dudeck had bounced up, hadn't even wiped the blood from his nose. Old hand. His eyes were blank with fury. He came in like a truck, a flurry of blows, all simple linear shit. Carl beat most of it, winced on a stray punch that scraped his cheekbone, then snagged the other man's right arm at the wrist. He locked up the arm, twisted it, and slammed down with his own forearm. Dudeck's elbow broke with a crunch, audible even over the sirens. The Aryan shrieked and went down for the last time. Carl kicked him as hard as he could in the ribs. He felt something give. He kicked again, twice, into the stomach. Dudeck threw up on the second impact, softly, like something rupturing. Carl stepped over the Aryan's twitching body to avoid the pool of vomit, stamped in the man's already bloodied face, and then bent over him. He grabbed Dudeck's head up by one ear.

"New rules, birdshit," he hissed. "I'm working for the man now. I can do what the fuck I want with you. I could kill you, and it wouldn't make any fucking difference now."

Dudeck foamed blood and spit. Fragments of a tooth on his smashed lower lip. He was making a low grinding noise somewhere deep in his throat.

Carl let go and stood up. For a moment, he thought he'd stamp on the crumpled form at his feet again, hard into the base of the spine to do some damage the infirmary wouldn't easily put right, into the face again to destroy it utterly. Maybe go back for the ribs until they snapped inward and punctured something. At least, he thought, he might spit on the Aryan. But the rage had drained abruptly away. He couldn't be bothered. The Guatemalan had what he'd asked for. Dudeck was out, infirmary-bound. Let the remainder of the Aryan's shitty Jesusland life take him the rest of the way down. Marsalis didn't need to see or inflict any more damage. He already knew, within parameters, how it would play out. They stacked men like Dudeck in cheap coffins five-deep outside the poor fund crematoria across the Republic every Sunday. Most of them never made it out of their twenties.

At the far end of F wing, the gate clanged back and the intervention squad piled through. Body armor, stunwrap carbines, and yells. Carl sighed, raised his hands to his head, and walked down the siren-screaming nanocarb hall to meet them.

"Cordwood Systems."

"Marsalis. Print me."

"Voiceprint confirmed. You are speaking to the duty controller. Please state your preferences."

"Jade, lattice, mangosteen, oak."

"Opening. What are your requirements?"

"I've just been hired out of custody by the Western Nations Colony Initiative. They want me to run a variant thirteen retrieval outside UNGLA jurisdiction."

"That is contrary to—"

"I know. I'll be in New York in a couple of days. Tell the perimeter crews to expect me. I'll be dumping my newfound friends as soon as practically possible."

CHAPTER 13

"Did you have to fucking hospitalize him?"

He shrugged. He'd dumped his prison jacket earlier—stripped off shoes and socks, too—and the beach sand under his feet was cool and firm. The night air brushed his neck and his bared arms like loose-drape silk.

"Couldn't see a good reason not to."

"No?" Ertekin had not taken off her shoes. "Well, it would have meant we got home tonight, instead of staying in this dump. Ever think of that?"

Her gesture took in the floodlit clutch of low-rise behind them, the coms tower, and behind it like some Godzilla parent the endless upward loom of the Perez nanorack. The rack's structure stood mostly in darkness, but red navigation lights blinked in dizzying stacked synchrony, dragging vision upward until the lights disappeared into the cloud cover.

"It's your dump," he said.

"It's leased."

"That must be heartbreaking for you. COLIN dependent on local state power. I'm surprised you don't just topple the government. You know, like you did in Bolivia back in the nineties."

She shot him a look he was beginning to recognize. Halfway to anger, locked down by something else. In another thirteen, he'd have read it as social aptitude training. Here, he wasn't sure what it might mean. Only one thing was clear. Something was scratching at the edges of Sevgi Ertekin, and had been since he met her.

"Marsalis, it's late," she told him. "I'm not going to get in a fight with you about something COLIN may or may not have done ten years before I joined them. The reason we're in *this dump* is because you let your much-vaunted thirteen tendencies get out of hand, and it cost us another six fucking hours of phone calls and negotiation. So don't push your luck. I'm close enough to sending you back as it is."

He grinned. "Now you're lying."

"Think so? The warden wanted to refer it all the way back up to Tallahassee and a convened Violent Crimes Committee assessment. He'd just love to have you locked down while that grinds through the legislature."

"I'd have thought he'd be glad to see the back of me."

"Well, you'd be wrong. Warden Parris is an ex-marine." Sevgi shot him another glance. "Just like Willbrink."

"Will who?"

"Yeah, right. Forget it."

He didn't know how much truth she was telling. Certainly, things had been fraught once they saw what he'd done to Dudeck. The intervention squad didn't quite stunwrap him on the spot, but it was a close thing. He spent three hours in the faintly ammoniac-perfumed gloom of the riot holding cells, was hauled out, marched summarily across to admin, and then marched just as rapidly back as, he supposed, competing authorizations whiplashed back and forth. It took another two hours to get him out of the hole permanently, by which time it was dark and the admin block was down to a skeleton crew of caretakers and security.

Norton and Ertekin came and went, in and out of doors to offices he never got to see inside. They barely glanced his way. Shift change came and went. At one point, a CO came and took his picture, took it away without comment. Carl let it all wash over him. When they were all done, he signed the documents they gave him, changed back into his own clothes, and, guessing it would be cold in New York, blagged an inmate jacket from the yawning night clerk. It was a use-faded gray-black, not a bad color in itself, but one sleeve was flashed with a line of orange chevrons and across the back was the customary SIGMA logo and name in the same glaring color. As with a lot of old stock, some tagging freak wit had taken a dye squirt to the lettering, dumping in a long jagged lowercase *t* after the S. He shrugged and took it anyway. Miami PD had impounded his gear from the hotel when they busted him, and he didn't suppose he'd ever see it again. UNGLA were apparently still negotiating for the return of the Haag gun and its load. Point of principle, point of pride. No one really believed they'd win. He shouldered his way into the jacket, rolled up the short personal effects strip that went with the clothes he'd been arrested in, and walked out.

Fuck the accessories, Carl. You're halfway home.

A grim-faced Norton stayed at his side all the way to the innocuous hired teardrop in the parking lot, opened the backseat for him, and closed it again as soon as he was in. Ertekin came out of the admin building a couple of minutes later, muttered something to her partner, and then got in behind the wheel. When Norton was in beside her, she fired up the engine and steered the car out of the prison gates on manual. Neither of the COLIN officers spoke to Carl at all.

Warden Parris, if he was still on site, never showed.

A couple of hundred meters down the exit highway, Norton was already on the phone, checking the Miami suborb terminal for departures north. Not surprisingly, there was nothing flying this late.

"Hotel?" he'd asked Ertekin.

She shook her head "Parris is way too pissed. I don't want to wake up to a VCC warrant tomorrow morning because he called some friend in Tallahassee during the night. We need to get back on our own turf."

Norton went back to the phone. A couple of hours later, they were rolling through a security gate and into the nanorack facility environs. Powered fences glinted off across the Florida flatland, watchful men and women in coveralls prowling back and forth in the gloom. The low-light headgear they wore made them look like insect aliens from a low-budget stage show. Carl spotted the COLIN insignia on an upper arm, on the badge of a beret. Safe haven. He could see the tension drain almost visibly out of his two rescuers.

Now, out on the beach with sand between his toes and his own clothes on his back for the first time in four months, he could feel a similar easing in himself. A sudden self-knowledge slopped in him, the awareness of how clenched he'd become, and the faintly scary slide as he let it go increments at a time. He'd been here before a few times: the bridge of the *Felipe Souza*, crackling suddenly with transmission from the incoming rescue boat; stepping off the elevator platform at the bottom of the Hawking nanorack and onto ground that sucked at him with a full g; getting out of the teardrop taxi in Hampstead and looking up at Zooly's new pad, checking the street corner sign, wondering if this could really be it, if maybe he'd gotten her instructions wrong—and then seeing her come to the huge picture window and grin down at him, dimly seen through the tree-shadowed glass. The slip in your guts that tells you it's okay, you can let go now.

"Tell me something, Ertekin." The words came out of his mouth like exhaled smoke, pure unguarded conversation. He didn't much care what she thought or said in reply—just talking and knowing it wasn't going to get him shanked was the point. "You've worked for COLIN a couple of years, right?"

"Two and a half."

"So who's senior? You or Norton?"

He got the look again, but muted. Maybe she could hear the lack of cabling in his voice. "It doesn't work like that."

"No? So how does it work?" He gestured. "Come on, Ertekin. We're just talk-ing here. It's a beach, for fuck's sake."

The twitched corner of a smile, but he got the feeling it wasn't for him. He ges-tured again.

"Come on."

"Okay, I'll tell you." She shook her head. "One in the morning, the man wants to talk office politics. Works like this. Norton's an accredited COLIN investigator, a troubleshooter. Got a dozen years in, he went straight to them after law enforce-ment training in some upstate college. It's a good career move: COLIN pay way over average and most of the work isn't what you'd call hazardous. You're looking at anticorruption task forcing, chasing down local government scams on COLIN property, Marstech licensing breaches, that sort of thing."

"Not much serial homicide then."

"No. When things get heavy, they mostly hire muscle from private military contractors like ExOp or Lamberts. Where it's legally messy, they pull local PD liaison. That was me. I came in on a couple of Marstech hijacks where COLIN staff got killed, seconded from NYPD Homicide. They liked the work I did for them, Norton was moving up to a senior post, he needed a permanent partner with bloodwork experience, so." She shrugged. "Like that. They offered me the job. The money was a lot. I took it."

"But Norton still ranks you?"

Ertekin sighed. Looked out to sea.

"What?"

"Thirteens. You're all so fucking wired for hierarchy. Who's in charge? Who's at the top? Who do I have to dominate? Every detective I ever shared an office with, it—"

She stopped.

For a moment, he thought Norton was there, coming down the beach toward them from the bunkhouse. The mesh cranked, rustily. He flicker-checked the beach, saw nothing. Went back to her face and found her still staring out at the ocean.

"It what?"

"It doesn't matter," she said evenly. "Yeah, Norton ranks me. Norton knows COLIN inside and out. But he's not a cop and I am."

"So he defers to you?"

"We cooperate." She left the sea and met his eyes. "Strange concept for some-one like you, I know. But Norton's got nothing to prove."

"*And a thick head of hair*, right?"

The lyric left her looking blank. He guessed she was too young to really remember Angry Young and the Men. Carl owned their last album because, hey, who over the age of forty didn't, the download went triple platinum as soon as it hit the open stacks. But Ertekin would have been barely out of diapers at the time. He'd only just been old enough himself to take it on board when Angry Young blew his brains out all over the fittings of a Kilburn recording studio. *Making a Mess.* Right. Black-comic sly and London-gutter cool to the last. He sometimes wondered if Angry Young had known what would happen to sales of *Making a Mess* when he put the barrel of the frag carbine in his mouth that afternoon, grinned—apparently—at the sound man, and flipped the trigger. Whether he had in fact begun to guess when he'd scrawled out the title track and lyrics a year earlier.

"What's his hair got to do with it?"

"Well, it's hardly male-pattern baldness, is it?"

"Hardly . . . ." She got it. "Oh you're fucking kidding me. You can*not* be serious. Marsalis, *you* don't have male-pattern baldness."

"No. But I'm not human."

It stopped her like a shot from the Haag gun. Even in the last gasp glow from the arc lamps back up on the asphalt, he saw the way her stare tautened as she looked up at him. Her voice, when it came, was exactly as tight.

"You quoting somebody there?"

"Well, yeah." He chuckled, mostly because it was so good to be out there on the beach with his hands in his pockets and his feet in the sand. "Your guys, for a start."

She raised an eyebrow. "My guys?"

"Yeah. You're Turkish, right? Sevgi? Which pretty much makes you a Muslim, I'd guess. Don't you listen to what your bearded betters tell you about my kind?"

"For your information," she said thinly, "the last imam I listened to was a woman. She doesn't have much of a beard."

Carl shrugged. "Fair enough. I'm just drawing on global media here. Islam, the Vatican, those Jesusland Baptist guys. They're all singing pretty much the same hymn."

"You don't know what you're talking about."

"Oh excuse fucking me." He caught the flapping edge of his mood and dragged it back into place. *You got out of jail today, pal. Tomorrow, you get out of the Republic. Day after that you're on a suborb home. Just grin and bear it.* He pushed out a laugh. "I pretty much do know what I'm talking about, Ertekin. See, I live inside this skin. I was there in '93 when Jacobsen came into force. And in case you think this is demob self-pity, it isn't. We're not just talking about the thirteens here. In Dubai I saw indentured Thai bonobos disemboweled and strung up outside the brothels they worked in when the *shahuda* hit town. The ordinary whores they just raped and branded."

"The *shahuda* are not—"

"Yeah, yeah. The *shahuda* are not representative. Heard it. Just like the *gladius dei* don't speak for all those peace-loving Catholics out there, and all those Jesusland TV freaks got nothing to do with Christianity, either. It's all just a big misunderstanding, right. All this slaughter and blind prejudice, these guys just didn't read promotional literature."

"You're talking about fanatical mino—"

"Look, Ertekin." He found this time the laugh was genuine. "I really don't care. I'm a free man tonight, got my feet in the sand and everything. You want to do the group-solidarity thing, run salvage on your broken-down patriarchal belief system, you go right ahead. I've believed some fucking stupid things in my time. Why should you be any different?"

"I'm not going to discuss my faith with you."

"Good. Let's not, then."

They stood in the sand and listened to the quiet. Surf boomed on a reef somewhere offshore. Closer in, the smaller waves broke creamily in the gloom, made a white-noise hiss as they sucked back.

"How come you knew I was Turkish?" she asked him finally.

He shrugged. "Been there a lot. One time, I had an interpreter called Sevgi."

"What were you doing in Turkey?"

"What do you think."

"The tracts?"

He nodded somberly. "Yeah, standard European response. If it's nasty or inconvenient, park it in eastern Turkey. Too far away to upset anyone who matters, and a long walk west if anybody gets out unauthorized. Which happens enough to keep me going back there a couple of times a year. You from the eastern end?"

"No, I'm from New York."

"Right." He nodded. "Sorry. I meant—"

He stopped as her gaze shuttled past him and up the beach. Turned to follow, though long-honed proximity sense already told him this time Norton was there for real. There on the low crest of the dunes, scuffing down through the sand toward them, and, by every physical sign Carl knew how to read, hauling bad news in bulk.

"Toni Montes. Age forty-four, mother of two." The images flipped up in sequence on the conference room wall-screen as Norton talked. Vaguely handsome Hispanic woman, identity card shot, a strong-boned face fleshing out a little with age, henna-red hair cut short and stylish. *flip*. Body a graceless tangle in disarrayed skirt and blouse, limned in crime scene white on a polished wood floor. "Shot to death in her home in the Angeline Freeport this evening." *flip*. Close-up morgue shot. Face bruised at the mouth, makeup smeared, eyes blown black by the pressure of the head shot that had killed her. The entry wound sat in her forehead like a crater. *flip*. "Children were out at a swimming class with the father. The house is smart, wired into a securisoft neighborhood net and upgrade-paid for the next three years. Either Merrin broke in with some very sophisticated intrusion gear, or Toni let him in." *flip*. Body detail, one mottled flank and the sexless sag of a breast. "There was a fight, he knocked her around, put her on the floor more than once. A couple of her ribs were broken, there's substantial bruising pretty much everywhere. You saw the face. Blood traces everywhere, too; CSI got it off the couch in the other room, the walls, too, in a couple of places." *flip*. Red smears on stucco cream. "Most of it's hers. Seems like he really went to town."

"Did he rape her?" Carl asked.

flip.

"No. No detectable sexual assault."

"Same as the others," said Sevgi quietly. "Baltimore, Topeka, that shithole little town in Oklahoma. Loam Springs? Whenever he's killed a woman, it's been the same thing. Whatever this is about, it isn't sex."

flip.

"Siloam Springs," Norton supplied. "Shithole little town in Arkansas in fact, Sev. Just over the state line, remember?"

"No, I don't remember." Ertekin seemed to regret the retort almost immediately. She gestured. The edge dropped out of her voice. "We wired in, Tom. It's not like there was much chance to get to know the place."

Norton shrugged. "Time enough to decide it was a shithole, though, right?"

"Oh shut up. It's all Jesusland, isn't it?" Ertekin rubbed at an eye and nodded at the projection wall. "Why'd they flag this one up?"

The sequence of images had frozen on another section of pale cream wall, Rorschach-blotched with blood and tissue. A tiny red triangle pulsed on and off in the corner of the screen.

"Yeah, Angeline PD couldn't work this one out." Norton prodded the dataslate on the table. On the screen, a block of forensic data floated down onto the picture. "When Merrin finally killed this woman, he shot her standing upright in the next room. High-velocity electromag round; it went right through her head and into the wall behind. The angle suggests he was standing right in front of her. That's what doesn't fit. Dying on her knees when she's finally got no more fight in her, yeah, that I can see. But standing up and just taking it, after the struggle she put up. It doesn't make a lot of sense."

"Yeah, it does." Carl paused for a moment, testing the intuition, the lines of force it flowed along. He knew the shape of it the way his hand knew the butt of the Haag gun. "She gave up before she was done, because he threatened her with something worse."

"Worse than beating her to death?" There was an icy anger in the rims of Norton's eyes as he spoke. Carl couldn't tell if it extended to him as well as Merrin. "You want to tell me what that would be, exactly?"

"The children," said Ertekin quietly.

He nodded. "Yeah. Probably the husband as well, but it's the children that would have clinched it. Playing to her genetic wiring. He told her he'd wait until the children came home."

"You can't know that," said Norton, still angry.

"No, of course not. But it's the obvious explanation. He got in through the house defenses. Either Montes knew him and let him in, or he gutted the software, in which case he'd been scoping the house well enough to know the systems, so he certainly would have known that there were children, that they'd be back soon. That was his leverage, that was what he used."

He saw the way a look went between them.

"It works, up to a point," Ertekin said, more to herself than anyone else. "But all it does is turn the question around. If he was prepared to use a threat like that, why not use it from scratch? Why bother dancing around the furniture in the first place?"

Carl shook his head. "I don't know. But to me, the shot looks like an execution. The fight must have been something else."

"Interrogation? You think this was about extracting a confession?"

Carl thought about it for a moment, staring into the border of glare and gloom where the side of the screen edged out on the wall. Recollection coiled loose like snakes—this woman seemed to dislodge memory in him practically every time she opened her fucking mouth. Back in the jail—*did you ever think that?*—it was the passageways of the *Felipe Souza* and the cold inevitability of his thoughts as he waited out the rescue. Now she had him again. The hot, tiny room in a nameless Tehran backstreet. Blocks of sunlight etched into the floor, the shadow of a single barred window. Stale sweat and the faint aroma of scorched flesh. Discordant screaming from down the hall. Blood on his fist.

"I don't think so. There are smarter ways of getting information."

"Then what?" pushed Norton. "Just straight sadism? Or is this some kind of *übermensch* thing? Brutalism by genetic right."

Carl met the other man's eyes for a moment, just to let him know. Norton held his gaze.

Carl shrugged. "Maybe it was rage," he said. "For whatever reasons, maybe this Merrin just lost control."

Ertekin frowned. "All right. But then he just, what? Just calmed down and executed her?"

"Maybe."

"That still doesn't make much sense to me," said Norton.

Carl shrugged again, this time dismissive. "Why should it?"

"What's that supposed to mean?"

"It means, Norton, that at a basic biochemical level, you're not like Merrin. None of you are. Down in the limbic system where it counts, across the amygdalae and up into the orbitofrontal cortex, Merrin has about a thousand biochemical processes going on that you don't have." Carl had meant to come across calm and detached—social aptitude routines had his body language and speech locked away from confrontational. But outside it all, the weariness in his own voice astounded him. He finished abruptly. "Of course it doesn't make sense to you. You don't have a map for where this guy is right now."

Quiet in the softly lit conference room. He could feel Ertekin's gaze on him like a touch. He looked at his hands.

"You said he's killed twenty others apart from this one."

Norton fielded it. "Seventeen confirmed, genetic trace material recovered at the scene. There are another four we're not so sure about. That's not including the people he murdered and ate aboard *Horkan's Pride*."

"Yeah. You got this stuff mapped out? Where he's been?"

He didn't look up, but he felt the glance run between them again.

"Sure," said Norton.

He worked the dataslate deck and the image of Toni Montes's blood went away. In its place, continental North America glowed to life, stitched with highways and slashed red along the excision lines of the Rim States and the Union. The map was punched through with seventeen black squares and four gray, each checked against a thumbnail victim photo. Carl got up and went to the wall for a closer look. The Angeline Freeport marker showed a laughing Toni Montes, hair styled up for some party and an off-the-shoulder gown. He touched it gently, and detailed data scrolled down beneath. Mother, wife, real estate feed host. Corpse.

He looked at the other images pockmarking the map. They were mostly similar, careless snapshots, lives caught in the living. In a couple of cases, the image was an ID holoprint, but mostly it was smiles and squints for the camera, close-cropped to cut family members or friends from the frame. The faces looking down were a mix of races and a range of ages, midthirties all the way up to one old man in his late sixties. Married, single, with children, without. Work ranging from datasystems specialties to manual labor.

They had nothing in common but the continent they lived on and the fact they were dead.

He moved back to the West Coast. Norton did something to the dataslate, and a Bay Area blowup slid out on top of the main map. The *Horkan's Pride* splash-down was marked in a not-to-scale box just off the coast, eleven faces and names stacked on top of one another beside it. Then three more red squares, all clustered around San Francisco and Oakland. Carl stared at the grouping for a moment, aware, at some level, that something didn't gel. He frowned, touched and read the scroll-down data.

Saw the dates.

"Yeah, that's right." Ertekin moved up behind him. Abruptly, he could smell her. "He came back. Two kills, same day *Horkan's Pride* hits the water. Then he's gone, across the frontier into the Republic. Next stop Van Horn, Texas, June 19. Eddie Tanaka, shot to death outside a cathouse on Interstate 10. And then he's back in the Bay Area again, nearly four months later, October 2, killing this Jasper Whitlock. What does that suggest to you?"

"He forgot his wallet?"

"There you go. I knew there was some reason we hired you."

Carl twisted and gave her a reproachful look. Something happened in the line of her mouth. He breathed in lightly, trying for her scent again. "He's working off partial data. However he came up with this hit list, he didn't have all the names at the start. Why cross into Jesusland in June when he's got to come all the way back and do this guy, uh, Whitlock, later. And now we've got Montes, she's down in the Angeline Freeport. That's a short run down from the bay, and no frontier checks. He's making this up as he goes along."

"Right. What we figured, too." Ertekin backed off a little, ended up close to where Norton was sitting. "If Jasper Whitlock had been another Eddie Tanaka type, you could maybe have sold me on Merrin not finding him first time around, needing to go back. But Whitlock was a medical services broker. All aboveboard, upright citizen, pillar of the community, ran his own business. Not the sort of guy that's too hard to find. Merrin shot him sitting behind the desk in his own office. So it's got to be, Merrin didn't know he had to kill this guy back in June. He found out later."

"Question is where from?" Carl stared at the continental map, the scattered black flags. "He crosses the border to ice Tanaka, goes all the way to Texas. Any sign that he was after information there?"

"No. Tanaka was strictly a small-time scumbag. Drugs, illicit abortions. The odd smuggled-organ deal."

Norton looked up from the dataslate, face deadpan. "In fact, the Jesusland version of a medical services broker."

"Well . . ."

Ertekin scowled. "We already chased that connection," she told Carl. "Tanaka's got no official medical standing, in the Republic or anywhere else. He was a bio-hazard engineer by trade—"

"Rat catcher," supplied Norton.

"Unemployed anyway for the last two years, living mostly off a string of women out of El Paso and points east. Before that, Houston, similar profile. Best guess is that's how he got into the abortion provision in the first place. There's a lot more money in it than—"

"Catching rats." Carl nodded slowly. "Right. So I'm looking at this map, we've got southeastern Texas, northern Texas, western Oklahoma, then two in Colorado, one suspected in Iowa, Kansas one suspected one dead cert, Ohio, Michigan, two in Illinois, South Carolina suspected, Maryland suspected, Louisiana, Georgia, and northern Florida. Have you got *any* ties between any of these victims? Anything that gels at all?"

The look on Ertekin's face was answer enough. She was staring at the map, too, and the scattered faces of the dead.

"He could be getting them out of the phone book for all we know," said Norton soberly.

CHAPTER 14

The sounds of shouting dragged her awake.

For a confused moment, she thought it was a theft or some excessive haggling down in the market. Then the rhythmic element in the voices made it through the wrap of sleep and she remembered where she was. She sat up sharply in the narrow barrack room bed. The inside of her head felt grimy with the lack of syn. On the other side of the room, dawn was seeping through at the edges of the moth-eaten varipolara curtain; pearl-gray light lay across the ceiling and down the far wall in blurred stripes. She looked at her watch and groaned. The chanting outside was too muffled to make sense of, but she didn't need to hear the words.

On the table beside the bed, her phone rang.

"Yeah?"

Norton's voice filtered into her ear. "Hear the fans?"

"I'm awake, aren't I?"

"Good call, Sev. If we'd stayed in town, we'd be fucked. That nasty cop mind of yours saves the day again."

"So." She flapped back the sheet, swung her legs out of bed to the floor. The skin on her thighs goosefleshed in the cool air. "Parris has friends in Tallahassee after all."

"Better than that." There was a sour grin in Norton's voice. "He went to the media feeds. We're all over *Good Morning South.*"

"Ah, *fuck.*" Groping around on the floor with her free hand for clothes. "You think we can still get out of here okay?"

"Well, not by suborb, that's for sure. Whatever was keeping the lid on Marsalis's genetic secrets at South Florida State is long gone now. He's blown. Either Parris talked, or somebody leaked higher up."

"Got to be Parris."

"Yeah, well, in any case, now you got Jesuslanders fifty-deep outside both gates and backing up down the access road for a couple of klicks at least. Real Die-for-the-Lord types by the look of it. I just got off the phone to our press liaison in Miami and she tells me there are bible thumpers lining up for airtime from here to Alaska." She could hear him grinning again. "We're not just trying to evade Republican justice anymore, Sev. We're harboring an abomination before the Lord."

"Great. So what do we do?" Sevgi stuck an arm into a shirtsleeve. "Fly home the old-fashioned way? COLIN's got to have a couple of flatline Lears down here, right? For short-hop VIPs."

"I would think so, yes."

"And they're not going to shoot us out of the sky when we hit Republic airspace, are they?"

Norton said nothing. Sevgi remembered her profiler cups halfway through seaming her shirt shut. She split the seam back open, peered around on the floor.

"Come *on*, Tom. You can't seriously think—"

"Okay, no, they probably won't shoot us down. But they might force the pilot back to a landing at Miami International and take us off the plane there. We're not popular in these parts, Sev."

"Not fucking popular anywhere," she muttered. She caught the translucent gleam of a p-cup at the foot of the bed. She fished it up between two fingers and pressed it up under the weight of her right breast. "All right, Tom. What do you want to do?"

"Let me talk to Nicholson." He rode out her snort. "Sev, he may be an asshole, but he's still responsible for operations. It doesn't look any better for him than for us if we end up slammed in some Miami jail."

Sevgi prowled the darkened room looking for the other p-cup. "Nicholson won't get in a fight at state legislature level, Tom, and you know it. He's too much of a political animal to upset people with that much clout. If Tallahassee gets in line behind this thing, we're going to be left twisting in the wind down here."

Another hesitation. Outside, the sounds of the crowd surged like distant surf. Sevgi found the cup under the bed, dug it out, and fitted it awkwardly, left-handed, under her left breast. She sat on the edge of the bed and started seaming her shirt shut again.

"Tell me I'm wrong, Tom."

"I think you are wrong, Sev. Nicholson is going to see this as interference with his COLIN Security authority, and at a minimum it's going to make him look bad. Even if he doesn't take on Tallahassee directly himself, he'll kick it upstairs with an urgent-action label attached."

"And meanwhile, what? We sit tight here?"

"There are more unpleasant places to be stranded, Sev." He sighed. "Look. Worst-case scenario, you get to spend the day on the beach with your new pal."

"*My* new . . ." Sevgi took the phone away from her ear and stared at it. The little screen was an innocent matte gray. Norton hadn't enabled the v-feed. "Fuck you, Tom."

"It was a *joke*, Sev."

"Yeah? Well, next time you're down on Fifth Avenue, get yourself a new fucking sense of humor."

She killed the call.

From the landward observation tower, it didn't look like much. Several hundred variously dressed men and women milling about in front of the facility gate while off to the left a suited, white-haired figure declaimed from behind a portable plastic ampbox podium. A couple of amateurish, hastily scrawled holo-placards tilted about in the air above the crowd. Teardrops and a few old-style IC vehicles were parked back along the access road, and people leaned against their flanks in ones and twos. Early-morning sunlight winked and glinted off glass and alloy surfaces. A couple of helicopters danced in the sky overhead, media platforms by the look of their livery.

It didn't look like much, but they were a good two hundred meters back from the gate here; the noise was faint, and detail hard to see. Sevgi had worked crowd control a few time as a patrol officer, and she'd learned not to make snap judgments about situations involving massed humanity. She knew how quickly it could turn.

". . . may have the form of a man, but do not be deceived by his form." The words rinsed up from the podium sound system, still relatively unhysterical. Whoever the preacher was, he was building up slowly. "Man is made in the image and love of God. This. *Creature.* Was made by arrogant sinners, by shattering the seed God gave us in His wisdom. The Bible tells us . . ."

She tuned it out. Squinted up at one of the helicopters as it banked.

"No sign of the state police?" she asked the tower guard.

He shook his head. "They'll show up if those clowns start charging the gate, not before. And only then because they know we're authorized to use lethal force if there's a line breach."

His face was impassive, but the sour edge in his voice was unmistakable. The name on his chest tag read KIM, but Sevgi guessed Korean American was close enough to Chinese for a common bitterness to find roots. Back before Secession, the Zhang fever mobs hadn't been all that selective in their lynchings.

"I doubt it'll come to that." She faked a breezy confidence. "We'll be out of your hair before lunchtime. They'll all go home after that."

"Good to know."

She left him staring out across the COLIN defenses at the crowd and made her way back down the caged staircase to the ground. There was an ominous quiet around the facility, in contrast with the noise outside. They'd suspended nanorack operations while the crisis lasted, and the storage hangars were all closed up. Tracked freight loaders ten meters broad squatted immobile on the evercrete aprons and access paths, like massive, scalped tanks, abandoned at the end of some colossal urban conflict. Their mortarboard lifting platforms were all empty.

At the other end of the complex, the 'rack thrust up into the cloud cover like a god-size fire escape. It made everything on the ground feel like toys. They'd built Perez early on, back when Mars was still a barely scratched desert and Brad-bury a collection of pressurized 'fabs. Now it looked used and grim, all mottled grays and blacks and overstated support structure. Compared with the cheery, brightly colored minimalism at Sagan or Kaku, Perez was a relic. Even for Sevgi, who didn't like the 'racks whatever fucking color they came in, it was a melancholy sight.

"Ever been up?"

She looked around and saw that Marsalis had gotten within two meters of her back without giving himself away. Now he stood watching her with a blank speculation that reminded her of Ethan so much, it sent shivers up from the base of her spine.

"Not this one, no." She nodded vaguely northward. "They trained me in New York. Kaku 'rack, mostly. I've been up Sagan and Hawking as well, and what they've built of Levin."

"You don't sound overenthusiastic."

"No."

It made him smile. "But the money's good. Right?"

"The money's good," she agreed.

He looked away, toward the gate. The smile faded out.

"Is all that noise out there for me?"

"Yes, it is." She felt oddly embarrassed, as if the Republicans on the other side of the wire were acquaintances whose bad behavior she had to cover for. "Blame your old friend Parris. Apparently he took exception to your departure after all. He's fed the whole thing to the local media."

"Smart of you to bring us here last night, then."

She shrugged. "I worked witness protection for a while. You learn never to take anything for granted."

"I see." He seemed to consider for a moment. "Are you people going to give me a gun?"

"That's not part of the deal. Didn't you read the fine print?"

"No."

It brought her up short. "You didn't?"

"Ever spent time in a Jesusland justice facility?" He put on a gentle smile, but his eyes were hard with memory. "It's not the sort of place you quibble over detail if they come to let you out."

"Right." She cleared her throat. "Well, the fine print says that you're retained by COLIN in an advisory capacity, not for actual enforcement. So, ah, you don't need a gun."

"I will if our Jesusland friends decide to storm the fences."

"That's not going to happen here."

"Your confidence is inspiring. Can we fly out of here?"

"It doesn't look like it. Tom's working the diplomatic angle, but it'll be awhile before we know if we can take the risk. In this part of the world, the Air Nationals tend to shoot first and sift wreckage afterward."

"Yeah, I've heard that." He turned away from the powered fences and the gate, looking out across the shimmering surface of the Atlantic. "Speaking of which, any idea why the skycops in the Rim didn't shove a heatseeker up *Horkan's* arse when it crossed the line? I hear those boys are pretty jumpy, too, and it must have profiled pretty much like a threat."

"Local COLIN liaison talked them out of it, apparently."

"Yeah?" Marsalis raised an eyebrow.

"Yes. Relations with the Rim are pretty good these days. It's not like down here. We negotiated a direct AI interface last year, high-level trust protocols, minimal buffering. The Sagan n-djinn mapped the trajectory and shunted it straight to the Rim Air Authority. No blocks, no datachecks above basic. It cleared the buffers in a couple of nanoseconds." Sevgi spread her hands. "Everyone's happy."

"Especially Merrin."

She said nothing. The sporadic chanting at the gate reached them between gusts of wind coming off the ocean. After a couple of seconds, Marsalis started away from her in the direction of the water. He didn't speak or look back. It took her his first three steps to understand he'd been waiting for her to continue the conversation, and now that she hadn't he was leaving.

"Where are you going?" It came out a lot less casually than she would have liked.

He stopped and turned back to her. "Why?" he asked gravely. "Am I in some kind of protective custody?"

Fuck it. "No, it's just." She gestured awkwardly. "In case I need to find you later, in a hurry."

He weighed it, the way he had the comment about her work for WP.

"I'm going for another walk on the beach," he said. "Want to come?"

"Ah . . . no." She hesitated. He was waiting. "I need to go over the Montes crime scene while we've got the time. See if there's anything that jumps out."

"Is that likely?"

"No, but you never know. I've been looking at Merrin's handiwork for the last four months, Angeline PD haven't. There might be something."

"No direct data interface there, then?"

"No. Technically, they're not part of RimSec. It's the Freeport legislation, Angeline PD have autonomy, they work pretty much like any city police department over in the Republic."

"And you're not sharing what you've got on this with any of those guys?"

"No. I told you, we don't want a panic on our hands." She threw out a weary signpost arm toward the chanting. "Listen to that. How do you think people like that are going to react to the news that there's a cannibal thirteen loose in North America, murdering selected citizens at his leisure. Remember Sundersen?"

"Eric Sundersen?" A shrug. "Sure. I spent a couple of months looking for him last year, just like everybody else."

"Then you'll remember what it was like. Seven weeks, and we nearly had martial law declared in five states of the Republic. Media screaming off the screen about clone monsters. Armed mobs trying to break into the tract at Cimarron and slaughter everyone there. Emergency measures all along the Rim frontier. If Sundersen hadn't broken cover when he did, it would have been Zhang fever all over again. And all he did was escape. He hadn't killed anybody. With this one, the mobs would go fucking crazy."

"Yeah, mobs. You humans have that trick down, don't you."

Sevgi ignored the jibe.

"We just don't want another bloodbath," she said doggedly. "We make local police aware that we have an interest, and we give them what help we can. But we can't afford anyone to know the whole picture."

He nodded. His walk on the beach seemed forgotten. "So what picture are they getting?"

"The cover story in the Republic is Marstech. A heist gang and a distribution network, squabbling over product." The words tasted stale on her tongue, as concocted and unconvincing as some corporate mission statement. She forced down a grimace and pressed on. "With scumbags like Eddie Tanaka that's been easy to sell. Elsewhere, when the victim's respectable, we're playing the collateral damage angle. Innocent bystanders caught in the crossfire, or cases of mistaken identity."

"Sounds a little creaky. What are you doing about the genetic trace?"

"Taking it off their hands. The COLIN n-djinns have access to police data-stacks right across North America; they fish out anything that fits the profile. That's usually long before Forensics get around to running a gene scan on the crime scene traces, so in most cases we get there before anybody knows there's been a thirteen at the scene."

"Most cases?"

"Yeah, been a couple of medical examiners we've had to lean on, get them to shut up." She looked away. "It isn't hard to do that with COLIN authority."

"No, I don't imagine it is."

She could feel herself flush a little. "Look, I have to get over to the upload building. You want to hit the beach, that's fine."

"No, it's okay. I'll walk with you."

She gave him a sharp look. He looked innocently back.

"May as well look at this Montes myself," he said. "Start earning my keep."

So they crossed the apron from the observation tower together, heading for the main complex. There was some heat in the day now, and Sevgi's own slightly stale scent pricked in her nostrils. She began to wish she'd had a shower before she tumbled out of the hospitality suite and into action.

"So, you were saying," Marsalis prompted. "The Republic don't know this is linked to *Horkan's Pride*."

"No. The media coverage said there were no survivors. We let them have the cannibalism angle, and told them anybody still alive would have been killed on impact. We let them have pictures."

"Ah."

"Yeah." Sevgi curled her lip. "Cannibal Ghost Ship Horror—click for further images. Worked like a dream, they ran with it, splashed it across every site on the net. They completely forgot to do any investigative journalism."

"Handy."

She shrugged. "Standard. American media's been taking sensation over fact for better than a hundred years now, and Secession just loaded the trend. Anyway, it *is* a miracle Merrin survived the crash. I mean, he had to find some way to trick the systems into accepting him back into his cryocap, which is glitched to fuck so the cryogen protocol doesn't work anymore. So he's got to beat that, he's got to persuade the cryocap to fill with gel anyway, to drown a live, unsedated body—"

"Not like he didn't have the spare time to work it all out."

"I *know*. But that's just the start. He's then got to lie there and *let* the system drown him, unsedated. He's got to *breathe* the gel, unsedated, awake, without his lungs revolting, for a good twenty minutes while *Horkan's Pride* programs its final approach, hits reentry, course-corrects, and comes down in the ocean."

A freight loader bulked dinosaur-like on their right, blocking out the angle of the early-morning sun. Sevgi shivered a little as they stepped into the long shadow it cast. She looked across at Marsalis, almost accusingly.

"You want to think what that must have been like—locked in an upright coffin with that shit filling your nose and your mouth and your throat, pouring in and filling up your lungs, pressing in on your eyeballs, and all around you the whole ship feels like it's shaking itself apart, maybe is shaking itself apart for all you know. Can you imagine what that would have felt like?"

"I'm trying not to," he said mildly. "Do we know how he got ashore?"

She nodded. "First victim in the Bay Area, Ulysses Ward. You saw him on the map last night. Tailored microfauna magnate, he had culture farms all over the Marin County shoreline and a bunch of those tethered plankton trays about a hundred klicks off the coast. We don't have the satellite footage to be sure, but it looks like he was out there doing maintenance when *Horkan's Pride* came down. Got curious, got too close, got himself killed."

"Or he went out there specifically to pick Merrin up."

"Yeah, we thought of that, too. RimSec did an n-djinn search, couldn't find any links between Ward and Merrin. We went back forty years. Unless they knew each other in a previous life, this is exactly what it looks like—a bad-luck coincidence."

"How'd he kill him?"

"Cressi sharkpunch. You ever see anyone killed with one of those things?" Sevgi gestured graphically. "Designed to stop a great white shark through ten meters of water, it's practically a handheld disintegrator. Blew Ward's belly out all over the surrounding furniture. Him plus another employee name of Emil Nocera, all in the same shot."

"Thanks for the ride."

"Right. CSI say there were another couple of employees around at the time, but they ran."

"Hard to blame them."

"Yeah, plus they were illegals. Apparently a lot of the casual labor up that way is. They see something, they're not going to hang around and make witness statements. RimSec are looking, but they don't hold out much hope."

"Do they know what this is about?"

"RimSec do, but that's as far as it's gone. There's no public knowledge, we can't afford it, and neither can they. Things are bad enough between Jesusland and the Rim without word getting out that this guy's treating their precious border security like a knee-high picket fence."

"But the Rim cops know he's killing in the Republic as well?"

"They've been apprised, yes."

"Nice of them to keep quiet about it for you."

"Well, like I said, there's no love lost across the fencelines. And it looks bad if the high-powered high-tech Rim States couldn't stop some psychotic killer crossing over and going on the rampage in the Republic. You can see how that'd play diplomatically."

"What price technology without God on your side?"

"Right. Plus, if word got out that said psychotic killer is a, uh . . ."

"A genetic monster?" he asked gently. "A twist?"

"I didn't say that."

"No. I guess you didn't."

"The Republic are already handing their people a line of shit about how the Rim is just a craven appeasement system for the Chinese. And with the stories coming out of China, the black lab escapees—" She shrugged again. "Well, you can see how that one'd play as well, right?"

"Pretty much. Nothing like a good monster scare."

They cleared the shadow of the freight loader. Sevgi turned her head to beat the sudden glare of the sun and thought she caught a smile slipping across the black man's lips. His gaze had rolled out to somewhere well beyond the gathering of buildings around the nanorack.

"Something funny?"

His attention reeled back in, but he didn't look at her. "Not really."

She stopped.

After a couple of paces, so did he, and turned to face her. "Something the matter?"

"If you've got something to contribute," she said evenly, "then I would like to hear it. This isn't going to work unless you talk to me."

He looked at her for a long couple of moments. "It's really not very important," he said easily. "I guess you'd call it a resonance."

She stood where she was. "Resonance with what."

He sighed. "A resonance with monsters. Do you know what a *pistaco* is?"

She dredged memory, pulled up something from a long-ago briefing on alti-plano training camp crimes. "Yeah, it's some sort of demon, right? Something the Indians believe in. Some sort of vampire?"

"Close. *Pistaco*'s a white man with a long knife who comes at night and chops up Indians to get at their body fat. Most likely, it's a cultural memory from the conquistadores and the Inquisition, because they certainly weren't averse to a bit of dismemberment in the name of Gold and Jesus Christ. But these days, up on the altiplano they've got a new angle on the story."

"Which is what?"

Marsalis grinned. She was appalled at how much it reminded her of Ethan, at how it reached inside and touched her in the place he used to.

"These days," he said, "the Andeans don't believe the *pistaco* is the white man as such anymore. That's gone. Still the same monster, still looks the same, but now the story they tell is, the *pistaco*'s something evil that the white man's *brought back*."

He nodded toward the dark towering webbed architecture of the nanorack.

"Brought back from Mars."

CHAPTER 15

The sweep and swoop of the codes took hold.

Sevgi felt herself dislodged from current reality, turned away from it like a small child guided away from a TV screen by warm parental hands. The couches at COLIN Florida were clunky, thirty-year-old military surplus stock, fully enclosed and soundproofed, and now, in the deadened stillness they created, there was a low chiming that seemed to resonate deep in her guts. From long habit, she let herself home in on it. Gentle steerage to the new focus. *Look at this, look at this.* The colors above her seemed to mesh into significance just out of reach. The chiming was the beat of her heart, the shiver of blood along veins and arteries, a cellular awareness. The swirling ebbed and inked back, glaring out like antique celluloid film melting through. The standard desert format inked in.

She looked around. Marsalis was not with her.

"Good afternoon, ma'am."

The Freeport PD 'face was a handsome black patrolman in his early twenties, insignia winking in the jarringly heatless Arizona sun. The fabric of his short-sleeved uniform had a perfect, factory-fresh texture to it, and so did his flawless, airbrushed skin. Muscle roped his forearms and bulked out his shoulders. He might have stepped, Sevgi thought sourly, out of the early stages of a porn experia, the storyline section before the clothes came off. She guessed the intention was to inspire confidence and respect for the symbols of Angeline law enforcement, but all it did was put her on the edge of a giggle and make her slightly warm.

Oh well, at least it isn't another fucking body-perfect überbitch.

More than slightly warm, in fact.

"Uh, I'm waiting—"

"For a colleague." The 'face nodded. "He's incoming, but it's taking some time. May I see your authorization?"

Sevgi lifted an open palm and watched as the skeins of bluish machine code fell out of it. They splashed on the ground with a faint crackling and disappeared into the dirt as if soaked up. Despite the color, it felt uncomfortably like watching herself bleed through a slashed wrist. At least, what she'd *imagined* it would when—

Stop that.

"Thank you, ma'am. You are cleared to proceed." Ahead of her, the familiar adobe datahomes swam rapidly into existence. The 'face stepped aside to indicate Sevgi's new status. "Your colleague also."

She hadn't noticed. Beside her, Marsalis was shading in. Looking at him as he solidified, she suddenly lost all interest in the patrolman. The attraction was in the flaws, the lines in the face, the faint and flattened scar across his left hand that looked like a burn, the barely perceptible tangles of gray in the hair. The way his mouth crimped slightly to the right when he looked at the patrolman. The way he took up space as if blocking a doorway to somewhere. The way—

She still wasn't sure why he'd suddenly opted to join her in the virtuality.

"You took your time," she said, a little more harshly than she'd intended.

He shrugged. "Blame the genes. Thirteens run high resistance to hypnotic technique. I knew some guys back in Osprey who had to be sedated before they could use a v-format at all. Shall we go have a look at Toni?"

The 'face led them across the sand to the closest of the datahomes. PRIMARY CRIME SCENE hung in the air beside it in holographic blue. Unusually, the adobe structure had a door. The patrolman worked the black iron latch and pushed the raw wood surface inward. It opened incongruously onto a prissily decorated suburban front hall.

"My name is Cranston," said the 'face as it stood back to let them pass. "If you need departmental assistance, please call me. The victim is in the dining room. Second door on the left. Feel free to touch or move anything, but if you wish the changes to be saved, you'll need to advise me."

They found Toni Montes sprawled on the dining room floor not far from the section of wall where her blood and brains were splashed. She'd rolled when she fell and landed on her side, head turned, displaying the soggy mess of the exit wound. Her limbs were a seemingly boneless tangle, her feet bare. The faintly shimmering white corpse outline seemed to isolate her from the surroundings of her home, as if preparatory to snipping her out of the picture. As they approached, supplementary data scrolled up over the body in neat holographic boxes. Tissue trauma, time of death. Probable causes of secondary injuries. Age, sex, race. Genetic salients.

"I hate that shit," said Sevgi, for something to say. "Fucking convenience culture, it just gets in the way of what you're trying to see."

"You can probably disable it."

"Yeah." She made no move to summon Cranston. "Back when I started on the
force, NYPD ran trials on this option where you could get the corpse to talk to
you."

"Jesus, whose fucked-up idea was that?" But it was said absently. Marsalis knelt
by the body, brow creased.

"I don't know. Some datageek with too much time on his hands, looking for a
creative edge. Rationale was, it was to prevent desensitizing. Supposed to bring
back to you the fact that this was once a living, breathing human being."

"Right." He took one of the dead woman's hands, which had fallen cupped
loosely upward, and lifted it gently. He seemed to be stroking her fingers.

Sevgi crouched beside him. "Well, they already had the models where you
could get the victim to reverse from moment of death, back up, and then walk
through the probable sequence of events. Guess it wasn't that much of a stretch."

He turned to look at her, face suddenly close. "Can we do that here?"

"You want to?"

Another shrug. "We've got time to kill, haven't we?"

"All right. Cranston?"

The 'face shaded undramatically into being across the room from them, like a
pre-millennial photo Sevgi had once seen developed chemically at a seminar.

"What can I do for you?"

Sevgi got up and gestured. "Can you run the crime event model for us? Last
few minutes only."

"No problem. You'll need to come through to the front room; that's where it
seems to have started. I'll engage the system now. Do you want sound?"

Sevgi, who'd watched a lot of this sort of thing, shook her head.

"No, just the motions."

"Then if you'll follow me."

Unnervingly, the patrolman stepped directly through the wall. They left
the body and took the more conventional route through the connecting door to
the front room, where Cranston was waiting. As they came in, the sky outside the
room's window darkened abruptly to night and the drapes drew themselves part-
way closed like some cheap horror-flick effect. An unharmed edition of Toni
Montes stood in for the ghost—she shaded back to life in the center of the room,
feet still shod in mint-and-cream espadrilles that picked up the colors in her skirt
and blouse. Her makeup was intact, and she looked impossibly composed.

A pace away from her, the system penciled in the perpetrator.

It was a black outline of a man, a figure with the smooth, characterless features and standardized body mass of an anatomical sketch, all done in shiny jet. But it breathed, and it swayed slightly, and it sprang at Toni Montes and hit her with a savage, looping backfist. The image of the woman flew silently backward, tripped, and fell on the couch. One espadrille came off, flipped ludicrously high, and landed on the other side of the room. The black figure went after Montes, seized her by the throat, and punched her in the face. She flopped and slumped. The other espadrille came off. She pushed herself away along the couch, stumbled toward upright while the black figure stood and watched with robot calm. When Montes got to her feet, it stepped in again and punched her high in the chest. She flew back into the drapes, rolled, staggered upright. She flailed with nails, got a backhand for her trouble that knocked her fully across the room. The edge of the opened door to the hall caught her in the back. This time she went down and stayed down.

The black figure stalked after her.

"At this point," said the 'face, "the model estimates the killer force-marched Montes into the other room, threw her back against the wall, and shot her through the head. Reasons for the change of tactic are still under consideration. It may be that he was concerned the killing would be seen through the window to the street."

The black figure bent over Montes and hauled her to her feet by the hair. It pinioned her arm into the small of her back and shoved her, struggling, toward the connecting door to the dining room. At the threshold, the two figures froze in tableau.

"Would you like to relocate to view the final sequence?"

Sevgi glanced at Marsalis. He shook his head. "No. Turn it off."

Montes and her black cutout killer blurred and vanished. Marsalis walked through the space where they'd been, leaving Sevgi in the front room. When she followed, she found him knelt once more by the corpse, apparently reading the scroll-ups.

"See something you like?" It was an old homicide joke, crime scene black humor. It was out of her mouth before she realized she'd said it.

He looked up and seemed to be scanning the room. "I'm going to need to see prior record."

She blinked at him. "Prior record of what?"

"Her prior record." He indicated the sprawled corpse. "Montes."

"Marsalis, she was a fucking housewife." Angry, she realized, with herself and the ease with which she'd slid back into crime scene macabre. She brought her voice down. "This is a suburban mother of two who sold real estate part-time. What record are you talking about?"

He hesitated. Got up and stared around the room again, as if he couldn't work out how Montes had come to be living with this décor.

"Marsalis?"

He faced her. "If this woman was a real estate saleswoman, I'm a fucking bonobo. You want to get some air?"

She cranked an eyebrow. "In a virtuality?"

"Figure of speech. There's got to be a briefing level somewhere in this format. How about we go there?"

The briefing level was cut-rate, a mesa top that you got to from anywhere in the construct by reciting a key code Cranston provided them with. The system switched without any transition you could feel to a viewpoint high up over the desert and the spread of datahomes on the plain below. Over time, it appeared various AFPD detectives had imported their own custom touches, and now the mesa top was littered with favorite armchairs in clashing upholstery, a couple of tatami mats, a hammock strung on two thick steel hooks embedded, startlingly, in floating patches of brickwork, another slung more conventionally between two full-size palm trees, a pool table, and, for some inexplicable reason, a tipped-over antique motorcycle with an ax buried in its fuel tank.

It was very quiet up there, just the wind catching on edges of rock in the cliff face below. Quiet enough that you thought if you listened carefully, you might be able to hear the faint static hiss of the base datasystems turning over. Carl stared down at the adobe structures for a while, not listening for anything, thinking it over. The datahomes seemed very distant, and he supposed that was appropriate. There was nothing here he needed to interest himself in more than superficially. He wondered how much to bother telling Ertekin, how much cooperation he needed to fake to keep her cop instincts cooled.

"Look," he said finally. "That fight they've modeled down there is bullshit. Montes wasn't a victim, she fought this guy all the way. She knew *how* to fight. That's why the slippers came off. She didn't lose them in the battering, she kicked them off so she could fight better."

"And you're basing this on what?"

"Initially, instinct." He held up a hand to forestall her protest. "Ertekin, this isn't some fucked-in-the-head serial killer we're talking about. Merrin came all the way to the Freeport just to kill this woman. That has to make her something special."

"Maybe so. But it doesn't make her a combat specialist."

"No. But her hands do." He raised both his own hands now, palms toward his face, fingers loosely curled, halfway to a double fist guard. "There's bone alloy marbling across the knuckles, you can feel it under the skin. Probably calcicrete. That's combat tech."

"Or part of a menopausal support regime."

"At forty-four?"

Ertekin shook her head stubbornly. "I looked through the file last night. There's nothing about combat training there. And anyway, it doesn't gel with the genetic trace material under her fingernails. You really think a combat pro would bother *scratching* her attacker?"

"No. I think she did that when she'd already given up. When she'd already made the decision to let him kill her."

"Why would . . ."

He saw the way it dawned on her, the way her brow smoothed out and the heavy-lidded eyes widened slightly. In the Arizona construct sunlight, he realized suddenly that they were irised in flecked amber.

"She knew we'd find it," she said.

"Yeah." He looked somberly down at the datahomes again. "Toni here was gathering evidence for us. Just think about that for a moment. This is a woman who knows she's about to die. A minute or less off her own death, she's calculating how to take this guy down posthumously. Now, *that* is either psychotic force of will, or training. Or a bit of both."

They both stood in silence for a while. He glanced at her again and saw how the wind twitched her hair around the lines of her jaw. Tiny motion, barely there at all, but something about it set off an itching in the pit of his stomach. She must have felt some of it, too, because she turned and caught him looking. He got the full sunlit force of the tiger eyes for a moment, then she looked hurriedly away.

"Gene analysis says no enhancement," she said. "Standard chromosome set, twenty-three pairs, no anomalies."

"I didn't say there would be." He sighed. "That's the fucking problem these days. Anything extraordinary shows up in anyone, we all go running to the augment catalog looking for correlation. Got to be something crammed into an Xtrasome, something fucking *engineered*. No one ever wonders if it might just be good old-fashioned heredity and formative conditioning."

"That's because these days it mostly isn't."

"Yeah, don't fucking remind me. Anyone wins anything these days, they're up there plugging some gene frame consortium as soon as the cameras roll." Carl lifted his arms in acceptance-speech burlesque. *"I'd just like to say I couldn't have done it without the good people at Amino Solutions. They truly made me what I am today.* Yeah, *fuck* off."

She was giving him an odd look, he knew.

"What?"

"Nothing. Seems like an odd stance for you to be taking, that's all."

"Oh, because I'm a thirteen I've got to like this pay-and-load excellence we're all living with. Listen, Ertekin, they rolled the dice with me just like with you. No one dumped an artificial chromosome into me in vitro. I got twenty-three pairs, just like you, and what I am is written all over them. There's no optional discard for shit like mine. No knockout sequencer in a hypo they can shoot me up with and make me safe to breed."

"In which case," she said quietly, "I'd have thought you'd see the Xtrasomes as a step forward. For the next generation at least."

For a moment, he could feel the rolling weight of his own pointless anger, back and forth through his chest cavity like a punching bag left swinging. Images from the past four *wasted* months flickered jaggedly through his head.

He put a clamp on it.

"I'm a little short on that kind of outlook right now. But let's stick with Montes, shall we? I'll bet you this much: she's got a combat history, at a minimum a combat training history. If it doesn't show up in the prior record, then she hid it for some reason. She wouldn't be the first person to wind up in the Angeline Freeport wearing a brand-new identity. Wouldn't be the first person to marry someone who knows nothing about who she used to be, either, so you're probably wasting your time talking to the husband."

"Yeah. Usually the way."

"How old were the kids?"

"Four and seven."

"His?"

"I don't know." Ertekin reached up and made a gesture that split the virtuality open. She tugged down a data scroll, gently glowing text written on the air like some angelic missive. She paged down with delicate middle- and ring-finger motions while the index finger kept the scroll open. "Yeah. First birth's Republic-registered, looks like they moved to the Freeport shortly after. Second child was born there."

"So she's from the Republic, too."

"Looks like it, yeah. You think that's relevant?"

"Might be." Carl hesitated, trying to put the rest of it into words, the vague intimations he'd had while he watched the replay death of Toni Montes. "There's something else. The children were the obvious leverage, the reason she let him kill her."

Ertekin made a gesture of distaste. "Yeah, so you said."

"Yeah, so the question has to be why did she believe him. He could have killed her and then still waited around and murdered the rest of her family. Why trust him to keep his word?"

"You think a mother put in that situation has a choice? You think—"

"Ertekin, she was making choices all the time. Remember the genetic trace under the nails? This isn't a civilian we're talking about, this is a competent woman making a series of very cold, very hard calculations. And one of those calculations was to trust the man who put a bullet through her head. Now, what does that say to you?"

She grimaced. The words came reluctantly.

"That she knew him."

He nodded. "Yeah. She knew him *well*. Well enough to know she could trust his word. Now, where does your suburban housewife mother of two part-time real estate saleslady make friends like that?"

He went and sat in one of the hammocks while she thought about it.

Norton was waiting for them when they surfaced.

Sevgi blinked back to local awareness and saw him watching her through the glass panel on the couch cover. It felt a little like staring up at someone from underwater. She thumbed the release catch at her side, propped herself up on her elbows as the hood hinged up.

"Any progress?" Her voice sounded dull in her own ears—hearing thickened with the residual hum of the soundproofing.

Norton nodded. "Yes. Of the slow variety."

"Do we get to go home?"

"Maybe tonight. Nicholson pulled in Roth and there's a full-scale diplomatic war in the making." He crimped a grin. "Roth is demanding a fully armed motorcade escort to Miami International, and fighter cover until we're out of Republican airspace. Really wants to rub their faces in it."

"That's our Andrea." Sevgi hauled herself off the couch and upright, groggy from the time in virtual and lack of k37. Despite herself, she felt a flicker of warmth for Andrea Walker Roth and the arrayed might of COLIN's diplomatic muscle. She didn't really like the woman, not any more than the rest of the policy board; she knew Roth was, like all of them, first and foremost a power broker. But—

But sometimes, Sev, it's good to have the big battalions standing behind you.

"Yeah, well, my guess is the real pressure's coming from Ortiz." Norton gestured at the other couch, where Carl Marsalis was just sitting up. "Secretary general nomination in the wind and all. He's going to be full of UN-friendly gestures for the next eight months. Luck and a following wind, he could be your boss next year, Marsalis."

The black man grimaced. "Not my boss. I'm freelance, remember."

"Fact remains, he's our best hope of not having to spend another night down here. There's a lot of COLIN subcontracting in this state. Lot of sensitive business-community leaders who won't want waves made. That's the angle Ortiz will play while Roth goes down the wires to Washington." Norton spread his hands, turned back mostly to Sevgi. "My guess is we'll wait till nightfall. Just a case of sitting tight."

Marsalis got up off the couch and winced. He worked one shoulder around in circles.

"Something the matter?" Sevgi asked.

He looked at her for a moment as if gauging the level of genuine concern in her voice. "Yeah. Four months of substandard betamyeline chloride."

"Ah," said Norton.

Marsalis flexed his right arm experimentally, a climber's stretch, palm to nape of neck, elbow up beside his head. He grimaced again. "Don't suppose you'd have any around?"

Norton shook his head. "It's unlikely. Human traffic through Perez is down to a minimum these days. Not much call for mesh-related product. Can you hold on until we get to New York?"

"I can hold on pretty much forever. I'd just rather not, if it's all the same to you. It's, uh, uncomfortable."

"We'll get you some painkillers," Sevgi promised. "You should have said something last night."

"It slipped my mind."

"Look, I'll check with supplies anyway," said Norton. "You never know. There might be some mothballed stock."

"Thank you." Marsalis glanced between the two COLIN officers, then nodded toward the door of the v-chamber. "I'm going to go for a walk. Be on the beach if you need me."

Norton waited until he was gone.

"Excuse me? If *we* need *him*? Is it just me or is he the one who needs something from *us* right now?"

Sevgi held down an unexpected smile. "He's a thirteen, Tom. What are you going to do?"

"Well, not look very hard for his betamyeline is what comes immediately to mind."

"He did say thank you."

"Yeah." Norton nodded reluctantly. "He did."

He hesitated, and Sevgi could almost hear what he was going to say before he opened his mouth. She found herself, suddenly, inexplicably saying it for him. "Ethan, right?"

"Look, I know you don't like to—"

She shook her head. "Doesn't matter, Tom. I. You know, maybe I'm way too sensitive around certain topics. Maybe it's time. Right? You were going to ask about Ethan? If he was like this?"

Small pause. "Was he?"

She sighed, testing the seals on her self-control. Breath a little shuddery, but otherwise *fuck it, Sev, it's four years gone, you need to . . .*

To what? Need what?

You need . . . something, Sev. Some fucking thing, you need.

Sigh again. Gesture at the door Marsalis just walked out of.

"Ethan was a different man, Tom. Ethan wasn't his gene code, he wasn't just a jazzed-up area thirteen and a custom-wired limbic system. He—"

Another helpless gesture.

"Do I see similarities? Yeah. Did Ethan have the same *hey-*cut*-my-fucking-throat-see-if-I-care* attitude? Yeah. Did Ethan make any normal male in the room itch up the way Marsalis is making you itch up? Yeah. Does that—"

"Sev, I'm not—"

"You *are*, Tom." She spread her hands, offered up the smile she'd repressed earlier. "You are. It's how they built them, it's what they're *for*. And your reaction— that's how they built you. It's just that it took evolution a hundred thousand generations to put you together, and it took human science less than a century to build them. Faster systems management, that's all."

"What's that, a quote from the Project Lawman brochure?"

Sevgi shook her head, kept the smile. "No. Just something Ethan used to say. Look, you asked me if Ethan and this guy are alike? How would I know? Ethan used to get up half an hour before me every morning and grind fresh coffee for us both. Would this guy do that? Who knows?"

"One way to find out," said Norton, deadpan.

Sevgi lost her smile. Leveled a warning finger. "Don't even go there."

"Sorry." There wasn't much sincerity in the way he said it. A grin hovered in one corner of his mouth. "Got to get down to Fifth Avenue, sort out that sense of humor."

"You got that right."

He grew abruptly serious. "Look, I'm just curious, is all. Both these guys do share some pretty substantial engineered genetic traits."

"Yeah, so what? Your parents engineered some similar genetic material into you and your brother way back at the start of Project Norton. Does that make the two of you similar?"

Norton grimaced. "Hardly."

"So why assume that because Ethan and Marsalis have some basic genetic traits in common, there'd be any similarity in what kind of men they are? You can't equate them just because they're both variant thirteen, any more than you can equate them because, I don't know, because they're both *black*."

"Oh come *on*, Sev. Be serious. We're talking about substantial genetic tendency, not skin color."

"I am serious."

"No, you're not. You're flailing, and you know it. It's not a good analogy."

"Maybe not for you, Tom. But take a walk out that gate and see what kind of thinking you knock up against. It's the same knee-jerk prejudice, just out of fucking date like everything else in Jesusland."

Norton gave her a pained look. His tone tugged toward reproach. "Now you're just letting your Union bigotry run away with you."

"Think so?" She didn't want to be this angry, but it was swelling and she couldn't find a way to shut it down. Her voice was tight with the rising pulse of it. "You know, Ethan tracked down his sourcemat mother once. Turns out she's this drop-dead-smart academic up in Seattle now, but she's from here originally."

"From Florida?"

"No, not from Florida." Sevgi waved a hand irritably. "Louisiana, Mississippi, someplace like that. Jesusland, however you want to look at it. She grew up in the southern US, before Secession."

Norton shrugged. "From what I hear, that's pretty standard. They got most of the sourcemat mothers from the poverty belt back then. Cheap raw materials, fresh eggs for quick cash, right?"

"Yeah, well, she was luckier. She let some West Coast clinic harvest her in exchange for enough cash to set up and study in Seattle. Point is, I went across there with Ethan to see her." Sevgi knew she was staring off into space, but she couldn't make herself stop that, either. It was the last trip they'd made together. "You wouldn't believe some of the shit she told us she went through, purely based on the color of her fucking skin. And that's a single generation back."

"You're talking about Jesusland, Sev."

"Oh, so who's pulling Union rank now?"

"Fine." For the first time, anger sharpened Norton's voice. "Look, Sev, you don't want to talk about this stuff, that's fine with me. But make up your mind. I'm just trying to get a lock on our newfound friend."

Sevgi held his gaze for a moment, then looked away. She sighed. "No, you're not, Tom. That's not it."

"No? Now you're a telepath?"

She smiled wearily. "I don't need to be. I'm used to this. From before, from when I was with Ethan. This isn't about Marsalis. It's about me."

"Hey, a telepath and modest, too." But she saw how he faltered as he said it. She shrugged.

"Suit yourself, Tom. Maybe you haven't spotted it yet, maybe you just don't want to see it. But what you're really trying to get a lock on is Marsalis *and me*. How I'm going to react to him, how I *am* reacting to him."

Norton stared at her for a long moment. Long enough that she thought he would turn away. Then he gave her a shrug of his own.

"Okay," he said quietly. "So how *are* you reacting to him, Sev?"

Norton was on the money about going home, if nothing else. It took the rest of the day to get clearance, and when it finally came, the crowds were still at the gate. Someone had set up big portable LCLS panels along the road, jacked into car batteries or run off their own integral power packs. From the tower, it looked like a bizarre outdoor art gallery, little knots of figures gathered in front of each panel, or walking between. The chanting had died down with the onset of night and the eventual arrival of three cherry-topped state police teardrops. They were parked now in among the other vehicles, but if the officers they'd brought were doing any crowd control, they were keeping a low profile while they did it. And the media had apparently all gone home.

"Seen it before," said the tower guard, a slim Hispanic just on for the graveyard shift. "Staties usually chase them off, so there's no adverse coverage if the shit hits the fan. Shit *does* hit the fan, everyone runs the same sanitized broadcast the next morning. Tallahassee got deals with most of the networks, privileged access to legislature and like that. No one breaks ranks."

"Yeah," rumbled Marsalis. "Responsible Reporting. I'm going to miss that."

The night wind coming off the sea was cool and faintly sewn with salt. Sevgi felt it stir strands of hair on her cheek, felt cop instinct twitch awake inside her at the same moment. She kept herself from turning to look at him, kept her tone casual. "Going to miss it? Where you going then?"

He did turn. She offered him a sideways glance, clashed gazes.

"New York, right?" he said easily. "North Atlantic Union territory, proud home of the free American press?"

She looked again, locked stares this time. "Are you *trying* to piss me off, Marsalis?"

"Hey, I'm just quoting the tourist guide here. Union's the only place they got

Lindley versus NSA still in force, right? Still got their statue of Lindley up in Battery Park, DEFENDER OF TRUTH chiseled on the base? Most places I've been in the Republic, they've pulled those statues down."

She let it go, let the cop twitch slide out of view for the time being, tagged for later attention. For the rest, she didn't know if she'd misread the irony in his voice or not. She was irritable enough to have done so; maybe he was irritable enough to have meant it. She couldn't be bothered to call it either way. After a full day of waiting, none of them was in the best of moods.

She shifted to the other side of the tower, swapped her view. Out at the far side of the complex, partially occluded by the towering bulk of the rack, the landing strip lights burned luminous green. They were far enough off for the distance to make them wink, as if they were embers the sea wind kept blowing on. COLIN were sending a dedicated transport, flatline flight so they'd be waiting awhile longer, but it was on its way and home was only a matter of hours away. She could almost feel the rough cotton sheets on her bed against her skin.

Marsalis, she'd worry about later.

After a couple of minutes, he left the tower top without comment and clattered back down the caged stairs to the ground. She watched him walk away in the flare of ground lighting, off toward the shore again. Casual lope, almost an amble but for the barely perceptible poise in the way he moved. He didn't look back. The darkness down to the beach swallowed him up. She frowned.

Later. Worry about it later, Sev.

She let her mind coast in neutral, watched the lights.

And presently, the COLIN jet whispered down from the cloud base toward them, studded sparsely with landing lights of its own. It kissed the ground, silent with distance, and taxied in like a jeweled shadow.

She yawned and went to fetch her stuff.

In flight, she dozed off and dreamed about the Lindley statue. Murat stood with her in winter sunlight—as he had when she was about eleven, but in the dream she was an adult—and pointed at the chiseled legend in the base. FROM THE DISCOMFORT OF TRUTH THERE IS ONLY ONE REFUGE AND THAT IS IGNORANCE. I DO NOT NEED TO BE COMFORTABLE, AND I WILL NOT TAKE REFUGE. I DEMAND TO KNOW.

See, he was saying. *It only takes one woman like this.*

But when she looked up at the statue of Lindley, it had transformed into the black-sketched perpetrator from the Montes CSI construct, and it leapt off the base at her, fist raised.

She fell back and grappled, one from the manual, cross-block and grab. The figure's arm was slick in her grasp and now ended, she saw, not in a fist but a

Greek theater mask cut out of metal. As she wrestled with the sketch, she understood with the flash logic of dreams that her opponent intended to press the mask
onto her face and that once it was done, there would be no way to get it off.

Across the park, a mother pushed a baby in a stroller. Two kids sat in the grass
and dueled their glinting micro-fighter models high overhead, fingers frantic on
the controls in their laps, heads tilting wildly beneath the blank-faced headsets.
Her own fight went slower, sluggish, like drowning in mud. The construct murderer was stronger than she was, but seemed disinclined to tactics. Every move
she made bought her time, but she could do no damage, could not break the
clinch.

The mask began to block out the sun on her face.

I have done everything I can, said Murat wearily, and she wanted to cry but
couldn't. Her breath came hard now, hurting her throat. Her father was walking
away from her, across the park toward the railings and the water. She had to twist
her neck to keep him in sight. She would have called after him, but her throat
hurt too much, and anyway she knew it wouldn't do any good. The fight started
to drain out of her, tiny increments heralding the eventual evaporation of her
strength. Even the sun was turning cold. She struggled mechanically, bitterly,
and overhead, the mask—

The plane banked and woke her.

Someone had lowered the cabin lights while she slept, and the plane's interior
was sunk in gloom. She leaned across the seat to the window and peered out.
Towers of crystalline light slid beyond the glass, red-studded with navigation
flash. Then the long dark absence of the East River, banded with bridges like jeweled rings on a slim and slightly crooked finger. She sighed and sank back in her
seat.

Home. For what it was worth.

The plane straightened out. Marsalis came through from the forward section,
presumably on his way to the toilet. He nodded down at her.

"Sleep well?"

She shrugged and lied.

CHAPTER 17

By the time they disembarked and came through the deserted environs of the private-carrier terminal at JFK, it was nearly 3 AM. Norton left them standing just inside the endless row of glass doors onto the pickup zone and went to get his car out of parking. The whole place was full of a glaring, white-lit quiet that seemed to whine just at the edge of audibility.

"So what's the plan?" Marsalis asked her.

"The plan is get some sleep. Tomorrow I'll take you over to Jefferson Park and get you hooked up with our chain of command. Roth, Ortiz, and Nicholson are all going to want to meet you. Then we'll look at Montes. If your theory checks out, there'll be some trace of a previous identity somewhere in the data record."

"You hope."

"No, I *know*," she said irritably. "No one disappears for real anymore, not even in the Angeline Freeport."

"Merrin seems to be managing."

"Merrin's strictly a temporary phenomenon."

They went back to staring averted angles around the terminal space until Norton rolled up in the snarl-grilled Cadillac. He'd held off putting the top up until a couple of weeks ago, but there was no way to avoid it now. The early-hours air beyond the terminal doors had a snap in it that promised the raw cold of the winter ahead.

"Nice ride," said Marsalis as he got in.

He'd taken the front seat. Sevgi rolled her eyes and climbed in the back. Norton grinned at her in the mirror.

"Thanks," he said, and gunned the magdrive as they pulled away. It didn't quite have the throaty roar of the vehicles from the period road movies he occasionally dragged Sevgi to at art-house theaters in the Village, but the car thrummed pleasantly enough and they took the exit ramp at rising speed. Norton drifted them across into the curve of the citybound highway. The airport complex fell away behind them like a flung fairy crown. Norton raised his eyes to the mirror again. "What are we doing about accommodation, Sev?"

"You can put me in a hotel," Marsalis said, yawning. "Wherever suits. I'm not fussy."

Sevgi faked a yawn of her own and slumped back in the seat. "Let's sort that out tomorrow. Too much hassle coordinating it all now. You can stay at my place tonight. Tom, I'll bring him in and meet you at the office for lunch. Somewhere on the mezzanine. Say about twelve?"

Peripheral vision showed her Norton trying to make eye contact in the mirror. His face was the carefully immobile deadpan she associated with his witnessing of mistakes made. He used it a lot in briefings with Nicholson. She gazed steadfastly out of the side window.

"He could stay with me, Sev. I've got the space."

"So do I." She made it come out casual. Still watching the dull metal ribbon of the crash barrier as it whipped smoothly along beside the car in the gloom. A teardrop taxi blipped past on the opposing side of the highway. "Anyway, Tom, it'd take you the best part of an hour just to clear out all that junk you keep in the spare room. All I have to do is crank down the futon. Just drop us off, it'll be fine."

Now she turned and met his eyes in the mirror. Matched him deadpan for deadpan. He shrugged and punched up some music on the car's sound system, ancient Secession-era punk no one played anymore. Detroitus or Error Code; Sevgi never could tell the two bands apart despite Norton's best efforts to instruct her. She settled back to the outside view again and let the vitriol of it wash over her, lulled by the familiar high-stepping bass lines and the stuttering, hacking guitars. She found her mouth forming fragments of lyrics:

> *Got what you want at last, got your*
> *Closed little world*
> *Got your superhero right and wrong*
> *And your fuckin' flag unfurled*

Marsalis stirred, leaned forward to read the player display, and sank back again without comment. Guitar fury skirled out of the speakers. The car slammed on through the night.

When they pulled up outside Sevgi's building, Norton killed the engine and got out to see them to the door. It was a nice gesture, but it felt wrong—Harlem hadn't seen serious crime in decades, and anyway, in among the carbon-fiber skeletons of the market stalls, figures were already moving around with crates, setting up. The place would be coming to noisy life in another couple of hours. Sevgi made a mental note to make sure the windows were all tight shut before she slept. She smiled wearily at Norton.

"Thanks, Tom. You'd better get moving."

"Yeah."

He hesitated.

"See you on the mez, then," she said brightly.

"Uh, yeah. Twelve o'clock?"

"Yeah, twelve's good."

"Where'd you want to eat? Henty's or—"

"Sure. Henty's." Backing away now. "Sounds good."

He nodded slowly and went back to the car. She raised a hand in farewell. He pulled out, looking back. They watched him out of sight before Sevgi turned to the door of the building and showed the scanner her face. The door cracked open on a hydraulic sigh.

"Sixth floor," she said, hefting her shoulder bag. "No elevator."

"Yeah? Why's that then?"

"Period charm. You coming?"

They took the stairs at a trudge. LCLS panels blinked awake on each floor as they climbed, then died to dimness in their wake. The bright white glow shone on pre-Secession grafitoform murals and embedded holoshots of the building in its various stages of growth. Sevgi found herself noticing them for the first time in months as consciousness of the man at her back lit everything for her the same way as the LCLS. She bit back the impulse to play tour guide.

In the apartment, she went from room to room, showing him where things were. He went to use the bathroom as soon as she was done. She checked the windows while he was in there, set the locks, organized herself. Fetched sheets and a quilt from the cupboard in the en suite. She caught a glimpse of herself in the mirror as she took the bed linen down, and didn't recognize the look on her face. There was a warm, irritable confusion rising in her as to how she should do this. Back in the living room, she powered up the futon and remote-extended it. She was putting on the sheets when he came out and joined her.

"All yours," she said, finishing and standing back up.

"Thank you."

They stood looking at the crisp, clean sheets. He seemed to be waiting for something. Maybe in response, a circuit clicked shut somewhere inside her. She put her hands in her jacket pockets and hooked his gaze.

"The door's double-locked," she said. "It's DNA-coded."

His brow creased. Silent query.

Ah fuck it, here we go. "You may as well know this now, Marsalis. You're going to find out sooner or later, so it may as well come from me. My last relationship was a thirteen. He's dead now, but I know how that shit works." She tapped fingertips to her temple. "I know how you work up here. Right now, you're probably mapping the shortest possible route across town to East Forty-fifth and First."

No visible reaction. She plunged on.

"And you're right, it's not far. Three, four klicks and cross the lines, you're home free. UN territory, right here in the heart of New York. I'm not sure how they'd get you out after that, but my guess is the powers-that-be here in the Union wouldn't kick much. They've got a better working relationship with the UN than with COLIN most of the time. Truth comes down, they don't like us much better than they do the Republic."

"That must be very upsetting for you."

"You're too kind. So, like I said, I know what's in your mind. I don't even blame you much. It's not like you're a free actor here—you're locked into something you'd probably rather not be a part of. You're under duress, and I know how badly that plays in the thirteen mind-set. You're looking for a way to pick the locks or smash down the door."

Ethan's words. He used to grin as he said them, that *something-burning* grin. She waited to see what he'd do. If he'd move.

He didn't. He raised an eyebrow instead, looked down at the open blade of his right hand. She recognized the displacement training, and a faint shiver ran through her.

He cleared his throat.

"Well, it's nice to know I'm so well understood. But you see, Ms. Ertekin, there seems to be a major flaw in your procedures here. If I'm the ravening, duress-shattering thirteen motherfucker you—"

"I didn't say—"

"—have me down as, then what's to stop me caving in your skull here and now, slashing you open to get some warm blood for your precious DNA locks, and then doing my predawn sprint across town after all?"

"The lock only works off saliva."

He stared at her. "I could always scrape it out of your dead mouth."

"Do you think you're going to scare me, Marsalis?"

"I couldn't care less if I scare you or not." For the first time since she'd met him, his voice tightened toward anger. "You were fucking some burned-out genetic augment who said he was a thirteen, and you want to delude yourself I'm him, that's your problem. I don't know what I symbolize to you, Ertekin, what you *want* me to symbolize, but I'm not up for it. I'm not a fucking number, I'm not a fucking gene code. I'm Carl Marsalis, I think we met already." He stuck out his hand bluntly, mock-offer of a clasp, then let it fall. "But in case it hasn't sunk in, that's *all* I am. Got a problem with that, then fuck off and deal with it somewhere I don't have to listen to you."

They faced each other either end of the stare, a couple of meters apart. To Sevgi, the room seemed to rock gently on the axis of their locked gazes.

"This is my house you're in," she reminded him.

"Then book me into a fucking hotel." He held her eyes for a moment, then looked down at the extended futon. "One with room service that doesn't lecture the guests." Another pause. "And an elevator."

Out of nowhere, the laugh broke in her. She coughed it up.

"Right," she said.

He looked up again. Grimaced. "Right."

She seated herself on one arm of the couch. Hands still tucked in her pockets, but she could feel the tension in her begin to ease. Marsalis raised an arm toward her and let it fall.

"I'm tired," he said. It wasn't clear if he meant it as an apology or information. "I'm not going anywhere, I'm not going to try and run out on you. I'm going to get some sleep and see if we can't make a fresh start in the morning. Sound okay to you?"

Sevgi nodded. "Sounds good."

"Yeah." He looked around, fixed on the futon again. "Well. Thanks for making up the bed."

She shrugged. "You're a guest."

"Could I get a glass of water?"

She stood up and nodded toward the kitchen. "Sure. Chiller on the counter. Glasses are in the cupboard above. Help yourself."

"Thanks."

"No problem. G'night."

She went to the bedroom and hooked the door closed behind her. Stood there for a while, listening to him move about in the kitchen.

Then she took her right hand out of her jacket pocket, opened her palm, and considered the Remington stunspike it held. It looked innocuous, a short thick tube in smooth matte gray. The charge light winked green at her from one end. Thrown hard or jabbed into the target by hand, it carried enough power to put anything human on the floor and leave it there for the best part of twenty minutes.

She hesitated for a moment, then slipped the spike under her pillow and began to get undressed.

He lay flat on his back on the futon, head pillowed on his crossed palms, and stared at the ceiling.

Still locked up, then.

Stupid fucking bitch.

Well, not really. She saw you coming a thousand meters out. That makes her pretty fucking smart.

He sighed and looked across at the window. Six floors up, probably jacked into the same security as the door anyway. Not a chance.

Could always—

Oh fuck off. Weren't you listening to Sutherland? Only do what you are happy to live with. She made your bed, for fuck's sake. You're out of the Republic, you're out of jail. How bad can it be? Sit it out, look at the case. Make some suggestions, let them get comfortable with you. If they want this to work, they can't keep a leash on you twenty-four seven.

He reached over for the glass and propped himself up to drink.

So she's an unluck-fucker. Doesn't seem the sort.

The sort being? Zooly?

Come on, that was a one-off.

A twice-off. So far.

Zooly's a friend.

Yeah, a friend who likes to fuck unlucks on an occasional basis.

Maybe it's me Zooly likes to fuck on an occasional basis. Ever think of that? Maybe my genetic status has fuck-all to do with it.

Right. And maybe this Ertekin woman just liked to fuck her unluck boyfriend for who he was, too.

Ah, go to sleep.

He couldn't. The mesh sent rusty twinges through him, out of time with his pulse.

Better deal with that tomorrow. Nearly four months of substandard chloride, you'll be lucky if it doesn't seize up on you soon.

Seemed to work on Dudeck and his pals.

Yeah, this isn't some bunch of neo-Nazi fuckwits you're dealing with now, this is another thirteen. An adapted thirteen, by the sound of it. You'll need to be wired all the way right if you're going to—

Hoy. Going to what? Couple of days and a dropped guard, we're out of here, remember.

He went back to staring at the ceiling.

CHAPTER 18

A bad chloride twinge kicked him awake, bone-deep aching along his left fore-arm and sudden sweat from the intensity of the pain. He'd curled up around it instinctively in his sleep, and there was a faint whimper trapped in his throat as he woke. Aunt Chitra's pain-management training, the silent imperative. Take the pain, breathe, breathe it under control, and *don't make a fucking sound*. He swallowed and rolled over, protecting the aching limb with his other arm.

Remembered he was in Sevgi Ertekin's home, and relaxed. The whimper got free as a low groan.

The room was full of barely filtered light—there were varipolara drapes at the windows, and someone had forgotten to opaque them the all the way down the night before. His watch said it was a little after nine. He grunted and flexed the fingers of his left hand, chased the pain to fading. The mesh, for reasons the Marstech biolabs apparently still didn't understand, "remembered" injury trauma and tended to overload the system in those parts of the body that had suffered it in the past. Fine so long as you fueled the system right; the worst you got was a faint warmth and itching at the site of previous wounds. But with the shit he'd been buying from Louie over the last few months, the neuromuscular interfacing would be ragged and inflamed. And Carl had once stopped a Saudi opsdog with that fore-arm. Some monstrous engineered hybrid, ghost-pale and snarling as it material-ized out of the desert night and leapt at his throat. The impact put him on his back, the jaws sank into the bone, and even after he killed the fucking thing, it took them nearly five minutes to break the bite lock and get it off him.

He listened for sound through the apartment, heard nothing. Evidently Ertekin was still out cold. No chance of going back to sleep now, and the door was still locked. He thought about it for a moment then got up, pulled on his pants, and padded through to the kitchen. A brief search of the cupboards pro-duced coffee for the espresso machine in the corner. OLYMPUS MONS ROBUSTA

BLEND—FROM ACTUAL MARSTECH GENE LABS! *Yeah, right.* He allowed himself a
sour grin and set up the machine to make two long cups, then went to the fridge
for milk.

There were a couple of LongLife cartons open, one weighing in at about half
full, the other a lot less. On impulse he sniffed at the torn cardboard openings on
both. Pulled a face and upended each carton carefully one after the other over
the sink. With the least full of the two, the contents came out slow and semi-solid,
splattered across the metal in slimy white clots. He shook his head and rinsed the
mess away.

"You and Zooly'd get on like a fucking house on fire," he muttered and went
back to the cupboards to find more milk.

"Who you talking to?"

He turned with the fresh carton in his hand. The kitchen had filled with the
smell of coffee, and either that or the noise he was making rummaging in the
cupboards had woken Ertekin. She stood in the kitchen doorway, eyes heavy-
lidded, hair stuck up in clumps, wearing a faded NYPD T-shirt several sizes too
big for her and, as far as he could tell, nothing much else. The look on her face
wasn't friendly.

"Singing," he said. "To myself. I made coffee."

"Yeah, so I fucking see."

He raised an eyebrow. "You're welcome."

She looked back at him for a moment, impassively, then turned away. He
caught the lines of her hips under the T-shirt, the length of her thighs as the
about-turn brought her legs together.

"What time is it?"

" 'Bout half past nine."

"Fuck, Marsalis." Her voice trailed away, back toward the bedroom. "What
you got, insomnia or something?"

Sounds of water splashing, a door closing it off. A sudden, unlooked-for image
opened in his head. Sevgi Ertekin strips off her T-shirt and steps into the shower,
hands gathered under her chin beneath the stream of warm water, arms pressing
breasts flat and—

He grinned wryly and derailed the internal experia script before it reached his
groin. Finished making the coffee anyway. It came out rich and creamed with
bubbles, steaming an aroma that kicked him straight back to the dusty bubblefabs
of Huari camp. The ominous itch on his skin of sunlight through an atmosphere
only recently made thick enough to breathe, the uneasy pull of Mars gravity, the
loose grip of a planet that didn't recognize him as its own and didn't really see

why it should hold on to him. Coffee in aluminium canisters, dust crunching underfoot, and Sutherland at his shoulder, rumbling speech like the reassuring turnover of heavy plant machinery. *Nothing human-scale around here, soak. Just shade your eyes and take a look.* And the staggering, neck-tilting view up Massif Verne, to drive the other man's point home.

He poured the coffee into two mugs, took one for himself and left hers to get cold on the kitchen counter. Serve her fucking right. He sipped from his mug, pulled a surprised face. FROM ACTUAL MARSTECH GENE LABS was right. He hated it when reality bore out the clanging boasts of the hype. He went back to the living room and peered out at the market below. He didn't know the city well, and this part less than most, but Ertekin's building was a pretty standard nanotech walk-up and he guessed the open plaza below had been a part of the same redevelopment. It had the faintly organic lines of all early nanobuild. He knew parts of southeast London that looked much the same. Buildings in a bucket—just pour it out and watch them grow.

He heard her come out of the bedroom, heard her in the kitchen. Then he could feel her in the room with him, at his back, watching. She cleared her throat. He turned and saw her on the other side of the room, dressed and somewhat groomed, coffee mug held in both hands. She gestured with the drink.

"Thanks." She looked away, then back. "I uh. I'm not great first thing in the morning."

"Don't worry about it." Randomly, for something to fill the quiet between them: "Possible sign of greatness. Nor was Felipe Souza, by all accounts."

Flicker of a smile. "No?"

"No. Did all his molecular dynamics work at night. I read this biography of him, once I got back to Earth. Seemed appropriate, you know. Anyway, book says, when they took him on at UNAM, he refused to lecture before midday. Great guy to have as a tutor, right?"

"Not for you."

"Well, my head starts to spin once you get past basic buckyball structure, so—"

"No, I meant the morning thing." She gestured with the cup again, one-handed this time, a little more open. "You wouldn't be—"

"Oh, that." He shrugged. "It's the training. Never really goes away."

Quiet opened up again in the wake of his words. The conversation, caught and scraping in the shallow waters of her continued embarrassment. He reached for something to pole them clear again. Something that had flared dimly in his mind the previous night as he finally arced downward toward sleep.

"Listen, I've been thinking. You guys debriefed the onboard djinn for *Horkan's Pride*, right? Back in June, when this all started."

"Yeah." Her voice stretched a little on the word, quizzical. He liked the sound it made. He fumbled after follow-up.

"Yeah, so who'd you have do it? In-house team?"

She shook her head. "I doubt it. We got transcripts handed down, probably some geek hired out of MIT's machine interface squad. They handle most of our n-djinn work. Why, you think there's something they missed?"

"It's always a possibility."

A skeptical look. "Something *you'd* pick up?"

"Okay, maybe not something they *missed*, as such." He sipped his coffee. Gestured. "Just something they weren't looking for, because I wasn't on the scene. A close link between Merrin and me. Something that'll put me next to him."

"A link? You said you didn't know him."

"I don't, directly. Come on, Ertekin, you were a cop. You must know something about complexity theory. Social webbing."

She shrugged. "Sure. We got the basics in our demodynamics classes. Yaroshanko intuition, Chen and Douglas, Rabbani. All the way back to Watts and Strogatz, all that small-world networks shit. So what? You know, once you get out on the streets for real, most of that demodynamics stuff's about as useful as poetry in a whorehouse."

He held back a grin. "Maybe so. But small-world networks work. And the variant thirteen club on Mars is a very small world. As is Mars itself. I may not know Merrin, but I'm willing to bet you can link me to him in a couple of degrees of separation or less. And if those links are there, then nothing's going to spot them out better than an n-djinn."

"Yeah. Any n-djinn. Why's it got to be *Horkan's Pride*?"

"Because *Horkan's Pride* was the last djinn to see Merrin alive. It stands to reason that—"

Soft chime from the door.

Ertekin glanced at her watch, reflexively. Confusion creased in the corners of her eyes.

"Guess Tom just doesn't trust the two of us together," Carl said, deadpan.

The confusion faded out, traded for a disdain he made as manufactured. She crossed to the door and picked up the privacy receiver.

"Yes?"

He saw her eyes widen slightly. She nodded, said yes a couple more times, then hung up. When she looked at him again, there was a fully fledged frown on her face. He couldn't decide if she was worried or annoyed, or both.

"It's Ortiz," she said. "He drove here."

He covered his own surprise. "What an honor. Does he collect all his new hires by limousine?"

"Not since I've been working there."

"So it must be me."

He'd intended it to come out light and supple with irony. But somewhere, sometime in the last four months, he'd lost the knack. He heard the weight in his own words, and so did she.

"Yeah." She looked at him over her coffee mug. "It must be you."

He'd met Ortiz a couple of times before, but doubted the man would remember him. Both meetings were years in the past, both had been swathed in the glassy-smile insincerity of diplomatic visits, and Carl had been only one of several variant thirteen trackers in a queue of agency staff lined up to press the visiting flesh on arrival. Munich II was in process, there was talk of COLIN coming back to the table to approve the Accords, fully this time, and everyone was walking on eggs. Back then—Carl recalled vaguely, he hadn't been that interested—Ortiz was a newly recruited policy adviser, fresh from a political career in the Rim States and not yet a major figure in the COLIN hierarchy. Detail had faded, but Carl remembered grizzled hair and a tan, a slim-hipped dancer's frame that belied the other man's fifty-something years. A slight lift to the serious brown eyes that might have been Filipino ancestry or just biosculp to suggest the same to voters. A good smile.

For his own part, Carl had been busy enjoying the comforts of his newly reacquired anonymity at the time. The media focus attendant on his rescue and return from Mars and the *Felipe Souza* had died down, to his relief, the previous year; the celebrity machine, in the absence of any attempt on his part to restoke the fires of its interest, had grown bored with him and moved on. Sure, he'd made it back alive and sane from a nightmarish systems breakdown in deep space, but what *else* had he done recently? UNGLA was sealed up tight, bureaucratically impassive, not the kind of brightly confected media play the networks liked at all. The high-profile cases were still to come. Meanwhile, some adolescent son of African royalty was up and about on the Euro scene, deploying his Xtrasome capacity at a Cambridge college and his polished-jet good looks in the dj-votional clubs of west London. The Bannister family were settling, amid some local acrimony, into their Union citizenship. A Thai experia star was getting married. And so on. The unblinking media eye rolled away, and Carl felt its absence like the sudden cool of shade from the Martian sun.

They went down to the street. Cold struck through the thin fabric of the S(t)igma jacket he'd blagged in Florida.

Ortiz was waiting for them on the other side of the thoroughfare, leaning against the flank of the COLIN limo in a plain black topcoat and sipping coffee from a stall up the street. Carl could see the yellow-and-black logo repeat, weak holoplay in the bright winter air of the market and again in stenciled micro on the Styrofoam in Ortiz's hand. Steam coiled up out of the cup and met the frost of the man's breath as he raised the coffee to his lips. An unobtrusive security exec stood nearby, hands lightly clasped, scanning the façade from behind lens-sheathed eyes.

Ortiz spotted them and stacked his coffee casually on the roof of the limo at his side. As Carl approached, he stepped forward to meet him and stuck out his hand. No wince, no sign of the internal steeling Carl was used to when he made the clasp with someone who knew what he was. Instead, there was a loose grin on Ortiz's lean bronzed face that shaved years off his otherwise sober demeanor.

"Mr. Marsalis. Good to see you again. It's been awhile, I don't know if you'll remember me from Brussels."

"Spring '03." Carl masked his surprise. "Yeah, I remember."

Ortiz made a wry face. "What a complete mess that was, eh? Two agendas, worlds apart and steaming steadily in opposite directions. Hard to believe we even bothered talking."

Carl shrugged. "Talking's always the easy part. Looks good, doesn't cost anything."

"Yes, very true." Ortiz shifted focus with the polished smoothness of the career politician. "Ms. Ertekin. I hope you'll forgive the intrusion. Tom Norton told me you'd be coming in, but I felt in view of the. Unpleasantness, it might be as well to provide an escort. And since I was on my way across town anyway . . ."

You thought you'd swing the opportunity to curry some potential UN favor. Right. Or maybe just gawk at the thirteen.

But underneath the sneer, Carl found himself unable to summon much dislike for Ortiz. Maybe it was the relaxed handshake and the grin, maybe just the contrast with the past four months down in the Republic. He turned to catch Ertekin's response, see what he could read in her face. The tiger eyes and—

—something invisible splits the air between them.

Carl was moving before he had time to consciously understand why.

—flicker of black motion in the corner of his eye—

He hit Ertekin with crossed arms, bore her to the pavement and crushed her there. One hand groping for a weapon he didn't have. Over his head, the air in the street erupted in spit-hiss fury.

Magfire.

He heard the coachwork on the limo go first, riddled from end to end—it sounded like a spate of sudden, heavy rain. Someone yelled, grunted as they were hit. Bodies tumbled behind him, dimly sensed. Screams. He was smearing himself on top of Ertekin, casting about for the—

There.

Out of the market, the pitch and panic of the surrounding multitude, three crouched, black-clad forms, and the sashaying gait of skaters. They hugged the stubby electromag spray guns to their bellies, cradled low in both hands as they surfed the crowd. Shoulder work opened their path—Carl saw bystanders shunted aside and sprawling. The mesh made it seem like slow motion. Chloride clarity gave him the lead skater, stance shifting as he lifted the muzzle of the spray gun, eyes wide in the pale skin gap of the black ski mask. Half a dozen meters at most, he was going to make sure of his shot this time.

Carl locked gazes and came up off the floor snarling.

Later, he'd never know if it was the matched stare, the noise he made, or just the mesh-assisted speed that saved his life. Maybe there was the edge of a flinch in the man's face as he hurtled forward; the ski mask made it hard to tell. By then Carl was already up and on him. Three—count them, *one! two! three!*—sprinted steps and a whirl of *tanindo* technique. The blade of his left hand slammed in under the lead skater's chin; his right just added lift and vectored spin. The two of them went over together in a tangle of limbs. The spray gun dropped and skittered. Carl got on top of the skater and started hitting him in the face and throat.

The other two were sharp. The right wing leapt cleanly over the tumbled bodies in his path, came down tight with a solid plastic smack, and kept going. Carl got a confused glimpse of the landing, too busy killing the lead skater to pay real attention. But he felt the other wingman fuck up the same maneuver and catch one skate on Carl's raised shoulder as he jumped. The black-clad form went headlong, almost graceful, hit and rolled on the pavement. Controlled impact, he'd be back up any second. The mesh strung moments apart like loops of cabling. Carl hacked down savagely with an elbow one more time and beneath him the lead skater went abruptly limp. As the tumbled wingman got almost back upright, Carl lunged, grabbed up the leader's electromag, clumsily, left-handed, squirmed sideways, getting line of fire, and emptied the gun.

The magload sounded like seething water as it left the gun. No recoil—*thank Christ*—and pretty much point-blank. Carl lay, awkwardly braced, and watched the slugs rip into their target. The wing skater seemed to trip forward again, but jerkily this time, no grace in it. He collapsed facedown, twisted once, and didn't move again.

The electromag's feed mechanism coughed empty and stopped.

Sound filtered through: voices raised and hysterical weeping. Still frosted into the mesh, Carl heard it as if through a long pipe. He picked himself up warily, still not convinced at a cellular level that the third skater wasn't coming back. He dropped the empty weapon, walked to the dead wingman. Crouched beside the body and tugged the man's spray gun free. He checked the load, almost absently, on autopilot now, and surveyed the damage around him.

The limo was a write-off, coachwork pockmarked gray on black with the raking impact of the magfire. The windows were punched through in a couple of dozen places, powdered to white opaque in spiderweb lines around each hole. Incredibly, Ortiz's coffee stood where he'd parked it, intact and steaming quietly on the roof of the limo. But Ortiz and his security were both down, tangled in each other's arms and motionless—it looked as if the bodyguard had tried to get his boss to the ground and cover him there. Blood pooling on the molded pavement where they lay suggested he'd failed. Other bodies lay at a distance, shoppers and stall traders caught in the magfire. Ertekin was up on her knees, staring dazedly around at the mess. Her olive skin was smeared sallow with shock.

"Got two of them," said Carl thickly as he helped her to her feet. "Third one was too fast leaving. Sorry."

She just stared at him.

"Ertekin." He flickered fingers in front of her face. "Are you injured? Are you *hurt*? Talk to me, Ertekin."

She shook herself. Pushed his hand away.

"Fine." It was a bare croak. She cleared her throat. "I'm fine. We'd better get. An ambulance. Get these people . . ."

She shook herself again.

"Who? Did you see . . . ?"

"No." Carl stared away in the direction the last skater had disappeared. He could feel a decision stealing over him like ice. "No, I didn't. But right after the meat van gets here, I think you'd better take me in to COLIN so we can start work and find out."

S evgi was still shaking when the cops showed up. She felt an odd shame when the detective in charge, a lean dark man with hard bones in his face, finished talking with patrol and made his way across to her. He was bound to notice. Wrapped in an insulene recovery shawl, seated in the open rear door of the murdered limo and watching CSI go about their business, she felt drenched in her civilian status.

"Ms. Ertekin?"

She looked up bleakly. "Yeah, that's me."

"Detective Williamson." He flipped his left palm open. The NYPD holo twisted to blue-and-gold life, glistened at her like lost treasure. "I'd like to ask you some questions, if you're feeling up to it."

"I'm fine." She'd taken the syn that morning, in the shower, but it wouldn't have kicked in yet even on an empty stomach. She groped after conventional resources, pulled herself together with a shiver. "I used to be on the force, I'm fine."

"That so?" Polite, speculative. Williamson didn't want to be her buddy. She could guess why.

"Yeah, eleven years. Queens, then Midtown Homicide." She managed a shaky smile. "You guys are from the Twenty-eighth, right? Larry Kasabian still attached there?"

"Yeah, Kasabian's still around, I think." No warmth in the words. He nodded at Marsalis, who sat starkly on the steps of the building in his South Florida State inmate jacket, watching the crime scene squad go about their business as if they were a stage play put on for his benefit. "Patrol says you told them this guy's a thirteen."

"Yes." She was cursing herself for it now. "He is."

"And." Brief hesitation. "Is that filed with anyone here in the city?"

Sevgi sighed. "We got in late last night. He's a technical consultant for COLIN Security, but we haven't had time to notify anybody yet."

"All right." But it clearly wasn't all right. Williamson's expression stayed cool. "I'm not going to pursue that, but you need to get him registered. Today. Is he, uh, staying with you?"

The implication sneered beneath the words. It felt like a slap. It felt like her father's tirade when he found out about Ethan. Sevgi felt her own expression tighten.

"No, he's not uh, staying with me," she parodied. "He's uh, staying in COLIN-account accommodation, just as soon as we can find him some. So do you think we can maybe just shelve the fucking Jesusland paranoia. And maybe get on with the police work at hand? How'd that be?"

Williamson's eyes flared.

"That'd be just fine, Ms. Ertekin," he said evenly. "The police work at hand is that this twist just killed two armed men in broad daylight, empty-handed, and he doesn't appear to have a scratch on him. Now, maybe this is just my paranoia running away with me, or maybe it's just good old-fashioned cop instinct, but something about that doesn't chime in time."

"He's carrying a Mars environment systemic biohoist. And he was combat-trained from age seven up."

Williamson grunted. "Yeah, I heard that about them. Bad to the bone, right? And you don't think the men he killed here were combat-proficient."

"You do?" Sevgi rapped her knuckles on the slug-riddled coachwork at her side. "Come on, Williamson, look at this shit. Combat-proficient? No, they just had guns."

"Any reason you can think of that someone would send a low-grade spray-for-pay crew after a COLIN executive?"

She shook her head wordlessly. *They weren't after Ortiz*, she knew inside. *Ortiz just got in the way. They were here to kill Marsalis. Kill him before he gets any kind of handle on Merrin.*

No reason to share that with Detective Williamson right now.

"And you told patrol you didn't see the actual fight at all?"

She shook her head again, more definitely this time, getting traction. "No, I said I didn't see much of it. Much of anything, I was on the ground—"

"Where he threw you, right?"

"Yes, that's right." The weight of his body on hers. "He probably saved my life."

"So he saw them coming?"

"I don't know. Why don't you ask him?"

Williamson nodded. "I'll get around to it. Right now, I'm asking you."

"And I told you I don't know."

There was a compressed pause. Williamson started again. "In the statement, you say you think there were three attackers. Or is that just what your twist friend over there told you?"

"No. I saw one take off toward the boulevard." She indicated the shrink-wrapped corpses of the men Marsalis had killed. The black skater rig was clearly visible through the plastic. "And I can count."

"Description?"

She looked up at him for a long moment. "Black-clad. Wearing a ski mask."

Williamson sighed. "Yeah. Okay. You want to tell me about this other guy?"

He gestured at the third bundle on the pavement. The pale, blood-speckled face of Ortiz's bodyguard gaped up wide-eyed through the plastic. They'd had to roll him onto his back to get Ortiz out from under and onto the wagon, and that was how CSI had wrapped him.

Sevgi shrugged.

"Security."

"Did you know him?"

"No. Not my section." It dawned abruptly on Sevgi why Williamson was so edgy. In theory, NYPD held the ground here, but under the Colony Initiative Act, she could take it from them pretty much at will. The sudden sense of the power she had gusted through her like insects in her belly. It wasn't a clean feeling.

Williamson moved a couple of paces to stand over the dead bodyguard. He stared down at the man's face. "So this guy covers Ortiz, right?"

"Yes, apparently."

"Yeah, that's his job. And our twist friend over there—"

"Do you want to *stop using that fucking word*?"

It got her a speculative look. The detective came back toward the limo. "All right. Security covers Ortiz. Your *genetically modified* friend over there covers you. You got any idea at all why he might have done that?"

Sevgi shook her head wearily. "Why don't you ask him?"

"Yeah, I will. But thirteens aren't known for their honesty." Williamson paused deliberately. "Or their self-sacrifice. Had to be something in it for him."

She glared back at the detective, and maybe it was the syn coming on now, but she thought she could have blown Williamson's head off if she had a weapon at hand. Instead she levered herself to her feet and faced him. "I'm done talking to you, Detective."

"I don't think—"

"I *said* I'm done talking to you." No maybe about it, it was the syn. The anger drove her forward, but it was the drug that gave her the poise. Williamson was a head taller than she was, but she stood in his personal space as if she wore body armor. As if the last forty minutes hadn't happened to her. The insulene shawl was puddled around her feet. "Someone a little less fucking Neanderthal, I'd be happy to liaise with. You, I'm done wasting time on."

"This is a murder investi—"

"Yeah, right now that's what it is. You want to see how fast I can turn it into a COLIN Security operation?"

His jaw tightened, but he said nothing.

"You back off, Detective, leave me the fuck alone, and you can keep your investigation. Otherwise I'm going to pull the COLIN act on you, and you can go back and tell them at the Twenty-eighth they'll be losing their jurisdiction."

Behind the syn, there was a tiny trickle of guilt as she watched Williamson crumble, an empathy from her own years on the other side of the fence.

She crushed it. Crossed the street to Marsalis.

COLIN arrived in modest force about ten minutes later. A secure transit Land Rover rolled quietly into the marketplace, parting the crowds with a low-intensity subsonic dispersal pulse that set Sevgi's teeth on edge even at distance. She hadn't called Norton, so someone must have authorized the roll-out when the news about Ortiz broke. The police had been holding back accredited film crews and solo shoulderscope artists in the crowd for a while, and it would be all over the feeds by now.

The Land Rover came to a halt at the edge of the crime scene, with scant regard for the incident barriers the NYPD had strung. One armor-swollen corner of its bodywork broke the bright yellow beams and set off the alarm. Police uniforms came running.

"Subtle," said Marsalis.

The Land Rover's forward passenger door cracked, swung open at a narrow angle. Tom Norton stood up on the running board behind it, scanning the crime scene. Even at a distance, Sevgi could see how ashen his face was.

"Sev?"

"Over here." She waved from the steps of the building, and Norton spotted her. He swung his door wider, stepped down, and closed it again. Brief words with the uniforms in his way, a display of badges, and they opened a path for him. Someone went to shut off the barrier breach alarm, and quiet soaked back into the street. The Land Rover backed up a couple of meters and sat there rumbling like the elegant tank it essentially was. The driver did not emerge.

"Overreacting a bit, aren't we?" Sevgi asked as Norton reached them.

He grimaced. "Tell that to Ortiz."

"Is he okay?"

"Relative to what? He isn't dead, if that's what you mean. They've got him hooked up to half the life-support machines available over at Weill Cornell. Major organ damage, but he'll have ready stock cultured somewhere. Family've been notified." Norton looked sick as he stared around at the shrink-wrapped corpses. "What the *fuck* was he doing over here anyway, Sev?"

She shook her head.

"I think he was here to see me," said Marsalis, rising to his feet for the first time since the assault. He yawned cavernously.

Norton eyed him with dislike. "All about you, huh?"

"NYPD are all over him, Tom," said Sevgi, defusing. "Detective in charge hardly gave a shit about Ortiz, all he wanted to talk about was how come we'd got an unlicensed thirteen on the streets."

"Right." Norton sharpened on the new task. "What's this detective's name?"

"Williamson. Out of the Twenty-eighth."

"I'll talk to him."

"He's already been talked to. That's not what I meant. I think it might play better if we let this look like an attempt on Ortiz."

"You think it wasn't?" Norton blinked. He gestured at one of the dead assassins. "Skater crew, Sev. Track the limo through traffic, that's standard gang operating procedure. Ten, twelve city murders a year the exact same way. What else are you going to make of this?"

Sevgi nodded at Marsalis.

"Oh come on. Sev, you've got to be kidding me. We've been in town less than a day. Who knew we were here?"

"Makes no sense the other way around, either, Tom. These guys were street. A real ground-level hit squad. What are they doing coming after someone fiftieth-floor like Ortiz? Man wouldn't know street if it bit him in the ass."

"It just did," Marsalis said, deadpan.

Norton spared him a hard look. Sevgi stepped in.

"Look, whatever just went down here, we had more than enough publicity we didn't need in Florida. Let's not have a repeat performance. Ask the cops to kill the thirteen angle, make sure the media don't run it. For public consumption purposes, Marsalis here can be just another heroic COLIN bodyguard, identity protected so that he can continue his good work."

"Yes," said Norton sourly. "As opposed to being a dangerous sociopath who hasn't actually done any work for us at all yet."

"Tom—"

Marsalis grinned. It was like a muscle flexing. "Well, I did save your partner's life for you. Does that count?"

"As far as I can see you saved your own skin, with some collateral benefits. Sevgi, if this Williamson is going to raise a stink about our friend here, we need to get you both out of here."

"Now, there's an idea."

Marsalis's voice was amiable, but something at the bottom of it made Sevgi look at him. She recalled the way he'd stared after the escaped assassin, the flat sound his voice made then as he told her *Right after the meat van gets here, I think you'd better take me in to COLIN so we can start work.* There was a finality to the way he'd said it that was like the silence following a single gunshot. And now, suddenly, she was afraid for Tom Norton and his dismissive flippancy.

"Sounds good to me, too," she said hurriedly. "Tom, can we wire up the n-djinn from *Horkan's Pride* at COLIN? Run a direct interface?"

Norton looked at her curiously, let his gaze slip to the black man at her shoulder and then back again. He shrugged. "Yeah, I suppose we *could*. But what the hell for? MIT already handed down the transcripts." He addressed himself directly to Marsalis. "They're on file at the office. You can go over them if you want."

"But I don't want." Marsalis was smiling gently. A small chill blew down Sevgi's spine at the sight. "What I *want*, Tom, is to talk to the *Horkan's Pride* n-djinn."

Norton stiffened. "So now suddenly you're an expert on the psychology of artificial intelligence?"

"No, I'm an expert on the hunting and killing of variant thirteens. Which is why you hired me. Remember?"

"Yeah, and don't you think that precious expertise might be—"

"Tom!"

"—better deployed going over the scenes of the crimes we're trying to bring an end to?"

Still the black man smiled. Still he stood relaxed, at a distance that Sevgi abruptly realized was just outside Norton's easy reach.

"No, I don't."

"Tom, that's *enough*. What the fuck is wrong with you this mor—"

"What's wrong with me Sev, is that—"

Two-tone rasp—a throat being ostentatiously cleared. They both stopped, switched their gazes back to Marsalis.

"You don't understand," he said quietly.

They were silent. The call for attention hung off the end of his words like a spoken command.

"You don't understand what you're up against." The smile came back, fleeting, as if driven by memory. "You think because Merrin's killed a couple of dozen people, he's some kind of serial killer writ large? That's not what this is about. Serial killers are *damaged* humans. You know this, Sevgi, even if Tom here doesn't. They leave a trail, they leave clues, they get caught. And that's because in the end, consciously or subconsciously, they *want* to be caught. Calculated murder is an antisocial act, it's hard for humans to do, and it takes special circumstances at either a personal or a social level to enable the capacity. But that's you people. It's not me, and it's not Merrin, and it's not any variant thirteen. We're not like you. We're the witches. We're the violent exiles, the lone-wolf nomads that you bred out of the race back when growing crops and living in one place got so popular. We don't have, we don't *need* a social context. You have to understand this: *there is nothing wrong with Merrin.* He's not damaged. He's not killing these people as an expression of some childhood psychosis, he's not doing it because he's identified them as some dehumanized, segregated extratribal group. He's just carrying out a plan of action, and he is *comfortable* with it. And he won't get caught doing it—unless you can put me next to him."

Norton shook his head. "You say Merrin's not damaged? You weren't there when they cracked the hull on *Horkan's Pride.* You didn't see the mess he left."

"I know he fed off the passengers."

"No. He didn't just *feed* off them, Marsalis. He ripped them apart, gouged out their eyes and scattered the *fucking* pieces from one end of the crew section to the other. That's what he did." Norton took a steadying breath. "You want to call that a plan of action, go right ahead. To me, it sounds like good old-fashioned insanity."

It was a fractional pause, but Sevgi saw how the news stopped Marsalis dead.

"Well, you'll need to show me footage of that," he said finally. "But my guess is there was a reason for whatever he did."

Norton grinned mirthlessly. "Sure there was a reason. Seven months alone in deep space, and a diet of human flesh. I'd be feeling pretty edgy myself under the circumstances."

"It's not enough."

"So you say. Ever consider you might be wrong about this? Maybe Merrin *did* crack. Maybe variant thirteen just isn't as beyond human as everybody thinks."

That got a sour smile out of Marsalis. "Thanks for the solidarity, Tom. It's a nice thought, but I'm in no hurry to be assimilated. Variant thirteen is not human the way you are, and this guy Merrin isn't going to be an exception. You judge what he does by normal human yardsticks, you'll be making a big mistake. Meanwhile, you hired me to echo-profile the guy, so how about we get on and do that, starting with the last living thing to see him alive. You going to let me talk to the *Horkan's Pride* n-djinn, or not?"

CHAPTER 20

The night sky lay at his feet.

Not a night sky you could see from Earth or Mars, or anywhere else this far out on a galactic arm. Instead the black floor was densely splattered with incandescence. Stars crowded one another's brilliance or studded the multicolored marble veins of nebulae. It might have been an accurately generated view from some hypothetical world at the core of the Milky Way; it might just have been a thousand different local night skies, overlaid one on top of the other and amped up to blazing. He took a couple of steps and stars crunched into white powder underfoot, smeared across the inky black. Over his head, the sky was a claustrophobic steel gray, daubed with ugly blob riveting in wide spiral runs.

Fucking ghosts in the machine.

No one knew why the shipboard djinns ran their virtual environments like this. Queries on the subject from human interface engineers met with vague responses that made no linguistic sense. *Flown from it-will, cannot the heavy, there-at, through-at, slopeless and ripe* was one of the famous ones. Carl had known an IF engineer on Mars who had it typed out and pasted above his bunk as a koan. The accompanying mathematics apparently made even less sense, though the guy insisted they had *a certain insane elegance,* whatever that was supposed to mean. He was planning a book, a collection of n-djinn haiku printed very small on expensive paper, with illustrations of the virtual formats on the facing pages.

It was Carl's opinion, admittedly not founded on any actual evidence, that the n-djinns were making elaborate jokes at humanity's dull-witted expense. He supposed that the book, if it ever saw print, could be seen as a punch line delivered.

In his darker moments, he wondered what might come after that. The joke over, the gloves off.

"Marsalis."

The voice came first, then the 'face, almost as if the n-djinn had forgotten it should manifest a focus the human could address. Like someone asking for a contact number, and then groping about for a pen to write it down. The 'face shaded in. A blued, confetti-shredded androgynous body that stood as if being continually blown away in a wind tunnel. Long ragged hair, streaming back. Flesh like a million tiny fluttering wings, stirring on the bone. It was impossible to make out male or female features. Under the voice, there was a tiny rustling, crackling sound, like paper burning up.

It was a little like talking to an angel. Carl grimaced.

"That's me. Been looking me up?"

"You feature in the flow." The 'face lifted one arm, and a curtain of images cascaded from it to the star-strewn floor. He spotted induction photos from Osprey, media footage following the *Felipe Souza* rescue, other stuff that lit odd corners of memory in him and made them newly familiar. Somewhere in among it all he thought he saw Marisol's face, but it was hard to tell. A defensive twinge went through him.

"Didn't know they were letting you hook up so soon."

It was a lie. Ertekin had shown him the release documentation from MIT— he knew to the hour when the n-djinn had been recalibrated and allowed back into the flow.

"It is potentially damaging for my systems to run without access to plentiful data," the blue figure said gravely. "Re-enabling a nanolevel artificial consciousness engine necessitates reconnection to local dataflows."

Unhumanly, the djinn had left the upheld arm where it was, and the downpour of images ran on.

Carl gestured toward the display. "Right. So what does the local dataflow have to say about me lately?"

"Many things. UNGLA currently defines you as a genetic licensing agent. *The Miami Herald* calls you a murderer. The Reverend Jessie Marshall of the Church of Human Purity calls you an abomination, but this is a generalized reference. News feeds abstracted from the Mars dataflow and currently held locally refer to you as this year's luckiest man on Mars, though the year in question is of course 2099. The *Frankfurter Allgemeine* called y—"

"Yeah, fine. You can stop there." Shipboard n-djinns were famously literal-minded. It was in the nature of the job they did. Minimal requirement for interface. Humans were deep-frozen freight. The djinns sat alone, sunk in black silence laced with star static, talking occasionally with other machines on Mars and Earth when docking or other logistics required it. "I came to ask you a couple of questions."

The 'face waited.

"Do you recall Allen Merrin?"

"Yes." Merrin's gaunt, Christ-like features evolved in the air at the 'face's shoulder. Standard ID likeness. "Occupant of crew section beta capsule, redesignated for human freight under COLIN interplanetary traffic directive c93-ep4652-21. Cryo-certified Bradbury November 5, 2106, protocol code 55528187."

"Yeah, except he didn't really occupy the beta capsule much, did he?"

"No. The system revived him at four hundred fourteen hours of trajectory time."

"You've told the debriefing crew that you shut down voluntarily at three hundred seventy-eight hours, on suspicion of corruptive material in a navigational module."

"Yes. I was concerned to prevent a possible viral agent from passing into the secondary navigational core. Quarantine measures were appropriate."

"And Merrin wakes up thirty-six hours later. Is that a coincidence?"

The blue shredded figure hesitated, face expressionless, eyes fixed on him. Carl guessed it was trying to calibrate his perceptions of relatedness and event, gleaning it from a million tiny shreds of evidence laid down in the details the dataflow held about him. Was he superstitious, was he religious? What feelings did he have about the role of chance in human affairs? The n-djinn was running his specifications, the way a machine would check the interface topography on a new piece of software.

It took about twenty seconds.

"There is no systems evidence to indicate a relation between the two events. The revival appears to have been a capsule malfunction."

"Were you aware of Merrin once he was awake?"

"To a limited extent, yes. As I said, it is potentially damaging for my systems to run without access to plentiful data. In a quarantine lockdown, the ship's secondary systems continue to feed into my cores, though it is impossible for me to actively respond to them in any way. The traffic is one-way; an interrupt protocol prevents feedback. You might consider this similar to the data processed by a human mind during REM sleep."

"So you dreamed Merrin."

"That is one way of describing it, yes."

"And in these dreams, did Merrin talk?"

The confetti-streaming figure shifted slightly in the grip of its invisible gale. There was an expression on its face that might have been curiosity. Might equally well have been mild pain, or restrained sexual ecstasy. It hadn't really gotten the hang of human features.

"Talk to whom?"

Carl shrugged, but it felt anything but casual. He was too freighted with the cold memories. "To the machines. To the people in the cryocaps. Did he talk to himself? To the stars, maybe? He was out there a long time."

"If you consider this talking, then yes. He talked."

"Often?"

"I am not calibrated to judge what would be considered *often* in human terms. Merrin was silent for eighty-seven point twenty-two percent of the trajectory, including time spent in sleep. Forty-three point nine percent of his speech was apparently directed—"

"All right, never mind. Are you equipped for Yaroshanko intuitive function?"

"Yaroshanko's underlying constants are present in my operating systems, yes."

"Good, then I'd like to run a Tjaden/Wasson honorific for links between myself and Merrin, making inference along a Yaroshanko curve. No more than two degrees of separation."

"What referents do you wish employed for the curve?"

"Initially, both our footprints in the total dataflow. Or as much of it as they're letting you have access to. You're going to get a lot of standard Bacon links, they're not what I'm after." Carl wished suddenly that Matthew were here to handle this for him, to reach quicksilver-swift and cool down the wires and engage the machine at something like its own levels of consciousness. Matthew would have been at ease in here—Carl felt clumsy by contrast. The terminology of complexity math tasted awkward on his tongue. "Cross-reference to everything Merrin said or did while he was aboard *Horkan's Pride*. Bring me anything that shows up there."

The blue shredded figure shifted slightly, rippling in the gale that Carl could not feel.

"This will take time," it said.

Carl looked around at the unending sky-floored desolation of the construct. He shrugged.

"Better get me a chair then."

He could, he supposed, have left the virtuality and killed the time somehow in the vaulted neo-Nordic halls of COLIN's Jefferson Park complex. He could have talked to Sevgi Ertekin some more, maybe even tried to massage Tom Norton back into a more compliant attitude with some male-on-male platitudes. He could have eaten something—his stomach was a blotched ache from lack of anything but coffee since Florida the previous night; he ignored it with trained stoicism—or just gone for a walk among the jutting riverside terraces of the complex. He had the run of the place, Sevgi said.

Instead he sat under the rivet-scarred metal sky and watched Merrin walk through the n-djinn's dreams.

The 'face had left him to his chair—a colliding geometry of comet trail lines and nebula gas upholstery, spun up out of the night sky as if flung at him—and disappeared into the dwindling perspectives of the wind that blew continually through its body. Something else blew back in its place—at first a tiny rectangular panel like an antique holographic postage stamp Carl had once seen in a London museum, fluttering stiff-cornered and growing in size as it approached until it slammed to a silent halt, three meters tall, two broad, and angled slightly backward at the base a handful of paces in front of where he sat. It was a cascade of images like the curtain where he'd seen his own face fall from the djinn's upheld arm. Silent and discoherent with the n-djinn's unhuman associative processes.

He saw Merrin wake from the beta capsule in the crew section, groggy from the revival but already moving with a recognizable focused economy. Saw him pacing the dorsal corridor of *Horkan's Pride*, face unreadable.

Saw him clean Helena Larsen's meat from between his teeth with a micro-gauge manual screwdriver from the maintenance lockers.

Saw him request a lateral vision port unshuttered, the ships' interior lighting killed. Saw him brace his arms on either side of the glass and stare out like a sick man into a mirror.

Saw him scream, jaw yawning wide, but silent, silent.

Saw him cut the throat of a limbless body as it revived, splayed palm held to block the arterial spray. Saw him gouge out the eyes, carefully, thoughtfully, one at a time, and smear them off his fingers against the matte-textured metal of a bulkhead.

Saw him talking to someone who wasn't there.

Saw him turn, once, in the corridor and look up at the camera, as if he knew Carl was watching him. He smiled, then, and Carl felt how it chilled him as his own facial muscles responded.

There was more, a lot more, even in the scant time it took the n-djinn to run the Tjaden/Wasson. The images juddered and flashed and were eaten over by other screen effects. He wasn't sure why the machine was showing it to him or what criteria it was using to select. It was the same sensation he knew from his time aboard *Felipe Souza*, the irritable feeling of trying to second-guess a capricious god he'd been assured—*no really, it's true, it's in the programming*—was watching over him. The feeling of sense just out of reach.

Maybe the djinn read something in him he wasn't aware of letting show, a need he didn't know he had. Maybe it thought this was what he wanted.

Maybe it *was* what he wanted. He wasn't sure.

He wasn't sure why he stayed there watching. But he was glad when it was over.

The floating blue shredded figure returned.

"There is this," it told him, and raised one restless, rippling arm like a wing. On the screen beneath, Merrin walked behind the automated gurney as it took Helena Larsen on her short journey from the cryocap chamber to the auto-surgeon. The second trip for her—just below the line of her leotard, her right thigh already ended in a neatly bandaged stump. She was mumbling to herself in postrevival semi-wakefulness, barely audible, but the n-djinn compensated and dragged in the sound.

". . . not again," she pleaded vaguely.

Merrin leaned in to catch the murmur of her voice, but not by much. His hearing would be preternaturally sharp, Carl knew, tuned up by now in the endless smothering stillness aboard the vessel as it fell homeward, honed in the dark aural shadow of the emptiness outside, where the abruptly deepened hum of a power web upping capacity in the walls would be enough to jerk you from sleep, and the sound of a dropped kitchen utensil seemed to clang from one end of the ship to the other. Your footfalls went muffled in spacedeck slippers designed not to scratch or scrape, and after a while you found yourself trying almost superstitiously not to break the hush in other ways as well. Speaking—to yourself, for sanity's sake, to the sentient and semi-sentient machines that kept you alive, to the dreaming visages behind the cryocap faceplates, to anyone or anything else you thought might be listening—speaking became an act of obscure defiance, a reckless violation of the silence.

"Again, yes," Merrin told the woman he was feeding off. "The cormorant's legacy."

The image froze.

"Cormorant," said Carl, memory flexing awake.

"Merrin uses the same word, out of context, on several occasions," said the djinn. "An association suggests itself. According to data from Wells region work camp rotations on Mars, both you and Merrin were acquainted with Robert P. Danvers, sin 84437hp3535. Yaroshanko-form extrapolation from this connects you both through Danvers to the Martian *familias andinas*, and, integrating with the term *cormorant* used here, with high probability to the sin-disputed identity Franklin Gutierrez."

Carl sat quietly for a while. The memories came thick and fast, the emotions he thought he'd discarded half a decade ago. He felt his fingers crook like talons at his sides.

"Well, well, well," he said at last. "Gutierrez."

"Never heard of him."

Norton, preparing to be unimpressed. He was standing, close enough to Carl for it to be a challenge.

"No, you wouldn't have," Carl agreed. He brushed past Norton, went to the office window, and stared out at the view. Smashed autumn sunlight lay across the East River in metallic patches, like some kind of chemical slick. "Franklin Gutierrez used to be a datahawk in Lima back in the mideighties. One of the best, by all accounts. In '86, he cracked Serbanco for upward of half a billion soles. Immaculate execution. It took them nearly a month to even realize he'd done it."

Norton grunted. "Couldn't have been that immaculate, if he ended up on Mars."

Carl fought down a sudden urge to remove Norton's vocal cords with his bare hands. He summoned patience from within, Sutherland style. *Hand over your responses to the man who triggers them, and you have already lost the battle for self. Look beyond, and find yourself there instead.* He focused on the details of the view below. COLIN New York, perhaps in conscious locational echo of the UN territory, stood a couple of long blocks south of Jefferson Park, vaulted and cantilevered over FDR Drive and looking out across the river. It was a fractal tumbling of structure that recalled nothing so much as a handful of abandoned segments from a huge peeled orange. Thin white nanocarb spidered over curves and angles of smoked amber glass, then swept down to brace elegantly amid the multi-level array of carefully tended walkways, paths, and gardens that linked each section into the whole site. You could stand here in the vaulted open-plan office suite Ertekin and Norton shared and look down across the whole thing, the gardens, the jutting edge of the mezzanine, and the river beyond. Carl's gaze reeled back out to the water, and he suffered a sudden resurgence of a feeling from his first days back on Earth eight years ago, a time when the sight of any large body of water came as an abrupt, visceral shock.

Time with the *Horkan's Pride* n-djinn had stirred him up, left him choppy and bleak with old memories.

So much for looking beyond.

"Yeah, they caught up with Gutierrez," he said neutrally. "But they caught him spending the money, not stealing it. Keep that in mind. This guy had his weak points, but getting away with the game wasn't one of them."

"So they offered him resettlement?" Ertekin asked.

"Yeah, and he took it. You ever seen the inside of a Peruvian jail?" Carl left the broad roofward sweep of the window, turned back into the office and his new colleagues. "He ended up in Wells, running atmospheric balance systems for the Uplands Initiative. When he wasn't doing that, he handled datacrime for the Martian *familias andinas*. I think it paid better than the day job."

Norton shook his head. "If this Gutierrez has links with Mars organized crime, then we've already run him and his association with Merrin."

"No, you haven't."

A swapped glance between Norton and Sevgi Ertekin. Norton sighed. "Look, Marsalis. One of the first things this investigation did was to—"

"Contact the Colony police, and ask them to run a list of associates for Merrin on Mars. Right." Carl nodded. "Yeah. Makes sense, I'd have done the same. Just that it wouldn't do any good. If Gutierrez had dealings with Merrin, they're gone now, wiped off the flow like shit off a baby's arse. All you'll be left with is some minor association with a low-level middleman like Danvers. And men like Danvers rub shoulders with practically everyone who's ever worked the Wells camps anyway. In other words, your business transaction is invisible. That's how it works when Gutierrez does something for you."

"And you know this how?"

He shrugged. "How do you think?"

"Gutierrez did something for you," Ertekin said quietly. "What was it?"

"Something I'm not going to talk to you about. The point is, in dataflow terms, my connection with Gutierrez no longer exists, and neither does Merrin's. Any associative search Colony ran on Merrin would have stopped at Danvers. The *Horkan's Pride* n-djinn only went farther because it didn't like the coincidence of two thirteens both making it back from Mars under uncommon circumstances *and* both having a separate, unrelated connection with a low-grade fence like Danvers. That's Yaroshanko intuition for you. Very powerful when it works, but it needs something to triangulate off."

"I still don't see," said Norton irritably, "how that gives you this Gutierrez."

"On its own, it doesn't. But the recollections the n-djinn has of Merrin include a couple of references to a cormorant."

Norton nodded. "Yeah, we saw that first time around. *The cormorant legacy, leavings of the cormorant, wring that fucking cormorant's neck.* We had our own reference n-djinns go over it. Checked out Martian slang, and got nothing—"

"No, it's not a Martian term."

"Might be now," Ertekin pointed out. "You've been back awhile. Anyway, we backed up into Project Lawman usage and thirteen argot in general. We still got nothing."

"It's Limeño."

Norton blinked. "Excuse me?"

"It's a Lima underground term. Pretty obscure, and old. Your n-djinn probably would have discounted it as irrelevant. Goes back to the early seventies, which is when Gutierrez was a young gun on the Andes coast datahawk circuit. Have you heard of *ukai*?"

Blank looks.

"Okay, *ukai* is a form of fishing where you use trained cormorants to bring up your fish. It's originally from Japan, but it got big in the Peruvian Japanese community about fifty years back when the whole designer-breeding thing really took off. *Ukai* is done at night, and the cormorants dive with a ring on their throat that stops them from swallowing the fish. They get fed when they bring the catch back to their handler. See the imagery?"

"Contracted datahawking." Ertekin's eyes lit up with the connection. "The *familias andinas.*"

"Yeah. In those days the *familias* here on Earth were still a force to be reckoned with. Anyone starting out as a hawk on the South Pacific coast worked for the *familias*, or they didn't work at all. You might end up a big-name *halcon de datos.* But you started life as a *cormoran.*"

Ertekin was nodding now. "Including Gutierrez."

"Including Gutierrez," he agreed, and something sparked between them as he echoed her words. "Later he got his rep, got his own gigs. Got caught."

"And when he got to Mars, he found the *familias* waiting for him all over again."

"Right. It's like stepping back in time half a century there. The *familias* have a hold they haven't had on Earth for decades. Apparently Gutierrez had to go right back into *ukai* work. Back to being a cormorant." Carl spread his hands, case-closed style. "He bitched to me about it all the time."

"That doesn't necessarily mean he'd do the same with Merrin," Norton said.

"Yeah, it does. Gutierrez had a thing about thirteens. A lot of people do on

Mars, there's a whole fetish subculture dedicated to it. It's like the bonobo fan clubs here. Gutierrez was a fully paid-up member, fascinated by the whole thing. He had this pet analogy he liked to draw, between the thirteens and the Lima datahawks. Both supermen in their own right, both feared and hated by the herd because of it."

Norton snorted. "Supermen. Right."

"Well, it was his theory," Carl said evenly. "Not mine. Point is, he went on and on about being reduced back to *ukai* status, about how I could understand that shit because of who I was, because of *what* I was. And he would have laid exactly the same line off on Merrin."

"So." Norton broke it up, stepped into the flood of light. "We call Colony, tell them to bring Gutierrez in and lean on him."

Carl snorted. "Yeah, lean on him from a couple of hundred million kilometers away. Ten-minute coms lag each way. That interrogation, I want to watch."

"I didn't say we'd lean on him, I said Colony would."

"Colony couldn't lean on a fucking wall. Forget it. What happens on Mars doesn't play this end. It's not a human distance."

Ertekin sank deeper into her chair, bridged her hands, and stared across the office. Light from the tall window fell in on her like the luminous sifting sunset rains on Mars. Carl's woken memories came and kicked him in the chest again.

"If the *familias andinas* helped get Merrin out of Mars," she said slowly, and mostly to herself, "then they could be helping him at this end as well."

"Not the South American chapters," Carl observed. "They've had a war with the Martian *familias* for decades. Well, a *state* of war anyway. They wouldn't be cooperating with anything at the Mars end."

Ertekin shook her head. "They wouldn't have to be. I'm thinking about the Jesusland *familias*, and what's left of them in the Rim. They pay lip service to the altiplano heritage, but that's about it. This far north, they run their own game, and a lot of it's human-traffic-related. I mean, the Rim squashed them pretty fucking flat after Secession, ripped their markets with the drug law changes, the open biotech policies. Sex slaves and fence-hopping's about all they had to fall back on. But they're still out there, just like they're still here. And in between, in the Republic, they still swing a hell of a lot of old-time weight."

She brooded for a while.

"Yeah, okay. They've got the human-traffic software Merrin would have needed to get in and out of the Rim like that. Maybe they've got something going on with the Martian chapters, some kind of deal that gets them this Gutierrez's services. The question is *why*? What's their end of something like this? Where's the benefit?"

"You think," Norton ventured, "these are *familia*-sanctioned hits he's carrying out?"

"They bring a thirteen all the way back from Mars to do their contract killing for them?" Ertekin scowled. "Doesn't make much sense. *Sicarios* are a dollar a dozen in every major Republican city. Prisons are full of them."

Norton flickered a glance at Carl. "Well, that's true."

"No, this has to be something else." Ertekin looked up at Carl. "You said this Gutierrez did something for you on Mars. Can we assume you had a working relationship with the *familias* as well?"

"I dealt with them on and off, yeah."

"Care to speculate on why they'd do this?" She was still looking. Tawny flakes in the iris of her eyes.

Carl shrugged. "Under any normal circumstances, I'd say they wouldn't. The *familias* run an old-time macho, conservative setup, here and on Mars. They've got all the standard prejudices against people like me."

"But?"

"But. Several years ago, I ran into a thirteen who tried to forge an alliance with what's left of the altiplano chapters. Guy called Nevant, French, ex–Department Eight Special Insertion Unit. Very smart guy, he was an insurrection specialist in Central Asia. Warlord liaison, counterintelligence, all that shit. Given time, he might have gotten something working up there, too."

"Might have," drawled Norton. "So it's safe to say he wasn't given time."

"No. He wasn't."

"What happened to him?"

Carl smiled bleakly. "I happened to him."

"Did you kill him?" Ertekin asked sharply.

"No. I tracked him to some friends he had in Arequipa, pulled the Haag gun on him, and he put his hands in the air sooner than die."

"Bit unusual for a thirteen, isn't it?" Norton cranked an eyebrow. "Giving up like that?"

Carl matched the raised brow, deadpan. "Like I said, he's a smart guy."

"Okay, so you busted this Nevant, this smart guy, and you took him back." Ertekin got to her feet and went to stare out the window. He guessed she could see where this was going. "So where is he now?"

"Back in the system. Eurozone Internment Tract, eastern Anatolia."

"And you want to go and talk to him there." It wasn't a question.

"I think that'll be more effective than a v-link or a phone call, yes."

"Will he see you?" Still she didn't turn around.

"Well, he doesn't have to," Carl admitted. "The Eurozone internment charter guarantees his right to refuse external interviews. If this were an official UNGLA investigation, we could maybe bring some pressure to bear, but on my own I don't carry that kind of weight. But you know, I think he'll see me anyway."

"You basing that on anything at all?" asked Norton.

"Yeah, previous experience." Carl hesitated. "We, uh, get on."

"I see. A few years ago you bust the guy, send him back to a lifetime in the Turkish desert, and as a result you're the best of friends?"

"Anatolia isn't a desert," said Ertekin absently, still at the window.

"I didn't say we were the best of friends, I said we get on. After I busted him, we had to kill a few days in Lima, waiting for transfer clearances. Nevant likes to talk, and I'm a pretty good listener. We both—"

A phone chirruped from Norton's desk on the other side of the office. He shot a last glance at Carl, then strode across to answer the call. Ertekin turned from the window and nailed Carl with a mistrustful look of her own.

"You think I should let you back across the Atlantic at this point?"

Carl shrugged. "Do what you like. You want to pursue another line of inquiry, be my guest and dig one up. But Nevant's the obvious lead, and I don't think he'll talk to me in virtual, because a virtual identity can be faked. Tell the truth, I wouldn't trust it in his place, either. Us genetic throwbacks don't like advanced technology, you know."

He caught the momentary twitch of her mouth before she locked the smile reflex down. Norton came back from the phone call, and the moment slid away. The COLIN exec's face was grim.

"Want to guess?" he asked.

"Merrin's holed up in the UN building with a nuclear device," suggested Carl brightly. "And enough delegates held hostage to eat his way through to Christmas."

Norton nodded. "I'm glad you're having a good time. Wrong guess. You're all over the feeds. Thirteen saves COLIN director, slaughters two."

"Oh fuck." Ertekin's shoulders slumped. "All we needed. How the hell did that happen?"

"Apparently, some anal little geek at one of the city feeds had a fit of total recall. Got our friend here's face off the crime scene footage, face reminded him of something, he matched it with the trouble down in Florida." Norton pointed. "Or maybe it was that jacket. Hard to miss, and it's not exactly high fashion. Anyway, the geek rings up the Twenty-eighth Precinct and asks some leading questions. Evidently he got lucky. He talked to either someone really cooperative or someone really dumb."

"Fucking Williamson."

Norton shrugged. "Yeah, or whoever. You've got to bet half an hour after Williamson got back to the Twenty-eighth, every cop in the precinct house knew they had a thirteen walking the streets. And probably saw no reason on Earth to shut up about it. In their eyes, it's a basic public safety issue. They know they've got no leverage with us, they'd be more than happy to let the feeds do their demonizing for them."

"Demonize?" Carl grinned. "I thought I was up there for saving Ortiz."

"And slaughtering two," said Ertekin wearily. "Don't forget that part."

"They're asking for a statement, Sev. Nicholson says he figures you're it. Former NYPD detective and all that, should make it easier to play down any anti-COLIN feeling the Twenty-eighth may have stirred up."

"Oh thanks, Tom." Ertekin threw herself back into her chair and glared up at Norton. "A fucking *press* conference? You think I haven't got anything better to do than talk to the fucking *media*?"

Norton spread his hands. "It isn't me, Sev. It's Nicholson. And the way he sees it, no, you don't have anything better to do right now. What do you want me to do, tell him you had to go out of town?"

Carl met her eyes across the room. He grinned.

part II

AWAY FROM IT ALL

The limited brief of this report notwithstanding, it is imperative to acknowledge that we are dealing here with actual human beings and not some theoretical model of human behavior. We should not then be surprised to encounter a complex and potentially confusing mass of emotional factors and interactions. Nor should it perplex us to discover that any genuine solution may well need to be sought beyond the current scope of our inquiry.

—Jacobsen Report,
August 2091

OLIN Istanbul was on the European side, up near Taksim Square and nestled amid a forest of similar purple or bronze glass towers inhabited mostly by banks. At night, a skeleton security staff and automated guns kept the base levels open, lit in pools of soft blue, for whatever business might crop up. The Colony Initiative, to paraphrase its own advertising hype, was an enterprise on which the sun never set. You never knew when or where it might need to flex itself fully awake and deploy some geopolitical muscle. Best always to remain on standby. Sevgi, who associated Taksim primarily with the murder of her grandfather and great-uncle by overzealous Turkish security forces, stopped in just long enough to collect keytabs for one of the COLIN-owned apartments across the Bosphorus in Kadıköy. Pretty much anything else she needed, she could access through her dataslate. Talking to Stefan Nevant was in any case not going to be a COLIN gig.

The less official presence he can smell on you, the better, Marsalis told her. *Nevant's special, he's one of the few thirteens I know who's come to an accommodation with external authority. He's emptied out his rage. But that doesn't mean he feels good about it. Be best if we don't poke a finger in that particular blister.*

The same limo that had collected them from the airport rolled them down to the Karaköy terminal, where the ferries to the Asian side ran all night. Sevgi shrugged off the driver's protests about security. Riding around via the bridge was going to take as long as or longer than waiting for the ferry, and she needed to clear her head. She hadn't wanted to come here, wanted still less to be here with Marsalis. She was beginning to wonder if she shouldn't have folded and taken the press conference after all.

They'd watched it broadcast on New England Net while the midafternoon THY suborb spun them up from JFK and dropped them on the other side of the globe, Norton looking sober and imposing in his media suit. TV audiences still

loved a solid pair of shoulders and a good head of hair above pretty much anything they'd actually hear coming out of a speaker's mouth, and Tom Norton excelled in both areas. He really could, Sevgi was convinced, have run for office of
some sort. He fielded the questions with exactly the right measure of patrician
confidence and down-home good humor.

*Dan Meredith, Republic Today. Is it true COLIN are now employing hyper-
males as security?*

No, Dan. Not only is it not true, it's also deeply flawed as an assumption. Inclu-
sive gesture to the whole room. *I think we're all aware what a hypermale would
look like, if anyone was actually criminally stupid enough to breed one.*

Ripple of muttering among the gathered journalists. Norton gave it just long
enough, then squashed it.

*Hypermale genetic tendency is, not to put too fine a point to it, autism. A hyper-
male would make a pretty poor security guard, Dan. Not only would he likely not
recognize signs of an impending attack from another human being, he'd probably
be too busy counting the bullets in his gun to actually fire them at anything.*

Laughter. The footage swung momentarily to Meredith's face in the crowd.
He offered a thin smile. Ladled urbane southern irony into his voice. *I'm sorry,
Tom. Leaving aside the fact we all know the Chinese have bred super-autists for
their n-djinn interface programs, that's not what I meant. I was referring to variant
thirteens, which most normal Americans would call hypermales. Hypermales like
the one you admit was present at today's attempt on Alvaro Ortiz's life. Are you employing any of those as security guards?*

No, we're not.

Then—

But Norton had already raised his head to scan the crowd, already signaled for
the next question.

*Sally Asher, New York Times. You've described this variant thirteen, Carl
Marsalis, as a consultant. Can you please tell us what exactly he is consulting on?*

*I'm sorry, Sally, I'm not currently at liberty to say. All I can tell you is that it has
nothing to do with the tragic events of this afternoon. Mr. Marsalis was simply a bystander who took the action any good citizen with the opportunity might.*

Any good citizen armed with an assault rifle, maybe. Asher's voice was light.
Was Mr. Marsalis armed?

Norton hesitated a moment. You could see the dilemma—data was out there,
it was loose in the flow by now. Footage of the crime scene, eyewitness accounts,
maybe even backdoor gossip from the path labs. No way to tell what was or wasn't
known, and Norton didn't want to get caught in a lie. On the other hand—

No. Mr. Marsalis was not armed.

Quiet but rising buzz. They'd all seen the bullet-riddled limo, at least.

How can a man, an ordinary man, possibly—

Meredith again, voice pitched loud before Norton's arm cut him off again, hauled in another question from the opposite side of the room. The feed didn't show Meredith's face, but Sevgi felt an ignoble stab of pleasure as she imagined the Jesuslander's chagrin.

Mr. Norton, is it true, I'm sorry, Eileen Lan, Rim Sentinel. *Is it true, Mr. Norton, that COLIN is training personnel on Mars in previously unknown fighting techniques?*

No, that's not true.

Then can you please throw light on this comment from an eyewitness at today's events. Lan held aloft a microcorder, and a male voice rinsed cleanly through the speaker. *The guy was like a fucking wheel. I've seen that stuff on Ultimate Fighting tapes from Mars, that's* tanindo. *That's stuff they won't teach back here on Earth, they say it's too dangerous to let ordinary people get to know because—*

The microcorder clicked off, but Lan left it upheld like a challenge. Norton leaned an arm across the lectern and grinned easily.

Well, I'm not really an Ultimate Fighting fan—polite laughter—*so obviously I can't comment accurately on what your eyewitness there is talking about. There is a Martian discipline called* tanindo, *but it's not a COLIN initiative. Tanindo has emerged spontaneously from existing martial arts in response to the lower-gravity environment on Mars. In Japanese, it means, literally, "way of the newcomer," because on Mars, as I'm sure I don't need to remind you, we are all of us newcomers. It's also known in some quarters as Float Fighting and, in Quechua, as—you'll perhaps forgive my pronounciation here—pisi llasa awqanakuy. Mr. Marsalis has served time on Mars, and may for all I know be an aficionado of the style, but really a martial art designed for a low-gravity environment isn't likely to be all that dangerous, or even useful, here on Earth.*

Unless you're inhumanly strong and fast, Sevgi qualified for him silently. Her gaze slipped sideways from the lap screen to Marsalis, dozing in the seat at her side. Norton had dug up fifty mil of COLIN-grade betamyeline and an inhaler just before they left, and Marsalis had dosed up in the departure lounge at JFK. He got some nosy sidelong glances, but no one said anything. Aside from a grunt of satisfaction as the chloride took, he made no comment, but as soon as they got to their seats he'd closed his eyes and a beatific grin split his face with ivory. He was asleep not long after.

Bonita Hanitty, Good Morning South. *You don't feel that by liberating a condemned criminal from a Florida penal institution, COLIN are flouting the very concept of American justice?*

More muttering, not all of it sympathetic. Republican journalists were a minority in the room, and the Union press wore *Lindley v. NSA* on their collective chest like a medal of honor. Cub reporters came up on the legend; senior staffers told pre-Secession war stories and talked about their Republican colleagues with either snide pity or disdain. Norton knew the ground, and rode with it.

Well, Bonita, I think you need to be careful there talking about justice. As the briefing disk you'll have received does specify, Mr. Marsalis had not actually been charged with anything during his four months of incarceration. And then there's the question of the initial alleged entrapment, no let me finish please, the alleged entrapment techniques used by the Miami police to arrest Mr. Marsalis in the first place. And this is without mentioning that Republican and state law in the matter of pregnancy termination both run counter to well-established UN principles of human rights.

Choked splutters from several quarters, muted cheers elsewhere. Norton waited out the noise with a stern expression, then trod onward.

So what I'd say is that COLIN has liberated a man who is in all probability innocent, and whom the state of Florida didn't really seem to know what to do with anyway. Yes, Eileen, back to you.

There was a lot more after that, of course. Hanitty, Meredith, and a couple of other Jesusland reps trying to dig back into Marsalis's prior record and the deaths in the Garrod Horkan camp. Mercifully nothing about Willbrink. Norton rode cautious and courteous herd on it all, didn't quite shut the Jesuslanders down, but leaned heavily toward Union journalists he knew and trusted enough not to throw curves. Sevgi yawned and watched it sputter to a close. Beside her in the suborbital, the object of all their fears and attentions dozed on unconcerned.

Sleep of her own was unforthcoming—the syn wouldn't allow it. She was still buzzing a couple of hours later as she slumped in the cheap plastic seating of the ferry hall, watching the few other waiting passengers with a cop's eye. The place was bare bones and drafty, lit from above by sporadic spotlights on the roof girders and at the sides by the ghostly flicker of a few LCLS advertising boards whose sponsors hadn't specified particular time slots for activation. EFES EXTRA!! JEEP PERFORMANCE!! WORK ON MARS!! The inactive panels between looked like long gray tombstones hung on the corrugated-steel walls.

Through rolled-back shutter doors at the side, the white-painted superstructure of the moored ferry showed like a sliced view of another age. More modern additions to Istanbul's diverse collection of water transport had a boxy, plastic look that made them out as no more than the seabuses they were, offering nothing at journey's end but the completion of the daily commute. But the high, wide bridge, hunched smokestack, and long waist of the antique ships still on the

Karaköy-Kadıköy run spoke of departure to farther-flung places, and an era when travel could still mean escape.

Marsalis came back from a prowl of the environs. She supposed in her grand-father's time, he'd have gotten more looks for his skin, but now he stood out no more than the half a dozen Africans waiting around the dock as passengers and the two who stood in coveralls on the deck of the ferry beyond the shutters. No one gave him more than a glance, and that mostly for his bulk and the bright or-ange lettering on the inmate jacket he still wore.

"Do you have to keep wearing that?" she asked irritably.

He shrugged. "It's cold."

"I said at the airport I'd buy you something else."

"Thanks. I like to buy my own clothes."

"Then why didn't you?"

Klaxons groaned in the girdered space over their heads. An LCLS arrow on a movable barrow lit up pointing to the cranked-back shutters, destinations in-scribed: HAYDARPAŞA, KADIKÖY. The two men on the ferry rolled out gangplanks, and a slow drift of humanity began moving toward the boat.

Impelled by memories of childhood visits, Sevgi moved along the starboard rail and seated herself on the outward-facing bench near the stern, propping her-self there with her booted feet on the rail's bottom rung. Thrum of the ship's mo-tors through the metal at her back. The mingled reek of engine oil and damp mooring ropes carried her back in time. Murat's hand ruffling her hair as she stood beside him at the rail, barely tall enough to see over the top rung. The soft, chuntered rhythms of Turkish pushing out the English in her head. The impact of a whole world she'd previously seen only in the photos, a city that wasn't New York, a place that was not her home but meant something vital—she sensed it in the way they looked around, exclaimed to each other, clutched each other's hands at her eye level—to her parents. Istanbul had shocked her to her four-year-old core, and each time she went back, it did it again.

Marsalis dropped into the seat beside her, copied her stance. The rail clanked dully as it took the weight of his legs.

"Now I'm really going to need this jacket," he said cheerfully. "See."

The engine thrum deepened, became a roar, and the stern of the ferry rose in a mound of seething water. Shouts from the crew, ropes thrown, and a rapidly widening angle of space opened between the ferry and the dock. The boat thrashed about and picked up a vector out across the darkened water. Karaköy fell away, became a festooned knot of lights in the night. A chilly sea breeze came slapping at Sevgi's face and hair. The city opened out around her, color-lit bridges and long low piles of skyline, all floating on a liquid black dotted with the running lights of other ships. She breathed in deep, held on to the illusory sense of departure.

Marsalis leaned toward her, pitching his voice to beat the engines and the wind of their passage. "Last time I came here, there was a delay at the suborb terminal, some kind of security scare. But I only found out about it after I'd checked out of my hotel. I had a couple of hours to kill before I needed to get out to the airport." He grinned. "I spent the whole two hours doing this, just riding the ferries back and forth till it was time to go. Nearly missed my fucking flight. Out here, looking at all this, you know. Felt like some kind of escape."

She stared at him, touched to shivering by the echo of her own feelings in his words.

His brow creased. "What's the matter? You getting seasick?"

She shook her head. Threw something into the gap. "Why'd you come back, Marsalis? Back to Earth?"

"Hey." Another grin. "I won the lottery. Would have been pretty ungracious not to take the prize."

"I'm serious." Fiercely, into the wind between them. "I know it's grim out there, but every thirteen I ever heard talk about it loved the whole idea of Mars. Escape to a new frontier, a place you can carve out something of your own."

"It isn't like that."

"I know. But that doesn't stop anyone believing it." She looked out across the water. "It's where they're all heading, isn't it. The ones you hunt down. They're heading for the camps and a one-way ticket to the Martian dream. Somewhere they've been told they'll be wanted, valued for their strengths. Not rounded up and kept on fenced ground like livestock."

"Most of them try for the camps, yeah."

"You ever ask yourself why UNGLA doesn't just let them run, let them hitch a cryocap ride out of everyone's hair?"

He shrugged. "Well, primarily because the Accords say they can't. The Agency exists to make sure every genetic variant on Earth is filed and monitored appropriate to their level of risk to society, and in the case of variant thirteens that means internment. If we start turning a blind eye to fence-breakers just because we think they're going to skip for Mars, pretty soon some of them *aren't* going to skip for Mars, they're just going to hole up somewhere here on Earth and maybe start breeding. And that puts the whole fucking human race back to pre-Munich levels of panic."

"You talk as if they weren't like you," she said, accusation rising in her voice. "As if you were different."

"I am different."

Just like Ethan, just fucking like him. Her own despair guttered upward on its wick. Her voice sounded dull in her own ears. "It doesn't matter to you that they're treated this way?"

Another shrug. "They're living the choices they made, Ertekin. They could have gone to Mars when COLIN opened the gates at Munich. They chose to stay. They could get on with their lives on the reservations. They choose to break out. And when I come for them, they've got the option to surrender."

Jagged memory of Ethan's bullet-ripped corpse on the slab. Called to make the identification, trembling and cold with the shock.

"Choices, yes," she snarled. "Every choice a fucking humiliation. Give up your freedom, roll over and do as you're told. You know full fucking well what kind of choice that is for a thirteen."

"It's a choice I made," he said mildly.

"Yeah." She looked away again, disgustedly. "You're right. You are different."

"Yeah, I'm smarter."

Another ferry passed them a hundred meters off, heading the other way. She felt an irrational tug toward the little island of lights and windowed warmth, the vaguely glimpsed figures moving about within. Then the stupidity of the situation came and slapped at her like the sea wind. Right behind her, pressing into her shoulders, were the window rims of an identical haven of lit and heated space, and she'd turned her back on it.

Yeah, much better that way, Sev. Turn away. Stay out in the cold and stare across the water at the fucking unattainable as it sails away from you.

Fucking idiot.

"So he went down fighting?"

She snapped around to face him again. "Who did?"

"The thirteen you were having a relationship with." The same mild calm in his voice. "You told me he's dead, you're angry about what I do for a living. Makes a certain kind of sense this guy got taken down by someone like me."

"No," she said tightly. "Not someone like you."

"Okay, not someone like me."

He waited, let it sit between them like the darkness and the noise of their passage through it.

She clenched her teeth.

"They sent the SWATs," she said finally. "A fucking dozen of them. More. Body armor and automatic weapons, against one man in his own home. They—"

She had to swallow.

"I wasn't there, it was morning and I'd already gone to work. He was off duty, just off a stack of night work. Someone in the department tipped him off they were coming, they found a call on the phone later, downtown number. He—"

"He was a cop?"

"Yeah, he was a cop." She gestured helplessly, hand a claw. "He was a *good* cop. Tough, clean, reliable. Made detective in record time. *He never did anything fucking wrong.*"

"Apart from faking his ID, presumably."

"Yeah. He got himself Rim States citizenship back before the internments started. Said he saw it coming way ahead of time. He bought a whole new identity in the Angeline Freeport, lived up and down the West Coast for a couple of years building it up, then put in for official immigration to the Union. They still weren't testing for variant thirteen then, and once he was in he had the Cross Act to protect him, the whole right-to-genetic-privacy thing."

"Sounds like the perfect vanishing act."

"Yeah?" She gave him a smile smeared with pain. "That your professional opinion?"

"For what it's worth. I guess he was smart."

"Yeah, well. Like Jacobsen says—*sociopathic tendency allied with dangerous levels of raw intelligence.* That's why we're locking thirteens up, right?"

"No. We're locking thirteens up because the rest of the human race is scared of them. And a society of scared humans is a very dangerous thing to have on your hands. Well worth a bit of internment to avoid."

She scanned his face for the irony. Couldn't tell.

"His name was Ethan," she said at last. "Ethan Conrad. He was thirty-six years old when they killed him."

The other ferry was almost gone now, fading amid the other flecks of traffic and the lights of the European side. She drew a deep breath.

"And I was six months' pregnant."

CHAPTER 23

On the Asian side, with Europe reduced to glimmering lights across the water, she got drunk and told him the rest.

He wasn't sure why—it might have been a by-product of the alcohol, or a desired result. Either way, it wasn't what he'd been expecting. He'd watched the way her mouth clamped shut behind the sudden admission of loss, and he recognized damage that wouldn't be healing anytime soon. They got off the ferry in Kadıköy without speaking, carrying a personal silence between them that deadened the clank and clatter of disembarkation. The same bubble of quiet stayed with them as they trudged the half a dozen rising blocks up from the waterfront, following the street-finder holo in the keytab, until they reached the winding thoroughfare of Moda Caddesi and the low-rise apartment tower that COLIN owned there. It was a residential neighborhood, long since put to bed, and they saw no one along the way.

There was a strange, secretive feeling of release and refuge in it all. Quietly, quietly, up and away from the lights of the ferry terminal, past the shuttered frontages of a market and the curtained windows of the sleeping world, the glimmering map in the hollow of Ertekin's palm and the pale bluish light it cast up into her face. When they arrived, she opened the door in from the street with exaggerated care, and they took the stairs rather than wake the machinery of the elevators. In the apartment—air infused with the slightly musty chill of no recent occupancy—they fetched up together in the kitchen, still without speaking, and found an open but barely touched bottle of Altınbaş rakı on the counter.

"You'd better pour me some of that," she told him grimly.

He searched for the appropriate long slim glasses, found them in a cabinet, while Ertekin filled a jug with water from the tap. He poured each glass half full with the oily transparent weight of the rakı and watched as she topped the measures off from the jug. Milky, downward-tumbling avalanche cloud of white as the water hit. She grabbed up a glass and drank it off without drawing breath. Set it down again and looked expectantly at him. He poured again, watched her top up. This one she sipped at and carried through to the abandoned chill of the living room. He took bottle and jug and his own glass, and followed her.

They were on the top floor, a broad picture-window vantage opening out over the rooftops of Kadıköy at a couple of stories' advantage. With the lounge lighting dimmed back, they had a clear view all the way to the Sea of Marmara and the minaret-spiked skyline of Sultanahmet back on the European side. Staring at it, Carl had the sudden, hallucinatory sensation of leaving something behind, as if the two shores were somehow drifting apart. They sat in squashy mock-leather armchairs facing the window, not each other, and they drank. Out on the Sea of Marmara, big ships sat at anchor, queuing for entry to the Bosphorus Straits. Their riding lights winked and shifted.

They'd killed well over half the bottle by the time she started talking again.

"It wasn't fucking planned, I can tell you that much."

"You knew what he was?"

"By then, yes." She sighed, but it got caught somewhere in her throat. There was no real relief in the noise it made. "You'd think we'd have terminated it, right? Knowing the risks. Looking back, I'm still not really sure why we didn't. I guess . . . I guess we'd both started thinking we were invulnerable. Ethan had that from the start, that whole thirteen thing. He always acted like bullets would have bounced off him. You could see it in him across a crowded room."

Her tone shifted, gusts of obscure anger rinsing through her voice.

"And once you are pregnant, well then the biology's there in you as well, ticking and trickling away inside, telling you this is *good*, this is *right*, this is what's supposed to *be*. You don't worry about how you'll manage, you just figure you will. You stop cursing yourself for that last inoculation you forgot to get, or for not forcing the guy to spray on before you fuck, for being weak and stupid enough to let your own biology get the better of you, because that same fucking biology is telling now it's going to be okay, and your critical faculties just take a walk out the air lock. You tell yourself the genetic-privacy laws are stronger in the Union than in any other place on Earth, and that the legislation's going to keep moving in the right direction. You tell yourself by the time it matters to the child in your belly, things will have changed, there'll be no more panic about race dilution and genetically modified monsters, no more Accords and witch hunts. And every now and then, when all that fails you and a doubt creeps in, you face it down by telling yourself hey, you're both cops, you're both NYPD. *You're* the ones who enforce the law around here, so who's going to come knocking on *your* door? You figure you belong to this massive family that's always going to look out for you."

"You met Ethan through the force?"

It got him a sour smile. "How else? When you're a cop, you don't socialize much with civilians. I mean, why would you? Half the time they hate your fucking guts, the rest of the time they can't fucking live without you. Who wants to buy drinks for a personality disorder like that? So you stick by your big adoptive family, and mostly that's enough." She shrugged. "I guess that was always part of the attraction for Ethan. He was looking to seal himself off from his past, and NYPD can be a cozy little self-contained world if you want it to be. Just like going to Mars."

"Not quite. You can always leave the police force."

She gestured with her drink, spilled a little. "You can always win the Ticket Home lottery."

"Yeah."

"Anyway, Ethan. I met him at a retirement party for my squad commander. He'd just made detective, he was celebrating. Big guy, and you could see from across the room how impressed he was with himself. The kind of thing you look at and want to tear down, see what's behind all that male control. So I went to have a look."

"And did you? Tear it all down?"

"You mean, did we fuck?"

"Actually, no. But—"

"Yeah, we fucked. It was an instant thing, we just clicked. Like that." She snapped her fingers loosely, to no real effect. Frowned and did it again. *Snac.* "Like *that.* Two weeks in, we were leaving overnight stuff at each other's places. He'd been seeing this cheerleader blond bitch worked Datacrime somewhere downtown, I had something going on with a guy who ran a bar out in Queens. I was still living out there, never managed to organize a move across the river when I made Midtown Homicide. Just an old neighborhood girl, see. So, anyway, I dumped my bar guy, he dumped the cheerleader." Another frown. "Bit of static with that, but anyway, a month later he moved in."

"Had he told you what he was?"

"Not then, no. I mean—" She gestured again, more carefully this time. "—not like he lied to me about anything. He just didn't say, and who'd think to ask? Thirteens are all locked away, right? In the reservations, or on Mars. They're not walking the city streets like you and me. They're certainly not walking around with a palmful of gold shield, are they?"

"Not generally, no."

"No." She nursed her drink for a while. "I don't know if he would ever have told me. But one night this other thirteen showed up, asking for Ethan by another name, and he sure as fuck filled me in."

"What did he want?"

Her lip curled. "He wanted money. Apparently, he was part of the same Lawman unit as Ethan when they deployed in some godforsaken corner of Central Asia back in the eighties. Bobby something, but he was calling himself Keegan. He was still aboveground when internment started, and he didn't rate Mars as an option, so they sent him to Cimarron. He went over the wire, hid out in Jesusland for a while till he found some gang to smuggle him into the Union. He'd been in the city for a couple of years when he showed up at our place, been making a living at this and that. Sheer bad luck he spotted Ethan coming out of a Korean noodle place in Flushing, followed him home."

"He recognized him? I'd have thought—"

"Yeah, Ethan got some facial surgery in the Rim states, but it wasn't deep, and this guy Keegan saw through the changes. Kept going on about how it wasn't the face, it was the whole package, how Ethan moved, how he talked. Anyway, he found out Ethan was a cop, figured it must be some kind of scam he was working. Blackmailing the right people. He couldn't." She clenched a fist in the low light. "He *wouldn't* believe Ethan had made NYPD detective the hard way. *That's not the way we do things*, he kept saying. *You're thirteen, man. You're not a fucking cudlip.*"

A darted look. "That's what you call us, isn't it. Cudlips. Cattle."

"It's been known."

"Yeah, well this Keegan had a hard time believing Ethan might have joined the cattle. But once he got his head around it, it just made things worse. Way he saw it, there were two possibilities now. Either Ethan had some scam going in the force, in which case he wanted in on it. Or Ethan had given up his thirteen self and settled for the herd life, in which case—" She shrugged. "Hey, fuck him like any other cudlip, right? Get what you can out of him. Squeeze him dry."

Quiet seeped into the room. She drank. Out at sea, the big ships sat at anchor, waiting patiently.

"So what happened?" he asked finally.

She looked away. "I think you know."

"Ethan solved the problem."

"Keegan started showing up regularly at the house." Her voice was a mechanical thing, less expression than a cheap machine. "Acting like he owned the place. Acting like a fucking caricature thirteen out of some Jesusland psychomonster flick. Acting like he owned *me*, when Ethan wasn't around."

"Did you tell Ethan about it?"

"I didn't need to. He knew what was going on. Anyway, you know what, Marsalis? I can pretty much take care of myself. I stopped that fucker dead in his tracks every time."

She paused. Picking words.

"But it wasn't stopping with Keegan, you know. It was just backing up. Like throwing stones at a biting dog. You throw a stone, dog backs up. Soon as you stop throwing, he's back showing you his teeth. There's only one way to really stop a thirteen, right?"

He shrugged. "So the psychomonster flicks would have us believe."

"Yeah. And we couldn't afford to risk the attention. Officer-involved death, Internal Affairs come poking around. There's an autopsy, maybe gene tests that turn up the thirteen variant. Big investigation. Keegan knew that, and he played off it. Like I said, one way or another he was going to squeeze us dry."

"Until."

She nodded. "Until I came home and found Ethan burning clothes in the yard. After that, we never saw Keegan again. We never talked about it, we didn't need to. Ethan had bruising all along the edge of his left palm. Skinned knuckles, finger gouges in his throat." A faint, weary smile. "And the house was cleaner than I'd seen it in months. Washed floors everywhere, bathroom like a screen ad, everything nanodusted. You could still hear the stuff working if you put your ear up close to the tub. He never cleaned up like that again in the whole time we were together."

More silence. She drained her glass and reached down to the floor for the rakı bottle. Offered it to him.

"You want?"

"Thanks, I'll pass."

He watched as, a little unsteadily, she built herself a new drink. When she was done, she held the glass without drinking from it and stared out at the ships.

"It seemed like we held our breath all summer," she said quietly. "Waiting to see. I knew a lot of cops in Queens from before I moved to Midtown, I started hanging out with them again, on and off, to see if there was a missing persons filed, or if a body had turned up. We checked the NYPD links to UNGLA's most wanted all the time for news. Keegan never made it onto the list. Ethan reckoned you guys had him down as such a fuckup he wasn't worth chasing, he'd dig his own grave soon enough if you'd just give him some time."

Carl shook his head. "No, we like the stupid ones. They're easy to track down, and that makes the Agency look good. If your guy wasn't listed, the most likely thing is whoever helped him over the wire at Cimarron found some way to keep it quiet. Or whoever had the contract to run the place at the time just hushed the whole thing up to keep the statistics sweet. Oversight provision for Cimarron is pretty fucking weak, even by Jesusland standards, and if the contract was up for a renewal bid, well." He spread his hands. "Every lag on that reservation knows the best time to plan an escape is just before tender. They know the operating corporation is going to try like crazy to squeeze maximum efficiency out of badly paid staff and end up with riot-level tension instead, and they know that if they do make it over the wire, there's going to be no public nationwide manhunt, because the contract holders can't afford the publicity. It's how half these guys keep getting away so easily."

"Fucking Jesusland," she slurred.

He gestured lazily. "Hey, I'm not complaining. It's the sort of thing keeps me in work. Come to that, Jesusland isn't the only place I've seen weak oversight."

"No. Only place they're fucking proud of it, though." She peered morosely into her drink. "Still can't fucking believe it sometimes, you know?"

"Believe what?"

"Secession. What America did to itself. I mean." She made an upward-groping gesture with her free hand. "We fucking *invented* the modern world, Marsalis. We modeled it, on a continental scale, got it working, sold it to the rest of the world. Credit cards, popular air travel, global dataflow. Spaceflight. Nanotech. We put all that in place, you know? And then we let a bunch of fucking Neanderthal Bible-thumping lunatics tear it all to pieces? What the fuck is that, Marsalis?"

"Don't ask me. Little before my time."

"I mean." She wasn't listening to him, didn't look at him. Her hand went on clenching and unclenching, making loose, gentle fists in the air one after the other. "If the Chinese or maybe the Indians had come and just chased us out of the driver's seat, you know I could maybe handle that. Every culture has to give way to something in the end. Someone fresher and sharper always comes along. But we fucking did this to ourselves. We let the grasping, hating, fearing idiot dregs of our *own society* tip us right over the fucking precipice."

"You live in the Union, Sevgi. That's hardly the abyss, is it?"

"But that's just the fucking point. That's what they always wanted, Marsalis. Separation from the North. Secession. Their own fucking mud puddle of ignorance to wallow in. It took them two hundred fucking years to do it, but in the end *they got exactly what they wanted.*"

"Come off it. They lost the Rim States. That's what, a third of American GDP?" He couldn't work out why he was arguing so hard with her. He knew the ground because anyone working for UNGLA had to, but it wasn't like he was an expert. It wasn't like he *cared*. "And look, from what I hear out of Chicago these days, they might not be able to hang on to the Lakes much longer either. Then you've got Arizona—"

"Yeah, right." She snorted, and sank deeper into her chair. "Fucking Arizona."

"They're talking about admission to the Rim."

"Marsalis, it's *Arizona*. They're more likely to declare an independent republic of their own than anything else. And anyway, if you think Jesusland is going to let either them or any of the Lake states secede the way the Northeast did, you're crazy. They'll put the national guard in there faster than you can say *Praise the Lord*."

Because he didn't care one way or the other—*right?*—he said nothing, and the conversation closed up on her final words with a snap. There was a long pause. They both looked out at the ships.

"Sorry," she muttered after a while.

"Skip it. You were telling me about Keegan. Waiting to hear if his body turned up."

"Yeah, well." She sipped her drink. "Nothing much to tell. We never heard anything. Come September, we started relaxing again. I think maybe that was how we ended up pregnant, you know. I mean, not there and then, but that was the beginning. That was when we started getting confident. Started not worrying about the situation, just living as if there were no danger, as if Ethan was just some regular guy. Year or so of that and, bang, oops." She smiled bleakly. "Biology in action."

"And they took it away from you."

The smile dropped off her face. "Yeah. Union law's pretty progressive, but they won't buck the consensus that far. No siring of offspring from variant thirteen stock, any and all incubated genetic material to be destroyed. I've got lawyers fighting it, claiming moral precedent from pre-Secession cases on late-stage abortion, right to life, all that shit. Been nearly five years now, and we're still fighting. Appeal, block, object, counterappeal. But we're losing. UNGLA have all the money in the world to fight this one, and their lawyers are better than mine."

"Sort of thing that makes a COLIN salary very attractive, I imagine."

"Yeah." Her expression hardened. "Sort of thing that makes working for an organization that doesn't give a fuck about UNGLA very attractive, too."

"Don't look at me. I'm freelance."

"Yes. But it was someone like you in UNGLA liaison at City Hall that came looking for Ethan, that put the SWATs onto him. It was someone like you that authorized inducing my fucking baby at six and a half months and sticking it in a cryocap until UNGLA's legal team can get a ruling to have it fucking murdered."

Her voice caught on the last word. She buried herself in her drink. Wouldn't look at him anymore.

He didn't try to disabuse her and deflate the jagged anger she'd fenced herself in with, because it looked like she needed it. He didn't point out the obvious flaws.

In fact, Sevgi, he didn't say, *it probably wasn't someone like me, because in the first place there aren't that many like me around. Four other licensed thirteens working UNGLA that I know of, and none of them in a liaison capacity.*

And more to the point, Sevgi Ertekin, if it had been someone like me hunting Ethan Conrad, that someone would have shown up in person. He wouldn't have handed it to a mob of SWAT cudlips and stood on the sidelines like some fucking sheep hierarch supervising.

Someone like me would have done his killing himself.

Instead he sat quietly and watched as Ertekin slid from brooding silence into a rakı-sodden doze. Awareness of where he was made its way back into his consciousness, the darkened apartment in the cloven city, the distant lights, the sleeping woman at barely arm's length but curled away from him now, the quiet—

Hey, Marsalis. How you been?

—the tidal fucking quiet, like swells of black water, the seeping silence and Elena Aguirre, back again, talking softly to him—

Remember Felipe Souza? Stars and silent, empty corridors and safely dreaming faces behind glass that locked you out in the alone. That little whining I made in the pits of your ears, the way I'd come up behind you and whisper up out of it. Thought I'd gone away, did you? No chance. I found you out there, Marsalis, and that's the way it's always going to be. You and me, Marsalis. You and me.

—and the ships out at anchor on the silent swell, waiting.

CHAPTER 24

They kept him waiting at reception. Not entirely an unpleasant experience; like a lot of Rim States v-formats, the Human Cost Foundation's site was subtly peopled with short-loop secondary 'faces, hardwired into the system to provide the environs with what product brochure enthusiasm liked to call *a more authentic feel*. Sitting across from him in the waiting area, a svelte young woman in a short business skirt crossed one long thigh over the other and gave him a friendly smile.

"Do you work for the foundation?" she asked.

"Uh, no. My brother does."

"You're here to see him?"

"Yes." The format sculpters had done their work well. He felt positively rude stopping on the dry monosyllable. "We don't see each other that much these days."

"You're not local then?"

"No. Wiring in from New York."

"Oh, that is a long way. So how do you like it out there?"

"It isn't out there for me, it's home. We both grew up in the city. My brother's the one who moved." Tiny flicker of sibling rivalry riding a base of Manhattan exceptionalism, and the tiny adrenal shock as he recognized both. He began to see how the interface psychiatry he'd always sneered at might work quite well after all.

"So, uh." The question rose to his lips; he tasted its idiocy but weariness let it through anyway, part challenge, part deflection from more talk about Jeff. "Where are *you* from?"

She smiled again. "That's almost a metaphysical question, isn't it. I suppose I'd have to say I'm from Jakarta. Conceptually, anyway. Have you ever been there?"

"Couple of times, wiring in. Not for real."

"You should go. It's beautiful now the nanobuild is finished. Best to try to see it in . . ."

And so on, effortlessly evading any conversational currents that might bring them up too hard against the fact of what she was. He guessed that this must be how high-class prostitution worked as well, but he was too tired to really care. He let go, let himself be lulled by the erudite flow of what she knew, the participative dynamic she ran the conversation on, the stocking-sheathed geometry of her elegantly crossed legs. There seemed to be a reactive subroutine that measured how much he wanted to talk and adjusted the response output accordingly. He found, oddly enough, that he wanted to talk quite a lot.

He wasn't aware of Jeff approaching until his brother stood almost over him, smiling wearily.

"Okay." He fumbled to his feet, recovered himself. "At last."

"Yeah, sorry. Whole boatload of washups came in from Wenzhou a couple of days ago, it's going to put us way over budget for the quarter. Been negotiating with the legislature all fucking day." He nodded at the still-seated woman. "I see you've met Sharleen."

"Uh, yeah."

"Lovely, isn't she. You know, sometimes I'll come out here and talk to her just for the fun of it."

Norton looked at the 'face. She smiled up at the two of them, head lifted, expression gone very slightly vacant, as if what they were saying was birdsong, or a played segment of some symphony she liked.

"Need to talk to you," he said uncomfortably.

"Sure." Jeff Norton gestured. "Come on through. Bye, Sharleen."

"Good-bye."

She smiled over her shoulder as they left, then swiveled and sat immobile and silent as they passed out of trigger range. Jeff led him past the reception island and down a truncated corridor with a watercooler at the end. Half a dozen steps along, the passageway grayed out around them and became Jeff's office. It was pretty much as Norton remembered the actual suite from a visit a couple of years back, a few décor differences in the pastel shades of the walls and fittings, maybe one or two ornaments on shelves that he didn't recall. A photo of Megan on the desk. He drew a compressed breath and seated himself on the right-angled sofa facing the window and the skyline view of Golden Gate Park. His brother leaned across the desk and punched something out on the deck.

"So?"

"I need some more advice. You heard about Ortiz?"

"No." Jeff leaned against the side of his desk. "What's he up to, more UN handholding tours?"

"He's been shot, Jeff."

"*Shot?*"

"Yeah. It's all over the feeds. Where have you been? I thought you'd know. I gave a COLIN press conference all about it yesterday afternoon."

Jeff sighed. Shook his head as if it weren't working properly. He crossed to the adjacent angle of the sofa and collapsed into it.

"Christ, I'm tired," he muttered. "Been on this Wenzhou thing for the last day and a half solid. I didn't even go home from the office last night. Been in virtual most of this morning. Is he still alive?"

"Yeah, holding up. They've got him wired into intensive-care life support over at Weill Cornell. Medical n-djinn says he's going to be okay."

"Can he talk?"

"Not yet. They're going to patch him into a v-format once he regains consciousness, but that might be awhile."

"Jesus fucking Christ." Jeff gave him a haggard look. "So what's this got to do with me? What do you need?"

"For Ortiz, nothing. I don't think you could help right now anyway. Like I said, he's not even conscious. They've got family and close friends at the hospital but—"

His brother gave him the corner of a smile. "Yeah, I know. Not my world anymore. Blew my chance at the Union power game, didn't I."

"That's not what I—"

"Ran west and ended up a bleeding-heart charity chump."

Norton gestured impatiently. "That's not what this is about. I want to talk to you about Marsalis. You know, the thirteen we levered out of South Florida State?"

"Oh. Right." Jeff rubbed at his face. "So how's that working out?"

Norton hesitated. "I don't know."

"You got problems with him?"

"I don't . . ." He lifted his hands. "Look, the guy signed up okay. You were right about that much."

"What, that he'd bite your hand off for the chance to get out of a Jesusland jail?" Jeff shrugged. "Who wouldn't?"

"Yeah, well I guess I owe you for the suggestion. And I've got to say, he lives up to the hype. He was there when they tried to hit Ortiz, and it looks like this guy's the only reason Ortiz is still breathing. He took out two of the three shooters and chased the third one off. Unarmed. You believe that?"

"Yes," said Jeff shortly. "I do believe that. I told you, these guys are fucking terrifying. So what's the problem?"

Norton looked at his hands. He hesitated again, then shook his head irritably and raised his eyes to meet his brother's curious gaze.

"You remember I told you I've got a partner now? Ex-NYPD detective, a woman?"

"Who you want to get horizontal with, but won't admit it. Yeah, I remember."

"Yeah, well, there's something I didn't tell you about her. She had a relationship with a renegade thirteen a few years back. Didn't work out, and there were some, uh, complications."

Jeff raised his brows. "Uh-oh."

"Yeah. I didn't give it much thought, even when we hired this guy."

"Bullshit."

Norton sighed. "Okay, I gave it some thought. But you know, I figured, she's tough, she's smart, she's got a handle on the situation. Nothing to worry about."

"Sure." Jeff leaned forward. "So what are you worrying about?"

Norton stared around the office miserably. "I don't know." He threw up his arms. "I don't know, I don't *fucking* know."

His brother smiled, sighed.

"You ever chew coca leaves, Tom?"

Norton blinked. "Coca leaves?"

"Yeah."

"What has that got—"

"I'm trying to help here. Just answer the question. You ever chew coca leaves?"

"Of course I have. Every time we have to go down to the prep camps for a Marstech swoop, they give us a big bag at the airport and recommend it for the altitude. Tastes like shit. So what has that got to do with—"

"Do you get high when you chew coca?"

"Oh come on—"

"Answer the question."

Norton set his jaw. "No. I don't get high. Sometimes your mouth goes numb, but that's it. It's just to give you energy, stop you feeling tired."

"Right. Now listen. That energizing effect is part of an evolved working relationship between humans and the coca plant. Coca gives humans medicinal benefits, humans ensure that there's plenty of coca being cultivated. Everybody wins. And human physiology copes very comfortably with the effects the leaf provides. It's a benefit that doesn't interfere with any of your other necessary survival dynamics. You're not going to do anything stupid just because you're chewing those leaves."

"Why is it," Norton asked heavily, "that every time I come to you for help, you have to lecture me?"

Jeff grinned at him. "Because I'm your older brother, stupid. Now pay attention. If you extract the alkaloid from the coca leaf, if you take it through the artificial chemical processes that give you cocaine, and then you slam that stuff into the human brain, well, then you're going to see a whole different story. You do a couple of lines of that shit, and you surely *will* get high. You'll also probably do some stupid things, things that might get you killed in a more unforgiving evolutionary environment than New York. You won't pay attention to the social and emotional cues of the people around you, or you'll misread them. Fail to remember useful personal detail. You'll maybe hit on the wrong woman, pick a fight with the wrong guy. Misjudge speeds, angles, and distances. And long-term, of course, you'll put your heart under too much strain as well. All good ways to get yourself killed. What it comes down to is that we're not evolved to deal with the substance at the level our technology can give it to us. Age-old story, same thing with sugar, salt, synadrive, you name it."

"And variant thirteen," Norton said drearily.

"Right. Though this is a software issue we're talking about now, rather than a hardware problem. At least to the extent that you can make that distinction when it comes to brain chemistry. Anyway, look—by all the accounts I've read, the Project Lawman originators reckoned that variant thirteens would actually have been pretty damn successful in a hunter-gatherer context. Being big, tough, and violent is an unmitigated plus in those societies. You get more meat, you get more respect, you get more women. You breed more as a result. It's only once humans settle down in agricultural communities that these guys start to be a serious problem. Why? Because they won't fucking do as they're told. They won't work in the fields and bring in the harvest for some kleptocratic old bastard with a beard. That's when they start to get bred out, because the rest of us, the wimps and conformists, band together under that self-same kleptocratic bastard's paternal holy authority, and we go out with our torches and our farming implements, and we exterminate those poor fuckers."

"Apart from the kleptocrats." Legacy of a lifetime in sibling rivalry, Norton tugged at the loose threads in his brother's theorizing. "I mean, they've got to be variant thirteen themselves, right? Otherwise, how do they get to be in charge in the first place?"

Jeff shrugged. "Jury's still out on that, apparently. The odd thing is the gene profiles for a kleptocrat and a thirteen don't look as similar as you might think. Thirteens don't seem to be much interested in material wealth for one thing. Anything they can't carry over one shoulder, they show very limited enthusiasm for."

"Oh come on. How are you going to measure something like that?"

"Wouldn't be that hard. Involuntary mental response to visual stimulus, maybe. We do that here with the washups when they come in. Helps us to profile them. Anyway, there's observational evidence as well—apparently before Jacobsen and the roundup, most of these guys were living in small apartments with not much more stuff than you'd fit in a decent-size backpack. So maybe the kleptocrats weren't thirteens at all, they were just smart guys like us who figured out a socially constructed way to beat the big bad motherfuckers to the pick of the women."

"Speak for yourself."

"Speaking for all of us, Tom. Because for the last twenty thousand years or so, these guys have been gone. We wiped them out. And by wiping them out, we lost any evolved capacity we might have had for dealing with them."

"Which means what?"

"Well, what's the preeminent quality of any good leader, any successfully dominant member of the group?"

"I don't know. Networking skills?"

Jeff laughed. "You are such a fucking New Yorker, Tom."

"So were you, once."

"Charisma!" Jeff snapped his fingers, struck a pose. "Leaders are charismatic. Persuasive, imposing, charming despite their forcefulness. Easy to follow. Sexually attractive to women."

"What if they *are* women?"

"Come on, I'm talking about hunter-gatherer societies here."

"I thought you were talking about now."

"Hunter-gatherer society *is* now, in terms of human evolution. We haven't changed that much in the last fifty to a hundred thousand years."

"Apart from wiping out the thirteens."

"Yeah, that's not evolution. That's civilization getting an early start."

Norton frowned. It was an abrupt bitterness you didn't often hear in Jeff's voice. "Kind of sour about it all of a sudden, aren't we?"

His brother sighed. "Yeah, what can I tell you? Work for Human Cost long enough, it starts to corrode your fucking soul. Anyway, point is variant thirteen seems to come with a whole suite of genetic predisposition toward charismatic dominance, and it operates at levels the rest of us haven't had to handle for twenty thousand years. It's like they carry around an emotional vortex that tears up everyone they touch. Women get pit-of-the-stomach attraction for them, men hate their guts. The weak and the easily influenced follow them, give in, do what they want. The violently inclined kick back. The rest of us quietly hate them but don't dare do anything about it. I mean, you're talking about so much force of personality that if one of these guys ran for any elected office, he'd flatten anyone you ran against him. They'd be pure political Marstech, guaranteed black-label winners every time. Why do you think Jacobsen wanted them interned and chemically castrated? The way he saw it, let them out into general population and within a couple of decades they'd be running every democratic nation-state on the planet. They'd demolish the democratic process, roll back everything feminized civil society's achieved in the last couple of centuries. And they'd breed right back into base humanity like rabbits, because any woman who's at all drawn to male sexuality is going to fall like a bomb for these guys." Jeff gave him another wry grin. "The rest of us wouldn't stand a chance. That what's bothering you, little brother?"

Norton gestured irritably "No, that's not what's bothering me. What's bothering me is that Marsalis is going to cooperate with us for just as long as it takes him to put a blind corner between us and him, and then he'll run. And what bothers me more is that my partner may be wandering around blind to that particular danger, giving Marsalis a long leash when we can least afford it. So what I really want to know is exactly how far I can rely on Sevgi Ertekin not to screw up while this guy's around."

"Well, how's she doing?"

"I don't know. But she's gone off to Istanbul with him, chasing a lead he came up with pretty much out of thin air. That was yesterday, and she hasn't called in yet."

"Exotic Istanbul, huh?"

"Oh shut up."

Jeff quelled his grin. "Sorry, couldn't resist it. Look, Tom, as far as it goes, I wouldn't lose any sleep over what you've told me so far. Chances are at some level she does want to fuck this guy raw—"

"Great."

"—but wanting to fuck a guy's brains out isn't necessarily the same thing as switching your own brain off. I mean, look—the bonobo thing is similar. They've got an amped-up feminine appeal that'll blast the average guy's sexual systems like a cocaine hit every time—"

"Yeah, you'd know all about that."

Jeff stopped and looked at him reproachfully. "Tom, I *said* I was sorry about the Istanbul crack. Give me a fucking break, will you? What I meant was, you don't see me leaving Megan and the kids for Nuying, do you. Risking divorce, separation from Jack and Luisa, maybe a lawsuit for professional misconduct, all because I'm crazy for some modified pussy. Those things are important to me, and I manage to balance them against what Nu does for me. And I come out ahead, Tom. In control, the best of both worlds. Sure, I've got a drug problem, and the drug is bonobo tendency. But I'm handling it. That's what you do, you deal with your weaknesses. You take up the strain. If this woman you're talking about really is professionally focused, serious about her work, knows who she is and what she's about, then there's no reason she can't do the same cost–benefit analysis and play the game accordingly. If anything, the genetic evidence suggests women are better at that shit anyway, so she's got a wired-in head start right there. I mean, I'm not saying I'd want to have to hand-wash the sheets in whatever Istanbul hotel they're in right now—"

"Oh *Christ*, Jeff."

Jeff spread his hands. "Sorry, little brother. You want me to make you feel better, tell you the field's clear for you to make your Manhattan urbanite move on this woman? I can't. But if what you're concerned about really is her professional grip on things—then I wouldn't worry."

They sat quietly for a few moments. To Norton, letting Jeff have the last word felt like a kind of defeat.

"Well, what about this Istanbul clue then? I mean, seriously, it doesn't come close to any of our current investigation, it's right out of left field. Some other thirteen the Europeans have interned in Turkey, who *might* have a connection to some Peruvian gangster who *might* have ties to the people who *maybe* had our renegade thirteen shipped back from Mars. I mean, am I supposed to trust that? It's pretty thin."

Jeff stared out of the window.

"Maybe it is," he said absently. "Thirteens don't think the same way as us. They have a whole different set of synaptic wiring. Some of that, the more extreme end, we just go ahead and label paranoia or sociopathic tendency. But often it just comes out as a different way of looking at things. That's why UNGLA employs guys like this Marsalis in the first place. In some ways, that's why I suggested you dig him out of Florida and hire him. Give you access to those other angles." A sudden, hard look. "You didn't tell anyone that was my suggestion, did you?"

"Of course not."

"Yeah? Not even this ex-cop you've got under the skin so badly?"

"I made you a promise, Jeff. I keep my promises."

"Yeah, okay." His brother pressed thumb and forefinger into tight closed eyes for a moment. "Sorry. I shouldn't get so harsh with you, just I'm stressed out of my fucking box right now. This job's a political tightrope act at the best of times, and now isn't the best of times. Someone gets to hear that the director of the

Human Cost Foundation is giving informal advice to a COLIN officer on matters relating to the genetically enhanced, I'm going to be looking for another job. We'll get the whole Rim-China-Mars superconspiracy bullshit blowing up in our faces all over again, probably lose the bulk of our funding overnight. Bad enough that we're taking in black lab refugees and giving them Rim citizenship. Arranging for dangerous genetic variants to be released from jail, that'd be the final straw."

"Yeah, well, like I said. Relax. No one knows." Norton felt an unaccustomed tightness in his throat as he looked at his brother. "I appreciate all this, Jeff. Maybe it doesn't come across that way sometimes, but I do."

"I know." Jeff grinned at him. "Been looking out for you since you were knee-high anyway. That's what big brothers are for, right? Whole stack of genetic predisposition right there."

Norton shook his head. "You've been working this field too long, Jeff. Why not just say you care."

"I thought I just did. Base reasons for caring about your siblings *are* genetic. I didn't have to join Human Cost to know that."

An image of Megan bloomed brightly in his mind. Long tanned limbs and freckled smile, sun and hair in her eyes. The recollection forced its way aboard, seemed to dim his vision. It felt as if the v-format and his brother had suddenly been tuned down into a muted distance. His voice sounded vague in his own ears.

"Yeah, so what about sibling rivalry? Where does that come in?"

His brother shrugged. "Genetic, too. At base, all this stuff is. Xtrasomes aside, everything we are is built on some bedrock genetic tendency or other."

"And that's how you justify Nuying."

Jeff's expression tightened. "I think we've had this conversation, and I didn't enjoy it much last time. I don't justify what I did with Nu. But I do understand where it comes from. Those are two very different things."

Norton let the memory of Megan fade. "Yeah, okay. Forget it. Sorry I started on you again. I'm feeling pretty stressed myself right now. Got my own genetic tendencies to handle, you know?"

"We all do," his brother said quietly. "Thirteen, or bonobo, or just base fucking human. Sooner or later, we all have to face what's inside."

CHAPTER 25

Morning came in laced with the sounds of traffic along Moda Caddesi and children shouting. Bright, angled sunlight along the sidewall of the room he'd chosen to sleep in and the reluctant conclusion that out here at the back of the apartment there was a school playground directly under the window. He pried himself out of bed, shambled about looking for the bathroom, stumbled in on a lightly snoring Ertekin in the process; she slept sprawled on her back with her mouth half open, long-limbed and gloriously inelegant in the faded NYPD T-shirt and tangle of sheets, one crooked arm thrown back over her head. He drank in the sight, then slid quietly out again, found the bathroom, and took a long, much-needed piss. A faint hangover nagged rustily at his temples, not nearly as bad as he'd been expecting. He stuck his head under a tap.

He left Ertekin to sleep, padded to the kitchen, and found a semi-smart grocery manager recessed in next to the heating system panel. He ordered fresh bread and *simits* both, not knowing Ertekin's preferences, milk, and a few other bits and pieces. Found an unopened packet of coffee—Earth-grown, untwisted—in a cupboard and a Mediterranean-style espresso pot on the counter. He fired up the stove and set up the pot; by the time it started burbling to itself, the breakfast delivery was buzzing for entry down at the main door. He let them in, found a screen phone, and carried it through to the kitchen table. He unwrapped the *simits*—gnarled rings of baked and twisted dough, dusted with sesame seeds, still warm—broke one up into segments, poured himself a coffee, and went looking for Stefan Nevant.

It took awhile.

The duty officer at the internment tract HQ in Ankara wasn't anyone he knew, and he couldn't pull UNGLA rank because his operating codes were six months out of date. Naming friends didn't help much. He had to settle for a referral to

one of the site offices, where, apparently, Battal Yavuz was putting in some over-
time. When he tried the site, Battal was out in a prowler and not answering his
radio. The best the woman on site could do was take a message.

"Just tell him he's a reprobate motherfucker, and a big bad thirteen's going to
fly right out there and steal his woman if he doesn't call me back."

The face on screen colored slightly. "I don't think—"

"No, really. That's the message. Thanks."

Noises from the corridor. He cut the call and broke another *simit*. Found
an unexpected grin in the corner of his mouth, frowned it away. Ertekin used
the bathroom, went back to the bedroom by the sound of it, and for a moment
he thought she was going to go back to sleep. Then he heard footfalls in the corridor again, approaching. He leaned back in his chair to watch her come into
the kitchen. Wondering if she'd still be in the T-shirt. His hangover, he noticed
vaguely, was receding.

She was dressed. Hair thickly untidy, face a freshly scrubbed scowl.

"Morning. Sleep well?"

She grunted. "What are you doing?"

"Working." He gestured at the phone. "Waiting for a callback on Nevant.
Why, what did you think? I'd skip out on you as soon as you passed out? Perfidi-
ous, self-regarding thirteen motherfucker that I am."

"I didn't pass out."

"Well, you dropped your glass while you were resting your eyes then. I figured
you'd finished drinking anyway, so I went to bed. How's your head?"

The look she gave him was answer enough.

"Coffee still in the pot, but it must be nearly cold. I can—"

The phone chimed. He raised an eyebrow and prodded it to life. Ertekin busied
herself with the coffee, and he dropped his gaze to the screen. A picture fizzled
into focus, grainy with patch-through. Wide angle on an arid backdrop through the
dust-plastered windshield and side window of an all-terrain prowl truck. Battal
Yavuz in the driver's seat, chubby features narrowed in peering disbelief.

"Carl? No fucking way that's you."

"The one and only."

"They had you in a Jesusland jail, man. Di Palma told us. Special powers in-
voked, indefinite retention without trial. How the fuck you get out of that?"

"I got out of Mars, Battal. What did you think, Jesusland was going to
hold me?"

"Man, you never know. They've got a history of that indefinite retention shit.
Fucking barbarians."

Across the table from him, Sevgi Ertekin snorted. Carl flashed her a quizzical look. She shrugged and sipped her coffee.

"So what are you doing in Istanbul, anyway? You coming out to visit?"

"Don't think I've got time for that, Battal. But listen, I was hoping you could do me a favor."

When he'd hung up, Ertekin was still slumped opposite, staring a hole in the bottom of her coffee cup. He eyed her curiously.

"So what was that about?"

"What was what about?"

He mimicked her snort. "That."

"Oh. Yeah. Just kind of amusing to hear a Turk talking about someone else's barbarism."

"Well, he *was* talking about Jesusland."

"Yeah, whatever." She sat up suddenly. "See, Marsalis, my father left this country for a reason. His father and his uncle both died back on that fucking square in Taksim because the illustrious Turkish military suddenly decided freedom of speech was getting a little out of hand. You know, you fucking Europeans, you think you're so fucking above it all with your secular societies and your soft power and your softly softly security forces that no one likes to talk about. But in the end—"

"In the end," he said, a little harshly because Battal was a friend, and he didn't have many, "Turkey's still in one piece. They had a psychotic religious element here, too, you know, and a problem with rabid patriotic dogma. But they solved it. The ones who stayed, the ones who didn't cave in to fundamentalist idiocy or just make a run for some comfortable haven elsewhere—in the end they made the difference, and they held it together."

"Yeah, with some judicious funding from interested European parties, is what I heard."

"None of which invalidates the fact that Jesusland is a fucking barbaric society, which you're not from anyway, so *what's your point?*"

She glared back at him. He sighed.

"Look. My head hurts, too, all right. Why don't you talk to Battal when he gets here? He's the one filled me in on local history, guy used to teach in a prison before he got this gig, he knows his stuff. He wrote his doctoral thesis on Turkey and the old US, how they were more similar than you'd think. Talk to him."

"You think he'll come here?"

"If Nevant comes, he'll have to have an escort. And I don't see Battal passing up the chance to see his teahouse friends in Istanbul at someone else's expense. Yeah, he'll come."

Ertekin sniffed. "*If* Nevant comes."

"Don't worry about Nevant. Just the fact I'm asking for his help is going to be enough to get him here. He's going to love that."

"Maybe he's going to love turning you down."

"Maybe. But he'll come here to do it. He'll want to see my face. And besides—" Carl spread his hands, gave her a crooked grin. "—there's a good chance this'll be his only opportunity to get off the internment tract for the next decade."

She nodded slowly, like someone assimilating a new concept. Gaze still on her coffee. He had the sudden, uneasy feeling that what she'd just grasped wasn't much to do with what he'd just been saying.

"Of course," she said, "there's really no need for either of them to come here at all. We could just as easily have gone out to them, couldn't we?" And her gaze flipped up, locked onto his face. "Out to the tract?"

It was only a beat, but she had him.

"Yeah, we could have," he answered, smoothly enough. "But we're both hung-over, and I like the view from this place. So—why bother going there, if we can get him to come to us?"

She got up from the table and looked down at him.

"Right."

For a moment, he thought she was going to push the point, but she just smiled, nodded again, and left him sitting there in the kitchen, memories of the tract and those he'd dragged back to it swirling through his mind in hungover free association.

He was still sitting there when Nevant called.

"Knew I'd come, eh?"

"Yeah."

Nevant drew on his cigarette, let the smoke gush back out of his mouth, and sucked it in hard through his nose. "Fuck you did."

Carl shrugged. "All right."

"Want to know why I did come?"

"Sure."

The Frenchman grinned and leaned across the table, mock confidential. "I came to kill your ass, Mars man."

Out beyond the glass-panel frontage of the restaurant, sunset bruised and bloodied the sky over the Sea of Marmara. Torn cloud, clotted with red. Carl met Nevant's gaze and held it.

"That's original."

"Well." Nevant sat back again, stared down at the tabletop. "Sometimes the old gene-deep reasons are the best, you know."

"Is that why you tried to persuade Manco Bambarén to give you house room? Gene-deep reasons?"

"If you like. It *was* a question of survival."

"Yeah, survival as a cudlip."

Nevant looked up. Carl saw the twitch of a suppressed fight instruction flowing down the nerves of one arm. Like most thirteens, the Frenchman was physically powerful, broad in chest and shoulders, long limbs carrying corded muscle, head craggy and large. But somehow, in Nevant, the bulk seemed to have whittled down to a pale, lycanthropic coil of potential. He'd lost weight since Carl saw him last, and his nose and cheekbones made sharp angles out of his flesh. The narrowed gray-green eyes were muddy dark with anger, and the smile when it came was a slow-peeling, silent snarl. He'd been fast, back in Arequipa three years ago—it had taken the mesh for Carl to beat him. If he came across the table now, it would be like a whip, like snake-strike.

"Don't like your jacket much. What is that, fucking incarceration chic?"

Carl shrugged. "Souvenir."

"That's no excuse. What'd it cost you?"

"About four months."

Brief pause. The Frenchman raised an eyebrow. "Well, well. What happened, your license expire?"

"No, that's still good."

"Still doing the same shit, huh?" Nevant plumed a lungful of smoke across the table. "Still hunting your brothers down for the man?"

"Oh, *please*."

"You know, it wouldn't just be for me, Mars man."

"Sorry?"

"Killing you. It wouldn't just be for me. You have a large fan club back there in the tract. Can hardly blame them, right? And if I killed you, and they knew about it." Nevant yawned and stretched, loosening the combat tension from his frame. "Well, I'd probably never have to buy my own cigarettes again."

"I'd have thought they'd want to kill me themselves."

The Frenchman gestured. "The limits of revenge. They can't *all* kill you, and stuck where they are right now none of them can. You learn a kind of wisdom in the tract—settle for what you can get, it's better than nothing."

"Am I supposed to feel bad about that?"

The wolfish grin came back. "Your feelings are your own, Mars man. Wallow in them as you see fit."

"They had their chance, Stefan. You all did. You could have gone to Mars."

"Yeah, it's not all red rocks and air locks, apparently. Saw the ads on my way in." Nevant touched the rakı glass on the table in front of him with one fingernail. He hadn't yet picked it up, or touched the tray of *meze* laid out between the two men. "Sounds great. Hard to see why you came back."

"I won the lottery."

"Oh, that's right, I forgot. It's so much fun on Mars that the grunts buy a ticket every month to see if they can't get the fuck out of there and home again."

Carl shrugged. "I didn't say it was paradise. It was an option."

"Look, man. *You* came back, and the *reason* you came back is that life on Mars is a pile of shit." Nevant blew more smoke at him. " Some of us just didn't need to make the trip to work that one out."

"You were busy making plans to spend the rest of your life up on the altiplano when I caught up with you. That's just Mars with higher gravity."

Nevant smiled thinly. "So you say."

"Why should I lie?"

Outside, streetlights were glimmering to life along the seawall walkway. Sevgi Ertekin sat with Battal Yavuz on tall stools at a *salep* stall a dozen meters down the promenade. They sipped their drinks in cupped hands and were apparently getting along okay. Nevant tipped his head in their direction.

"Who is she, then?"

"No, I'm not his partner." Sevgi struggled to keep the edge out of her voice. "This is strictly a temporary thing."

"Okay, sorry. My mistake. Just the two of you seem, you know . . ."

"Seem *what*?"

Yavuz shrugged. "Connected, I guess. That's unusual with Marsalis. Even for a thirteen, he's pretty locked up. And it's not like it's easy getting close to these guys in the first place."

"Tell me about it."

"Yeah. I don't want to sound like those Human Purity fuckwits, but I've been working the tract for nearly a decade now, and I've got to say variant thirteen are the closest thing to an alien race you're ever going to see."

"I've heard the same thing said about women."

"By men, yeah." Yavuz slurped at his *salep* and came up grinning. He cut a cheery figure in the evening gloom and the yellowish lights from the stall. His jacket collar framed a tanned, well-fed face, and there was a small but unapologetic paunch under his sweater. Life at UNGLA Eurozone seemed to be treating him well. His hair was academic untidy, his eyes merry with reflected light. "Naturally. The way you people are wired, compared with the way we are."

"*You people*?"

"I'm joking, of course. But the same way male and female genetic wiring is substantially different"—Yavuz jerked a casual thumb back toward the lit interior of the restaurant, and the two men who sat facing each other in the window—"that's the way those two are substantially different from you and me both."

"Bit closer to *you people*, though," said Sevgi sourly. "Right?"

Yavuz chuckled. "Fair point. In testosterone chemistry, in readiness for violent acts and suspension of basic empathy, yes, I suppose so. They are more male than female, of course. But then, no one ever tried to build a female thirteen."

"That we know of."

"That we know of," he echoed, and sighed. "From what I understand, readiness for violent acts and suspension of empathy were exactly the traits the researchers hoped to amplify. Small surprise they opted for the male model, then."

For just a moment, his gaze drifted out past her shoulder to the sea.

"At times," he said quietly, "it shames me to be male."

Sevgi shifted uncomfortably on her stool. She turned her *salep* mug in both hands. They were speaking Turkish, hers a little creaky with lack of use, and for some reason, some association maybe with childhood misbehavior and scolding, the Turkish phrasing of that sentiment—*it shames me*—lent an obscure force to Yavuz's words. She felt her cheeks warm against the cold air in sympathy.

"I mean," he continued, still not looking at her. "We index how civilized a nation is by the level of female participation it enjoys. We fear those societies where women are still not empowered, and with good cause. Investigating violent crime, we assume, correctly, that the perpetrator will most likely be male. We use male social dominance as a predictor of trouble, and of suffering, because when all is said and done males are the problem."

Sevgi's eyes flickered away to the restaurant window. Stefan Nevant was leaned across the table, gesturing, talking intently. Marsalis looked back at him, impassive, arms draped on the back of his chair, head tilted slightly to one side. The same intensity seemed to crackle off both men for all the differences in their demeanor. The same raw sense of force. It was hard to imagine either of them ever talking about a sense of shame. For anything.

Deep in the pit of her stomach, despite herself, something warmed and slid. She felt her cheeks flush again, harder. She cleared her throat.

"I think there's another way to look at it," she said quickly. "Back in New York, I've got a friend, Meltem, who's an imam. She says it's a question of stages in social evolution. You're Muslim, right?"

Yavuz put tongue in cheek, grinned. "Nominally."

"Well, Meltem says—she's Turkish, too, Turkish American, I mean, and she's a believer, of course, but—"

"Yeah," Yavuz drawled. "Comes with the job, I imagine."

She laughed. "Right. But she's a feminist Sufi. She studied with Nazli Valipour in Ahvaz before the crackdown. You've heard of the Rabia school?"

The man in front of her nodded. "Read about them. That's the Ibn Idris thing, right? Questions all authorities subsequent to the Prophet."

"Well, Valipour cites Idris, yeah, but really she's tracing a line right back to Rabia al-Basri herself, and she's arguing that Rabia's interpretation of religious duty purely as religious love is uh, is you know, the prototypical feminist understanding of Islam."

And then she dried up, suddenly self-conscious. Back in New York, she wasn't used to talking about this stuff. She was rarely at the mosque these days, never found the time for it. Her conversations with Meltem had stopped soon after Ethan died. She was too angry, with a God she wasn't at all sure she believed in anymore, and in his echoing absence with anybody who made the mistake of taking his side.

But Battal Yavuz just smiled and sipped at his *salep*.

"All right, that sounds like an interesting angle," he said. "So how does your imam square her Islamic feminism with all that inconvenient textual shit in the hadiths and the Book?"

Sevgi frowned, mustering her rusty Turkish. "Well, it's cycles, you know. The way it looks from the historical context, the male cycle of civilization *had* to come first, because there was no other way outside of male force to create a civilization in the first place. To have law and art and science, you have to have settled agrarian societies and a nonlaboring class that can develop that stuff. But that kind of society would have to be enforced, and pretty brutally in the terms we look at things today."

"That's right." Yavuz nodded at the two thirteens in the restaurant window. "You'd have to wipe out all those guys, for a start."

"She's the client." Carl picked up a fork and helped himself to a slice of eggplant from the *meze* tray. "Are we going to eat some of this?"

Deep, final draw on the cigarette, raised brow. Nevant stubbed out the butt. "You freelancing now?"

"I always was, Stefan. UNGLA hold the license, but they only call me when they need me. Rest of the time, I've got to make a living like everybody else."

"So what does *the client* want with me?"

"We're chasing some *familia andina* connections. Trying to bust a Marstech ring in the induction camps."

"There's some reason that I'd help you do that?"

"Apart from the fact that Manco Bambarén sold you out to me three years back? No, no reason I can think of. I always did have you down as the forgiving sort."

Nevant skinned a brief grin. "Yeah, *tayta* Manco sold me out. But it was you that came to collect."

"Blame the messenger, huh?"

"Oh, I do."

Carl helped himself to more *meze*. "You really think a cut-rate godfather with delusions of ethnicity was ever going to go up against UNGLA for you? Were you really that desperate to believe you'd found a bolt-hole, Stefan? There's a reason Manco made it to *tayta* level, and it's not his charitable nature."

"What the fuck do you know about it, Mars man? As I recall, you were on urban fucking pacification detail most of your time in the Middle East."

"I know tha—"

"Do you know that they've got warlord alliances operating in Central Asia *still* that I fucking built from nothing back in '87? Do you know how many of those puppet presidents you see mouthing the words on Al Jazeera *I helped launch?*"

Carl shrugged. "Works in Central Asia doesn't mean it'll fly in South America. That's a whole different continent, Stefan."

"Yeah, and a whole different goal." Nevant shook a new cigarette out of the packet. He fit it in the corner of his mouth, drew it to life, and raised his eyebrows. "You want one of these?"

"I'm eating."

"Suit yourself." He leaned forward, blew smoke across the table, and grinned. "See, the *familias* aren't like those warlord motherfucks, they never were. Warlord wants the same thing any cudlip politician wants—legitimacy, recognition, and respect from the rest of the herd. The whole nine-car motorcade."

Carl nodded, chewing. He'd had pretty much the same lecture from Nevant three years ago, waiting for the paperwork to clear so he could take the Frenchman out of Lima in restraints. But let Nevant lecture. It was Carl's best chance of gleaning something he could use.

"So habitually, you've got a lawless vacuum and a bunch of these assholes fighting to put their stamp on a new order that lets them ride up front in the lead limo. Now, with the *familias*, that's never going to be the case. There's *already* a structure in place, and it's already full of legitimized scumbags, *criollo* whites, and trained token *indigenas* who've got the parliament, the military, the banks, the landowners, all that good shit right there in their pockets. The *familias* are locked out, all they've got is crime and this faint echo of an ethnic grievance." Nevant cupped a hand at his ear. "And the echo's fading, man. COLIN's shipped so many altiplano natives out to Mars over the past fifty years, poured so much money into the region, the *familias* just can't recruit like they used to. Only places they're strong anymore are ghetto populations in the Republic. No one else can be bothered. Nobody's scared of them anymore."

"So you were going to provide the fear."

More smoke, billowing. Nevant gestured through it. "Play to your strengths. Everybody's scared of the thirteens."

"Yeah, would be, if they weren't all locked up."

The Frenchman grinned. "You wish."

"Oh come on." Carl waved the fork. "We've got a couple of dozen out there at any one time, at most."

"Not the point, Mars man. Not the point at all."

"No? Then what is the point?"

Nevant toyed with the cutlery on his side of the table, just touching it with the fingertips of his right hand. "The point is that we exist. We're a perfect fit for all those atavistic fears they have. They've been desperately looking for witches and monsters ever since they wiped us out the first time around. Now they've got us back."

"Okay, so male force and hierarchy nail the human race into a coherent social order, weed out the worst of the loose cannons, and provide a stable base, all so that thousands of years later female principles can emerge to govern with a modicum of civilized decency. That's your imam's stance?"

Sevgi nodded. "It's Valipour's stance as well, give or take. And a valid Sufi stance, too, insofar as it represents a continuing revelation."

"Sort of explains the backlash, though, doesn't it." Yavuz grinned. "*Thanks, guys, you've done a bang-up job, given your gender limitations, but we'll take it from here.* I mean, it's hard to imagine the *shahuda* sitting still for that."

"Well." She shrugged. "They didn't, no."

"Yeah, I remember the mobs here, chanting in the streets when I was a kid." Yavuz put a raised, droning note into his voice. "*Men have authority over women because Allah hath made the one of them to excel the other.* So forth."

Sevgi snorted. "That tired old shit."

"That tired old shit's the Qu'ran, as I recall. Is the Qu'ran not a part of Islam in New York?"

"Very funny. Is historical context not a part of intelligent human thought around here?"

The impish grin again. Yavuz seemed to be shrugging off his sudden bout of male guilt. "Around here, sure. But you don't have to go too far southeast before intelligent human thought is pretty severely frowned on. Come to that, from what I hear you don't have to go too far southwest of New York before the same thing applies."

She laughed. "Fair comment. Marsalis told me you wrote a thesis on that stuff. Similarities in the US before Secession and Turkey, something like that?"

" 'Psychosocial Parallels in Turkish and American Nationalisms,' " Yavuz quoted with mock-bombast. He gestured modestly, undercut the effect. "Nothing's ever that simple, of course, but there *were* a lot of similarities. Both big, stroppy nationalisms founded in very shallow cultural soil. Both constitutionally secular societies with a resentful fundamentalism snapping at their heels. Both running a massive cultural gap between urban and rural society. Both very uneasy with the New Math, both trying to beat back the virilicide with draconian drug laws and wishful thinking. You know this place might have fractured apart, too, the way the US did, if we hadn't had the Europeans sneaking about pulling levers from the outside."

"You don't sound that pleased about it."

The Turk sighed. "Yeah, I know. And I should be, I guess. Certainly don't want the fucking *shahuda* prowling the streets here, stoning my daughters if they go out unchaperoned or showing more flesh than a wrapped corpse. But it's no fun, either, knowing your whole country's just the new backyard for a bunch of over-the-hill ex-imperial cynics."

"Now you sound almost patriotic."

"Not me." He shook his head grimly. "Did Carl tell you I used to teach in the prison system before I got this gig?"

"He mentioned it."

"Yeah, well you get to see some unpleasant things in the Turkish penal system. I've met a few too many torture-scarred political prisoners to be much of a Turkish patriot anymore. The way I see it, anyone who's proud of their country is either a thug or just hasn't read enough history yet."

"I like that." Sevgi smiled into her *salep.* "So you think the US might have held together the way Turkey did. I mean, if there'd been an outside force to apply the right pressure?"

"Not necessarily, no." Yavuz looked unaccountably sad as he said it. "I mean, you've got the whole states' rights issue, which we never had. Two centuries of southern resentment and cultural abrasion, religious fury, racial tension. Those are pretty deep fissures. Plus the anti-drug laws meant less chance for the virilicide to do its weeding out the way it was elsewhere."

He put his *salep* mug down on the counter, sat back, and held his open palms toward it, as if in obscure invocation.

"But anyway, it's academic, isn't it. Because there never *was* an outside force big enough to make you people behave. COLIN didn't exist as such back then, the UN was still a toothless tiger trying to find its dentures, the Chinese just didn't give a shit. Homegrown corporate interests were all behaving like thugs, they just wanted the cheap resources and labor for as long as it lasted. You've got the environmental lobby screaming, Zhang fever scaring the shit out of the Asian populace. Pacific Rim commercial interests don't want a fight, they just step in and make their offer, and pretty much everyone on the West Coast breathes a big sigh of relief when they do. Los Angeles goes first, toe in the pool, and then the whole coast takes the plunge when it works."

Sevgi nodded. Somewhere in a box on top of a wardrobe, she still had a replica scroll of the Angeline Freeport charter. Murat had brought it back from a West Coast medical conference for her when she was still in junior high. Like most successful first-generation immigrants, he'd been passionate about his adoptive homeland, even after it fractured apart under his feet almost as he stepped off the plane.

"Yeah," she said grayly. "And anything the fucking *West* Coast can do . . ."

Yavuz nodded, teacher-like. "Just so. The northeastern states seize the precedent and walk away as well. And on all sides, the rhetoric has been stoked so high that there can be no climb-down for anyone. It's the classic male impasse. Honor satisfied, and everybody loses. A textbook case. Have you ever read Mariela Groombridge? *Evolving States?*"

She shook her head.

"You should. She's brilliant. Taught at the University of Texas until they threw her out for signing an anti-creationist petition. She's in Vienna these days. Basically, she argues that the Secession was an example of a nation-state going extinct because it failed to adapt. America couldn't cope with modernity, it died from the shock and was torn apart by more adaptive entities. Though I think she tends to skate around the edge of what America really died of."

"Which is what?"

Yavuz shrugged. "Fear."

"It's a power beyond numbers." Nevant still hadn't touched the *meze*, but he was a couple of fingers down the rakı glass now. He sneered. "You think the cudlips give a shit about *facts*? Statistics and formal studies? It's the knee-jerk, man. That's what these people live and breathe. There *are* monsters, there *is* evil, and it's *somewhere out there in the dark.* Whoo-oo-oo. You know, before I got out to Peru, Manco was putting out a rumor that he had *pistacos* working for him. Settling scores for that turf squabble they had back in '03."

Carl nodded. On Mars, he'd seen the *familias* run a similar dynamic among the less educated end of the Uplands Initiative workforce. He'd been offered *pistaco* work himself a couple of times, lack of pale skin notwithstanding.

"Whatever works, I guess."

"Yeah, well. Worked for a while." Nevant snorted disgustedly and knocked back another chunk of his rakı. "Manco was so fucking pleased with himself, he couldn't see it'd crash and burn soon as one of his fake *pistacos* got called and couldn't cut it. I told him—the way I had it mapped out, he could have that monster threat *for real.* Real, honest-to-DNA monsters doing his enforcing for him. Something to scare everybody, not just the illiterates. Just think what would have happened if the word got around: *Cross the* familias *and they'll send a fucking thirteen to visit you.*"

"Always assuming you and your future army of thirteens could cut it any better than *tayta* Manco's fakes."

Nevant looked at him. "You lose many fights to a normal human recently?"

"No. But like you just got through telling me, it isn't the facts that do it for humans. Maybe Manco didn't need a real threat. Or at least, he didn't need it badly enough to cuddle up with a bunch of fucking twists."

"Didn't have any problem cuddling up to that hib cunt Jurgens," said Nevant sourly. "Amazing how your prejudices can go out the window when there's a decent rack in the equation."

"Greta Jurgens?" Carl summoned vague recollection of a languid, gray-eyed blonde from his inquiries after Nevant three years back. She'd been running front-office operations for Manco in Arequipa. "She was a hibernoid?"

"Yeah, she was. Why?"

Carl shrugged. "No reason. Just the way Manco was about the whole twist thing, it's strange he'd tolerate one that far up the ladder on the inside."

"Like I said, check out the rack. The ass. And hey, for all I know, hibs do some dickshift tricks you can't get out of a human woman."

Carl sipped his drink, shook his head. "That's bonobos, and even then it's bullshit hype. Anyway, Manco wants that kind of thrill, he can go down to Lima and have his pick of twist brothels. Come on. It doesn't add up."

"Well then, maybe it's just that there are twists and twists." Nevant's lip curled. "Not many people are scared of the ones whose party piece is curling up and sleeping for four months at a time. Doesn't threaten your masculinity much, that. It's only people like us they feel the need to lock up and stop breeding."

Carl gazed at the cutlery on the table. He nodded, a little sadly. "People like *you.* They lock people like *you* up. Me, I'm licensed."

"Domesticated, you mean."

"Call it what you like. You can't turn the clock back twenty thousand years, Stefan."

Nevant unsheathed the wolf-snarl grin again.

"Can't you?"

"See, once upon a time," Yavuz was saying, "fear was a unifying force. Back then, you could make a country strong with xenophobia. That's the old model, the nation-state fortress thing. But you can't live in a fortress when your whole way of life depends on globalized interdependence and trade. Once that happens, xenophobic tendency becomes a handicap, in Groombridge's terms a non-adaptive trait. She cites—"

Down the promenade, the splintering crack of glass. Sevgi whipped about in time to see the restaurant window shattered outward around two grappling bodies. Someone shrieked.

"Ah, *fuck*."

She grabbed after the gun she wasn't permitted to carry here, blind fingers registering the lack ahead of conscious thought. Flung herself off the stool—it teetered and toppled behind her, she heard it go down clattering—and toward the fight. Yavuz was at her side, brandishing an authorized pistol . . .

On the floor, the pale thirteen had Marsalis pinned. His arm hauled up, something in it, slashed down. Somehow, Marsalis twisted aside, did something with his legs that shifted the balance of the fight. Nevant reeled, shaking a hand that must have hit the concrete floor with killing force, must have broken bones. He was trying to keep the black man down with his other arm, but the lock wasn't working. Marsalis skated sideways by fractions, his shoulder slipped loose. His hand flapped, grabbed, pulled the Frenchman down toward him. He hinged upward from the stomach, hard, met Nevant's face with the crown of his skull. Sevgi heard the noise it made, and her teeth went on edge.

They arrived.

"That's it, motherfucker." Yavuz, in English. Voice shocked hoarse, pistol jammed in Nevant's ear. "Game over."

Nevant swaying, one hand clutched to his face, blood dripping between fingers from a nose that had to be broken. Coughing, bubbling, but through it came laughter. Marsalis grunted and tugged himself out from beneath, folded a leg, and shoved the Frenchman sideways with his knee. Nevant went halfway to collapsing, still clutching his face. Still chuckling. The hand he was using was the same one he'd just broken on the concrete.

"Going to have to." He sucked a breath, wetly. "Buy my own cigarettes after all."

"Looks like it, yeah." Marsalis rolled to his feet, one smooth coiling motion. He was checking himself for cuts from the glass.

"I did warn you."

"Yeah, and you made a real pig's ear of palming that cutlery knife as well." The black man's tone was absent. He turned his right hand, frowning, and Sevgi saw tear-track ribbons of blood in the cup of it. Marsalis lifted the hand to eye level, twisted it palm-outward, and pulled back his sleeve. He grimaced. There was a long cut, narrow sliver of glass still embedded, in the flesh on the outer edge of his palm.

"You stay there, you *fuck*," Yavuz was telling Nevant shakily. The pistol muzzle floated about close to the pale thirteen's forehead. "You sit there, and you *don't fucking move*."

He fished in his jacket with his spare hand, brought out a phone, and punched a speed-dial number. Beyond, in the cave made by the hole through the window, people stood about and gaped at the tumbled chairs and table. Waiters hovered, uncertain. A big downward-jagged triangular chunk of glass dropped suddenly from among its fellows in the top of the frame and broke undramatically in three pieces on the ground.

At the apex of the narrowest fragment, as if indicated by an arrowhead of glass, Sevgi saw the glint of the cutlery knife where Nevant had dropped it. The words the two thirteens had just traded caught up with her. She stared at Marsalis.

"You. *Knew* he was going to do this?"

The black man pinched the glass sliver between finger and thumb and tugged slowly until it emerged whole from the wound. He turned it curiously this way and that in the dim light for a moment, then dropped it.

"Well." He flexed the injured hand and grimaced again. "There was always a risk he'd get genetic about it, yeah."

"*You told us the two of you were friends.*"

Choked chortle from Nevant where he now sat with his back to the undamaged neighboring window panel. Marsalis looked at Sevgi levelly over his wound.

"I think I said we got on okay."

Sevgi grew aware of the thuttering in her chest and temples. She took a long breath, took stock. Gestured around her.

"And you call this *okay*?"

Marsalis shrugged. "Hey, what can I say? Blame the wiring."

On the floor, Nevant chuckled again, through blood and broken bone.

CHAPTER 27

His hand needed glue, and there were still minute fragments of glass in the wound. He sat in a UN medical unit in Fenerbahçe and waited patiently while a nurse cleaned him up. Glare of overhead lighting and—something he could have lived without—a screen in one corner with a microscopic blowup of the wound as it was treated. He looked fixedly elsewhere.

Ertekin had wanted the COLIN facilities on the European side instead, but couldn't argue with the immediacy of the UN hospital's location. It took them less than five minutes in a taxi—the bloodied promenade and gathering, gawping crowds dumped for the quiet residential streets of Fenerbahçe and the welcome-beacon lamps out front at the medical center's modestly appointed nanobuild façade. Now Ertekin was gone, along with Battal Yavuz and Nevant, down the corridor to wherever they were treating the Frenchman's injuries. He guessed she wanted a shot at hearing the other thirteen's side of the story. He also judged she was still a little numb from the action, and couldn't blame her much. The strain of the encounter with Nevant still twanged in his own blood, more than he showed.

The door opened and a Turk in a suit slipped in, yawning. Grizzled hair and matching, close-clipped mustache, not quite clean-shaven slate-gray chin. The suit was expensive and came with a carefully knotted silk tie. Only the sleep-swollen eyes and the yawn suggested the bed he'd been called out of. The sleepy gaze calibrated Carl for a moment, then the newcomer murmured something to the nurse, who immediately laid down his microcam-enhanced tools and excused himself. The door shut quietly behind him. Carl raised an eyebrow.

"Am I going to have to pay for this?"

The Turk smiled dutifully. "Very droll, Mr. Marsalis. Of course, as a licensed UNGLA accountant, you have a health plan with us. That's not why I'm here."

He came forward and offered his hand. "I am Mehmet Tuzcu, UNGLA special liaison."

Carl took the hand, careful of his wound. He stayed seated. "And what can I do for you, Mehmet bey?"

"Your Colony Initiative escort is on the next floor." Tuzcu's gaze flicked toward the ceiling. "There is transport waiting for you in the street at the back of this building. We will leave by the bulk elevator, unseen. In half an hour we can have you on a suborbital to London, but"—a glance at a heavy steel watch—"we will have to hurry."

"You're. Rescuing me?"

"If you like." The patient smile again. "They expected you in New York, but events seem to have overtaken us. Now we really must—"

"I, uhm." Carl gestured with his nearly repaired hand. "I don't really need rescuing. COLIN aren't holding me under any kind of duress."

The smile paled out. "Nevertheless, you are part of an unauthorized retrieval operation. COLIN are in breach of the Munich Accords by employing you in this capacity."

"I'll mention it to them."

Tuzcu frowned. "You are refusing to come with me?"

"Yeah."

"May I ask why?"

Ask away, he was tempted to say. *Been asking myself the same thing, don't have an intelligent answer yet.*

"Do you know Gianfranco di Palma?"

Tuzcu's eyes were careful. "Yes. I have met Signor di Palma a number of times."

"Slimy piece of shit, isn't he?"

"What is your point, please?"

"You were asking me for a reason. Tell di Palma this is what happens when you run your licensed operatives on a no-win/no-fee bounty and a three-month delay on expense reimbursement. They start to have loyalty issues."

The UNGLA man hesitated. He glanced back at the door. Carl stood up.

"Don't let's force this, Mehmet," he said easily.

Sevgi found him later, seated in the ground-floor waiting area watching some low-grade global music show on an overhead screen. A miked-up and dyed blonde pranced back and forth on stage in clothing that wasn't much more than slashed ribbons, stances, and motion designed to maximize the display of the tanned flesh beneath. A dance troupe of young men and women, similarly unclad, followed her in mindless body echo. The song wittered on, backed by instruments you couldn't see being played.

"See anything you like?" she asked.

"It's better than what I was watching earlier." He glanced past her. "What did you do with Nevant?"

"He's coming down."

"Right." Marsalis's eyes drifted back to the screen. "Got to hand it to you people, this is something you do really well."

"*You people?*"

"Humans. Look at that." He waved his bandaged hand up at the gaily colored images. "Perfect lockstep. Group mind. No wonder you guys make such good soldiers."

"Kind of ironic, coming from you," she said waspishly. "Compliments from the state-of-the-art gene warrior."

He smiled. "Ertekin, you don't want to believe everything they tell you on the feeds."

The elevator chimed, and Battal Yavuz exited, shepherding Nevant. The pale thirteen wore a mask of bandaging across the middle of his face and a similar wrapping on his broken hand. He seemed in good spirits.

"See you again," he said to Marsalis. He lifted the damaged hand. "When this is back to functional, maybe."

"Sure. You know where I live. Look me up soon as you get out."

Yavuz looked sheepish. "Sorry about this, Carl. If I'd known he was going to—"

"Skip it. No harm done." Carl got up and clapped the Turk on the shoulder. "Thanks for coming out. Been good to see you."

Sevgi hovered, watching Nevant peripherally.

"You want me to come with you to the heliport?" she asked Yavuz.

He shook his head. "No need."

"But if—"

Marsalis grinned. "Show her your ankle, Stefan."

As if they were all sharing a joke, the Frenchman pulled up the left leg of his pants. Tight at the bottom of his shin, a slim band of shiny, pored black fiber wrapped around. It wasn't much larger than a man's watch, but a tiny green light winked tirelessly on and off at one edge. She shouldn't really have been surprised, but her breath still hitched to a halt for a moment as she saw.

"Excursion restraint," said Yavuz. "No one comes off the tract without one. Stefan here's not going to give me any trouble."

"And if he slips it? Finds a way to cut it loose?"

"It's anti-tamper," said Nevant, curiously gentle. "Wolf-trap-formatted. Any interference, it triggers. Want to know what happens then?"

She already knew. The wolf-trap cuffs had a long and unpleasant history, made worse in her case by close personal connection. News stories of mutilated Muslim prisoners of war in American custody had dogged her father in his choice of émigré destination—his mail in the last weeks before he left Istanbul for good had been sprinkled with badly spelled death threats. Controversy raged in the feeds, cheap and violent vitriol overshadowing Murat's personal struggle with culture and conscience—Western pundits retorted angrily to the war-crime accusations with detail on modified cuff use for Sharia punishments in many of the self-declared Islamic republics, a rebuttal that stood for a while, then rang increasingly hollow as it became apparent who was selling the Islamic purists their mutilative technology. Murat, tasting a sour expedient hypocrisy whichever fruit he bit into, stormed out of Turkey anyway, and never looked back.

But later, as if they were some kind of family curse, Sevgi ran across the wolf-trap cuffs herself.

"She's a cop, Stefan." Marsalis, there at her shoulder, filling in for her sudden drop into silence. "I reckon she'll be familiar with the hardware."

She had been a cop, but only just, less than two years in, when she developed her *familiarity with the hardware*. Internal Affairs landed on the 108th like a bomb, brought a case against a group of detectives she knew who'd used the cuffs on hard-core suspects, apparently—but who the fuck could *really* fathom the logic of it—in an attempt to scare up a usable confession. During the interrogation, the pressure got cranked up a little too high. A young Sevgi Ertekin got dragged into the mix by association, was rapidly cleared, but still had had to stand in a field in upstate New York at dawn, watching mist cling just above the fallow earth, listening to the precise scrape–crunch rhythm of machine spadework, and, finally, gagging as the IA digging robot gently exhumed the three nine-week-old corpses and their cuff-severed hands.

Welcome to NYPD.

Small consolation—*look at it this way, Sev*, an uninvolved brother officer suggested at the time—that the cuffs, long outlawed in the Union, had come surreptitiously to the 108th via a Jesusland brother-in-law to one of the convicted detectives, a senior officer for a private policing outfit in Alabama, Republican law enforcement—of course—still making widespread use of the cuffs in defiance of three international treaties and a nominal federal ruling yet to be ratified anywhere except Illinois.

Look at it this way, Sev;

IA backed off from her speedily enough to avoid Officer Ertekin being tarred as a collaborator; better yet, her exemplary balancing act between loyalty to her fellow officers and duty to her calling was noticed by senior heads who would, years down the line, smooth her entry into Midtown Homicide.

Look at it this way, Sev;

The dead men in the field would not be much missed—all three had prior convictions as cross-border sex traffickers, hoodwinking young women from the Republic with promises of lucrative casual labor among the bright lights, then disciplining them via rape and battery until most went numbly to work providing orifices for New York's low-end paying males.

She looked to the small consolations, as advised. All that spring she looked at it *that way*, but in the end it still came down to the remembered reek of decomposed human flesh in the early-morning mist. Something changed in her that day—she saw the recognition of it in Murat's eyes when she came home to him afterward. It was the day he stopped trying to persuade her there were better career paths than the police, perhaps because he saw that if she didn't quit for this then she never would.

Nevant dropped his pants leg over the cuff, and she blinked back to the present. A small bubble of quiet expanded in the waiting area.

"I thought those were illegal in Europe," she said, to break the silence.

"On humans," agreed Nevant, darting a glance at Marsalis. "With thirteens, though, well, you can't be too careful. Isn't that right, Mars man?"

The black man shrugged. "Depends how bright they are, I'd say."

He watched Yavuz take the Frenchman out and put him in the dedicated UN teardrop without speaking again, or moving. His face could have been carved from anthracite. Only when the vehicle pulled softly away did he glance up at the dance troupe on the screen above his head, and something happened in the lines around his eyes. Sevgi made it for disgust, but she couldn't have said with any certainty at what or whom it was aimed, and she wondered if Marsalis could, either.

So they went back to the apartment, and there was a kind of gathering potential in that, a sense that they'd left something back there that needed to be collected. They walked, because it wasn't really cold outside or really late, and maybe because they both needed the time and the sky. They got lost, but neither minded much, and rather than use the street-finder holo in the keytab, they navigated vaguely for the waterfront, followed it as closely as was feasible until they wound up at the far end of Moda Caddesi and a slight but steady slope back down toward the COLIN-owned block. The glue along Carl's wound itched in the cool air.

At one point, Ertekin asked him the obvious question. "When did you know he was going to try for you?"

He shrugged. "When he told me. Couple of minutes after you and Battal left us alone."

"And that didn't bother you enough to call us back?"

"If I'd done that, he would have kicked off there and then. Without telling me anything."

They walked in silence for a while. The apartment blocks of Fenerbahçe loomed over them, balconies trailing foliage, some of it still dripping stealthily from recent watering. One blank-sided wall bore a massive artist's impression of Atatürk, sharp-eyed, clean-browed, and commanding, head haloed with the proclamation he'd seen enough times in other visits to know the meaning of. NE MUTLU TURKUM DIYENE. What joy to say I am a Turk. Someone else had climbed up, probably using gecko gloves, and drawn a speech bubble filled with jagged black spray-can Turkish he couldn't read.

"What's that say?" he asked her.

She groped after a translation. "Uhm, 'male-pattern baldness—it's a bigger problem than you think.' "

He stared up at the national hero's receding hairline and chuckled.

"Not bad. I was expecting something Islamic."

She shook her head. "Fundamentalists don't have much of a sense of humor. They would have just defaced it."

"And you?"

"It's not my country," she said flatly.

At a second-story balcony ahead, an old man leaned amid pipe smoke and watched the street. Carl met his eye as they passed underneath, and the old man nodded an unforced greeting. But it was clear his eyes were mostly for the woman at Carl's side. Carl glanced sideways, caught the line of Ertekin's nose and jaw, the messy hair. Gaze tipping downward to the unapologetic swell of her breasts where they pushed aside the edges of the jacket she wore.

"So *did* you get anything useful out of Nevant?" He wasn't sure if she'd caught him looking, but there was haste in the tone of her voice. He went back to watching the pavement ahead.

"I'm not sure," he said carefully. "I think we need to go and talk to Manco Bambarén."

"In Peru?"

"Well, I don't see him taking up an invitation to New York in a hurry. So yeah, we'd have to go there. Apart from anything else, it'll suit his sense of things. It's his ground."

"It's your ground, too, isn't it?" He thought she smiled. "Planning to disappear into the altiplano on me?"

"If I was going to disappear on you, Ertekin, I would have done it awhile ago."

"I know," she said. "I was joking."

"Oh."

They reached the end of the block, took a left turn in unison to beat an obvious cul-de-sac. He wasn't sure if he'd followed her lead, or vice versa. A hundred meters farther on, the street ended at a steep bare slope set with dirty white ever-crete steps and a cryptic sign inscribed with the single word MODA. They climbed in hard-breathing silence.

"That cuff," she said as they spilled out at the top, then had to grab her breath back before she went on. "You knew Nevant was wearing it."

"Never really thought about it." He thought about it. "Yeah, I guess I knew it'd be there. It's standard tract procedure."

"It didn't stop him trying to kill you."

"Well, those things are slow acting. Probably take the best part of twenty minutes to sever his foot completely. Sure, I might have gotten my hands on it in the tumble, tried to trigger it, but while I was wasting my time doing that, old Stefan would have buried that knife in my spine." He paused, reviewing the fight. "Or my eye."

"That's not what I mean." There was a hot exasperation in the way she came back at him, an edge of tone that tugged in the base of his belly and dripped a slow, pooling tumescence into the length of his prick.

"Well, what do you mean then?"

"I mean he knew there was a risk he'd lose a foot, not to mention bleed to death trying to get away. And he still tried to kill you."

It was on the tip of his tongue to ask her *Are you sure you dated a thirteen, I mean a real one?* He bit it back, walked on. Modest gene-stunted cottonwood trees sprouted at intervals from squares cut out of the pavement along this end of Moda. Their branches broke the streetlighting as it fell, formed a soft mosaic of light and dark underfoot.

"Look," he said experimentally. "First of all, Stefan Nevant wasn't planning on getting away anywhere. He came to kill me, that's all. Us genetic warriors are pretty focused about these things. If he had managed to ice me, he would have stood up afterward as quiet as a Jesusland housewife while you and Battal restrained him, and he would have gone back out to the tract a happy man."

"But that's fucking stupid," she flared.

"Is it?" This time he stopped on the pavement, turned toward her. He could feel his own control coming unmoored, feel it seep into his voice, but he couldn't tell how much was this, how much was the mouth-itching display of her standing there wrapped in streetlight and shadow, tumbled hair and long mobile mouth, jut and swell of breasts under the dark sweater, tilt of hips, long-legged in the canvas jeans despite the flat-soled boots she wore them with. "I put Nevant in the tract. He was out and I brought him back, to a place he'll never leave except hobbled the way he was today. He'll never breed, or have sex with anyone who isn't a paid tract whore or an UNGLA employee cruising for twist thrills. He knows, to within a couple of thousand square kilometers, exactly where he'll die. You think about that, and then you ask yourself whether it might not be worth the risk of losing a foot—which he'd get a biocarbon prosthetic for anyway, under the rules of internment—you ask yourself whether that might not be a price worth paying to put out the light in the eyes of the man who fenced him in."

"Worth dying for?"

"You forget: there's no death penalty in Europe, even for thirteens."

"I meant you might have killed him."

Carl shrugged. "I might. You're also forgetting that Nevant was a soldier. *Kill or be killed* is pretty much the job description."

She locked her gaze on his.

"Would you have killed him? If we hadn't gotten there first?"

He stared at her for a moment, then, swift as the fight, he stepped in and hooked an arm to her waist. Her feet shifted on the pavement, she leaned back and lifted one long fingered hand. For fragments of a second he thought she would strike him, then the fingers clenched in the collar of his jacket and dragged his face close. She bit into his mouth, thrust in a coffee-tasting tongue. Made a deep, soft sound as his free hand molded to her breast, and dragged him back into the shadows of an apartment house entryway.

It was like the mesh, a rising tide in blood and muscle. He tore at her clothing, unseamed the canvas jeans and forced them down to her knees, got his hand inside the slip of lace cotton she wore beneath. She gasped at the touch, already moist. With his other hand, he pushed up the sweater, forced it over the swell of the breasts, and fingered loose one of the profiler cups. The breast sagged into his hand. He buried his face in the flesh, as if drinking water out of his cupped palm. His mouth slurped up the nipple, sucked it to the roof of his mouth. In the tight trap of her cotton panties and inner thighs, his fingers worked the moistness apart. She shuddered, groped vaguely at the swollen lump in his trousers, finally got both hands on his belt and opened it. He flopped out, tightened to fully erect in the cool air. She laughed, short and throaty as she felt the length of his prick, ghosted an open palm up and down the underside of it.

Four months in Florida jails, nothing female you could touch. He felt himself sliding down the long hard slope of it, made his mouth unfasten from her breast with an effort of will, left the fingers of his other hand where they were and squatted, trying to pull one of her boots off. She saw what he was trying to do, laughed again, shook her leg impatiently up and down, stamping the air, angling her foot to get it loose. No luck—the boot stayed on. He caught a glancing blow from her knee in the side of his face. Grunted and shook his head.

"Oh shit, I'm sorry." She stopped, bent toward him. His fingers slipped loose, damp. "Look, stop, wait."

She twisted away, something that was almost judo, pushed him upright and against the wall in her place. She tore her jacket off arm by arm, stowed it in a wad at his feet, and dropped to her knees on it. Wide, split-mouth grin up at him, and then she bent over the head of his prick and sucked it in. Her curled fingers slipped up and down the shaft. Her mouth moved. His hands slapped flat on the shadowed wall at his sides, crooked as if he could claw into the evercrete with his nails. He thought then that was it, grabbed the moment, but something had hitched up inside him, would not let go. The orgasm subsided, rocked away, just out of reach.

She felt the change, made a muffled, querying noise and went to work in earnest, mouth and fingers; he felt himself climbing the curve again, but knew again he would not make it. His hands uncurled, came loose from the wall, hung there. He stared at the shadows.

"Hey," she said softly.

"Look, I'm—"

"No, *you* look." Sudden instruction in her voice, it hooked his gaze downward and she grinned up at him. With her left hand, she gathered her exposed breasts up and together. She gripped his shaft hard in the other hand, pushed the glans back and forth in the press of her cleavage. He felt something leap violently in his chest. She grinned again, bent her head and spat gently, drooled spit onto the head of his prick and then, still gripping hard, pushed the wet-gleaming flesh back between her breasts, rubbed it there, in and out, in and out, for the ten or twenty more seconds it took before he felt the furious heat come raging up through him, no hitch now, no stopping . . .

And out.

He made a noise like a drowning man hauled back aboard, like the sound he'd made the day the rescue ship hailed *Felipe Souza* for the first time, and he sagged back against the wall, then slid down it, as if shot. He felt her fingers let go, stick-ily, felt her gathering her disordered clothing together, and put out his hand.

"Wait."

"We should go, it's—"

"You're going. Nowhere," he said unsteadily. "Stand up."

He pushed her upright again, where she'd been, against the wall, and this time he crouched, slid hands up the insides of the long thighs to part them, pulled the scrap of lace cotton firmly to one side, and sank his tongue in her as deep as it would go.

Back at the apartment, he did it again, this time on the bed where he'd seen her asleep that morning. Pulled up close to breathe her scent, one hand raising the cushion of her buttocks up so the lips of her cunt met his mouth like a mis-matched kiss, the fingers of his other hand deep inside her and the breadth of his tongue lapping up against the rubbery switch of her clit. He felt a carnivore itch rising in him, a deep thirst that was only partly slaked when she bucked and flexed across the bed and clamped hands and thighs around his head as if she could push him by sheer force inside her.

She flopped, panting, face rolled sideways, eyes closed, gone, and he gathered her under him and slid into her to the hilt of his newly swollen-tight erection. Her eyes flew open, and she said *oh*, just that single sound, lightly, delightedly, fresh hunger rolling on the edge of the syllable.

And then it was like the hard evercrete steps they'd taken up to Moda, steep and stiff breathing and no speech at all on the long, steady climb together to the top.

CHAPTER 28

"**H**e did *what?*"

Norton glowered out of the screen at her, disbelief and anger struggling for the upper hand on his face.

"Ended up in a fight with Nevant," said Sevgi patiently. "Relax, Tom, it's already happened. There's nothing anybody could have done."

"Yes there is. You could have refused to let him have his way."

"Let him have his way?" She felt the faint stain of a blush start in her neck. All the places Marsalis had bitten softly into her flesh were suddenly warm again. "What's that supposed to mean?"

"It means Marsalis suddenly decides he needs to fly out to the other side of the globe, and you just lie down for it. Our cannibal friend is killing people in America, not Europe. I don't suppose it's occurred to you that Marsalis is looking for a way to get home without fulfilling his contract."

"Yes, that occurred to me, Tom. Quite awhile ago in fact, back when you were happy to stick him in an unguarded New York hotel for the night."

Pause. "As I recall, I was going to put him up at my place."

"Whatever, Tom. The point is, we hired Marsalis to do a job. If we aren't going to trust him to do it, then why did we bother springing him in the first place?"

Norton opened his mouth, then evidently thought better of what he was going to say. He nodded. "All right. So having beaten up Nevant, what does our resident expert want to do now?"

"He's talking about Peru."

"*Peru?*"

"Yes, Peru. *Familias andinas*, remember. He got leads from Nevant that point back to the altiplano, so that's where we need to go."

"Right." He cleared his throat. "So, Sevgi, you think we're actually going to do any investigating at all in the places the crimes are being committed? You know, I was never a cop, but—"

"Fuck it, Tom." She leaned into the screen. "What's wrong with you? This is the twenty-second century. You know, global interconnection? The integrated human domain? We can be in Lima in forty-five minutes. Cuzco a couple of hours later at worst. And back in New York before the end of the day."

"It is the end of the day," said Norton drily. "It's past midnight here."

"Hey, you called me."

"Yeah, because I was getting kind of alarmed at the silent running, Sev. You've been gone two days without a word."

"Day and a half." The retort was automatic, but in fact she wasn't sure who was closer. Her sense of time was shot. Crossing the Bosphorus seemed weeks in the past, New York and Florida months before that.

Norton didn't seem disposed to argue the toss, either. He glanced at his watch, shrugged.

"Fact remains. You stay gone much longer, Nicholson and Roth are going to start barking."

She grinned. "So that's what you're pissed about. Come on, Tom. You can handle them. I saw the press conference. You played Meredith and Hanitty like a pair of cretins."

"Meredith and Hanitty *are* a pair of cretins, Sev. That's the point. Whatever you say about Nicholson, he's not stupid, and he's our boss, and that goes double for Roth. They won't wear this for long. Not without more payback than your new playmate's hunches." Norton's gaze flickered across the quadrants of the screen, scanning the space over her shoulders. "Where is wonderboy, anyway?"

"Asleep"—she caught herself—"I'd guess. It's a pretty antisocial hour here as well, you know."

In fact, when the phone rang, she'd rolled over in the bed and felt a shivery delight as she found the bulk of him there at her side. The frisson turned into a jolt as she saw, at a distance of about ten centimeters, that he was awake, eyes open and watching her. He nodded in the direction of the ringing. COLIN *apartment,* he said, *I figure that's for you.* She nodded in turn, groped over the side of the bed for her T-shirt, and sat up to pull it over her head. She could feel his eyes on her, on the heavy swing of her breasts as she completed the move, and it sent another quiver of jellied warmth through her. The feeling stayed as she blundered out to the phone.

"*On COLIN's endeavor, the sun never sets,*" quoted Norton, deadpan. "Anyway, if you're going to Peru, you'll need an early start."

"Have you talked to Ortiz?"

He grew somber. "Yeah, earlier today. They put him through to a v-format for about ten minutes. Doctors won't run it for longer than that, they say the mental strain's the last thing he needs. They've got nanorepair fixing the organ damage, but the slugs were dirty, some kind of trace carcinogen, and it's fucking up the new cell growth."

"Is he going to die?"

"We're all going to die, Sev. But from this, no, he won't. They've got him stabilized. Still a long road out, but he'll make it."

"So what did he say, in the virtual?"

A grimace. "He told me to trust your instincts."

They got a late-morning suborb to La Paz—like most nations aligned with the Western Nations Colony Initiative, Turkey ran connections to the altiplano hubs every couple of hours. Sevgi had the COLIN limo pick them up at the door. No leisure to ride the ferries this time around.

"We could have waited for the Lima hook," Marsalis pointed out as they neared the airport at smooth, priority-lane speed. "Less rush that way. I'd have time to buy those clothes you were bitching about."

"I'm under instructions to rush," she told him.

"Yeah, but you know there's a good chance Bambarén might be in Lima, anyway. He does a lot of business down the coast."

"In that case, we'll go there."

"That'll take some time."

She gave him a superior grin. "No, it won't. You're working for COLIN now. This is our backyard."

To underline the point, she had a reception detachment meet them at the other end. Three unsmiling *indigenas*, one male, two female, who brought them out of the terminal with hardened, watchful care to where an armored Land Rover waited under harsh lighting in the no-parking zone. Beyond was soft darkness, a smog-blurred moon and the vague bulk of mountains rising in the distance. As soon as they were all inside the Land Rover, the female operative gave her a gun—a Beretta Marstech, with two clips and a soft leather shoulder holster. She hadn't requested it. *Welcome to La Paz*, the woman said, with or without irony Sevgi could not decide. Then they were in motion again, shuttled smoothly through the sleeping streets to a dedicated suite in the new Hilton Acantilado, with views out across the bowl of the city, and Marstech-level security systems. A beautifully styled Bang & Olufsen data/coms portal sat unobtrusively in the corner of every section but the bathroom, which had its own phone. The beds were vast, begging to be used.

They stood at opposite ends of the floor-to-ceiling window and stared out. It was, once again, obscenely early in the morning—they'd outrun the sun, dumping it scornfully behind them as the suborbital bounced off its trajectory peak and plunged back down to Earth. Now the predawn darkness beyond the windows jarred, and the inverted starscape bowl of city lights below them whispered up a weightless sense of the unreal. It all felt like too much time in virtual. Thin air and hunger just added to the load. Sevgi could feel herself getting vague.

"Want to eat?" she asked.

He shot her a glance she recognized. "Don't tempt me."

"Food," she said primly. "All I've eaten in the past day is that *simit*."

"Price of progress. On a flatline flight, they would have fed us twice at least. The untold downside of the suborb-traveler lifestyle."

"Do you want to eat or not?"

"Sure. Whatever they've got." He went to the Bang & Olufsen, checked the welcome-screen protocol, and fired the system up. She shook her head, took a last look at the view, and went to order from the next room.

Midway through scanning the services menu, she accidentally brought up the health section. Her eye caught on the subheading TAB STIMULANTS AND SYNAPTIC ENHANCERS, and she realized with a slight jolt that she hadn't taken any syn for the best part of twenty-four hours.

Hadn't wanted any.

The first time Carl wanted Manco Bambarén's attention, three years back, he'd gotten it by the simple expedient of sounding out the *tayta's* business interests and then doing them as much rapid damage as he easily could. It was an old Osprey tactic from the Central Asian theater, and it transferred without too much trouble.

Bambarén's particular limb of the *familias* were moving exotic fabric out of prep camp warehouses in quantities small enough not to trigger a COLIN response, amassing the scavenged gear in isolated village locations and then trucking it down to Lima to feed the insatiable maw of the Marstech black market. It wasn't hard to get detail on this—pretty much everyone knew about it, but bribes and kickbacks kept the much-vaunted but badly paid Peruvian security forces out of the equation, and Bambarén was smart enough to limit his pilfering to relatively commonplace tech items no longer sensitive at a patent level. The corporations claimed on their insurance, made the right noises but no great effort otherwise to plug the leaks. In tacit quid pro quo, Bambarén stayed out of their hair on the more vexing issue of local labor relations, where the *familias* had a traditional influence that could have been problematic if it were ever deployed. Local loyalties and Bambarén's ferocious Cuzco slum street rep did the rest. It was a sweet-running system, and since it kept everyone happy, it showed potential to run that way for a long time to come.

Carl had entered the equation with no local ax to grind and nothing to lose but his bounty for Stefan Nevant. For two quiet weeks, he'd done his research, and then one night he held up one of *tayta* Manco's trucks on the precipitous, winding highway down from Cuzco to Nazca and the coast. The armed muscle in the passenger seat took exception, which from a logistical point of view was a blessing in disguise. Carl shot him dead, then gave the driver the option of either joining his companion in the white powdered dirt by the side of the road or helping Carl roll the vehicle over the edge with an incendiary grenade—Peruvian army stock, he'd bought it from a friendly grunt—taped to its fuel tank. The driver proved cooperative, and the hardware worked. The truck exploded spectacularly on its first cartwheeling bounce, trailed flame and debris down into the canyon below, and burned there merrily for an hour or so, releasing enough exotic long-chain pollutants into the atmosphere to attract the attention of an environmental monitoring satellite. Not many things burned with that signature, and the things that did had no business being on fire outside of COLIN jurisdiction. Helicopters gathered in the night, like big moths around a campfire. With them came the inevitable journalists, and not far behind *them* a sprinkling of local politicians, environmental experts, and Earth First reps, all keen to get some media profile. Presently, an official recovery team made its painstaking way down into the ravine, but not before a lot of embarrassing spectrographics had been shot and a lot of equally embarrassing questions sharpened to a fine edge on the whetstone of starved journalistic speculation.

By then, Carl was long gone. He'd given the truck driver a lift down to Nazca and a message to hand on to *tayta* Manco with a number to call. Bambarén, who was no fool, called the next day, and after a certain amount of male display rage asked what exactly the *fuck* Carl wanted, motherfucker. Carl told him. Thirty-six hours after that, Stefan Nevant walked back into his Arequipa hotel room and found himself looking down the barrel of the Haag gun.

Subtlety, Carl had discovered, was a much overrated tool where organized crime was concerned.

In the Bolivian predawn, he dialed accordingly.

"This had better be life or fucking death," Greta Jurgens said coldly when she finally answered. The screen showed her settling in front of the phone, pulling a gray silk dressing gown closer about her. Her face was puffy. "Do you know what time it is?"

Carl made a show of consulting his watch.

"Yeah, it's October. I figure that gives me another couple of weeks before it's your bedtime. How's things, Greta?"

The hibernoid squinted at the screen, and her face lost all expression. "Well, well. Marsalis, right? The bogeyman."

"The very same."

"What do you want?"

"That's what I like about you, Greta. Charming small talk." Carl floated a casual, open-handed gesture. "It's nothing much. Wanted to talk to Manco. Strictly a chat, old-times stuff."

"Manco's not in town right now."

"But you know how to get hold of him."

Jurgens said nothing. Her face wasn't just puffy, it was rounder than he remembered it, smooth-skinned and chubby with late-cycle subcutaneous fat uptake. He guessed her thinking was groggier than usual, too—silence was the safe option.

Carl grinned. "Look, we can do this one of two ways. Either you can tell Manco I want a word and we arrange a friendly sitdown, or I can start making your lives difficult again. What's it going to be?"

"You might find that a little harder to do these days."

"Really? Made some new Initiative friends, have we?" He read the confirmation in the hibernoid's face. "Do yourself and Manco both a favor, Greta. Trace this call and find out whose wafer I'm running on. Then decide whether you want to piss me off."

He killed the line and Greta Jurgens blinked out in midretort.

Carl got up and went to stare down at the lights of La Paz. A couple of hours at worst, he reckoned. Jurgens had specialists a phone call away who could run the trace, and it wouldn't take them very long to nail it to COLIN's dedicated Hilton suite. Marstech-level systems showed up in the dataflow like implanted metal on an X-ray plate. The *familia* datahawks probably wouldn't be able to get past the tech; Jurgens in any case probably wouldn't ask them to. But it would still be pretty fucking clear what they were looking at, thank you very much. Say an hour to do all that. Then, allow that Jurgens had been telling the truth and Manco Bambarén wasn't with her in Arequipa. Wherever he was, he could be reached, and that wouldn't take long, either. And with what Jurgens had to tell him, he'd call back.

Ertekin came back through from the other room. She'd changed into the NYPD T-shirt and a pair of running sweats.

"Food's here," she said.

In the buffered quiet of the suite, he hadn't heard it arrive. He nodded. "Shouldn't eat too much at this altitude. Your body's working hard enough as it is."

"Yeah, Marsalis." She gave him a hands-on-hips sort of look. "I have been on the altiplano a couple of times before. COLIN employee, you know?"

"That's not what it says on your chest," he told her, looking there pointedly.

"This?" She pressed a hand to one breast and tapped the NYPD logo with her fingertips. A grin crept into the corner of her mouth "You got a problem with me wearing this?"

He grinned back. "Not if you let me take it off you after breakfast."

"We'll see," she said, unconvincingly.

But after breakfast, there was no time. The phone chimed while they were still talking, sitting with the big clay mugs of *mate de coca* cupped in both hands. *Outside call*, the system announced in smooth female tones. Carl took his mug through to the next room to answer. He dropped into the chair in front of the Bang & Olufsen and thumbed the accept button.

"Yeah?"

Manco Bambarén's weather-blasted Inca features stared out at him from the screen. His face was impassive, but there was a slow smoking anger in the dark eyes. He spoke harsh, bite-accented English.

"So, black man. You return to plague us."

"Well, historically, that ought to be a change for you guys." Carl sipped the thin-tasting tea, met the other man's eyes through rising steam. "Better than being plagued by the white man, right?"

"Don't play word games with me, twist. What do you want?"

Carl slipped into Quechua. "I'm only quoting your oaths of unity there. *Indigenous union, from the ashes of racial oppression*, all that shit. What do I want? I want to talk to you. Face-to-face. Take a couple of hours at most."

Bambarén leaned into the screen. "I no longer concern myself with your scurrying escapee brothers and their bolt-holes. I have nothing to tell you."

"Yeah, Greta said you'd gone up in the world. No more fake-ID work, huh? No more low-level Marstech pilfering. I guess you're a respectable criminal these days." Carl let his voice harden. "Makes no difference. I want to talk anyway. Pick a place."

There was a long pause while Bambarén tried to stare him down. Carl inhaled the tea steam, took down the damp, green-leaf odor of it, and waited.

"You still speak my language like a drunken peasant laborer," said the *familia* chief sourly. "And act as if it were an accomplishment."

Carl shrugged. "Well, I learned it among peasant laborers, and we were often drunk. My apologies if it offends. Now pick a fucking place to meet."

More silence. Bambarén glowered. "I am in Cuzco," he said. Even in the lilting altiplano Quechua, the words sounded bitten off. "I'll see you out at Sacsayhuamán at one this afternoon."

"Make it three," Carl told him lazily. "I've got a few other things I want to do first."

CHAPTER 29

He still had the deep oil-and-salt scent of Sevgi Ertekin on his fingers later as he sat in the COLIN jeep with his chin propped up on his thumb, staring glumly at the scenery and waiting for Manco Bambarén. It was his sole source of cheer in an otherwise poisonous mood. Jet lag and the showdown with Nevant were catching up with him like running dogs. He'd bought two new sets of clothes through the hotel's services net, didn't much like any of them when they arrived, could not be bothered to send them back and start again. They were black and hard wearing—*like me*, he thought sourly—and top-of-the-line. The latest generation of declassified Marstech fabrics, released to the high-end public amid a fog of testimonials from global celebrities and ex-Mars personnel. He hated them, but they'd have to fucking do.

Out of sheer contrariness, he kept the S(t)igma jacket.

"He's late," she said, from behind the jeep's wheel.

"Of course he's late. He's making a point."

Through the windshield, the grassy terraces of Sacsayhuamán rose on walls of massive, smoothly interlocking stone, dark under a glaring white-clouded sky. This late in the day, they had the ruins almost to themselves, and the emptiness lent the ramparts a brooding air. There were a few late-season tourists wandering about the site, but the scale of the Inca building blocks dwarfed them. Similarly reduced, a small knot of locals in traditional dress had withdrawn to the margins, women and children minding long-suffering llamas done up in ribbons, all waiting for a paying photo opportunity. They made tiny flecks of color against the somber stone.

It wasn't the first time Carl had seen Sacsayhuamán, but as always the stonework fascinated him. The blocks were shaped and finished but hugely irregular, echoing the slumped solid enormity of natural rock formations. The jigsaw lines between them drew your eye like detail in a painting. You could sit there just looking at it all for quite a while, which—he glanced at his watch—they had been.

"You think he's making a point with this as well?" Ertekin nodded forward at the walls. "Land of my fathers, that kind of thing?"

"Maybe."

"But you don't think so?"

He shot her a side glance. "Did I say that?"

"You might as well have."

He went back to staring at the stonework. Ghostly beyond, Nevant grinned at him out of a bloodstained, broken-nosed face, pale with hospital lighting. *Your feelings are your own, Mars man. Wallow in them as you see fit.*

He made an effort.

"You could be right," he admitted. "The guy does talk like a fucking poet half the time, and he's seriously impressed with himself. So yeah, maybe he is getting all cultural on us."

Ertekin nodded. "Thought so."

Ten more minutes crept by. Carl was thinking about getting out to stretch his legs when an armored black Range Rover rolled bumpily across the rough turf parking area to their left. Smoked-glass windows, glossy curved flanks, anti-grenade skirt almost to the floor. Carl dropped his introspection. The jet lag folded away.

"Here we go."

The new arrival braked to a halt, and a door cracked in the black carapace. Manco Bambarén stepped out, immaculately attired in a sand-colored suit and flanked by bodyguards in Ray-Bans that matched his own. No visible weapons, but there didn't need to be. The stances and blank, reflective sun-shade menace were old-school South America; Carl had seen the same thing deployed all over, on streets from Buenos Aires to Bogotá. The mirror patches Bambarén and his guards had in place of eyes talked up the same exclusive power as the shiny bombproof flanks on the Range Rover. You saw yourself thrown back in the reflecting surfaces, sealed outside and of no importance to the eyes within.

Carl climbed out of the jeep.

"I'm coming with you," said Ertekin quickly.

"Suit yourself. It's all going to be in Quechua anyway."

He crossed the turf to the Range Rover, pushing down an unnecessary surge from the mesh. He intended to lean on Bambarén, but he didn't think it'd come to a fight, however much he'd have liked to smash the mirror shades back in splinters into the eyes behind, take a limb from the bigger of the two guards, and—

Whoa, Carl. Let's keep this in perspective, shall we?

He reached the *familia* chief and stopped, just out of reach.

"Hello, Manco. Thanks for coming. Could have left the kids at home, though."

"Black man." Manco jerked his chin. "Nice coat you have there. Jesusland threads?"

Carl nodded. "South Florida State."

"Thought so. Got a cousin had one just like it."

Carl touched finger and thumb to the lapel of the S(t)igma jacket. "Yeah, going to be a major fashion anytime now."

"It was my understanding," said the *familia* chief urbanely, "that in Jesusland it already is. Highest incarceration rate on the planet, they say. So who's your tits and ass?"

Carl turned casually and saw that Ertekin had gotten out as well, but hadn't followed him. As he watched, she leaned back on the jeep beside the COLIN decal and put her hands in her pockets. The movement shifted her jacket aside, showed the strap of her shoulder holster. She'd put on her shades.

He held down a grin. "That's not tits and ass, that's a friend."

"A thirteen with friends." Bambarén's eyebrows showed above the curve of the sunglasses. "Must go against the grain for you."

"We adapt to circumstance. Want to walk?"

Manco Bambarén nodded at his security and they relaxed, opening space around their *tayta*. He took a couple of paces away from the Range Rover, in the direction of the stone walls. Carl fell into step. He saw the *familia* chief squinting sideways behind his sun lenses, toward the jeep and Ertekin's casual watchfulness.

"So you work for COLIN now?"

"With." Carl let his grin out. "I work *with* COLIN. It's a cooperative venture. You should understand that."

"Meaning?"

"Meaning you've made a niche career out of coexisting with the Initiative, and from what Greta said it's a flourishing relationship."

Bambarén shook his head. "I don't believe Greta Jurgens discussed my business associations with you."

"No, but she tried to threaten me with them. The implication was that you have bigger friends these days, and you keep them closer."

"And this is what you wanted to talk about?"

"No. I want to talk about Stefan Nevant."

"Nevant?" A frown wrinkled the *tayta*'s forehead. "What about him?"

"Three years ago, he was trying to talk your people up here into an alliance. I want to know how far that went."

Bambarén stopped and looked up at him. Carl had forgotten how short and stocky he was. The palpable force of the *familia* chief's personality wiped the physical factors away.

"How far it *went*? Black man, I *gave* Nevant to you. How far do you think it went?"

"You gave him to me because it was less trouble than having me disrupt your business in the camps. That doesn't mean he wasn't offering you something of value."

The *tayta* took off his sunglasses. In the harsh glare from the altiplano sky, his eyes barely narrowed. "Stefan Nevant was up here scrabbling for his miserable twist life. He had no friends and no allies. He had nothing I could use."

"But he might have, given time."

"I do not have the luxury of dealing in what might have been. Why don't you ask these questions of Nevant himself?"

Carl grinned. "I did. He tried to kill me."

Bambarén's eyes flickered to the glued-up wound on Carl's hand. He shrugged and put on his sunglasses again. Resumed walking.

"That is not an indication that he had anything to hide," he said tonelessly. "In his place, I would very likely have tried to kill you as well."

"Quite."

They reached the wall. Carl put up a hand to brush along the smooth, dark surface of interlocking blocks, each the size of a small car. It was instinctive: the edges of the stone sections curved inward to meet each other with a bulged organic grace that made him think of female flesh, the swell of breasts and the soft juncture of thighs. You wanted to run your hands over it, your palms twitched with the desire to touch and cup.

Manco Bambarén's ancestors had put together this jigsaw of massive, perfectly joined stonework with nothing for tools but bronze, wood, and stone itself.

"I'm not suggesting you personally bought in to Nevant's plans," Carl offered. *Though if you didn't, why did he choose you to deal with?* "But you're not the only *tayta* around here. Perhaps someone else saw the potential."

Bambarén paced in silence for a while.

"My *familiares* share a common dislike of your kind, Marsalis. You cannot be unaware of this."

"Yes. You also share a sentimental attachment to ties of blood, but that didn't stop you all going to war with each other in the summer of '03, or cutting deals with Lima afterward. Come on, Manco, business is business, up here the same as anywhere else. Racial affectation's got to come a poor second to economics."

"Well, it's not really a race thing where thirteens are concerned," said the other man coldly. "More of a species gap."

Carl coughed a laugh. "Oh you *wound* me, Manco. To the core."

"And in any case, I see no fruitful business application, for myself or any other *tayta*, to be had from association with your kind."

"We make very convenient monsters."

Bambarén shrugged. "The human race has more than enough monsters as it is. There was never any need to invent new ones."

"Yeah, like the *pistacos*, right? I heard you were busy playing that card back in '03 as well."

A sharp glance. "Heard from who?"

"Nevant."

"You told me Nevant tried to kill you."

"Yeah, well, we had a little chat first. He told me he applied to be your tame *pistaco*, maybe funnel some more thirteens in to do the same trick. Form some sort of elite genetic monster squad for you. Ring any bells?"

"No." The *familia* chief appeared to consider. "Nevant talked a great deal. He had schemes for everything. Streamlining for my ID operation, leverage tricks in the camps, security improvements. After a while, I stopped listening."

Carl nodded. "But you still kept him around."

Bambarén spread his hands. "He'd come to me like his fellow escapees before him, for documentation and fresh identity. That takes time if you're going to do it right. We don't operate like those chop shops on the coast. So yes, he was around. Somehow he stayed around. Now, when I ask myself how he managed that, I have no answer. He made himself useful in small ways, he had a skill in this."

Carl thought of warlords and petty political chess pieces across Central Asia and the Middle East, making use of Nevant making himself useful, without ever seeing how the insurgency specialist maneuvered them deftly into geopolitical place even as they were using him. *A failure to understand social webbing at an emotional level*, Jacobsen had found, *and so a lack of those emotional restraints that embedding within such webbing requires.* But Carl didn't know a single thirteen who hadn't laughed like a fast-food clown construct when they read those lines. *We understand*, he told Zooly one drunken night. Fingers snapped out one by one, enumerating, like stabbing implements, finally the blade of a hand. *Nationalism. Tribalism. Politics. Religion. Fucking soccer, for Christ's sake.* Pacing her apartment living room, furious, like something caged. *How could you not understand dynamics that fucking simplistic. It's the rest of you people who don't understand what makes you tick at an emotional fucking level.*

Later, hungover, he'd apologized. He owed her too extensively to freight her with that much genetic truth.

Beside him, Bambarén was still talking.

". . . cannot tell, but if his schemes did include this genetic *pistaco* fantasy, then he was a fool. You do not need real monsters to frighten people. Far from it. Real monsters will always disappoint. The unseen threat, the rumor, is a far greater power."

Carl felt an abrupt surge of contempt for the man at his side, a quick, gusting flame of it catching from the fuse of remembered rage.

"Yeah, that plus the odd object lesson, right? The odd exemplary execution in some village square somewhere."

The *tayta* must have heard the change in his voice. He stopped again, pivoted abruptly to face the black man, mouth smeared tight. It was a move that telegraphed clear back to the parked vehicles. Peripheral vision gave Carl sight of the two bodyguards twitching forward. He didn't see if Ertekin moved in response, but he felt the flicker of a sudden geometry, the lines of fire from the Range Rover to where he stood, from the jeep to the Range Rover and back, the short line that his left hand would take on its way to crush Manco Bambarén's throat while he grabbed right-handed at the *tayta*'s clothing and spun him for a shield, all of it laid out like a virtuality effect in predictive, superimposing red, distance values etched in, the length of ground he couldn't possibly cover in time when the guards drew whatever probable high-tech hardware they had under their leather coats, he'd have to hope Ertekin could take both men down in time . . .

He saw her falling, outgunned, or just not fast enough . . .

"Easy, Manco," he murmured. "You don't want to die today, do you? Shit weather like this?"

The *tayta*'s upper lip lifted from his teeth. His fists clenched at his sides. "You think you can kill me, twist?"

"I know I can." Carl kept his hands low, unthreatening. Open. The mesh ticked in him like a countdown. "I don't know how it'll boil down after that, but it won't be your problem anymore, that's a promise."

The moment hung. A quiet wind snuffled along the massive stone rampart at his back. He stared into Manco's mirror lenses. Saw the motion of gray cloud across the sky, like departure, like loss.

Oh fuck . . .

The *familia* chief drew a hard breath.

His fists uncurled.

His gaze lowered, and Carl lost the view of the moving cloud in the sunglasses, saw himself twinned there instead.

The moment, already past, accelerated away. The mesh sensed it, stood down.

Bambarén laughed. The sound of it rang forced and uncertain off the jigsaw blocks of stone.

"You're a fool, black man," he said harshly. "Just as Nevant before you was a fool. You think I need to put out rumors about the *pistacos?* You think I need an army of monsters, real or imagined, to maintain order? *Men* will do that for me, ordinary men."

He gestured, but it was a slack motion, a turning away toward the huge jigsaw walls. His anger had thinned to something more general and weary.

"Look around you. This was once an earthquake-proof city built to honor the gods and celebrate life in games and festivals. Then the Spanish came and tore it down for the stone to build churches that fell apart every time there was a minor tremor. They slaughtered so many of my people in the battle to take this place that the ground was carpeted with their corpses and the condors fed for weeks on the remains. The Spanish put eight of those same condors on the city coat of arms to celebrate the fact of those rotting corpses. Elsewhere, their soldiers tore nursing infants from the breast and tossed them still living to their attack dogs, or swung them by the heels against rocks to smash their skulls. You do not need me to tell you what was done to the mothers after. These were not demons, and they were not genetically engineered abominations like you. These were men. Ordinary men. We—my people—invented the *pistacos* to explain the acts of these ordinary men, and we continue to invent the same tales to hide from ourselves the truth that it is ordinary men, always, who behave like demons when they cannot obtain what they want by other means. I pass no rumors of the *pistaco*, black man, because the lie of the *pistaco* is already in us all, and it comes to life time and time again on the altiplano without any encouragement from me."

Carl glanced back toward the two enforcers and the Range Rover. They stood at ease again, hands clasped demurely before them at waist height, studiously ignoring him. Or perhaps, it occurred to him, simply trying to stare down Sevgi Ertekin. It was hard to tell at this distance.

"So," he said breezily. "Those two attack dogs back there got much Spanish blood in them?"

Bambarén drew a breath through his teeth. But he wasn't going to bite, not now. The soft, indrawn hiss was the sound of control.

"Is it your intention to spend the afternoon offending me, black man?"

"It's my intention, *tayta*, to get some straight answers out of you. And speechi-fying on atrocities past isn't going to cut it."

"You dismiss—"

"I dismiss your carefully cultivated sense of racial outrage, yeah, that's right. You are a fucking criminal, Manco. You talk like a poet, but your enforcers are a byword for brutality from Cuzco to Copacabana, and the stories they tell about you coming up on the street make me think you probably take a personal interest in training them that way. Not unlike those Spanish dogs of war you feel so dread-fully sensitive about."

"I have to have the respect of my men."

"Yes, as I said. Not unlike dogs. You humans are just so fucking predictable."

Beneath the sunglasses, Bambarén's mouth stretched in an ugly sneer. "What do you know about it, black man? What do you know about human life in the favelas? What do you know about struggle? You grew up in some cotton-wool-wrapped Project Lawman rearing community, catered to, cared for, provided with every—"

"British. I'm British, Manco. We didn't have a Project Lawman."

"It makes no difference. You." The *familia* chief's face twitched. "Nevant. All of you. You all had the same treatment. No expense spared, no nurturing too ex-cessive. You all got born into a place scarcely less protected than the rented wombs you grew in, sucking on the bought-and-paid-for milk and maternal affec-tions of colonized women too poverty-stricken to afford children of their own—"

"Go fuck yourself, Manco."

But it was out of his mouth too quickly to be the studied irritation he'd in-tended, his voice was too bright and jagged with the unlooked-for memory of Marisol. And Manco smiled as he heard it, gangster's attuned sense for vulnera-bility homing in on the shift.

"Ah. You thought perhaps she loved you for yourself? What a shock it must have been that day—"

"Hey, fuck you, all right. Like I said." Now he had the tone, the drawl. "We're not here to discuss my family history."

But *tayta* Manco had grown up a knife fighter in the slums of Cuzco, and he knew when a blade had gone home. He leaned in and his voice dripped, low and corrosive. "Yes, the little steel debriefing trailer, the men in uniforms, the awful truth. What a shock. The knowledge that somewhere out there, your real mother had sold out her half of you for cash, let herself be *harvested* of you, and that some other woman, for cash, had taken on her role for fourteen years and then, on that day, walked away from you like a prison sentence served. How did that feel, *twist*?"

And now it came pulsing down on him, the killing fury, the black tidal swell of it in the back of his brain like faint fizzing, like detachment. Harder by far to hold out against than the cold calculations he'd made two minutes ago, the certain knowledge of Manco Bambarén's death at the edge of his striking hand. There was no art in this; this was thumbs hooked into the *familia* chief's eyes and sunk brain-deep, a snapping reflex in the hinge of the jaws, the surf-boom urge to smash and bite—

If we are ruled by what they have trained into us, said Sutherland, somewhere distant behind the breaking waves of his rage, *then we are no more and no better than the weapon they hoped to make of us. But if we are ruled instead by our limbic wiring, then every bigoted, hate-driven fear they have of us becomes a truth. We must seek another way. We must think our way clear.*

Carl flexed a smile and put his rage away, carefully, like a much-loved weapon in its case.

"Let's not worry about my feelings right now," he said. "Tell me, how are you getting along with your Martian cousins?"

He'd intended it to come out of the blue, and from the look on the other man's face, it had. Bambarén blinked at him as if he'd just asked where the long lost treasure of the Incas was kept.

"What are you talking about?"

Carl shrugged. "I'd have thought it was a simple enough question. Have you had much contact with the Martian chapters recently?"

Bambarén spread his hands. His brow creased in irritation. "No one talks to Mars. You know that."

"You'd talk to each other if there was something in it for you."

"They walked away from that possibility back in '75. In any case, at present it would be pointless. There is no practical way to beat nanorack quarantines."

Sure, there is. Haven't you heard? Just short-circuit the n-djinn on a ship home, climb inside a spare cryocap—you can always eat the previous occupant if you're hungry—and dive-bomb the Pacific Ocean with the survivable modules. Piece of cake.

"You don't think it's also pretty pointless having a declared war across those quarantines? Across interplanetary distance?"

"I wouldn't expect you to understand that."

Carl grinned. "Hate will find a way, huh? That old *deuda de sangre* magic."

The *familia* chief studied the ground. "Did you really come all the way to Cuzco to discuss the *afrenta Marciana* with me?"

"Not as such, no. But I am interested in anything you and your colleagues might know about a resurgence."

Again, the flicker of irritation across Manco's face. "A resurgence of *what*, black man? We are at war. That's a given, a state of affairs. Until technology gives us a new way to wage that war, the situation will not change."

"Or until you curry enough favor with COLIN to get some nanorack leverage."

Manco looked pointedly back toward the jeep that had brought Carl to the meeting place.

"COLIN is a fact of life," he said somberly. "We all reach an accommodation of one sort or another with the realities, sooner or later."

"Yeah, very fucking poetic."

Sevgi drove back down the twisting road into Cuzco, taking the curves with a deliberate lack of care. Marsalis held on to the rough-ride strap above his door.

"Well, he has a point."

"I didn't say he didn't. I'd just like to know what you got out of him—apart from cheap poetics—that was worth coming all this way for."

Marsalis said nothing. She shot him a sideways glance. The jeep drifted a little with her inattention, back toward the center of the corkscrew curve on the road, and they met an autohauler rig head-on. Sick, sudden jump of adrenaline and sweat through her pores. But slow—she was still a little soggy from the near showdown with Bambarén's men. She dragged the wheel back, they swerved out of the rig's path, bumped a curb. The autohauler's collision alert blasted at them as it crawled past, machine-irate. People on the pavements stood and looked. The man sitting next to her said nothing still.

"Well?"

"Well, I think you should keep your eyes on the road."

She slammed the heel of her palm into the autocruise button. Let go of the wheel. The jeep's navigational system lit blue across the dashboard and chimed.

"Please state your destination." Fucking Asia Badawi's perfect dulcet tones again.

"City center," she snapped. They'd come direct from the airport, had no hotel as yet. She evened her voice, turned across the space between the seats to face him. "Marsalis, in case you hadn't noticed, we came close to a firefight up there. I got your back."

"I know that."

"Right. Now I don't mind taking risks, but I want to know why I'm doing it. So you start fucking telling me what's in your mind before it explodes all over us."

He nodded, mostly, she thought, to himself.

"Bambarén's clean." He said it reluctantly. "I reckon."

"But that's not all?"

He sighed. "I don't know. Look, I sprang the Martian angle on him, he didn't blink. Or rather, he looked like I was talking in tongues. The war's still on, and I'd bet everything I made last year that no one up here has seen or heard anything to change that. I don't think he knows anything about our pal Merrin's trip home."

She heard the raised tone at the end. "But?"

"But he's jumpy. Like you said, we nearly got into it up there. Last time I had to deal with Manco Bambarén, I'd just blown up a truckful of his product and killed one of his thugs, and I was promising to do it again if I didn't get what I wanted. He was about as emotional about it as that wall of stone up there. This time around, all I want to do is ask him some questions and he nearly gets us all killed for it. It doesn't make any fucking sense."

She grunted. She knew what it felt like, the nagging, loose-thread itch of *something not right*. The sort of thing that kept you awake and thinking last thing at night, stole your mind from elsewhere in your caseload during the day, and had you staring a hole in the detail while your coffee went cold. You just wanted to pull on that thread until it unraveled or snapped.

"So what do you want to do about it?" she asked.

He stared out of the side window. "I think we'd better talk to Greta Jurgens. She's getting near the sleepy end of the season, and hibernoids generally aren't at their best when that happens. She might let something slip."

"That's Arequipa, right?"

"Yeah. We could drive it overnight, be there in the morning."

"And be approximately as fried as Jurgens when we talk to her. No thanks. I'm sleeping in a bed tonight."

Marsalis shrugged. "Suit yourself. Just, it takes us off the scope if we go by road. Chances are Manco's going to have someone at the airport checking when we leave, checking where we leave to. And if he sees it's Arequipa, well, it doesn't take a genius to work out what we want there."

"You think he'd try to stop us seeing Jurgens by force? You think he'd risk that with accredited COLIN reps?"

"I don't know. A couple of hours ago, I'd have said no. But you were there when the mirror-shade twins got twitchy. What did you think was going to happen?"

Long pause. Sevgi recalled the way it had gone, like her reaction to the near collision a couple of minutes ago, the sudden, pore-pricking sweat as the *familia* bodyguards moved, the surge of adrenal overdrive in her guts and up the insides of her arms. It had taken conscious will to keep her hand away from the butt of her gun, and she'd been afraid, rusty with too long away from the brink and not trusting her judgment, not knowing if she'd be fast enough or just call it wrong.

She sighed.

"Yeah, okay." She sank back into her seat, thudded an irritable elbow into the padding a couple of times. "*Insha'Allah*, we can get a halfway decent recline out of these things."

Then she pitched her voice louder, for the jeep.

"Course-correct. Long haul, Arequipa."

Scribbles awoke on the displays.

"This journey will take until the early hours of tomorrow morning," Asia Badawi told her coolly.

"Yeah, fucking tell me about it."

CHAPTER 30

The center of Cuzco was solid with traffic, most of it driven by humans. No cooperation, no overview—the late-afternoon air rang with irate hornblasts and the queues backed up across intersections. Drivers went to the brink in duels to change lanes or inject themselves from filter systems into already established traffic flow. Windows were down to facilitate yelled abuse, but most people just sat rigidly behind the wheel and stared ahead as if they could generate forward motion through sheer willpower. That, and continual, frustrated blasts on the horn. Traffic cops stood amid it all with arms raised as if stuck in a swamp, gesturing like manic orchestra conductors and blowing whistles incessantly, to no appreciable effect. Perhaps, Sevgi thought sourly, they just didn't want to be left out of the noisemaking process.

The jeep was a carpool standard. Its automated systems, safety-indexed down to a patient deference, could not cope. After they'd sat at a particularly fiercely contested intersection for twelve minutes by the dashboard clock, Marsalis shifted in his seat.

"You want to drive?"

Sevgi looked out gloomily at the unbroken chain of nose-to-tail metal they were trying to break into.

"Not really."

"You mind if I do?"

The lights changed, and the truck blocking the intersection crept out of the way. The jeep jerked forward half a meter, then jerked to a halt again as the vehicle behind the truck surged to take up the slack. The opening vanished.

Behind them, someone leaned on the horn.

"Right."

It was the matter-of-fact tone that slowed her down. Before she realized what was going on, he'd cracked the passenger door and swung down onto the street. The sound of the horn redoubled. He looked back, toward the car behind them.

"Marsalis, don't—"

But he was already gone, striding back toward the car behind them. She twisted in her seat and saw him reach the vehicle, take two steps up and over the hood—she heard the clunk as his foot came down each time—and then jump lightly down again beside the driver's-side window. The hornblast stopped abruptly. He leaned at the window a moment, she thought he reached in as well, but couldn't be sure.

"Ah, *shit.*"

Checked her gun in its holster, was turning to open her door when he appeared there beside the window. She scrabbled it open.

"What the fuck are you—"

"Scoot over."

"What did you just do?"

"Nothing. Scoot over, I'm going to take it on manual."

She threw another look back at the vehicle behind them, couldn't see anything through the darkened glass windshield. For a moment, she opened her mouth to argue. Saw the lights change back to their favor again and shook her head in weary resignation.

"Whatever."

He took down the automation, engaged the drive, and rolled the jeep out hard, angling for a narrow gap in the opposing flow. He got the corner of the jeep in, waved casual thanks to the vehicle he'd cut off, and then levered them into the gap as it opened. They settled into the flow, crept forward a couple of meters and away from the intersection. She looked at his face and saw he was smiling gently.

"Did you enjoy that?"

He shrugged. "Had a certain operational satisfaction."

"I thought the point of going by road was to keep a low profile. How's that going to work with you starting fights all the way across town?"

"Ertekin, there was no fight." He looked across and met her eye. "Seriously. I just told the guy to please shut up, we were doing our best."

"And if he hadn't backed down?"

"Well." He thought about it for a moment. "You people usually do."

It took the best part of another hour to get through to the southern outskirts and pick up the main highway for Arequipa. By then the day was thickening toward dark and lights were coming on in the buildings on either side of the road, offering little yellowish snapshots into the lives of the people within. Sevgi saw a girl no older than nine or ten leaned intently on the edge of an opened truck engine in a workshop, peering down while an old man with a white walrus mustache worked on the innards. A mother seated on a front step, smoking and watching the traffic go by, three tiny children clinging about her. A young man in a suit leaning into a shop doorway and flirting with the girl behind the counter. Each scene slipped by and left her with the frustrated sense of life escaping through her fingers like sand.

On the periphery, they pulled into a Buenos Aires Beef Co. and ordered pampaburgers to go. The franchise stood out in the soft darkness like a grounded UFO, all brightly colored lights and smoothly plastic modular construction. Sets of car lights docked and pulled away in succession. Sevgi stopped for a moment on her way back to the jeep, bagged food hot through the wrappings against her chest, Cuzco's carpet of lights spread out across the valley. Sense of departure colliding with something else, something that hurt like all those passing yellow-lit moments of life she'd seen. She thought of Murat, of Ethan, of her mother somewhere back in Turkey, who knew the fuck where. Couldn't make sense of any of it—just the general ache.

Supposed to get better at this with age, Sev.

Right.

Marsalis came up behind her, clapped her on the shoulder. "You okay?"

"Fine," she lied.

At the jeep, he got into the driver's seat then powered up the autopilot. Sevgi blinked. Ethan would have kept the wheel until his eyelids were sagging.

"You don't want to drive anymore?"

"No point. Going to be dark out there, and I don't speak the same language as most of the long-haul traffic."

He was right. As they pulled away from Cuzco, the autohaulers began to materialize out of the gloom, routed straight out from corporation depots and warehouses on the city periphery. They seemed to come out of nowhere, like breaching whales beside a rowboat, no warning, no white wash of headlights from behind, surging up alongside with a sudden dark rush of air, hanging there for moments with high steel sides vibrating and swaying in the faint gleam from their running lights, then pulling ahead and away into the night. The jeep's systems chirruped softly in the dashboard-lit cabin space, talking to each rig, interrogating, adjusting. Maybe bidding farewell.

"You get used to that on Mars?" she asked him. "The machine thing?"

He frowned. "Got used to it from birth, just like everybody else. Machine age, you know?"

"I thought on Mars—"

"Yeah, everybody does. It's the reflex image. Machines keeping everyone alive, right? I guess it's got to be a hangover from the early years, before they got the environmental stuff really rolling. I mean, from what I read about it, back in the day even the scientists thought the terra-forming would take centuries. Guess they just never saw what the nanotech was going to do to our time scales. Technology curve accelerates, we all spend our lives playing catch-up." He gestured. "So now we're still stuck with the red-rocks-and-air-locks thing, all those images from back before the air was breathable. Takes a long time for stereotypes like that to change. People form a picture of something, they don't like to let it go."

"Ain't that the fucking truth."

He paused, looked at her. Cracked a smile. "Yeah, it is. Plus of course Mars is a long way off. Little too far to go and see for yourself, dispel the illusion. It's a lot of empty black to cross just for that."

The smile faded out on the last of his words. She saw the way his gaze slipped out of focus as he spoke, heard the distance he was talking about in the shift of his voice, and suddenly a door seemed to have blown open somewhere, letting in the chill of the space between worlds.

"It was bad, huh?" she said quietly. "Out there?"

He shot her a glance. "Bad enough."

Quiet settled into the cabin, the blue display-lit space, rocking gently with the motion of the jeep through the darkness.

"There was this woman," he said at last. "In one of the cryocaps. Elena Aguirre, I think she was from Argentina. Soil technician, coming home off tour. She looked sort of like . . . someone I used to know. So anyway, I used to talk to her. Started out as a joke, you know, you say a lot of stuff out loud just to stay sane. Asking her how her day'd been, like that. Any interesting soil samples recently? Trouble with the nanobes? And I'd tell her what I'd been doing, make stupid shit up about meetings with Earth Control and the rescue ship crew."

He cleared his throat.

"See, after a while, when you're on your own out there, you start to make patterns that aren't there. The fact that you're fucked starts to seem like more than an accident. You're asking yourself, *Why me? Why this fucking statistical impossibility of a malfunction on* my *watch?* You start to think there's some kind of malignant force out there, someone controlling all this shit." He grimaced. "That's religion, right?"

"No, that's not religion." Sudden asperity in her voice.

"It's not?" He shrugged. "Well, it's the closest I ever came. Got to the point, like I said, I was starting to believe there was something *out there* trying to take me down, and then it seemed like maybe if that were true, there'd be something else as well, a kind of opposed force, something *in there* with me, something maybe looking out for me. So I started looking for it, started looking for signs. Patterns, like I said. And it didn't take me long to make one—see, every time I stopped by Elena Aguirre's cryocap, every time I looked in at that face and talked to her, I felt better. Pretty soon feeling better came to seem like feeling protected, and pretty soon after that I decided Elena Aguirre was put on the *Felipe Souza* to watch over me."

"But she was." Sevgi gestured. "A person. Just a human being."

"I didn't say it made any sense, Ertekin. I said it was religion."

"I thought," she said severely, "thirteens were supposed to be incapable of religious faith."

Ethan certainly had been. She remembered his incurious, stifled-yawn incomprehension whenever she tried to talk about it, as if she were some Jesusland fence-hopper stood on his doorstep trying to sell him something plastic and pointless.

Marsalis stared into the blue glow of the dashboard displays. "Yeah, they say we're not wired for it. Something in the frontal cortex, same reason we don't take direction well. But like I said, it got pretty bad out there. You're stuck in the empty dark, looking for intent where there's only incidence. Feeling powerless, knowing you'll live or die dependent on factors you can't control. Talking to sleeping faces or the stars because it beats talking to yourself. I don't know about the cortical wiring argument, all I can tell you is that for a couple of weeks aboard *Felipe Souza* it felt like I had religion."

"So what changed?"

He shrugged again. "I looked out the window."

More silence. Another autohauler droned by, buffeting them with the wind of its passage. The jeep rocked in its wake, adrift on the night.

"*Souza* had vision ports let into the lower cargo deck," Marsalis said slowly. "I went there sometimes, got the n-djinn to crank back the shields. You have to kill the interior lights before you can see anything, and even then . . ."

He looked at her, opened his hands.

"There's nothing out there," he said simply. "No meaning, no mindful eye. Nothing watching you. Just empty space and, if you travel far enough, a bunch of matter in motion that'll kill you if it can. Once you get your head around that, you're fine. You stop expecting anything better or worse."

"So that's your general philosophy, is it?"

"No, it's what Elena Aguirre told me."

For a moment, she blanked. It was like those moments when someone talked to her in Turkish out of the blue and she was still working in English, a failure to process the words she'd heard.

"I'm sorry?"

"What I said. Elena Aguirre told me to stop believing all that shit and face up to what you can see out the window."

"Are you laughing at me?" she asked him tautly.

"No, I'm not laughing at you. I'm telling you what happened to me. I stood at that window with the lights off, looking out, and I heard Elena Aguirre come up behind me. She'd followed me down to the cargo deck and she stood there behind me in the dark. Breathing. Talking into my ear."

"That's impossible!"

"Yeah, I know that." Now he did smile, but not at her. He was looking into the light from the dashboard again, eyes blind, washed empty with the electric blue glow. "She'd have left tank gel all over the deck, wouldn't she. Not to mention, she would have rung every alarm on the ship climbing out of the tank in the first place. I mean, I don't know how long I stood frozen to the window after she'd gone, you tend to lose track of time out there, and I was pretty scared, but—"

"Stop it." She heard the jagged edge on her tone. Felt the urge to shudder creep up her neck like a cold, cupped hand. "Just stop it. Be serious."

He frowned into the blue light. "You know, Ertekin, for someone who believes in a supreme architect of the universe and a spiritual afterlife, you're taking this remarkably hard."

"Look." Thrown down like a challenge. "How could you know it was her? This Elena Aguirre. You'd never even heard her voice."

"What's that got to do with it?"

There was a quiet simplicity in the question that tilted her, suddenly, weightlessly, like sex the first time she got to do it properly and came, like her first dead-body crime scene by the tracks off Barnett Avenue. Like watching Nalan's breathing stop for the final time in the hospital bed. She shook her head helplessly.

"I—"

"See, you asked if it got bad," he said softly. "So I'm telling you how bad it got. I went down deep, Sevgi. Deep enough for some very strange shit to happen, genetic wiring to the contrary or not."

"But you can't believe—"

"That Elena Aguirre was the incarnation of a presence watching over me? Of course not."

"Then—"

"She was a metaphor." He breathed out, as if letting something go. "But she got out of hand, like metaphors sometimes can. You go that deep, you can lose your grip on these things, let them get free. I guess I'm lucky whatever was waiting for me down there spat me out again. Maybe my genetic wiring gave it indigestion after all."

"What are you talking about?" Flat anger. She couldn't keep it out of her voice. "Indigestion? Metaphors? I don't understand anything you're telling me."

He glanced across at her, maybe surprised by her tone.

"That's okay. I'm probably not explaining it all that well. Sutherland would have done better, but he's had years to nail it all down. Let's just say that out there in transit I talked myself into something at a subconscious level, and it took an invented subconscious helper to talk me back out. Does that make more sense?"

"Not really. Who's Sutherland?"

"He's a thirteen, guy I met on Mars, what the Japanese would call a sensei, I guess. He teaches *tanindo* around the Upland camps. He used to say humans live their whole lives by metaphor, and the problem for the thirteens is that we fit too fucking neatly into the metaphorical box for all those bad things out beyond the campfire in the dark, the box labeled MONSTER."

She couldn't argue with that. Memory backed it to the hilt, faces turned to her full of mute accusation when they knew what Ethan had been. Friends, colleagues, even Murat. Once they knew, they didn't see the Ethan they'd known anymore, just an Ethan-shaped piece of darkness, like the perp sketch that served in virtual for the man who'd murdered Toni Montes.

"Monsters, scapegoats." The words dropped off his tongue like cards he was dealing. His voice was suddenly jeering. "Angels and demons, heaven and hell, God, morality, law and language. Sutherland's right, it's all metaphor. Scaffolding to handle the areas where base reality won't cut it for you guys, where it's too cold for humans to live without something made up. We codify our hopes and fears and wants, and then build whole societies on the code. And then forget it ever was code and treat it like fact. Act like the universe gives a shit about it. Go to war over it, string men and women up by the neck for it. Firebomb trains and skyscrapers in the name of it."

"If you're talking about Dubai again—"

"Dubai, Kabul, Tashkent, and the whole of fucking Jesusland for that matter. It doesn't matter where you look, it's the same fucking game, it's humans. It's—"

He stopped abruptly, still staring into the blue-lit displays, but this time with a narrowed focus.

"What is it?"

"I don't know. We're slowing down."

She twisted in her seat to look through the rear windows. No sign of an autohauler they might be blocking. And no jarring red flashes anywhere on the display to signify a hardware problem. Still the jeep bled speed.

"We've been hacked," Marsalis said grimly.

Sevgi peered out of the side windows. No road lighting anywhere, but a miserly crescent moon showed her a bleached, sloping landscape of rock and scrub, mountain wall to the right, and across on the far side of the highway what looked like a steep drop into a ravine. The road curved around the flank of the mountain, and they were down to a single lane each way. The median had shrunk to a meter-wide luminous guidance marker painted on the evercrete for the autohaulers. No lights or sign of human habitation anywhere. No traffic.

"You're sure?"

"How sure do you need me to be?" He took the wheel and tried to engage the manual option. The system locked him out with a smug triple chime and pulsing orange nodes in among the blue. The jeep trundled sluggishly on down the gradient. He threw up his hands and kicked the pedals under his feet. "See? Motherfucker."

It wasn't clear if he was talking to the machine or to whoever was reeling them in. Sevgi reached for her pistol, freed it from the shoulder holster, and cleared the safety. Marsalis heard the click, fixed on the gun in her hands for a moment. Then he leaned across the dashboard and hit the emergency shutdown stud. The display lit red across, and the brakes bit. They still had solid coasting velocity. The jeep's tires yelped at the abuse and locked. They slewed, but not far. Jerked to a tooth-snapping halt.

Silence—and the blink, click of the hazard lights on automatic. Cherry-red glow pooled at each corner of the jeep, vanished. Pooled, vanished. Pooled, vanished.

"Right."

He fumbled the mechanism of his seat so it sank and allowed him access to the back of the jeep. Dived over and hung from the seat back by his hips, groping around. His voice tightened up with the pressure on his stomach muscles. "Seen this before in the Zagros. Mostly from the other side of the scam. We used to flag down the Iranian troop carriers like this for ambush. Hook them well before they could see you." A blanket rose and fell in his hand, tossed away. "Once you've cracked the pilot protocols, you can do pretty much what you like with them." Rattle of something plastic spilling. He reached harder. "Crash them into each other, drive them off the edge of a cliff, if there is one. Or over a carefully placed mine *fuck*."

"What are you *doing*?"

"Looking for a weapon. I figure you're not going to share that Beretta with me, right? Contractual obligations and all that." He bounced back into the seat, teeth tight in frustration, glared around him, and then threw open the door. He ran around to the back of the jeep. Road dust from the emergency stop caught on a soft breeze and blew forward over and around them in a cloud. It floated away, ghostly quiet and intermittently lit up red by the hazard lights. Sevgi looked back and saw Marsalis working to loosen something from the rear hatch. The jeep rocked on its suspension with every tug. The flashing lights lit him amid the dust, turning his face demonic with tension and focused effort. She thought she heard him grunt. Something clanked loose.

He came back to the door, hefting a collapsible shovel.

"All right, listen," he said, suddenly calm. "If we're lucky, these are local thugs, used to flagging down easy-mark trucks and the odd tour bus. If they are, I'm guessing we've got a couple more minutes before they realize what we've done. Maybe another three or four minutes after that for them to mount up and come find us. Not long, however you look at it. So, textbook response, we need to get out of the vehicle and find some cover, fast."

Sevgi nodded mutely, suddenly aware of how dry her mouth was. She snapped the slide on the Beretta, textbook style, tilting it to the horizontal so she could read the load display on the side. Thirty-three, and one in the pipe. The Marstech guns took state-of-the-art expansion slugs, pencil-slim, accurate at long range, and explosive on impact. She cleared her throat and lifted the Beretta.

"You think we'll be able to chase them off?"

He stared at her. The hazards painted him red, dark, red, dark, red, dark. He looked down at the folded shovel in his hands. Snapped the blade out into the functional position. Then he looked up at her again, hands tightening the locking mechanism in place, and his voice was almost gentle.

"Sevgi, we're going to have to kill these guys."

CHAPTER 31

There were seven of them.

From his limited vantage point, Carl made them for Peruvian regulars and relaxed a little. *Familia* hit men would have been worse. He let the mesh come on, felt it seep into his muscles like rage. His vision sharpened on the lead soldiers. They were walking three-abreast on the opposite lane, ten paces ahead of a slow-crawling open army jeep that carried the other four and a mounted machine gun. The vehicle moved with the main lights doused—that much, at least, they were doing right—and the vanguard party held their assault rifles ready for use. A gawky tension in the way they moved screamed *conscript nerves*. These guys could have been the same easy-grin, soccer-talking uniforms he'd blagged a ride from months back on his way to kill Gray. With luck, they'd be as young and unprepared.

They came to a halt twenty meters from the red hazard flash pooling and fading at each corner of the stranded COLIN jeep. Muttered Spanish, too far off to catch. The curve on the road was gentle—they'd have been able to see the lights for the last hundred meters at least, but they'd chosen now to stop and discuss tactics. Carl smiled to himself and gripped the shaft of the shovel. The eroded metal edge of the blade touched his face, cold and notched with use against his cheek.

The jeep backed up a little. The vanguard soldiers crossed the luminous median, looking both ways like well-trained children. Carl thought he could hear the distant drone of an autohauler somewhere in the night, impossible to tell how far off or which direction it was headed. Otherwise there was nothing but thin moonlight on porous rock and jagged mountain backdrop. Stars shingled across the sky, almost as clear as on Mars. It was quiet enough to hear the scuff of booted feet across the evercrete now that they were close, the follow-up grumble of the jeep's antique engine.

Fucking seven of them. Christ, I hope you're up for this, Ertekin.

He'd asked her if she knew how to kill someone with the matte-gray Beretta, if she'd ever shot anyone dead. Half hoping she'd crumble and give him the weapon. The look he got in return was enough. But she hadn't answered his question and he still didn't know.

The vanguard arrived at the COLIN vehicle. They crept up crabwise and peered inside the cabin. Tugged at the door handles and barked surprise when the doors pulled open on smooth hydraulic servos. Poked their weapons nervously inside. Now he could hear them talking. Forced bravado rinsing through the soft coastal Spanish accents like grit through a silk screen. Young-boy talk.

"You check the back, Ernesto?"

"Already done it, man. They're fucking gone. Run off. Told the sarge we should have pulled them over old style. Flashing lights, roadblock, it never fails."

"That's all you fucking know." A third voice, from around the other side of the jeep. It sounded a little older. "This isn't some Bolivian strike leader, this is a fucking thirteen. He would have driven right through us, fucked us in pieces."

"That gringa cunt, that's what I'll fuck in pieces when we catch up with them."
Laughter.

"She's not a gringa, Ernesto. Didn't you see the photo? I got a sister-in-law in Barranca got lighter skin than that."

"Hey, she's from Nueva York. That's good enough fucking for me."

"You know something, you guys disgust me. What if your mothers could hear you now?"

"Ah, come on, Ramón. Don't be an altar boy your whole fucking life. You seen the photos of this bitch or not? Tits on her like Cami Chachapoyas. Don't tell me you don't want a piece of that."

Ramón said nothing. The slightly older one filled in for him.

"Tell you what, you do fuck her, either of you, you'd better spray on first. Those gringas got a dose of everything going. I got a cousin in Nueva York says those bitches are out fucking everything that moves."

"Man, you got fucking family all over, don't you. How come—"

An NCO bellow from the jeep: "Report, Corporal!"

"Nothing here, sir," the older voice called back. "They're gone. Have to quarter the area."

In the jeep, something indistinct was said about fucking infrareds. Probably, Carl guessed, that they didn't have any.

"Ground search. Oh for fuck's sake. I'm telling you, when we catch up with this twist and his bitch—"

And time.

He let the rage drive him, rolled, braced himself off the edge of the molded roof storage pan, and came down a meter clear, on the side opposite the other jeep. The heat-resistant elastic tarpaulin that had hidden him stretched taut as he rolled, let him free, and then snapped back with a flat slapping sound.

It was all the warning they ever had.

He hit the evercrete amid uniformed bodies. Sent them staggering and sprawling—no time to count. The one in front had his back turned, did not quite go down—

"Fuck, Ramón, what are you *doing?*"

He hadn't understood what was happening. Was turning, unguarded, no worse than irritated, when Carl swung the shovel blade into his face. Blood splattered, warm and unseen in the dark, but he felt it on his cheek. The man dropped his assault rifle and clutched at his shattered cheekbone, made a wet sound, fell down screaming. Carl was already spinning away. A second uniform, struggling on his hands and knees. Ramón the altar boy? Carl hacked down with the shovel, into the soft top of the skull. The man made a noise like a panicked cow and collapsed prone. More blood spritzed, painted his face with its warmth.

The third soldier was still on the far side of the COLIN jeep. He came around the back of the vehicle at speed and Carl met him head-on, grinning, black and splattered with the other men's blood. The soldier panicked, yelled. Forgot to raise his rifle.

"He's here—"

Carl lunged. Jabbed hard with the shovel, blade end into the soldier's throat. The warning shout died to a choked gurgle. Carl zipped up the gap between them, blocked off the late-rising barrel of the assault rifle with one splayed hand, smashed the butt end of the shovel into the man's nose. The fight died, the soldier went down choking. Carl reversed the shovel and hacked down with the point of the blade, into the throat until the other man stopped making a noise.

The night flared apart with headlight beams from the other jeep. Shouts of alarm from the other side. *Four more*, he knew. No way to be sure how many were still sitting in their vehicle, how many deployed by now . . .

Come on, Ertekin. Pick it up.

Gunfire—the flat, high crack of the Marstech gun, six rapid shots in succession. The lights doused. Panicked yells from the jeep.

Fuck. Nice shooting, girl.

"Open fire!"

Carl hit the asphalt. Kicked the screaming, rolling victim with the shattered face out of his way, snagged the man's assault rifle. Dimly he registered it as a use-worn Brazilian Imbel, not exactly state-of-the-art but—

From somewhere, the mounted machine gun on the army jeep cut loose. The noise ripped the night apart. Stammering thunder from the gun, and the shattering clangor as the .50-cal rounds smashed themselves apart on the COLIN vehicle's armored flank. *Marstech, Marstech, we got the Marstech.* The idiot rhyme marched through his head, flash image of the kids who used to chant it out back of the bubblefabs at Wells. Carl grinned a tight combat rictus, crabbed about in the cover the jeep gave him, and poked the Imbel under the vehicle. He sprayed a liberal burst of return fire through the gap, then cut it off. Confused yelling. The machine gun coughed, suddenly silent. Carl pressed his face flat to the road surface and peered. Nothing—his vision was still blasted from the headlamps. He squeezed both eyes shut, tried again.

"Motherfucking twist piece of—"

The injured soldier was on him, flailing with fists, face hanging off in flaps where the shovel had sliced it apart. His voice was a high weeping torrent of abuse, a boy's fury. Carl smacked him under the chin with the butt of the Imbel, then again in the region of the wound. The soldier screamed and cringed back. Carl brought the barrel of the assault rifle to bear. Short, stuttering burst. The muzzle flash lit the boy's ruined face, reached out and touched him on the chest like fizzling magic—kicked him away across the road like rags.

The machine gun cut loose again, died just as abruptly at yelled orders from the jeep. Still grinning, Carl got to his feet and crept to the wing of the COLIN vehicle. He crouched and squinted, squeezed detail from his flash-burned vision. Saw the silhouette of the soldier manning the mounted gun. About forty meters, he reckoned. It hurt to hold on to the detail through aching pupils, but—

Better get this done.

As if she'd heard him, Ertekin's Marstech pistol cracked again across the night, three times in rapid succession. The soldier on the mounted gun pivoted his weapon about, chasing the sound. Carl put the Imbel to his shoulder, popped up over the jeep hood, cuddled the weapon in, and squeezed the trigger. Clattering roar at his ear and the muzzle flash stabbed out again in the cool air. Long burst, drop back into cover, don't stop to see . . .

But he already knew.

The mounted machine gun stayed silent.

He gave it another minute, just to be safe—*just to beat that bullshit thirteen arrogance, right, Sutherland?*—then poked the weapon up over the hood again, butt-first. No returning fire. He moved to the rear of the COLIN jeep and eased his head out far enough to see the other vehicle.

Silent, tumbled figures in and alongside the open-topped jeep. The mounted gun, stark and skeletal amid the carnage, unmanned and tilting butt-first at the sky. Carl stepped out of cover. Paused. Moved slowly forward, mesh-hammer ebbing along his nerves now that the fight was done. He covered the distance to the other jeep in a cautious, curving arc. Peripherally, he was aware of Ertekin climbing up onto the road from the ravine side where she'd hidden. He got to the jeep well ahead of her, circled it once, warily, and then stood looking at his handiwork.

"Well, that seemed to work," he said, to no one in particular.

It looked as if the sergeant had gotten clear of the jeep, was on the way to support his men when he ran into the hail of fire from the Imbel. Now he lay flung back against the forward wheel arch like a drunk who'd just tripped on a curb. Above his slumped form, the jeep's driver was still behind the wheel, hands folded neatly in his lap, face ripped away, brains dripping down his shirtfront like spilled gravy. The soldier manning the mounted gun hung twisted over the back of the jeep, one foot tangled in something that had prevented the impact of the Imbel's rounds from knocking him bodily out of the vehicle. His head was almost touching the evercrete surface of the road, boy's face slack with shock, staring from frozen, upside-down eyes as Carl moved past him.

The remaining man lay huddled in the back of the jeep like a child playing hide-and-seek. In the low light, blood shone wet and dark on his battledress, but his chest still rose and fell. Carl reached in and gripped his shoulder. The soldier's eyes flickered open drowsily. He blinked at Carl for a moment, bemused. Blood-irised spit bubbles moved at the corner of his mouth as his lips parted.

"Uncle Gregorio," he muttered weakly. "What are *you* doing here?"

Carl just looked at him, and presently the soldier's eyes slid closed again. His head tipped a little to one side, came to rest against the inside trim of the jeep. Carl reached in again and felt for a pulse. He sighed.

Ertekin reached his side.

"You okay?" he asked her absently.

"Yeah. Marsalis, you've got blood—"

"Not mine. Can I see that Marstech piece of yours for a second?"

"Uh. Sure."

She handed the weapon to him, took the Imbel as he offered it over in return. He weighed the Beretta for a moment, checking the safety and the load display. Then he raised it and shot the young soldier through the face. The boy's head jerked back. Lolled. He knocked the safety back on, palmed the warmth of the barrel, and handed the pistol back to Ertekin.

She didn't take it. Her voice, when it came, was leashed tight with anger. *"What the fuck did you do that for?"*

He shrugged. "Because he wasn't dead."

"So you had to *make* him that way?" Now the anger started to bleed through. Suddenly she was shouting. "Look at him, Marsalis. He was no threat, he was injured—"

"Yeah." Carl gestured around at the deserted road and the empty landscape beyond. "You see a hospital out there anywhere?"

"In Arequipa—"

"In Arequipa, he'd have been a fucking liability." Running a little anger of his own now. "Ertekin, we need to hit Greta Jurgens fast, before she finds out what went down here tonight. We don't have time for hospital visits. This isn't a . . . what?"

Ertekin was frowning, anger shelved momentarily as she reached into her jacket pocket. She fished out her phone, which was vibrating quietly on and off, pulsing along its edges with pale crystalline light.

"Oh, you've got to be fucking kidding me." Carl looked away down the perspectives of the road in exasperated disbelief. "At this time of night?"

"Rang before," she said, putting the device to her ear. "Just before the fireworks kicked off. Didn't have time to pick up. Ertekin."

Then she listened quietly. Made monosyllabic agreement a couple of times. Hung up and put the phone away again, face gone calm and thoughtful.

"Norton," he guessed.

"Yeah. Time to go home."

He gaped at her. "*What?*"

"That's right." She met his eye, something harder edging the calm. "RimSec called. They've got a body. We've got to go back."

Carl shook his head. Twinges of the firefight backed up in his nerves, fake-fired the mesh. "So they've got a body. Another body. Big fucking deal. You going to pull out now, just when we're getting somewhere?"

Ertekin gazed around at the carnage. "You call this getting somewhere?"

"They tried to stop us, Sevgi. They tried to kill us."

"They tried to kill us in New York as well. You want to go back there? Come to that, Nevant tried to kill you in Istanbul. Violence follows you around, Marsalis. Just like Merrin, just like—"

She clamped her lips.

Carl looked at her and felt the old weariness seeping in. He cranked up the rind of a smile for cover.

"Go ahead, Sevgi, say it. *Just like Ethan.*" He gestured. "Go on, get it off that gorgeous chest of yours. It's what you're thinking anyway."

"You have *no* fucking right to assume—"

"No?" He paused for effect. "Oh yeah, I forgot. You get some kind of perverse thrill out of fucking unlucks, and that makes you think you don't see us the same way the rest of the whole fucking human race does. Well, it takes more than a Cuban wank and a few sheet stains to—"

Abruptly, he was on the ground.

He lay there on his back in the road dust, staring up while she stood over him, clutching her right fist in her left hand.

"Mother*fucker*," she said wonderingly.

She'd stepped in before she threw the punch, he realized. Right hook, or an uppercut, he couldn't work out which. He never saw it coming.

"You think I haven't been where you are now, Marsalis?"

He propped himself up on an elbow. "What, flat on the your back in the road?"

"*Shut up.*" She was trembling visibly. Maybe with comedown from the fire-fight. Maybe not. "You think I don't know what it's like? Think again, fuckwit. Try growing up Muslim in the West, while the Middle East catches fire *again*. Try growing up a woman in a Western Muslim culture fighting off siege-mentality fundamentalism *again*. Try being one of only three Turkish American patrol-women in a New York precinct dominated by male Greek American detectives. Hey, try *sleeping with* a thirteen, you'll get almost as much shit as being one, not least from members of your own fucking family. Yeah. People are *stupid*, Marsalis. You think I need lessons in that?"

"I don't know what you need, Ertekin."

"No, that's right, you don't. And listen—you got some fucking problem with what we did back in Istanbul, then deal with it however you need to. But don't you ever, *ever* call into question my relationship with Ethan Conrad again. Because the next time I swear I will put a fucking bullet in you."

Carl rubbed at his jaw. Flexed it experimentally left and right.

"Mind if I get up now?"

"Do what you fucking like."

She stood away from him, staring off somewhere beyond the corpses and the arid landscape. He climbed carefully to his feet.

"Ertekin, just listen to me for a moment. Look around you. Look at this mess."

"I am looking at it."

"Right. So it's got to mean something, right?"

Still she didn't look at his face. "Yeah, what it probably means is that Manco Bambarén's tired of you pushing him around in his own backyard."

"Oh *come on*, Ertekin. You're a cop, for fuck's sake."

"That's right, I'm a cop." Suddenly she whipped around on him. Fast enough to halfway trip a block reflex. "And right now, while I get dragged around the globe watching you fulfill your genetic potential for wholesale slaughter, other cops elsewhere are doing real police work and getting somewhere with it. Norton was right about this, we're wasting our time. We are going back."

"You're making a mistake."

"No." She shook her head, decision taken. "I made a mistake in Istanbul. Now I'm going to put it right."

part IV

OUT TO SEA

We must at all times guard against any illusory sense of final achievement. To recommend change, as this report does, is not to suggest that the problems we address will disappear or no longer require attention. At most they will disappear from view, and this may very well be a counter-productive outcome, since it cannot fail to encourage a complacency we can ill afford.

**—Jacobsen Report,
August 2091**

CHAPTER 32

Greta Jurgens came to work early, shuffling across the deserted white stone courtyards just off the Plaza de Armas before the sun got high enough to make them blaze. Still, she wore heavy-framed sunglasses against the light, and her pace was sluggish enough for summer heat or a woman twice her age. She wasn't small-boned, or even especially pale given her Germanic ancestry, but the tanned, muscle-freighted bulk of the two Samoan bodyguards detailed to escort her from the limousine each day made her seem delicate and ill by comparison. And as she reached the cloistered edge of the courtyard where her office was, stepped under the cloister's stone roof and up to the office door, she shivered, harder than most humans would. October was a knowledge, a cold creeping tide in her blood. Darker, colder days, coming in.

Back in Europe, the seasonal cycle her metabolism had originally been calibrated for was already well into autumn and winding slowly down to winter. *And you never could quite get it together to get recalibrated, could you, Greta.* Too little faith in the local service providers—it was a complicated procedure, went very deep—and too little disposable income or time to go back and pay someone she'd trust. *Yeah, and if you're honest, just never the* right *time, either: too fucking busy, then too fucking depressed, then just too fucking asleep.* It was a pretty standard hib complaint—along with the more obvious physiological factors, the hibernoid hormonal suite lent itself to mental fluctuations that were almost bipolar in their intensity. All through the waking segment of the cycle, she whirred like an overloaded magdrive dynamo, working, dealing, brokering, *living* but always too busy, too busy, too busy to rest or relax or sleep or worry about minor considerations like changing her life for the better. Then, as the hormonal tide began to ebb and such considerations finally managed to creep to the front of her conscious concerns, they came in freighted with such a surging sense of weariness in the face of insurmountable odds that it was all she could do not to weep at the pointlessness of trying to do anything about a thing like that now. *Better just to sleep on it, better just let it go this time around, pick up again in spring and . . .*

And around she went again.

An unfortunate psychological side effect, went the arid, tut-tutting text of the Jacobsen Protocol, *and somewhat debilitating for those implicated, but not a failing this committee need concern itself with unduly, nor a social threat as such.*

Somewhat debilitating. Right. Her fingers mashed at the door code panel, slow and clumsy, as if they weren't really hers. The Samoans stood by. Isaac and Salesi, both of them *familia* enforcers since their youth, long schooled in a sort of hard-faced butler's diplomacy where escort duties were concerned—they knew better than to offer her help. She'd been in a foul mood for days now, snappish and strung out at the wrong end of her waking tether. Judgment fraying, social skills barely operational. Under normal circumstances, she'd already have handed over operations here to one of Manco's brighter minions, given in to the inevitable changes in her blood chemistry, and let the cold tide turn opiate-warm along her veins. She'd already be housebound, down at the Colca retreat, pottering about, prepping for the long sleep ahead. Under normal circumstances, she wouldn't have to—

He came out of nowhere.

She still had her sunglasses on, blurry early-morning vision, and not much peripheral sense at all this late in the cycle—no surprise she didn't see it happen. Her first warning was the sound of a solid, untidy impact behind her. The door, coded open, was already swinging inward off the latch. She felt the huge hand of one of the bodyguards hit her in the small of her back, shoving her bodily inside. She stumbled, caught the corner of a desk in the cramped office space, struggled foggily to comprehend.

We're being hit.

Impossible. Her mind rejected it out of hand, objections in a blurry rush. Manco had put his stamp on the Arequipa gangs a decade ago, made his allegiances, wiped out the rest. No one—*no one*—was stupid enough to buck the trend. And the courtyard, the white stone courtyard, was pristine when they crossed, empty this early.

The sound behind her played back in her head. Shock jumped in her blood as she put it together.

Someone had come off the paved walkway above the cloister, jumped better than five meters directly down and onto one of her escorts. Was outside now, finishing the job . . .

Isaac cannoned into the doorjamb and sagged there, clinging. Blood matted his hair and poured down his face between the eyes. He made a convulsive effort to gain his feet again, failed, went down in a heap.

Behind him in the doorway, a black figure silhouetted against the gathering glare of the early-morning sun. Something flopped in her sluggish blood, deep jolt of instinctive fear just ahead of recognition.

"Morning, Greta. Surprised to see me?"

"Marsalis." She spat it out, temper snapping across. "What the *fuck* do you think you're doing?"

He stepped carefully into the office, skirting Isaac's toppled bulk with cat-like care and a wary sideways glance. Behind him, through the open door, she saw Salesi stretched out unmoving on the chessboard white-and-gray pavement of the courtyard like a beached whale. Marsalis didn't have a mark on him; didn't even appear to be breathing heavily. He stood just inside reaching distance and looked impassively at her.

"I haven't had much sleep, Greta. I'd bear that in mind if I were you."

"I'm not afraid of you."

He saw it was true. Smiled a little. "I guess not. Welcome to the twist brotherhood, right? All just monsters together."

"I repeat." She stepped away from the desk corner, straightened up to him. "What the fuck do you think you're doing?"

"I might ask Manco the same question. See, I've been pretty polite so far. Couple of quick conversations and I'm out of your hair for good. No damage, no disruption, everybody's happy. That's the way I wanted it, anyw—"

"We don't always get what we want, Marsalis. Didn't your mummy ever tell you that?"

"Yeah. She also told me it was rude to interrupt." He reached in, whiplash-swift, and her sunglasses were gone, plucked into his hand. Her vision watered and swam. "Like I said, Greta, I could have been out of everyone's hair in nothing flat. Instead, last night, while I was on my way here to talk to you, someone paid a bucketful of your illustrious local military to have me disappeared."

She blinked hard to clear her vision. Silent curse at the tears it squeezed visibly out at the corners of her eyes.

"What a shame they didn't manage it."

"Yeah, well, you just can't get the help these days. Point is, Greta, who do you think I should blame?"

She tipped her head to look past him at the crumpled form by the door. "Looks to me like you've already decided that one."

"You're confusing purpose with necessity. I don't think your islander friends would have been overkeen on us all having a sitdown chat."

She met his gaze. "I don't seem to be sitting down."

For a moment, they stared at each other. Then he shrugged and tossed her sunglasses onto the desktop. He nodded at the chair behind the desk.

"Be my guest."

She made her way around the edge of the desk and seated herself. At the door to the little office, Isaac stirred, shook his head muzzily. Marsalis glanced his way, looked back at Greta and pointed a warning finger, then crossed to where the Samoan lay. Isaac snarled and spat blood, glaring up at the black man in disbelieving rage. He braced his arms at his sides, and pressed huge hands flat to the floor.

"You stand up," Marsalis said without passion, "I will kill you."

The Samoan didn't appear to hear. His arms flexed, his mouth formed a grin.

"Isaac, he means it." Greta leaned over the desk, put urgency into her tone. "He's thirteen. Unluck. You stay where you are. I'll square this."

Marsalis shot her a glance. "Generous of you."

"Fuck you, Marsalis. Some of us got loyalties past getting paid." Sudden, unstoppable, cavernous yawn. "Wouldn't expect you to understand that."

"Am I keeping you up?"

"Fuck off. You want to ask me questions, ask me. Then get the fuck out."

"You talk to Manco today?"

"No."

He seated himself on the edge of the desk. "Yesterday?"

"Before he went to meet you. Not since."

"Why would he use the army and not *familia* talent?"

"You're assuming it was him."

"He came close to greasing me himself, up at Sacsayhuamán. Yeah, I'm assuming this was him."

"You got no other enemies?"

"I think we agreed I was asking the questions."

She shrugged. Waited.

"Manco got any interests up in Jesusland?"

"That I know of? No."

"The Rim?"

"No."

"He had a cousin did jail time in Florida. Wore a jacket just like this one, apparently. Know anything about that?"

"No."

"You guys move medical tech at all?"

She held down another yawn. "If it pays."

"Heard of a guy called Eddie Tanaka?"

"No."

"Texan. Strictly small-time."

"I said no."

"What about Jasper Whitlock?"

"No."

"Toni Montes?"

"No."

"Allen Merrin?"

She threw up her hands. "Marsalis, what the fuck is this? *Gone Walkabout*? Do I look like Shannon Doukoure to you? We're not a fucking missing persons agency."

"So you don't know Merrin?"

"Never heard of him."

"What about Ulysses Ward?"

She sat back in the chair. Sighed. "No."

"Manco treat you okay, Greta?"

She flared again, for real this time. "That's none of your motherfucking business."

"Hey, I'm just wondering here." He gestured. "I mean, you're good looking and all, but in the end you're a twist, just like me, and—"

"I am nothing like you, unluck," she said coldly.

"—we all know how the *familias* feel about twists. I don't imagine Manco's any different from the other *taytas*. Must be tough for you."

Greta said nothing.

"Well?"

"I didn't hear you ask me a question."

"Didn't you?" He grinned mirthlessly. "My question, Greta, was how does a gringa hib twist like yourself end up working front office for the *familias*?"

"I don't know, Marsalis. Maybe it's because some of us *twists* can transcend what it says in our genes and just get on and do the work. Ever think of that?"

"Greta, you're asleep four months out of every twelve. That's going to put a serious dent in anyone's productivity. Add to that you're white, you're a woman, and you're not from here. The *familias* aren't known for their progressive attitudes. So I don't see any way this works, unless my sources are right and you're fucking the boss."

Across the room, Isaac's eyes widened with disbelieving fury. She caught his gaze and shook her head, then fixed Marsalis with a stare.

"Is that what you'd like to believe?"

"No, it's what Stefan Nevant tells me."

"Nevant?" Greta sneered. "That shithead? Fucking wannabe *pistaco*, too stupid to realize—"

She stopped, sat silent.

Fucking end-of-cycle slippage, she knew dismally. *Fucking traitorous genetic bullshit modifi—*

Marsalis nodded. "Too stupid to realize what?"

"To realize. That he needed us, and we didn't need him at all."

"That's not what you were going to say."

"Oh, so now you're a fucking telepath?"

He got off the edge of the desk. "Let's not make this more unpleasant than it's got to be, Greta."

"I agree. In fact, let's stop this shit right now."

The new voice held them both frozen for a pair of seconds. Greta locked onto the figure in the doorway, then looked back just in time to see Marsalis's face slacken into resignation. His lips formed a word, a name, she realized, and realized at the same moment, confusedly but surely, that it was all over.

Sevgi Ertekin stepped into the room, Marstech Beretta in hand.

In the taxi, they sat with a frigid thirty centimeters of plastic seat between them and stared from opposite side windows at the passing frontages. Outside, the sun was on its way up into a sky of flawless blue, striking the early-morning chill out of the air and lighting the white volcanic stonework of the old town almost incandescent. Traffic already clogged the main streets, slowed passage to a jerky crawl.

"We're going to miss our fucking flight," she said grimly.

"Ertekin, this place has a dozen flights a day to Lima. We've got no problem getting out of here."

"No, but we've got a big fucking problem making the Oakland suborbital out of Lima if we miss this flight."

He shrugged. "So we wait in Lima, catch a later bounce to Oakland. This guy they've found is dead, right? He's not in a hurry."

She swung on him. "What the fuck were you doing back there?"

"Working a source, what did it look like?"

"To me? Looked like you were winding up to beat a confession out of her."

"I wasn't looking for a confession. I don't think she knows about our little reception committee last night."

"Shame you didn't think to find that out before you cut loose on the hired help."

Carl shrugged. "They'll live."

"The one out in the courtyard may not. I checked him on my way in. At a guess I'd say you fractured his skull."

"That's hardly the point."

"No, the point is that I told you we were *done* here. I told you we were going to stay put in the hotel until we were ready to fly out. The point is that you told me you would."

"I couldn't sleep."

She said something in Turkish under her breath. He wondered whether to tell her the truth: that he had slept, but not for very long. Had stung himself awake with dreams of Elena Aguirre muttering behind him in the gloom of *Felipe Souza*'s cargo section, had thought for one icy moment that she stood there beside the bed in the darkened hotel suite, staring down at him glitter-eyed. He'd dressed and gone out, itching to do violence, to do anything that would chase out the remembered powerlessness.

Instead, he told her: "She knows Merrin."

Momentary stillness, a barely perceptible stiffening, then the scant shift of her profile from the window, a single, sidelong glance.

"Yeah, right."

"I ran a long list of names on her, mostly victims from your list. Merrin's was the only one that got a reaction. And when I moved on to the next name, she relaxed right back down again. Either she knew him before he went to Mars, or she knows him now."

"Or she knows someone else with that name, or did once." She'd gone back to looking out of the window. "Or it sounded like something or someone she knew, or you're mistaken about the way she reacted. You're chasing shadows and you know it."

"Someone tried to kill us last night."

"Yeah, and on your own admission Jurgens knows nothing about it."

"I said she didn't *seem* to."

"Like she *seemed* to know Merrin, you mean?" She looked at him again, but this time there was no hostility. She just looked tired. "Look, Marsalis, you can't have it both ways. Either we trust your instincts or we don't."

"And you don't?"

She sighed. "I don't trust *this*."

"What's that supposed to mean, this?"

"It means this fucking dive back to the visceral level all the time. This throwing your weight around and pissing people off and pushing until something breaks loose and gives us someone new to fight. Confrontation, escalation, fucking death or glory." She gestured helplessly. "I mean, maybe that worked for Project Lawman back in the day, but it isn't going to cut it here. This is an investigation, not a brawl."

"Osprey."

"What?"

"Osprey. I'm not American, I was never part of Project Lawman." He frowned, flicker of something recalled, too faint now to get back. "And another thing I'm not, Ertekin, just so you keep it in mind. I'm not Ethan."

For a moment, he thought she'd explode on him, the way she had the night before on the highway, with the corpses draped across the stalled and blinded jeep. But she only hooded her gaze and turned away.

"I know who you are," she said quietly.

They didn't speak again until they reached the airport.

They made the Lima flight with a couple of minutes to spare, got into the capital on time, and confirmed their places on the Oakland suborb an hour before it lifted.

Time to kill.

Quiet amid the bustle and vaulted space of the Lima terminal, Sevgi faced herself in a washroom mirror. She stared for what seemed like a long time, then shrugged and fed herself the syn capsules one at a time.

Dry-swallowed and grimaced as they went down.

CHAPTER 33

Alcatraz station. Special Cases Division.

By the time she got there, the superfunction capsules had kicked in with a vengeance. Her feelings were her own again, vacuum-packed back into the steel canister she'd made for them. An icy detachment propped up focus and attention to the detail beyond the mirror.

Another fucking mirror, she noted.

But this time she sat behind the glass and watched the scene in the interview room on the other side. Coyle and Rovayo and a woman who sprawled leggily in the chair provided, wore formfitting black under a heavy leather jacket she hadn't bothered to take off, and watched her interrogators with energetic, gum-chewing dislike. She was young, not far into her twenties, and her harsh-boned, Slavic face carried the sneer well. The rest was pure Rim mix—short blond hair hacked about in a classic Jakarta shreddie cut that didn't really suit her, crimson Chinese characters embroidered down the leg of her one-piece from hip to ankle, the baroque blue ink of a Maori-look skin-sting curled across her left temple. Her voice, as it strained through the speaker to the observers' gallery, was heavily accented.

"Look, what you fucking want from me? Everything you ask me, I give you answers. Now I got places I got to be." She leaned across the table. "You know, I don't show up for shift tonight, they don't pay me. Not like you public sector guys."

"Zdena Tovbina," said Norton. "Filigree Steel co-worker. They got her off video archive from the building where this guy used to live. Seems she came looking for him when he didn't show up for work two shifts running."

"Nice of her. Shame Filigree Steel didn't think to do the same thing."

Norton shrugged. "Fluid labor market, you know how it is. Apparently they did call him a couple of times, but when he didn't call back, they just assumed he'd moved on. Hired someone else to fill his shifts. These security grunts make shit, staff turnover's through the roof. What are you going to do?"

"I don't know. Unionize, maybe?"

"Ssssh."

In the interview room, Alicia Rovayo was pacing about. "We'll inform your shift manager if we need to keep you much longer. Meantime, let's go over it one more time. You say you didn't actually *know* anything was wrong with Driscoll."

"No, I knew was something wrong. Something wrong was he saw inside of that ship." For just a moment, Zdena Tovbina looked haunted. "When we saw, we all got sick. Joey was first, but we all saw what was there."

"You actually saw Driscoll vomiting?" Coyle asked from his seat.

"No, we heard." Tovbina tapped her ear twice, graphically. "Squad net. Radio."

"And later, when you saw him?"

"He was quiet. Would not talk." A phlegmatic, open-handed gesture. "I tried, he turned away from me. Very male, you know."

"These guys went in masked," Norton murmured. "Minimal stuff, upper-face goggle wrap, but they were smearing anticontaminants as well. You beginning to see where this is going?"

Sevgi nodded glumly. She glanced across the gallery at Marsalis, but he was focused wholly on the woman beyond the glass.

"When was the last time you actually saw Joseph Driscoll?" Coyle asked patiently.

Tovbina all but ground her teeth in frustration. "I have *told* you. He went back on Red Two shuttle. Climbed in by mistake. We were all shaken. Not thinking right. When we're back at base, I looked for him in squad room. He was already gone."

"Oh yeah," breathed Marsalis. "He was gone all right."

"Where'd they find the body?" Sevgi asked.

"Caught up in deep-water cabling a hundred and something meters down, on the edge of one of these bioculture platforms they've got out there. It's pretty much the area where *Horkan's Pride* came down, allowing for drift. Whoever threw Driscoll over the side weighted him around the legs with a couple of bags of junk from the *Horkan's Pride* galley. Probably made them up in advance. Took him down fast and clean, heading for the seabed until he hit something that snagged him. Pure chance a repair crew was out that way yesterday."

"Did he drown?"

"No, looks like he was dead before he went into the water. Crushed larynx, snapped neck."

"Fuck. Weren't these guys wearing vital signs vests?"

"Yeah, but no one checks them, apparently. Staffing cuts, Filigree Steel eliminated the deck medics on their shuttles sometime last year when they went up for retender."

"Great."

"Yeah, market forces, don't you just love them. Oh yeah, and there are a lot of smaller contusions on Driscoll, some abrasions, too. Forensics reckon he was stuffed inside one of the disposal chutes up near the kitchen section, then dumped straight out into the ocean. A couple of those hatches at least would have been on the submerged side of the hull. No one would have noticed."

Sevgi shook her head. "Blowing an outer hatch should have shown up on a scanner somewhere. Takes power. Either that, or you have to use the explosive bolts like he did with the access hatches, and that would have made a noise, even submerged."

"There'd be plenty of power in the onboard batteries," said Marsalis distantly. "You wouldn't need the bolts. And by the look of it, these people were too busy puking their guts up to be watching their screens for low-level electrical activity."

He sat back and puffed out his cheeks.

"Our boy Merrin really played this one." He shook his head. "A thing of beauty, really."

Norton shot him an unfriendly look.

"So." Sevgi wanted to hear someone say it, even if it was her. "Merrin walks out of there as Driscoll. Steals his gear, masks up, and slips aboard the wrong transport in the general confusion. Think that was deliberate, or did he just luck out?"

Marsalis shook his head again. "Deliberate, absolutely. He'd be paying attention for that stuff."

"He makes it back to the base, gets *off* the base somehow. I'd guess that's not hard. Got to be a hundred different outs for someone with Merrin's training. Security's going to be focused on incoming personnel anyway, not the graveyard shift going home. And with all this breaking loose, everyone's running around like a Jesusland snake-handling meet." She stopped. "Wait a minute, what about the quarantine?"

Norton sighed. "Fudged. They applied it, made the announcement on the way back. Everyone through the nanoscan. Apparently"—irony lay heavy on the word—"no one at Filigree Steel realized Driscoll didn't take the scan."

Marsalis grunted. "Or by the time they realized, it was too late and they just covered their arses."

"Yeah, well, in any case, quarantine cleared inside the first couple of hours.

Some biohazard outfit down from Seattle, they checked the hull for contaminants before it was towed. If someone at Filigree Steel was covering their asses, they knew they were safe by lunchtime."

Sevgi nodded gloomily. "And by the time we'd get to digging any deeper with Filigree Steel, Ward shows up dead so we assume that's how Merrin got ashore, and we don't bother. What a fucking mess."

"It's classic insurgency technique," Marsalis said. "Misdirect, cover your tracks."

"Can you sound a little less fucking impressed, please."

In the interview room, they were done. Zdena Tovbina was escorted out, ostentatiously checking her watch. Rovayo stayed behind, played a long, weary glance through the one-way glass to the gallery as if she could see the three of them sitting there.

"That's all, folks," she said.

"He planned this." Sevgi was still talking to make herself believe it. "He opened up the cryocaps and ripped the bodies apart to create a fucking *diversion*."

"Yeah." Marsalis got up to leave. "And you guys thought he'd just gone crazy."

Coyle and Rovayo had been busy. There was a full CSI virtual up and running for Joey Driscoll's death, including a gruesomely modeled corpse-recovery site. They stood, briefly, in fathomless, lamplit blue and Driscoll peered down at them out of the tangled cabling, one puffy hand waving gently in the current. A CSI 'face reached up helpfully and pulled in magnified detail that Sevgi, syn or no syn, could really have done without. Driscoll's eyes were gone, and the earlobes, the mouth eaten back to a lopsided harelip snarl, and the whole swollen face gone waxy with adipocere seepage through the skin from the subcutaneous fat layers beneath. Sevgi'd seen worse, much worse, fished out of the Hudson or the East River every so often, but it was all a long time ago, and now the illusion of floating beneath the waterlogged corpse in the depths of the ocean kept triggering an impulse to hold her breath.

"You said Forensics have been over the apartment," she said. "Any chance of seeing that?"

Coyle nodded. "Sure. We all done here?"

"I think so," said Norton uncomfortably.

Marsalis nodded impassively.

"Full shift, datahome six," Coyle told the 'face, and the drowned blue murk amped up to a blinding flash of white, then soaked back out into the somber colors of cheap rental accommodation. Driscoll'd either been saving for something better, or maybe didn't rate home environment as much of a budget priority. The furniture was functional and worn; the walls carried generic corporate promo artwork from what looked like a string of different employers. A window gave them a view of what must be an identical apartment building twenty meters away across an alley.

Sevgi breathed in relief.

"You got matching genetic trace?" she asked.

"Yeah." Rovayo pointed, and all around the room tiny scuffs of transparent red lit up on the furniture and fittings. "He was definitely here. Used the place for a couple of days at least."

Marsalis went to the window and peered out. "Any sightings? Eyewitnesses?"

The female Rim detective frowned. "Not much from witnesses, no. These blocks are purpose-built for immigrant labor. Tenant turnover's high, and people keep pretty much to themselves. There's some security video from the corridors, but not much of that, either. It looks like he took out most of the surveillance equipment in the building right after he got here. They didn't get around to fixing it for a couple of weeks."

"Pretty standard," Marsalis muttered.

"Yeah, right," Coyle growled. "And I suppose you don't got immigrant labor slums in the Euro-fucking-Union."

The black man flickered a glance at him.

"I was talking about the surveillance takedown. Pretty standard urban penetration procedure."

"Oh."

"You want to see some of what we did get?" Rovayo asked. She was already gesturing a viewpatch screen into existence on the empty air. Marsalis shrugged and shifted from the window.

"Sure. Can't hurt."

So they all watched at a foreshortening camera angle as Merrin walked gaunt and hollow-eyed through the lobby, stared thoughtfully up at the lens for a moment, and then walked on again. Sevgi, watching Marsalis as well, thought she saw the black man stiffen slightly as Merrin seemed to look up at them all from the screen. She wasn't sure what he saw there to tighten him like that; maybe just a worthy opponent. For her, the moment flip-flopped abruptly in her head, Merrin looking up, the corpse of Joey Driscoll looking down, corpse and killer, little windows opening out of time to let the dead and destructive peer in. Fucking virtual formats. Copied worlds, no place for anything but ghosts and the machine perfection of the 'faces drifting between, administering it all with the inhuman competence of angels.

She wondered suddenly if that was what the paradise the imams talked about would be like. Ghosts and angels, and no place for anything human or warm.

"We've got a problem here," she said to dispel the sudden, creeping sense of doom. "If this is how Merrin got off *Horkan's Pride*, then—"

"Yeah." Coyle finished it for her. "How does he end up at Ward BioSupply the same afternoon, painting the dock with Ulysses Ward's blood?"

"More important than *how*," said Marsalis quietly. "You might want to wonder *why*?"

Coyle and Rovayo shared a look. Sevgi wrote the subtitles. *Who knows why the fuck an unluck twist does anything?* She wasn't sure if Marsalis caught it, too.

Norton cleared his throat. "Ward *was* out there. The satellite footage and the filed sub plans prove it. We've assumed that was coincidence, his bad luck he happened to be in the region. He rescued Merrin from the wreck and got murdered for his kindness."

"Big assumption," said Marsalis, less quietly.

"We didn't assume anything." Irritable tiredness in Rovayo's voice. Now that Sevgi thought about it, neither of the Rim cops looked as if they'd had a lot of sleep recently. "We ran background checks on Ward at the time. COLIN-approved security n-djinn. There's no evidence of a link to Merrin, or Mars generally."

"There is now. Maybe you just didn't dig deep enough."

Coyle bristled. "What the fuck do you know about it? You some kind of cop all of a sudden?"

"Some kind of, yeah."

"Marsalis, you're full of shit. You're a licensed hit man at best, and from what I hear you weren't even very good at that. They bailed your ass out of a Florida jail for this job, right?"

Marsalis smiled faintly.

"We'll go back to Ward," Rovayo said quickly. She'd stepped subtly into the space between the two men, body language a blend of backing Coyle up and defusing the situation. Sevgi made it as instinctive—you couldn't brawl in a virtuality, but Rovayo seemed to have forgotten where they were. "We'll change the protocols, maybe run it through a different n-djinn. We'll go deeper until we find the link. Now, it's a given that they knew each other. So it's probably a safe bet that Ward went out there with the specific intention of bringing Merrin back."

Coyle nodded. "Only Merrin won't play ball. He doesn't show, after what's happened to him in transit from Mars, he doesn't trust Ward or anybody else who's in on this thing. And Ward has a limited window before Filigree Steel shows up; he doesn't have time to search the hull for the guy he's supposed to be collecting."

"Or," offered Rovayo, "Ward climbs down into the hull and when he sees the mess, he freaks and runs."

"Yeah, could work that way, too." Coyle grimaced. "Either way, Merrin finds his own way out, then goes looking for Ward anyway. You know what that sounds like to me? Revenge."

Sevgi turned to look at Marsalis. "That make sense to you?"

"Well, you know us thirteens." Marsalis glanced across at Coyle. He burlesqued a caricature Jesusland drawl. "We're all *real* irrational when someone pisses us off."

Coyle shrugged it off. "Yeah. What I heard."

"Merrin's just endured seven months in transit," Norton pointed out. "He's had to resort to cannibalism to survive. All because someone messed up his cryo-cap thaw. If he blamed Ward for that—"

"Or if Alicia here is right, and Ward did freak and run—" Coyle gestured. "Come on, however you look at it, this twi . . . this guy isn't going to be in the most forgiving of moods. This is payback, pure and simple."

"Marsalis." Sevgi tried again. "I asked you what you think. You want to answer my question?"

He met her eyes. Face unreadable. "What do I think? I think we're wasting our time here."

Coyle snorted. Rovayo laid a hand on his arm. The black man barely looked in their direction. He took a step across the virtual apartment, faced the screen where Merrin was locked in freeze frame walking away, slipping out of the security camera's angle of capture.

"He was clear," he said slowly. "He'd beaten your half-arsed private sector security effort, he'd left them puking their guts up exactly as planned. He'd run rings around them, misdirected everyone's attention, and then disappeared into local population, just the way he was trained. Going back for Ward meant exposing himself, coming out into the open again." A long, speculative stare across at Coyle. "When you're operational in enemy territory, you don't take risks like that for some kind of revenge kick."

"Sure," said Coyle. "Your kind, you'd just let that be. Let the people who abandoned you out there in space get away with it."

"Who said anything about getting away with it?" Marsalis grinned unpleasantly. "My *kind* know how to wait, cudlip. My *kind* would let the people who did this live with the knowledge that we're coming, let them wake up every day knowing—"

"What did you call me?" It had taken Coyle a moment or two to grasp the unfamiliar insult he'd just been handed.

"You heard me."

"Will you two knock it off," snapped Sevgi. "Marsalis, you're saying this isn't revenge. Then what is it?"

"I don't know what it is," the black man said irritably. "I'm not Merrin, and contrary to what our friend here thinks, not everyone with a variant thirteen geneprint thinks exactly alike."

Norton stepped into the breach. "No, but you were trained similarly, and that must count for something. You say his training wouldn't allow an impulse of revenge. What would it dictate in this situation?"

"Maybe he just needed to shut Ward up," Rovayo said. "Cover his retreat. If Ward talked—"

Sevgi shook her head. "Doesn't fit. Ward isn't far enough up the chain of command. Self-made biosupply magnates don't swing the weight to get things done on Mars, even in California. If Ward was a part of this, he was a small cog. They hired him to fish Merrin out of the Pacific and hand him on. End of function. He didn't know anything that he hadn't already been told."

"Right," said Coyle slowly. "But he must have known his chain of command, or at least his nearest contact. We're looking at this the wrong way around. Merrin didn't go to Ward to shut him up, he went to make him talk. To get the names of the people who were giving the orders."

Norton looked suddenly hopeful. "You think Merrin got his hit list out of Ward?"

"Unlikely." Marsalis prowled the virtual apartment like someone looking for a hidden exit somewhere high up. "The way Merrin's been hopping the border back and forth, he's working off either partial or sequential knowledge. Whatever he got out of Ward, it wasn't his hit list."

"Or maybe just not the whole list," said Norton hopefully. "Maybe Ward had the first couple of names."

"There are no links from Ward to Whitlock," Rovayo pointed out.

"Or Montes," said Coyle.

Norton sighed. "Right. Or any of the Jesusland kills, as far as we can tell. Shame, it would have been nice to find ourselves getting somewhere for a change."

"Yeah, well, for that you've got to be looking in the right place." Marsalis gestured around the apartment. "And like I said before, we're wasting our time here."

Coyle's lip curled. "Then perhaps you'd care to tell us how we could more profitably employ that time."

"Outside of going back to the altiplano and coming down hard on Manco Bambarén?" A shrug. Marsalis caught Sevgi's eye, clashed gazes like swords. "Well, you could start by asking yourselves why this corpse shows up now, all of a sudden, just as we're cracking the ice off the *familias*. You could wonder why it's taken nearly six months for someone to go sniffing around the aquaculture environs of the crash site—"

"Who the fuck is Bambarén?" Rovayo wanted to know. She shuttled a glance between Norton and Sevgi. Sevgi shook her head wearily. *Don't ask.*

Meanwhile, Coyle's sneer had made it to a full-blown grin. "The reason it's taken *four* months to find this corpse—fucked-up, gene-enhanced paranoia aside—is that the outfit that run routine maintenance on Ward BioSupply's deep-water platforms are mobile contractors with a biannual contract. Daskeen Azul. They're based out of a co-op factory raft called *Bulgakov's Cat*, and they come by here just about every six months to do the work. They just got here."

"You think I'm paranoid?" asked Marsalis, with the same gentle smile he'd used on Coyle earlier.

The big Rim cop snorted. "Are you shitting me? You people were fucking *designed* paranoid, Marsalis."

Norton cleared his throat. "I think—"

"Nah, let's just lay this out where we can all see it." Coyle jabbed a finger at the thirteen. "In case you missed it, Marsalis, I don't like your kind. I don't like what you are, and I don't think you should be walking around in public without a wolf-trap cuff on. But that's not my call."

"No, it's not," said Norton. "So why don't we—"

"I'm not done yet."

Marsalis watched the Rim cop quietly. Measuring, Sevgi realized. He was measuring the other man.

"This is a Rim States police investigation," Coyle said. "Not some black ops slaughter ground out in the Middle East. We're in the business of catching criminals, not murdering them—"

"Yes. You don't seem to have caught Merrin yet, though, do you?"

Coyle bared his teeth. "Cute. No, we haven't caught this one yet. But we will. And when we do—"

"Roy." It was the first time Sevgi could remember hearing Rovayo use her partner's first name. "Crank it down, huh?"

"No, Al, I'm sick of the assumptions here. This has got to be said." Coyle looked pointedly at Sevgi and Norton on his way back to staring down the thirteen. "If your COLIN masters here decide they want Merrin summarily executed when we've done our job and brought him in, well then I guess we'll come to you for your professional expertise. Meantime, why don't you just curb your fucking twi . . . gene-enhanced tendencies and let us work?"

Wall of silence. The last of the words seemed to hit it like pebbles off evercrete. It was a space, Sevgi realized with syn-sharpened surety, that outside virtual would have filled with violence the way blood rises to fill a wound. Marsalis and the Rim cop were wired eye-to-eye, like nothing else existed around them. She caught something in Rovayo's face she couldn't define. The other woman seemed locked up, an impossible step away from doing something. Norton wavered, helpless exasperation in the way he twitched. And she, Sevgi, watching the situation decay like —

"Okay," said Marsalis, very softly.

Sevgi thought he'd finished. She opened her mouth, but the black man went on speaking.

"A couple of things." Still soft, like the touch of cotton-wool wadding on fingertips. "First, if you think you'll bring Allen Merrin down in any condition other than dead, then you're not living in the real world. None of you are. And second, *Roy*, if you ever speak to me like that again, in the real world, I'll put you in intensive care."

The Rim cop flared up. "Hey, you want to fucking step outside with me?"

"Very much, yes." But Sevgi had the curious sensation that Marsalis was imperceptibly shaking his head as he said it. "But it isn't going to happen. I want you to remember a name, Roy. Sutherland. Isaac Sutherland. He saved your life today."

Then he was gone.

Scribbled out in a flicker of virtual light as he left them to the empty virtual apartment, Merrin's viewpatch freeze-frame portrait walking away, and the hundred red glow traces of his forensic passing.

CHAPTER 34

Oddly enough, it was Rovayo who came looking for him. By the time she tracked him down, he'd stopped prowling angrily about the Alcatraz station and drifted instead to an irritable halt on an outside gallery at the western end of the complex. She found him leaning on the rail, staring across the silver-glinting chop of the sea toward the mouth of the bay and the rust-colored suspension span that bridged it. There was a towering bank of fog rolling in against the blue of the sky, like a pale cotton-candy wave about to break.

"Enough water for you?" she asked.

Carl shot her a curious glance. "I've been back a long time."

"Yeah, I know." Rovayo joined him at the rail. "I got this cousin down in the Freeport, he did six years on Mars when he was younger. Soil engineer. Two three-year qualpro stints back-to-back. He told me you never get used to the size of the water again, doesn't matter how long ago you went."

"Well, that's him. Everyone handles it differently."

"You ever miss it?"

He looked at her again. "What do you want, Rovayo?"

"Says he misses the sky," she went on neutrally, as if Carl hadn't spoken. "Sky at night, you know. All that landscape on that tiny horizon, says it looks like furniture crammed into a storeroom that's too small for everything to fit. And all the stars. He says it was like you were all camping out together, like you were all part of the same army or something. You and every other human being you knew was on the planet with you, all with the same reason for being there, like you were all doing something that mattered."

Carl grunted.

"You ever feel like that?" she asked.

"No."

It came out more abrupt than he'd meant. He sighed and opened his hands where they rested on the rail. "I'm a thirteen, remember. We don't suffer from this need to feel useful that you people have. We're not wired for group harmony."

"Yeah, but you don't always let your wiring tell you what to do, right?"

"Maybe not, but I'd say it pays to listen to it from time to time. If you plan on ever being happy, that is."

Rovayo rolled over on the railing, put her arched spine to it, and hooked her elbows back for support. "I seem to remember reading somewhere we're none of us wired for that one. Being happy. Just a chemical by-product of function, a trick to get you where your genes want you to go."

His gaze slipped sideways, drawn by the lithe twist she'd used to reverse her position on the rail. He caught her profile, lean high-breasted body and long thighs, the dark flaring facets of her face. The wind off the bay fingered through the curls in her hair, flattened it forward around her head.

"You don't want to worry too much about Coyle," she said, not looking at him.

"I'm not."

She smiled. "Okay. It's just. See, we don't get a whole lot of thirteens out here on the Rim. They crop up occasionally, we just bust 'em and ship 'em out. Dump them in Cimarron or Tanana. Jesusland's always a good place to export the stuff you don't want in your own backyard. Nuclear nondegradables, nanotech test runs, cutting-edge crop research. The Republic takes it all at a fraction what it'd cost us to do the processing ourselves."

"I know."

"Yeah, you worked a couple of Cimarron breaks, right?"

"Six." He considered. "Seven if you count Eric Sundersen last year. He escaped en route, never actually got to Cimarron itself."

"Oh yeah, I remember that one. The guy who shorted out the autocopter, right?"

"Right."

"You the one who brought him in?"

"No," he said shortly. Eric Sundersen had died in a hail of assault rifle fire on the streets of Minneapolis. Standard police ordnance and tactics; apparently he'd been mistaken for a local drug dealer. Carl was chasing false leads down in Juarez at the time. He went home with day-rate expenses and minor lacerations from a razor fight triggered by one too many questions in the wrong bar. "I missed out on that one."

"Yeah?" Rovayo hitched herself up on the rail. "Well, anyway, like I said. Having guys like you around isn't something any of us are used to. Coyle's got a pretty standard Rim mentality about what a good thing that is. And with the mess Merrin made on that ship . . . well, Coyle's a cop, he just doesn't want to see any more blood in the streets."

"You trying to apologize for him? That what this is about?"

She grimaced. "I'm just trying to make sure you two don't kill each other before we get the job done."

He cocked an eyebrow at her. "I can guarantee you Coyle won't kill me."

"Yeah." She nodded and her mouth tightened. "Well, just so you know, he's my partner. It's not a fight I'll stay out of if it cuts loose."

He let it sit for a while, waiting to see if she was finished, if she'd leave him alone with the threat. When she didn't, he sighed again.

"Okay, Rovayo, you win. Go back and tell your good, honest, compassionate cop partner that if he can keep the word *twist* hedged a little tighter behind his teeth next time, I'll cut him some slack."

"I know. I'm sorry about that."

"Don't be. You're not the one who said it."

She hesitated. "I don't like that word any more than you do. It's just, like I said, we don't get—"

"Yeah, I know. You don't get many like me in the Rim, so Coyle gets to throw the words around without repercussions. Don't worry, it's not much different anywhere else I've been."

"Apart from Mars?"

He hunched around to look at her properly.

"Mars, huh? This cousin of yours really planted some seeds, didn't he? What's the deal, you thinking about going yourself?"

She didn't meet his gaze. "Nothing like that. Just Enrique, my cousin, he talked a lot about how no one had a problem with the thirteens there. Like they had this kind of minor celebrity status."

Carls snorted. "Pretty fucking minor, I'd say. Sounds to me like your cousin Enrique's having a bad attack of qualpro nostalgia. That's pretty common once you get safely back, but you notice most of these guys don't sign up for another tour. I mean, he didn't, right?"

She shook her head. "I think part of him wanted to, part of him would have stayed out there longer, maybe not come back at all. But he got scared. He didn't exactly tell me that, but you could pick it up from what he said, you know."

"Well, it's an easy place to get scared," Carl admitted grudgingly.

"Even for a thirteen?"

He shrugged. "We're not that good at fear, it's true. But this is something deeper, it's not an actual fear *of* anything. It's something that comes up from inside. No warning, no trigger you can work out. Just a feeling."

"Feeling of what?"

Carl grimaced, remembering. "A feeling that you don't belong. That you shouldn't be there. Like being in someone else's home without them knowing, and *you* know they might be coming home any minute."

"Big bad Martian monsters, huh?"

"I didn't say it made any sense." He stared out at the bridge. The southern tower was almost lost in the encroaching fog bank now, wrapped and shrouded to the top. Tendrils crept through under the main span. "They say it's the gravity and the perceived horizon that does it. Triggers a survival anxiety. Maybe they're right."

"You think you handled it better?" She made an embarrassed gesture. "Because. You know, because of what you are?"

He frowned. "What do you want to hear from me, Rovayo? What's this really about?"

"Hey, just making conversation. You want to be alone, say the word. I can take a hint if you hit me upside the head with it."

Carl felt a faint smile touch the corners of his mouth.

"You work at it, you can reach a balance," he said. "The fear tips over into exhilaration. The weakness turns into strength, fuels you up to face whatever it is your survival anxiety thinks it's warning you about. Starts to feel good instead of bad." He looked down at the backs of his hands where they rested on the rail. "Kind of addictive after a while."

"You think that's why they're happy to have you on Mars?"

"Rovayo, they're happy to have *anyone* on Mars. The qualpro guys mostly go home as soon as their stint's up—to be fair to your cousin, he's a tough motherfucker if he stayed even for a second tour—and you've got a high rate of mental health problems in the permanent settlers, that's the grunts *and* the ex-grunts who've upskilled, doesn't seem to make much difference either way. End result—there's never enough labor to go around, never enough skilled personnel or reliable raw human material to learn the skills. So yeah, they can put up with the fact you're a born-and-bred twist sociopath if they think you'll be able to punch above your weight." A thin smile. "Which we mostly can."

The Rim cop nodded, as if convincing herself of something.

"They say the Chinese are breeding a new variant for Mars. Against the Charter. You believe that?"

"I'd believe pretty much anything of those shitheads in Beijing. You don't keep a grip on the world's largest economy the way they have without stamping on a few human rights."

"You see any evidence? When you were there, I mean?"

Carl shook his head. "You don't see much of the Chinese at all on Mars. They're mostly based down in Hellas or around the Utopia spread. Long way from Bradbury or Wells, unless you've got some specific reason to go there."

They both watched the silvered chop of the water for a while.

"I did think about going," Rovayo said finally. "I was younger when Enrique came back with all his stories, still in my teens. I was going to get some studies, sign up for a three stint."

"So what happened?"

She laughed. "Life happened, man. Just one of those dreams the logistics stacked up against, you know."

"You probably didn't miss much."

"Hey, *you* went."

"Yeah. I went because the alternative was internment." A brief memory of Nevant's jeering slipped across his mind. "And I came back as soon as I got the chance. You don't want to believe all your cousin's war stories. That stuff always looks better in the rearview mirror. A lot of the time, Mars is just this cold, hardscrabble place you won't ever belong to no matter how hard you scrabble at trying."

Rovayo shrugged.

"Yeah, well." A hard little smile came and went across her mouth, but her voice was quiet and cop-wisdom calm. "You think it's any different here on Earth, Marsalis? You think down here they're ever going to let you belong?"

And for that, he had no answer. He just stood and watched the disappearing bridge until Rovayo propped herself upright off the rail and touched his arm.

"C'mon," she said companionably. "Let's get back to work."

They were working the *Horkan's Pride* case out of a closed suite in the lower levels of the Alcatraz station. Shielding in the superstructure above them ensured a leak-tight data environment, the transmission systems in and out ran Marstech-standard encryption, and all the equipment in the suite was jacked together with python-thick coils of black actual cable. It gave the offices a period feel that sat well with the raw, sandblasted stone walls and the subterranean cool that soaked off them. Sevgi sat in a commandeered desk chair and stared at a rough-hewn corner, keeping her eyes off Marsalis and furious with herself for the feeling that had snaked across her belly when Rovayo came back with the black man in tow.

"Coyle and Norton went to talk to Tsai," she told them. "Going to book some n-djinn time, run a fresh linkage model on Ward and the victims, soon as we can get on the machine."

Rovayo nodded and went to her desk, where she stood prodding through a pile of hardcopy with limited enthusiasm. Sevgi turned to Marsalis.

"There's a Mars datafile you might want to take a look at here. Seems Norton got on to Colony while we were in Istanbul, had them pull Gutierrez in. You want to screen it?"

She thought she saw a subtle tightening go through him. But he only shrugged. "Think it's worth looking at?"

"I don't know," she said acidly. "I haven't seen it yet."

"The chances Colony got anything useful out of an old *familia* hand like Gutierrez are pretty thin."

"Not really the main point," said Rovayo absently from across the room without looking up from her paperwork. "Cop'll tell you it's what the guy doesn't say as often as not gives you the angle."

"Uh, exactly," said Sevgi, startled.

Marsalis shuttled a sour look between the two women.

"All right," he said ungraciously. "So let's all watch the fucking thing, shall we."

But in the screening chamber, she saw how the quick-flaring irritation damped down to an intent stare that might have passed for boredom if she hadn't seen him looking the same way after the third skater in New York, the man he'd failed to kill. She had no way of knowing where exactly Marsalis's attention fell—the file was a standard split-screen interrogation tape, six or seven facets slotted together on the LCLS display, frontal on Gutierrez, face and body from the table-top up, vital signs in longitudinal display below, minimized footage of the whole interview room from two or three different angles, voice profiles in dropdown to the left. Cop custom had her skimming detail from the whole thing in random snatches. But if she'd had to guess, she'd say the thirteen at her side was riveted on the slightly gaunt, sun-blasted features of the *familia* datahawk as he sat unimpressed and smoking his way through the interrogation.

"They let him take fucking *cigarettes* in there?" asked Rovayo, outraged.

"It's not a cigarette as such," Sevgi told her patiently. She'd been a little shocked the first time she saw it, too. "That's a gill. You know, like in the settler flicks. Chemical ember, gives off oxygen instead of burning it. Like a lung supercharger."

Rovayo snapped her fingers. "O-kay. Like, Kwame Oviedo's always got one stuck in the corner of his mouth, practically every scene in that *Upland Heroes* trilogy."

Sevgi nodded. "Yeah, same with Marisa Mansour. Even in *Marineris Queen*, which when you think about it, is pretty—"

"Weren't we supposed to be watching this," said Marsalis loudly.

Sevgi cocked an expressive eyebrow at the Rim cop, and they turned back toward the screen. Gutierrez was settling comfortably into his role of career criminal cool. Upland-dialect Quechua drawled out of him—the language monitor tagged it in the lower right-hand corner of the screen, provided a machine-speed simultaneous subtitle in Amanglic, but for the original interrogators it would have been hard work. They'd have some street Quechua, Sevgi supposed, you'd have to have, be a decent cop out there, but you could see they were uncomfortable with it. Instead, they fell back repeatedly on Amanglic or Spanish—both of which the file said Gutierrez spoke well—and listened constantly to their sleek black earplug whisperers. The datahawk smirked through it.

"Look, let's cut the bouncing about, Nicki," he said, apparently. "There is no motherfucking way you have anything on me. You'll have to give me my phone call sooner or later. So why not save us all a lot of fucking around and do it now?"

The ranking officer on the other side of the table sat back in her chair and fixed the ex-datahawk with a somber stare.

"I think you've forgotten which planet you're on, Franklin. You'll get to make a phone call when I say you can."

Her companion got up out of his chair and began to pace a slow circle around the table. Gutierrez tipped his head back a little to watch the move, drew on his gill and puffed a long feather of fumes up into the air, then went back to looking at the woman. He shook his head.

"They'll come and dig me out of here before breakfast, Nicki. You know that."

The other cop hit him, dropped body weight into the swing, one cupped striking hand to the datahawk's ear and side of the head. The gill went flying. In the slack grip of Mars gravity, so did Gutierrez and the chair. Clatter of plastic on evercrete, soft human yelp. Rovayo flinched—Sevgi caught it peripherally from two seats over. On screen, Gutierrez rolled to a halt and the cop was on him. The datahawk was shaking his head muzzily, trying to pick himself up—his assailant locked a thick muscled arm around his throat, hauled him upright by it. The ranking officer watched impassively.

"Wrong guess, fuckwit," hissed the strong-arm cop into the ear he hadn't deafened. "See, we got a lot of leeway on this one. You really fucked up with *Horkan's Pride*, and I mean big-time. There's a lot more juice coming down from COLIN right now than your buddies over in Wells know how to soak up. I'd say we've got you down here for a fortnight at least."

The datahawk choked out a reply. "Reyes," said the subtitles. "You're confusing your wet dreams with reality again."

The cop bared his teeth in a grin. He reached down and grabbed Gutierrez by
the crotch. Twisted. A suffocated screech made it up the datahawk's throat.

"Can he—" Rovayo began numbly.

Marsalis rolled his head slightly in her direction. Met her eye. "Colony police.
Oh yeah. He can."

The ranking officer made a tiny motion with her head. Her companion let go
of Gutierrez's testicles and dumped the datahawk forward onto the tabletop like
a load of laundry. He lay there, face to one side, breath whistling hoarsely in and
out of his teeth. The cop called Reyes pressed a flat palm down hard against their
suspect's cheek, leaned on it, and then closer, over him.

"You'd better fucking learn to behave, Franklin," he said conversationally.
"What they tell me, we can blow this whole year's compensation budget on you
if we have to." He looked at the woman. "What's the rate for testicular damage
these days, Nick?"

The ranking officer shrugged. "Thirty-seven grand."

Reyes grinned again. "Right. Now, that's for each one, right?"

"No, that's for both." The woman leaned forward a little. "I hear the restora-
tive surgery's a bitch, Franklin. Not something you'd want to go through at all."

"Yeah, so how about you speak *English* to us for a change." Reyes marked the
emphasis, skidding his palm hard off the datahawk's face, as if wiping it clean. His
face wrinkled up with disgust. "Because we all know you can, sort of. Just wrap
the fucking Upland chatter for a while. Do us that small favor, huh? Maybe then
I leave your *cojones* intact."

He stepped back. A thin sound trickled out of Gutierrez. Sevgi, disbelieving,
made it as laughter. The datahawk was chuckling.

Reyes hooked back around to stare. "Something amusing you, *pendejo*?"

Gutierrez got up off the table. He straightened his clothes. Nodded, as if he'd
just had something entirely reasonable explained to him. His ear, Sevgi knew,
must still have been singing like a fire alarm.

"Only the dialogue." His English was lightly accented, otherwise flawless.
"You say you got me down here indef. Okay, I'll bite. Nicki, you want to put a
leash on your dog?"

Reyes tensed, but the woman made another barely perceptible motion with
her head, and he slackened off again. Gutierrez lowered himself gingerly back
into his chair, wincing. He patted his pockets for the pack of gills, found them,
and fit a new one into his mouth. He twisted the end till it tore open, puffed it to

life. Breathed the fumes out of his mouth and up his nose. Sevgi made it for buying time. The datahawk shrugged.

"So what do you want to know?"

"*Horkan's Pride*," said Reyes evenly.

"Yeah, you mentioned it. Big spaceship, went home last year. Crashed into the
sea, they say." He plumed pale smoke "So what?"

"So why'd you do it?"

"Why'd I do what?"

The two Colony cops swapped a glance of theatrical exasperation. Reyes took
a couple of steps forward, hands lifting.

"Hold it," said the woman. It rang staged, patently false after the imperceptible signals the two cops had exchanged before.

"Yeah, hold it," agreed Gutierrez. "You're going to tie me to some systems crash
on another fucking *planet*? I mean, back in the day I was good. But not that good."

"That's not what we hear," growled Reyes.

"So what do you hear, exactly?"

"Why don't you tell us, *pendejo*?"

Gutierrez cocked his head. "Why don't *I* tell *you* what *you've* just heard? What
am I, telepathic now?"

"Listen, fuckwit . . ."

Marsalis groaned, a little theatrical exasperation of his own. It was hard for
Sevgi not to sympathize. Colony were fucking it up beyond belief.

They sat it out, nonetheless. The interrogation cycled a couple more times,
reasonable to third degree and back again, but spiraling downward all the way.
Gutierrez drew gill fumes and strength in the soft spells, weathered Reyes's brutality when it came around. He didn't give a millimeter. They took him out limping, broken-mouthed, and bruised around one eye, nursing a sprained wrist.
He gave one of the cameras a bloodied smile as he was led away. The vital signs
monitors collapsed as he left the room; the ranking officer signed off formally.
Fade to black.

Marsalis sighed. "Happy now?"

"I will be when you tell me what you think."

"What do I think? I think short of professional torture with electrodes and
psychotropics, Gutierrez isn't going to tell Colony anything worth knowing. How
long ago did this happen?"

"Couple of days. Norton put in the arrest order the night we flew out to
Istanbul."

"They worked on him since?"

"I don't think so. This is all we have. I don't think they'll go to the next level with him until they get something solid from us."

"Yeah, and they'll probably still be wasting their time. Earth or Mars, the *familias* have too much invested in guys like this. They get in early on with the good ones, give them the same synaptic conditioning you see in covert ops biotech. Stuff where the brain'll turn to warm porridge sooner than give up proscribed information."

"You think he'd really be wearing something like that?" Rovayo asked, slightly wide-eyed.

"If I were running him, I'd have had it built in years ago." Marsalis yawned and stretched in his seat. "Plus, you want to remember Gutierrez is a datahawk. Those guys live for the virtual, they spend their whole lives switching off exactly the kind of physical realities torture involves. If they're good at one thing, it's distancing themselves from their own bodies. Back in the early days, back when the technology was fresh and the hookups were a lot more jack-and-pray than they are now, lot of 'hawks died from stupid shit like dehydration or burning to death because they missed a fire alarm. I remember Gutierrez telling me once, *Hey, pain, that's just your body letting you know what the thing you're doing is going to cost—just got to get in there and pay the bill, soak.* At that level, he's as tough a motherfucker as you'll ever see walk into an interrogation chamber. And with the *familias* behind him, he's not much scared of physical damage, either, because he knows it can be repaired."

"Scared of dying, though, I guess," Sevgi said snappishly.

"Yeah, and that's part of your problem. See, Colony are a real bunch of thugs, but they can't actually kill you, except maybe by accident. But the people Gutierrez works for, the *familias*—now, that's a whole other skyline. If *they* think he's talked, or even that he *might* talk, then they got no problem putting him away. None at all, and he knows that. So yeah, Gutierrez is scared of dying, just like anybody else. But you've got to be able to deliver on the threat."

They sat for a couple of moments, facing the dead LCLS screen. Sevgi looked across at Rovayo.

"You mind giving us a couple of minutes?" she asked.

"No," he said, as soon as they were alone.

"I'm not saying—"

"I know exactly what you're saying, and you can just fucking forget it. They're on *Mars*, Ertekin. You saw the footage. You think I can scare Gutierrez any worse than that from two hundred fifty million kilometers out?"

"Yes," she said steadily. "I think you can."

He shook his head. Voice creased with irritation. "Oh, based on *what?*"

"Based on the fact you and Gutierrez have history. I'm a cop, Marsalis. Eleven years in, so give me some fucking credit, why don't you. I saw the way you were when his name popped out of the n-djinn scan. I saw the way you watched him up on that screen just now." She drew a deep breath, let it go. "Gutierrez wired you to wake up midway home on *Felipe Souza,* didn't he?"

"Did he?" Now there was nothing in his voice at all.

"Yeah, he did." Gathering certainty, the way he sat like stone. "It's too much of a coincidence, you *and* Merrin. The way I figure it, you did some kind of deal with Gutierrez for the lottery win, but Gutierrez didn't like his end when it paid off. He sent you home with a little farewell kick. Fuck with your head, wake you up out there and hope you maybe go insane before recovery can get to you. That how it was?"

He rolled his head toward her on the back of the seat, looked at her, and suddenly for the first time in days she was afraid of him again.

"Well, you're the cop," he said tonelessly. "You got it all worked out, what do you need me for?"

She threw herself to her feet, paced toward the screen and turned to look back at him. Told herself it was not a retreat.

"What I need you for is to look at Gutierrez like you just looked at me. Look him in the eye and tell him you'll kill him if he doesn't tell us what we need to know."

"That standard operating procedure for the NYPD these days, is it?"

She was back in the field, upstate New York at dawn and the gagging stench of disinterred flesh. The speculative stare of the IA detectives.

"Fuck you."

"See. I can't even scare you. And you're right here in the room with me. How am I going to scare Gutierrez on Mars?"

"You know what I'm talking about."

He sighed. "Yeah, I know what you're talking about. Talking about the mythos, right? You think that because Gutierrez was a thirteen aficionado, he bought in to this whole implacable gene-warrior bullshit that goes with it. But it's Mars, Sevgi. It's hundreds of millions of kilometers of empty fucking space and no way to cross it without a license. Don't you understand what that does to all those fucking human imperatives Jacobsen goes on about? What it does to love and loyalty, and trust, and revenge? Mars isn't just another world, it's another fucking *life.* What happens there, stays there. You come back, you *leave it behind.* It's like a dream you wake up from. Gutierrez helped send me home. He isn't going to believe in a million years that I'd go back there just to kill him for what he did, let alone just to shake him down for you people."

"He might believe you'd order it done. Pay for someone else to do it at the other end."

"Someone who isn't scared of the *familias?*"

She hesitated a beat. "There are options that—".

"Yeah, yeah, I know. I don't doubt COLIN could rustle up a hit squad for me if your pal Norton makes the right calls. But I do my own killing, and Gutierrez knows that. I can't fake him out on that one. And Sevgi, you know what? Even if I thought I could do it—I won't."

The last word grated in his mouth, like braking on gravel. Sevgi felt her expression congeal. "Why not?"

"Because this is bullshit. We are being led around by the dick here, and it's got nothing to do with what may or may not have happened back on Mars. We are looking in the wrong places."

"I am not going back to Arequipa."

"Well then, let's start closer to home. Like maybe looking a little harder at your pal Norton."

Quiet dripped into the room. Sevgi folded her arms and leaned against the back of a chair.

"And what the fuck is that supposed to mean?"

He shrugged. "Work it out for yourself. Who else knew where I was sleeping in New York the morning the skaters jumped us? Who called you the same time we were getting hijacked on the way to Arequipa? Who dragged us all the way back here to look at a fucking four-month-drowned lead when we were just about to start getting somewhere?"

"Oh," She gestured helplessly. "*Fuck* off, Marsalis. Coyle was right, this is pure thirteen paranoia."

"Is it?" Marsalis came to his feet with a jolt. He stalked toward her. "Think about it, Ertekin. Your n-djinn searches have failed. They didn't find the link between Ward and Merrin, they didn't find Gutierrez. Everything we've found since I started shaking the tree points to a cover-up, and Norton is ideally placed to pull it off. He's fucking perfect for it."

"You shut the fuck up, Marsalis." Sudden rage. "You know *nothing* about Tom Norton. *Nothing!*"

"I know men like him." He was in her face, body so close she seemed to feel the warmth coming off it. "They were all over the Osprey project from as young as I can remember. They dress well and they talk soft and they smile like they're doing it for the society pages. And when the time comes, they'll order the torture and slaughter of women and children without blinking because at core they *do not* give a shit about anything but their own agenda. And *you*, you people hand control over to them every *fucking* time, because in the end you're just a bunch of fucking sheep looking for an owner."

"Yeah, well." The anger shifted, sluggish in her guts. Intuitive reflex, maybe the years with Ethan, told her how to use it, kept her voice nailed-down detached. "If they ran Osprey, then I'd say *you* people handed over control to them pretty neatly, too."

It was like pulling a plug.

You can feel a good shot, an NYPD firearms instructor told her once, early on in training. *Like you and the target and the gun and the slug are all part of this one mechanism. Shoot like that, you'll know you've hit the guy before you even see him go down.*

Like that. The anger drained almost visibly out of Marsalis. Though he didn't move at all, somehow he seemed to step away.

"I was eleven," he said quietly.

And then he did walk away, without looking back, and closed the door and left her alone with the dead LCLS screen.

CHAPTER 35

"**S**he's not your mother," *the pale-eyed uncle in the suit tells him.*

"Yes," *he says, pointing through the chain link at Marisol.* "That one."

"No." *The uncle places himself in Carl's line-of-sight, leaning back against the fence so that it sags, makes a springy, shivery sound as it takes his weight. There's a careless, hard-buffet wind coming in off the sea, and the uncle pitches his voice to beat it.* "None of them is a mother, Carl. They just work here, looking after you. They're just aunts."

Carl looks up at him angrily. "I don't believe you."

"I know you don't," *the uncle says, and there seems to be something in his face, as if he's not feeling very well.* "But you will. This is a big day for you, Carl. Climbing that mountain was just the start of it."

"Have we got to go up there again?" *He tries to ask the question casually, but there's a tremor in his voice. The mountain was scary in a way none of the uncles' games so far has been. It wasn't just that there were parts where you could easily fall and kill yourself, and that this time they had no ropes; it was the feeling he had that the uncles were watching him closely when it came to those parts, and that they weren't watching to see if he was okay, that they didn't really care if he was okay, they only wanted to know if he was scared or not. And that was even scarier because he didn't know whether he should be scared or not, didn't know if they'd want him to be scared or not (though he didn't think that was likely). And besides, now it's getting late and while Carl's pretty confident he can do the climb again, he doesn't think he could do it in the dark.*

The uncle forces a smile. "No. Not today. But there are some other things we have to do. So you've got to come back inside with the others now."

On the other side of the chain link and the multiple razor-wire coils beyond, Marisol has moved across the helicopter landing apron so he can see her past the uncle's obstructing bulk. She's staring at him, but she doesn't raise her hand or call out. She stood and kissed him that morning, he recalls, before the uncles came to collect him, held his head between her hands and looked into his face intently, the way she sometimes did when he'd gotten cuts and scrapes from fighting. Then, hurriedly, she let him go and turned away. She made a soft sound in her throat, reached up and fiddled with the way she'd fixed her hair, as if it were coming loose, and then of course it was coming loose because she'd fiddled with it and now she really did have to fix it again the way she always . . .

He recognized the signals. But he just couldn't see how he'd made her cry this time. He hadn't been in a fight with any of the other kids for at least a week. He hadn't mouthed off to an uncle for even longer. His room was tidy, his schoolwork was gold-starred in everything except math and blade weapons, and both Uncle David and Mr. Sessions said he was improving even in those. He'd helped in the kitchen most evenings that week, and when he burned himself on the edge of a pan the day before, he'd shrugged it off with one of the control techniques they were working through in Aunt Chitra's pain-management class, and he could see in Marisol's eyes how proud she was of that.

So why?

He racked his brains on the way out to the mountain, but couldn't find an answer. Marisol didn't cry often, and she didn't cry without reason at all, except that once, he would have been about five or six, he came home from school with a raft of questions about money, how did some people end up with more than others, did uncles get more than aunts, did you *have* to have it, and would you ever do something you really, *really* didn't like to get some. That time she cried out of nowhere, suddenly, still talking to him at first as the tears rushed up out of her, before she could turn away and hide them.

He knows, knew then as well, that the other mothers cried like this sometimes, for reasons no one could work out, and of course Rod Gordon's mother had to go away in the end because she kept doing it. But he'd always been vaguely sure that Marisol wasn't like that, that she was different, the same way he was absently proud of how dark her skin was, how her teeth glowed white in her face when she smiled, the way she sang in Spanish about the house. Marisol is something special, he knows. Discovers it, in fact, for the first time now, wisps of knowledge, taken for granted, taken on trust, coalescing suddenly into a solid chunk of understanding that sits in his chest like damage. She jumps into sudden focus in his mind. He sees her across the chain link and razor wire, as if for the first time.

She raises her hand, slowly, as if she's in a class and not sure whether she really knows the answer or not. Waves to him.

"I want to talk to her," he says to the uncle.

"I'm afraid you can't, Carl."

"I want to."

The uncle straightens up off the fence, frowning. The chain link rebounds with another metallic shiver. "You already know not to talk like that. Your wishes are very small things in this world, Carl. You are valuable because of what you can do, not because of what you want."

"Where are you taking her?"

"She's going away." The uncle stands over him. "They all are. She's done her job now, so she's going home."

It's what he already knew, somehow, but still the words are like the slap of the wind in his face, buffeting, robbing him of breath. He feels the strength in his legs drain out, his stance shift fractionally on the worn concrete beneath his feet. He wants to fall down, or at least sit down somewhere, but knows better than to show it. He stares out across the huddled structures of the Osprey Eighteen settlement, the cottages in tidy rows, the schoolhouse and dining hall, lights just starting to come on here and there as the afternoon tips toward evening. The bleak undulations of coastal moorland under a darkening pewter sky, the distant rise of mountains worn smooth and low with age. The cold Atlantic behind it all to the north.

"This is her home," he tries to convince himself.

"Not anymore."

Carl looks suddenly up into the man's face. At eleven, he's already tall for his age; the uncle tops him by barely half a head.

"If you take her, I'm going to kill you," he says, this time with conviction as deep as all his sudden knowledge about Marisol.

The uncle punches him flat.

It's a short, swift blow, into the face—later he'll find it's split the skin across his cheekbone—and the surprise alone puts him on the ground. But when he bounces to his feet, the way he's been taught, comes back with his rage fully unleashed, the uncle blocks him and hits him again, right fist deep in under the base of his ribs so he can't breathe. He staggers back and the uncle follows, chops left-handed into the side of his neck with a callused palm edge and puts him down a second time.

He hits the ground, whooping for air he can't find. He's fallen facing away from the helicopter apron and Marisol. His body hinges convulsively on the asphalt, trying to turn over, trying to breathe. But the uncle knows his pressure points and has found them with effortless accuracy. Carl can barely twitch, let alone move. Behind him, he thinks Marisol must be rushing toward him, but there's the razor wire, the chain link, the other aunts and uncles . . .

The uncle crouches down in his field of vision and scrutinizes the damage he's done. He seems satisfied.

"You don't talk to any of us like that, ever again," he says calmly. "First of all be-

cause everything you have ever had, including the woman you think is your mother, was provided by us. You just remember that, Carl, and you show a little gratitude, a little respect. Everything you are, everything you've become, and everything you will become, you owe to us. That's the first reason. The second reason is that if you ever do speak to one of us like that again, I personally will see to it that you get a punishment beating that'll make what we had to do to Rod Gordon look like a game of knuckles. Do you understand that?"

Carl just glares back at him through brimming eyes. The uncle sees it, sighs, and gets back to his feet.

"In time," he says from what seems like a great height, "you will understand."

And in the distance, the waxing, hurrying chunter of the helicopter transport, coming in across the autumn sky like a harvester scything down summer's crop.

He drifted awake in a bed he didn't know, among sheets that emanated the scent of a woman. A faint grin touched his mouth, something to offset the bitter aftertaste of the Osprey memories.

"Bad dream?" Rovayo asked him from across the room.

She sat a couple of meters off in a deep sofa under the window, curled up and naked apart from a pair of white briefs, reading from a projected display headset. Streetlight from outside lifting a soft sheen from the ebony curves of her body, the line of one raised thigh, the dome of a knee. Recollection slammed into him like a truck—the same body twined around him as he knelt upright on the bed and held her buttocks in his hands like fruit and she lifted herself up and down on his erection and made, again and again, a long, deep noise in her throat like someone tasting food cooked to perfection.

He sat up. Blinked and stared at the darkness outside the window. Sense of dislocation—it felt wrong.

"How long was I out?"

"Not long. An hour, maybe." She tipped off the headset and laid it aside on the back of the sofa, still powered up. Tiny panels of blue light glowed in the eye frames, like the sober gaze of a robot chaperone. She shook back her hair and grinned at him. "I figured you earned the downtime."

"Fucking jet lag." He remembered vaguely the last thing, long after her hands and mouth could no longer get him to rise to the occasion, lying with his head pillowed on her thigh, breathing in the odor of her cunt as if it were the sea. "My time sense is shot to pieces. So looked like I was having a bad dream, huh?"

"Looked like you were wrestling Haystack Harrison for the California title, if you really want to know. You were thrashing all over the place." She yawned,

stretched, and stood up. "Would have woken you up myself, but they say it's better to let something like that play out, let the trigger images discharge fully or
something. You don't remember what you were dreaming?"

He shook his head and lied. "Not this time."

"Well then, maybe you were dreaming about me." She put her hands on her
hips. Another grin. "Going a fifth round, you know."

He matched the grin. "Don't know, I think I'm pretty fully beaten into submission right now."

"Yeah, I guess you are," she said reflectively. "You certainly seemed like a guy
knew what he wanted."

He couldn't argue with that—self-ejected from the screening room, tight with
anger at Ertekin, he'd stood in the center of the operations space and when he'd
spotted Rovayo propped on the edge of her desk and watching him, he'd drifted
toward her like a needle tugging north.

"Problems?" she asked neutrally.

"You could say that."

She nodded. Leaned back across her desk space to the datasystem and
punched in a quit code. Looked back at him, dark eyes querying.

"Want to get a drink?"

"That's exactly what I want," he said grimly.

They left, rode an elevator stack up through the levels of the Alcatraz station
until they could see sky and water through the windows. It felt like pressure easing. On the upper balconies, Rovayo led him to a franchise outfit called Lima
Alpha that had chairs and tables with views across the bay. She got heavily loaded
pisco sours for them both, handed him his, and sank into the chair opposite with
a fixed, speculative gaze. He sipped the cocktail, had to admit it was pretty good.
His anger started to ebb. They talked about nothing much, drank, soaked in the
late-afternoon sunlight. Slipped at some point from Amanglic into Spanish.
Their postures eased, sank lower in their chairs. Neither of them made an obvious move.

Finally, Rovayo's phone wittered for attention. She grimaced, hauled it out,
and held it to her ear, audio only.

"Yeah, what?" She listened, grimaced again. "On my way home, why?"

A male voice rinsed tinnily out of the phone, distant and indistinct.

"Roy, I haven't been home in thirty, no wait"—she checked her watch—
"thirty-five hours. I haven't slept in twelve, and that was ninety minutes on the
couch in operations . . ."

Crackled dispute. Rovayo glowered.

". . . No, it fucking wasn't . . ."

Coyle crackled some more. She cut him off.

"Look, don't try to tell me how much sleep I've had, Roy. You don't . . ."

Spit, spit, crack.

"Yeah, you're right, we *are* all tired, and when you're this fucking tired, Roy, you know what you do? You get some sleep. I'm not going to pull another macho all-nighter just so you can play at old-school cop with Tsai. Outside of all those pre-mil period flicks you love so much, nobody cracks a case like that. You guys want to act like the New Math never fucking happened, be my guest. I'm going home."

A more muted crackling. Rovayo glanced across at Carl and raised an eyebrow.

"No," she said flatly. "Haven't seen him. Doesn't he have a phone? No? Well, try his hotel, maybe. See you in the morning."

She killed the call.

"People are looking for you," she said.

"Oh."

"Yeah. You want to be found?"

"Not particularly."

"What I thought." She drained what was left in her glass and gave him the speculative look again. "Well, I'd say your hotel is a bust right now. Want another drink at my place?"

He gave her back the look. "Is that a trick question?"

Alcatraz station ran smart-chopper shuttles for its staff, twenty-four seven to both sides of the bay. The Oakland service dropped off at a couple of points within an easy walk of Rovayo's apartment. They walked, easily, pisco sours and the shared sense of truancy, laughing in the early-evening air. She asked him how come he spoke Spanish, he told her a little about Marisol, a little more about Mars and the Upland projects. As before, she seemed hungry for the detail. They touched, far more than her Hispanic background could write off as a cultural norm. Signals coming through clear and tight. They got up the stairs and in the door of her second-floor apartment a couple of grins short of the clinch.

The door swung shut behind them with a solid snap and the burble of electronic security engaging.

Their restraint shattered in hungry pieces on the floor.

"So what do you want to do now?"

Still standing in front of him, hipshot, wide grin. Despite everything, he felt his sore and shrunken prick twitch at the sight.

"I thought you were tired."

She shrugged. "So did I. Cyclical, I guess. Give me another couple of hours, I probably will be again."

"You're not Xtrasoming on me, are you?"

"No, I'm not fucking Xtrasoming on you." Suddenly there was a real edge in her voice. "Do I look like I come from that kind of money? You think if my parents had the finance for built-in, I'd be working for RimSec?"

He blinked. Held up his hands, palms out. "Okay, okay. It was just a thought. Rim States have got a reputation for that stuff, you know."

She wasn't listening. She gestured at herself with one splayed hand, motion robbed of any sensuality by the look on her face. "What I've got, I was either born with or I fucking worked to build. I came up through the ranks, it's taken me eight years to make detective, and I didn't take any fucking genetic shortcuts along the way. I didn't have—"

"I said *okay*, Detective."

It stopped her. She sank back onto the sofa, sat hunched at the edge with her arms resting on her thighs, hands dangling into the space between. She lifted her head to look at him, and there was something hunted in her expression.

"Sorry," she muttered. "We're all just a little fucking tired of the Asia Badawis and the Meredith Changs around here."

"Badawi's New York Sudanese," he pointed out.

"Yeah? You want to see the house she's got down the coast. Lot of fucking acreage for a foreigner. Anyway, that's not what I meant."

"No?" Suddenly the postcoital intimacy was too tight, like binding on his limbs and a masking film across his face. Rovayo was abruptly the stranger she'd always been, but naked and in too close. He felt an unlooked-for visceral surge of nostalgia for sex with Sevgi Ertekin. "So you're not a big fan of enhancement generally, then?"

She snorted. "You think *anyone's* a big fan of Xtrasomes that doesn't have them?"

"I am" But he knew at base he was trying to provoke her. "You think I'd be in this fucking mess if they'd had working artificial chromosome technology for humans forty years back? You think we'd be running around looking for some superannuated supersoldier turned cannibal fucking survivalist if thirteen tendency could be platform-loaded and switched on and off at need? Take a good look at me, Rovayo. I'm the walking fucking embodiment of last century's pre-Xtrasome jump-the-gun genetics."

"I know."

"I seriously doubt that." Carl lifted fingertips to his face, brushed at his cheek-bones. "You see this? When you're a variant, people don't look at this. They go right through the skin, and all they see is what's written into your double helix."

The Rim cop shrugged. "Perhaps you'd prefer them to stop at the skin. What I hear about the old days, we're both the wrong color for that to be a better option. Would you really prefer it the way things were? A dose of good old-fashioned skin hate?"

"I already had my dose of that. I was banged up in a Jesusland jail for the best part of four months, remember."

She widened her eyes. It made her look frighteningly young. Ertekin, he thought, would have just raised one quizzical eyebrow.

"You did *four months* in there? I thought—"

"Yeah, long story. Point is, you talk too easily about this shit, Rovayo. Until you've lived inside a locked and modified gene code, you can't know what it's like. You can't know how happy you'd be to have an Xtrasome on-off switch to fall back on."

"You don't think?" Rovayo bent and swooped an arm to the floor beside the sofa, hooked up her discarded shirt, and shouldered her way into it. Her eyes never left his face the whole time. It made him feel suddenly untrustworthy, an intruder into her home. She thumb-pressed the garment's static seam halfway closed, enough to pull it over her breasts and hide them. "What do you really know about me, Marsalis? I mean, *really* know?"

He tasted the smart-mouth retorts on his tongue, swallowed them unspoken. Maybe she saw.

"Yeah, I know we've fucked. Please tell me you don't think *that* means anything."

He gestured. "Well, I wasn't planning to propose."

It got him a thin, unamused smile. "Yeah. Thing is, Marsalis." She sat back in the sofa. "I'm a bonobo."

He stared. "No, you're fucking not."

"No? What did you think, we're all sari-wrapped housewives or geisha bunnies? Or maybe you were expecting the giggly slut model, like that stupid fucking whore ranch they got down in Texas?"

"No, but—"

"I'm not full. My mother's the hundred percent deal, she used to work escort for a Panama agency, met my father when he was on a fishing trip down there. He smuggled her out."

"Then you're not a bonobo."

"Half of me is." Said defiantly, jaw tight, eyes locked with his. "Read your Jacobsen. *Inherited traits will be an unknown factor for generations to come.* Quote, unquote."

Something happened to the room. A dense, deafening quiet sat behind her voice, washed in like a tide when she stopped talking.

"Does Coyle know?" he asked, for something to break the stillness.

"What do you think?"

And quiet again.

Finally, her mouth crimped at one corner. "I don't know," she said slowly. "I look at what I am, the way I react to things, and then I look at *her*, and I just don't know. My old man tells me she never fit in down there, never was submissive the way bonobos are supposed to be. He says that she was different from all the others, that's why he picked her out. I don't know whether to believe that shit or write it off to rose-tinted romantic fucking nostalgia."

Carl thought back to the bonobos he'd seen in the transit camps in Kuwait and Iraq, the ones you couldn't get away from on R&R in Thailand and Sri Lanka. Some that he'd talked to, one or two he'd fucked. And back in London, Zooly's friend from the club, Krystalayna, who always claimed she was but never showed him any proof that wasn't fan-site fantasy bullshit.

"I think," he said carefully, "you don't want to confuse submissive with maternal or nonviolent. Most of the bonobos I ever ran into knew how to get what they wanted about as well as anyone else."

"Yeah." Violence rose simmering in her voice. "I know how to give a pretty good blow job myself. Don't you think?"

"That's not what I meant."

"You know what it feels like, Marsalis? Constantly testing your actions against some theory of how you think you might be supposed to behave. Wondering, every day at work, every time you make a compromise, every time you back up one of your male colleagues on reflex, wondering whether that's you or the gene code talking." A sour smile in Carl's direction. "Every time you fuck, the guy you chose to fuck *with*, even the *way* you fuck him, all the things you do, the things you want to do, the things you want done to you. You know what it feels like to question all of that, *all the time*?"

He nodded. "Of course I do. You just pretty much described where I live."

"I'm a good cop," she said urgently. "You don't last in RimSec if you're not. I've shot and killed three men in the line of duty, I don't lose sleep over any of them. I mean, I got sick at the time, went through the counseling like everyone else, but after that I was fine. I've got commendations, early promotion to special cases, clearance rates that—"

"Rovayo, stop it." He held up a hand, surprised at how weary the sudden mirroring of his younger self in her was making him feel. "I told you, I know. But you're going about this the wrong way. You don't have to justify yourself to anyone except you. In the end, that's all that matters."

She smiled the hard, humorless smile again. "Spoken like a true variant thirteen. Pretty obvious you've never had to face a genetic suitability assessor."

"I thought in the Rim—"

"Yeah, Rim States citizens have a lot of rights that way. But citizen or not, I've still got my Jacobsen license to live with. And before you say it, yes, that is confidential data, Charter-protected up the ass. But you waive your right to that protection when you sign up for RimSec."

"And Coyle still doesn't know about you?"

"No. Assessment comes as part of the standard officer vetting procedure. There's no way for anyone to know I went through anything different from all the other grunts. Tsai knows, he's my commanding officer, he'll have the file. And there are a few others at divisional level, the ones who were on the vetting committee. But it's more than any of their jobs are worth to let something like that leak."

"You think if Coyle knew, he'd care?"

"I don't know. You tell all your friends what you are?"

"I'm a thirteen," he said with a straight face. "We don't have any friends."

She made the effort, laughed. There was some genuine amusement in it this time. "That why you're here?"

"I'd have thought my reasons for being here were transparently obvious."

"Well." She tilted her head to one side. "I guess you did explain yourself pretty thoroughly earlier, yeah."

"Thanks."

"Question remains, though." Her stance opened a little. She crossed one long ebony thigh over the other, bounced her foot up and down lightly at the end of the raised leg, and spread her arms cruciform along the back of the sofa. "What do you want to do now?"

He smiled.

"Got an idea," he said.

CHAPTER 36

Seen from the descending autocopter, *Bulgakov's Cat* had the blunt, blocky look of a nighttime skyscraper chopped off across its base and floated lengthwise on the ocean. Lights festooned every segment of the factory raft's structure, studded its aerials and dishes, marked out landing pads and open-air sports arenas along the upper levels. Carl picked out a baseball diamond, a soccer pitch, a scattering of basketball courts and softly underlit swimming pools, some half of which appeared to be in use. Like most of its floating sisters, the raft sold itself on being a twenty-four-hour city, a pulsing engine of production, employment, and leisure whose reactor-powered heart never missed a beat. The publicity specs said she was home to thirty thousand people, not including the tourists. Just looking down at her made Carl feel itchy and sociopathic.

In the next seat, Alicia Rovayo yawned cavernously and shot him a sour look over her turned-up jacket collar. "I can't fucking believe I let you talk me into this."

"You asked what I wanted to do."

"Yeah." She leaned across his lap to peer out of the cabin port. "Not quite what I had in mind at the time."

The autocopter swung closer, made a courtesy circuit before touchdown so its decals could be read by sight and not just by machines. Carl picked out individual figures on a basketball court, shadowed forms plowing laps up and down in the tranquil, rippling lights of the pools.

"Think of it as an intuitive leap," he said absently.

"I'm thinking of it as a paranoid fantasy outing. Which is exactly the way it's going to look when I have to write up the chopper time. I told you, Donaldson and Kodo came down here yesterday and talked to these people. Got the interviews and the report on file. We're wasting our time. Long flight for nothing."

"Yeah, that's something else you might want to think about. *Cat* there is still a couple of hundred klicks off optimum range for maintenance on Ward's spread. How come they rushed up here to do it now instead of waiting until next week?"

"How the fuck would I know?" she grumbled. "Maybe if you'd accessed the file instead of insisting on coming down here personally, you'd already have an answer."

"Yeah, I'd have an answer. I'd have whatever lie Daskeen Azul have decided to tell you to cover themselves. That's not what I want."

Rovayo rolled her eyes. "Like I said. Fucking paranoid."

The autocopter found its designated landing pad, exchanged brief electronic chatter with the traffic-management systems, and floated down to land with characteristic, inhuman perfection. The cabin hatch hinged open, and Carl jumped down. Rovayo followed him, still mutinous.

"Just don't break anything," she said.

Daskeen Azul had an unremarkable mall frontage somewhere amidships for direct client contact and a couple of elevator-served workshops down in the hull where they kept the submarine hardware. They subcontracted landing pad time and aircraft support through a secondary provider, but had their own surface and sub vessels moored in dry dock, aft and starboard. This much Rovayo could tell him off the top of her head, detail skimmed from what she remembered of Donaldson and Kodo's briefing. There was more in the file, and in theory they could have requested it via the autocopter's datahead, but the Rim cop seemed disinclined to use the machine systems more than they already were—was already, it seemed, regretting the way they'd requisitioned the transport with her Special Cases badge—and Carl didn't much care one way or the other. He had more than enough to work with.

So they flagged their business aboard *Bulgakov's Cat* as simple follow-up investigation, which the autocopter told the factory raft's datahead, and the Rim Security protocols did the rest. Technically, vessels like the *Cat* were autonomous nation-states, but any nation-state that lived so solidly from niche entry into the hyperdynamic Rim States economy had to live with the political realities the relationship entailed. *Bulgakov's Cat* cruised freely in and out of the Rim's coastal jurisdiction, its citizens had right of access to Rim States soil, its contracts were legally enforceable in Rim courts—but it all came at a stiff colonial price. Rovayo led Carl along the promenades and corridors of the factory raft with a proprietorial lack of self-consciousness and an authorized, loaded gun beneath her jacket. They might have been taking a stroll inside Alcatraz station for all the tension she showed. They'd spoken to no one when they came aboard, notified no one, taken no courtesy measures whatsoever at a human level. Somewhere in the walls, the machines whispered to one another about them in incomprehensible electronic tones, but beyond that they came on Daskeen Azul unannounced.

"And at this time of night," the Daskeen Azul front desk agent complained, with barely disguised irritation. "I mean, our usual hours of business—"

"—are not my problem," Rovayo told him crisply. "We're here for follow-up on a RimSec murder investigation, and the last I heard *Bulgakov's Cat* was a twenty-four-hour service community. You've seen my ID, so how about you roll out some of that twenty-four-hour service and answer my questions."

The agent switched his eyes to Carl. "And he is?"

"Getting impatient," Carl said impassively.

"I've seen no ID," the agent insisted. Below the smooth upper shelf of the reception desk, his hands were busy pressing buttons. "I have to see ID for both of you."

Rovayo leaned on the shelf.

"Did your mother get you this job?" she asked curiously.

The agent gaped at her, belated anger dropping his jaw for a retort he wasn't fast enough to make.

"Because it appears to be a job you don't feel any pressing need to do properly. This man is a private consultant for Rim Security and his liaison is with me, not you. I've shown you my fucking ID, sonny, and in about another ten seconds I'm going to be showing you the front end of a RimSec probable-cause shutdown order. Now either you're going to answer my questions or you're going to get someone better paid out of bed to do it for you. I don't much care either way, so which is it going to be?"

The man behind the desk flinched as if slapped.

"I'll just see," he muttered, prodding more buttons on the screens beneath his hands. "Just, please, just, uhm, have a seat."

"Thank you," said Rovayo with heavy irony.

They folded themselves into the utilitarian bank of chairs opposite the desk. The reception agent fit a phone hook to his ear, muttered into it. Outside, on the broad sweep of the mall, a thin but unending nighttime herd of shoppers browsed past the open storefronts, clothing bright, gait unhurried and undirected, like sleepwalkers or the victims of some multiple hypnotic trick. Carl sat and tried, the way Sutherland had taught him, not to feel the usual seeping contempt. It wasn't easy.

On Mars . . .

Yeah, like fuck.

On Mars, things are different because they have to be, soak. Lopsided grin, like he was giving away some secret he shouldn't. *But that's strictly temporary. No more long-term truth in it than all that bullshit they sell in the qualpro ads. Day's going to come, this place'll be just like home only less gravity. It's them, Carl. It's the humans. Take 'em wherever and give 'em time, they'll build you the same fairy fucking playground as ever was. And that's the construct you got to live inside, soak, like it or like it not.*

A slim, elegantly dressed woman emerged from an inner door behind the front desk. Tailored jacket and slacks in olive green and black, just a chic hint of work coveralls about the ensemble. Striking looks, strong on Chinese genes but salted with something else. She leaned down beside the reception agent, spoke briefly in low tones, then looked up again. Carl met her eyes from across the room and saw a depth of calm there that told him they'd just gone up an entire level. He saw something that might have been an acknowledgment in the return gaze; then the woman straightened up and came around the side of the desk toward them. She walked like a dancer, like a combat pro.

Carl came to his feet, on automatic, the way he would have if someone in the room had pulled a gun.

The new arrival saw it and smiled a little. It hit him secondarily, riding in past the wave of caution, that she was very beautiful in that Rim-blended, Asia Pacific fashion you saw in Freeport movie stars and major female political figures up and down the West Coast. She put out her hand, offered to Carl first. The grip and the look that backed it up were both coolly evaluative. Shaking hands with Rovayo was strictly a side issue, a formality dealt with and then set aside.

"Good evening," she said. "I'm Carmen Ren, assistant duty manager. I must apologize for the way you've been received. We're all still a little shaken from our discovery up at Ward BioSupply. But of course, we want to cooperate fully with the investigation. Please come with me."

She led them back through the door she'd used, through cramped storage space racked with shelves of underwater equipment and other less identifiable hardware. On the far side of one sparsely loaded freestanding unit, Carl glimpsed two commercial-size elevator hatches set into a sidewall. A faint sea-salt dampness hung about in the air. At the back, the storeroom had another door that opened into an office cubicle where Carmen Ren gestured them to the two visible chairs and pulled down a third, folding seat from the wall. They sat with knees almost touching. The Chinese woman looked back and forth between them.

"So then," she said brightly. "I'd been given to understand that your colleagues had all the information they needed, but clearly that's not the case. So what is it I can do for you?"

Rovayo looked over at Carl and nodded with ironic largesse. She was still visibly fuming from their reception at the front desk and the subtle relegation Ren had dealt her. Carl shrugged and stepped up.

"Ward BioSupply's fields are a good two hundred kilometers northwest of here," he said. "Nearer three hundred, when you went up there two days ago. You mind telling us why you didn't hold off until the *Cat* got a little closer?"

"Well." Carmen Ren gestured apologetically. "I wasn't the duty manager for that shift, so it's not a question I can answer fully. But we quite often do attend to a contract ahead of time that way. It depends more on staffing rotations, hardware overhaul, that kind of thing, than actual proximity. As you'll probably know from our promotional literature, Daskeen Azul has an operational deployment radius of up to five hundred kilometers should the need arise."

"And the need arose here."

"So it appears, yes. Though, as I said—"

Rovayo joined the play. "Yeah, you weren't on duty. We heard you. So who was?"

"I would really need to check the duty logs to be certain." A hint of reproach tinged Ren's voice. "But I'm reasonably sure that the officers who visited us yesterday will already have that information."

Carl ignored the significant look he was getting from Rovayo.

"I'm not concerned with what you told Donaldson and Kodo," he said bluntly. "I'm looking for Allen Merrin."

Ren frowned, genuine puzzlement or immaculate control. "Alan . . . ?"

"Merrin," said Rovayo.

"Alan Merrin." Ren nodded seriously, kept to the slightly vowel-heavy mispronunciation of the first name. "I'm afraid we don't have an employee of that name. Or a client, as far as I'm aware. I could—"

Carl smiled. "I'm not a policeman, Ren. Don't make that mistake with me. I'm here for Merrin. If you don't give him up, I'll go through you to get him. Your choice but one way or another, it's going to get done. He can skulk about America, hiding in the crowd like a cudlip if he wants, but it isn't going to save him. This game is over. Next time you hear from him, you can tell him that from me."

Ren let go a small, sliding breath, the sound of politeness embarrassed. "And you are, exactly?"

"Who I am isn't very important. You can call me Marsalis, if it matters. *What* I am, well." He watched her face closely. "I'm a variant thirteen, just like your pal Merrin. You can tell him that, too, if you like."

A defensive smile hesitated at the corners of the woman's mouth. Her eyes slipped sideways to Rovayo, as if in appeal.

"I'm afraid I really don't know who you're referring to with this Merrin. And, Detective Rovayo, I have to say that your colleague here is being considerably less well mannered than the two officers who preceded you."

"He's not my colleague," said Rovayo indifferently. "And I don't think he's that bothered about manners, either. I'd start cooperating if I were you."

"We are already cooperating fully with—"

"You put in to Lima on your way up here," Carl asked her. "Right?"

This time, he thought the frown was genuine. "*Bulgakov's Cat* very rarely *puts in*, as you express it, anywhere. We are dry-docked in the Angeline Freeport on average every five years, but otherwise—"

"I'm not talking about the *Cat*. I'm talking about Daskeen Azul. You got friends on the Peruvian coast, right?"

"I, personally, do not. No. But it may be that some of our employees do. *Bulgakov's Cat* is, as I'm sure you're aware, licensed for the whole of the Pacific Americas Rim. And Daskeen Azul certainly has contracts along the Peruvian segment. As do many of our fellow companies aboard. But this, all of this, is common knowledge—you could have ascertained it using any corporate commerce register for the region."

"Seen Manco Bambarén recently? Or Greta Jurgens?"

Another elegant furrowing of the clean white brow. Lips pursed, regretful shaking of the head. Her long glossy hair shifted in sheaves. "I'm sorry, these names. None of them is familiar to me. And I'm still not clear exactly what—if anything—you are accusing us of."

"What are they paying you, Ren?"

Pause. The brief smile again. "I really don't think, Mr. Marsalis, that my salary is any of your—"

"No, really. Give it some thought. I think the people I represent would make it worth your while to turn. And this is coming down around you anyway. We don't have enough yet, but we will. And when Merrin breaks cover, I'll be there. You don't want to get caught in that particular crossfire, believe me."

"Are you trying to scare me, Mr. Marsalis?"

"No, I'm appealing to your sense of reality. I don't think you scare easily, Ren. But in the end, I think you're smart enough to recognize when it's time to cut cable and bounce." He held her gaze. "That time is now."

The polite, sliding-breath sound again. "I don't really know how to respond to that. You're attempting to . . . bribe me?" Another shuttled glance at Rovayo. "Into what, exactly? Is this standard RimSec procedure these days?"

"I already told you I'm not a cop, Ren. I'm just like you. For hire and—"

Ren shot to her feet, clean and rapid motion, no leverage with either arm on the furniture around her. In the confined office space, it was a remarkable piece of physical precision. She brought loosely cupped fists together at her chest, a formal stance that echoed dojo training.

"That's it," she flared. "This conversation is over. I have been as cooperative as possible, Detective Rovayo, and all I have received in return are innuendo and insult. I will not be compared to some . . . *variant* in this way. Take your offensive, genetically enhanced friend, and get out. If you wish to speak to me again, you will contact our legal representatives."

"Think that was for real?" Rovayo asked him as they walked back to the landing pad. She was still fingering the tiny lawyer's card Ren had handed her.

Carl shook his head. "She wanted us out of there, and she hooked the best opportunity there was to shut us down fast."

"Yeah. What I thought."

"If she's a Daskeen Azul duty manager, then I'm a fucking bonobo. You see the moves on her?"

Rovayo nodded reluctantly.

"Still think I'm paranoid?"

"I think you—"

And out of nowhere, a corner in the mall, shoppers still around them, out of the fractured crowd, out of the sweet piped Muzak and murmur, suddenly a panicked bystander screamed, and then the figure leaped, tall and lean, distorted face around the gut-deep yell, eyes blown wide with hate, and gunmetal glint of the machete hacking down.

CHAPTER 37

Scott Osborne had seen and heard enough.

Nearly five months of sitting on his hands, waiting because Carmen told him that was how it had to be. Months while *Bulgakov's Cat* churned up and down the coast of the Americas, coastline always out of sight, just below the horizon, like the harrowing that Carmen had promised was to come but hadn't still. Months adrift. Scott had never seen the ocean for real before he came to the Rim, and living afloat in the middle of it, week after landless week, didn't seem natural, never would. He bore it because he must, and because when Carmen came to him, it all seemed worth it. Lying with her afterward, he seemed to feel the approaching storm, and to accept it with the same comfortable ache he'd felt that last summer before he left for Bozeman and the fence run. It was the sense of your time running out, and the sudden value in everything you'd ordinarily take for granted, everything that would soon be swept away.

But the storm never came.

Instead they waited, and life aboard the factory raft took on the same dismal proportions as life anywhere else you tried to survive that wasn't home. He hung around Daskeen Azul, looking for things to do and taking on whatever work they'd give him. He kept out of the stranger's way—even now that he'd learned to call him Merrin, now that his knees no longer trembled when he looked into the hollow eyes—and he didn't ask when Merrin and Carmen disappeared together for long periods of time. But something was happening to the exhilaration he'd felt on the deserted airfield all those months ago, and it was something bad.

He didn't want to believe it was lack of faith, not again. He prayed, more now than he ever had even back home, and what he prayed for mostly was guidance, because what had seemed so clear back at the airfield with his head still bandaged and the fear fresh in his heart was slowly but surely giving way to a mess of conflicting voices in that selfsame head and heart. He *knew* the judgment was at hand, had at first derived an almost smug superiority among the other workers and shoppers aboard the *Cat* as he watched them living out what were probably the last months of their lives in ignorance. But that was fading fast. Now that same blissful ignorance rubbed at him like a badly fitting boot, irritated something deep inside that made him want to grab them by the throat as they browsed sheep-like through the glittery-lit glass storefronts of the mall, or sat on a break in the bowels of *Bulgakov's Cat* guffawing and barking like subnormals about what they'd give that slinky bitch Asia Badawi if they ever got in an elevator with her. He wanted to choke them, slap them, smash down their idiot complacency, scream into their faces *Don't you understand, it's time! He is coming, don't you see! You will be weighed in the balance and found wanting!*

He forced it down, deeper inside him. Prayed for patience, talked to Carmen.

But these days, even Carmen was not the refuge she had once been. When they slept together now, he sometimes felt an impatience smoking off her in the act, as if he were some awkward tangle of weed around a marker buoy on the Ward estates. She'd snapped at him a couple of times postcoital, apologized immediately of course, told him she was sorry, she was tired, yes, she was tired of waiting, too, but that was the way it had to be, it was a hard path for the, uh, the righteous.

And there was Merrin.

Now the terror of precarious faith came sweeping in for real, up along his arms, lifting the hair with a ghost caress. It pricked out sweat on his palms and swathed him in a cool dread, like standing over a precipice. *What if he was wrong?* What if Carmen was wrong, what if they all were? Merrin was out of sight so much, Scott had no way of knowing what he did with his time. But when he was there, it didn't feel like the presence of a Savior, of the King of Heaven come again in triumph. It was more like sharing v-time with a stripped-protocol 'face, one of the bare-bones chassis models you could buy off the rack and customize the way those kids he'd once shared a flop with in the Freeport were always doing. Merrin spoke little, answered questions even less, sat mostly wrapped in his own silence and staring out at the sea from whatever vantage point there was. It was like he'd never seen the ocean before, either, and for a while that gave Scott a warm feeling of kinship with the other man. He thought it might mean he could be a more worthy disciple.

Of course he knew to leave Merrin alone; Carmen had been clear on that if on nothing else. But every now and then, in the tight corridors and storage spaces of Daskeen Azul, he caught the stranger's eye and the returned gaze did nothing but chill him. And he never told Carmen, didn't dare tell her, about the time he'd come up behind Merrin at one of his ocean vigils and said, in as steady and respectful voice as he could manage, *Yeah, it got me that way when I first saw it, too. Just didn't seem possible, that much water in one place.* And Merrin whipped around on him like some bar tough whose drink he'd just spilled, only faster, so much inhumanly faster. And said nothing, nothing at all, just glared at him with the same blank unkindness in those eyes that Nocera had sometimes had, the same but not, because this time there was something in the eyes so deep, so cold, so distant that whatever else Scott believed about this man, he knew for certain that what Carmen Ren had told him was true, that Merrin really had come here across a gulf that nothing human could cross unprotected. He looked back into those eyes for the scant seconds he could bear to, and he felt the cold of it blowing over him as if Merrin's gaze were an open door into the void he'd crossed to get here.

Scott winced, he turned away, mumbling half-formed apologies.

He moved like a snake.

Walking away, he heard Merrin say something that sounded like *cunt lips,* knew it couldn't be those words, tried to put the encounter out of his mind. But the way the stranger had turned on him, the whiplash-speed and venom of it, would not go away. *He moves like a snake* ran in his thoughts like dripping poison. He could not reconcile it with what he wanted to believe.

Judgment means what it says, Pastor William had always warned them. *You think the Lord is gonna come like some bleeding-heart UN liberal and make us all love one another? No, sir, He will come in judgment and vengeance for those who defile His gifts. Like it says in the Good Book itself* —the big, black, limp-cover Bible brandished aloft— *Think not that I am come to send peace on earth; I come not to send peace but a sword. Yes, sir, when the Lord comes, He will be wrathful and those who have not walked in righteousness will know the terror of His justice.*

Terror, Scott could accept, could understand, but should the Savior of mankind really *move like a snake?*

Questions and doubts, coiling back and forth in his head, and Carmen withdrawing, cooler now with every time they lay together, drifting away from him. There'd been times recently when she simply didn't want him, shrugged him off, made excuses that convinced him less and less. He could see the time coming when—

And then, instead, the black man came.

"You stay out of it," Carmen snapped at him as she threw on clothes. "You don't make a move unless I call it, right?"

At the door of the tiny lower-deck apartment, she turned back, softened her voice with an effort he saw on her face.

"Sorry, Scott. It's just, you know how hard this is for all of us. Just let me handle it. It'll be fine."

So he watched on the monitors instead, and he saw the black man for himself. No doubt in his mind anymore; he felt the thud of certainty in his blood. The black man, betraying himself in his arrogance. *I'm not a policeman, Ren. Don't make that mistake with me. I'm here for Merrin. If you don't give him up, I'll go through you to get him. Your choice, but one way or another, it's going to get done.* Scott felt his previous confusion shrivel away. Regained conviction was a solid joy in his throat, a pulsing in his limbs.

And Carmen, showing no fear—his heart swelled with love and pride for her—but he knew the terror she must feel, there alone, facing the darkness. Carmen, brave enough to keep silent in the face of the black man's threats, to stand his presence, but not strong enough to do what needed to be done.

We have a part to play in this, Scott. You have a part.

And now he knew what it was.

The machete was cling-padded to a panel under the bed. He hadn't told Carmen, but he'd seen how it might come down, the enemy smashing in the door like the faceless helmeted UN police in End Times Volume I Issue 56, dragging them naked and defenseless from the bed.

He wouldn't go that way.

He dressed, pulled on a midlength deck coat with DASKEEN AZUL logos across back and sleeves. He freed the machete from its cling-pads, tucked it under the coat, under one arm. Checked himself in the mirror and saw that it worked—not enough to get past any kind of door with security on it, but in the incessant crowds of the shopping decks, more than enough to let him get close.

The rest was in God's hands.

He looked into the mirror, saw the taut determination his face threw back, and for just a moment it was as if it were Him, Merrin, looking out from behind Scott's eyes, lending him the force of will he'd need.

Scott murmured a swift prayer of thanks, and walked out to face the black man.

It was like the fucking Saudi opsdog all over again. Like Dudeck and the Aryans. Carl saw the eyes, locked with them on instinct, and it was the same blank, driven hatred that filled them. Who the fuck—

No time—the machete swung down. His attacker was a big guy, tall and reachy, the response wrote itself. Carl hurled himself forward, inside the chopping arc, blocked and stamped, took the fight to the ground. Against all expectation, the other man flailed like an upturned beetle. Carl got in with an elbow, stunning blow to the face, *tanindo* grasp on the machete arm, twist and the weapon clattered free. A knee came up and caught him in the groin, not full force but enough to half kill his strength. The other man was screaming at him, weird invective and what sounded like religious invocation. Hands came clawing for his throat. It was no kind of fighting Carl knew. He fended, expecting a trick. Got feeble repetition instead. He did the obvious thing, grabbed a finger and snapped it sideways. The invocation broke on a scream. Another long leg lashed at him, but he smothered it, kept hold of the snapped finger, twisted some more. His attacker screamed again, quivered like a gaffed fish. Carl had time to look down into the eyes again, saw no surrender there. He chopped down, into the side of the throat, pulled it a little at the last moment—he'd need to talk to this guy.

The fight died.

Rovayo circled in, gun drawn, leveled on the unmoving figure on the floor. Carl grunted around the ache in his balls, shot the pistol an ironic glance.

"Thanks. Little late for that."

"Is he dead?"

"Not yet." Carl levered himself to his feet, groaned again, glanced around. The gathered crowd gaped back. "Just him, huh?"

"Looks that way." Rovayo hauled an arm aloft, showed the holo in her palm to the spectators.

"RimSec," she stated it like a challenge. "Anyone work security around here?"

Hesitation, then a thickset uniform with blunt Samoan features shouldered his way through the others.

"I do."

"Good, you're deputized." She read the name off his chest ID. "Suaniu. Call this in, get some backup. The rest of you, give me some space."

On the floor, Carl's attacker coughed and flopped. They all looked. Carl saw suddenly that he was young, younger even than Dudeck had been. Barely out of his teens. He cast about and saw a cluster of carbon-fiber chairs and tables around a sushi counter that had closed for the night. He hauled the boy up by the lapels and dragged him toward the nearest chair. The crowd skittered back out of his path. The boy's eyes fluttered. Carl dumped him into the chair, settled him there, and slapped him hard across the face.

"Name?"

The boy gagged, tried to rub at his neck where Carl's stunning chop had gone home. The black man slapped him again.

"Name," he said again.

"You can't do that," said a woman's voice from the crowd. Australian twang to it. Carl turned his head, found her with a narrow look. Elegant olive-skinned shopper, early fifties, stick-thin. A couple of bags, ocher and green parcels, black cord handles, flicker ad for some franchise or other across the ocher in black Thai script.

His lip curled. "Haven't you got some shoes to go buy?"

"Fuck you, buddy." She wasn't backing down. "This isn't the Rim. You can't walk all over us like this."

"Thanks, I'll bear that in mind." Carl went back to the boy in the chair, back-handed him and got blood. "*Name.*"

"Marsalis," Rovayo was at his side. "That's enough."

"You think?"

Her voice dropped to a mutter. "She's right, this isn't the Rim. There's only so far we can push this."

Carl looked around. The Samoan security guard was talking into a phone, but his eyes were fixed on the boy and the black man standing over him. And the crowd had shuffled back when Rovayo ordered them to, but beyond that they were staying put. Carl guessed maybe one in ten had actually seen the fight, even less the machete attack that preceded it. The scenario was wide open for interpretation.

He shrugged. "You've got the gun."

"Yeah, I do. And I'm not about to start shooting these people with it."

"I don't think it'd come to that."

"Marsalis, forget it. I'm not—"

Spluttering cough. The boy in the chair floundered there, grasping the carbon-weave arms. His gaze was locked on Carl's face.

"Black man," he spat.

Carl glanced sideways at Rovayo. "Observant little fucker, isn't he."

The Rim cop grimaced and put herself between Carl and the chair. She showed the RimSec holo to the boy. "See that? Do you know how much trouble you're in, son?"

The boy glared back at her. "I know you lie for him. Authority out of Babylon, and black lies that shield the servants of Satan. I know who your master is."

"Oh great."

"Marsalis, shut up a minute." Rovayo closed her hand, stowed her gun, and scrutinized their prisoner with hands on hips. "You're from Jesusland, right? You're a fence hopper? You got any idea how quickly I can have you sent back there?"

"I do not answer to your laws. I do not bow down before Mammon and Belial. I have been chosen." In the crystalline lighting of the mall, the boy's face was pale and slick with sweat. "I have gone beyond."

"You certainly have," said Carl wearily.

"Marsalis!"

"Hey, he didn't come at *you* with the fucking machete."

The boy tried to stand. Rovayo stiff-armed him impatiently in the chest, sent the chair skidding back a little as he collapsed back into it.

"Sit down," she advised him.

Rage detonated in his eyes. His voice scaled upward.

"You are *false judges. False lawgivers, money changers, sunk in stinking sins of flesh and corruption.*" It was as if he were vomiting up something long suppressed. "*You will not lead me astray, you will not pre—*"

"You want me to shut him up?"

"*—vail, I am beyond your traps. Judgment—*"

"No, I fucking don't. I want—"

"*—is coming. He is* here! *He lives, in the flesh,* among us! *You know Him as* Merrin *but you know* nothing, *He is—*"

The tirade ebbed a little, lost some of its shrill rage, as Carl and Rovayo both stared down at the boy with fresh interest.

"*—the Commander of the legions of Heaven,*" he finished uncertainly.

"Merrin's *here?*" jerked out of Carl. "Aboard the *Cat?* Now?"

The boy's lips tightened. Carl switched gazes to Rovayo. She reached for her phone.

"Can you lock this place down?"

"On it." She was already dialing. She put the phone to her ear, looked at him as she listened. "Alcatraz can authorize a block on traffic in and out. Might have to get a couple of people out of bed to do it, but—"

The phone crickled audibly with scrambler protocols and then a voice. Rovayo cut across it.

"Alicia Rovayo, Special Cases. Print me, and then get me the Alcatraz duty officer."

Pause. Very deliberately, Carl turned his back on the boy in the chair. Casually, he asked, "Is that going to be satellite-enforceable?"

Rovayo nodded. "There's bound to be something overhead. One of ours, or something we can rent the time on. Special Cases can usually. Hello? Yeah, this is Rovayo, listen—"

"Hey! No!"

Carl didn't really need the anonymous yell. *Tanindo*, as taught by Sutherland, worked up a high level of proximity sense, and the mesh tuned it tighter still. He felt the boy come out of the chair without needing to turn and see it. He turned anyway, at a leisurely rate, and caught the escape bid with a peripheral glimpse, the same peeled awareness that had saved him from the machete attack in the first place. The boy was already out of tackle range, heading for the refuge of a side access walkway. Pumping limbs, head thrown back, a spurt of desperate speed. Not bad, all things considered.

He saw Rovayo stiffen, stop speaking to Alcatraz. Reach for her stowed gun. He put out an arm to forestall her, shook his head.

"Let him go. I'm on it."

"But you—"

"Relax. Running after idiots is what I do for a living."

He turned away. Would have liked the gun, but it wasn't like there was the time to talk it through—

"He's getting away," shouted the Australian woman.

Carl spared her a murderous look, then he was in motion. Slow run building to a sprint, gathering speed and purpose, the fine focal intensity of the hunt.

Time to find Merrin and shut him down.

CHAPTER 38

Wide awake, jet-lagged to pieces even the syn didn't seem able to fix, she sat in the window of the hotel room and stared out over the bay. COLIN privileges—top-floor suite, unobstructed views. The marching lights of the Bay Bridge led her gaze inexorably across to where Oakland's own nighttime display glowed from the waterline and twinkled up into the hills.

Cheap fucking piece of shit.

Norton wanted to put out a citywide search and detain, but neither she nor Coyle was interested. They both knew damn well where Marsalis was, and the fact that he was technically absent without authorization was the least of it. Rovayo wasn't answering her phone, and what that meant was punched onto the other Rim cop's face like bruising from a street fight. Sevgi couldn't be sure if Coyle and Rovayo had ever been an item as such, but they were partners and most of the time that ran deeper. Higher loyalty stakes—the people you accepted into your bed weren't likely to have to save your life on any given day. Back with NYPD, Sevgi'd had her share of ill-advised co-worker liaisons, but she never, never crossed that particular line with anybody she partnered, not because she hadn't occasionally been tempted, but because it would have been stupid. Like taking one of harbor patrol's big powerboats into the shallow waters off some white sand tourist beach. You just knew that you were going stick and tip.

Not like now, huh, Sev, the syn sneered at her. *This one, you've got well under control, don't you? Deep water and an even keel all the way.*

Oh shut up.

She wasn't sure how long she'd been sitting there, disconnected into the sprinkle-lit night, when someone started hammering on the door.

"Sevgi?"

She blinked. It was Norton's voice, muffled through the soundproofing on the door, and slightly slurred. They'd sat up in the hotel bar for a while earlier, barely touched drinks and not much to say. At least she'd thought the drinks were barely touched until, out of nowhere, he said to her quietly, *Just like cocaine, right. No evolved defenses, too much strain on your heart.* She stared back at him, aware that he'd nailed her somehow but unable to make exact rational sense of the words. *I don't know what you're thinking about, Tom,* she answered stiffly. *But I'm sitting here thinking about Helena Larsen and how we still haven't caught the mother-fucker who murdered her.* It was only halfway to a lie. The promises she'd made to herself and the mutilated corpse back in June weighed heavily whenever she gave them headroom.

So she'd fled the bar, left Norton sitting there with a brief good night. Now it seemed he'd stayed for the long haul.

"Sev. You in there?"

She sighed and levered herself off the window shelf to the floor. Padded across to the door and opened it. Norton leaned on the door frame with one raised arm, not as drunk as she'd feared.

"Yeah, I'm in here," she said. "What's going on?"

He grinned. "This you are going to love. Coyle just called."

"Yeah?" She turned away, left the door open. "Come on in. So what happened? He storm over to Rovayo's place and drag Marsalis out of her bed?"

"No, not quite." Norton followed her in, waited until she turned back to face him. He was still grinning. She folded her arms.

"So?"

"So Rovayo and Marsalis stormed *Bulgakov's Cat* this evening, bullied their way into Daskeen Azul's offices, and made a mess. Someone took exception and came at Marsalis with a machete."

"*What?*"

"That's right. Now Rovayo's called a RimSec lockdown on the whole raft, and Marsalis is somewhere down in the belly of the beast, chasing the machete artist because he thinks it's all part of some grand conspiracy that'll lead him to Merrin."

"Oh you've got to be fucking kidding me."

"I wish I were."

"Well—where's Coyle?"

"On his way here, now. He's heading out to the party with a detachment of RimSec's public order thugs in tow. I sort of insisted he stop by and pick us up."

Sevgi grabbed her jacket off the bed and shouldered her way into it.

"Would have settled for him just fucking her," she muttered, then suddenly remembered she was no longer alone.

Norton pretended not to hear.

In the bowels of *Bulgakov's Cat*, Carl found a curious relief. There were at least no fucking stores down here.

His short-term memory spilled recall of endless smooth-floored covered thoroughfares and changing frontages in such volume that their individuality finally blurred into perceptible patterns of appeal. Clothing under glass, museum exhibit sober or in shout-out garish display, depending on the prey it was designed to hook. Little chunks and slices of hardware under soft gleaming lights. Food and drink laid out in holo-real impressionistic tumbles of plenty designed to imitate some ghost memory of a street market. Psychochemicals blown up in holodisplay to sizes where pills and the molecules they were made of each started to resemble the fetishized pieces in the hardware shops. Services and intangibles sold with broad cinematic images that offered almost no intelligible connection with the product. Level after level after level of it, walkway after walkway, maze of corridors, of elevators and staircases, all bright and endless.

He tuned it out and chased the machete boy, as close as the sparse nighttime crowds would allow.

He'd long ago learned that when the untrained are chased, they look back a lot in the early stages of the pursuit, but rapidly gain confidence if no pursuer is readily apparent. He supposed it was evolved tendency—if the big predator doesn't get you in the first few minutes, you're probably clear. In any event, the trick was to hang back and let your quarry build up that confidence, then tighten up and follow until they take you where you want to go. It rarely failed.

Of course, he would have liked more cover. The late shoppers were a thin crowd and to make matters worse a typical Rim mix, which meant black or white faces were a lot less common than Asian or Hispanic. And the boy with the machete seemed curiously fixated on Carl's skin color. That might just have been standard, antiquated race hate—the boy was after all from Jesusland and spouting religious gibberish to match, so anything was possible—but even if it wasn't, machete boy would be looking back for a black face, and there weren't that many in the crowd. Carl needed him to see a few, suffer the jolt-drop of terror and then the relief as he wrote the sighting off. The more times that happened, the more the boy's adrenal response to a black face was going to decay, and the more he'd relax.

He hung back, he used the mirrored surfaces, the camera playback-and-display narcissism of the mall space, and he watched as his quarry's frantic, spinning, backward staring run damped down to a slower, purposeful threading through the crowd. The full-body turns became frequent over-the-shoulder glances, and then not so frequent. Carl eased forward, keeping behind knots of shoppers and going bent-kneed where there was no one tall enough to give him cover.

Then the stores ran out.

They'd been dropping levels slowly but steadily, taking gleaming marbled stairways and the odd gleaming jewel-box elevator, all consistently downward. At first Carl thought they might be heading back to Daskeen Azul, but they'd already gone too low for that, and he didn't think the boy had the skills or presence of mind to lay a double-back track. In the frontages, prices came down. Empty rental space began to interpose itself between the taken units. The holodisplays got ragged, the merchandise and the way it was sold took on an imitative quality, a not-quite-good copy of what the upper decks carried. The services on offer became less wholesome, or at least less smoothly packaged. KILLBITCH AVAILABLE, he saw in cheap neon, wasn't sure what it referred to, wasn't sure he wanted to. Elsewhere, someone had spray-canned a huge empty rectangle on the glass front of an untenanted unit and filled it with the words BUY CONSUME DIE—ARTWORK TO FOLLOW. No one had cleaned it off.

The boy flickered left out of the flow of shoppers and took another staircase. This time it was a utilitarian unpolished metal affair, and no one else was using it. When Carl got to it, he could hear his quarry's steps clattering down in the well.

Fuck.

He waited until the metallic footfalls stopped, then went down after them, trying to make as little noise as possible. At the bottom of the well, he found himself in a low-rent residential section, simple green security doors set in bleak gray corridor walls whose ragged graffiti scars were almost a relief. A steady thrum in the structure suggested heavy-duty engines somewhere close. The floor was dirty, stains and patches of dust that crunched underfoot, neat lines of detritus swept to the sides either by mechanical cleaning carts or possibly the residents themselves. Clear evidence, if he'd been in need of it, that the nanohygiene systems didn't make it down here much. Nor, he supposed, did anyone else who didn't either live here or know someone who did.

Which, of course, made it perfect for Merrin.

The corridor was deserted. Receding rows of closed doors and no sign of machete boy anywhere. Branch corridors up ahead to left and right, the same story again when he reached them and peered down the dingy perspectives they offered. Meshed-up tension sagging slowly into the realization that his quarry had gone to ground. He held off the settling feeling as best he could, prowled down the left-hand branch passage, ears tuned past the engine thrum for the sound of

voices or footsteps. Well aware—*I know, I fucking* know—that the doors would
have security cameras and that each one he passed upped the risk of being spotted if his quarry was in one of the apartments behind, watching the screen.

He did it anyway. Maybe machete boy had gotten hold of another weapon and
was up for another shot at killing the black man.

He found a zone plan screwed to a wall at the next intersection, studied it, got
a sense of how the area was laid out. The wall next to the map offered the deadpan grafittoed legend: YOU ARE HERE I'M AFRAID—DEAL WITH IT. He grinned despite himself and prowled back the way he'd come, aiming to start a proper
search pattern. Something to do until RimSec got there in force. He'd have to
hope the lockdown worked.

Behind him, the clank-punt of a door disengaging its locks. He spun about,
combat crouch in the making when he saw the woman backing out of the open
doorway. She wore nondescript coveralls, some logo he didn't recognize, and had
her corkscrew-unruly hair gathered up in a tight band. Mestiza complexion, unlit
spliff tucked into the corner of her mouth. By the time she'd fully turned, he was
casual again.

"Hey there."

She appraised him with a head-to-foot look. "What's the matter, you lost?"

"Next best thing." He built her a smile. "I'm supposed to meet some guy down
here works for Daskeen Azul, think either I've taken a wrong turn or he has."

"That right?"

She was looking at the S(t)igma jacket, he realized. Maybe the corporation
and what it did wasn't standard knowledge out this far west, but unless you were
immune to continental American news digests, it was hard to misunderstand the
style of the jacket and the bright chevrons down the sleeve. He sighed.

"Chasing a job, you know," he said, faking weariness. "Guy says he can maybe
get me some hours."

Another flickered assessment. She nodded and took the spliff out of her
mouth, turned and gestured with it, back to the corner with the map. "See that
right turn there. Take that, two blocks straight then one left. Takes you through
the bulkhead to starboard loading. Think Daskeen got a couple of berths there.
You're not far out—probably just got the wrong stairwell down off Margarita
thoroughfare."

"Right." He let the renewed pulsing of the mesh leak through as eagerness.
"Hey, thanks a lot."

"No problem. Here." She handed him the spliff. "You get the work, celebrate
on me."

"Oh hey, you don't have to do—"

"Take it, man." She held it out until he did. "Think I've never been where you are now?"

"Thanks. Thank you. Look, I'd better—"

"Sure. Don't want to be late for your job interview."

He grinned and nodded, wheeled about, and stalked rapidly back to the corner. As soon as he rounded it, he broke into a flat run.

"Who is this?"

"This is Guava Diamond. We are blown, Claw Control. Repeat, we are blown. Heaven-sent is endangered at best, fully exposed at worst. I don't know what the fuck you're playing at over there, but this is out of nowhere. We have no cover and no exit strategy I can guarantee. Request immediate extraction."

The bulkhead was a lustrous nanofiber black, raw and shiny and as distinct from the gray walls of the residential section as his Hilton-bought shirt was from the inmate jacket he wore over it. Bright yellow markings delineated the access hatches. By the look of it, they could be simply coded shut at a molecular level, hinges and locks turning to an unbroken whole with the surface of the hatch. He passed through, stabbed suddenly with memories of Mars. It hit him that ever since he'd gotten down from the shopping levels, that was what this place brought to mind. Life on Mars. Right down to the camaraderie of the helpful mestiza, the freely offered spliff.

Don't think you're going to miss all this, Sutherland had grinned at him. *But you will, soak. You wait and see.*

Beyond lay starboard loading.

He'd been on factory rafts a few times before this, but it was always easy to forget the scale of the things. Looking over the rail of the gantry he'd stepped onto was like viewing some immense factory testing rank for cable cars. The loading space was a fifty-meter slope up from the ocean and a vast roof of the same nanofiber construction as the bulkhead, vaulted so high overhead it could almost have been the night sky. Cut into this base, a dozen or more cable-crank slipways led up out of the water to the undersides of the perched docking sheds they served. The nanofiber cables shone in their channels like roped licorice, new and wet looking in the overhead blast of LCLS arcs. Poised at various points between the underbelly entrances of the sheds and the sea, heavy-duty cradles held a variety of seagoing vessels secure on their respective slipways. Latticed steel gantries and stairs ran up and down the sides of the slips for maintenance and clung to the outer edges of the dock facilities above. Cranes and pylons bristled off the sloping surface. Dotted figures scrambled about, and faint yells lofted back and forth across the cavern-cold air. Carl scanned the roofing of the sheds for the Daskeen Azul logo, found it on the sixth unit in line, and started to run.

"Guava Diamond?"

"Still holding."

"We are unable to assist, Guava Diamond. Repeat, we are unable to assist. Suggest—"

"You what? You bonobo-sucking piece of shit, you'd better tell me I misheard that."

"There are control complications at this end. We cannot act. I'm sorry, Guava Diamond. You're on your own."

"You will be fucking sorry if we make it out of this in one piece."

"I repeat, Guava Diamond, we cannot act. Suggest you implement Lizard immediately, and get off Bulgakov's Cat while you can. You may still have time."

Pause.

"You're a fucking dead man, Claw Control."

Static hiss.

Carl was almost to the Daskeen Azul unit when the crank cables leading up to it whined into sudden life. Shifting highlights on the nanofiber black in its recessed channel, it looked more like something melting and running than actual motion. He heard the change in engine note as the cables engaged a load. Somewhere down the line, a cradled minisub jerked and started to climb.

Here we go.

He was still at the initial access level he'd come in on, behind and three meters above the roofing of the line of docking sheds. Long, shallow sets of steps ran out from the walkway he stood on, sank between the units, and joined with a lower-level gantry that fringed each shed. He made for the access level to the doors and hatches leading inside the facilities. Below again, further sets of steps snaked down on themselves and connected to the slope the slipways were built into.

There were hatches set into the roof of the Daskeen Azul unit, but they were very likely sealed from the inside, and even if they weren't, going in that way was a good recipe for getting shot in the arse. Carl slowed to a crouched jog, made the corner of the shed, and started down the flight of stairs at its side. The murmur of the winch engine came through the wall at his ear. A couple of small windows broke the corrugated-alloy surface, and there was a closed door at the bottom of the stairs. No easy way in. He paused and weighed the options. He had no weapon, and no sense of the layout within the unit. No idea how many Daskeen Azul employees he might be up against, or what they'd be armed with.

Yeah, so this is where you back off and wait for Rovayo's cavalry.

But he already knew he wasn't going to do that.

He crept under one of the windows and eased his head up beside it, grabbed a narrow-angled view into the space on the other side of the wall. Cleanly kept flooring, stacked dinghy hulls and other less identifiable hardware, LCLS panels shedding light from the walls and ceiling. The squat bulk of the winch machinery at the head of the slipway and four gathered figures. He narrowed his eyes—the glass was filthy, and the winch system blocked a lot of the room's light. The four were all wearing Daskeen Azul jackets, and the face he could see clearly was a stranger, a man. But the profile of the figure next to him was machete boy, gesticulating frantically at a woman whom Carl identified as Carmen Ren by poise and stance before he made out her face. She had a phone in her hand, held low, not in use.

The fourth figure had his back turned to the window, had long hair gathered into a loose tail that hung below the collar of his jacket. Carl stared at him and a solid slab of something dropped into his chest. He didn't need to see the face. He'd watched the same figure walk away from him in the mind's eye of the *Horkan's Pride* n-djinn, along the deadened quiet of the spacecraft's corridors. Had seen him stop and turn and look up at the camera, look through it as if he knew that Carl was there.

He looked around now, as if called.

Carl jerked his head back, but not before he'd seen the gaunt features, a little more flesh on the bones now maybe, but still the same slash-cheeked, hollow-eyed stare. He was checking the door, twitched around on some whisper of intuition from the weight of Carl's gaze.

Allen Merrin. Home from Mars.

Carl sank back to the step, fuming. With the Haag gun, Rovayo's gun, *any* fucking gun, he would have just stormed through the door and gotten it over with. Merrin's mesh and thirteen instincts, Carmen Ren's combat poise, the unknown quantity that the other Daskeen Azul employee represented, any weapons the four of them might have—it wouldn't matter. He'd fill the air with slugs going in, looking for multiple body hits, clean up the mess after.

Unarmed, he was going to end up dead.

Where the fuck are you, RimSec?

Rovayo's words rinsed back through his mind. *Alcatraz can authorize a block on traffic in and out. Might have to get a couple of people out of bed to do it, but—*

But nothing. Merrin and his pals here are going to bail out before RimSec's dozy fucking authorities get the sleep out of their eyes . . .

The cradled sub came on up the slipway.

And stopped.

Carl peered down through the steel lattice of the gantry he stood on. The haul cradle was still a good twenty meters down the slope, frozen there. Inside the docking shed, the winding engine ran on but its sound had shifted. The licorice black of the cable was frozen in its channel. The winch had disconnected.

He peered across the sweep of the loading slope and saw the same story all the way along. No motion: none of the cables was working.

Lockdown. He'd done RimSec an injustice.

He saw it coming, just ahead of time. Moved off the wall, shifted stance for the combat crouch, and then the door ahead clanked open, three steps down. The mesh pounded inside him. Ren came out, the others crowding behind.

". . . yank the cradle releases and ride it down. There's no other—"

She saw him. He jumped.

Their numbers made it work for him. He cannoned into Ren, knocked her flying back along the walkway and to the floor. Machete boy roared and swung at him, hopelessly wide. Carl blocked, locked up an elbow, and shoved the boy back into the two other men behind him. All three staggered back through the confines of the doorway. The nameless Daskeen Azul employee yelped and brandished a weapon awkwardly, one-handed. Yelling *Get out of the way, get out of the fucking way.* Carl made it as a sharkpunch and his flesh quailed. He rode the attack momentum through the door, sent them all stumbling. He got his hands on the gunman's arm and wrenched, forced him to the floor, followed him down, knee into the stomach. Found the pressure point in the wrist, wrenched again. The sharkpunch went off once, symphony of dull metallic plinks and clanks as the murderous load punched ragged holes in the roof. Then he had possession and the former owner was flailing under him disarmed. Carl twisted, pointed down point-blank, and pulled the trigger. The other man turned abruptly to shredded bone and flesh from the waist up. Blood and gore splattered, drenched him from head to foot.

Proximity sense signaled left. Carl rose and twisted at mesh speed, still blinking the blood from his eyes. Machete boy ran onto the sharkpunch, screaming abomination and hellfire. This time, Carl pulled the trigger in sheer reflex. The impact kicked the boy back toward the open door and tore him apart in midair.

The screaming died in midsyllable, the wall and doorway suddenly painted with gore. Carl gaped at the damage the weapon had done—

—and Merrin hit him from the side. Locked out the gun in exactly the same way Carl had taken it from its original owner. Carl grunted and let the other thirteen's attack carry the two of them around in a stumbling dance. Kept the gaping muzzle of the sharkpunch angled hard away as best he could. He tried for a *tanindo* throw, but Merrin knew the move. They lurched again, feet on the edge of the opening in the shed floor where the slipway ran in.

"Been looking for you," Carl gritted.

Merrin's fingers dug into his wrist. Carl heaved and let the sharkpunch go, through the hole in the floor. It hit the slope below and clattered heavily away downward. Better than leaving it lying around for Ren to pick up and use. He tried another technique to get loose, worked his feet back from the hole and hitched an elbow strike at Merrin's belly. The other thirteen smothered the blow, hooked out Carl's ankle with a heel, and brought both of them down. He got in an elbow of his own, blunt force into the side of Carl's face. Vision flew apart. Merrin got on top. Grinned down at the black man like a wolf.

"I did not cross the void to be killed like a cudlip," he hissed. "To die like meat on the slab. You have not *understood* who I am."

He drove a forearm up into Carl's throat, bore down and began to crush his larynx. Carl, vision still starry, took the only option left: levered with one leg, rolled, and tipped them both over the edge.

It wasn't a long drop, the height of the haulage cradle when it slotted into place at the top of the ramp, three meters at most. But the impact broke their holds on each other and they rolled down the slope apart. Twenty meters farther down, the solid steel bulk of the locked-up cradle waited to greet them. Impact was going to hurt.

Carl got himself feetfirst in the tumble and tried to jam a foot into the crank-cable channel. The sole of his boot skidded off the nanofiber, braked him, but not a lot. Merrin came plowing past at his shoulder, grabbed at him, and tugged him loose again. He kicked out, missed, slithered after the other thirteen. The cradle loomed, smooth curve of the sub's hull held in its massive forked iron grasp. Merrin hit, shrugged it off at mesh speed, braced himself upright against one of the forks. He turned to face Carl with a snarling grin. Carl panicked, jammed his foot hard into the cable space again, tried to sit as his knee bent. He must have hit a bracket or a support brace. His fall locked to a halt a couple of meters off impact with the cradle. The momentum flipped him almost upright, hurled him down to meet Merrin like a bad skater fighting to stay upright. The other thirteen gaped: Carl was coming in impossibly high. Carl snapped out a fist, some reflex he didn't know he owned, and drove into the side of Merrin's neck with all the force of his arrival.

It nearly broke his wrist.

He felt the abused joint creak with the impact, but it was lost in the surge of savage joy as Merrin choked and sagged. He pivoted off the punch and cannoned into the side of the sub. Merrin made some kind of blocking move, but it was weak. Carl beat it down, seized the other thirteen's head in both hands, and smashed it sideways as hard as he could against the edge of the cradle fork. Merrin made a strangled, raging noise and lashed out. Carl shrugged off the blow, smashed the thirteen's head into the metal again—and again—and again—

Felt the fight go finally out of the other man. Didn't stop.

Didn't stop until blood made a sudden blotched spray across the gray hull of the sub, and sprinkled warm on his face again.

CHAPTER 39

S evgi came down the gantry stairs through a flood of CSI lighting and experts setting up their gear. RimSec had cordoned off the whole of starboard loading, shepherded everyone out for questioning, and then locked the place down. There were uniforms along the upper walkways at every entry point, and a sharkish black patrol boat prowled the ocean alongside the open bay. Smaller inflatables fringed the water's edge at the bottom of the slipway like orange seaweed, wagging back and forth with the slop of the waves against the slope. There was a sense of hollowness under the vaulted roof, of something emptied out and done.

Sevgi fished her COLIN identification from a pocket and showed it to a supervising officer at the Daskeen Azul docking shed. Surprised herself with the faint stab of nostalgia for the days of her palm-wired NYPD holobadge. Being a cop, back in the day. The officer looked back at her blankly.

"Yeah, what do you want?"

"I'm looking for Carl Marsalis. I was told he's still down here."

"Marsalis?" The woman stayed mystified for a moment, then the light dawned. "Oh, you're talking about the twist? The guy that did all this damage?"

Sevgi was too churned to up to call the Rim cop on her terminology. She nodded. The officer pointed down the slope.

"He's sitting down there on that empty cradle, one across from this slip. Was going to have him forcibly removed for questioning, but then some Special Cases badge calls down and says to leave him be, the guy can sit there all night if he wants." She made a weary gesture. "Who am I to argue with Special Cases, right?"

Sevgi murmured something sympathetic and headed on down the stairs beside the Daskeen Azul slipway. When she got level with the empty cradle on the other slip, she had to pick her way awkwardly across the sloping surface, once or twice teetering and dropping to a crouch to stop herself from falling. She reached the cradle and hung on to one of the forks with relief.

"Hey there," she said awkwardly.

Marsalis glanced down, apparently surprised to see her. It was the first time she'd seen him so unaware of his surroundings, and it jolted her more than the surprise had shaken him. She wondered, briefly, if he was in shock. His clothes were covered with drying blood in big uneven patches, and there were smeared specks and streaks still on his face where he'd washed but apparently hadn't scrubbed hard enough.

"You okay?" she asked.

He shrugged. "Few bruises. Nothing serious. When did you get here?"

"Awhile ago. Been upstairs, shouting at Daskeen Azul's management." Sevgi hauled herself up onto the cradle, propped herself against the fork next to him, and slid her legs out in front of her. "So. Turns out you called it right after all."

"Yeah. Thirteen paranoia."

"Don't gloat, Marsalis. It's not attractive."

"Well, I'm not looking to get laid."

She shot him a sideways glance. "No, I guess you've probably had enough of that for one night."

He shrugged again, didn't look at her.

"Daskeen Azul are denying any knowledge," she said. "As far as they're concerned, Merrin, Ren, and Osborne were all casual employees, automatically renewed contracts every month unless there's a problem, and there never was. They're lying through their teeth, but I don't know if RimSec are going to be able to prove that."

"Osborne?"

"The guy who jumped you with the machete. Scott Osborne, Jesusland fencehopper. RimSec Forensics reckon he was one of the Ward BioSupply employees who ran when Merrin showed up there. DNA match with genetic trace leavings from here and Ward's place."

He nodded. "And Ren?"

"That's a tougher one. There was no genetic trace for her at Ward's place, so looks like she or someone else went over there and cleaned up after they left. But we're working off witness description composites and yeah, looks like she was there, too."

"What about gene trace here. Have they run that?"

"Not yet." She looked at him again, curiously. "You don't seem very happy about any of this."

"I'm not."

She frowned. "Marsalis, it's over. You get to go home now. You know, back to London and your smug European social comfort zone."

He raised an eyebrow, stared out at the water. "Lucky me."

Abruptly, there was a light tripping pulse in her throat. She tried for irony. "What, you going to miss me?"

He turned to look at her now.

"This isn't over, Sevgi."

"It isn't?" She felt a little crime scene macabre creep into her tone. "Well, you could have fooled me. I mean, you did just kill them all. Osborne and the other guy are all over the walls and floor up there. Merrin, you just brained. I'd say we're pretty much done, wouldn't you?"

"And Ren?"

Sevgi gestured, throwaway. "Pick up her up, sooner or later."

"Yeah? Like you did after she split from Ward BioSupply?"

"Marsalis, you're fucking up the victory parade here. Ren's aftermath, she's a detail at most. Merrin's dead, that's what counts."

"Yeah. Suppose we should be celebrating, right?"

"That's right, we should."

He nodded and reached into his inmate jacket. Produced a well-made blunt and held it up for her approval.

"Want some?"

"What is it?"

"Don't know. Someone gave it to me. In case I needed to celebrate." He put the blunt in his mouth and crunched the ember end to life. Drew in smoke, coughed a little. "Here, try. Not bad."

She took it and drew her own toke. The smoke went down sweet and silty, enhanced dope and an edge of something else on it. She held it in, let it go. Felt the cool languor of the hit come stealing along her limbs. All sorts of knots seemed to loosen in her head. She drew again, let it up quicker this time, and handed the blunt back to him.

"So tell me why you're not happy," she said.

"Because I don't like being played, and this whole fucking thing was a setup from the start." He smoked in gloomy quiet for a while, then held the blunt up and examined the burning end. "Fucking monster myths."

"Eh?"

"Monsters," he said bitterly. "Superterrorists, serial killers, criminal masterminds. It's always the same fucking lie. Might as well be talking about werewolves and vampires, for all the difference it makes. We are the good, the civilized people. Huddled here in our cozy ring of firelight, our cities and our homes, and out there"—a wide gesture, warming to his theme now—"out in the dark, the monster prowls. The Big Evil, the Threat to the Tribe. Kill the beast and all will be well. Never mind the—"

"You going to smoke that, or not?"

He blinked. "Yeah, sorry. Here."

"So you don't think we've killed the beast?"

"Sure. We've killed it. So what? That doesn't give us any answers. We still don't know why Merrin came back from Mars, or what the point of all these deaths was."

"Should have asked him."

"Yeah, well. Slipped my mind at the time, you know."

She stared at the toes of her boots. Frowned. "Look, maybe you're right. Maybe we don't have the answers yet. But the fact we don't know what this was about doesn't mean we shouldn't be happy we've stopped it."

"We didn't stop it. I already told you, this whole thing was set up."

"Oh come on. Set up how? Rovayo says you took Daskeen Azul totally by surprise. They weren't expecting this to happen."

"We were early."

"What?"

He took the blunt from her. "We were early. They didn't expect me to push so hard, they were maybe going to let this play out sometime next week."

"Let *what* play out next week?" Exasperation slightly blurred by whatever they were smoking. "You think Merrin planned to *let* you kill him?"

"I don't know," he said thoughtfully. "He certainly didn't fight as hard as I expected him to. I mean, I got lucky in the end, but the whole thing felt, I don't know. Slack. Anyway, that's not the main point. Ren could have come in at any point and tipped the balance. She wasn't injured; all I did was knock her on her back."

"So? She just cut her losses, got out while she could."

"After partnering this guy for the last four months? I don't think so. Ren was a pro, it was stamped right through her. The way she moved, the way she stood. The way she looked at you. Someone like that doesn't panic. Doesn't mistake one unarmed man for a RimSec invasion."

"Did you tell her you were a thirteen?"

He gave her a tired look.

"Well? Did you?"

"Yeah, I did, but—"

"There you are then." She bent one knee, eased around to face him more.

"That's what panicked her. Look, Marsalis, I've been around you when the fighting starts, and it scares *me*. And I know what a thirteen really is."

"So did she. She'd been caretaking one for the last four months, remember."

"That's not the same as facing one in combat. She'd have a standard human response to that, a standard—"

"Not this woman."

"Oh, you think you're an expert on women, do you?"

"I'm an expert on soldiers, Sevgi. And that's what Ren was. She was someone's soldier, the same someone who hired Merrin out of Mars. And whoever that someone was, for whatever reasons, they were getting ready to sell him out. Maybe because he'd served his purpose, maybe because we were getting too close to the truth down in Cuzco. Either way, this"—he nodded back toward the CSI buzz on the slope above them—"all this was a planned outcome. COLIN with its boot on the corpse of the beast, big smiles for the camera, congratulations all around. Fade out to a happy ending."

"Doesn't sound so bad to me," she muttered.

"Really?" He plumed smoke up at the nanofiber vault. "And there I was thinking you were a cop."

"Ex-cop. You're confusing me with Rovayo. You really ought to try and keep the women you fuck separate in your head."

She took the blunt from him, brusquely. He watched her smoke for a couple of moments in silence. She pretended not to notice.

"Sevgi," he said finally. "You can't tell me you're happy to walk away, knowing we've been played."

"Can't I?" She met his eyes. Exploded a lungful of smoke at him. "You're wrong, Marsalis. I *can* walk away from this happy, because the fucked-up psycho who cut Helena Larsen into pieces and ate her is dead. I guess for that, at least, I should thank you."

"Don't mention it."

"Yeah. And maybe we don't know why Merrin came back, and maybe we'll never know. But I can live with that, just like I lived with more unsolved cases than you'll ever know when I worked Homicide. You don't always get a clean wrap. Life is messy, and so is crime. Sometimes you just got to be happy you got the bad guy, and call time on the rest."

He turned away to look at the sea. "Well, that must be a human thing."

"Yeah. Must be."

"Norton'll be pleased."

She rolled her head sideways, blew smoke, nailed him through it with another look. "We're not going to talk about Tom Norton."

"Fine. We're not going to talk about Norton, we're not going to talk about Ren. We're not going to talk about anything inconvenient, because you've got your monster and that's all that matters. Christ, no wonder you people are in such a mess."

Anger ignited behind her eyes.

"Us people? Fuck you, Marsalis. You know what? *Us people* are running a more peaceful planet now than the human race has ever fucking seen. There's prosperity, tolerance, justice—"

"Not in Florida, that I noticed."

"Oh, what do you want? That's Jesusland. *Globally*, things are getting better. There's no fighting in the Middle East—"

"For the time being."

"—no starving in Africa, no war with China—"

"Only because no one has the guts to take them on."

"No. Because we have learned that *taking them on* is a losing game. *No one* wins a war anymore. Change is slow, it has to come from within."

"Tell that to the black lab refugees."

"Oh, spare me the fucking pseudo-empathy. You could give a shit about some Chinese escapee you never met. I know you, Marsalis. Injustice is personal for guys like you—if it didn't happen to you or someone you think belongs to you, then it doesn't touch you at all. You don't—"

"*It did fucking happen to me!*"

The shout ripped loose, floated away in the immensity of the vaulted space. She wondered if the RimSec CSI crew heard it. His hands were on her shoulders, fingers hooked into her flesh, head jutting close, eyes locked into hers. They hadn't been this close since they fucked, and something deeply buried, some ancestor subroutine in her genes, picked up on the proximity and sent the old, confused signals pulsing out.

It was the part of herself she most hated.

She kept the locked stare. Reached up and jabbed the lit ember of the blunt into the back of his hand.

Something detonated in his eyes, inked out just as fast. He unhinged his fingers with a snap. Backed off a fraction at a time. She drove him back with her eyes.

"Keep your fucking hands off me," she hissed.

"You think—"

His voice was hoarse. He stopped, swallowed and started again.

"You think I can't empathize with someone out of the black labs, some gene experiment made flesh? I *am* them, Sevgi. I mean, what do you think Osprey was? I *am* a fucking experiment. I grew up in a controlled environment, managed and checklisted by men in fucking suits. I lost—"

He stopped again. This time, his eyes slid away from hers. A faint frown furrowed his brow. For a split second she thought he was going to weep, and something prickled at the base of her own throat in sympathy.

"Motherfucker," he said softly.

She waited, finally had to prompt him. "What?"

Marsalis looked at her, and his eyes were washed clean of the rage. His voice stayed low.

"Bambarén," he said. "Manco fucking Bambarén."

"What about him?"

"He was fucking with me, back at Sacsayhuamán. He thought they took Marisol—my surrogate—away from me when I was fourteen. But that's Lawman. In Osprey, they did it at eleven. Different psych theory."

"So?"

"So he was too close to the detail. It wasn't just the age, it was the other stuff. He was talking about men in uniforms, debriefing in a steel trailerfab. Osprey's handlers all wore suits. And we never had any trailers, the whole place was purpose-built and permanent."

She shrugged. "Maybe he's read about it. Seen footage."

"That's not how it sounded, Sevgi. It sounded personal. As if he'd been involved." He sighed. "I know. Thirteen paranoia, right?"

She hesitated. "It's pretty thin."

"Yeah." He looked away from her. Seemed to make an effort: she saw his mouth clamp. He met her eyes again. "I'm sorry I grabbed you like that. Thought I had that shit locked down."

" 'sokay. Just don't do it again. Ever."

He took the blunt from her, very gently. It was down to the stub and smoldering unequally from where she'd stabbed his hand with it. He coaxed a little more from it, drew deep.

"So what's going to happen now?" he asked, voice tight with holding down the smoke.

She grimaced. "Aftermath, like I said. We're going to be chasing the detail for months, but they'll start to fold the case priority away. Someone somewhere's going to figure out how to knock off some major unlicensed Marstech again, and we'll get switched to that. File Merrin for a rainy day."

"Yeah. What I thought."

"Look, let it go, Carl." Impulsively, she reached out and took his hand, the same hand she'd scorched. "Just let go and walk away. You're home free. We'll look at the *familia* thing, who knows, maybe we'll get somewhere with it."

"You go down there without me, all you'll get is killed." But he was smiling as he said it. "You saw what happened last time."

She flickered the smile back at him. "Well, maybe we'll be a bit less full-frontal in our approach."

He grunted. Held up the dying blunt, querying. She shook her head, and he just held it there between them for a moment or two. Then he shrugged, took one last toke, and pitched it out through the cradle forks, down the long slope to the water.

"You chase that aftermath," he said.

"We will."

But out beyond the vault of starboard loading, the waves were starting to pale, black to gunmetal, as the early light of a whole new day crept in.

CHAPTER 40

Back at the hotel, he opaqued the windows against the unwelcome dawn. Jet lag and fight ache stalked him through the darkened suite to the bed. He shed his clothes on the floor and stood staring down at them. S(T)IGMA, the back of the inmate jacket reminded him in cheery orange. Sevgi Ertekin stood in his thoughts and waved—she'd walked him up to the helipad on *Bulgakov's Cat* and seen him off. Was still standing there with one arm raised as the *Cat* dropped away below and behind the autocopter, visible detail blurring out.

He grimaced, tried to shake the memory off.

He ripped the bed open irritably, crawled in, and tugged a sheet across his shoulder.

Sleep came and buried him.

The phone.

He rolled awake in the still-darkened room, convinced he'd only just closed his eyes. Steady blue glow digits at the bedside disputed the impression: 17:09. He'd slept through the day. He held up his wrist, peering stupidly at the watch he'd forgotten to take off, as if a hotel clock could somehow be wrong. The wrist ached from the fumbled blow he'd hit Merrin with. He turned it a little, flexing. Might even be—

Phone. Answer the fucking—

He groped for it, dragged the audio receiver up to his ear.

"Yeah, what?"

"Marsalis?" A voice he should know but, sleep-scrambled, didn't. "Is that you?"

"Who the fuck is this?"

"Ah, so it is you." The name came just ahead of his own belated recognition of the measured tones. "Gianfranco di Palma here. Brussels office."

Carl sat up in bed, frowning.

"What do you want?"

"I have just been speaking to an agent Nicholson in New York." Di Palma's perfect, barely accented UN English floated urbanely down the line. "I understand that COLIN have no further use for your services, and that they have arranged that all charges against you in the Republic will be dropped forthwith. It seems you will be returning to Europe very shortly."

"Yeah? News to me."

"Well, I don't think we need to wait around on formalities. I'll have an UNGLA shuttle dispatched to SFO tonight. If you would care to be at the suborbital terminal around midnight—"

"No I wouldn't."

"I am sorry?"

South Florida State swirled up into his mind, like dirty water backing up from a blocked drain. A sudden decision gripped him, cheery as the lettering on his S(t)igma jacket.

"I said you can fuck off, di Palma. Write it down. Fuck. Right. Off. You let me sit in a Jesusland jail for four months and I'd still be there for all the fucking efforts you made to get me out. And you still owe me expenses from fucking *January.*" And just like that, out of nowhere he was furious, trembling with the sudden rage. "So don't think for one fucking moment I'm going to jump into line just because you finally got your dick out of your own arse. I am not done here. I am very far from done here, and I'll come home when I'm fucking good and ready."

There was a stiff pause at the other end of the line.

"You understand, I assume," said di Palma silkily, "that you are not authorized to operate without UNGLA jurisdiction. Of course, your time is your own to dispose of, but we cannot agree to you having any further professional contact with COLIN or the Rim States Security Corps. In the interests of—"

"What's the matter with you, di Palma. Don't you have a pen there? I told you to fuck off. Want me to spell it?"

"I strongly advise you not to take this attitude."

"Yeah? Well, I strongly advise you to go and get a caustic soda enema. Let's see which of us takes direction best, shall we."

He broke the connection. Sat staring at the phone for a while.

So. Planning to pay for our own suborb ticket, are we? And look for a new job when we get back?

It won't come to that. They need me worse than di Palma's dented pride.

They don't need you worse than a breach of the Accords. Which is what it's going to be if you pick up that phone again and call Sevgi Ertekin. You heard the man. Any further professional contact.

The phone sat in his hand.

Just go home, Carl. You gave them their monster, got another notch on your belt, right up there next to Gray. Thirteen liquidator, top of your game. Just take that and ride it home, maybe even bluff it into a raise when you get back.

The phone.

Come on, leave her alone. You're not doing her any favors, pushing this. Let her walk away like she wants to.

Maybe she doesn't really want to walk away.

Oh, how very alpha-male of you. What's next, form an Angry Young tribute band? People got to lead their own lives, Carl.

He tightened his fingers on the smooth plastic of the receiver. Touched it to his head. His whole body ached, he realized suddenly, a dozen different small, jabbing reminders of the fight with Merrin.

Merrin's done, Carl. All over.

There's still Norton. Lying fuck tried to have you killed in New York, maybe down in Peru as well.

You don't know that.

He's right next to her still. She starts asking awkward questions, he could have her hit the same way he tried with you.

You don't know he did that. And anyway, he's a little too dewy-eyed around Sevgi Ertekin to let anything like that happen to her, and you know it.

He grunted. Lowered the phone and stared at it again.

Give it up, Carl. You're just looking for excuses to get back inside something you never wanted to be a part of in the first place. Just cut it loose and go home.

He grimaced. Dialed from memory.

Sevgi took the call on her way through a seemingly endless consumer space. Late-afternoon crowds clogged the malls and the open-access stores, crippled her pace to limping. She had to keep slowing and darting sideways to get past stalled-out families or knots of dawdling finery-decked youth. She had to queue on escalators as they cranked their slow, ease-of-gawking trajectories up and down in the dizzying cathedral spaces of racked product. She had to shoulder through gathered accretions of bargain hunters under holosigns that screamed REDUCED, REDUCED, REDUCED TO THIS.

It had been the same fucking thing all day, everywhere she went in the upper levels of *Bulgakov's Cat*. The temptation to produce badge and gun to clear passage was a palpable itch in the pit of her stomach.

"Yeah, Ertekin."

"Alcatraz Control here. I have a patched call for you, will you take it?"

"Patched?" She frowned. "Patched from where?"

"New York, apparently. A Detective Williamson?"

She grappled with memory—saw again the tall, hard-boned black man amid uniforms and incident barriers and the shrink-wrapped corpses outside her home. Marsalis, seated on the front steps, gazing at it all like a tourist, as if the dead men were nothing to do with him at all. Crisp October air, and the never-stilled sounds of the city getting on with life. New York seemed suddenly as far away as Mars, and the gun battle some part of her distant past.

"Yeah, I'll take it."

Williamson came through, wavery with the patch. "Ms. Ertekin?"

"Speaking." A little breathless from her pace through a bookstore with mercifully few browsing customers.

"Is this a bad time?"

"No worse than any other. What can I do for you, Detective?"

"It's more what I can do for you, Ms. Ertekin. We have some information you might like." He hesitated for a moment. "I ran into Larry Kasabian. He speaks very highly of you."

She blinked back to the mist-deadened sounds of the IA digging robot, the field at dawn, and the sudden waft of the bodies. Kasabian at her side, blunt and silent, an occasional flickered glance under knotted brows. Once, he nodded grimly at her, some barely perceptible amalgam of solidarity and weariness, but he never spoke. It was the habit of weeks now—they were all watching their words. IA were all over the place, authorized to listen electronically who knew where.

"That's very kind of Larry." She fended off a bovine gaggle of shoppers grazing amid menswear, hopped half to a halt, and dodged around them. "And kind of you to call me. So what have you got?"

"What I've got, Ms. Ertekin, is your third shooter for Alvaro Ortiz."

She nearly stopped again, in clear space. "Is he alive?"

"Very much so. There's a hole in his shoulder, but otherwise he'll be just fine. Got into a fight in a bar over in Brooklyn, pulled a piece, and it turns out the place is full of off-duty cops." Williamson chuckled. "You believe that luck?"

"Not a local boy then?"

"No, he's from the Republic, someplace out west. Dirk Shindel. Right of residence in the Union, he's got a grandparent up in Maine somewhere, but no official citizenship. We can't put him at the scene with genetic trace, but he's copped to it anyway."

"How'd you manage that?"

"We're sweating him pretty hard," Williamson said casually. "Got one of the Homicide psych teams on it. Thing is, our boy Dirk was all fucked up on hormone jolts and street syn when the Brooklyn thing went down. You know what a cocktail like that'll do. He's babbling like a snake handler."

Along her nerves, Sevgi felt the subtle thrum of her own decidedly nonstreet syn dosage. She summoned a dutiful chuckle. "Yeah, seen that before. So what's he said about Ortiz?"

"Said a whole lot of stuff, I can file it over to you if you want. Boils down to he was hired out of Houston by some front guy he's never met, friend of the other two in the crew. Quite a lot of money, which I guess for a hit on a guy like Ortiz you'd expect, but it doesn't explain why the low-grade hires. Shindel says he's whacked guys before, in the Republic, but the psych team think he's lying. At best, they reckon he was maybe a driver or a backup man."

"What about the others?"

"Yeah, Leroy Atkins. That's the guy your, uh, enhanced friend put down with the machine pistol. Turns out he's got some record in the Republic, but strictly spray-and-run stuff. Cop I talked to in the Houston PD said he thought Atkins might have upped his game in the last couple of years, gone out of state for the work. Nothing they can touch him for, it's just street rumor and implied Yaroshanko links from some West Coast n-djinn Houston rent time on. Same with the other guy, uh, Fabiano, Angel Fabiano. Houston resident, some gang affiliations down there. Been doing time since he was a kid, but they never got him for worse than possession of abortifacients with intent to sell, and some aggravated assault. But Houston reckon he might have upgraded as well. He's a known associate of Atkins."

"Okay." Disloyalty for Norton snaked in her, deep enough to force a grimace onto her face. She asked anyway. "Did Shindel have anything to say about Marsalis?"

"Marsalis? The thirteen guy?" Pause while Williamson presumably scrolled through the report. "No. Nothing here outside of *we would have brought the whole thing off, too, that fucking nigger twist hadn't been there. No offense.*"

"No offense?"

"Yeah." Williamson's tone shifted into sour amusement. "One of the psych team's the same color as me. This is one sensitive Jesuslander we're dealing with here."

Sevgi grunted. "Probably the syn talking. He tell you how they ended up outside my front door?"

"Yeah, he was pissed about that, too. Told us they'd been watching Ortiz for weeks, mapping his moves. Seems he always went by this coffeehouse he liked on West Ninety-seventh, they were going to track him across there on the skates and light him up outside. The skates, that's an old Houston *sicario* standby, apparently. Good for city-center hits where you've got high-volume, slow-moving traffic. Anyway, the way Shindel paints it, Ortiz breaks his routine and heads uptown suddenly, they go after him but it nearly kills them to keep up. By the time they get to Hundred eighteenth, they're panting like dogs, they just want to get this thing finished."

"Very pro." She could hear the lightness in her own tone. The vindication of Norton blew through her like a cool breeze. She even found a smile for some face-painted idiot who collided with her coming around a support column and then backed off all apologies and smiles.

"Right," Williamson agreed. "Not quite Houston's finest, it seems."

"No."

"Yeah." The New York detective hesitated again. "So like I said, I talked to Kasabian. He told me you'd want to know. Was going to hang on to this until you were back in town, but then I caught you on that news flash out of the Rim this morning. So I figure the Rim, that's where Ortiz is from originally, maybe this ties in to whatever you're dealing with out there."

The press conference, hastily called in a deck-level government garden amidships, her dry lack-of-progress report buffered by wooden professions of coordinated effort from RimSec and the *Cat*'s security services, a brief, sonorous pronouncement from a local political aide—it all seemed to be sliding into the past at alarming speed as well. She made a fleeting match with the feeling she'd had on the highway out of Cuzco, the sense of time slipping through her fingers. Marsalis at her side like a dark rock she could maybe cling to. She grimaced. Shouldered the image aside, like another drowsy shopper getting in her way.

"Well, listen, Detective, I appreciate you taking the trouble to hand me this. See if I can't return the favor someday."

"No need. Like I said, saw the news flash. Lot of talk about agency cooperation in America these days, a lot of talk. I figure maybe it's time there actually started to *be* some, too."

"I hear that. Can you wire the Shindel file across to RimSec at Alcatraz? I'll pick it up there later."

"Will do. Hope it helps."

The New York patch clicked out, taking Williamson's accent and the winter city with it. Left her with the star-static almost-hush of satellite time, and then nothing at all.

"Nothing. That's what I'm telling you."

Carl shook his head irritably. "Matthew, I told you this guy just doesn't feel right. Are you sure?"

"I am better than sure, Carl. I am mathematically accurate. Tom Norton's associational set is as close to perfectly behaved citizenship as it's possible for a human to get. The worst blemish I can find is a data-implication that his brother may have helped him get his job at COLIN. But you're talking about a good word in the right ear, not outright nepotism. And it's years in the past, no sense of a continuing influence."

"You certain about that?"

"Yes, I am certain. In fact, the data suggests that he and his brother don't get on all that well. Same-sex sibling relationships are often combative, and in this case the Nortons seem to have resolved theirs by living at opposite ends of the continent."

Carl stared at the hotel window, where evening was already starting to shut down the sky. His reflection stared back, hemmed him in. He put a crooked elbow to the glass and leaned on it with his forearm over his head, fingers stroking through his hair. It was something Marisol used to—

"And the New York hit? The fact he was the only person who knew where I was sleeping?"

"Is coincidence," said Matthew crisply.

He met his reflection's eyes in the glass. "Well, it doesn't feel much like it from where I'm standing."

"Coincidence never does. It's not in the nature of human genetic wiring to accept it. And as a thirteen, you have your own increased predisposition toward paranoia to contend with as well."

Carl grimaced. "Has it ever occurred to you Matt, that—"

"Matthew."

"Yeah, Matthew. Sorry. Has it ever occurred to you that for a thirteen, for someone who doesn't connect well with group dynamics, paranoia might be quite a useful trait to have?"

"Yes, and evolutionarily selective, too." The datahawk's didactic tone had not shifted. It almost never did; didactic was part of the way Matthew was wired. "But this is not the point. Human intuition is deceptive, because it is not always consistent. It is not necessarily a good fit for the environments we now live in, or the mathematics that underlie them. When it does echo mathematical form, it's clearly indicative of an inherent capacity to detect the underlying mathematics."

"But not when they clash." Carl leaned his forehead against the glass. They'd had this discussion before, countless times. "Right?"

"Not when they clash," Matthew agreed. "When they clash, the mathematics remain correct. The intuition merely indicates a mismatch of evolved capacities with a changed or changing environment."

"So Norton's clean?"

"Norton is clean."

Carl turned his back on his reflection. Leaned against the window and looked around the room that caged him. He recognized the reflex—seeking exits. Stupid, there was the fucking door, right there.

So use it, fuckwit.

"Does it ever bother you?" he asked into the phone.

"Does what bother me, Carl?"

"This whole thing." He gestured as if Matthew could see him. "Jacobsen, the fucking Accords, the Agency and the enforcement. Having to be licensed like some fucking hazardous substance."

"To the extent that personal identification records are a form of social licensing, we are all licensed, base humans and variants alike. If the type of licensing reflects certain gradients of social risk, is that a bad thing?"

Carl sighed. "Okay, forget it. I'm asking the wrong person."

"In what way?"

"Well, no offense, but you're a gleech. Your whole profile is post-autistic. This is an emotional thing we're talking about."

"My emotional range has been psychochemically rebalanced and extended."

"Yeah, by an n-djinn. Sorry, Matthew, I don't know why I'm fronting you with this stuff. You're no more normal than I am."

"Leaving aside for a moment the question of what exactly you would consider to be a normal human, what makes you think you would receive a more valid answer from one? Are normal humans especially gifted in discovering complex ethical truths?"

Carl thought about that.

"Not that I've noticed," he admitted gloomily. "No."

"So my perception of the post-Jacobsen order is probably no more or less useful than any other rational human's."

"Yeah, but that's just the big fat point." Carl grinned. There was a solid pleasure in showing up the datahawk and his hyperbalanced mind-set, mainly because he didn't get to do it very often. "This isn't *about* rational humans. The Jacobsen Report wasn't about a rational response to genetic licensing, it was about a group of rational men trying to broker a deal with the gibbering mass of irrational humanity. The religious lunatics, the race purists, the whole doom-of-civilization crew." For a moment, he stared off blindly into a corner of the room. "I mean, don't you remember all that stuff back in '89, '90? The demonstrations? The vitriol in the feeds? The mobs outside the facilities and the army bases, crashing the fences?"

"Yes. I remember it. But it did not bother me."

Carl shrugged. "Well, you didn't scare them like we did."

"And yet Jacobsen was not a capitulation to the forces you describe. The report is critical of both irrational responses and simplistic thinking."

"Yeah. But look who ended up in the tracts anyway."

Matthew said nothing. Carl saw Stefan Nevant's lupine grin, rubbed at his eyes to make it go away.

"Look, Matt, thanks—"

"Matthew."

"Sorry. Matthew. Thanks for the check on Norton, 'kay? Talk to you soon."

He hung up. Tossed the phone on the bed and got rapidly dressed in the least used and bloodied garments from among his limited wardrobe. He let himself out of the hotel room, paused briefly on his way past Sevgi Ertekin's door, then made an exasperated noise in his throat and stalked on. He waited ten impatient seconds at the elevator, then stiff-armed the door to the emergency stairwell open instead and went down the steps two at a time. Crossed the lobby at a fast stride and went out into the city. He walked a single block to get the feel of the evening, then flagged down an autocab.

The interior was low-lit and cozy, an expansive black leatherette womb with slash-narrow views to the passing street. In the gloom on the front panel, an armored screen blipped into life and showed him a rather idealized female driver interface. Generic Rim beauty, the classic Asian-Hispanic blend. Pinned dark hair, a hint of a curl in it, chic high-collar jacket. Something of Carmen Ren in the features and the poise, but machined up to an inhuman perfection. The voice was an Asia Badawi rip-off.

"Good evening, sir. Welcome to Cable Cars. What will be your choice of destination this evening?"

He hesitated. Sutherland, he knew, would not have been impressed with this.
Sutherland's on fucking Mars.
"Just take me somewhere I can get in a fight," he said.

Switched off and careless from jet lag, long sleep, and yesterday's combat,
he never noticed the figure on the corner that watched him leave the hotel, or
the nondescript teardrop that slid out from parking on the opposite side of the
street and dropped into the traffic behind his cab.

CHAPTER 41

Dougie Kwang's week had been shaping up for shit ever since it started, and tonight didn't look any better. He was three games down to Valdez already, stalking the angles of the table, pumping violent, crack-bang shots to take his mind off it all. The technique—*if you want to call it that,* he fumed—mostly just rattled the balls in the jaws, and they sat out more often than he sank them. He knew his anger was the exact reason he was losing, but he couldn't shake it loose. There was too much else gone to shit around him.

Wundawari's shipment never made it through MTC in Jakarta; Wundawari herself was now banged up in an Indonesian jail on trumped-up holding charges until some scummy Seattle-based rights lawyer she used could wire across and get her out. The money was gone. *Write it off,* the Seattle guy advised drily down the line, *what you maybe claw back from the Maritime Transit guys in compensation, you're going to be paying me in fees.* Dougie might have called him on that one, but Wundawari wouldn't do the time, and both he and Seattle knew it. She was too soft, came from Kuala Lumpur money and a whole crèche of spoiled-brat connections down in the Freeport. She'd pay whatever Seattle wanted.

On the street, things were no better. Alcatraz station were coming down hard and heavy all over the fucking place, big-ass RimSec interventions at levels those guys mostly didn't bother with. He still couldn't find out why. Some shit about a factory raft bust last night and the fallout, but none of his few bought-and-paid-for touches inside the RimSec machine ranked high enough to know any more than that. More importantly, they were too fucking scared of Alcatraz to risk sniffing around any closer. End result was, he couldn't move shit anywhere north of Selby or west of the Boulevard, and even in the yards at Hunter Point, he was getting heat he didn't need. And the border had been sticky for fucking *months* now, none of the gangs he knew could get more than the odd fence-bunny across, mostly straitlaced white girls out of the Dakotas who took fucking forever to break in and even then didn't play too well to popular demand.

Mama was still coughing. Still wouldn't take her fucking pills.

Now Valdez was lining up in the wake of another too-hard-too-fast fuckup, two spots floating nice and loose over open pockets, clean backup angles everywhere, and then the eight-ball doubled into the side, one of Valdez's favorite cheap trick shots, he'd do it with his fucking eyes closed if he wanted. Another fifty bucks. He'd—

But Valdez frowned instead and lifted his chin off the cue. Got up and came around the table to Dougie, eyes narrowed.

"Hey, *pengo mio.* You say Elvira *wasn't* working tonight?" He nodded across the gloom to the bar. "Because if that ain't work, then you got a problem."

So Dougie slanted a glance across the gloom to where Valdez was looking, and like the rest of it wasn't fucking enough, here's Elvie on her stool with her back to the bar, elbows down and tits cranked out in that red top he bought her back in May, legs making all kinds of slit-skirt angles on the frame of the stool, and all for this big black guy draped over the next stool and just looking her over like she's fruit on some Meade Avenue street stall.

Too fucking much.

He hefted the cue up one-handed through his own grip, half a meter down from the tip where it thickened, reversed his hold, and carried it low at his side across to the bar. Elvira saw him coming, made that dumb fucking face of hers, and stopped gabbing. Dougie let the silence work for him, came on a couple more steps and locked to a halt a meter and a half off the black guy's shoulder.

"That's a mistake you're making, pal," he said, breathing hard. Anger slurred through his tone like smeared paint on a cheap logo. "See, Elvira here isn't working tonight. You want some cheap fucking pussy, you'd better come around and see her another fucking day. Got that?"

"We're just talking." The black guy's tone was low and reasonable, almost bored. Weird fucking accent as well. He didn't even look at Dougie. "If Elvira's not working, I guess she's free to do that, right?"

Dougie felt the weight of the day come down on him like demolition.

"I don't think you're paying attention," he told the guy tightly.

And then the black guy did look at him, a sudden switch so his eyes collected Dougie's stare like third base snapping up a low ball out at Monster Park.

"No, I am," he said.

It stopped Dougie dead in his tracks, knocked him back and kept the cue at his side, because at some level he couldn't quite nail he knew this guy was actively looking for what came next. It felt like a skid, like ice under his wheels when he least expected it. He knew he had to keep going, no one much in the place tonight but Valdez was watching, so were the barkeep and a couple of others, whatever went down, street feed would have it out to everyone by morning, he *had* to fuck this guy up, but the ground under his feet had shifted, was no longer safe, he couldn't fucking read this guy or what he'd do.

He tightened his grip on the cue.

"Try to hit me with that thing," said the black man softly. "I will kill you."

Dougie's heart kicked in his chest. He felt the rage flicker, overstoked, held too long, suddenly unreliable. Tiny, rain-drip voice of caution in the gap. He drew breath, forced the knowledge down.

"Door's over there," he said. "Just walk the fuck away."

"My feet are tired."

So Dougie just swung that fucking cue like he'd always known deep down he'd have to. Lips peeled back off a snarl and the shaky lift of the held-too-long adrenal surge.

Situation like that, what else was he going to fucking do?

Even as the fight bloomed, Carl could feel the small seep of disappointment at the back of it all. This swaggering low-grade gangster in front of him, a little more spine than most pimps maybe, but in the end no competition, no real threat.

Yeah, like you expected anything else out here, black-walled bunker bar in a derelict neighborhood on the edge of an all but fully automated navy yard. Not like he hadn't discussed it carefully enough with the autocab, walked the deserted streets for long enough looking. *Face it, soak, this is* exactly *what you've been prowling for. This is what you wanted. Enjoy.*

The fight was so mapped out in his head, it was almost preordained. He already had his weight braced off the stool he'd been using, some in the forearm where he leaned on the bar, more in his legs than he showed. He saw the intention tremor down the other guy's arm, grabbed a leg of the stool and yanked the whole thing savagely upward. The leg ends hit and gouged, face and chest. Swing momentum on the seat end hooked the thing around and blocked out the cue completely—the strike never made it above waist height. He let go, stepped in as the pimp reeled back, hand up to the rip in his face. The stool tumbled away. Carl threw a long chop, hard as he could make it, into the unguarded side of the throat. The pimp hit the floor, dead as far as he could tell. Elvira shrieked.

At the pool table, the pimp's shaven-headed friend stood shocked and motionless, cue held defensively across his body in both hands. Carl stalked forward a couple of steps, proximity sense peeled for the rest of the room.

"Well?" he rasped.

It was half a dozen meters at most; if the skinhead had a gun, he wasn't going to have time to clear it before Carl was on him. Carl saw in his face that he knew it.

Peripheral vision, left. The barkeep, fumbling for something, phone or weapon. Carl threw out an arm, finger raised.

"Don't."

On the floor, the pimp moaned and shifted. Carl checked every face in the room, calibrated probable responses, then kicked the downed man in the head. The moaning stopped.

"What's his name?" he asked of the room.

"Uh, it's Dougie." The barkeep. "Dougie Kwang."

"Right. Well anyone here who's a big friend of Dougie Kwang's, maybe wants to stay and discuss this with me, you can. Anyone else had better leave."

Hasty shuffle of feet, graunch of chair legs jammed back in a hurry. The thin crowd, scrabbling to leave. The door swung open for them. He felt the cold it let in touch the back of his neck. The barkeep snatched the opportunity, went too. Left him with Elvira, who'd started grubbing about on the floor next to Dougie in tears, and the skinhead, whom Carl guessed just didn't trust getting safe passage to the door. He gave him a cold smile.

"You really want to make something of this?"

"No, he doesn't. Look at his face. Stop being an asshole and let him go."

Control and the mesh stopped him whipping around at the voice, the cool amusement and the iron certainty beneath. He already knew from the tone that there was a gun pointing at him. That he wasn't on the floor next to Dougie, shot dead or dying, was the only part that didn't make sense.

He shelved the wonder, stepped aside with ironic courtesy, and gestured the skinhead to pass him. Momentary flashback to the chapel in South Florida State, the sneering white supremacist walking past him up the aisle. Suddenly he was sick of it all, the cheap postures and moves, the use of stares, the whole fucking mechanistic predictability of the man-dance.

"Go on," he said flatly. "Looks like you get a free pass. Better take Elvira there with you."

He watched Dougie Kwang's friend drop the pool cue he was clutching and come forward a hesitant step at a time. He couldn't work out what was going on, either. His eyes flickered from Carl to whoever the new arrival was and back. A numb failure to catch up was stamped across his face like a bootprint. He knelt beside the off-duty whore and tried to manhandle her to her feet. She wriggled and wept, refused to get up, hands still plastered on Dougie's motionless form, long dark-curling hair shrouding his eyes-wide, frozen face. She keened and sobbed, half-comprehensible fragments, some Sino-Spanish street mix Carl couldn't follow well.

Enjoying our handiwork here, are we?

He wondered momentarily if, when the time came, there'd be a woman, any woman, to weep like this for him.

"We don't have all night," said the voice behind him.

Carl turned slowly, fear of the bullet prickling at the base of his neck. Time to see what the fuck had gone wrong.

Right. Like you don't already know.

There was a tall man at the door.

A couple of others, too, neither of them small, but it was this one who drew attention the way you vectored in on color in a drab landscape. Carl's mesh-sharpened senses fixed on the heavy silver revolver in the raised and black-gloved hand, the bizarre, consciously antiquated statement it made, but it wasn't that. Wasn't the oily, slicked-back dark hair or the slight sheen on the tanned and creased white features, telltale marks of cell-fix facial and hair gel for an assassin who had no intention of leaving genetic trace material at the scene of his crime. Carl saw all this and set it aside for what really mattered.

It was the way the man stood, the way he looked into the room as if it were a stage set purely for his benefit. It was the way his dark clothes were wrapped on his body as if blown there by a storm, as if he didn't much care whether he wore them or not. The way his tanned face had some vague familiarity to it, some sense that you must have met this person before somewhere, and that he had meant something to you back then.

Thirteen.

Had to be. Paranoia confirmed. Merrin's back-office crew, come for payback. It wasn't over.

Beside Carl, the pool player spoke urgently to Elvira, finally succeeded in getting her to her feet, and shepherded her past Carl with an arm around her shaking shoulders. The same dazed mix of shock and incomprehension on his face as before. Carl nodded him past, then turned slowly to watch him half carry Elvira to the door. The new arrivals stood aside to let the couple out, and one of them closed the door firmly afterward. All the time, the silver gun never shifted from its focus.

Carl gave its owner a sardonic smile and moved a few casual steps forward.

The other man watched him come closer, but he didn't move or make any objection. Carl breathed. He wasn't going to get shot just yet, it appeared.

But it's coming.

He took the bright flicker of fear, broke it, and folded it away. The mesh and a sustained will to do damage pulsed brighter.

Push it, see how far it goes.

It went almost to touching distance.

The tall man let him come on that far, even gave him a gentle, encouraging smile, like an indulgent adult watching a child in his charge do something daring. Close enough that Carl's assessment of the situation began to flake apart, to leave him abruptly uncertain of how to play this. But then, a couple of meters off the muzzle of the revolver, the tall man's smile shifted on his face, never quite left it, settled into something hard and careful.

"That'll do," he said softly. "I'm not that careless."

Carl nodded. "You don't look it. Do I know you from somewhere?"

"I don't know. Do you?"

"What's your name?"

"You can call me Onbekend."

"Marsalis."

"Yes, I know." The tall man nodded toward a nearby table. "Sit down. We've got a little time."

So. Cool gust of confirmation down the back of his neck, down the muscles of his forearms.

"You sit down. I'm fine right here."

The revolver's hammer clicked back. "Sit down or I'll kill you."

Carl looked in the eyes and saw no space there, not even for the snappy one-liner—*Looks like you're going to do that anyway.* This man would put him down right here and now. He shrugged and stepped across to the table, lowered himself into one of the abandoned chairs. It was still warm from its previous occupant. He leaned back and set his feet apart, as far off the table edge as he thought he could get away with. Onbekend glanced at one of his shadows, nodded at the door. The man slipped quietly outside.

The remaining backup stood immobile, fixed Carl with a cold stare, and folded his arms. Onbekend checked him with another glance and then moved across and seated himself opposite Carl at the table.

"You're the lottery guy, aren't you?" he said.

Carl sighed. It wasn't entirely faked. "Yeah, that's me."

"The one who woke up halfway home?"

"Yeah. You looking for an autograph?"

He got a thin smile. "I'm curious. What was it like, being stuck out there all that time, waiting?"

"It was a riot. You should try it sometime."

Onbekend didn't react any more than a stone. The sense of familiarity grew—Carl was certain it was specific. He knew this face, or one very like it, from somewhere.

"Did you feel abandoned? Like when you were fourteen all over again?"

Fourteen?

Carl grinned. The tiny piece of advantage felt adrenal in his veins. He cocked his head, elaborately casual.

"So you were a Lawman, huh? Fortress America's final set of southern-fried chickens coming home to roost."

Just there, just as tiny, but there nonetheless, there in the corners of Onbekend's eyes. Loss of poise, siphoned sip of anger. For just that moment, Carl had him backed up.

"You think you know me? You don't fucking know me, my friend."

"I'm not your fucking friend, either," Carl told him mildly. "So there you go. We all make these mistakes. What do you want from me, exactly?"

For a moment so brief it was gone before he even registered it, Carl thought he was dead. The barrel of the revolver didn't shift, but it seemed to glimmer with intent in the lower field of his vision. Onbekend's mouth smeared a little tighter, his eyes hated a little more.

"You could start by telling me how it feels to hunt down other variant thirteens for the cudlips at the UN."

"Remunerative." Carl stared blandly back into the other thirteen's narrowed eyes. One of them was going to die in this bar. "It feels remunerative. What are *you* doing for a living these days?"

"Surviving."

"Oh." He nodded, mock-understanding. "Playing the outlaw, are we?"

"I'm not working for the cudlips, if that's what you mean."

"Sure you are." Carl yawned—sudden, tension-driven demand for oxygen, out of nowhere, but it played so fucking well he could have crowed. "We're all working for the cudlips, one way or another."

Onbekend set his jaw. Tipped his head a little, like a wolf or a dog listening for something faint. "You talk very easily about other men's compromises. Like I said, you don't fucking know me at all."

"I know you bought food today. I know you traveled here in some kind of manufactured vehicle, on city streets built and paid for in some shape or form by the local citizenry. I know you're holding a gun you didn't build from raw metal in your spare time."

"This?" Onbekend raised the gun slightly, took the muzzle fractionally out of line. He seemed amused. Carl forced himself not to tense, not to watch the wavering weapon. "I took this gun from a man I killed."

"Oh, well there's a sustainable model of exchange. Did you kill the guy who served you breakfast this morning as well, so you wouldn't have to pay for that, either? Going to murder the guy who sold or rented you your transport option, and the guy who runs the place you sleep tonight? Got plans for the people who employ them, too, the ones who run the means of production, the managers and the owners, and the people who sell for them and the people who buy from them?" Carl leaned forward, grinning hard against the cool proximity of death. It felt like biting down. "Don't you fucking get it? They're all around us, the cudlips. You can't escape them. You can't cut loose of them. Every time you consume, you're working for them. Every time you travel. On Mars, every time you fucking *breathe* you're part of it."

"Well." Onbekend put together another small smile of his own. "You've learned your lesson well. But I guess if you whip a dog often enough, it always will."

"Oh *please*. You know what? You want to pretend there's some other way? You want to escape into some mythical pre-virilicide golden age—go live in Jesusland, where they still believe in that shit. I was there last week, they love guys like us. They'd burn us both at the stake as soon as look at us. Don't you understand? *There is no place for what we are anymore.*" Sutherland's words seemed to rise in him, Sutherland's quiet, amused, bass-timbre voice like thunder, like strength. "They killed us twenty thousand years ago with their crops and their craven connivance at hierarchy. They won, Onbekend, and you want to know why? They won because it *worked*. Group cooperation and bowing down to some thug with a beard worked better than standing alone as a thirteen was ever going to. They ran us ragged, Onbekend, with their mobs and leaders and their fucking strength in numbers. They hunted us down, they exterminated us, and they got the future as a prize. And now here we are, standing in the roof garden of the cudlip success story, and you're telling me no, no, you didn't take the elevator or the stairs, you just fucking flew up here all on your own, all with your own two fucking wings. You are *full* of shit."

Onbekend leaned forward, mirroring, eyes flaring. It was instinctive, anger-driven. The revolver shifted fractionally in his hand to allow the shift in posture. Angled minutely to one side. Carl saw, and held down the surge of the mesh. *Not yet, not yet.* He met the other man's eyes, saw his own death there, and didn't much care. There was a rage rising in him he barely understood. The words kept him alive, warmed him as long as he could spit them out.

"They *built* us, Onbekend, they fucking built us. They brought us back from the fucking dead for the one thing we're good at. Violence. Slaughter. You, me." He gestured, slashing, open-handed disgust. "All of us, every fucking one. We're *dinosaurs.* Monsters summoned up from the deep dark violent past to safeguard the bright lights and shopping privileges of Western civilization. And we *did* it for them, just like they wanted. You want to talk about cudlips, how they bow and fold to authority, how they let the group dictate? Tell me how we were different. Project fucking Lawman? What does that sound like to you?"

"Yeah, because they fucking *trained* us." For the first time, Onbekend's voice rose almost to a shout, was almost pain. He flattened it again, instantly, got it down to a cold, even-tempered anger. "They locked us up from fucking child-hood, Marsalis. Beat us down with the conditioning. You know that, Osprey must have been the same. How were we supposed to—"

"*We did, as we, were told!*" Carl spaced his words, leaned on them like crow-bars going into brickwork. "Just like them, just like the cudlips. We *failed,* just like we failed twenty thousand years ago."

"That was then," Onbekend snapped. "And this is now. And some of us aren't on that path anymore."

"Oh don't make me fucking laugh. I already told you, *everything about you* is part of the cudlip world. If you can't come to some kind of accommodation with that, you might as well fucking shoot yourself—"

A ghost grin came up across Onbekend's face. "It was your suicide I was sent to arrange, Marsalis. Not mine."

"Sent?" Carl jeered it, leered across the scant space between them. "*Sent?* Oh, I rest my fucking case."

"Thirteens have had an unfortunate propensity for death by their own hand." The other man's voice came out raised, words rushed, trampling at Carl's scorn, trying to drive home a winning point he hadn't embedded quite as well as he'd hoped. "Violent suicide, in the tracts and reservations. And a thirteen carrying as much guilt as you—"

"Guilt? Give me a *fucking* break. Now you're *talking* just like them. Variant thirteen doesn't do guilt, that's a cudlip thing."

"Yes, all the ones you've hunted down, murdered, or taken back to a living death in the tracts." But Onbekend was calmer now, voice dropping back to even. "It stands to reason you couldn't live with it forever."

"Try me."

A bleak smile. "Happily, I don't have to. And as for the suicide, you've made it easy for me."

"Really?" Carl looked elaborately around him. "This doesn't look much like a suicide scene to me."

But under the drawl, he already saw the angle and something very like panic started to ice through him. He'd played all his cards, and Onbekend just hadn't loosened enough. The other thirteen was watching him minutely again, back to the cold control he'd walked in with. Awareness of the place they were in congealed around him—ancient grimy fittings, the long arm of the bartop, scars and spill stains gleaming in the low light and the piled-up glassware and bottles behind. The worn pool tables in their puddles of light from the overheads. Dougie Kwang faceup on the floor, head rolled to one side, eyes staring open across the room at him. Waiting for company, for someone to join him down there in the dust and sticky stains.

"Suicide would be hard to fake here," Onbekend agreed. "Would have been harder to fake wherever we did it. But you've been kind enough to let your drives get the better of you and so here we are, a mindless bar brawl in a low-grade neighborhood with low-grade criminals to match, and it seems Carl Marsalis just miscalled the odds. Pretty fucking stupid way to die, but hey." A shrug. Onbekend's voice tinged suddenly with contempt. "They'll believe it of you. You've given them no reason not to."

The oblique accusation stung. In the back of his head, Sutherland concurred. *If we are ruled by our limbic wiring, then every bigoted, hate-driven fear they have of us becomes a truth.*

Ertekin might not buy it.

Yeah, but she might. You don't always get a clean wrap, Marsalis. Remember that? Life is messy, and so is crime.

Kwang seemed to wink at him from the floor.

Could be this'll be just messy enough for her, soak.

As if he didn't have enough with his own thoughts beating him up, Onbekend was still going strong.

"They'll believe you were too stupid to beat your own programming," he said matter-of-factly, as if he'd been there for Sutherland's musings, too. "Because you are. They'll believe you went looking for trouble, because you did exactly that, and they'll believe you found a little too much of it down here to handle alone. So they'll do a little light investigating, they'll talk to some people, and in the end they'll decide you got shot at close range with a nondescript gun that'll never be found, in the hand of some nameless street thug who'll also never be found, and they'll walk away, Marsalis, they'll walk away because it'll fit right in with this idiocy you've spontaneously generated for us. I couldn't have arranged it better myself."

Carl gestured. "That's hardly a nondescript gun."

"This?" Onbekend lifted the revolver again, weighed it in his hand. "This is—"

Now.

It wasn't much—the fractionally lowered reflexive response in the other man, neurochemical sparks lulled and damped down by Carl's previous open-handed gestures and the descending calm after all the shouting. Then the fractional shift of the revolver's muzzle, the few degrees off and the brief lack of tension on the trigger. Then Onbekend's standard-issue thirteen sense of superiority, the curious need he seemed to have to lecture. It wasn't much.

Not much at all.

Carl exploded out of the chair, hands to the table edge, flipping it up and over. Onbekend got one shot off, wide, and then he was staggering back, trying to get out of the chair and on his feet. The shadow by the door yelled and moved. Carl was across the empty space where the table had been, into Onbekend, palm heel and hooking elbow, turning, try for the gun, lock in close, too close to shoot at. He had the other thirteen's arm in both hands now, twisted the revolver up and around, looking for the man by the door. Tried for the trigger. Onbekend got his finger out, blocked the attempt, but it didn't matter. The other man yelled again, dodged away from the slug he thought was coming. The door flew inward on its hinges, the other half of Onbekend's human backup burst into the room. Carl yanked at the revolver, couldn't get it free. The new arrival didn't make the same mistake as his companion. He stepped in, grinning.

"Just hold him there, Onbee."

Desperate, Carl hacked sideways with one foot, tried to get the fight on the ground and jar the revolver out of Onbekend's stubborn grip. The other thirteen locked ankles with him, stood firm, and Carl tumbled instead, pulled off balance by his own weight and a *tanindo* move that hadn't worked. Onbekend timed it just right, stepped wide and shrugged him off like a heavy backpack. He went down, clutching for the revolver, didn't get it. Onbekend kicked him in the groin. He convulsed around the blow, tried frantically to roll, to get up—

Onbekend leveled the revolver.

The world seemed to stop, to lean in and watch.

In the small unreal stillness, he knew the impact before it came, and the knowledge was terrifying because it felt like freedom. He felt himself open to it, like spreading wings, like snarling. His eyes locked with Onbekend's. He grinned and spat out a final defiance.

"You sad, deluded little fuck."

And then the gunblasts, the final violence through the quiet, again—again—again, like the repeated slamming of a door in a storm.

CHAPTER 42

The Beretta Marstech had a burst function that allowed three shots for every trigger pull. Sevgi Ertekin came through the door with it enabled, gun raised and cupped in both hands, and she squeezed the trigger twice for each figure in her sights. No time for niceties: she'd seen through the window what was about to go down. The expansion slugs made a flat, undramatic crackling sound as they launched, but they tore down her targets like cardboard.

Bodies jerked and hurled aside. Two down.

The third one was turning, tiger-swift, the first burst missed him altogether. A big, heavy silver revolver tracking around in his hand. She squeezed again and he flipped over backward like a circus trick.

Marsalis flopped about on the ground, struggled to sit up. She couldn't see if he was hit. She advanced into the room, gun swinging to cover angles in approved fashion. Peering down at the men she'd just hit, no, wait—

—she took in staring eyes and crumpled, awkward postures, one of them slumped almost comically in the arms of a chair, legs slid out from under him, one on the floor in a sprawl of limbs like some tantrum-prone child's doll—

—the men she'd just killed. The Marstech gun and its load, unequivocal in its sentencing as a Jesusland judge.

The third one hit her from the side. Flash glimpse of a bloodied face, distorted with rage. She hit the floor, arms splayed back to break the fall, lost the fucking Beretta with the impact. For a moment the third man lurched above her, growling through lips skinned back off his teeth, empty hands crooked like talons. The look in the eyes was savage, stripped of anything human. She felt the terror thrust up like wings in her stomach and chest.

He saw the fallen gun. Stepped past her to get it.

"Onbekend!"

Her attacker twisted around, bent halfway over to the Beretta, saw the same as her—Carl Marsalis, propped up off the floor with the big revolver in his hand.

Onbekend wheeled around and the shot went wide. Deep bellow of the heavy caliber across the room. Marsalis snarled something, swung and fired again. The door slammed shut on the other man.

Sevgi grabbed up her gun.

"You okay?"

Grim nod. He was getting unsteadily to his feet. She gave him a tight grin and went to the door. Pushed it open a crack and peered out. The teardrop she'd taxi-trailed from the hotel was still there on the other side of the deserted, dilapidated street. The injured third man fumbled at its door, got it open. No time. She ran through and took up her firing stance again on the sidewalk. A thousand memories from the streets and back alleys of Queens and Manhattan, eleven years of pursuits and arrests—it pulsed through her, anchored her, steadied her hands.

"Police officer! Put your hands on your head, get down on the ground!"

He seemed to kneel at the opened door of the car. She trod closer.

"I said get your hands—"

He spun, yanked a weapon clear from somewhere. Came up firing. She shot back. Clutch of three—saw him punched back on the teardrop's high-sheen flank, but knew at the same time she'd gone too high. Felt something kick her in the left shoulder, staggered with it and fell back against the wall of the bar. One leg shot out from under her, she flailed not to go all the way down. She braced herself on the wall, saw him reel off the car, leave smears of blood on the shiny bodywork of the teardrop, stagger and collapse inside the vehicle. She fought to get upright again, watched him lean out to haul the door closed after him, knew she was going to be too late. She threw up the Beretta one-handed and snapped off a shot. The three-slug burst was too powerful to hold down; the bullets pinged off the teardrop, nowhere near. The door hinged and snapped shut with a clunk she heard clear across the street. The engine whined into instant life. She stumbled forward, tried to straighten up, tried against the numbness in her shoulder to get a clean bead on the teardrop as it took off.

Three times, she came down on the trigger. Nine shots, solid pulsing kick each time into the wounded shoulder from the two-handed firing stance she held. The teardrop slewed side to side, then straightened up, reached a corner and took it at speed, disappeared from view on a screech of abused tires. She let her arms drop, blew out a disgusted breath, and just stood there for a moment.

"Fuck it," she said finally. Her voice sounded loud in the suddenly silent street. "Two out of three, anyone got a problem with that?"

Apparently no one did.

She walked back to the bar, pushed open the door, and leaned there in the doorway, surveying the mess. Marsalis had gotten himself upright in the midst of it, had the revolver in his hand. He jolted as she came in, then just stood there looking at her. A faint smile twitched at her lips.

"I take it there's no one back there in the restroom."

"You take it right."

"Good. I'm tired." She put the Beretta away in its shoulder holster, wincing a little at the pain the movement caused her.

"You okay?"

She looked down at her left shoulder, where the slug had torn through. Blood leaked slowly down the arm of her ruined jacket. The numbness was fading out now to a solid, thumping ache. She flexed her left hand, lifted it and grimaced a little at the pain.

"Yeah, he tagged me. Flesh wound. I'll live."

"You want me to take a look at it?"

"No, I don't fucking want you to take a look at it." She hesitated, gestured what might have been apology. Her voice softened. "RimSec are on their way. It'll wait."

"I heard the car. Did he get away?"

She grimaced. "Yeah. Hit him a couple of times, but not enough to put him down. Thirteens, huh."

"Yeah, we're tough motherfuckers you know."

And then the breath seemed to come out of Marsalis as if he'd been punctured. He went to the bar, got behind it, and laid the revolver carefully down on the scarred wood.

"Thank Christ that's over," he said feelingly. "You need a drink."

"No, I don't need a fucking drink. He got away."

Marsalis turned to survey the piled assortment of bottles behind him. His eyes found her in the mirror.

"Yeah, but look on the bright side. We're neither of us dead, which is a big fucking improvement on what I was expecting ten minutes ago."

She shivered a little. Shook it off. Marsalis picked out a bottle from the multitude and a couple of shot glasses from below the bar. He set the glasses up on the bartop and drizzled amber-colored liquor into them.

"Look, humor me. Least I owe you for saving my life back there is a couple of stolen whiskeys. And you look like you could use them."

"Oh hey, thanks a lot. I save your fucking life, you tell me I look like shit?"

He made a wobbling plane of his hand, tilted it back and forth. "Bit pale, let's say."

"Fuck you." She picked up the glass.

He matched her, clinked the glasses together very gently. Said very quietly, "I owe you, Sevgi."

She sipped and swallowed. "Call it quits for the skaters. You don't owe me a thing."

"Oh but I do. Those guys in New York were trying to kill me as well as you. That was self-defense. This is different. Cheers."

They both drained their glasses. Sevgi leaned on the bar opposite him and felt the warmth work its way down into her belly. He lifted the bottle, querying. She shook her head.

"Like I said, RimSec should be here any minute," she said. "I called them back around the time your friends made their entrance. Would have stormed in a little earlier but I was hoping for some backup."

"Well." He looked at his hands and she saw they were trembling a little. It did something to the pit of her stomach to see that. He looked up again, grinned. "Pretty good timing anyway. How the hell did you wind up here?"

"I saw you walk out of the hotel. I was just arriving." She nodded at the corpses on the floor between them. "Saw the teardrop with these guys pull out and go after your taxi. Took me a few seconds to flag one down myself. Then when I got down here, I saw them sit outside the bar and wait. I didn't know what the fuck was going on, what you'd be doing all the way out of town like this, if these guys were with you or not. Only called it in when I heard shots and then headed on over. Which reminds me, what the fuck *were* you doing down here?"

He looked away from her, into a corner. "Just looking for a fight."

"Yeah? Looks like you found a good one."

He said nothing.

"So who were they?"

"I don't know."

"You called him something." A sudden cop sharpness spiked in her mind, ruined the moment with its objections. "Back when he went for the gun. I heard you. *On*-something."

"Onbekend, yeah. It's his name. He introduced himself while he was getting ready to kill me." Marsalis frowned to himself. "He was a thirteen."

"He told you that?"

"It came up in the conversation, yeah."

She shivered again. "Bit of a coincidence."

"Isn't it. Speaking of which, what were *you* doing back at the hotel watching me?"

"Oh yeah. That." She nodded, let the satisfaction of being right warm her into a faint smile of her own. "Came to tell you. NYPD tracked down the third skater and brought him in. He says their target was Ortiz all along. Not you."

Marsalis blinked. "Ortiz?"

"Yeah. Seems you and me just got caught in the crossfire. Sort of puts Norton in the clear, doesn't it. Paranoia aside, I mean."

"Are you sure about this? I mean, did NYPD check if—"

"Marsalis, just fucking drop it." Her weariness seemed to be building. Or maybe the whiskey had been a bad idea. Either way, her eyes were starting to ache. "Better yet, just think about apologizing, if you know how that's done. You were fucking wrong. End of fucking story."

"Don't gloat, Ertekin. It's not attractive, remember."

And she had to laugh then, even through the crushing weight of the tiredness. In the distance, she heard a RimSec siren approaching.

"And I'm not looking to get laid," she said.

"Yeah, you are."

She chuckled. "No, I'm fucking not."

"You are."

"Am fucking not, you—"

She coughed hard, caught off guard by the abrupt violence of it. Shook her head and found her eyes flooded with sudden tears. She heard Marsalis produce a chuckle of his own.

"Well, maybe not, then. I wouldn't want to—"

Another shiver ripped through her, stronger. In the wake of the coughing, her head was suddenly aching. She frowned and put a hand to the side of her brow.

"Sevgi?"

She looked up, gave him a puzzled smile. The shivering was still there; she hadn't shaken it at all. The siren was louder now, but it seemed to get stuck inside her head and the noise it made there scraped. "I don't feel too good."

His face went mask-like with shock.

"What did he shoot you with, Sevgi?"

"I don't—"

"*Did you see the gun he shot you with?*" He was around the bar, at her side as she shook her head sleepily.

"No. He got away. Like I said."

He turned her, put his hands on either side of her face. His voice was tight and urgent. "Listen to me, Sevgi. You have to stay awake. You're going to start feeling very tired in the next—"

"*Going* to?" She giggled. "Fuck, Marsalis, I could sleep for a month right here on this fucking floor."

"No, you *stay awake*." He shook her head. "Listen, they're coming, they'll be here. We'll get you to the hospital. Just don't fucking flake on me."

"What are you *talking* about? I'm not going to—"

She stopped because she noticed groggily that his eyes were tear-sheened like her own. She frowned, and the skin on her face felt hot and thick and stiff, she had to force expression into it like pushing a hand into a tight new glove. She made a small, amused sound.

"Hey, Marsalis," she slurred, trying not to. "What's the matter? You feeling bad as well?"

The RimSec medical team took her out in a stretcher, got her in the helicopter. She wasn't quite sure how that had happened; one minute Marsalis was cradling her in the corpse-strewn shithole bar, the next they were out in the chilly air and she was looking straight up at the shrouded stars. Awareness was a flapping cloth behind her eyes, there then gone, gone then back again. She tried to crane her neck and see what was going on around her, but it was all a blur of shouts and lights and hurrying busy figures. The clatter of the helicopter rotors just added to what was now a splitting headache.

"Sevgi?"

Oh, Marsalis. There he was.

"It's okay, sir. We'll take it from here."

"You tell them it's a Haag slug." She couldn't work out why he was shouting, unless it was the racket of the rotor blades. Nothing seemed to connect up the way it should. She thought maybe she'd lost a lot of blood after all. "You tell them they've got to get the smartest antivirals they have into her, right now."

"We know that, sir. We've called ahead."

She squinted in the glare from the helicopter's landing lights. It hurt to do it. She just about made out Marsalis's bulk. He had one of the paramedics by the shoulders, was shaking him.

"Don't you fucking let her die," he was yelling. "I will kill you and everyone you care for if you let her die."

Scuffling. The helicopter shifted about, lifted, and wheeled away. Studded lights all over the hills of the city, the rise and fall of it, the tilting horizon. As if she weren't fucking dizzy enough already.

And she seemed to have been hanging on forever. Not just this shit, whatever it was, the whole *Horkan's Pride* case. The whole fucking thing with Marsalis, the wrecked attempt to make something of it. The repeated calls to her father, the stilted, carefully polite conversations and the barrier she could no longer break through. The memories of Ethan, the battle for custody and reimplantation of Murat-to-be, the serried ranks of lawyers and their fucking waiting rooms. The struggle to hold on to faith, to go back to the mosque and find whatever it was that welled up out of Rabia's poetry and Nazli Valipour's writing, and Meltem's kindly smiling patience. The search for reasons to go on that didn't come in bottles or foil wafers.

It marched through her mind in tawdry procession, and she was suddenly sick of it all, sick of the effort. Better to just watch the sway and twinkle of the city lights below, go where the ride was taking her, listen to the motors hammering out their white-noise refrain, like lying next to a waterfall that smelled ever so slightly of oil and hot metal. The tilting night sky, sense of the sea, flat and black beyond. Not so bad, when you thought about it, not really. Not so hard.

She gave up holding on not long after that, just let go and slid away down the gradient of her own immense tiredness.

part V

HOME TO ROOST

The problems we address here are general to humanity. No amount of privileged withdrawal, segregation, or hierarchical exclusion will serve to insulate any of us from a process of fallout that has already begun. If we are arrogant, if we fail to acknowledge this generality and to act on it while there is still time—then the price that we pay for our failure will be horrific, and it will be levied on us all.

**—Jacobsen Report,
August 2091**

CHAPTER 43

Dawn crept up on the Stanford campus like a cautious painter, mixing color into the monochrome gloom overhead so it faded through shades of gray toward a clean morning blue, layering beige back onto the sandstone angles of the hospital buildings one pale coat at a time, working from the top down. In the gardens, the hedges and trees got back their green and people started to come through on the gravel paths in ones and twos. A few of them glanced at the black man seated alone on the bench, but none stopped. There was a curious immobility to him that drove off any impulse for human contact, and stilled conversational voices as they approached. Those whose work was in the acute wards at the medical center knew at a glance what it meant. This was a man undergoing surgery without anesthetic—the slow, sawtoothed severing of himself from another human being somewhere inside the hospital.

Out on Highway 101, the occasional brushing sound of nighttime traffic was building to a steady background murmur. Birdsong made self-important, twittering aural counterpoint, like handfuls of brightly colored pebbles tossed continually onto a broad gray conveyor belt. Human voices splashed between with increasing strength and frequency, feet crunched in gravel like a grave being dug. Day stormed the walls Carl had built around himself in the cold hours, smashed and battered down the simplicity of his vigil with human detail. He looked up out of the wreckage with a quiet and implacable hatred for everything he could see and hear.

"Happy now?"

Norton stood in front of him, not in reach. He'd slept in his clothes somewhere; even the Marstech jeans were creased.

He seemed to be genuinely waiting for an answer.

"No. You?"

There was a stone bench on the other side of the path, twin to the one Carl was using. Norton lowered himself onto it.

"You're not going to get away with this," he said woodenly. "I'm going to have you sent back to South Florida State. I'm going to have you sent to Cimarron or Tanana for the rest of your fucking life."

By the look of him, he'd been crying. Carl felt a brief stab of envy.

"How is she?" he asked.

"You're joking, of course. You *fuck.*"

The mesh pounded up out of his desolation. He lifted a shaky, loose-fingered hand, pointed it. "Don't push me, Norton. I could do with killing something right now, and it might as well be you."

"You took the words right out of my mouth." Norton stared down at his own hands as if assessing their suitability for the task. "But that isn't going to help Sevgi."

"Nothing's going to help Sevgi, you fucking prick!" There was a brutal pleasure somewhere in the snapped words, like biting down on a mouth ulcer until it split and bled. "Didn't they tell you? It's a Haag slug."

"Yes, they told me. They also tell me Stanford has the best immune system repair clinic on the West Coast. Cutting-edge techniques."

"It won't matter. It's Falwell. Nothing short of death stops that motherfucker."

"That's right, give up why don't you? Very fucking British."

Carl stared at him for a couple of seconds, made a disgusted spitting noise, and looked away. A young woman went by pushing a bike. The small black backpack she wore had a smiley face pinned to it, winking a merciless yellow in the fresh morning light. WHATEVER YOU ARE, a tinselly patch above the badge suggested brightly, BE A GOOD ONE.

"Norton," he said quietly. "How is she?"

The COLIN executive shook his head. "They've stabilized her. That's all I know. They've got an n-djinn mapping the viral shift."

Carl nodded. Sat in silence.

Finally, Norton asked him. "How long has she got?"

"I don't know." Carl drew breath. Let it out by shuddering increments. "Not long."

More quiet. More people went past, talking intimate irrelevancies. Living their lives.

"Marsalis, how the fuck did this guy get hold of a Haag gun in the first place?" There was a high, desperate note in Norton's voice now, like a child protesting an unfair punishment. "They're illegal everywhere I know, incredibly expensive to get hold of on the black market. Lethally dangerous in the wrong hands. There can't be more than a couple of hundred people on the planet with a Haag carry permit."

"Yeah. For anyone with major male tendency, you just described the perfect object of desire." Carl drew on the collateral detail like dying embers in a fire, huddling to the warmth and distraction it offered. "Haag gun's infinitely attractive to anyone even remotely enamored of weaponry. Guy I knew in Texas once offered me half a million dollars for mine. Cash in a suitcase."

"Okay, look." The COLIN exec rubbed hands over his face. Dragged his head up through his fingers. "Say this guy, this Onbekend, he somehow gets hold of a Haag gun because it makes his dick hard. He carries it into a situation where he runs the risk of arrest or a shoot-out with RimSec, and just before the action starts he leaves the damn thing in the *car*? There's no sense in that."

"Yes there is." He'd had the whole night to think it through, sitting in a chair outside the intensive-care unit and fitting together the irreversible march of events that put Sevgi Ertekin in a support cocoon on the other side of the biosealed doors. He had his solution before dawn, and it stared him in the face like a skull, drove him out of the cleanly kept corridors and away, down into the gardens and their graying light. "Onbekend brought the Haag gun for me, because he thought he was going to have to walk me out of the hotel and get me somewhere they could fake my suicide. They couldn't afford a murder, they're trying to run silent right now. And Onbekend couldn't afford to sedate me, because it might show up in an autopsy. He was looking to back me up and push me around fully conscious, and that's a tricky thing to do with a thirteen. We don't scare easily, and we're generally not that afraid of dying. But there are ways and ways to die. I might have tried to jump almost any ordinary weapon, even against the odds. Not the Haag gun."

"He told you that. That he was planning to fake your suicide?"

"Yeah, he told me." Carl stared back into the memories. "Above and beyond anything he was hired to do, Onbekend hated me. I'm used to that from other thirteens, it's standard. But this was a little more. He wanted me stripped down before I died. Wanted me to know how stupid I'd been, how far ahead and above me he was. How pitiful I was going to look with my brains blown out by my own hand somewhere."

"But they shelved the suicide."

"Yeah." Carl drew another hard breath. Onbekend's remembered scorn cut through him. "They didn't need it. I went walkabout, and the plan changed. It was going to be enough to fake a street death instead. No need for the Haag as a threat, and it would have been entirely the wrong weapon to actually kill me with. Onbekend left it in the teardrop, only used it on Sevgi because he didn't have anything else at hand."

Norton stared at him. "I'm sure that'll be a great comfort to her."

Carl looked tiredly back at him. "You want to blame me for this, Norton? Need a target for your impotent male rage? Go right ahead, hate me. I'm used to it, I'm not going to notice the extra weight. Just don't push your luck, because I'm tired and I will break you in half if you cross the line."

"If you hadn't—"

"If I hadn't gone out, it would have been different. I know. They would have taken me in the hotel, walked me out, and Sevgi Ertekin would still have been there when it happened because, Norton, she was coming to see me anyway. Maybe that's what's really eating you, huh?"

"Oh fuck you." But it was said wearily, and he looked away.

"You want to know the truth, Norton? Why she was coming to see me?"

"No, I don't."

"She was coming to clear your name."

The COLIN exec looked back at him as if Carl had just slapped him. "What?"

"I didn't trust you, Norton, any more than a Jesusland presidential address. Those skaters were outside Sevgi's place that morning, and you were the only one who knew where I was. I figured you had some agenda that involved wiping me off the landscape."

"*What?* I fucking got you out of jail in the first place, Marsalis. It was *my* call, *my* initiative. Why the hell would I—"

"Hey, call it thirteen paranoia." Carl sighed. "Anyway, seems last night Sevgi got a call from NYPD: they'd picked up the third skater and he talked. I was never the target. Ortiz was. Sevgi was coming to tell me that, because she couldn't bear the idea of your name being smeared."

Norton said nothing.

"Feel any better now?"

"No." It was a whisper.

"She never wore it as a theory anyway. Slapped me down when I tried to sell it to her. I don't know if you guys were ever an item—"

"We weren't." Snapped out, brittle and harsh.

"No, well, whatever you had, it still went pretty deep, apparently."

Long silence. Norton looked around the garden as if he might see some kind of explanation hanging up in a shrub, sparkling there in the fountain.

"She was a cop," he muttered finally. "Two and a half years in COLIN, but I don't think she ever really changed."

"Yeah. She was a cop. That's why she backed you, her partner, against anything I could sell her. And that's why she went out into the street after Onbekend, and that's why she got shot."

More quiet. Direct sunlight reached the bottom of the buildings, gilded the gravel. There was some real warmth seeping into the day now. A group of students went past in a hurry, late for something. A woman in a blue doctor's tunic came toward them from the acute unit building.

"Which of you is Marsalis?" she asked peremptorily. Under close-cropped black hair, her Chinese features were smudged with tiredness.

Carl raised his hand. The doctor nodded.

"You'd better come in. She's asking for you."

Norton looked away.

The v-format was state-of-the-art and took less time than he'd expected to cajole his thirteen nervous system into relaxing and accepting the illusion. He blinked in behind floor-to-ceiling sliding glass doors. On the other side there was a garden, less arid and stylized than the one he'd been sitting in back in the real world. Here, there was a border of lush growth around the well-kept lawn, nodding ferns and draped foliage, tall, straight trees beyond. A pair of wooden easy chairs were set out in the center.

Sevgi Ertekin sat in one of them, loosely robed in a slate-and-blue kimono with embroidered Arab characters, waiting. There was a book in her lap, but she held it closed, fingers loosely inserted between the pages; her head was lifted, as if listening. She was staring at something else, as if someone already stood there on the other side of the garden, waiting as well.

The glass slid back soundlessly, and he stepped through. The motion caught her eye, or the system was wired to chime the arrival of visitors. She saw him, lifted an arm in greeting.

"Nice, isn't it," she called out. "No expense spared for dying COLIN executives, you know."

"So I see." He walked to her, stood looking down into her face. The system had allowed no trace of her illness into its imaging.

She gestured. "Come on, then. Sit down, soak it up."

He sat.

"I guess I'm looking a lot better in here than I do for real," she said brightly, treading on the heels of his own thoughts with an accuracy that made him blink. "Right?"

"I don't know. They haven't let me in to see you yet."

"Well, they haven't shown me a mirror yet, either. Then again, I haven't asked. I figure the idea is to make you feel as good about yourself as possible, hope that kicks your will to live into high gear, boosts your immune system, and gets you out of their expensive acute-care unit as soon as humanly possible." She stopped abruptly, as if unplugged, and he saw for the first time how scared she really was. She licked her lips. "Of course, that's not a dynamic that applies to me."

He said nothing, could think of nothing to say. A brook chuckled to itself somewhere beyond the foliage. A couple of small birds hopped about on the grass, closer to the humans than would have been likely in the real world. Sunlight struck through the surrounding trees at a high angle.

"My father's flying in from New York," she said, and sighed. "I'm not looking forward to that."

"I don't suppose he is, either."

She ghosted a chuckle, barely louder than the brook. "No, I guess not. We haven't been getting along all that well the last few years. Don't see each other much, don't really talk. Not the way we used to, anyway." Another faint laugh. "He's probably going to think I did this just to get his attention. Deathbed reconciliation. What a fucking drama queen, huh?"

Carl felt his mouth tighten, back teeth locking down with involuntary force. It cost him more effort than he'd thought to keep looking at her.

"Norton here?" she asked.

"Yeah." He tried to smile. It was as if he'd forgotten which muscles to use. "I think he's kind of hurt you asked to see me first."

Ertekin pulled a face. "Yeah, well. Be time for everybody, it's not like I've got a lot of friends."

He took an interest in one of the brightly colored birds around his feet.

"Marsalis?"

He looked up reluctantly. "Yeah?"

"How much time *have* I got?"

"I don't know," he said quickly.

"But you know how the Haag system works." Urgency in her voice like pleading. "You've used the fucking thing often enough, you must have some idea."

"Sevgi, it depends. They're treating you with state-of-the-art anti-virals here—"

"Yeah, just like fucking Nalan."

"Sorry?"

She shook her head. "Doesn't matter. Look, you're not going to scare me any more than I already am. Tell me the truth. They can't stop it, can they?"

He hesitated.

"Tell me the fucking truth, Carl."

He met her eyes. "No. They can't stop it."

"Good. Now tell me how long I've got."

"I don't know, Sevgi. Honestly. They can probably back it up with what they have here, maybe model it enough to . . ."

He saw the look on her face and stopped.

"Weeks," he said. "A couple of months at most."

"Thank you."

"Sevgi, I—"

She raised a hand, made a smile for him. She got out of the chair.

"Going to walk down to the river. Want to come? They told me I'm not supposed to exert myself, even in here. Stimulus feedback, apparently it affects the nervous system almost like the real thing. But I think I'd like to walk a little while I still can." She held up the book. "And there's only so much fifteenth-century poetry you can handle without a break, you know."

He read the title off the antique russet-and-green binding. *The Perfumed Garden* by Ibn Muhammad al-Nafzawi.

"Any good?"

"The aphrodisiac recipes are shaky, but the rest is pretty solid, yeah. Always promised myself I was going to get around to reading it one day." Again the brief flicker of fear in her eyes, rapidly quashed. "Better late than never, right?"

Again, he had no answer, not for what she said or for what he'd seen in her eyes. He followed her across the lawn toward the sound of the water and helped her hold back the hanging branches that blocked passage. They eased through, bent-backed, and stood up in sun-dappled foliage on the bank of the shallow stream. Sevgi stared down at the flow for a while as it slipped past them.

"I need to ask you a couple of favors," she said quietly.

"Sure."

"I need you to stay on here. I know I said you were free to go, I know I more or less sent you away, but—"

"Don't worry." His voice thickened. He had to damp down the surge of fury. "I'm not going to just walk away from this. Onbekend is a dead man walking. And so is whoever sent him."

"Good. But that's not what I meant."

"No?"

"No. With what's happened now, there's more than enough to keep the case wide open. It'd be good if you were there to help out after I'm . . ." She made a limp gesture at the flow of the stream. "But that's not what I'm asking you for. This is, well, it's more selfish."

"I'm alive because of you, Sevgi," he said tonelessly. "That buys you a lot of indulgence."

She turned. She touched his hand.

There was a brief, visceral shock to it; tactile contact was one of the wrinkles the technology still hadn't really ironed out, and format etiquette tended against it as a result. Outside of the crude and curiously unsatisfying porn virtuals he'd used on base in the military, he doubted he'd touched anyone in format more than half a dozen times in his life, and most of those would have been accidental collisions. Now he felt Sevgi Ertekin's hand as if through gloves, and a twitching sense of frustration rose to fan the embers of his fading anger.

"I need you to stay with me," she said. She looked down at where their hands met, as if trying to make out some detail she wasn't sure was there. "It's going to be hard. Murat—that's my father—he's going to be hurting too much. Norton's too conflicted. Everyone else is too far off, I've pushed them all away anyway, since Ethan. I wouldn't know what to say to them. That leaves you, Carl. You're clean. I need you to help me do this."

Clean?

"You said two favors," he reminded her.

"Yeah." She dropped his hand, went back to staring at the flow of the water. "I think you know what the other one's going to be."

He stood beside her and watched the stream flow.

"All right," he said.

He waited for Norton in the corridor outside the visiting station and the v-format cubicles. The COLIN exec came out puffy-eyed and blinking, as if the light in the corridor was too harsh to deal with.

"I need to talk to you," Carl told him.

Norton's face twitched. "And you think now's the time?"

"She isn't going to improve, Norton. You'd better get used to operating under these conditions."

"What do you want?"

"Have you read the statement I gave to RimSec?"

"No, I." Norton closed his eyes for a moment. "Yes. I skimmed it. So what?"

"Someone sent Onbekend to take me out. Probably the same someone who hired Carmen Ren to partner Merrin, the same someone who had Merrin brought back to Earth in the first place. We're not done here, we're not even half done."

Norton sighed. "Yes, I've just spent the last twenty minutes with Sevgi telling me the same thing. I don't need you to ram it home. COLIN will step up the inquiry, RimSec are already covering bases here. Right now, though—"

"I'm not going home until this is done."

"Yes, Sevgi made that quite clear to me as well." Norton tried to brush past him. Carl fought down a desire to snag his arm and snap him around. He backed up a couple of rapid paces instead and put his arm out across the corridor to the wall, so the COLIN exec had to stop. Norton's teeth clenched, his fists balled at his sides.

"What, do you want, from me, Marsalis?"

"Two things. First, you need to get on to Ortiz and have him put a stopper on my release back to UNGLA jurisdiction. I had a call from the Brussels office last night and they're very keen to have me back in the fold."

"Ortiz is barely out of intensive care. He's in no condition—"

"Then talk to whoever is. I don't want to have fight UNGLA as well as whoever's running Onbekend."

Norton pulled in a compressed breath. "Very well. I'll pass this on to Nicholson when I speak to him this afternoon. What else?"

"I want you to lean on Colony. I want to talk to Gutierrez."

COLIN ran a small administrative unit out of two blocks in downtown Oakland, with facilities for a Mars coms link. Norton got a RimSec autocopter detailed to fly them back up and across the bay, and a COLIN limo to meet them at touchdown. He did it all with the remote command of a preoccupied man driving a familiar route home. In the limo, he called ahead to the coms link duty technician and set up the call.

Sevgi burned in his head like a brand, dry-eyed beside the small stream, all the things she didn't say. All the things he didn't, either.

The red tape from the Colony police administration at the Mars end was fierce and self-referential. Having Gutierrez arrested and interrogated had been easy by comparison—Colony knew, in their own cloddish way, how to do that. But authorized off-world communication, from custody, with non-COLIN personnel was apparently just too exotic to have precedent or established procedure. It took three levels of rank before he reached someone who'd do what he told them. And the distances didn't help—Mars currently sat just less than 250 million kilometers away, and transmission time was around thirteen and a half minutes each way. Almost a full half hour between each act of communication. It seemed somehow emblematic.

Marsalis prowled outside the chamber, occasionally visible through the head-height windows on the door. There was a small, mean-spirited pleasure in excluding the thirteen from the early proceedings, an impulse that Norton knew only too drearily well was the human equivalent of a tomcat pissing to mark his territory.

He was too tired to combat the urge, too nonspecifically furious to feel embarrassed by his behavior. He battered down the red tape at Colony with a cold, controlled anger he hadn't known he owned, appealed to reason where he could, bullied and threatened where he could not. He waited out the long delay silences that punctuated the whole process with the patience of an automaton. None of it seemed to matter, except as a way to stave off the knowledge that Sevgi would die, was dying right now by stages as her immune system staggered under the repeated blows from the Falwell viruses and their mutating swirl.

Finally, he let Marsalis in. Ceded the operational seat and folded himself into an off-scope chair at the side of the chamber. Stared emptily at the thirteen as he settled himself.

"You really think this is going to work?"

His voice was slack and careless in his own ears, run flat with emotional overload.

"That depends," said Marsalis, studying the countdown clock above the lens-and-screen array in front of him.

"On what?"

"On whether Franklin Gutierrez wants to go on living or not."

The last digits blinked through, the receiving announcer chimed, and the screen rezzed up to an image of a similar transmission chamber at the Mars end. Gutierrez sat there, cleaned up since Norton had last seen him dragged out of interrogation. There was a clean white plaster wrap on his damaged hand, and the bruising around his face and eye had been treated with inflammation suppressants. He frowned into the camera a little, glanced aside to someone off screen, then cleared his throat and leaned forward.

"Till I see who the fuck's on the other end of this, I don't say anything. Got that? You get these morons to pull their claws out of me, we can maybe do some kind of deal. But that's when I see your face, not before."

He sat back. The transmission-locked seal blipped across the screen in green machine code, and the image froze. The online light glowed orange. Marsalis sat looking at the screen, moved no more than a corpse.

"Hullo, Franklin," he said flatly. "Remember me? I'm pretty sure you do. So now that you know who's on the other end, listen carefully to me. You will give me everything you know about Allen Merrin and why you helped send him home. You get one chance to do this. Don't disappoint me."

He snapped the arm control and the transmission sealed, fired off. Above their heads, the counter started down again.

"You'll forgive me if I'm not impressed yet," Norton said.

Marsalis barely shifted in the seat, but his eyes tracked around and out of nowhere, through all the weariness and grief, Norton saw something there that sent a small chill chasing around the base of his skull like cold water rinsing around a basin.

They waited out the counter. It reached zero, started counting up again into time used before transmission at the other end.

"Hey, the lottery man!" Gutierrez came back sneering, but behind it Norton could see the chill, the same jolt he'd felt when Marsalis looked at him half an hour earlier. And the counter told its own tale in glowing frozen digits. They were

up around two and a half minutes over base transmission-and-turnaround time—
and unless the datahawk had made a speech to the camera, the time overspill was
hesitation. Gutierrez had jammed up, had had to put a reply together on hold.
The bravado rang false as a Tennessee Marstech label. "Yeah, how's your luck
holding back home, Marsalis? How you doing? Missing the girls from the Dozen
Up club?"

After that, Gutierrez switched into Quechua. The screen fired up stilted subtitles to cover. *You are three hundred million kilometers away from me. That is a
long way off for making threats. What will you do, take the long sleep? Come all
the way back here, just to kill me? You don't scare me anymore, Marsalis. You make
me laugh.* It went on, derisory, building the bravado up. It boiled down to *fuck off
and die.*

It still rang false.

Marsalis watched it all with a thin, cold smile.

When the transmission ended, he leaned forward and started speaking, also in
Quechua. Norton had no knowledge of the altiplano tongue beyond counting
one to twenty and a handful of food items, but even through the blanket incomprehension, he felt a dry-ice cold coming off the black man and what he was saying. The words husked out of him, rustling and intent, like something reptilian
breaking out of an egg. In the fog of sleeplessness that was gradually shutting
down his senses, Norton had one moment of clarity so supreme he knew it had
to be a lie; but in that moment it was as if something else was speaking through
Marsalis, something ancient and not really human using his mouth and face as a
mask and a launch point to hurl itself across the gulf between worlds, to reach out
and take Franklin Gutierrez by the throat and heart, as if he were sitting across a
desk and not a quarter of a billion kilometers of empty space.

It took little more than a minute to say, whatever it was, but for Norton the
whole thing seemed to happen outside real time. When Marsalis was finished
speaking, the COLIN exec opened his mouth to say something—say anything, to
break the creaking, something-has-left-the-building silence—and then stopped
because he saw that Marsalis had not thumbed for transmission. The message
was still open, still waiting to be sealed, and for what seemed like a very long time
the black man just looked into the facing lens and said nothing at all, just looked.

Then he touched the button and, in some way Norton could not define, he
seemed to slump.

It was a solid minute before the COLIN exec found words of his own.

"What did you say?" he asked, through dry lips.

Marsalis twitched like someone waking from a doze. Shot him a normal,
human look. Shrugged.

"I told him I'd go back to Mars and find him if he didn't tell me what I wanted to know. Told him COLIN would fund the ticket, there and back. Told him I'd kill him and everyone he cares about."

"You think he'll buy it?"

The black man's attention drifted back to the screen. He must also, Norton suddenly realized, be very tired. "Yes. He'll buy it."

"And if he doesn't? If he calls your bluff?"

Marsalis glanced at him again, and Norton knew what the answer was going to be before the quiet, matter-of-fact words fell into the quiet room.

"This isn't a bluff."

They waited, down to zero on the glowing counter and then minutes clocking up beyond. Neither of them said anything; Norton at least could think of nothing to say. But the lack was almost companionable. Marsalis met his eye once or twice, and once he nodded as if the COLIN exec had said something, so securely that Norton wondered if he hadn't in the extremities of his grief and weariness vocalized some random internal thought.

If he had, he couldn't recall what it was.

The quiet in the room settled in around him like a blanket, warming and soothing, inviting escape, exit from the mess and the grief, the slide down into the soft oblivion of long-deferred sleep . . .

He jerked awake.

The chime of the receiver, and his neck, cricked and aching.

The screen rezzed up again.

Gutierrez came through, panic-stricken and babbling.

CHAPTER 45

You're clean.

He couldn't work out what she meant, not really. He tried. He tugged at the tightly knotted intricacies of it while he sat in a pool of lamplight in the darkened offices at COLIN and played back the transcript of Gutierrez cracking wide open. He gave up exasperated, left it alone. Came back and tugged at it some more.

That leaves you. Carl. You're clean.

He felt around the rough contours of it, but it was like searching for holds on one of the improbably towering cliff faces in the Massif Verne. Your fingers told you what was there, gave you something to hold on to or lever off, but that was immediate applicability, not the shape of the whole. It wasn't understanding. He knew the moves that were coming, what *That leaves you, you're clean* meant in terms of what she wanted him to do, but that no more told him what she believed about him, what she thought they were to each other, than a successful series of moves back on that Verne rock gave you a topographic map of the face.

It was like being back in the Osprey compound, puzzling over one of Aunt Chitra's more obscure training koans.

You're clean.

The phrase ticked in his head like a bomb.

Norton left, presumably to get some sleep before he collapsed. He offered no comment other than *See you in the morning.* His tone was hesitant, if not friendly then a close analog, buffered soft by exhaustion. Somewhere in the last few hours, the tension between them had shifted in some indefinable way, and something else was emerging to take its place.

Carl sat in the empty offices, listening to the transcript over and over, staring into space, until the floor he was on started to shut itself down for the night. Over-head lighting blinked out panel by panel, and the darkness beyond the floor-to-ceiling windows washed quietly in to fill the work spaces like dark water. Unused systems dropped into standby mode, screens locked to the COLIN acronym, and small red lights gleamed to life in the gloom. No one came up to see what he was doing. Like most COLIN facilities, the Oakland offices were manned around the clock, but by night the staffing went down to skeleton levels and an enabled smart system in the basement. Security was down there—Norton must just have told them to leave him alone.

Gutierrez confessed, hasty and disjointed, backing up, self-correcting, proba-bly lying and embellishing along the way. A picture emerged anyway.

. . . *someone in the* familias . . . *had to break ranks sooner or later . . . the war's just fucking stupid . . .*

. . . *I don't know, Marsalis, they didn't feed me that much fucking informa-tion . . . just had to fake the guy through, that's what I do, you know . . .* At some point in the protracted, half-hour-gapped interrogation, something tipped over in Gutierrez. Fear, the dangled promise of COLIN protection, maybe some griping sense of betrayal for his time in custody, waiting for a *familia* rescue that hadn't yet come—resentment built from smoldering, sparked, and finally flared into open, angry revolt . . . *Look, I'm a fucking cormorant, man, a wire hire, it's not like I've got blood with any of them, why are they going to tell me a fucking thing they don't have to . . .*

. . . *well, obviously someone who stands to gain from a cessation of hostilities with Mars . . . you don't need me to tell you that, right . . .*

. . . *yeah, yeah, jump the docking protocols, put the guy down off the California coast . . .*

. . . *no, they didn't say why . . . like I said . . .*

. . . *yeah, of course I showed him how to jump-start the cryocap gel . . . how else was he going to survive a splashdown . . .*

And with the resentment, a steadily leaking pool of self-pity and justifica-tion . . . *yeah, fucking right, that was an accident. You think I planned to send him home awake like that? Think that's the kind of work I do from choice? Should have woken up two weeks from home, not from Mars . . . fucking would have, too, if I'd had my way. I told them it was risky, killing the n-djinn two weeks into the trajec-tory, told them it might knock on and trigger the other stuff, but hey, why the fuck listen to the expert, what does he fucking know . . .*

. . . *because, if you shut the n-djinn down two weeks from home, COLIN Earth sends a rescue ship up to find out what the fuck happened. Guaranteed. They don't want to take the risk of a docking fuckup, can't afford the bad publicity. But if it shuts down two weeks into the trajectory, and then the ship runs silent but smooth all the way home, then they're going to trust the auto systems and let it go. You know how those fuckers are about costs . . .*

There were a couple of hours of it, even when you cut out the transmission delay. The datahawk's resistance had gone like a dam wall failing. Carl went back through it, time after time, because the alternative was to start thinking about Sevgi Ertekin. He listened until what Gutierrez was saying started to rub smooth in his head, until it was just patterned noise, with no more meaning than the stamped geometric light and dark of windows, lit and not, in the other buildings outside the window.

He saw her walk back in through the door of the bar once more, wry grimace and the slow ooze of blood on her shoulder and sleeve. The kick in his throat when he saw it, the relief when she said she was okay, the—

. . . blood, said the transcript for the nth time.

. . . not like I've got blood with any of them . . .

He frowned. Hit pause, rewind. The transcript gibbered backward, rolled again.

Gutierrez sulked once more. *Look, I'm a fucking cormorant, man, a wire hire, it's not like I've got blood with any of them . . .*

He heard his own voice and Bambarén's, worried at by the wind across Sacsayhuamán.

My familiares share a common dislike of your kind, Marsalis. You cannot be unaware of this.

"*Yes. You also share a sentimental attachment to ties of blood, but that—*

He sat up suddenly straight from his slump. He played it back again, listened once more to the juxtaposition he'd never spotted before.

That's got to be it.

He reeled back some more, backed up through the datahawk's rambling.

. . . obviously someone who stands to gain from a cessation of hostilities with Mars . . . you don't need me to tell you that, right . . .

Fucking got to be. He stared at the revelation as it unfolded in the LCLS blast of the desk lamp. Bambarén's image-tight knowledge of Project Lawman's weaning procedures. Greta Jurgens, boasting, Bambarén's suave understated confirmation when called on it. The two items collided in his head.

. . . you've made a niche career out of coexisting with the Initiative, and from what Greta said it's a flourishing relationship.

I don't believe Greta Jurgens discussed my business associations with you.

No, but she tried to threaten me with them. The implication was that you have bigger friends these days, and you keep them closer.

. . . someone who stands to gain . . .

. . . a sentimental attachment to ties of blood . . .

Fucking *had* to be.

The realization of how close to the mystery he'd been digging at the time came in across waves of tiredness and made him giddy with exhilaration.

All the time, all the fucking *time we were that close. Just fucking wait till I tell—* Sevgi.

And then, abruptly, it was all worth nothing again, and all he had was rage.

He checked the files, rang Matthew with it.

"Gayoso." The datahawk seemed to be tasting the name. "Okay, but it may take awhile, especially if people have been hiding things the way you say they have."

"I'm not in a hurry."

Slight pause at the other end of the line. "That's not like you, Carl."

"No." He stared at his reflected self in the nighttime glass of the office windows. Grimaced. "I don't suppose it is."

More silence. Matthew didn't like change, at least not among his human colleagues. Carl could feel his discomfort crawling on the line.

"Sorry, Matt. I'm kind of tired."

"Matthew."

"Yeah, Matthew. Sorry again. Like I said, tired. I'm waiting for some things to shake out at this end, so I'm in no rush for this stuff. That's all I meant."

"Okay." Matthew's voice went back to sunny as if he'd thrown a switch. "Listen, you want to know a secret?"

"A secret?"

"Yes. Confidential data. Would you like to know it?"

Carl frowned. He didn't often use video when he talked to Matthew; the datahawk didn't seem to like it much, for one thing, and for another the calls were usually purely functional, so it seemed pointless. But now, for the first time, he wished he could see Matthew's face.

"Confidential data's usually the reason I ring you," he said carefully. "So, yeah. Let's hear it."

"Well, you're in trouble with the Brussels office. Gianfranco di Palma is very angry with you."

"He told you that?"

"Yes. He told me not to communicate with you anymore, not until you come back from the Rim."

A slow-leaking anger trickled in Carl's belly. "Did he now."

"Yes, he did."

"I notice you're not doing what he told you."

"Of course not," Matthew said serenely. "I don't work for UNGLA, I'm part of the interagency liaison. And you are my friend."

Carl blinked.

"That's good to know," he said finally.

"I thought you'd be pleased."

"Listen, Matthew." The anger was shifting, colored with something altogether less certain. The flush of understanding he'd had earlier seemed to recede, drowning out by new factors. "If di Palma talks to you again—"

"I know, I know. Don't tell him I'm checking on Gayoso for you."

"Yeah, that." Creeping sense of unease now. "But you tell him also that we're friends, okay. That you're my friend."

"He'll know that already, Carl. It's obvious just looking at the data that—"

"Yeah, well he may not have looked too closely at the data, you know. You tell him you're my friend. You tell him I said that, and that I told you to tell him that, too." Carl stared somberly at the night outside. "Just so he's clear."

A little later, he let himself out of the building, looking for a cab to get him back to the hotel. He walked down through the cool of the evening on big successive rectangles of crystalline violet light from the street's LCLS overheads. It felt like crossing a series of small theater stages, each one lit for a performance he refused to stop and give. His head was fogged with lack of sleep. Weary speculative whirl in there that just wouldn't quit, still jostling for position with an expansive, freewheeling anger.

Fucking di Palma.

He didn't realize how much rage must show on his face until he knocked into a street entertainer coming the other way and loaded down with what seemed like random pieces of junk. They cannoned, shoulder-to-shoulder, and his bulk sent her sprawling. The junk clattered and scattered right across the pavement. A single steel wheel from a child's bike rolled away glinting in the LCLS, hit the curb, and keeled over abruptly in the gutter beyond. The entertainer looked up at him from where she'd fallen, face-painted features sullen.

"Why don't you . . ."

And her voice dried up.

He stood looking down at the garish clown-masked face and rigid copper page-

boy wig for a silent moment, then realized that his mouth was tight, jaw still set
with undischarged anger at di Palma, at Onbekend, at a whole host of shadowy
targets he still couldn't clearly make out.

Yeah, none of whom is this girl. Get a grip, Carl.

He grunted and offered her his hand.

"Sorry. Wasn't paying attention. My fault."

He hauled her to her feet. The fear stayed in her eyes, and she snatched her
hand away as soon as she was upright. He moved to help her gather up the scattered bits and pieces of her act from the pavement, saw how she flinched, was still
afraid of this big, black man on the violet-paneled, deserted street. Gritty irritation flared through him.

"I'll leave you to it," he told her curtly.

He got the feeling she was watching him out of sight as he walked away.
Something nagged at him about the encounter, but he couldn't be bothered to
chase the thread. A cab cruised by on the cross-street ahead, and he yelled and
signaled. The sensors registered him and the cab executed a natty, machine-
perfect U-turn across the oncoming traffic, pulling sedately in to collect him.
The door hinged out.

He got in, low light and slit windows, leatherette fittings. The rush of memory
from his cab ride the night before, the one that Sevgi Ertekin had spotted him
getting into and followed, came and did him some tiny, inexplicable harm inside.

The generic female interface rezzed up. "Welcome to Merritt Cabs. What
will—"

"Red Sands International," he said roughly.

"The Red Sands chain operates on both sides of the bay. Which do you require?"

"San Francisco."

"In transit," the 'face said smoothly. The features composed, once again he
thought of Carmen Ren and her generic Rim States beauty, the smooth—

The clown.

The fucking clown.

"Stop the cab," he snapped.

They glided to a halt. He wrestled with the door.

"You want to fucking let me out?"

"The engagement fee is outstanding," said the cab diffidently. "Regardless of
trajectory, Merritt Cabs reserves—"

"I'm coming back, I'm fucking *coming back.* Just hold it here."

The door clunked free and hinged. He spilled out, sprinted back up the cross-street for the corner. Before he reached it, he already knew what he'd find. He cornered at speed anyway, ran on, back up the long line of crystalline violet stage panels, back toward the COLIN block.

The street was empty, just the way he'd known it would be. Bits and pieces of junk lay unrecovered exactly where they'd fallen. The bicycle wheel sat gaunt and canted, in the gutter. The face-painted woman was gone.

He pivoted about, scanned the street in both directions.

Pale crystalline stages, lit for performance, marching away in both directions. He stood in the pale violet fall of the LCLS, utterly alone. Tilting sense of the unreal. For one fragmented moment, he expected to see Elena Aguirre come drifting toward him over the narrow bands of gloom that interspersed the panels of light.

Come to collect him after all.

CHAPTER 46

They went over it in the garden.

Sevgi Ertekin's choice: she would not be left out of the briefings. *Still my fucking case*, she said tightly when Norton protested. Carl guessed it had to be better for her than contemplating what was coming, and she seemed to have either finished or gotten fed up with al-Nafzawi. So they sat in the wooden chairs in the soft sunlight, listened to the brook behind them, and they all acted like Sevgi wasn't going to die.

"Fucking face-painted," she exploded, when Carl told them about his encounter the night before. "That bitch did the exact same thing to me back on *Bulgakov's Cat*. She slammed into me coming around a support pillar. Had to be her. Why the fuck would she do that?"

"Listening in," said Carl. "I went over to Alcatraz last night, immediately after. Set off every alarm in the place when I tried to get down to the shielded suites. They took a pinhead mike off my jacket. Size of a bread crumb, chamelachrome casing. Sticks on impact, practically everlasting battery."

"Then there'll be one on my clothing, too."

"Most likely, yeah."

"So this is Ren, still in the game?" Norton frowned. "That doesn't make much sense. You'd think she'd be running. Down to the Freeport to get a new ID and a face change."

Carl shook his head. "She's smarter than that. Why go for major surgery when you can just slap on a layer of paint and a wig?"

"Yeah," said Sevgi sourly. "You know how many street entertainers there's got to be in this city. You see them fucking everywhere."

"That doesn't answer the question of what she's doing hanging around," Norton pointed out. "If her original assignment was to back Merrin up, then I'd say she's out of a job."

"I told you this wasn't finished," Carl said. "We took down Merrin a little early, but apart from that, whoever set this thing up is running exactly according to plan."

Norton gave him a dubious look.

"Yeah, but according to *what* plan?" Sevgi said. "You say Gutierrez claims he was sending Merrin back as a Martian *familia* hit man—revenge killings for the enforcement violence back in the seventies. Manco Bambarén gets in on the act because he could use a change of leadership, get the chance to make the most of his relationships with the Initiative corporations. And then instead of taking down the Lima bosses, Merrin goes and hits a couple of dozen random citizens in Jesusland and the Rim. It doesn't join up at all."

"Gutierrez *thought* he was sending back a *familia* hit man." Carl geared up for the revelation. "But there's obviously another agenda here. For one thing, Bambarén's tied in to this with a lot more than business interests."

Another cranked eyebrow from Norton. "Meaning?"

"Meaning that Merrin's genetic donor mother, Isabela Gayoso, is also Manco Bambarén's real mother. Bambarén and Merrin were brothers. Well, half brothers."

Sevgi sat upright in her chair, staring.

"No, fucking, way."

"I'm afraid so. Isabela Rivera Gayoso, slum mother in Arequipa, gave genetic material to a visiting US Army medical unit who were on the scrounge down there with Elleniss Hall Genentech. I think they paid her fifty dollars. She gave her second family name, her mother's surname, probably because she was ashamed. She also seems to have given a false sin, because the one on record with Elleniss Hall is a dead end. Or maybe they scrambled it somehow. I think back then they weren't all that fussed about keeping tight records. The whole project was off the books anyway. On paper, Project Lawman didn't exist."

"I don't believe this," Norton said evenly. "The n-djinn searches would have turned it up."

"Well, yeah, they might have, if there hadn't been so much deliberate data-fogging going on at the time. Like I told you when I came on board, Sevgi, we were all ghosts back then. Nothing concrete, nothing some overzealous journalist might be able to nail down. And they used early n-djinn technology to do the fogging, so it's solid. When Jacobsen came along, some of the fog got lifted, but most of the Project Lawman records still belong to the Confederated Republic and they weren't overly cooperative back when UNGLA were setting up. Our covert research guys are always turning up some fresh dirty little secret the US military buried somewhere and forgot about."

"If that's true, then how did you find all this out?"

"I asked one of our covert research guys. He did some digging for me last night, daytime back in Europe, came back to me this morning just before he went to bed. He says it looks like there was some covering at the other end of things as well, cheap datahawk stuff, probably Bambarén trying to bury the unpleasant family history once he got some influence. Having a mother who cooperated with the gringo military, opened her legs for them right up to the ovaries, so to speak—well, it isn't exactly a good thing to have on your résumé if you're planning to make it big in the *familias* down there."

Norton sniffed. "I still fail to see how this research guy of yours could do something our n-djinns couldn't."

"Well, there are a couple of reasons. The first is that I was going in from the far end. Something Bambarén said to me, something about blood, just a feeling I had. I started with the assumption and asked my researcher to chase Gayoso down. I already had my connection. Your n-djinns would have been working the other way, probably off a broad-sweep trawl through the general dataflow with Merrin as their starting point, then a filter for relevance and more detailed followup. N-djinns aren't human, they don't do cognitive leaps the way we do. Like I said last week, Yaroshanko intuition's a wonderful thing, but you have to have something to triangulate off. Your n-djinn data trawl's only as good as your chosen filters, and I'm guessing they were Mars- or Rim-States-related."

"Yeah, and Lawman-related."

"Sure, and Lawman-related. But think about what that means—do you really think an n-djinn search running into the Project Lawman protocols is going to pay any attention to genetic source material? You're talking about people who never met their offspring, never had anything to do with them. In Gayoso's case, you're talking about someone who was never even in the same country, never came within a thousand kilometers of the thing they made with her donated ovum. Genetic material is cheap as fuck, even now with Jacobsen in force. Back then, it meant less than nothing. No machine is going to see that as a lead worth pursuing; it never would have made it through the filters for follow-up analysis. You have to *already* know that the genes Isabela Gayoso handed on to her son are important before you can get the n-djinn to make the link. And like I said, she was never anywhere near him."

Norton frowned. "Hold it. There was a deployment in Bolivia, wasn't there? Back in '88, '89?"

" 'Eighty-eight," said Sevgi. "Argentina and Bolivia. But it's disputed, a lot of the data says he might not have been there at all. It's also got him down as leading a platoon in Kuwait City around the same time."

"Yeah, but if he *was* there," Norton argued, suddenly enthused, "that'd be a point of contact. That's maybe when Bambarén finds out he's got a brother he didn't know about, and . . ."

"And what, Tom?" Sevgi shook her head irritably. "They meet, they have a few beers, and Merrin heads out for urban pacification duties in the Rim. Six years later he goes to Mars, and *twelve* years after that some Mars-end *familia* head cooks up some crackpot revenge assassination plan, chooses Merrin for the job, and Merrin turns around and says, *Oh hey, I've got a half brother back on Earth who can help out with that.* Come on, that's not it. There has to be something else, something that ties it in tighter than that."

"There probably is," Carl told them. "I said there were a couple of reasons why your n-djinns failed and my researcher didn't. Well, the second reason is that there's been a whole lot more datafogging, and it dates from a lot more recently than all this ancient history. Someone out there is still very much concerned to keep this whole thing under wraps."

"Someone who's using Carmen Ren," mused Sevgi. "Keeping her deployed."

"That's an angle," Carl admitted.

"Did they destroy your pinhead bug?"

"No, still holding it. We could try to put it back in play, I guess. See if we can draw Ren in. But I don't see it working, she's too sharp for that. This much silence, she'll know she's been blown."

"So where does that leave us?" Norton asked.

"It leaves us with Bambarén," Carl said grimly. "We go down there and we stamp on him until he tells us what we want to know."

"And Onbekend?" Sevgi asked, with a strange light in her eye.

Silence. Norton hurried in to fill it. "Checked that yesterday. I talked to Coyle. No record that fits with the descriptions you both gave. But *Onbekend*'s a name from the Netherlands, apparently it was Dutch bureaucracy's get-out for anyone who didn't have a fixed family name to go on their identity documents." He grimaced. "It means 'unknown.' "

Sevgi coughed out a laugh. "Oh very good."

"Yeah, seems quite a few Indonesians ended up with it in the last century, because they didn't have family names in the sense the Dutch understand the concept. It's pretty common all over the Pacific Rim these—"

He stopped, because Sevgi's cough hadn't died away. It picked up, intensified until it shook her, feedback from the stimulus in the format triggering the real thing back in her hospital bed. The force of it bent her almost double in the chair, and then she flickered in and out of existence as her mental focus slipped. Carl and Norton exchanged a silent glance.

Sevgi's presence flickered once more, then settled. She wheezed and seemed to get control.

"Are you okay, Sev?"

"No, Tom, I'm not fucking okay." She drew a hard breath. "I'm fucking *dying,* all right? Sorry if it's causing problems."

Carl looked at Norton again, surprising himself with the sudden jolt of sympathy he felt for the other man.

"Maybe we'd better take a break," he said quietly.

"No, it's . . ." Sevgi closed her eyes. "I'm sorry, Tom. That was unforgivable. I had no call to snap at you like that. I'm fine now. Let's get back to Onbekend."

They did, after a fashion, but the incident sat among them like another presence. The conversation ran slow, grew diffident, finally fell apart. Sevgi wouldn't meet Norton's eyes, just sat and twisted her fingers in her lap until finally the COLIN exec cleared his throat and excused himself with the pretext of calling New York. He blinked out with obvious relief. Carl sat and waited.

The twisted fingers again. Finally, she looked up at him.

"Thanks for staying," she said softly.

He nodded at the surroundings. "It beats the garden they've got outside. Too arid, too stylized. This is very British, makes me feel at home."

It got a short laugh, but carefully deployed this time.

"Has your father arrived?"

"Yeah." Jerky nod. "He came in to see me this morning, before you and Tom got here. For real, in the hospital. They're giving him a suite over in the staff dorms. Professional courtesy."

"Or COLIN influence."

"Well, yeah. That, too."

"So how'd you get on with him?"

She shook her head. "I don't know. He, you know, he cried a lot. We both did. He apologized for all the fights about Ethan, the distance. A lot of other stuff. But—"

"Yeah."

She looked at him. "I'm really scared, Carl."

"I think you're entitled to be."

"I, I mean, I keep having these dreams where it's all been a mistake. It's not really a Haag slug. Or it's not as bad as they thought, they've got an antiviral that can keep up. Or the whole thing was just a dream and I've woken up back in New York, I can hear the market outside." Tears leaked out of her eyes. Her voice took on a desperate, grinding edge. "And then I wake up for real, and I'm here, in that fucking bed with the drips and the monitors and all the fucking equipment around me like relatives I don't want to fucking see. And I'm dying, I'm fucking *dying*, Carl."

"I know," he said hollowly, voice stupid in his own ears. Numb for something to say, to meet her with.

She gulped. "I always thought it'd be like a doorway, like standing in front of a door you've got to go through. But it isn't. It isn't. It's like a fucking wall coming at me and I'm strapped in my seat, can't fucking move, can't touch the controls or get out. I'm just going to fucking lie there and *die*."

Her teeth clenched on the last word. She looked emptily out across the garden at the foliage on the fringes of the lawn. Her hands tightened to fists in her lap. Loosened, tightened again. He watched her and waited.

"I don't want you to go down there after Bambarén and Onbekend," she said quietly. She was still staring away into the sun-splashed foliage. "I don't want you to end up like me, like this."

"Sevgi, we all end up like this sooner or later. I'd just be catching you up."

"Yeah, well there are ways and ways of catching up. I don't recommend the Haag shell method."

"I can handle Onbekend."

"Sure, you can." Her gaze switched back to him. "Last time you went up against him, as I recall, I had to bust in and save your life for you."

"Well, I'll be more careful this time."

She made a compressed sound that might have been another laugh. "You don't get it, do you? I'm not scared that Onbekend might kill you down there. This is selfish, Carl. I'm scared that you won't come back. I'm scared you'll leave me here, dying by fucking increments with no one to help."

"I already told you'd I'd stay."

She wasn't listening. Wasn't looking at him anymore. "Saw my cousin die that way, back when I was still a kid. Sex virus, one of the hyperevolved ones, she caught it off a soldier in the East. Nothing they could do. I'm not going to go through that. Not the way she went."

"Okay, Sevgi. Okay. I won't go anywhere. I'm right here. But I think it's time you let me in to see you for real. In the ward."

She shivered. Shook her head. "No, not yet. I'm not ready for that yet."

"Staying in v-format is going to put a lot of strain on your nervous system. A lot of stress."

Sevgi snorted. "That's all you fucking know. You want to know what the strain is? I'll tell you. Strain is lying back there in that fucking bed, staring up at the ceiling and listening to the machines they've got me hooked up to, feeling my lungs clogging up and all the needles they've stuck in me, aching every fucking place I can feel and no way to move unless someone comes to do it for me. Compared with that"—she gestured weakly at the garden—"this is fucking paradise."

She looked at the hanging branches in silence for a while.

"They say it is a garden," she muttered. "Paradise, you know. Garden full of fruits and the sound of water."

"And virgins. Right? Seventy virgins each, or something?"

"Not if you're a woman. Anyway, that's for martyrs." She pulled a face. "*Anyway,* it's a crock of shit. Simple-minded post-Qu'ranic desert Islam propaganda. No one in the modern Muslim world with two brain cells to rub together believes that shit anymore. And who wants a fucking virgin anyway? You got to teach them every fucking thing. Like having sex with a fucking mannequin with its motion circuits shot up."

"Sounds like you're talking from experience there." He grabbed the change of subject, glad of the chance.

It drew a crooked smile from her. "I've broken in one or two in my time. You?"

"Not that I know of."

"That's not very public-spirited of you. Somebody's got to do it."

He shrugged. "Well, you know, maybe I'll still get out there and do my share, later on in life."

Her smile faded, shaded out at the mention of the future, like the passing of cloud cover across the sunlit lawn. She shivered and hunched her body a little in the chair. He cursed himself for the slip.

"I was reading somewhere," she said quietly. "They reckon in another thirty or forty years they'll have v-formatting so powerful you'll be able to live inside it. You know, the n-djinn just copies your whole mind-state into the construct and then runs you as part of the system. You just sedate the body and step through. They say you'll even be able to go on living there after your body actually dies. Forty years away, they're saying, maybe not even that long." She grinned desperately. "Bit late for me, though, huh?"

"Hey, you're not going to need that shit." Floundering for a response. "You're going to heaven, right? Paradise, like you said."

She shook her head. "I don't think I really believe in paradise, Carl. You want to know the truth, I don't think any of us do really. Deep down, down where it counts I think we all know it's a crock of shit. That's why we're all so fucking determined to spread the good news, to shove it down other people's throats. Because if we can't make other people believe it, how are we going to stamp out the doubt in ourselves. And it's cold, that doubt." She looked at him, shivered as she said it. Her voice dropped to a whisper. "Like November in the park, you know. Like winter coming in."

He got up and went to where she sat, and tried as best he could to hold her. Blunt, glove-skinned sensation, like fistfuls of crushed velvet, like nothing real. No feeling of warmth, but as she shivered again he pulled her close anyway, and he held her head against his chest so she wouldn't see how his jaw was clenched tight and his mouth had become a savage down-drawn line.

Like winter coming in.

CHAPTER 47

Sevgi lived four more days.

They were the longest days he could remember since the week he waited for Marisol to come back, believing somehow against everything the uncles told him that she would. He'd sat blankly then, as he did now at the hospital, detached for hours at a time, staring into space in classes he'd previously excelled in. He took the punishment beatings from the uncles with a stoic lack of response that bordered on catatonic—fighting back would do no good, he knew, would only ensure that he took more damage. Aunt Chitra's pain-management training had come just in time.

Many years later, he wondered if that particular course hadn't been deliberately scheduled for the months leading up to the removal of the surrogate mothers. There wasn't much that happened in Osprey Eighteen without carefully considered planning. And pain, after all, as Chitra began the series of classes by telling them, came in many forms. *Pain is unavoidable*, smiling gently at their group, shaking each of them formally by the hand. Something of an unknown quantity after their other teachers, this small, hawkish-featured woman with skin like some fire-scorched copper alloy, cropped black hair, a figure that sent vaguely understood signals out to their prepubescent hormones, and dry, callus-edged hands that told those same hormones exactly how they'd better behave around her. Her grip was firm, her eyes direct and appraising. *Pain is all around us. It takes many forms. My job will be to teach you how to recognize all those forms, to understand them, and to not allow any of them to keep you from your purpose.* Carl had learned the lessons well. He dealt with the careful brutality the uncles were applying exactly as if it were one of Chitra's worked examples. He knew they would not damage him beyond repair because all the Osprey Eighteen children had been told, time and time again, how valuable they were. He also knew the uncles would have preferred not to use physical violence to this extent. It was never a preferred method of discipline at Osprey, was only ever used to punish serious breaches of respect and obedience, and only then as a last resort. But every other punishment task they set Carl that week, he simply refused to carry out. Worse, he spat back his refusal in their faces, savoring the tug of disobedience like the pain of pushing himself on a run or a cliff climb. And when the measured violence came, he embraced it, shrugged himself into Chitra's training like a harness, and faced the uncles with a blank fury they could not match.

In the end, it was Chitra who unlocked his efforts, just as she'd given him what he needed to shore them up. She came to him one gray afternoon as he sat, bruised and bleeding from the mouth, aching back propped against a storage shed near the helipad. She stood for a while without saying anything, then stepped into his direct field of vision, hands in her coverall pockets. He tried to look around her, shifted sideways, but it hurt too much to sustain the posture. She didn't move.

In the end he had to look up into her face.

What's your purpose, Carl? she asked him quietly. There was no judgment in either tone or expression, only genuine inquiry. *I understand your pain, I see the ways in which you've tried to make it external. But what purpose do you have?*

He didn't answer. Looking back he didn't think she ever expected him to. But after she'd gone, he realized—allowed himself to realize—that Marisol really wasn't coming back, that the uncles were telling the truth, and that he was wasting his own time as well as theirs.

Waiting with Sevgi was different. He had her there with him. He had purpose.

He was still going to *fucking* lose her.

He met her father in the gardens, a big, gray-haired Turk with powerful shoulders and the same tigerish eyes as his daughter. He wore no mustache, but there was thick stubble rising high on his cheeks and bristling at his cleft chin, and he had lost none of his hair with age. He would have been a very handsome man in his youth, and even now—Carl estimated he must be in his early sixties—even seated on the beige stone bench and staring fixedly at the fountain, he exuded a quiet, charismatic authority. He wore a plain dark suit that matched the thick woolen shirt beneath it and the purplish smudges of tiredness under his eyes.

"You're Carl Marsalis," he said as Carl reached the bench. There was no question mark in his voice. It was a little hoarse but iron-firm beneath. If he'd been crying, he hid it well.

"Yeah, that's me."

"I am Murat Ertekin. Sevgi's father. Please, join me." He gestured at the empty space beside him on the bench, waited until Carl was seated. "My daughter has told me a lot about you."

"Care to give me specifics?"

Ertekin glanced sideways at him. "She told me that your loyalty cannot be easily bought."

It brought him up short. The received wisdom about variant thirteen was that they had no loyalties at all beyond self-interest. He wondered if Ertekin was quoting Sevgi directly or putting his own spin on what she'd said.

"Did she tell you what I am?"

"Yes." Another sidelong look. "Were you expecting disapproval from me? Hatred, perhaps, or fear? The standard-issue prejudices?"

"I don't know you," Carl told him evenly. "Aside from the fact that the two of you don't get on and that you left Turkey for political reasons, Sevgi hasn't told me anything about you at all. I wouldn't know what your attitude is to my kind. Though my impression is that you weren't too happy about Sevgi's last variant thirteen indiscretion."

Ertekin sat rigid. Then he slumped. He closed his eyes, hard, opened them again to face the world.

"I am to blame," he said quietly. "I failed her. All our lives together, I encouraged Sevgi to push the boundaries. And then, when she finally pushed them too far for my liking, I reacted like some village mullah who's never seen the Bosphorus Bridge in his life and doesn't plan to. I reacted exactly like my fucking brother."

"Your brother's a mullah?"

Murat Ertekin laughed bitterly. "A mullah, no. Though perhaps he did miss his vocation when he chose secular law for a career. I'm told he was never more than an indifferent lawyer. But a self-righteous, willfully ignorant male supremacist? Oh yes. Bulent always excelled at that."

"You talk about him in the past. Is he dead?"

"He is to me."

The conversation jerked violently to a halt on the assertion. They both sat for a while staring into the space where it had been. Murat Ertekin sighed. He talked as if picking up the pieces of something broken, as if each bending down to retrieve a fragment of the past was an effort that forced him to breathe deeply.

"You must understand, Mr. Marsalis, my marriage was not a successful one. I married young, and in haste, to a woman who took her faith very seriously indeed. When we were still both medical students in Istanbul, I mistook that faith for a general strength, but I was wrong. When we moved to America, as it still was then, Hatun could not cope. She was homesick, and New York frightened her. She never adjusted. We had Sevgi because at such times you are told that having a child will bring you together again." A grimace. "It's a strange article of faith— the belief that sleepless nights, no sex, less income, and the constant stress of caring for a helpless new life should somehow alleviate the pressures on a relationship already under strain."

Carl shrugged. "People believe some strange things."

"Well, in our case it didn't work. My work suffered, we fought more, and Hatun's fear of the city grew. She retreated into her faith. She already went head-scarfed in the streets; now she began to wear the full chador. She would not receive guests in the house unless she was covered, and of course she had already quit her job to have Sevgi. She isolated herself from her former friends and colleagues at the hospital, frustrated their attempts to stay in touch, eventually changed mosques to one preaching some antiquated Wahhabi nonsense. Sevgi gravitated to me. I think that's natural in little girls anyway, but here it was pure self-defense. What was Sevgi to make of her mother? She was growing up a streetwise New York kid, bilingual and smart, and Hatun didn't even want her to have swimming lessons with boys."

Ertekin stared down at his hands.

"I encouraged the rebellion," he said quietly. "I hated the way Hatun was changing, maybe by then I even hated Hatun herself. She'd begun to criticize the work I did, calling it un-Islamic, snubbing our liberal Muslim or nonbelieving friends, growing more rigid in her attitudes every year. I was determined Sevgi would not end up the same way. It delighted me when she started asking her mother those simple child's questions about God that no one can answer. I rejoiced when she was strong and determined and smart in the face of Hatun's hollow, rote-learned dogma. I egged her on, pushed her to take chances and achieve, and I defended her to her mother whenever they clashed—even when she was wrong and Hatun was right. And when things finally grew unbearable and Hatun left us and went home—I think I was glad."

"Does her mother know what's happened?"

Ertekin shook his head. "We're not in contact anymore, neither Sevgi nor I. Hatun only ever called to berate us both, or to try to persuade Sevgi to go back to Turkey. Sevgi stopped taking her calls when she was fifteen. Even now, she's asked me not to tell her mother. It's probably as well. Hatun wouldn't come, or if she came she'd make a scene, wailing and calling down judgment on us all."

The word *judgment* went through Carl like a strummed chord.

"You are not a religious man, are you?" Ertekin asked him.

It was almost worth a grin. "I'm a thirteen."

"And thus genetically incapable." Ertekin nodded. "The received wisdom. Do you believe that?"

"Is there another explanation?"

"When I was younger, we were less enamored of genetic influence as a factor. My grandfather was a communist." A shrewd glance. "Do you know what that is?"

"Read about them, yeah."

"He believed that you can make of a human anything you choose to. That humans can become what they choose. That environment is all. It's not a fashionable view any longer."

"That's because it's demonstrably untrue."

"And yet, you—variant thirteens everywhere—were thoroughly environmentally conditioned. They did not trust your genes to give them the soldiers they wanted. You were brought up from the cradle to face brutality as if it were a fact of life."

Carl thought of Sevgi, tubes and needles and hope withering away. "Brutality *is* a fucking fact of life. Haven't you noticed?"

Ertekin shifted on the bench, turned toward him. Carl sensed that the other man was close to reaching out, to taking his hands in his own.

Groping for something.

"Do you really believe that you would have become this, that you were genetically destined to it, however you were raised as a child?"

Carl made an impatient gesture. "What I believe isn't important. I *did* become this; how I got here is academic. So let the academics discuss it at great length, write their papers and publish, get paid to agonize. In the end, none of it affects me."

"No, but it might affect others like you in the future."

Now he found he could smile—a thin, hard smile, the rind of amusement. "There aren't going to *be* any others like me in the future. Not on this planet. In another generation, we'll all be gone."

"Is that why you don't believe? Do you feel forsaken?"

The smile became a laugh of sorts. "I think you'll find, Dr. Ertekin, that the technical term for that is *transference*. You're the one feeling forsaken. I haven't ever expected to be anything other than alone, so I'm not upset when I find it to be true."

Marisol sat in his head and called him a liar. Elena Aguirre ghosted past, whispering. He held down a shiver, talked to stave it off.

"And you're missing a rather important point about my lack of religious convictions as well. To be a believer, you have to not only believe, you also have to *want* someone big and patriarchal around to take care of business for you. You have to be apt for worship. And thirteens don't do worship, of anyone or anything.

Even if you could convince a variant thirteen, against all the evidence, that there really was a God? He'd just see him as a threat to be eliminated. If God were demonstrably real?" He stared hard into Ertekin's eyes. "Guys like me would just be looking for ways to find him and burn him down."

Ertekin flinched, and looked away.

"She's chosen you well," he murmured.

"Sevgi?"

"Yes." Still looking away, fumbling in a jacket pocket. "You will need this."

He handed Carl a small package, sealed in slippery antiseptic white with orange flash warning decals. Lettering in a language he couldn't read, Germanic feel, multiple vowels. Carl weighed it in his palm.

"Put it away, please." Ertekin told him. The garden was starting to fill as students and medical staff came out on lunch break to enjoy the sun.

"This is painless?"

"Yes. It's from a Dutch company that specializes in such things. It will take about two minutes from injection."

Carl stowed the package.

"If you brought this," he said quietly, "why do you need me?"

"Because I cannot do it," Ertekin told him simply.

"Because you're a Muslim?"

"Because I'm a doctor." He looked at his hands again. They hung limp in his lap. "And because even if I had not taken an oath, I do not think I would be capable of ending my own daughter's life."

"It's what she wants. It's what she's asked for."

"Yes." There were tears gathering on Ertekin's eyelids. "And now, when it most matters, I find I cannot give her what she wants."

He took Carl's hand suddenly. His grip was dry and powerful. The tiger-irised gaze burned into Carl's, blinked tears aside so they trickled on the leathery skin.

"She's chosen you. And deep in my hypocritical, doubting soul, I give thanks to Allah that you've come. Sevgi is getting ready once more to push the boundaries, to cross the lines drawn by others that she will not heed. And this time I will not fail her, as I did four years ago."

He wiped away the tears with quick, impatient gestures of his hand.

"I will stand with my daughter this time," he said. "But you must help me, thirteen, if I am not to fail her again."

The Haag complex rips through Sevgi's system like vacuum in a suddenly holed spacecraft. Cells rupture, leak vital fluids. Debris flies about, her immune system *staggers, flushes itself desperately, clings to the antiviral boosters Stanford fed her, and still it fails. Her lungs begin to fill. Her renal functions slow and must be artificially stimulated if her kidneys are not to explode. Tubes in, tubes out. The creep of waste products through her system begins to hurt.*

She finds it harder to think with clarity for any length of time.

Only when the v-format was no longer viable, when she sputtered in and out of existence there like a disinterested ghost, did she let him see her for real.

He sat by the bed in shock.

For all he'd prepared himself, it was a visceral blow to see how the flesh had burned off her, how her eyes had grown hollow and her cheeks drawn. He tried to smile at her, but the expression flickered on and off his face, the way she'd flickered in virtual. When she saw, she smiled back at him and hers was steady, like a lamp burning through the stretched fabric of her face.

"I look like shit," she murmured. "Right?"

"You've been skipping meals again, haven't you?"

She laughed, broke up into coughing. But he saw the look in her eyes, saw she was grateful. He tried to feel good about that.

He sat by the bed.

He held her hand.

"Tell me a secret."

"What?" He'd thought she was sleeping. The little room was dim and still, adrift in the larger quiet of the hospital at night. Darkness pressed itself to the glass of the window, oozed inward through the room. The machines winked tiny red and amber eyes at him, whispered and clicked to themselves, made vaguely comprehensible graphic representations, in cool shades of blue and green, of what was going on inside their charge. The night lamp cast a faded gold oblong on the bed where Sevgi made mounds in the sheet. Her face was in shadow.

"Come on," she croaked. "You heard me. Tell me what really happened on Mars. What did Gutierrez do to you?"

He blinked, cleared his eyes from long aimless staring into the gloom. "Thought you'd already worked that out."

"Well, you tell me. Did I?"

He looked back at it, bricks of his past he hadn't tried to build anything with in years. *It's another world, it's another time,* Sutherland had said once. *Got to learn to let it go.*

"You were close," he admitted.

"How close? Come on, Marsalis." A laugh floated up out of her, like echoes up from a well. "Grant a dying woman a last wish."

His mouth tightened.

"Gutierrez didn't fix the lottery for me," he said. "There's too much security around it, too much n-djinn presence. And it's a tough thing to do, fix a chance event so it does what you want and still looks like chance. Something like that, you've got to look for the weak point."

"Which was?"

"Same as it always is. The human angle."

"Oh, humans." She laughed again, a little stronger now. "I guess that makes sense. Can't trust them any farther than a Jesusland preacher with a choirgirl, right?"

He smiled. "Right."

"So which particular human did you finesse?"

"Neil Delaney." Faint flare of contempt as he remembered, but the years had bleached it back almost to amusement. "He was Bradbury site administrator back then."

"He's on the oversight council now."

"Yeah, I know. Mars works well for some people." Carl found himself loosening up. Words were flowing easier now, here in the low light at her bedside, just the two of them in the gloom and quiet. "Delaney was selling to the Chinese. Downgrading site reports, writing them off as low potential, so COLIN wouldn't bother filing notice of action. That way, the New People's Home teams could get in and stake their claim instead, without having to do the actual survey work."

"Mother*fucker!*" But it was the whispered ghost of outrage; you could hear how she didn't have strength for the real thing.

"Yeah, well. Helps if you just think of it as outsourcing—NPH buying COLIN expertise under the table, probably cheaper than they could afford to do the surveys themselves. In market terms, it makes perfect sense. There's a lot of planet to cover, not many people to do it. And the Chinese were just doing what they've always done—dangling enough dollars in the right places to get the West's corporate qualms to go belly-up."

"Somehow I don't think the feeds would have seen it that way."

"No. That's the way we put it to Delaney." Carl reflected, found he still got a faint warm glow from the recollection. "It was a good sting. He caved in completely. Gave us everything we asked for."

"He sent you home."

"Well, he opened up the security on the lottery system for us. Gave Gutierrez a clear run at it. So yeah, I won the lottery."

"And what did Gutierrez get?"

Carl shrugged. "Cash. Favors. We had a few other players on the team as well, they all got paid."

"But only you got to go home."

"Yeah, well. Only one cryocap up for grabs, you know. And it was my sting, my operation from the start. I put the crew together, I made it pretty clear from the start what I wanted out of the deal."

"So." She wheezed a little. He reached for the glass, held it to her lips, and cradled her head. The actions felt smooth with custom. "Thanks, that's better. So you think Gutierrez was jealous. Fucked you after the event?"

"Maybe. Or Delaney asked him to do it, hoped I'd flip out before the rescue ship got there. You remember that guy who woke up on the way back from the Jupiter moon survey, back in the eighties? Spitz, or something?"

"Specht. Eric Specht. Yeah, I remember."

"He went crazy waiting for the rescue. Maybe Delaney hoped the same thing'd happen to me. Who knows?"

"You don't know?"

"I know Gutierrez sent me a very scared mail once I made it back to Earth, said he'd had nothing to do with it. So maybe it was just a glitch. Or maybe Delaney hired another datahawk. Then again, Gutierrez always was a lying little fuck, so like I said, who knows?"

"You don't care?"

He twisted a little in his seat, smiled at her. "There's no *point* in caring, Sevgi. It's a different planet. Another world, another time. What was I going to do—go *back* there? Just for revenge? I'd put the whole of my last year on Mars into scamming my way back to Earth. Sometimes, you know, you've just got to let go."

Beneath the covers, she drew into herself a little. "Yeah," she whispered. "I guess that's the truth."

They sat in silence for a while. She groped for his hand. He gave it to her.

"Why'd you come back, Carl?" she asked him softly.

He made a crooked grin in the gloom. "Listen to what the Earth First people are telling you, Sevgi. Mars is a shithole."

"But you were free there." She let go of his hand, gestured weakly. "You must have known there was a risk you'd be interned when you got back. It's pure luck they didn't put you straight into the tracts."

"Not quite. I bought some machine time before all this went down, before I

put the Delaney sting together. I asked the n-djinn to look at the way lottery winners were treated when they got back, then extrapolate for a thirteen. The machine gave me a seventy–thirty chance they'd work some kind of special
exemption in view of my celebrity status." He shrugged. "Pretty good odds."

"And what if the n-djinn got it wrong?" She craned forward in the bed, halfway
to sitting up. The pale gold light fell on her face. Eyes intense and burning into
his. "What if they just went ahead and interned your ass?"

Another shrug, another crooked grin. "Then I guess I would have had to break
out and run. Just like all the other saps."

She lay back, puffing a little from the effort.

"I don't believe you," she said when she'd gotten her breath back. "All that
risk, just because Mars is a shithole? No way. You could have had the cash instead. Milked Delaney for pretty much anything you wanted out there. Set yourself up. Come on, Carl. Why'd you really come back?"

He hesitated. "It's not that important, Sevgi."

"It is to me."

Footsteps down the corridor outside. A murmur of voices, receding. He sighed.

"Sutherland," he said.

"Your sensei."

"Yeah." He lifted his hands on his lap, trying to frame it for himself. "See,
there's a point you get to with *tanindo*. A level where it stops being about *how* to
do it, becomes all about *why*. Why you're practicing, why you're learning. Why
you're living. And I couldn't get there."

"You didn't know why?" She puffed a breathless laugh. "Hey, welcome to the
club. You think any of us know why we're doing this shit?"

Carl let an echo of her amusement trace itself onto his lips, but absently. He
stared across the shadowed bed and her form beneath the sheet as if it were a
landscape.

"Sutherland says it's easier for basic humans," he said distantly. "You people
build better metaphors, believe in them more deeply. He said I'd have to find
something else. And until I did, I was blocked."

"Sutherland's a thirteen, too, right?"

"Yeah."

"So how come he managed it?"

Carl nodded. "Exactly. He gave me a path. A functional substitute for belief."

"And that was?"

"He told me to make a list, keep it to myself, and focus on it. Eleven things I
wanted to do at some point in what was left of my life. Things it was important for
me to do, things that mattered."

"You didn't go for the round dozen?"

"The number's not important. Eleven, twelve, nine, doesn't matter. Best not to make too long a list, it defeats the point of the exercise, but otherwise you just pick a number and make your list. I chose eleven." He hesitated again, looked at her almost apologetically. "Nine of those, I realized I needed to be on Earth to do."

The hospital quiet closed in again. He saw in the gloom how she turned to look out the window.

"Have you done them all yet?" she asked quietly.

"No. Not yet." He cleared his throat, frowned. "But I'm getting through them. And it does work. Sutherland was right."

For a few moments, she seemed not to be listening, seemed to have lost herself in the darkness outside the glass. Then, dry slide of her hair on the pillow, her head switched around to face him again.

"You want to hear a secret of mine?"

"Sure."

"Three years ago, I planned to have someone murdered."

"Yeah?"

"Yeah, I know. Everyone thinks about killing someone every now and then. But this was for real. I sat down and I mapped it out. I knew people back then, cops and ex-cops who owed me. There was this accidental-killing incident back when I was a patrol officer, only a couple of years in, all wide-eyed and innocent." She coughed a little. "Ah, it's a long story, not going to bore you with the details. Just this interrogation that went over the line one time. I was there, saw it go down. Guess you'd say I was complicit. Internal Affairs were certainly looking to paint it that way. Pressure came down, they wanted me to roll over in return for immunity. But they couldn't prove I was in the room, and I didn't leak. Stuck at that, half their case collapsed. So nine years later, that's three years ago like I was telling you, there were guys walking around New York with a badge they owed me for. Other guys who didn't go to jail when they should have. I could have done it, Carl. I could have set it in motion."

She started coughing again. He lifted her, held a tissue to her lips until she cleared the shit that was sitting in her lungs, cleaned her mouth after. He fed her sips of water, laid her gently back down. Wiped the sweat of effort from her brow with another tissue, waited while her breathing stabilized again.

He leaned in closer. "So who'd you want to kill?"

"Amy fucking Westhoff," she said bitterly. "Fucking bitch who killed Ethan."

"You told me the SWATs took Ethan down."

"Yeah. But someone had to leak this shit, someone had to find out what Ethan was and notify UNGLA liaison up at City Hall. You remember I told you in Istanbul, Ethan was seeing this cheerleader blonde in Datacrime?"

"Vaguely."

"That was Westhoff. She showed up in the corridor outside my office the week Ethan moved in with me, screaming abuse, telling me I didn't know what I was getting into. Saying she'd fuck with my life and Ethan's if I didn't back off."

"You think she knew what he was?"

"I don't know. Not then, I don't think. If she'd known, I think she would have used it on him when he tried to move out."

"Maybe she did, and he didn't tell you."

That stopped her, pinned her to a long pause while she thought about it. He tilted his head, trying to work a kink out of his neck.

"I don't believe she knew back then," Sevgi said finally. "Maybe she had her suspicions on and off. I think I did, too, if I'm honest about it, even before Keegan showed up and blew the whole thing. You know, if you're a woman, it's one of those things you can't help thinking about sometimes. I mean, there's so much scare stuff out there. All the warnings, all the sexy panic every time someone gets out of Cimarron or Tanana. *The Truth About Thirteens*, how to recognize one, what you guys are supposed to be like, how you'd act that's different from a regular guy. Warning signs, free phone snitch numbers, public information postings, and then the fucking media aftermath every time. You know, I saw a woman's magazine article once while I was waiting to see my lawyer. 'Are You Sleeping with a Thirteen—Thirteen Telltale Signs That Let You Know.' Fucking bullshit like that."

She twitched about in the bed with the force of her frustration. Her breath came hoarse and agitated. Voice impatient.

"Anyway, whether she knew then or not, I know damn well she was keeping tabs on Ethan. And then, when we fucked up, when we got complacent after Keegan, she had her chance."

"She knew about the pregnancy?"

"Yeah, well, we weren't hiding that. I started showing seriously at three months, went on reduced duties at four. Of course she knew, everybody knew by then." Sevgi stopped, waited until her breathing evened out again. "That wasn't it. When we got pregnant, something in Ethan shifted. That was when he started trying to track down his genetic mother. He'd always talked about doing it, all this stuff about wanting to know who his real mother was, but with the baby—"

"So, not his surrogate then?"

"No. That was finished business, as far as he was concerned. He never wanted

to see her again. Never talked about her to me. But he was hung up about finding Patti. The baby really kicked him into action."

Carl saw the link. "You think he went to Westhoff to do the searches?"

"I don't know. But he went to Datacrime, I know that much because he told
me he was going to. They've got the best machines in the city for that kind of
work, and he knew quite a few people there, not just Amy." He saw the way her
fists clenched where they lay on the bed. "But Amy knew. She came up to me on
the street, congratulated me on the baby, said something about how it was great
Ethan was getting back in touch with his family. I *told* Ethan that, but—" She
rolled her head back and forth on the pillow. "—like I said, we got so fucking
complacent about everything."

"Is there any actual evidence Westhoff tipped off UNGLA?"

"Enough to make a case?" He thought she smiled in the dimness. "No. But
you remember I told you someone in the department tipped Ethan off that they
were coming for him?"

"Yeah, you said a downtown number."

"Yeah." She was smiling, bleakly. "Datacrime is downtown. I talked to a Datacrime sergeant said Amy Westhoff was acting weird all that day. Upset about
something, in and out of the office all the time. The call went out from another
floor in the building, an empty office up on fifth, but she could have gotten there
easily enough."

"Could have. You said he had a lot of friends in Datacrime."

"No one knew about the SWAT deployment. No one except whoever it was
that tipped them off in the first place."

"Did Ethan have any friends in the SWAT chain of command? Or in City
Hall, maybe?"

"Sure, and they waited until the morning it was due to go down before they
called. And they went all the way across the city to do it, to a downtown NYPD
precinct house and a fifth-floor office that they just happened to know would be
empty. Come on, Carl. Give me a fucking break."

"And no one else picked up on this?"

Another weak smile. "No one wanted to. First off, it's not a crime to turn in a
thirteen to the authorities. You still see screen ads encouraging good citizens to
do exactly that, every time someone gets out of Cimarron or Tanana. And then
there's the fact that Ethan was a cop, and to all appearances it looks like another
cop ratted him out. That's the kind of thing most people in the department would
rather just forget ever happened."

He nodded. He thought it might be starting to get light outside.

"So you planned to kill her. Have her killed. What stopped you?"

"I don't know." She closed her eyes. Voice small and weary with the effort she'd been making. "In the end, I couldn't make myself go through with it, you know. I've killed people in the line of duty, had to, to stay alive myself. But this is different. It's cold. You've got to be so fucking cold."

Beyond the window, the night was definitely beginning to bleach out. Carl saw Sevgi's face more clearly now, saw the desolation in it. He leaned over and kissed her gently on the forehead.

"Try to get some rest now," he said.

"I couldn't," she muttered, as if trying to explain herself before a judge, or maybe to Ethan Conrad. "I just couldn't do it."

Rovayo showed up, off duty, with flowers. Sevgi was barely polite. The jokes she made about casual fucking, in a hoarse whisper of a voice, weren't funny, and no one laughed. Rovayo toughed it out, spent the time there she'd announced she could, promised awkwardly to return. The look in Sevgi's eyes suggested she didn't much care one way or the other. Outside in the corridor afterward, the Rim cop grimaced at Carl.

"Bad idea, huh?"

"It was a nice thought." He sought other matters, shielding from the coming truth behind the door at their backs. "You get anything from the crime scene?"

Rovayo shook her head. "Nothing that doesn't belong to you, the dead guys, or a dozen irrelevant Bayview lowlifes. This Onbekend must have been greased up pretty good."

"Yeah, he was." Carl brought recall to life, surprised himself with the stab of fury that accompanied the man's half-familiar face. "You could see it in the light, shining in his hair pretty fucking thick as well. No way he was going to be leaving trace material for the CSI guys."

"Right. Makes you wonder why Merrin didn't do the same thing. Instead of leaving his fucking trace all over everything for us to track him with."

"Yeah, I guess that's why we caught him so easily."

Rovayo blinked. "I see you're in a great mood."

"Sorry. Haven't had much sleep." He glanced back at the closed door of Sevgi's room. "You want to get a coffee downstairs?"

"Sure."

Across the scarred plastic tabletop from her in the cafeteria downstairs, he asked mechanically after the *Bulgakov's Cat* bust. There wasn't much. Daskeen Azul weren't shifting from their position. Merrin, Ren, and the others were employees who had usurped company policy and practice for their own illicit ends. Any attempt to incriminate owners or management would be fought right into court and out the other side. Warrants resisted, bail set and paid, legal battle joined.

"And we'll probably lose" was Rovayo's sour assessment. "Same day we made the arrests, some very heavy legal muscle showed up from the Freeport. Tsai's going to take them on anyway, he's pissed about the whole thing. But no one's talking, they're all either too scared or too confident. Unless someone in this crew rolls over for us, and fast, we're going to end up dead in the water."

"Right." It came out slack. He couldn't make himself care.

Rovayo sipped her coffee, eyed him grimly across the table, and said: "I'm only going to ask this once, because I know it's stupid. But are they sure they can't beat this thing she's got?"

"Yeah, they're sure. The viral shift moves too fast, we're just playing catch-up. There isn't an n-djinn built that has the chaos-modeling capacity to beat this. Haag system's designed to take down a thirteen, and my immune system's about twice as efficient as yours, so they had to come up with something pretty unstoppable."

Rovayo grunted. "Nothing ever fucking changes, huh?"

"Sorry?"

"Arms industry, making a living scaring us all. You know a couple of hundred years ago, they built a whole new type of bullet because they thought ordinary slugs wouldn't take down a black man with cocaine in his blood?"

"Black man?"

"Yeah, black. Black-skinned, like you and me. First they tie cocaine use to the black community, make it a race-based issue. Then they reckon they need a bigger bang to put us down, because we're all coked up." The Rim cop made an ironic gesture of presentation. "Welcome to the .357 magnum round."

Carl frowned. The terminology was only vaguely familiar. "You're talking about some Jesusland thing, right?"

"Wasn't called Jesusland then. This is a cased round I'm talking about. Two hundred years ago, I did say."

He nodded and rubbed at his eyes with thumb and forefinger. "Yeah, sorry. You did. I forgot."

"Same thing happened another couple of hundred years before that. Automatic fire this time." Rovayo sipped at her coffee. "Guy called Puckle patented a crank-action mounted machine gun designed to fire square bullets at the advancing Turkish hordes."

Carl sat back. "You're winding me up."

"No. Thing was supposed to fire round bullets if you were fighting Christians, square if you were killing heathens."

"Come on! There's no fucking way they could build something like that back then."

"No, of course they couldn't. It didn't work." The Rim cop's voice tinged grim. "But the .357 magnum did. And so does Haag."

"Monsters, huh," said Carl quietly. "How come you know all this stuff, Rovayo?"

"I read a lot of history," said the black woman. "Way I see it, you don't know anything about the past, you got no future."

They aspirate her lungs, try to bring her breathing back up. She just lies there while they do it, before, during, and after, puddled on the bed in her own lack of strength. The whole process feels like the kicks of a midterm pregnancy, but higher up and much more frequent, as if in tiny, hysterical rage.

Memory brings tears, but they leak out of her eyes so slowly she runs out of actual feeling before they stop. She doesn't have a lot of fluid to spare.

Her mouth is parched. Her skin is papery dry.

Her hands and feet feel swollen and increasingly numb.

When the endorphins they give her wear thin, she can track the passage of her urine by the tiny scraping pains it makes on its way to the catheter.

Her stomach aches from emptiness. She feels sick to its pit.

When the endorphins come on, it feels like going back to the garden, or the nighttime ride of the ferries across the Bosphorus to the Asian side. Black water and merry city lights. She hallucinates once, very clearly, coming into the dock at Kadıköy and seeing Marsalis waiting for her there. Dark and quiet under the LCLS overheads.

Reaching out his hand.

Surfacing from the dosage is pain, dragging her back like rusty wires, and sudden, sick-making fear as she remembers where she is. Lying drained, and seeping slowly in and out of bags. Stale sheets and the gaunt sentinels of the machines around her. And through it all, a racking, overarching, frustrated fury with the body she's still wired and tied and bedded down into.

He tried to work.

Sevgi was out on the swells of endorphin a lot of the time, drifting there in something that approximated peace. He found he could step out and leave her in these periods, and he conversed with Norton in low tones, sitting in waiting rooms, or leaned against walls in the night-quiet hospital corridors.

"I remembered something this afternoon," he told the COLIN exec. "Sitting in there, shit going through my head. When Sevgi and I went to talk to Manco Bambarén, he recognized this jacket."

Norton peered at the arm Carl held out to him, the orange chevrons flashing along the sleeve.

"Yeah? Standard Republican jail wear, I guess any criminal in the Western Hemisphere's got to know what that looks like."

"It's not quite standard." Carl twisted to show Norton the lettering on the back. The COLIN exec shrugged.

"Sigma. Right. You know how many prison contracts those guys have in Jesusland? They've got to be the second or third biggest corporate player the incarceration industry has. They're even bidding on stuff out here on the coast these days."

"Yeah, but Manco told me he had a cousin who did time specifically in South Florida State. Now, maybe we can't hack the datafog around Isabela Gayoso so easily, but we ought to be able to chase prison records and maybe dig this guy up. Maybe he'll tell us something we can use."

Norton nodded and rubbed at his eyes. "All right, we can look. God knows I could use the distraction right now. You get a name?"

"No. Bambarén, maybe, but I doubt it. The way Manco was talking, this wasn't anyone that close to home."

"And we don't know when he did time?"

"No, but I'd guess recently. Sigma haven't held the SFS contract more than five or six years max. Sigma jacket, you've got to be looking at that time frame."

"Or Bambarén misremembered, and his cousin did time in some other Sigma joint, somewhere else in the Republic."

"I don't think there's anything wrong with Manco Bambarén's memory. Those guys aren't big on forgive and forget, especially not when it's down to family."

"All right, leave it with me." Norton glanced back down the corridor toward Sevgi's room. "Listen, I've been up since yesterday morning. I've got to get some sleep. Can you stay with her?"

"Sure. That's why I'm here."

Norton's gaze tightened on his face. "You call me if anything—"

"Yeah. I'll call you. Go get some rest."

For just a moment, something indefinable passed between the two of them in the dimly lit width of the corridor. Then Norton nodded, clamped his mouth tight, and headed away down the corridor.

Carl watched him go with folded arms.

Later, sitting by her bed in the bluish gloom of the night-lights, flanked by the quiet machines, he thought he felt Elena Aguirre slip silently into the room behind him. He didn't turn around. He went on watching Sevgi's sallow, washed-out face on the pillow, the barely perceptible rise and fall of her breathing beneath the sheet. Now he thought Aguirre was probably close enough to put a cool hand on the back of his neck.

"Wondered when you'd show up," he said quietly.

Sevgi washed awake, alone, left beached by the receding tide of the endorphins, and she knew with an odd clarity that it was time. The once vertiginous terror was gone, had collapsed in on itself for lack of energy to sustain it. She was, finally, more weary, more miserably angry, and more in pain than she was scared.

It was what she'd been waiting for.

Time to go.

Outside the window of her room, morning was trying to get in. Soft slant of sunlight through the gap in the quaint hand-pull curtains. Waiting between endorphin surges for night to drag itself out the door had seemed like an aching, gritty forever. She lay there for a while longer, watching the hot patch of light creep onto the bed at her feet and thinking, because she wanted to be sure.

When the door opened and Carl Marsalis stepped into the room, the decision was as solid in her head as it had been when she woke.

"Hi there," he said softly. "Just been up the hall for a shower."

"Lucky fucking bastard," she said throatily, and was dismayed at how deep, how bitter her envy of that simple pleasure really was. It made her feelings over Rovayo look trivial by comparison.

Time to go.

He smiled at her, maybe hadn't caught the edge in her voice, maybe had and let it go.

"Can I get you anything?" he asked.

The same question he asked every time. She held his gaze and mustered a firm nod.

"Yeah, you can. Call my father and Tom in here, will you?"

The smile flickered and blew out on his face. He stood absolutely still for a moment, looking down at her. Then he nodded and slipped out.

As soon as he was gone, her pulse began to pound, up through her throat and in her temples. It felt like the first couple of times she ever had to draw her weapon as a patrol officer, the sudden, tilting comprehension that came with a street situation about to go bad. The terror of the last decaying seconds, the taste of irrevocable commitment.

But by the time he came back with the other two, she had it locked down.

"I've had enough," she told them, voice a dried-up whisper scarcely louder in the room than it was in her own head. "This is it."

None of them spoke. It wasn't like this was a surprise.

"Baba, I know you'd do this for me if you could. Tom, I know you would, too. I chose Carl because he can, that's all."

She swallowed painfully. Waited for the ache it made to subside. Hiss-click of the machines around her across the silence. Outside in the corridor, the hospital's working day was just getting under way.

"They've told me they can keep me going like this for at least another month. Baba, is that true?"

Murat bowed his head. He made a trapped sound, somewhere between throat and chest. He jerked a nod. Tears fell off his eyes onto the sheets. She found suddenly, oddly, that she felt worse for him than she did for herself. Abruptly, she realized that the fear in her was almost gone, squeezed out of the frame with pain and tiredness and straightforward irritation with it all.

Time to go.

"I'm not going to go on like this for another month," she husked. "I'm bored, I'm sick, and I'm tired. Carl, I told you this felt like a wall rushing at me?"

Carl nodded.

"Well, it isn't rushing anymore. It's all slowed down to sludge. I'm sitting here looking at where I have to go, and it looks like fucking kilometers of hard ground to crawl on my hands and fucking knees. I won't do that. I don't want to play this fucking game anymore."

"Sev, are you—" Norton stalled out.

She smiled for him. "Yeah, I'm sure. Been thinking it through for long enough. I'm tired, Tom. I'm tired of spending half my time stoned, and the other half waking up in pain to realize I'm still not fucking dead, that I've still got that part to go. It's time to just get on with it, just get it done."

She turned to Carl again.

"Have you got it?"

He took out the slippery white packet and held it out to her. Light from the brightening morning outside came in and glimmered on the slick plastic covering. Letting go of the light was going to be the hardest thing. Sunlight broke in and danced about the room when they pulled the curtains each morning, and it was almost worth not quite being dead each morning because of it. It was what she clung to as she rode the long troughs and swells of dreaming and back-to-real every night. She'd hung on this long because of it. Might even have hung on a little longer, a few more mornings, if she wasn't so *fucking* weary.

"Baba." Her voice was tiny, she had to struggle to keep it even. "Is this going to hurt me?"

Murat cleared his throat wetly. He shook his head.

"No, *canım*. It'll be like." He gritted his teeth to keep from sobbing. "Like going to sleep."

"That's good," she whispered breathlessly. "I could use some decent sleep."

She found Carl with her eyes. She nodded, and watched him tear open the package. His hands moved efficiently, laying out the component parts of the kit. He barely seemed aware of the actions—she guessed he'd done similar on enough battlefields in the past. She glanced across to Tom Norton, found him weeping.

"Tom," she said gently. "Come here and hold my hand. Baba, you come 'round here. Don't cry, Baba. Please don't cry, any of you. You've got to be happy I'm not going to hurt anymore."

She looked at Carl. No tears. His face was black stone as he prepped the spike, held it up one-handed to the light, while his other hand touched warm and callus-fingered on the crook of her arm. He met her eyes and nodded.

"You just tell me when," he said.

She looked around at their faces once more. Made them a smile each, squeezed their hands. Then she found his face again, and clung to it.

"I'm ready," she whispered.

He bent over her. Tiny, cold spike into her arm, held there a moment by the overlaying warmth of his fingers, and then gone. He swabbed, applied something cool, and pressed down. She arched her neck to get closer to him, brushed her paper-dry lips across the rasp of his unshaven cheek. Breathed in his scent and lay back as the beautiful, aching warmth spread through her body, inking out the pain.

Waited for what came next.

Sunlight outside.

She wanted to look sideways at the slanting angle it made, but she was just too sleepy now to make the effort. Like her eyes just wouldn't move in their sockets anymore. It felt like a weekend from her youth in Queens, *crawling into bed Sunday morning just past dawn, weary from the long night out clubbing across the river. Taxi home, girlish hilarity leaching out to a reflective comedown quiet as they cruised through silent streets, dropping off along the way. Creeping up to the house, scrape of the recog fob across the lock, and of course there's Murat in pajamas, already up and in the kitchen, trying to look scandalized and failing dismally. She grins her impish grin, steals white cheese crumbs and an olive off his plate, a sip of tea from his glass. His hand cuffs through her hair, tousles it, and tugs her head gently into an embrace. Bear-hug squeeze, and his smell, the rasp of his stubble across her cheek. Then, climbing the stairs to her room, yawning cavernously, almost tripping over her own feet. She pauses at the top, looks back, and he's standing there at the foot of the stairs, watching her go with so much pride and love in his face that out of nowhere it shunts aside the comedown weariness and makes her heart ache like a fresh cut.*

"Better get some sleep, Sevgi."

Still aching as she stumbles into bed, still half dressed. Curtains not properly drawn, sunlight slanting in, but no fucking way that's going to stop her sleeping, the way she feels now. No fucking way . . .

Sunlight outside.

Aches and pains forgotten. The long, warming slide into not worrying about anything at all.

And the room and all that was in it went away gently, like Murat closing her bedroom door.

When it was done, when her eyes slid finally closed and her breathing stopped, when Murat Ertekin bent over her, sobbing uncontrollably, and checked the pulse in her neck and nodded, when it was over and there was, finally, no more left for him to do, Carl walked away.

He left Murat Ertekin sitting with his daughter. He left Norton standing trembling like a bodyguard running a high fever but still on duty. He left and headed down the corridor alone. It felt as if he were wading in thigh-deep water. Humans brushed past, moving aside for him, cued in by the blank face and the forced gait. There was no panic, no buzz of activity in his wake—Murat knew how to bypass the machines so they wouldn't scream for help when Sevgi's vital signs sank to the bottom.

They would know soon enough. Norton had promised to deal with it. That was his end—Carl had done what he did best.

He walked away.

The memories scurried after him, anxious not to be left behind.

"Don't know what's next," she says, smiling as the drug takes hold. "But if it feels anything like this, it'll do."

And then, as her eyelids begin to sag, "I'll see you all in the garden, I guess."

"Yeah, with all that fruit and the stream running under the trees there," he tells her, through lips that seem to have gone numb. Voice suddenly hoarse. He's the only one talking to her now. Norton is silent and rigid at his side, no use to anyone. Murat Ertekin has sunk to his knees beside the bed, face pressed into his daughter's hand, holding back tears with an effort that shakes him visibly as he breathes. He summons strength to keep speaking. Squeezes her hand. "Remember that, Sevgi. All that sunlight through the trees."

She squeezes back, barely. She sniggers, a gentle rupturing of air out through her lips, barely any actual sound. "And the virgins. Don't forget them."

He swallows hard.

"Yeah, well you save me one of those. I'll be along, Sevgi. I'll catch you up. We all will."

"Fucking virgins," she murmurs sleepily. "Who needs 'em? Gotta teach 'em every fucking thing . . ."

And then, finally, just before the breathing stops.

"Baba, he's a good man. He's clean."

He smashed back the doors out of the ward, along the corridors people got out of his way. He found the stairs, plunged downward, looking for a way out.

Knowing there wasn't one.

CHAPTER 48

A fterward, the COLIN exec came to find him in the garden. Carl hadn't said he was going there, but it wouldn't have taken a detective to work it out. The benches around the fountain had become a standard haunt for all of them over the past few days, familiar with habitual use. It was where they went when the weight of the hospital pressed down on them, when the antiseptic-scented, nano-cleansed air grew too hard and arid to breathe. Norton slumped onto the bench beside him like someone getting home to a shared house and hitting the sofa. He stared into the sunlit splash of the fountain and said nothing at all. He'd cleaned up, but his face still looked feverish from the crying.

"Any trouble?" Carl asked him.

Norton shook his head numbly. His voice came out mechanical. "They're making some noise. The COLIN mandate should cover it. Ertekin's talking to them."

"So we're free to go."

"Free to . . . ?" The exec's brow furrowed, uncomprehending. "You've always been free to go, Marsalis."

"That's not what I mean."

Norton swallowed. "Listen, there's the funeral. Arrangements. I don't know if—"

"I'm not interested in what they do with her corpse. I'm going to find Onbek-end. Are you going to help me?"

"Marsalis, listen—"

"It's a simple question, Norton. You watched her die in there. What are you going to do about it?"

The COLIN exec drew a shuddering breath. "You think killing Onbekend is going to make things better? You think that'll bring her back?"

Carl stared at him. "I'm going to assume that's rhetorical."

"Haven't you had enough yet?"

"Enough of what?"

"Enough of killing whatever you can get your *fucking* hands on." Norton came off the bench, stood over him. The words hissed out like vented poison gas. "You just took Sevgi's *life* in there, and all you can think of to do is go look for someone else to kill? *Is that all you fucking know how to do?*"

Across the gardens, heads turned.

"Sit down," Carl said grimly. "Before I break your fucking neck for you."

Norton grinned hard. He sank onto his haunches, brought his face level with Carl's.

"You want to break my fucking neck." He gestured up. "Here it is, my friend. Right fucking here."

He meant it. Carl closed his eyes and sighed. Opened them and looked at Norton again, nodded slowly.

"All right." He cleared his throat. "There are two ways to look at this, *my friend.* See, we can do the civilized, feminized, constructive thing and work a long by-the-book investigation that may or may not lead us eventually back to Manco Bambarén and the altiplano and Onbekend. Or we can take your COLIN authorization and a little hardware, and we can fly down there and set fire to Manco's machine."

Norton levered himself upright again. He shook his head. "And you think that's going to make him cave in? Just like that?"

"Onbekend is a thirteen." Carl wondered fleetingly if he shouldn't try harder with Norton, lever his voice up out of the dead tone he could hear in it. "Manco Bambarén may have hired him, or he may just be doing business with the people who did, but whatever the connection is, it's not blood the way it was with Merrin. Manco's going to see Onbekend and me as two of a kind, monsters he can play off against each other for whatever best result there is. He gave me Nevant three years ago to get me off his back, and he'll give me Onbekend for the same reason. In the end, he's a businessman, and he'll do what's good for business. If we make it bad enough for business to hold out, then he'll cave in."

"We?"

"Slip of the tongue. I'm going anyway. You can come with me or not, as your nonvariant conscience sees fit. Be easier for me if you did, but if you don't, well." Carl shrugged. "I promised Gutierrez I'd go back to Mars to kill him, and I meant it. The altiplano's a lot easier gig than that."

"I could stop you."

"No, you couldn't. First sign of trouble from you, I'm on an UNGLA bounce out of here. They practically tried to drag me onto the shuttle last week. They'll jump at the chance if I call them. Then I'll just double back to Peru on my own ticket."

"COLIN could still make your life very tough down there."

"Yeah, they usually do. Occupational hazard. It never stopped me before."

"Hard man, huh?"

"Thirteen." Carl looked at him levelly. "Norton, this is what's wired into me, it's what my body chemistry's good for. I am going to build a memorial to Sevgi Ertekin out of Onbekend's blood, and I will cut down anyone who gets in my way. Including you, if you make me."

Norton sank back onto the bench.

"You think that's just you?" he muttered. "You think we don't all feel that way right now?"

"I wouldn't know. But *feeling* and *doing* are two very different things. In fact, there's a guy back on Mars called Sutherland who tells me humans have built their entire civilization in the gap between the two. I wouldn't know about that, either. What I *do* know is that an hour ago in there"—Carl gestured toward the hospital—"Murat Ertekin *felt* he wanted to put his daughter out of her misery. But he couldn't or wouldn't do it. I won't judge him for that, just like I won't judge you for not coming with me, if that's the choice you make. Maybe this stuff just isn't wired into you people as deep. That's what they told us at Osprey, anyway. That we were special because we were able to do what the society that created us no longer had the stomach for."

"Right," Norton said bitterly. "Believe everything the recruiting poster says, why don't you."

"I didn't say I did, I said that's what they told us. I don't necessarily think they were right. This much is true—it certainly didn't work out well, not for us or for you people." Carl sighed. "Look, I don't know, Norton. Maybe the fact that you don't have the stomach for single-minded slaughter anymore, the fact that you're forgetting how to do it—maybe that's a good thing. Maybe it makes you a better human being than me, a better member of society, a better *man* even. I wouldn't know, and I don't care because for me it isn't relevant. I am going to destroy Onbekend, I am going to destroy anyone who stands in my way. Now, are you coming with me or not?"

In the hotel, he found mundane things to do. The last four days of Sevgi's life had frozen his own existence in its tracks; he'd done nothing awake but sit by her and wait. He'd been in the same set of clothes since the night she was shot, and even the Marstech fabrics were starting to look shabby. He bundled them up and sent them for cleaning. Ordered something similar from the hotel catalog and wore it out into the street when he went looking for a phone. He supposed that he could have gotten phones easily enough from the hotel along with the clothing, but a habitual caution stopped him. And besides, he needed to walk. Away from or toward what, he wasn't quite sure, but the need sat in the pit of his empty stomach like tiny bubbles, like frustration rising.

"Bambarén's cousin's a bust," Norton had told him on their way back into town. The COLIN exec slumped in the back of the autocab as if broken at the joints. "So if you're looking for a way in, that isn't it. We got a name, Suerte Ferrer, street hook Maldición, string of small-time stuff on the fringes of the Jesusland *familias*. Did his three years in South Florida for gang-related, but he's out right now and he's dropped right off the scope."

"The n-djinns can't find him?"

"He's gone to ground somewhere in the Republic, and I can't get an n-djinn search in there without causing a major diplomatic incident. We're not exactly flavor of the month since we sprung you from South Florida State."

"You don't think you can get local PD to cooperate?"

"Which local PD?" Norton stared emptily out of the window. "As far as our information goes, Ferrer could be in any of about a dozen different states. And besides, Jesusland PD don't have the budget to run their own n-djinns."

"So they hire one out of the Rim."

"Yeah, they do that. But you're talking about major expenditure, and half these departments are struggling just to make payroll and keep their tactical equipment up to date. You're looking at decades of slash-and-burn tax cuts in public services across the board. There is no way, in that climate, I can start ringing up senior detectives across the Republic and asking them to buy n-djinn time to track down some minor-league gangbanger they've never heard of with no warrant out and no suspicion of anything other than being related to someone we don't like."

Carl nodded. Since leaving the hospital, he'd found himself thinking with a faintly adrenalized clarity that was like a synadrive hit. Sevgi was gone now, shelved in some space he could access later when he'd need the rage, and in her absence he was serene with vectored purpose. He looked back down the chain of association to Ferrer and saw the angle he needed.

"Norton."

The COLIN exec grunted.

"How easy would it be for you to get access to unreleased Marstech?"

On the northern fringes of Chinatown, more or less at random, he found an unassuming frontage with the simple words CLEAN PHONE picked out on the glass in green LCLS lozenges. He went inside and bought a pack of one-shot audio-phones, walked out again and found himself standing in the cold evening air, abruptly alone. In the time he'd been in the shop, everyone else seemed to have suddenly found pressing reasons to get off the street. He suffered an overpower-ing sense of unreality, and a sudden urge of his own to go back into the shop and see if the woman who'd served him had also disappeared, or had maybe ceded her place behind the counter to a grinning Elena Aguirre.

He grimaced and glanced around, picked out Telegraph Hill and the blunt finger of the Coit Tower on the skyline. He started walking toward it. The smoky evening light darkened, and lights began to glimmer on across the vistas of the city. He reached Columbus Avenue, and it was as if the city had suddenly jerked back to life around him. Teardrops zipped past in both directions, the muted chunter of their motors filling his ears. He joined other human beings at the crosswalk, waited with them for a space in the traffic flow, hurried with them when it came, across to Washington Square. More life here, more lives being lived. There was a softball match just packing up in the center of the grass, peo-ple headed home from under the spread of the trees. A tall, gaunt man dressed in ragged black stopped him and held out a begging bowl in hands that spasmed and shook. There was a sign in Chinese characters pinned to his shirt. Carl shot him a standard-issue *get-the-fuck-out-of-my-way* look, but it didn't work.

"Bearliunt," the man said in a hoarse voice, pushing the bowl at him. "Bearliunt."

He met hollowed-out eyes in a stretched parchment face. He held down the easy-access fury with an effort.

"I don't understand you," he told the derelict evenly. He jabbed a finger at the Chinese script. "I can't read this."

"Bearliunt. Rike you. Needy Nero."

The eyes were dark and intelligent, but they darted about. It was like being watched by something avian. The bowl came back, prodding.

"Bearliunt. Brack Rab from."

And Carl felt understanding pour down the back of his neck like cold water, like Elena Aguirre's touch. The man nodded. Saw the recognition.

"Yes. Brack Rab from. Bearliunt. Rike you."

Chilled out of nowhere, fucked up in some indefinable way, Carl reached into his pocket and fished out a wafer at random. He dumped it into the bowl without checking for denomination. Then he shouldered past the man and headed away fast, toward the rising slope of Telegraph Hill. When he got out of the park, he looked back and the man was staring after him, standing awkwardly with one arm raised stiffly like some kind of scarecrow brought barely to life. Carl shook his head, not knowing what he was denying, and fled for the tower.

He got to the top, out of breath from the speed he'd climbed.

The tower was closed up; he had the place to himself apart from a young couple propped against the seaward viewing wall in each other's arms. He stood and watched them balefully for a while, wondering how much he might also look like a living scarecrow in their eyes. Finally they grew uncomfortable, and the girl tugged her boyfriend away toward the exit stair. He was a muscular boy, tall and handsome in a pale Nordic fashion, and at first he wasn't going to go. He stared back at Carl, blue eyes marbled wet with tension. Carl concentrated on not killing him.

Then the girl leaned up and murmured in the blond boy's ear, and he contented himself with a snort, and they left.

Somewhere inside Carl, something clicked and broke, like ice in a glass.

He went to the wall and looked out across the water. Watched the lights glimmer on the Alcatraz station, out along the bridge, over at the shoreline on the Marin side. Sevgi was there in all of it, a thousand memories he didn't need or want. He blew hard breath through his nose, pulled one of the phones loose from the pack, and dialed a number he'd never expected to need.

"Sigma Frat House," said a jeering voice. "This ain't the time to be calling neither, so you leave a message and it better be a fucking good one."

"Danny? Let me speak to the Guatemalan."

The voice scaled upward, derisive. "Guatemalan's sleeping, motherfucker. You call back in office hours, you hear?"

"Danny, you listen to me very carefully. If you don't go and wake the Guatemalan up *right fucking now*, I'm going to hang up. And when he hears that you took some fucked-up decision about what he did and didn't need to hear, all on your own pointed little head, he'll have you bunking with the Aryans for a reward, I fucking guarantee you."

Incredulous silence.

"Who the fuck is this?"

"This is Marsalis. The thirteen. Couple of weeks back I carried one of your shanks into the chapel after Dudeck, remember? Then I walked out the front gate. I've got something out here for the Guatemalan he's going to like. So you go wake him up and tell him that."

The voice at the other end went away. Soft, prison-wall static sang in the space it left. Carl stared across the hazed evening air in the bay, screwed up his eyes, and rubbed a tear out of one corner with his thumb. Grumbling voices in the background, then the bang of someone grabbing the phone. The Guatemalan rumbled down the line, amused and maybe slightly stoned.

"Eurotrash? That you?"

"Like I told Danny, yeah." Carl picked his angle of entry with care. "Dudeck out of the infirmary yet?"

"Yeah, he is. Moving a little slow right now, though. You do good work, Eurotrash, I gotta give you that much. Dudeck what this is about? You feelin' nostalgic, calling to talk about old times?"

"Not exactly. I thought we could do a little business, though. Trade a little data. They say you're a good man to see for that. So I've got something I need to know, you can maybe help me with it."

"Data?" The other man chuckled. "Seems to me you told me you'd hooked up with the Colony Initiative. You telling me I got data that COLIN don't?"

"That's what I'm telling you, yeah."

There was a long pause.

"Want to tell me what my end of this is, Eurotrash?"

"Let's see what you've got first. You remember a low-grade *familia* gangbanger came through SFS on a three-spot, got out a couple of years ago?"

Another rumbling chortle. "Niggah, I remember a whole graveyard of those *andino* boys. They bounce in and out of this place like they tied to it on a rubber line. Muscle up *sooooo* proud to the brothers and the Aryans and every other fucker that'll look them in the eye, and mostly they get stretchered out again. So which particular skull you picking over?"

"Name of Ferrer, Suerte Ferrer. Likes to call himself Maldición. He went out walking, so he's either tougher or smarter than average. That ought to ring some bells."

"Yeah, Maldición. Smart, I'm not convinced on, but he certainly fit tough. Sure. Think I could be induced to remember that boy."

"Good. You think you could be induced to tell me where he is now?"

"You talking about where he is *outside* population?"

"Yeah, it looks that way."

A thoughtful, spreading pool of quiet on the line again. Carl could smell the reek of mistrust it gave off. The Guatemalan's voice came back slow and careful.

"I been in here nine long years, Eurotrash. Terror *and* organized crime, they slammed me away for both. What makes you think I'm in any position to know anything about what goes on outside?"

Carl let his tone sharpen. "Don't get stupid on me, I'm not in the mood. I cut a deal with COLIN, not drug enforcement or the morals committee. This isn't some hick Jesusland entrapment number. I want Ferrer found, and if possible delivered over the fenceline to the Rim. I'm willing to pay COLIN prices for the service. Now can we do each other some good, or not?"

The Guatemalan missed a beat, but only just. "I heard . . . COLIN prices?"

"Yes, you did."

Another pause, but this time it thrummed with purpose. He could almost hear the whir as the Guatemalan made calculations and guesses.

"Moves on the outside come a lot higher-priced than in population," the other man said finally, and softly.

"I imagined they would."

"And cross-border delivery, well." The Guatemalan made a noise with indrawn breath that sounded like spit steaming off a hot griddle. "That's topping out the favors list, Eurotrash. Big risks, very high stakes."

"Unreleased Marstech." Carl dropped the words into the pool of quiet expectation at the other end of the line. "You hear what I'm saying?"

"Not a lot of use to me in here." But now you could hear the excitement cabled beneath the Guatemalan's casual tone.

"Then I guess you'll have to spend it outside somehow. Maybe buy yourself some big favors at legislature level. Maybe just lay down a little future growth here and there. Man like you, I'm sure you'd know better than me how to find the best investment options for your capital. Now, you going to find Maldición for me or not?"

Silence again, tight with the promise of its own brevity. Carl twitched a sudden look over his shoulder, tingle of alarm. Gloom across the space behind him back to the steps up to the tower. Dark bordering shrubs and foliage. Nothing there. He worked his shoulders and felt the unreleased tension of days locked up there. The Guatemalan came back.

"Call me in two days," he said calmly. "And think of a very big number."

He hung up.

Carl folded the phone and listened to the faint crackle as the internal circuitry fired and melted. He let out a long breath and leaned on the wall, shoulders hunched. The tension gripped his neck like muscled fingers. The soft mounds of the Marin coast rose on the other side of the bay. He stared at the final orange leavings of dayglow on their flanks, filled with an obscure desire he couldn't pin down. The phone casing was warm in his hand from the meltdown, the air around him suddenly chilled in contrast.

"You're looking in all the wrong places, thirteen."

The voice sent him spinning about, combat stance, gripping the phone in his hand as if it could possibly serve him as a weapon.

She stood at the borders of the trees, and he knew the shiver of alarm he'd picked up earlier was the sensation of her watching him. She came forward, arms spread, hands open, palms turned upward with nothing on them. He knew the poise, knew the voice. Looked for the face paint and saw that this time she hadn't bothered.

"Hello, Ren."

"Good evening, Mr. Marsalis."

Carmen Ren came to a halt about three meters away. Feet set apart on the evercrete in cleated boots that promised steel beneath the curve of the toes. Black pilot-style pants with thigh pockets sealed shut, plain gray zipped jacket with a high collar that pointed up the elevated planes of her face, hair gathered simply back off the pale narrow face. He looked her up and down for weaponry, saw none she could access in a hurry.

He straightened out of the fighting crouch.

"Very wise," she said. "I'm here to help."

"So help. Sit down cross-legged with your hands on your head and don't move while I call RimSec."

She peeled him a brief smile. "I'm afraid I'm not feeling that generous."

"I didn't say you had a choice."

Something moved in her eyes, the way she breathed. The smile floated back onto her face, but this time it was the adrenal veil, the prelude to fight-or-flight. She telegraphed it to him with an odd, careless abandon that was curiously like the offer of open arms. Abruptly he wasn't very sure that he'd be able to take her.

He cleared his throat. "That's very good. How'd you do that?"

"Practice." The smile went away again, pocketed for later use. "Are we going to talk, or are you going to get all genetic on me?"

He thought back to Nevant. Broken glass and blood. The nighttime streets of Istanbul, walking back to Moda and —

He put a tourniquet on it, twisted hard. Grimaced. "What do you want to talk about?"

"How about I hand you this case in a bento box?"

"I told you already I'm not a cop. And anyway, why would you do that? Last time I checked, you were playing on Manco Bambarén's team."

He was watching her face. No flicker on the name.

"The people I work for hung me out to dry," she said. "You want to ask yourself why I left you and Merrin to fight it out?"

He shrugged. "Off the sinking ship in your little rat life vest. I assume."

"You assume wrong."

"Want to back that up? You know, with evidence?"

"Right here." She patted her jacket pocket. "We'll get to it in a moment. First, why don't you play back the fight in starboard loading for me. Think it through."

"I think I'd rather just see this evidence."

A thin smile. "You knock me down, take the others back inside, and use their numbers against them." She mimed a pistol grip. "You take Huang's sharkpunch, use it on him and Scotty, that's Osborne to you, the Jesusland kid. So I hear both of them go down while I'm still on the floor, but that's all it takes me to get back on my feet and there you are, mixing it up with Merrin and all that Mars-side *tanindo* shit. Now, you really think I didn't have time to swing back in there and pull you off him? Come on, Marsalis. Work the gray matter. I had all the time in the world, and keeping Merrin alive was my job."

Hairline crack of unease. "Keeping Merrin alive?"

"That's what I said."

"Someone paid you to shadow him?"

"Shadow him?" She raised an elegant eyebrow. "No, just get him aboard the *Cat*. Hook up with Daskeen Azul and keep him there, look after him until further notice."

The crack ran out, split wide, from unease to splintering confusion.

"You're saying . . . you're telling me Merrin's been locked down on *Bulgakov's Cat* the last four months? He hasn't been anywhere else?"

"Sure. Took us about a week to get him there from Ward's place, but since then? Yeah. Just a handling gig. Why?"

The quarry face of what he knew blew up. Detonated from within, multiple blasts in the thin Martian air and the building roar after, rock shattering and slumping, sliding down itself into rubble and dust. He glimpsed the new face of what was behind, the new surface exposed.

Onbekend's face.

The trace familiarity about the features, the certainty he knew them from somewhere, had seen them before or features very like them.

Rovayo's voice floated back through his head. *This Onbekend must have been greased up pretty good.*

Yeah, he was. You could see it in the light, shining in his hair pretty fucking thick as well. No way he was going to be leaving trace material for the CSI guys.

Right. Makes you wonder why Merrin didn't do the same thing. Instead of leaving his fucking trace all over everything for us to track him with.

The enormity of it towered above him like the sky.

I've seen data, said Sevgi, the first day he met her, *that puts Merrin in combat zones hundreds of kilometers apart on the same day, eyewitness accounts that say*

*he took wounds we can't find any medical records to confirm, some of them wounds
he couldn't possibly have survived if the stories are true.* Sevgi in the prison interview room. He remembered the scent of her as she spoke and his throat locked
up. Her voice ran on, wouldn't get out of his head. *Even that South American deployment has too much overlap to be wholly accurate. He was in Tajikistan, no he
wasn't, he was still in Bolivia; he was solo-deployed, no, he was leading a Lawman
platoon in Kuwait City.*

The idiot pattern of the murders. Death in the Bay Area, then Texas and
beyond, and then back to the Rim all over again, months later. No sense to the
double-back, unless . . .

Unless . . .

"Onbekend," he said tightly. "Do you know him?"

"Heard the name." Amused quirk in the corner of her mouth. "But it means—"

"I know what it means. Are you working with anyone who has that name?"

"No. I was working with a guy called Emil Nocera, and with Ulysses Ward, before Merrin went genetic and slaughtered them both. After that, I used Scotty to
ride shotgun and pulled some contacts elsewhere."

"What contacts?"

"Just contacts. No one I see any reason to hand over to you. They're peripheral, they don't count. Rimside plug-ins for the people who hired me."

Carl thought back to the boy with the machete, the gibbering religious abuse.
"You sold Osborne some story about me?"

"Not as such." Ren looked suddenly tired. "I told him Merrin was the, what do
you call it, the second coming? Christ returned and hiding because a black man
was out there, coming to do him harm. Mix-and-match imagery, cooked it up
from what I knew about Jesusland ideology and the way Osborne was rambling."

Very Christ-like, he remembered saying when he saw Merrin's file photo. *Very
Faith Satellite Channel.*

He nodded. "I can see how that would work."

"Yeah, well. Jesuslander, you know. Seemed like a nice enough kid deep
down, but you know what that old-time religion will do. Wasn't hard to sell him
the concept, half those people live their whole fucking lives waiting for their Savior to show up. They'd jump at the chance for a walk-on role." She shrugged, perfectly. "Plus, he was hot for me and concussed from a smack in the head he got
from Merrin in the fight at Ward's place. Poor little fucker never stood a chance."

"So I'm the black man."

She pulled a face. "Yeah, you just showed up and fit the role a little too well."

"Tell me about." Carl stirred through his recollections again, the fight in the
nighttime mall. "You didn't send him after me then?"

"No, that was all his idea." Ren's tone was sour. "Thought it up all on his own, and I wasn't there to stop him. Wasn't for that, we might all have gotten off the *Cat* quietly while RimSec were still clumping about up on deck trying to lock us down."

"You have any idea why you were supposed to bodyguard Merrin?"

"None. I'm strictly for hire. Got the word he'd be coming in, emergency splash-down, and Ward goes out to collect. My end was just keep him safe for a few months, they were going to need him later. We were going to do that at Ward's place, but it seems Merrin had a few trust issues after what he went through aboard *Horkan's Pride*."

"Yeah. Understandable. So how'd you talk him down?"

"Initially?" Ren grinned. "With ninjutsu."

"And after that?"

The grin stayed. "How do you think?"

"Really? Osborne *and* Merrin? How'd you make that work?"

Another elegant shift of the gray-fleeced shoulders. "Playing handmaiden to Christ, I get to do what I like in Scotty's eyes. Or at least, he sells it to himself that way as long as he can, because he doesn't want the rest of it to go away. Maybe that's what really went wrong when you showed up. Who can tell?"

"And Merrin?"

"Well, I'd say Merrin never quite came back from that ride he took home on *Horkan's Pride*. I'd been bracing myself for all the usual arrogant thirteen bullshit when he arrived." She shook her head. "Not much sign of it. I wouldn't say he was broken, but I'm not sure he ever straightened out what was really going on. I rammed it home that if he made waves, he was just going to blow cover, and I guess he was smart enough to take that much in. He had covert training, right?"

"Yeah. Field experience, too."

"So. Something to hang on to, I guess."

Carl felt the sequence of the fight rise up in his mind again. Slurred *tanindo*, the slack, not-quite-committed feel to the moves, the lack of force. Almost as if Merrin were still half back on Mars and living a lesser gravitational pull. As if he'd never really made it home after all.

"So, *you* had any field experience?" he asked Ren.

"Not as such."

"Not as such, huh?" Carl glanced out across the bay to Marin. The light was almost gone now. "Who the fuck are you, Ren?"

"That's not what matters here."

"I think it is."

She stared at him for a couple of seconds in the gloom. Put together a throw-away gesture.

"I'm just some guy they hired."

"Just some guy. Right. With ninjutsu technique good enough to beat an ex-Lawman. Try again. Who are you?"

"Look, it's simple. Forget whatever skills I picked up on my way around the Pacific Rim. I got hired here, in California, to do a handling job, because that's what I do. I did my job, I handled the mess when Merrin boiled over, and I kept him covered. Then, when the heat got turned up high again, my scumbag client cut me loose. And now I'm looking for payback."

"I thought you were here to help."

"I am. My payback is handing you the people who cut me loose."

"Not good enough."

"I'm sorry, it'll have to do."

"Then go peddle your grudge to someone else."

He turned his back and leaned on the seaward wall. Stared at the lights out across the water, tried hard not to think of Istanbul, and failed. Under certain superficial differences, the two cities shared an essence you couldn't evade. Both freighted with the same distilled dream of shoreline, hills, and suspension spans, the same hazy sunlit air and rumble by day, the same glimmer on water at evening as ferries crisscrossed the gloom and traffic flowed in skeins of red and pale gold light across the bridges and through the street-lamp-studded veins of the city. What was in the air there was here as well, and he felt it catching in his throat.

He heard her boots move behind him. Footfalls on evercrete, closing the gap. He looked out at the glimmer of lights.

"Kind of careless tonight, aren't you?' She draped her arms on the wall, mimicked his posture about a meter off to his left.

He shrugged, didn't look at her. "I figure if you want to feed me some information, it doesn't pay you to take me out. You were going to do that, you would have done it awhile ago."

"Fair analysis. Still a risk, though."

"I'm not feeling very risk-averse right now."

"Yeah, but you're being fucking choosy about who you take your leads from. Mind telling me why?"

He tipped a glance at her.

"How about because I don't trust you any farther than I would a Jesusland preacher with a choirboy? You're handing me what looks like half a solution,

Ren. And it doesn't match up with what I already know. To me, that stinks of deflection. You want me to believe you're really ready to sell out your boss? Tell me who you are."

Quiet. The city breathed. Reflected light trembled across the water.

"I'm like you," she said.

"You're a variant?"

She squinted at the blade of her outstretched hand. "That's right. Harbin black lab product. Nothing but the best."

"You some kind of bonobo then?"

"No, I am not some kind of fucking bonobo." There were a couple of grams of genuine anger in the way her voice lifted. "I had sex with Merrin and Scotty for *my* operational benefit, not because I couldn't keep my hands off them."

"Well, you know what?" He kept his voice at a drawl, not really sure why he was pushing, just some vague intuitive impulse to feed the anger and keep Ren off balance. "The real bonobo females, the pygmy chimps in Africa? That's what they do a lot of the time, too. Fuck to calm the males down, keep them in line. I guess you could call that operational benefit, from a social point of view."

She got off the wall and faced him.

"I'm a fucking thirteen, Marsalis. A thirteen, just like you. Got that?"

"Bullshit. They never built a female thirteen."

"Right. Tell yourself that, if it makes you feel better."

She stood a meter off, and he saw her force the anger back down, iron it out of her stance, and put it away. Shiver of unlooked-for fellow feeling as he watched it happen. She leaned on the wall again, and her voice came out cool and conversational.

"Has it ever occurred to you, Marsalis, to wonder why Project Lawman failed so spectacularly? Has it occurred to you that just maybe cramming gene-enhanced male violent tendency into a gene-enhanced male chassis is overloading the donkey a little?"

Carl shook his head. "No, that hasn't occurred to me. I was there when Lawman blew apart. What went wrong was that thirteens don't like to do what they're told, and as soon as the normal constraints come off, they stop doing it. You can't make good soldiers out of thirteens. It's that simple."

"Yeah, like I said. Overloading the donkey."

"Or just misunderstanding the concept of soldier." He brooded on the outline of the Marin Headlands against the sky, watched the neat, corpuscular flow of red dotted lights funneling off the bridge and into a fold in the darkened hills. "Anyway, speaking of soldiering, if Harbin put you together, gave you the genes and the ninjutsu, I've got to assume that means you belong to Department Two."

He thought she maybe shivered a little. "Not anymore."

"Care to explain that?"

"Hey, you asked who I was. No one said anything about a full fucking résumé."

He found he was smiling in the gloom. "Just sketch it out for me. Bare bones, enough to convince. One thing I don't intend to be is a cat's paw for the Chinese security services."

"You're starting to piss me off, Marsalis. I told you I don't do that shit anymore."

"Yeah, but I'm a naturally untrusting motherfucker. You want me to murder your boss for you? Indulge my curiosity."

He heard her breath hiss out between her teeth.

"Late '96, I worked undercover to crack a Triad sex-slave operation in Hong Kong. When we finally hit them, it got bloody. Department Two aren't overly concerned about innocent bystanders."

"Yeah, I heard that about them."

"Yeah, well I took the opportunity of all that blood and screaming to step out quietly. Disappeared in the crossfire, crossed the line. Used the contacts I'd made to hook a passage to Kuala Lumpur, and then points south." An odd weariness crept into her voice. "I was an enforcer in Jakarta for a while, played in the turf wars they had going against the yakuza, built myself an Indonesia-wide rep. Headed south again. Sydney and then Auckland. Corporate clients. Eventually the Rim States, because that's where the real money is. And here we are. That sort out your curiosity for you?"

He nodded, surprised once again by the twinge of kinship he felt. "Yeah, that'll do for the CV. But I do have one more question, general point of information you could clear up for me."

Weary sigh. "And that is?"

"Why bother with me? You're lethal as shit, well connected, too. Staying one step ahead of RimSec and making it look easy. Why not go in and take this faithless fuck out for yourself. Not like you don't know where he is, right?"

She was silent for a while.

"It's a simple question, Ren."

"I think I've told you enough. In the end, you're an UNGLA bounty hunter. You take me down, it puts food on your table."

"I already know what you are," he said roughly. "You see me reaching for a Haag gun?"

Voice not quite even on those last two words. Her head tilted, as if she maybe caught the tremor. She examined the blade of her hand again.

"You've made a career of betraying your own kind. No reason why you'd stop now, is there?"

"Ren, let me tell you something. I'm not even sure I still have my license." Memories of di Palma flitted through his head, the prissy bureaucratic superiority of the Agency. "And even if I do, first thing I plan on doing when I get back is turn it in."

"Change of heart, huh?" It wasn't quite a sneer.

"Something like that. Now answer the question. Why me?"

More quiet. He noticed the chill in the air for the first time. His eyes kept sliding back to the Marin hills, the disappearing stream of traffic headed north. As if there were something there waiting for him. Ren seemed to be making calculations in her head.

"Two reasons," she said, finally. "First, he's likely to be expecting me. You, he's got no reason to watch for."

"If I were standing where you are, that kind of risk wouldn't be enough for me to hand things over to a proxy."

"I know. But you're a *male* thirteen. I'm a little smarter than that. For me it's enough to know that it'll get done. I don't have to be there and smell the blood."

"Maybe I'm smarter than you think. Maybe I just won't do it."

He saw her smile. "Well, we'll see."

"You said two reasons."

"That's right." Now she was the one looking out across the water. Her voice tinged with something that might have been embarrassment, might have been pride. "It seems I'm pregnant."

The silence seemed to rush them, like dark fog coming in off the bay. The noises of the city, already faint, receded to the edge of perception. Carl placed his hands flat on the stonework of the wall, peered down at them in the gloom.

"Congratulations."

"Yeah, thanks."

"Is it Merrin's? Or machete boy's?"

"I don't know, and I don't much care. And neither will your Agency friends. It's enough that the mother's a certified thirteen, without worrying about the father as well. They'll send everything they've got after me. I need to be leaving, Marsalis. Bowing out and heading somewhere safe."

"Right." He folded his arms against the chill, turned to face her. "On the other hand, you do have one major advantage over the Agency."

"Which is."

"They don't even know you exist."

And somewhere in his head, Sevgi Ertekin's voice.

Baba, he's a good man. He's clean.

Carmen Ren regarded him narrowly. "That's right. Right now, they don't know I exist."

Carl looked away across the bay again. Something was aching in his throat. Sevgi, Nevant, all the others. His whole life seemed to pulse with grief.

"They aren't going to hear it from me," he said.

t felt strange, walking into the Human Cost Foundation's offices for real. Memories of the v-format clashed with the actual architecture of the reception space and the corridors leading off it. There was no Sharleen sitting there, no one in the waiting area at all, and the walls were a paler, colder blue than he recalled. The artwork he remembered wasn't there, and the prints and Earth First shout-out posters that had replaced it seemed grubby and tired. Jeff, when he came out to greet them, looked similarly worn.

"In the flesh," he said, hugging Norton briefly at the shoulders. "Nice surprise."

Norton hugged back. "Yeah, strictly business, I'm afraid. Come to pick your professional brains again. This is Carl Marsalis. Marsalis, my brother Jeff."

Jeff shook the thirteen's hand without a blink. "Of course. Should have recognized you from the feed photos. Do you want to come through?"

They took a different corridor from the one Norton remembered in the virtual offices, and of course it didn't blur out the way it had in the format. They passed doors with cheaply lettered plastic signs that hinted at the foundation's daily round: TRAUMA COUNSELING, COAST GUARD LIAISON, HARASSMENT RESPONSE, FUNDING . . . Through one open office door, Norton glimpsed a stout Asian woman looking sleepily into the middle distance and drinking from a Styrofoam coffee cup. She half raised a hand as they passed, but said nothing. Otherwise, the place seemed to be deserted.

"Quiet this morning," Marsalis said.

Jeff glanced back across his shoulder. "Yeah, well, it's early yet. We've just ridden out a major funding crisis, so I sent everyone home with instructions to celebrate and come in late. In here."

He let them into the office marked with the simple word DIRECTORATE, closed the door carefully behind them. Changes from the virtual here, too: the décor was a higher-powered blend of reds and grays; the sofa was the same but had been turned so its back was to the window and there was space to walk around behind it, a low coffee table in front. Ornaments had moved around, been replaced. The photo of Megan was gone from the desk, there was a smaller one of the kids instead. Jeff gestured at the sofa.

"Grab a seat, both of you. How are COLIN treating you, Mr. Marsalis?"

The thirteen shrugged. "Well, they got me out of jail in Jesusland."

"Yeah, I guess that could count as a pretty good opening offer." Jeff came around to the sofa and seated himself facing both of them. He put on a weary smile. "So what can I do for you guys?"

Norton shifted uncomfortably. "How much do you know about the Harbin black labs, Jeff?"

Raised brows. His brother blew out a long breath.

"Well, not a whole lot. They keep that end sewn up pretty tight. Long way north, a long way from the sea. Very high security, too. From what we can piece together, it's where the high-end product comes out."

"You ever meet a variant from the Harbin labs?" Marsalis asked. "Human Cost ever handle any?"

"Christ, no." Jeff sat back and rested his head on one hand. He seemed to be giving it some thought. "Well, certainly not since we've been set up in our current form anyway. I mean, before we got state funding, back before my time, they might have, I could check the files. But I doubt it. Most of the escapees we get are failed variants from the experimental camps. They don't quite let them go, but they don't much care what happens to them, either, so it's easier for them to slip out, grab a fishing boat or something, maybe stow away. Anyone coming out of Harbin, though, they'd be very highly valued, and probably very loyal as well. I doubt they'd be interested in running, even if security was lax enough to let them."

"I met one last night," said Marsalis.

Jeff blinked. "A Harbin variant? Where?"

"Here. In the city."

"*Here?* Jesus." Jeff looked at Norton. "You see this as well?"

Norton shook his head.

"Well." Jeff spread his hands. "I mean, this is fucking serious, Tom. If someone out of Harbin is here, chances are they work for Department Two."

"No." Marsalis got up and went to the window. "I had quite a long talk with her. She bailed out of Department Two awhile back."

"So." Jeff frowned. "Who's she working for now?"

"She's working for you, Jeff," said the black man.

The moment hung in the room, creaked and turned like a corpse at the end of a rope. Norton was watching his brother's eyes, and all he needed to see was there. Then Jeff jerked his eyes away, twisted about, stared up at Marsalis. The thirteen hadn't turned from the window. Jeff looked at the broad back, the jacket lettered with s(t)igma, the lack of motion. He swung back to his brother.

"Tom?"

Norton reached into his pocket and produced the phone. He looked into Jeff's face and thumb-touched the playback.

"*Guava Diamond?*"

"*Still holding.*"

"*We are unable to assist, Guava Diamond. Repeat, we are unable to assist. Suggest—*"

"*You what? You bonobo-sucking piece of shit, you'd better tell me I misheard that.*"

"*There are control complications at this end. We cannot act. I'm sorry, Guava Diamond. You're on your own.*"

"*You will be fucking sorry if we make it out of this in one piece.*"

"*I repeat, Guava Diamond, we cannot act. Suggest you implement Lizard immediately, and get off Bulgakov's Cat while you can. You may still have time.*"

Pause.

"*You're a fucking dead man, Claw Control.*"

Static hiss.

They all listened to the white-noise emptiness of it for a couple of moments, as if they'd just heard the last transmission of a plane going down into the ocean. Norton thumbed the phone to off.

"That's you, Jeff," he said quietly. "Tell me it's not."

"Tom, you know you can fake a voice like that as easily as—"

He jammed to a halt as the black man's hands sank weightily onto his shoulders from behind. Marsalis leaned over him.

"Don't," he said.

Jeff stared across the sofa space at Norton. "Tom? Tom, I'm your fucking *brother*, for Christ's sake."

Norton nodded. "Yeah. You'd better tell us everything you know."

"Tom, you can't seriously—"

"Sevgi is *dead!*" Suddenly he was yelling, trembling, throat swollen with the force of it, memories of the hospital swirling. "She is fucking *dead*, Jeff, because you hid this from me, *she is dead!*"

Marsalis's hands stayed where they were. Norton gritted his teeth, tried to

master the shaking that would not stop. He clamped his mouth tight, breathing
hard.

"Bonobo-sucking piece of shit," he got out. "She called you right, didn't she,
Jeff. She knew you well."

"Tom, you don't understand."

"Not yet, we don't," said Marsalis. He lifted one hand, slapped it down again
on Jeff's shoulder, encouraging. "But you are going to tell us."

"I." Jeff shook his head. "You don't understand, I can't."

Marsalis lifted his head and looked directly at Norton. Norton felt something
kick in his stomach, something that made him feel sick but was somehow a release as well. He nodded.

The black man hooked one hand into Jeff Norton's throat, dragged him
back against the sofa. His fingers dug in. His other arm wrapped around Jeff's
chest, pinning one arm, holding him in place. Jeff made a shocked, choking
sound, flailed about on the sofa, tugged at the thirteen's grip with his only free
hand. Marsalis grabbed the flapping arm at the wrist and held it out of the way.
Jeff heaved, flopped, could not get loose.

"You're the one who doesn't understand," said Marsalis coldly. It was the same
voice that Norton had heard him use, in Quechua, on Gutierrez. "Someone is
going to bleed for Sevgi Ertekin. Someone's going to die. Right now, we've got
you. You don't give us someone else, then you're it. You try keeping what you
know from me, RimSec are going to find you floating in the bay with every bone
in your body broken and both your eyes put out."

Norton watched, made himself watch. Jeff's gaze clawed frantically at him,
out of a face turning blue. But Sevgi's fading was crowded into his head like
someone shouting herself hoarse, and it kept him pinned in his seat, watching.

"You killed her, Jeff," he said, and his voice had a quiet, reasonable tone to it
that felt like the rising edge of madness. "Someone's got to pay."

"Onbekend!"

It was a strangled grunt, barely recognizable. Marsalis caught it while Norton
was still sorting meaning out of the crushed syllables. He unhinged his grip on
Jeff's throat and chest, hauled on the arm he'd captured at the wrist, dragged it up
and around so Jeff was forced flat to the sofa. Marsalis leaned over and pressed the
side of Jeff's head down hard into the fabric, dug into the other man's temple with
his knuckles. Jeff coughed and gagged, whooped for breath, eyes flooded with
tears.

"What about Onbekend?" Norton asked.

The dizzying sense of insanity had not gone. It circled him like a street gang.

He wondered, in the midst of the revolving horror of it all, if this was what it felt like to be a thirteen, if this was what you had to embrace to live the way Marsalis did and Merrin had. He wondered how easy it would be to let go, and if you could ever find your grip again afterward.

Jeff made raw panting sounds.

"What about Onbekend?"

"All right, I'll tell you, I'll fucking tell you." Jeff's voice cracked. He stopped trying to get loose. He lay on the sofa, swallowing breath, leaking slow tears onto the fabric. "Just let me up. Please."

Again, Marsalis flickered a glance at Norton. Norton nodded. *My brother's not a soldier or a thug,* he'd told the thirteen the previous night. *He's not physically tough that way, he won't stand up. Just let me call it. We'll get everything we need from him.*

Marsalis hauled Jeff into a sitting position on the sofa. He moved and took up a position by the desk. Folded his arms.

"Let's hear it, then."

Jeff's eyes went from the black man to his brother. Norton stared back.

"Tom . . ."

"You heard him, Jeff. Let's hear it."

Jeff Norton seemed to collapse in on himself. He shuddered. Marsalis and Norton exchanged a glance. Norton lifted a hand in his lap. Wait. Jeff rubbed his hands over his face, dragged them back through his hair. He sniffed hard, wiped his eyes. *Yeah, cry, Jeff,* Norton caught himself thinking, with a violence that rocked him to the core. *Cry like the fucking rest of us have been. Like Sevgi and me and Marsalis and Megan and Nuying, for all I fucking know, and who knows how many others. Want to play alpha male, big brother? Welcome aboard.*

Jeff dropped his hands. He dredged up a weak smile, pinned it in place. Playing himself to the cheap seats once again.

"Look, you have no idea how deep this goes, Tom. Onbekend's not just some random thirteen—"

"Yeah, he's Merrin's twin," Marsalis said flatly. "We already got that far. You had Carmen Ren hold Merrin safe while Onbekend went around leaving genetic trace at crime scenes all over Jesusland and the Rim. Come the right time, Merrin shows up conveniently dead and takes the rap for it all. The question is why? Who were all these people?"

Jeff closed his eyes. Sighed. "Can I have a drink, please?"

"No, you can't have a fucking drink," said Marsalis. "We just got through agreeing to let you live. Count your fucking blessings and talk."

Jeff looked at his brother, pulled a weary face. Norton made the connection—Jeff had to have his props. Cheap-seat appeal.

"Sure. I'll get you a drink, Jeff," he said gently. He met the black man's disbelieving look, made the tiny raised-hand gesture again. "Where d'you keep it?"

"Wall cabinet. There's a bottle of Martell in there and some glasses. Help yourselves." Jeff Norton turned to look at Marsalis. "He's got you jumping pretty neatly to the line for a thirteen, hasn't he?"

Marsalis looked down at him. A faint frown creased his brow. "You want to get that looked at."

"Get what looked at?"

Norton looked around from the open bar cabinet just in time to see the black man's fist snap out from the waist. Short, hard, and full force into Jeff's nose. He heard the cracking sound it made as the cartilage broke. Jeff bucked and screamed. His hands flew to his face again. Blood streamed out between them.

"Get that looked at," said Marsalis tranquilly.

Norton spotted a box of tissues on the desk. He hooked it up and carried it across to the sofa with the bottle of cognac and a single glass. He set everything down on the coffee table, tugged a tissue loose, and handed it over to his brother.

"Don't fuck around, Jeff," he said quietly. "He wants you dead bad enough to taste, and I'm not that far behind him. Here, clean yourself up."

Jeff took the tissue, then a couple more from the box. While he stanched the blood flow from his nose, Norton poured into the single glass. He pushed the cognac across the tabletop.

"There's your drink," he told his brother. "Now make it good."

"Scorpion Response," he told them.

Carl nodded. "Claw Control. Right. You're still using the call signs, you sad fuck. What were you, Jeff, backroom support? You sure as fuck weren't the front end of anything as nasty as Scorpion."

"You've heard of these guys?" Norton asked him.

"On the grapevine, yeah. Ghost squad in the Pacific Rim theaters, supposed to be one of the last covert initiatives before the Secession." Carl looked speculatively down at Jeff Norton. "So let's hear it, Jeff. What was your end?"

"Logistics," the Human Cost director said sulkily. "I was the operations coordinator."

"Right."

"When the fuck was this?" Norton stared at his brother. "You didn't even move out here until '94. You were in New York."

Jeff Norton shook his head wearily. "I was out here all the time, Tom. Back and forth, Union to the Rim, Rim to Southeast Asia. We had offices all over. Half the time, I wasn't home more than one weekend in five." He took the blood-clotted tissues away from his nose, dumped them on the coffee table, and grimaced. "Anyway, how would you have known? We saw you what, once a month, if that?"

"I was busy," said Norton numbly.

"The way I heard it," Carl said. "Secession should have been the end of Scorpion Response. Supposed to have been wound up like all the other dirty little bags of deniability the American public didn't need to be told about. That's the official version, anyway. But this is the seventies, a good few years before they would have been employing you, Jeff. So what happened? They go private?"

Jeff shot him a startled look. "You heard that?"

"No. But it wouldn't be the first time a bunch of sneak op thugs couldn't face early retirement and went to the market instead. That what happened?"

"Scorpion Response were retained." Jeff was still sulking. More tissues, tugged up from the box on the table. Carl watched him impassively.

"Retained by who?"

Norton had the answer for that already. "The Rim States. Got to be. They've just cut loose, the Pacific arena's their future. Anything that gave them an edge had to be worth hanging on to, right?"

"That's right, little brother." Jeff moved the tissues from his nose long enough to knock back a chunk of the cognac. "Starting to see the big picture now?"

"Toni Montes," Carl said. "Jasper Whitlock, Ulysses Ward, Eddie Tanaka. The rest of them. All Scorpion personnel?"

"Yeah. Not those names, but yeah."

"And Onbekend."

"Yeah." Jeff Norton's voice shaded with something. Carl thought it might be fear. "Him, too. Some of the time. He came and went, you know. On secondment."

"But not Merrin?"

The Human Cost director sneered. "Onbekend *was* Merrin to us. We didn't know about the other one, no one knew there were two." He looked down into his glass. "Not until now."

Carl paced across the office to the bar. He stared down at the assembly of bottles and glasses. The Bayview tavern mapped itself onto his vision, drinking with Sevgi Ertekin, stolen whiskey from behind the bar, and the stink of gunfire still hanging in the air. He felt the swift skid of anger in his guts, wanted to smash everything in the cabinet, take one shattered bottle by the neck, go back to Jeff Norton with it and—

"N-djinn search on the victims turned up no connections among them," he said tonelessly. "Which means you must have used some very high-powered Rim n-djinn capacity of your own to bury these people in their new lives. Now, I can only see one reason why anybody would bother to do that."

"You were winding up." Realization etching wonder into Tom Norton's tone. "Shutting the whole operation down and scattering."

Carl turned back to face the sofa, empty-handed.

"When, Jeff? When, and why?"

Jeff Norton glanced across at his brother. "I'd have thought you'd be able to work that one out for yourself, Tom."

The COLIN exec nodded. "You came out here, took up the Human Cost job in '94. They were burying you, too. Had to be sometime around then."

Jeff put down his latest clump of bloodied tissue, reached for more. There was a thin smile playing about his lips. A little more blood trickled down into the grin before he could soak it up.

"Little earlier in fact," he said. "Thing like that has quite a momentum once it's rolling, it takes awhile to brake. Say '92 for the decision, early '93 to cease operations. And we were all gone by the following year."

Carl stepped closer. "I asked you why."

The Human Cost director stared back up at him, dabbing at his nose. He seemed still to be smiling.

"Can't you guess?"

"Jacobsen."

The name fell off his lips, dropped into the room like an invocation. The era, '89 to '94, blazed across his memory in feed-footage flicker. Riots, the surging crowds and lines of armored police, the vehicles in flames. Pontificating holy men and ranting political pundits, UNGLA communiqués and speeches, and behind it all the quiet, balding figure of the Swedish commissioner, reading from his report in the measured tones of the career diplomat, like a man trying to deploy an umbrella in a hurricane. Words swept away, badly summarized, quoted, misquoted, taken out of context, used and abused for political capital. The awful, creeping sense that it did, after all, have something to do with him, Carl Marsalis, Osprey's finest; that, impossible though it had once seemed, some idiot wave of opinion among the grazing cudlips really did matter now, and his life would be affected after all.

Jacobsen.

Oh yes, affected after all.

Covert heroes to paraded monsters in less than five years. The bleak pronouncements, the bleaker choices; the tracts, or the long sleep and exile to the endless tract of Mars, jostled toward one or the other by the idiot mob, like a condemned man swept forward toward a choice of gallows.

And the cryocap, chilly and constraining, filling slowly with gel as the sedatives took his impulse to panic away from him, the same way they'd taken his discarded combat gear at demob. The long sleep, falling over him like the shadow of a building a thousand stories tall, blotting out the sun.

Jacobsen.

Jeff Norton leaned forward for his glass again. "That's right, Jacobsen. We weren't sure what the Accords would actually look like in '92; it was all still at a draft stage. But the writing was pretty fucking clearly on the wall. Didn't take a genius to see the way things were going to fall."

"But." Tom Norton, shaking his head. "What's that got to do with anything? Okay, you had Onbekend. But all these other people—Montes, Tanaka, and the rest. They weren't variants, they were ordinary humans. You were an ordinary human. Why should Jacobsen have mattered?"

Carl stood over the Human Cost director and saw, vaguely, the shape of what was coming.

"It mattered," he said evenly, "because of what they were doing. Right, Jeff? It wasn't the personnel, was it? It was what Scorpion Response did. What was your purview, Jeff? And don't ask me to guess again, because I will hurt you if you do."

Jeff Norton shrugged and drained his cognac.

"Breeding," he said.

His brother blinked. "Breeding what?"

"Oh for *fuck's sake, Tom, what do you think?*" Jeff gestured violently, nearly knocked over the bottle. The cognac seemed to have gone to his head. "Breeding *fucking variants.* Like your friend here, like Nuying. Like everything we could lay our hands on over there."

"Over there?" Carl asked from the depths of an immense, rushing calm. "You're talking about the Chinese mainland?"

"Yeah." Jeff kept the tissues loosely pressed to his nose, worked the cork on the bottle one-handed, poured himself another tumblerful. "Scorpion Response had been running covert operations into Southeast Asia and China since the middle of last century. It was their playground, they got in and out of there like a greased dick. The new mandate just meant going in and getting what looked like promising material. Pre-Jacobsen, variant science still looked like the way to go. The

Chinese were still doing it full-on, no human rights protest to get in the way, they were getting ahead of the game. We aimed to even up the race."

Carl saw the way Tom Norton was looking around the office, dazed, stark disbelief smashed through with understanding.

"Human Cost. Promising material. You're talking about people? Jesus Christ, Jeff, you're talking about fucking *people*?"

His brother shrugged and drank. "Sure. People, live tissue culture, cryocapped embryos, lab notes, you name it. Small-scale, but we were into everything. We were a big unit, Tom. Lot of backing, lot of resources."

"This is not possible." Norton made a two-handed gesture as if pushing something away. "You're telling us Human Cost was . . . you *ran* Human Cost as a, as some kind of pirate genetic testing program?"

"Not exactly, no. Human Cost was the back end, shell charity to cover the operation here in the Rim. It was a lot smaller then, back before we had official state funding, before I came out here to run it officially. Back then it was a guerrilla outfit. Couple of transit houses here and there, some waterfront industrial units down in San Diego. Scorpion Response were the sharp end, gathering the intelligence, going in and getting the goods." Jeff stared through his brother at something else. "Setting up the actual labs and the camps."

"Camps," Norton repeated sickly. "Black labs, here in the Rim? I don't believe you. Where?"

"Where do you think, little brother? Where do the Rim stick anything they don't like the smell of?"

"Jesusland." Carl nodded to himself. "Sure, why not? Just preempting Cimarron and Tanana, after all. Where'd you set up shop? Nevada? That's nice and close to the fenceline. Utah, maybe?"

Jeff shook his head. "Wyoming. Big place, barely any population. No one to see what's going on, no one to care, and state legislature in that part of the world will take your hand right off at the wrist if you offer good money for use of the land. We just told them it was another gene-modified crop project." Still, the glassy, through-everything stare. "I guess that's even the truth when you get right down to it, right? So. We took a couple of hundred square kilometers, power-fenced it in. Minefields and scanners, big corporate KEEP OUT notices." His voice dropped to a whisper. "I saw it once. I saw it working, all working perfectly, and no one out there knew or cared."

"What happened to it all when you folded?" Carl asked quietly.

"Can't you guess?"

The black man kicked out, smashed into Jeff Norton's shin just below the knee. The Human Cost director yelped and hunched over. Carl grabbed his head by the hair and smashed his face down on the coffee table. Pulled back, smashed again—

Then Tom Norton was in his way. Restraining hands on him, pushing him back.

"That's enough," the COLIN exec said.

Carl nailed him with a look. "Get your hands off me."

"I said that's enough. We need him conscious."

At their feet, Jeff huddled away from the blows, curled up fetally on the floor space between coffee table and sofa. Carl stared at Norton a moment longer, then jerked a nod. He dragged the Human Cost director back to the sofa and dumped him there. Bent so he was eye-to-eye with him.

"I told you not to make me guess again," he said evenly. "Now what happened to the Wyoming camp when Scorpion folded?"

"All right." The words burst out of Jeff Norton like a dam breaking. His nose had started bleeding again, was leaking into his cupped hands. "We torched it, we fucking torched it, all right? Scorpion went in, they killed everyone, the subjects and the hired staff. Then they mined it, blew it up, and burned everything to the ground. Left nothing but the ashes."

In his mind, Carl saw how it would be, the sporadic clatter of small arms, the wailing panic and truncated shrieks, dying away to quiet and the crackle of flames. The ripcord string of crunch-thump explosions through the camp as the placed charges went up. And later, walking away, the fire on the darkened skyline in the distance when you turned to look back. Like Ahvaz, like Tashkent, like the hotels in Dubai. The age-old signal. The beast is out.

"And no one said anything?" Norton asked, disbelieving.

"Oh Jesus, Tom, have you been listening to any fucking thing I've said?" Jeff sobbed out a snot-thickened laugh. "This is the *Republic* you're talking about. You know, Guantanamo syndrome? Do it far enough away and *no one gives a shit.*"

Carl moved back to the desk and leaned against its edge. It wasn't interrogation procedure; he should keep proximity, keep up the pressure. But he didn't trust himself within arm's reach of Jeff Norton.

"Okay," he said grimly. "Scorpion Response ties all these people together, gives them a dirty little secret to keep, and Scorpion Response buries their details so there are no links left on the flow. None of that explains killing them all now, fourteen, fifteen years later. Someone's cleaning house again. So why now?"

The Human Cost director lifted his bloodied face and bared his teeth in a stained grin. He seemed to be shaking, coming apart with something that was almost laughter.

"Career fucking progression," he said bitterly. "Ortiz."

CHAPTER 50

They caught a crack-of-dawn Cathay Pacific bounce to New York the following morning. Carl would have preferred not to wait, but he needed time to make a couple of calls and plan. Also, he wanted Tom Norton to sleep on his choices—if he could sleep at all—and face the whole thing in the cold light of a new day. All things considered, he was playing with better cards than he'd expected, but Norton was still an unknown quantity, all the more so for the way things had finally boiled down at the Human Cost Foundation.

At the airport, Norton's COLIN credentials got them fast-tracked through security and aboard before anyone else. Carl sat in a preferential window seat, waiting for the shuttle to fill, and stared out at an evercrete parking apron whipped by skirling curtains of wind-driven rain. Past the outlines of the terminal buildings, a pale, morose light was leaking across the sky between thick gunmetal cloud. The bad weather had blown in overnight and looked set to stick around.

Forecasts for New York said cold, dry, and clear. The thoughts in his head were a match.

The suborb shuttle shifted a little on its landing gear, then started to back out. Carl flexed his right hand, then held it cupped. Remembered the smooth glass weight of the ornament from the Human Cost director's desk. He glanced across at Tom Norton in the seat next to him. The COLIN exec caught his eye—face haggard with the demons that had kept him from sleep.

"What?"

Carl shook his head. "Nothing. Just glad you're along."

"Leave me the fuck alone, Marsalis. I made a promise. I'll keep it. I don't need your combat bonding rituals."

"Not about bonding," Carl looked back at the window. "I'm glad you're here because this would have been about a hundred times harder to do without you."

Brief quiet. In the window, the terminal building slid out of view as the shuttle turned to taxi. He could feel Norton hesitate.

"That wouldn't have stopped you, though," he said finally. "Would it?"

Carl rolled his head to face front, pressed back into the seat's cushioning. He hadn't had a lot of sleep, either. Elena Aguirre had sat in the darkened corners of his hotel room on and off all night, pretending to be Sevgi Ertekin and not quite pulling it off.

"Not in the end, no."

"Is that how you do it?" Norton asked him.

"Do what?"

"Become a thirteen. Is that what it's about, just not letting yourself be stopped?"

Carl shot him a surprised look. "No. It's about genetic wiring. Why, you feeling left out?"

"No." Norton sank back in his seat as well. "Just trying to understand."

The shuttle trundled steadily out toward the runway. Rain swept the windowpane, smeared diagonal with the wind. Soft chime—the FASTEN WEBBING sign lit on the LCLS panel above their heads, complete with animated instructions. They busied themselves with the thick, padded tongues of fabric. Like the siren-song lull of v-format prep, Carl usually had a hard time with how it felt once the webbing had him in its grip—it triggered tiny escape impulses across his body that he had to consciously hold down with Osprey-trained calm. But this time, he finished smoothing the cross-folds over one another, drew a deep breath, and found, with a shock like trying to walk up a step that wasn't there, that he felt nothing at all. Only the sense of anchored purpose, soaking coldly through him like the woken mesh.

"I'm sorry," he said to the man at his side. "About your brother. I'm sorry it had to work out this way."

Norton said nothing.

Across the aisle and back, a soft but urgent chiming signaled that some idiot had failed to web up correctly. An attendant appeared and hurried down past them to help out. The shuttle's motors picked up their idling whine, began to build force. On the LCLS panel, soft purple lettering in Chinese, then English, then Spanish, then Arabic, swelling forward, fading out. On station.

Carl glanced at the silent COLIN exec. "That's part of the reason you're here, right?"

"Sevgi's the reason I'm here." Norton's voice came out tight.

The engines outside reached shrieking pitch; the shuttle unstuck and hurled itself down the runway. Carl felt himself pressed back into the cushioning once more, this time with outside force beyond his own strength.

He closed his eyes and gave himself up to it.

They hit the sky on screaming turbines. The suborbital fuel lit and kicked them up around the curve of the world. The webbing hugged them tight and close.

"Fucking Ortiz," said Norton loudly, beside him.

In the judder and thrum of the trajectory, it wasn't clear if he was talking to the man or just about him. And this time his tone was loose and hard to define, but somewhere at the bottom of it Carl thought he could hear something like despair.

Norton hadn't really been surprised when Jeff spat the name out, but not because it wasn't a shock. Simply, surprise wasn't an option anymore: the glandular wiring that would have supplied it was running surge-overloaded, had been since the previous evening when Marsalis played him Jeff's phone conversation and told him about Ren. And it certainly shouldn't have mattered to him more than his own brother's betrayal.

Somehow it did.

He still remembered the change when Ortiz came fully aboard at Jefferson Park, when the slim, dynamic Rim politician's post morphed from consultative policy adviser to actual Americas policy director. He remembered the sudden sense of stripping down as layers of bureaucracy were lashed into efficiency or simply fired down to skeleton staffing levels. He remembered the way the little fiefdom people like Nicholson and Zikomo ran for cover. The new hires and promotions, Andrea Roth, Lena Oyeyemi, Samson Chang. Himself. The tide of change and the clean air it seemed to bring in with it, as if someone had suddenly opened all the windows facing the East River.

On another day, some other time, he would have called the bringer of this news a liar to his face, would have refused to believe.

But there was too much else now. The old landscape had burned down around him, Sevgi, Jeff, the aftermath of the Merrin case—it was all on fire, too hot to touch anywhere without getting hurt.

"It was Tanaka's fucking idea from the start." Jeff, laying it out. Bloodied nose stanched once more, this time with torn twists of tissue pushed up each nostril, a freshened tumbler of cognac, and, now, slightly slurring tones. "He comes to me two, two and a half years ago with this stupid fucking scheme. We can take Ortiz for some serious extra cash if we just threaten to go public on Scorpion Response."

"Why you?" Marsalis asked.

Jeff shrugged. "I was all he had. When we scattered back in '94, there were no links, no looking back. I was the only one apart from Ortiz who kept my identity, the only one with any public profile. Tanaka—he was called Asano back then, Max Asano—sees me on the feeds, this conference in Bangkok on the Pacific Rim refugee problem. So he sneaks across the fenceline, tracks me to the house over in Marin, and lays it out for me. He's got it all set up, the discreet clearing accounts in Hawaii, the back-sealed financial disconnect, the whole method. It's all there for the taking."

"Ortiz?" Norton still could not make it fit. "Alvaro Ortiz ran Scorpion Response? Why the hell would he get involved in something like that?"

Jeff shot him a weary look. "Oh grow up, Tom. Because he's a fucking politician, a power broker with an eye to the main chance. He always has been. Back then, just after Secession kicked in, he was just a junior Rim staffer looking for an edge. He got Scorpion Response handed to him and he worked it as far as it would carry him, which was pretty much up to policy level. When Jacobsen came in and the oversight protocols looked too stiff to risk anymore, he folded Scorpion up ahead of time and moved on to getting elected to the assembly instead. That's how you do it, Tom. Stay ahead of the game, know when to get out and keep your eyes open for the next opportunity."

"The next opportunity being COLIN."

"Yeah, that's right, little brother." Jeff's expression turned hooded and resentful. "Fucking Ortiz does seven years of elected office in the Rim, which he then bargains into a consultancy with the Colony Initiative. Another six years there, he climbs to the top of that tree as well, and now they're talking about the UN."

"Ripe for the plucking," said Marsalis.

"Yeah, well, that's what Tanaka thought." Jeff swallowed brandy, shivered. "See, he figures there are twenty or thirty ex-Scorpion personnel scattered about North America with their new identities, so Ortiz can't know who the blackmail's coming from, and he can't very well set out to find and kill them all. Plus he's got access to COLIN-level funds these days, he can skim a few million off here and there, make the payments easily. It's the line of least resistance."

"But that's not Ortiz," said Norton automatically, startled.

"No. That's what Tanaka missed."

"And so did you," Marsalis pointed out. "Why did Tanaka need you in the first place? Why not take his demands straight to Ortiz?"

Another shrug. "He said he wanted a buffer. I don't know, maybe he just wanted a friend, someone to work with. It's got to be tough, right? Living a cover identity for the rest of your life. Covering for a past you can't ever tell anyone about."

Marsalis stared at Jeff like something he wanted to smash. "Oh, you're breaking my fucking heart. So how come it took this Asano-Tanaka-whatever guy over a decade to get around to blackmail?"

"I don't know," Jeff said tiredly. "Scorpion personnel all got seed money for going away, all part of the deal. But not everyone knows how to handle that. Maybe a decade was what it took for Tanaka to piss his stake away. Or maybe he just got unlucky a couple of years back and lost what he'd made. You slip financially in the Republic, there's not a lot of help out there to get you back on your feet."

"Right. So this washed-up ex-sneak-op petty crook comes to you with some wild-eyed scheme for putting pressure on one of the most powerful men in American corporate and political life. And you just go along with it?"

Jeff drained his glass again, sat hunched forward over it. "Sure. Why not? It could have worked."

"This I've got to fucking hear. Worked how?"

Jeff reached for the bottle. "Tanaka's idea was, he sends the blackmail demand to me, and I take it to Ortiz as if I'm scared. I steer Ortiz toward paying up, point out the smart move, and offer to act as a conduit so he stays clean."

Norton shook his head. "But that's not Ortiz. He wouldn't just . . . Christ, you should have known that, Jeff. Why didn't you see it?"

Jeff gave him a hunted look. He uncorked the cognac.

"Why do you think, little brother? I wanted the fucking money."

"Yeah, but you must have—"

"Just fucking *don't*, Tom. All right?" The bottle slammed down, the pale liquid slopped and splashed up through the open neck. Jeff's voice scaled upward, defensive to bitter fury. "What do you know about my life anyway? It's okay for you, with your fucking COLIN badge, your promotion that I set up for you, your fucking loft apartment on Canal Street, and your no-ties, no-costs jet-set fucking life. You know what I make here at Human Cost? For fourteen-hour days, six and sometimes seven days a week, you know what I fucking make? I've got two kids, Tom, a wife with expensive tastes, no pension plan yet. What do you know about all this, Tom? You *float*, you fucking float through life. So don't come to me telling me what I should or shouldn't have known. I wanted the money, that's it. I was in."

Norton stared at him, too numb to pick up pieces and make them fit. It was too much, too much of his world blown open.

"I don't live on Canal Street, Jeff," he said stupidly. "I never did. It's Lispenard. You should know that."

"Don't fucking tell me what I should know!"

"Why don't you tell us what went wrong," Marsalis suggested. "Ortiz wouldn't roll over, right?"

"No." Jeff reached for the bottle again. "At first, yes. He transferred some funds of his own, told me to make an interim payment and play for more time. Then, when Tanaka's next demand came in, he just sat me down and told me what we were going to do."

Marsalis nodded. "Wipe out everyone who could be doing it."

"He." A helpless gesture. "He'd kept tabs on them all. I didn't know that, but he knew where every single one of them was. Or where they'd started out from, anyway. Some of them had moved around, he said, so it'd take a little time to track them down. But one way or another, they all had to go. I sat there, Tom, I couldn't fucking believe what I was hearing. I mean." Jeff's voice turned almost plaintive. "We hadn't asked for that much, you know."

"It wasn't the money," Norton said distantly.

Marsalis reached over and took the bottle out of Jeff's trembling hands. He poured into the tumbler. "UN nomination a step away. You fucked with the wrong patriarch just when he could least afford it."

"Yeah." Jeff sat and looked at the drink the thirteen had just made him. "That's what he said. *There's too much at stake here, Jeff. We can't be exposed now. We have to get tough.* I tried to talk him down, tell him it wasn't so much money. But he didn't care. I told him he'd get caught, that nobody could get away with killing that many people, that many ex-special-op guys. You'd need a whole team of people to bring it off, and then they'd have the same goods on you as the original blackmailers."

"Or," said Marsalis, "you bring in the one member of the old team you can trust to get it done. The one person who also can't afford the word to get out, and who won't let nostalgia and camaraderie get in the way of doing the job. The one person who's wired for it—a thirteen."

Jeff just nodded, let the black man talk. He was emptied out.

"Everyone thinks Merrin's gone to Mars," Marsalis went on, nodding what might have been approval. "A thirteen called Merrin *did* go to Mars. So that makes the other Merrin, Onbekend, pretty invisible back here on Earth. He's pulled his own disappearing act, found a surrogate brother down on the altiplano, a safe haven. A sideline in playing *pistaco* for his brother now and then, when the local bad guys need scaring, but the rest of his time's his own. Until suddenly here's his old boss banging on the door, telling him it's all about to end. Some ungrateful fuck from the old team is threatening to blow everything wide open, and the only way to ensure that doesn't happen is to go back and wipe out every member of the old team left alive. Does Onbekend want the work?" Marsalis spread his hands. "Probably not, but what choice does he have? If Ortiz isn't going to pay, the blackmailers are going to get angry and the word on Scorpion Response is going to get out. And there's just no telling how far that thread can unravel. Whatever Onbekend's managed to swing for himself down on Manco Bambarén's patch is under threat. There's a good chance he's going to the tracts, because if they do find him it's that or a bullet. Feel free to contribute, Jeff, if I'm getting any of this wrong."

"No, you're right." Jeff sipped at his drink, held it in both hands before him, staring into space. "When Ortiz went to Onbekend with it, he saw what had to happen right away."

Marsalis grinned. It wasn't a pleasant sight. "Clean sweep, huh? Just like Wyoming all over again."

"It was the only way," said Jeff.

"Okay, but Onbekend isn't stupid. He knows he isn't going to get away with murdering thirty-odd ex-sneak-op soldiers and not leave some trace of himself at least at a couple of the crime scenes. And once that genetic trace gets into the system, he's as fucked as if he'd let Ortiz's blackmailers go ahead and blow the whistle. Because the only living thirteen who's supposed to have that geneprint is on Mars. So if it shows up around a stack of murder victims in the Rim or the Republic, all hell is going to break loose. That's what he fronts Ortiz with, that's the sticking point."

"And Ortiz is at COLIN," said Norton wonderingly.

"Right. So he hatches the perfect alibi for Onbekend. Not only will they bring Merrin back from Mars to account for any genetic trace that crops up, they'll set him up as the fall guy for the whole set of murders. Hold him in reserve while Onbekend gets the killing done, and then have him die in some plausible way and leave him for RimSec to find. With finesse, they could even set it up so RimSec get him pinned and kill him themselves. Medals all around, and no one looks too closely at the aftermath, because it's so fucking neat. After all, you can't argue with genetic trace, and there's your monster, dead in the dirt."

Norton looked at his brother and could not name the feeling that seeped into him. He hoped it was pity.

"No wonder Ortiz paid up at the start, Jeff," he told him. "He had to have time to put all this in place. He had to get Merrin back here, before Onbekend could go to work."

"And Onbekend came over the Texas border and started with Tanaka."

Marsalis nodded. "He could have stopped right there, if he'd only known. But he doesn't know, doesn't get the chance to get it out of Tanaka, maybe wouldn't even have been able to afford to trust him even if he did, so he's committed. He kills his way across the Republic, because those are the easiest ones—underfunded police departments, low-grade data tech, highest murder rate on the planet, and a massive underclass to hide out in. He only heads on to the Rim when the easy work is done, moving slower now because he's got RimSec to contend with. But still, Jasper Whitlock and Toni Montes, he's getting through them, probably only a handful left, and then . . ."

They both turned to look at Jeff Norton.

"What happened?" Marsalis asked him softly. "You lose your nerve, playing both ends against the middle? Thought maybe Ortiz had worked you out, knew you were part of it after all? You start to think maybe Onbekend's last bullet was going to be for you?"

"No!"

"Don't fucking lie to me."

"Then what happened in New York?" Norton peered at his brother's face. "Someone had Ortiz shot. Sure as hell wasn't Tanaka, he was already in the ground. That leaves you, Jeff."

Jeff looked away.

"They were Tanaka's," he muttered. "Dead hand insurance. If anything went wrong, he'd given me this Houston number, in case he didn't have time to set it off before he ran. Or in case he . . . didn't make it. The contract was already paid, I just had to call to set it in motion."

"Waited long enough, didn't you?" Marsalis coughed out a laugh. "Or did it take this crew of geniuses four months to get from Texas to the Union?"

Norton snapped his fingers. "Whitlock."

He saw the way his brother flinched at the name. *Oh Christ, Jeff.* Made it into words so he'd have to hear it, so he'd believe it.

"Onbekend came across the fenceline into the Rim States and he killed Whitlock, October 2. You must have caught it on the feeds, recognized Whitlock's face."

"Yeah, right here in the Bay Area." Marsalis whistled long and low, mock concerned. "Just a little too close for comfort, right, Jeff?"

"So you made the call," Norton said flatly.

"All right, yes, I made the fucking call!"

Marsalis grunted. "And it all comes grinding to a halt. Onbekend on hold, at least until he finds out if Ortiz is going to live or die."

"It was right after Whitlock you called me," Norton realized suddenly. "Suggested I get Marsalis out of Jesusland and hire him. What was that, just a little added pressure, keep Onbekend on his toes?"

Amazement on the black man's face. "*You* got me out of South Florida State, Jeff? I owe *you* for that?" A chuckle broke out of him. "Oh man, you've got to be fucking kidding me."

"I got sick of waiting," Jeff snapped, voice tight with sudden, puny fury. "A week after I called the Houston crew and nothing. I didn't know anything about them, how good they'd be—"

"They weren't very good," said Marsalis somberly.

"Yeah, well, I thought maybe they'd gotten caught at the fence, trying to get into the Union. Or maybe just faded with the cash and walked. I had no fucking way of knowing, Tom. I was scared. I knew you wouldn't bring UNGLA in, I tried to persuade you, thought maybe that'd scare Ortiz into pulling the plug. But you wouldn't do it." Jeff looked across at Marsalis. "I thought maybe he'd scare Ortiz instead."

Norton saw the black man walk to the desk and pick up a paperweight Jeff had brought back from a trip to England when he and Megan were first married. He weighed it in his hand.

"There's just a couple more things I'd like to know, Jeff," he said absently. "Then we're done."

"Yeah?" Jeff tugged at his drink. Grimaced as it went down. "What's that?"

"Ren. She didn't know anything about Onbekend. Where does she come into this?"

"No. She's freelance, we've used her in the past. I pulled her in because we needed someone who knows the Rim systems. Ortiz wanted to keep the Merrin end of things separate from the rest."

"And Daskeen Azul. They're your people?"

A shrug. "Associates. You know how it works, Human Cost did them some favors in the past, they owed us."

"So who sent them up to find that corpse in the nets? You?"

Jeff shook his head. "Onbekend. He heard from down south that you and this COLIN cop were poking around. Told me to bring the denouement forward."

Marsalis came back to the sofa, paperweight in his hand. He was frowning. "Against Ortiz's orders?"

"Ortiz was in the hospital." Jeff gestured wearily. "No one knew which way to jump. You ever met Onbekend?"

"Briefly."

"Yeah, well, when he tells you to do something, you don't argue with him."

Marsalis hadn't lost his frown. "And the soldiers?"

"What soldiers?"

"Someone sent a uniformed death squad after Ertekin and me. They pulled us over between Cuzco and Arequipa."

"I don't know anything about that. Maybe someone panicked down there."

"Bambarén," the thirteen said softly. He crouched to Jeff's eye level. "Do you think Manco Bambarén knows that Merrin existed? The other Merrin?"

"I don't know Manco Bambarén from a hole in the fucking ground." Jeff stared bitterly back at Marsalis. He seemed completely drunk now. "How the fuck would I know what he does or doesn't know?"

"That's unfortunate," said the black man softly. "Tell me, Jeff, did you set On-bekend on me when I got back from *Bulgakov's Cat?*"

"No! That wasn't me, I swear. Onbekend wanted you out of the picture, I think he'd maybe talked to Ortiz, but he was furious about something else anyway. I told him it was better to let things lie, but he wouldn't listen. You don't understand what he's like. Once he's decided, he doesn't listen to anything or anyone who gets in his fucking way."

"Right. And I don't suppose you know where I can find him now, do you?"

Jeff knocked back the rest of his drink. Shrugged. "You guess right. Last I heard, he was on his way back to the altiplano with a shoulderful of holes from a Marstech gun."

"You treated him here?"

"At a Human Cost walk-in clinic, yeah. Over on Carmel."

Marsalis came smoothly back to his feet. Norton saw how the thirteen's fingers tightened on the paperweight, saw the heft in the arm. He stepped swiftly across, blocked Marsalis body-to-body. His eyes locked with the black man's stare.

"No," he said, very quietly. "Please."

Marsalis stood coiled. His voice came back, also barely above a murmur. "Don't get in my way, Norton."

"He didn't kill Sevgi." Norton looked back at where Jeff sat slumped in one corner of the sofa, staring listlessly into his empty glass. He barely seemed aware of the other two men. "Look, you want to go after Onbekend, I'm with you. Ortiz, too, if that's what you want. But this is my brother, Marsalis."

"He's going down anyway, Norton. He'll do thirty years in a RimSec facility for this, minimum. I'd be doing him a favor."

But a little of the tension seemed to drain from the thirteen's stance. Norton raised his hand, palm-out. The small gesture for *enough*.

"Marsalis, *please*. I'm asking you for this. He's my fucking brother."

Marsalis stood there locked for a moment longer. It was like facing off against a wall.

"Ortiz, and Onbekend," he said, as if checking a list.

Norton nodded. "Whatever you need."

And the moment passed. Marsalis let go; Norton saw it go out of him like dark water down a drain. He shrugged and lobbed the paperweight down into Jeff's lap. Jeff jolted with the shock, dropped his empty glass, fumbled with both hands to catch the spherical ornament before it rolled to the floor.

"Fuck d'you do that for?" he mumbled.

"You'll never know," Marsalis told him. Then, turning away to the door, voice trailing back. "Keep him here, Norton. Don't touch the phones, or use yours in here. We'll need to freeze and store their whole net as it is. I'll clean-call Rovayo from the street, get a RimSec CSI squad over here. Going to make her day—this should be enough to lever the *Cat* bust wide open all over again."

"Right."

He paused at the door, looked back. "And don't forget. We've got an arrangement now."

Norton listened to him walk away down the corridor. Then he turned back to face his brother. Jeff looked disinterestedly up at him.

"What now?"

Sudden, pulsing rage, up from the soles of his shoes and into the space behind his eyes. He bit it back as well as he could.

"You know," he said, almost evenly. "I told Megan about you and Nuying."

Jeff gaped up at him, eyes cognac-veiled and confused.

"Maybe that's simplifying it. I guess you could say she got it out of me. Or maybe not that, either, maybe we both wanted it said and we just helped each other get it out. If I'm honest, I think she already had a pretty good idea something was going on."

Clumsily, his brother started to get up.

"You fucking traitor," he said thickly.

"Stay in your seat, Jeff." Suddenly, the rage came washing up out of him, would not be contained. "Because if you don't, *I will fucking kill you myself.*"

And now, here it was. The moment that had been festering inside him for over two years. His brother blinking at him, like a deer staring into the headlights.

He drew in breath. He really was going to do this.

"You want to know what Megan did when she found out?" Another hard breath. "She fucked me, Jeff. We went to some motel up near Novato, and she fucked me raw. All afternoon and night. Best sex I ever had."

And now Jeff came flailing up out of the sofa, roaring, fists swinging. Norton blocked, twisted, and punched his brother in the side of the face. The first time he'd used his enforcement training in better than a year. It felt creakily unaccustomed, but it felt unexpectedly good as well. The blow connected solidly, put Jeff down, crawling half on the sofa, half on the floor. Norton grabbed him by the back of the collar, balled fist raised again.

And stopped.

No. You're not Carl Marsalis.

Fist slowly unflexing, dropping away. He let go of the collar. Overpowering urge to shake himself, like a drenched dog. Instead he stepped away, leaned against the edge of his brother's desk.

"This is going to be hard on her," he said, still breathing unevenly. "Megan and the kids. But don't worry. When they send you up to Quentin Two for what you've done here, I'll make sure she's okay. I'll take care of her."

A low, grinding howl came up out of his brother's throat as he propped himself up on the sofa, as if he'd swallowed broken glass. Norton felt a peculiarly comfortable calm settling into place on his shoulders. His breathing eased.

"We're good together, Jeff. She laughs when she's around me. We'll work something out."

"*Fuck you!*" Spat out like blood.

There was a timid tap at the door. Norton glanced up, surprised. "Yeah?"

The door opened and the stout Asian woman peered around the edge. "Mr. Norton, are you . . . ?"

She stared, eyes wide.

"It's okay," said Norton hurriedly. "I'm Jeff's brother, Tom. Jeff's been under a lot of strain recently. I'm sure you'll have noticed. It's, uh, it's gotten pretty bad."

"I, uhm—"

"He really needs to be alone right now, just with family, you know. We've made the calls. If you could—"

"Yes, of course, uhm . . ." She looked across at Jeff where he now sat on the floor with his back to the sofa. Blood-flecked tissue in his nose, face smeared with tears and rage, uncapped bottle on the table in front of him. "Mr. Norton, I'm so sorry, if there's anything at all I can do . . ."

Jeff Norton stared back at her.

"It's okay, Lisa," he said dully. "Everything's going to be fine. Could you show my brother where we keep our medical records from the Carmel clinic."

"Yes, of course." Imbued with a solid purpose, Lisa seemed to grow visibly stronger again. "You're quite sure that—"

Jeff dragged up the husk of a smile. "Quite sure, Lisa."

He turned to look at his brother, and there was an odd note of triumph suddenly in his voice. "Go ahead, little brother. You want to see something I kept back from your thirteen friend?"

Lisa vacillated in the doorway. Norton stared at Jeff.

"This is about Onbekend?"

"Just go look, Tom." He saw Norton's hesitation and chuckled. "What am I going to do, make a dash for the airport while you're gone? Seriously, go look. This is something I saved just for you. You're going to love it."

"It's, uh." Lisa gestured along the corridor. "This way."

"Jeff, if you knew something else about Onbekend, you should have—"

"Just go fucking look, will you!"

So he went, left the door ajar and followed Lisa out into the corridor. In the doorway, he paused and turned, looked hard at his brother, pointed at him.

"You stay right there."

Jeff snorted, rolled his eyes, and reached for the bottle of Martell.

Down the angled corridor, tracking Lisa's stolid progress, floating behind the eyes with all that he was still trying to assimilate. He wondered vaguely if Marsalis hadn't gone out into the street as much to clear his head as to keep the call to RimSec clean.

They were almost at the door marked CARMEL STREET CLINIC when the single shot slammed behind them, so flat and undramatic that at first he mistook it for the sound of the door to Jeff's office, the exit he hadn't bothered to close.

CHAPTER 51

They had Alvaro Ortiz in a monitored convalescence suite on the newly nanobuilt upper levels at the Weill Cornell Medical Center. He was tagged with microdoc subdermals that would broadcast a scream to the hospital system if his life signs dipped in any way, the receptionist explained with an enthusiastic smile, and he had panic buttons in the bathroom, next to his bed, and on his wheelchair. A full crash team and a dedicated emergency room doctor were retained at all times on idle, specifically for the patients on these levels. Norton thanked her, and they went upstairs. A COLIN Security detachment was on duty outside the suite, two hard-faced men and a woman who met them out of the elevator with professional tension that evaporated when they recognized Norton. Carl let them pat him down anyway, not sure if it was his thirteen status or just procedure that made them do it. The more relaxed they were, the better. Norton told the squad leader not to bother seeing them in, they'd be fine. Mr. Ortiz knew they were coming.

The doors to the suite hummed smoothly back and they walked through. Ortiz was in a wheelchair in the living room, parked by the floor-to-ceiling windows. He wore loose gray silk pajamas, held a book apparently forgotten in his hands, was lost instead in contemplation of the view out across the cubist thickets of the city to the park. He looked thin and breakable in the chair, the tanned face hollowed out to a worn gray, the grizzled hair gone to white in places. He didn't appear to have heard the door open, and he didn't turn as they stepped into view from the entryway hall. Carl wondered if he already knew why they'd come.

"Ortiz," Norton said harshly, moving a step ahead.

Ortiz prodded at the chair's arm controls, and it coasted silently around on the spot to face them. He smiled, a little forcedly.

"Tom Norton," he said, as if it were a philosophical question that had been

troubling him. "I'm so very sorry to hear about your brother, Tom. I've been meaning to call you. And Carl Marsalis, of course. I still haven't had the chance to
thank you for saving my life."

"Don't thank me yet."

"Ah." Something happened to the planes of the ravaged face. "Well, I didn't
imagine that this was a social call."

"Jeff talked." Norton was trembling with the force of what he'd carried inside
him across the continent. "Scorpion Response. Wyoming. The whole thing. So
don't you tell me you're sorry, you piece of shit. You did this, all of it. You're the
reason Jeff is dead."

"Am I?" Ortiz didn't seem to be disputing it. He placed his hands palm-to-
palm in his lap, pressed them together, maybe to hold down his fear. "And so
you've brought your avenging angel with you. Well, that is fitting, I suppose, but
I should warn you this chair has—"

"We know," Carl said bleakly. "And I'm not here for Norton's benefit. I came
for Sevgi Ertekin."

"Ertekin?" A frown crossed Ortiz's face, then cleared. "Oh yes, the officer you
stayed with in Harlem when we had you released. Yes, she died, too, didn't she.
A few days ago. I'm afraid I've not been keeping up very closely with—"

"She didn't die." Carl held down the fury with distant, trained reflex. His voice
was quiet and cold, like the faint bite of winter in the New York air outside. "Sevgi
Ertekin was killed. By *your* avenging angel, Ortiz. By Onbekend. Merrin. Whatever you call him. She died saving my life."

"I am . . . very sorry about that as well."

"That's not good enough."

"For you? No, I don't imagine it would be. I assume there was some." Ortiz
frowned. "Some connection between you and this Ertekin."

Carl said nothing. The words would take him nowhere.

"Yes, there must have been. You people care about so little in the end, *need* so
little, of the material world and of other people. But when you do choose to own
something or someone, when you consider that something or someone to be
yours . . ."

"Yes, then," said Carl. "Nothing else matters."

He met the COLIN director's eyes, saw the way they flinched away.

"I'm afraid," said Ortiz shakily, "that events have run rather out of control in
my . . . my absence from the bridge, as it were. Your involvement, Onbekend,
other changing factors. Had I not been removed so unexpectedly from managing
the operation, perhaps things would not have become so tangled. I truly regret
that, you must believe me."

"You still would have murdered over twenty men and women," said Norton violently. "Just to save your political fucking neck."

Ortiz shook his head. "No, Tom, that isn't—"

"Don't fucking use my name like we're friends, you piece of shit!"

Carl put a hand on Norton's arm. "Keep it down, Tom. We don't want your security breaking the door down on us."

The COLIN exec jerked away from him, looked at him as if he were contagious. In front of them, Ortiz was talking again.

"—was not for me, personally. You must understand that. I'm a wealthy man, and I have access to even greater wealth through other channels if I need it. I could have afforded to pay off your brother and his accomplice—"

Norton stared. "You knew? You knew he was part of it?"

"I suspected." Ortiz coughed a little, hunched over in the chair. He cleared his throat. "His story seemed feeble, I thought it was likely he was involved, but . . . we were once close associates, Tom. Friends, even. You must know I promoted you on his request, just the way I promoted him to Scorpion Response twenty years ago."

Norton's voice came through his teeth. "Am I supposed to be fucking grateful to you now?"

"No, of course not. That's not what I'm saying. Listen to me, please. I suspected Jeff, I didn't know for sure. But I did know that if I unleashed Onbekend on the others, whoever they were, Jeff would fold. If he had been involved, I knew he'd give me no more trouble. Even in the old days, even with Scorpion Response, he was a logistical manager, a facilitator. Not an operative, not a killer. Jeff never had the stomach for those things."

Norton grinned savagely down at him. "That's all you know. My brother sent those skaters to kill you. My brother got me to hire Marsalis out of South Florida State to crank up the pressure on you and Onbekend. He was playing you just like you played him."

"Is that so?" An attempted smile wavered on the COLIN director's face for a moment. "Ironic, then, that he provided both the agents of my death and the means to foil them. Ironic, too, that you, Mr. Marsalis, should both save my life and then bring everything tumbling down around me. But then, that has always been the double-edged blade that your kind offered us, from the very beginning. Variant thirteen, the avatars of purified violence, our saviors and our nemeses."

Carl listened to the lilt of imagery in Ortiz's voice and thought abruptly of Manco Bambarén's mannered speeches on *pistacos* and human history. He wondered idly what genes the two men might share.

"Where is Onbekend?" he asked bluntly.

"I'm afraid I don't know." Maybe Carl twitched forward, because Ortiz's voice tightened a little with anxiety. "Really, I don't. Believe me, if I knew—"

"Jeff Norton said he'd gone back to the altiplano. Back to Bambarén. That's where you would have contacted him in the beginning to set this up, right?"

"Yes, but through Bambarén's organization. In the end, I could only leave messages. It was he who came to me, here in New York one night, like a ghost through the security around my home." Ortiz stared away through the window and shivered a little. "Like something I had summoned up. I should have known then, all those lessons our myths and legends scream at us, time and again. Never summon up what you cannot control."

"You must have had direct contact with him after that," Carl said pragmatically. "You set him on me in San Francisco, after the *Bulgakov's Cat* arrests."

Ortiz tried another smile. It guttered and died. "Believe me, Mr. Marsalis, I tried harder than you'll ever know to prevent that. I am not an ungrateful man, and you had saved my life. But once decided, Onbekend is a force of nature. You had already threatened the object of his affections in Arequipa; he would not take less than your death. I tried to move you out of range, I had UNGLA attempt to recall you, but it seems you are in your way no less stubborn than any other of your kind. You would not shift. And Onbekend was closing on you too fast for me to do anything else."

The shock sparked in him. "*You* had di Palma call me?"

"Yes, Mr. Marsalis." Ortiz sighed. "And not only then. From the very beginning, Gianfranco di Palma had instructions to remove you from the proceedings as rapidly as possible. We had simply not expected you to be so tenacious in a fight that was not your own."

Carl remembered the UNGLA clinic in Istanbul. Mehmet Tuzcu and his diplomatic attempts at extraction. His own refusal to shift, the weak fistful of reasons he threw out, like sand in his own eyes. But it had always been Sevgi Ertekin, he knew, even then.

"Greta Jurgens is Onbekend's?" he asked distractedly.

"So it would appear. A curious match, is it not? But then they do at least have in common that they are both objects for the hormonal hatred the rest of humanity seems constantly to need a target for."

Norton was dealing with something else, staring at Ortiz. "You're pulling favors with UNGLA already? You've got your hooks in that far?"

"Tom, I have a secure nomination for secretary general. There will be no dispute, it's decided at all the levels that matter. I will hold the post by this time next year, if you let me live." The pressed palms raised, almost like prayer. "Don't you understand, either of you, that this is what I have been trying to safeguard? You think this was about me personally? It was not, please believe me. I have spent the last six years of my life trying to bend the Colony Initiative closer to a rapprochement with the UN. To reach agreements on Martian law and cooperative governance. To leash corporate greed and harness it to a European social model. To break down the barriers between us and the Chinese instead of building walls and fences. I've done all of that in the hope that we don't have to take our insular nation-state insanities to the first new world we've reached and build the same stupid hate-filled structure from the ground up all over again."

Ortiz's face was flushed and animated, passion briefly imitating health while it filled him. Carl watched the COLIN director as if he were something behind glass in an insect vivarium. *See the humans. Watch the patriarchal male justify his acts to his fellows and to himself.*

"One more year," said Ortiz urgently. "That's all I need, and I can continue that work from the other side of the fence. I can restructure the idiot posturing in the General Assembly, force reforms, make promises, all built on the work I've already done here with COLIN. That's what was under threat from this stupid petty blackmail out of the past—not some quick cash that I could have filtered through a COLIN account for less than the cost of a single nanorack elevator. That's not why I did this. I did it for the future, a hope for the future. Isn't that worth the sacrifice? It was a handful of used-up, counterfeit lives, tired, superannuated men and women of violence hiding from their own pasts, set in the balance against the hope of a better future for all of us."

Carl thought briefly of Toni Montes, imagined her fighting Onbekend with the decayed vestiges of her combat skill, then letting go and dying to keep the thirteen away from her husband and children. He wondered if she'd thought of smoking ruins in Wyoming as she stood there waiting for the bullet, or only the children she would never see walk through the door again.

He wondered what he'd have to picture when the time came for him.

Elena Aguirre, whispering behind him.

The quiet, filling him up . . .

"You're full of shit, Ortiz." The rasp of Norton's voice pulled him out of it. "You didn't have a problem with using these men and women of violence when you were running Scorpion Response."

"No, that's true, Tom. But it was a different time." Ortiz, pitching his tone raised but reasonable. Arguing his point in good faith. "You have to remember that. And back then, those men and women themselves would gladly have given their lives in the causes I'm talking about, because they also believed in a better future."

Norton jolted forward, face tight with rage. He gripped the arms of Ortiz's wheelchair, pushed it back half a meter before the autobrake cut in. Carl saw tiny specks of spittle hit Ortiz in the face as the COLIN exec yelled at his boss.

"A better fucking future? And what exactly was your bright new future going to be, you motherfucker? Covert ops in other people's countries? Corrupt corporate practice? A genetic concentration camp in Wyoming?"

Carl pulled him back. "Get a grip, Tom. This isn't what we're here for."

But the force had already gone out of Ortiz's face, like a candle flame blown out by Norton's rage. Suddenly the wheelchair held only an ill old man, shaking his head in weary admission.

"I . . . was . . . young. Foolish. I have no defense. But I believed what we were doing was right, at the time. You have to understand what it was like. In the West we were losing the edge, terrified of the gene research that needed to be done, held back by moral panic and ignorance. China was doing work that *our* universities and technology institutes should have been pursuing. They still are." Ortiz shifted his gaze to Carl, grew animated once more. "There is a future on Mars, Mr. Marsalis, but it's not a human future the way Jacobsen and UNGLA understood it. You've been there, you know what it's like. We will *need* the variants, we will have to *become* a variant of some sort if we plan to stay. The Chinese understand this, that's why they haven't stopped their programs. I only sought to equalize the pressure, so when the explosion, the *realization* finally came, it would not rupture our society apart from the differential."

Carl nodded. "Yeah. Let's get back to Onbekend."

"You don't believe me?"

"What does it matter what I believe? It won't change what you've done. How did Onbekend find out he was Manco Bambarén's half brother?"

Ortiz sighed. "I really don't remember details of that sort. It was a long time ago. Yes, possibly, he used Scorpion Response time and resources to track down his sourcemat mother, discovered who she was, and saw the angle. The work we were doing in Wyoming may have sparked his interest. It is through Scorpion channels that he discovered he had a twin, that I do know, so quite possibly he found Isabela Gayoso the same way. And I know that when he wasn't seconded to us, Project Lawman deployed him in a covert capacity in Bolivia on at least one occasion, so he would perhaps have had opportunity then as well. All I can tell you is that when the time came to dissolve the Scorpion operation, he already had his place in the sun prepared. He knew that his twin had accepted Mars resettlement, and that Scorpion Response would be wiped from the flow by n-djinn. And Bambarén had made a place for him in his organization. It was a perfect disappearing act."

Yeah, until Stefan Nevant shows up trying to sell Bambarén a pistaco *threat he already has blood-related access to and drawing down attention they could really all do without. Poor old Stefan, right on target. Better intuition than you ever knew. No wonder Bambarén turned you over so fucking fast. All you were going to do was lead an UNGLA squad right to his half brother's door.*

And no wonder Bambarén freaked when we showed up, set it all in motion all over again. I thought I'd offended him when I talked about exemplary executions in some village square somewhere. Must have nailed something Onbekend did for him, too close to the truth for comfort.

He thought I was playing with him. Thought I'd come for his brother.

He thought of Sevgi Ertekin, propped against the side of the COLIN jeep, hands in pockets, jacket hooked back. The casual reveal of the shoulder-holstered Marstech gun, the telegraphed warning to Bambarén not to fuck up.

Sevgi, you should have been here to hear all of this. We were so fucking close after all.

But you would have told me not to gloat, it's not attractive.

He focused hard on the man in the wheelchair. "Is Isabela Gayoso still alive?"

"No, she died some years ago. Onbekend mentioned it to me in passing when we met in New York. She grew up in crushing poverty, it seems, and of course these things tend to take their toll later in life. From what I hear, Bambarén himself was lucky to survive his childhood. Neither of his siblings did."

"Does Bambarén know he has a second half brother?"

"No. We did not involve him. Onbekend has enough *familia* presence these days to make the contacts we needed at Bradbury and Wells, and to be convincing when he did. It took some time, but he convinced the Martian chapters that there is a wedge opening between the Lima clans and the altiplano." Ortiz's shrunken shoulders lifted under the gray silk of the pajamas. "From what I understand, it's not far from the truth."

"And Merrin never knew who was hiring him, either?"

"Merrin was never aware that he had a twin in the first place. As I said, it was only through Scorpion Response intelligence that Onbekend discovered what had been done. Merrin never would have had access to the data. And you've seen Onbekend; he changed his face when he went underground back in '94. No resemblance any longer."

Carl thought about the echo in the features he'd seen the night Sevgi was shot. "No, there is a resemblance. If you look for it."

"Well, as I understand it the actual hiring was filtered through the Martian *familia* machine anyway. I doubt Merrin and Onbekend ever actually saw each other across the screen. The *familias* knew only that this was a personal matter, that the people at this end had chosen this particular man, Merrin, and that if they could not recruit him, there would be no deal."

"And Merrin?" Norton wanted to know. "What was he told?"

Another fragile shrug. "That he had friends here on Earth who wanted him back, who would provide him with a new identity and the resources to disappear in comfort. We made it a very attractive package."

The COLIN exec shook his head numbly. "So Onbekend just sold out his brother? His twin?"

"Sacrificed him, yes. What of it?" Ortiz gestured. "They had never known each other, never met. What bond could there be?"

"That's not the point!" But now Norton was looking at Carl. "He was his brother, for Christ's sake!"

"That is the point, Tom," Carl told him quietly. "Thirteens don't do abstract allegiance. It's not part of our makeup."

"But . . . Bambarén." Norton held out his hands. "That's an abstract blood tie."

Ortiz made an arid chuckling sound. "Yes, one that Onbekend has exploited to great benefit."

"Bambarén got used," said Carl, looking down at Ortiz. "Just like everybody else. Just like Scorpion Response, just like Human Cost. Just like Onbekend and Merrin. You got everybody dancing."

"Mr. Marsalis, please understand—"

Enough.

Carl grabbed Ortiz under the arms and hauled him out of the chair in a single violent motion. The other man seemed to weigh almost nothing, but that might have been the mesh kicking in, or the rage. Ortiz kicked and struggled, but feebly. Carl held him in what felt for a moment like an embrace, stepped back clear of the panic-wired wheelchair, and laid the COLIN director carefully down on the polished wood floor.

"Wait, you can't—"

But Ortiz's voice was as weak as his struggles. Carl knelt and pressed a hand to the COLIN director's chest to hold him still. He leaned over him, face impassive.

"I know you, Ortiz," he said. "I've seen your kind making your speeches from every pulpit and podium on two planets, and you never fucking change. You lie to the cudlips and you lie to yourself so they'll believe you better, and when the dying starts you claim regret and offer justification. But in the end, you do it all because you think it's your right, and you *do not care.* If you really suspected Jeff Norton, if you knew what kind of man he was, you could have squeezed him for the names, dealt with whoever it was—"

"It was Tanaka," Norton said, standing over Ortiz. "Only Tanaka."

Carl nodded. "You could have stopped this thing as soon as it started. But what Tanaka and Jeff Norton could do, so could someone else sooner or later. So could any of the ones who knew about Wyoming, any of the ones who were left, and it could happen at any time. No matter what position you achieved, Scorpion Response was going to hang over you to the grave. You'd never be safe. So you saw a chance to clean house, and you took it, at whatever cost."

And now Carl found a small truth seeping up inside him, an understanding.

"You know, Ortiz, you would have made a pretty good thirteen. All you ever lacked was the strength, the power, and that, well, I guess you can always find a mob of cudlips to supply that for you."

"All right." Ortiz stopped struggling. The force came back into his voice. He spoke clearly and urgently. "Listen to me, please. If you kill me now, I have alarm systems attached to my body. They're under the skin, inside me, you'll never find them. There'll be a crash team here in minutes."

"I won't need that long," Carl told him.

Ortiz broke. His face seemed to crumple, his eyes closed, blinked open moist with tears.

"But I want to live," he whispered. "I want to go on, I have work to do."

Cold, cold pulse of rage. He felt his face move with it. "So did Sevgi Ertekin."

"Please believe me, Mr. Marsalis, I truly do regret—"

Carl leaned closer. "I don't want your regret."

Ortiz swallowed, mustered control from somewhere.

"Then, I have a request," he husked. "Please, at least may I phone and speak to my family first. To say good-bye."

"No." Carl hauled the COLIN director up onto his lap, locked an arm around the man's neck, positioned his free hand against the skull. "I'm not here to ease your passing, Ortiz. I'm here to take what you owe."

"Please . . ."

Carl jerked and twisted. Ortiz's neck snapped like rotten wood.

Soft, chiming sirens went off everywhere in the suite, the wail of distressed cudlip society. *Man of substance down.* Rally, gather, form a mob.

The beast is out.

CHAPTER 52

The crash team were fast—less than two full minutes from when the micro-docs tripped under Ortiz's skin and the sirens went off. But well before that, the COLIN Security detachment had heard the alarms and come through the door on general principles. They found Ortiz in his wheelchair, slumped over to one side, Norton and Marsalis standing staring at him.

"Sir?" The squad leader looked at Norton.

"Lock this whole floor down," Norton told her absently. "Call in some more support to do it. I don't want anyone, not even NYPD, getting up here without my say-so."

"But, but—"

"Just do it." He turned to Carl. "You'd better get moving."

Carl nodded, looked once more at Ortiz, and then stepped outside the unconsciously tightening ring the security detachment had formed around the body. He headed out of the room without looking back, out of the suite and into the corridor where he met the crash team head-on, all lifesaving speed and resuscitation gear, gurney and white coats, dedicated emergency room doctor and all.

He stood aside to let them pass.

Outside the hospital, he walked rapidly away, two blocks west and four south, lost himself in the sun-glinting brawl and bustle of the city. He peeled off his S(t)igma jacket, pulled his pack of phones from it, then balled it up inside out and dropped it into the first recycling bin he saw. The cold bit through his shirt, but he had COLIN-approved credit in his pockets, and he had time.

He stopped on a street corner, checked his watch, and calculated traveling time to the JFK suborb terminal. Hoped Norton could hold up his end.

Then he pulled a new phone loose from the pack, clicked it on, and waited for

Union cover to catch up with it. With his other hand, he dug in his trouser pocket and tugged out the photo and list of scribbled numbers Matthew had hooked for him the night before.

"Okay, Sev," he murmured to himself. "Let's do this."

She stepped into the gloom of the bar uncertainly, but with a certain confidence as well. They were, after all, on her home ground, Lower Manhattan, only a couple of blocks north of Wall Street and the NYPD dedicated Datacrime HQ. She hadn't had to come far.

Two short steps in to let the door hinge shut behind her, and she scanned the room. He raised a hand as her gaze passed down the line of booths along the side-wall opposite the bar. She didn't respond to the wave, but she headed over. The single sodden suit, marooned on a stool at the end of the bar with his nth martini and no friends, gave her an unsubtle once-over as she passed him. Carl supposed she was worth the look. Long-limbed and well-shaped under her casual wear, shown off in her stride and the way she held herself. The single old-style bulb lamp in the middle of the ceiling burnished her hair golden as she passed beneath it, briefly lit the cheerleader good looks as well. She hadn't changed much from the photo.

"Amy Westhoff?"

He raised himself out of his seat as she reached his booth, offered her his hand. She took it, gave him a searching look.

"Yeah. Agent . . . di Palma, is it?"

"That's right." He flashed his UNGLA ID, carefully held so she'd see the photo but not the name. Feigned a querying frown to distract her as he put the badge away again. "But I see you've come on your own?"

She made a dismissive gesture as she seated herself on the other side of the table. The lie hurried out. "Yeah, well, my partner's wrapped up with, uh, some other stuff right now. He couldn't make it. Now, you said this is about the bust on Ethan Conrad four years back. I don't really see how that can have anything to do with me, or with Datacrime."

"Well, it is only a stray lead. But then . . . can I get you a drink, maybe?"

"No, thank you. I've got to go back on duty. Can we make this quick?"

"Certainly." Carl sipped at the Red Stripe in front of him. "In fact, my own jurisdiction in this matter is, should I say, rather loose. Obviously we're not on UN territory here."

"Not far from it, though."

"No, true enough." Carl put his drink down, let his hands drop into his lap. "Well then, I guess you're familiar with the case. I understand you had some kind of relationship with Ethan Conrad, back before it was known what he was."

Tautly. "That's right, I did. *Well* before anybody knew what he was."

"Ah, yes, quite. Well, it's just that I've received information from an NYPD officer, an ex-officer in fact, Sevgi Ertekin. Would you have heard of her?"

The waitress sauntered over, eyebrows raised, notepad not yet out of her apron pocket. It was early yet. Aside from the lonely broker, they had the place to themselves.

"Get you guys any—"

"We're fine," said Amy Westhoff curtly.

The waitress shrugged and backed off. Carl gave an apologetic look. Westhoff waited until she'd gone back to the bar before she spoke again.

"I knew Ertekin, vaguely, yeah. So what's she been saying?"

"Well, she said that you tipped off UNGLA about Conrad's thirteen status because you were jealous that he'd left you, and that you then tried to call and warn him at the last minute. But were too late, obviously. Now—"

"That fucking bitch!" But even in the low light, he could see that Amy Westhoff's face had gone ashen.

"You'd deny that then, I assume."

Westhoff lifted a trembling finger. "You go back to that raghead bitch, and you tell her from me—"

"I'm afraid that won't be possible. Sevgi Ertekin is dead. But she did give me a message for you, something she meant to do but couldn't manage."

The blond woman's eyes narrowed. "What message?"

Then she flinched, yelped, reared back in the booth, and looked down at her trouser leg. She pressed on her thigh with both hands.

"What the fuck was that?"

"That was a genetically modified curare flechette," Carl said coldly. "It's going to paralyze your skeletal muscle system so you can't breathe or call for help."

Westhoff stared at him. Tried to get up from the table, made a muffled grunting sound instead and dropped back into her seat, still staring.

"It's a vastly improved variant on natural curare," he went on. "You might call it the thirteen of poisons. I think you'll last about seven or eight minutes. Enjoy."

He slid the Red Stripe over so it stood in front of her. Westhoff's mouth twitched, and she slumped against the wall. Carl got up to go. He leaned in close.

"Sevgi Ertekin wanted you dead," he told her softly. "And now you are."

Then he eased out of the booth and headed for the door. On the way out, he looked across at the bar, where the waitress sat on a stool, fiddling with some aspect of her phone. As she glanced up at him, Carl fielded her gaze, rolled his eyes expressively, put on *jilted, hurt, and weary*. The girl pulled a sympathetic face, smiled at him, and went back to her phone. He reached the door, pushed it open, and let himself back out into the late-afternoon chill.

He dropped the flechette gun down a grate on Wall Street, a little sad to see it go after the trouble Matthew had gone to in tracking down a suitably disreputable dealer for him, and the price the suitably disreputable dealer had screwed out of him when it became clear that Carl was in a hurry.

Then again, it had served its purpose.

Hope that was what you wanted, Sevgi.

He called Norton from a cab on the way to JFK.

"Can you talk?"

"Yeah, I'm back at Jefferson Park. Where are you?"

"Queensboro Bridge. On my way to the airport."

"You're still *here*, in *town*?" Norton's voice punched out of the phone. "What the fuck are you playing at, Marsalis?"

"I had a couple of things to do. Am I still safe to fly?"

Norton blew out a long breath. "Yeah, should be. I've got the NYPD hammering on my door and Weill Cornell screaming about lawsuits, but so far the COLIN mandate is holding. Always knew there was some reason I took this job."

"That old-time corporate power, huh?" Carl grew serious. "Think they'll try and nail you, though?"

"Well, for now it's my train set, so I'm fine. And anyway, I was in the bathroom, remember. No idea what was going on till you called me and there's Ortiz, dead in his chair."

"Sounds kind of thin."

"It is kind of thin. But this is the most powerful nongovernmental body on the planet we're talking about, and right now they've got my back. Quit worrying about me, Marsalis. You want to help, just get your ass out of Union jurisdiction right now."

"On my way."

He hung up and looked out the taxi window. Ribbed light blipped through the steel lattices of the bridge structure as they headed out over the span, strobed across his face and turned the air in the cab alternately dusty and dimmed. Back across the East River, Manhattan made its block graph skyline against a cold, perfect blue. The sun glowed and dripped like broken yolk off the top and down the side of one of the new black nanobuild towers. Departure clung to the shrinking scene like mist.

The same obscure desire he'd felt staring at the Marin Headlands two nights ago came and stabbed him in the heart all over again. He could not pin down what it meant, could only give it a name.

Sevgi.

coda

PISTACO

CHAPTER

CHAPTER **53**

The path down into Colca was a foot-pounded dusty white, in places barely an improvement over the loose scree and scrub it cut through. Initially, it straggled and twisted along the rim of the canyon like a recently unwound length of cable with the worst of the kinks still not out. It headed out of the village in a relatively straight line, followed the line of the canyon more or less, brushed up to the edge here and there, close enough to offer a dizzying view downward, then slid away again as if unnerved by the drop. A couple of kilometers out of town, the path skirted a desolate cleared space with a paint-peeled rusting goal iron at either end. It kinked a couple more times and then found and dropped into a wide basin-shaped bite in the canyon wall, riding the curve around and down like the track of a roulette ball made visible on its fall toward the luck of the numbers. Thereafter, it fell abruptly off the edge of the canyon, spilled down the flank of the valley in a concertina of hairpin turns that made grudging concession to the steep angle of descent, and arrived at last, in dust and sliding pebbles, at an ancient wooden suspension bridge across the pale greenish flow of the river.

The bridge was not much more user-friendly than the path that led to it. The materials employed in its construction didn't look to have been renewed in decades, and where the planking had cracked and holed, the locals had placed rocks so there was no downward view into the water that might scare the mules—which were still the only viable means of heavy transport down from the towns on the canyon rim. Infrastructural neglect was a general feature of the region—significant distance from the nearest prep camps meant no possible return on corporate funds deployed here, tourism was the only staple, and the tourists liked their squalor picturesque—but here the process had been allowed to run a little farther than elsewhere. Here visitors other than known locals were not encouraged, and tour companies had been persuaded to route their itineraries away to other sections of the canyon. Here, comings and goings on the path were watched by men carrying weapons whose black and metal angles gleamed new and high-tech in the harsh, altiplano sun. Here, it was rumored, there lived a witch who, lacking the normal human capacity to survive the whole of the dry season awake, must fall into an enchanted sleep before the end of each year and could only be roused when the rains came, and only then by the call and ministrations of her *pistaco* lover.

"You cannot seriously be planning to go down there *now."* Norton was shaking his head, but his tone carried less disbelief than weary resignation. He seemed to have lost all capacity for shock over the previous few days.

"Better now than later," Carl told him soberly. "The more the dust settles, the more chance Bambarén and Onbekend have to take stock, and for them I'm a big black mark in the negative asset column. They don't know about Sevgi, but they know the work I do for UNGLA, and they know I know about Onbekend. And they're both cautious men. Leave it long enough, they're going to start wondering where I am and what I'm doing. But right now, they figure I'm scrambling for cover just like everybody else."

"Yeah, you should be."

"Getting hard to hold the line, is it?"

"No, and that's not what I meant. I'm just saying you need to think about what you're going to do when this is over."

Carl stared out at the slow nighttime crawl of the cross-border traffic in the checkpoint lanes. "I'll worry about that when it is over. Meantime—you made me a promise."

"And I came running, didn't I?" Norton gestured around the stark, utilitarian space they had to themselves. "I'm sitting here, aren't I? Not like I haven't got other things to do, or more attractive places to be doing them."

He had a point. RimSec's Immigration Division was widely recognized as the shitty end of the organization's sprawling jurisdiction, and the unlovely interior of the observation lodge offered mute testimony. Gray pressed-carbon lockers stood ranked along the back wall; a random scatter of cheap tables and chairs crowded one half of the limited floor space, and a pool table clothed in garish orange baize took up the rest. A plastic rack held the warped and battered cues pinned to the wall like suspects, alongside a couple of vending machines whose wanly glowing display windows were racked with items that looked more like hazardous material in an isolation chamber than food or drink. Bleak LCLS panels in the roof, the long window of the observation port commanding its three-meter elevated view of the traffic. An unobtrusive back door led out to the cells.

They'd been sitting there since before it got dark.

Carl got up and prowled the room for the fifteenth time. He was beginning to think he could feel the soul of the place breathing, and it didn't improve his mood much. The yellow-painted walls were institutionally uncared for, scarred in a hundred places at the pool table end with the memory of overzealous windup for irritable, jaw-rattling shots. Elsewhere forlorn-looking posters attempted to break up the monotony, everything from RimSec information flyers and mission statements to soft-porn printouts and announcements of local gigs and fiesta nights at clubs up the road in Blythe. None of it looked very appealing, less so than ever fifteenth time around.

It wasn't much of a place to say his farewells to Norton.

"NYPD still giving you a lot of grief?" he asked.

Norton gestured. "Sure, they're pushing. They'd like to know where the hell you are, that's for sure. Why you walked out like that. I've got you down as officially helping COLIN with its internal investigation, witness-protected as part of the deal. They don't buy it, but hey, they're just cops. They don't get to argue with us about stuff like this."

"They ask about anything else?"

The COLIN exec looked away. He'd never asked what Carl had found to do in Manhattan the rest of that day. "No, they haven't. Why, is there something else I should know about?"

Carl gave the question a moment's honest consideration. "That you should know about? No. Nothing else."

The death of NYPD sergeant Amy Westhoff had made some headlines across the Union, he'd checked for it, but he doubted Norton had the spare time or energy to make any connection there still might be with Sevgi Ertekin. Four years was a long time, and he was pretty sure he'd covered his tracks when he called Westhoff. The woman's guilt had done most of the heavy lifting for him.

"If I'm honest," said Norton tiredly, "I'm more worried about the Weill Cornell people than the police. There's some serious finance lying about in that place, some people with access to high-level ears, and some seriously dedicated medical staff who don't like losing their patients under mysterious circumstances. Not to mention the fact that the Ortiz family's personal physician has a consultant residency there."

"Did you have to pay off the crash team?"

"No, they're not the problem. They're all juniors, looking to build careers, and they know what a malpractice suit can do to a résumé, even by association. I had them pronounce Ortiz dead at the scene and then chased them out, told them it wasn't their responsibility any longer. You should have seen their faces—they were all very relieved to get out of that room."

Carl paused by a gig listing. FAT MEN ARE HARDER TO KIDNAP—BLYTHE MARS MEMORIAL HALL, NOVEMBER 25. Nearly three weeks away. He wondered briefly where he'd be when the Fat Men took the stage. Put the thought away, barely looked at.

"Got an exit strategy for Ortiz yet?"

Norton peered into the dregs of coffee gone two hours cold. "Variations on a theme. Unsuspected late-stage viral contamination from the bioware slugs he was shot with. Or interface incompatibilities; his body rejected the nanorepair suite he was implanted with, and he was too weak to survive the shock. Either way, you can be damn sure there'll be no postmortem worth worrying about. Alvaro Ortiz is going to get a statesman's funeral, eulogies over a tragic untimely death, and his name on a big fucking plaque somewhere. None of this is ever going to come out. That's how we buy the family's silence."

Carl gave him a curious look from across the room. Something had happened to Norton since he'd seen him last, something that went beyond the weary lack of capacity for surprise. It was hard to pin down, but the COLIN exec seemed to have taken to his new role as the Initiative's fixer with a bitter, masochistic pleasure. In some obscure way, like a driven athlete with pain, he looked to be learning to enjoy the power he'd been handed. In the vacuum vortex created by the death of Ortiz and his brother, Tom Norton was the man of the hour, and he'd risen to it like a boxer to the bell, like the reluctant hero finally called to arms. As if, along with the young-patrician demeanor and the studied press-conference calm, this was just part and parcel of what he'd been made for after all.

"And the feeds?" Carl asked him. "The press?"

Norton snorted. "Oh, the *press*. Don't make me fucking laugh."

Carl came back to the table and stood staring out of the observation port. Up and down the lines of traffic, breath frosted from the mouths of uniformed immigration officers as they moved briskly about in the chilled desert night, bending and peering into vehicles at random with long tubular steel flashlights raised to the shoulder like some kind of mini bazooka. The queues stretched all the way back to the bridge, where Interstate 10 came across the Colorado River from Arizona under a frenzy of LCLS and wandering spotbeams. The prickly, piled-up fortifications around the bridge were blasted into black silhouette by the light.

"Come on, Suerte," he muttered. "Where the fuck are you?"

There were two armed guards hanging about at the far side of the suspension bridge in the canyon, both of them bored to distraction, yawning and cold, weapons slung. One, the younger of the two, a lad barely out of his teens called Lucho Acosta, sat on a rock where the path began again, tossing pebbles idly out into the river. His somewhat older companion was still on his feet but propped casually back against the rope cabling on one side of the bridge, smoking a hand-made cigarette and tipping his head back occasionally to look up out of the canyon at the sky. Miguel Cafferata was sick of this gig, sick of being buried down here a day's hard drive from the lights of Arequipa and his family, sick of the chafing bulk of the weblar jacket, slimline though it was supposed to be, and sick of Lucho who didn't seem to have a single interest in life outside soccer and porn. Miguel had the depressing sense when he spent time with the boy that he was looking at a premonition of his own son ten years hence, and the impression was making him irritable. When Lucho got to his feet and pointed upward to the path, he barely bothered following the gesture.

"Mules coming down."

"Yeah, so I see."

Conversation was exhausted between the two of them. They'd both been on the same duty every day for the last two or three weeks, the same dawn-to-midafternoon shift. The boss was twitchy; he wanted the place locked down tight, no unnecessary changing of the guard. The two of them watched in silence as the solitary figure and the two mules picked their way down the concertina turns of the path in the early-morning sun. It was a common enough sight, and anyway, you couldn't be surprised down here in daylight, except maybe by snipers or a fucking airstrike.

Even when the mule driver and his animals made it onto the last few hairpin twists before the bridge, Miguel didn't tense as such. But a flicker of interest woke on his weathered face. Behind him, he heard Lucho get to his feet off the rock.

"Isn't that Sumariva's mule, leading?"

Miguel shaded his eyes. "Looks like it. But that sure isn't Sumariva. Way too big. And look at the way he's walking."

It was a fair comment. The tall figure clearly didn't have the hang of coming down a mountain path. He jolted heavily, scudding up powdery white dust every couple of steps. Seemed to be walking with a limp, too, and he didn't appear to have much idea of how to lead the mules. Big, modern boots and a long coat plastered with the dust of his ungainly descent, battered leather Stetson. Beneath the brim of the hat, a face flashed pale. Miguel grunted.

"It's a fucking gringo," he said curiously.

"You think . . ."

"Don't know. Supposed to be looking out for some black guy, not a gringo and a couple of mules. Maybe this is someone from the university. A lot of those guys are from the north, doing survey experiments down here for Mars. Testing equipment."

The mules did appear, now that he looked, to be loaded with small, shallow-draft crates that winked metallic in the high-angled slant of the sun.

"Well, he ain't fucking testing it around here," said Lucho, unshipping his shotgun with a youthful glower. He pumped a round into the chamber and stepped onto the bridge planking. Miguel winced wearily at the sound.

"Just let him come to us, all right? No sense rushing up to meet him, and there's no space to do a search on that side anyway. Let him get across to this side, then we'll see who he is, turn him around, and send him on his way."

But when the gringo got to the bridge, he didn't come out onto the planks immediately. Instead he stopped and sent one of the mules across ahead of him. The animal made the crossing with accustomed docility, while back on the other side the gringo in the hat seemed more concerned with searching his pockets and fiddling with the webbing straps across the other animal's back.

"This is Sumariva's mule," Lucho said as the animal clopped solemnly up to them, then past and onto the solid ground of the riverbank, where it stood and waited for its owner to catch up. "You think he'd loan it out like that?"

"For enough cash, yeah. Wouldn't you?" Miguel shifted to Spanish, raised his voice. "Hoy you, you can't come down here. This is private property."

The figure at the other end of the bridge waved an arm. The voice came back in Quechua. "Just give me a minute, will you."

Then he started to lead the other mule out onto the bridge. Hat tilted down over his eyes.

"All right, you stay here," Miguel told the boy. The language had floored him; he'd never met a gringo before who spoke it. "I'll go see what this is about."

"You want me to call it in?"

Miguel glanced at the mule standing there like the most ordinary thing in the world. It blinked back at him out of big liquid eyes. He grunted impatiently.

"Nah, don't bother. Not like they won't hear it if we have to shoot this guy."

But he unslung his shotgun, and he went out to meet the new arrival with the vague crawl of unease in him. And he slowed as he closed the last few meters of the rapidly shrinking gap between himself and the advancing stranger. Came to a stop near the middle of the bridge, stood athwart, and pumped a round of his own into the shotgun in his hands.

The stranger stopped at the dry rack-clack of the action.

"That'll do," Miguel said, in Quechua. "Didn't you hear me? This is private fucking property."

"Yeah, I know that."

"So what the fuck are you doing down here, gringo?"

"I'm here to see the witch."

That was when the stranger tipped up his head so Miguel could see his face properly. It was also when he realized he'd made a mistake The white they'd seen flashing under the hat brim as he came down the path above was pasty and unreal, clotted and streaked on the face like a poorly applied clown's mask or a half-melted Day of the Dead candy skull. The eyes were dark and impassive, and they stared out of the disintegrating white face with no more humanity than a pair of gun muzzles.

Pistaco.

Miguel had time for that single quailing thought, and then something erupted behind him in a string of firecracker fury. He locked up, tugged both ways at once, and the stranger's long dusty coat split open and he had a flash glimpse of some stubby, ugly weapon cradled there in the *pistaco*'s arms.

Deep, throat-clearing cough, spiteful shredding whine.

Then there was only impact, a sense of being tugged violently backward, a split second of the sky and Colca's steep-angled sides tilting and spinning, and then everything was gone.

Carl Marsalis sprinted past the ruins of the first *familia* gunman, closed the gap with the second while the other man raised his shotgun and snapped off a useless blast from the hip. This one was already panicked beyond any professional combat training he might have had, the remote-triggered firecrackers in the lead mule's panniers, the sudden explosive death of his comrade. Carl ran in firing, too far out for the sharkpunch to have any serious impact yet, but the boy ahead of him flinched and staggered with the few shards that found their mark.

It wasn't an ideal weapon for the circumstances, and out of the water it was too fucking heavy for comfort. He'd had to drape the long elastic sling it came with around his neck, and stick a cling patch on his right thigh to hold the damn thing still under his coat. His leg ached with the extra effort of walking with the weight. But the patented Cressi sharkpunch had the sterling advantage that it was classed as sub-aqua sports equipment, which meant he'd gotten it through security in his baggage without a second look, when second looks were the last thing he needed. And a gun that punched razor-sharp spinning slivers of alloy through water hard enough to eviscerate a great white shark did have some considerable reach in air, even if the spread made accuracy a joke. The young guard had blood running down his face as he fumbled at the slide on his shotgun, he was probably dazed from the sound of the explosions, and he was clearly terrified.

Carl closed the gap, pulled the trigger on the sharkpunch again. The boy slammed back against the side cables of the bridge. Large chunks of him slopped through and fell into the river; the rest collapsed skeletally onto the suddenly blood-drenched planking.

Over.

The mule carrying the firecrackers had, not unreasonably, panicked as much as anybody else. It was headed up the path along the riverside, bucking and snorting. No time to hang about. Carl loped after the animal, ears open for the sounds of other humans.

He met a third gunman a couple of hundred meters along the river, hurrying down the path toward the sounds of gunfire, a matte-gray Steyr assault rifle held unhandily across his body as he jogged. The man saw the mule, tried to get out of its way, and Carl darted around one side of the animal, threw out the sharkpunch, and fired more or less blind. The other man went down as if ripped apart by invisible hands. Carl scanned the path up ahead, saw and heard nothing, and stopped by the ruins of the man he'd just killed. He crouched and scooped up the Steyr left-handed out of the mess, dumped it immediately with a grunt of frustration. The guy had still been holding it across his body when Carl shot him, and the anti-shark load had smashed the breech beyond repair.

"Fuck!"

He picked and prodded his way around the shattered carcass, sharkpunch still leveled watchfully over his knee at the path ahead. Came up finally with a blood-soaked holster holding a shiny new semi-automatic. He tugged the gun loose and held it up to the light—Glock 100 series, not a bad gun. Pricey, shiny ordnance for backwoods muscle like this, but Carl supposed even here the power of branding must hold sway.

Tight, adrenaline-crazy grin. He put down the sharkpunch for a moment to work the action on the other weapon. It seemed to be undamaged, would be accurate to a point, but . . .

Still no decent longer-range weapon. The shotguns they'd been packing back at the river had no more reach than the sharkpunch, and he still had no clear idea how many more of Bambarén's security there were between him and Greta Jurgens's winter retreat. Outside of actual location, Suerte Ferrer had been hopelessly vague.

He shrugged and got back to his feet. Tucked the Glock into his waistband, hefted the sharkpunch again, and moved past the shattered man on the ground. Up ahead, the path seemed to rise slowly out of the rock-walled groove where it ran along the riverside. The mule had bolted on ahead, seemed to have finally found open ground off to the right.

Carl settled the leather hat a little more carefully on his head and followed. The combat high pounded through him. The mesh picked up the beat, fed it. The grin on his face felt like it would never come off.

"You need to get a sense of geography about this, Suerte."

Suerte Ferrer glowered up from the holding cell chair as Carl walked around him. Immigration had cuffed him there. "Don't need no fucking geography lessons from you, nigger."

The insult twanged through him, freighted with memories from South Florida State. It was the first time he'd heard it since Dudeck.

Of course, he'd heard the word *twist* a few times in the interim.

"I see you're acclimatizing to Jesusland culture pretty well." Carl completed his circuit and leaned on the table at Ferrer's level. Their captive was still grimy and tired looking from his border transit in a false-bottomed crate purporting to contain experimentally gene-modified rapeseed oil. He flinched back as Carl went face-to-face with him. "You want to go back there, maybe, Suerte? That what you want?"

"Quiros said—"

Carl slammed the table. "I don't know this Quiros. And I don't fucking want to know him. You think we pulled your autohauler out of the line for luck? You have been sold, to me, and by someone a lot farther up the food chain than your pal Quiros. So if you think you're going get some slick down-the-wire Seattle lawyer come pull you out of here, you're wrong."

He went around the table and took a seat again, next to Norton, who'd done nothing but sit with his legs thrust out in front of him and stare somberly the whole time. Carl jerked a thumb toward the cell door, which they'd left promisingly ajar when they came in.

"Out there, Suerte, you've got a highway that goes in two directions. It goes west to the Freeport, or it goes east back into Jesusland and a bust for illegal crossover. Your choice which direction you get to take."

"Who the fuck are you people?" Ferrer asked.

Norton exchanged a look with Carl. He leaned forward and cleared his throat. "We're you're fairy godmothers, Ferrer. Surprised you didn't recognize us."

"Yeah, we're looking to grant all your wishes."

"See, this identity is blown." Norton gestured at the tabletop, where the documents Ferrer had been carrying were spread out. "Carlton García. RimSec have a warrant out on you under that name from San Diego to Vancouver and back. Even if we hadn't fished you out here, you'd get about three days into the Rim before you tripped something and ended up either busted or yoked to some gangmaster who'd put you to work fifteen hours a day in a trench and expect you to suck his dick for the privilege."

Carl grinned skullishly. "Was that the Rimside dream you had in mind, Suerte?"

"Go west, young man, go west," Norton said piously. "But go with some cash and a decent fake ID."

"Both of which we'll give you," Carl told him. "Together with a bus ticket right into the Freeport. And all you've got to do is answer a couple of questions we have about your cousin Manco Bambarén."

"Hey!" Suerte Ferrer backed up in the chair. His hands chopped a flat cross out of the air in front of him. "I don't know nothing about Manco's operation, they didn't tell me shit about any of that. I didn't live down there more than a couple of years on and off anyway."

Carl and Norton swapped another look. Carl sighed.

"That's a shame," he said.

"Yeah." Norton started to get up. "We'll tell the *migra* boys not to rough you up too bad before they dump you back over."

"Hope you've enjoyed your brief stay in the Land of Opportunity."

"Wait!"

Greta Jurgens's hibernation retreat was an environment-blended two-story lodge built right into the side of a cliff face set back a couple of dozen meters from the riverbank. Fifteen meters or more of scrubby open ground from where the path from the bridge rose out of the groove it followed along the river, rounded a worn rock bluff, and petered out in the scrub a handful of paces from the front door. The upper-story windows were blanked with carbon-fiber security shutters, but downstairs there was activity. Motion visible through a wide picture window, and men darting in and out of the open door with weapons in their hands. Carl counted five before he slid back into cover, none of them yet fitted out in the weblar jackets the three down by the river had worn. One of them, older and apparently in charge, was already on the phone for further orders. Carl crouched where the rock wall on the right of the path still rose over a meter high and listened to the reports of his coming.

". . . sounds like a whole fucking squad." Voice panicky and small across the distance and the steady white-noise pour of the river in the background. "I can't raise Lucho or Miguel down at the bridge. There's a fucking mule here with panniers that look like they fucking blew up or something. I don't know if—"

Pause.

"All right then, but you'd better make it quick." A shouted aside. "You fucking idiots get your jackets on."

Shit.

Well, not like you weren't expecting this.

He went around the corner of the shallowing rock wall at a taut, bent-kneed run, sharkpunch slung and cling-padded to his thigh once more, Glock held out in both hands at head height before him like some kind of venerated icon.

It took them the first three meters to spot him, another two before they realized he wasn't one of their own. He held fire until they realized, didn't want to waste the shots. But as the yells erupted and weapons came up, he squeezed the trigger and the pistol yapped in his hands like a badly behaved little dog. He came on in, same rapid pace, straight line toward them, *Make the shots count.*

The older guy with the phone, jittering in front of his own men's guns, tugging a pistol loose from somewhere. Carl's third and fourth shots put him down, staggering back against the wall and doorjamb behind him, clawing for support, sinking fast. *One down.* More yelling, boiling confusion. Someone got off return fire—*At fucking last, Jesus where'd you get these guys, Manco*—but it crackled nowhere near, and the mesh made him ignore it. No time, no time, still firing, the steady, flat smack of the Glock rounds, the picture window starred and cratered, had to be security glass. Another guy with a Steyr, shooting wildly from the hip, correct right with the Glock and knock him off his feet like some tugging trick with a wire. *Two down.* The others were in the game now, cacophony of gunblasts, automatic stutter, and the dull boom of shotguns. Pale dry earth erupted from the ground to his right and in front, he darted left, lost some focus, thought he tagged a third target as the guy darted back inside the lodge, couldn't be sure. The two remaining outside huddled back toward the door as well, weapons held higher; they'd be getting the range. Shotgun blast, he caught the outer edge of the spread, felt a couple of pellets sting through in his legs. He sprinted the rest of the way in, emptying the Glock as he came. A slug finally caught him somewhere low in the ribs, hammer-blow impact, and he staggered, jerked to a halt, nearly went over. His hat came off, bared his face to the light and his remaining opponents. He saw the shock in their eyes. He snarled and got the Glock back in line, kept pulling the trigger. One of the two men jolted, stumbled backward, firing wildly, one-handed, winged but not down. The Glock locked out on the last round, he threw it away. Less than half a dozen meters now, he ripped the sharppunch clear and up, aimed vaguely for both men, pulled the trigger.

The picture window shattered in the center, became a sudden, jagged-toothed mouth. The two men were both hurled back off their feet and hard against it, the remaining glass suddenly awash with red and clots of gore; the bodies fell in shredded chunks. Carl got to within two meters of the door, put another shot through on general principles, and then stopped.

Listen.

Faint scrabbling sound from within, off to the right. He threw himself inside, falling and twisting in the air, saw vague movement above the rise of a breakfast bar, and fired at it. Another gun went off at the same time, and he felt a second impact in the ribs. But the edges of the bar ripped apart in flying splinters, and the darkened form in the kitchenette behind blew backward. Wet, uncooked meat noise and a shriek. He hit the ground, skidded painfully into the back of a wood-frame armchair.

And everything stopped again.

This time for real.

"It's simple enough," he told Norton, after the interrogation was done. They were playing an inept game of pool on the garish orange table. "I don't have to find Onbekend now. He'll come to me."

"If he doesn't just have you picked off at whatever airport you're planning to use."

"Yeah, well, like I said they're kind of busy right now. And I'll be going in under a fresh identity. No COLIN badge, no UNGLA accreditation, no weapons, nothing to ring any bells."

Norton paused, chin hovering over the cue. "No weapons?"

"Not as such, no. I aim to look like a tourist."

"And this fresh identity." The COLIN exec rammed his shot home. "I assume you're looking to me for that."

"No, I've got a friend back in London can handle that for me, have the stuff couriered across inside a day. What I need from you is the cash. Free wafers, untraceable back to COLIN. My credit still good for that?"

"You know it is."

"Good. And can you persuade RimSec to keep Ferrer locked up somewhere until end of next week? Make sure he doesn't have a change of heart and go squawking down the wires to Bambarén?"

"I suppose so." Norton looked vainly for position, tried a double, took it too fast and missed. "But look. You don't know this Jurgens will be there. What if she's not sleeping yet?"

"It's November, Norton." Carl chalked his cue. "Jurgens was almost flaking out when I talked to her three weeks ago. She's got to be under by now."

"I thought they had drugs that'll unlock the hibernation."

"Yeah." Carl lined up his shot, eased back with due regard for the scarred yellow wall behind him. Sharp snap and the target ball disappeared into a corner pocket as if sucked there by vacuum. The cue ball stood solid in its place. "I knew this hibernoid back on Mars, we used to go the same *tanindo* classes. He was a private detective, occasional enforcer, too. Very tough guy, always getting into scrapes. I don't think I ever knew him when he wasn't carrying some kind of injury. And he told me that no beating he ever took hurt as much as the time he dosed himself with that wake-up shit."

"Yeah, but if they're worried about—"

"Norton, they don't know any reason why I'd be coming after them like this. They don't know Ertekin was anything to me. And if there's going to be any COLIN fallout in the air, the very best thing Onbekend can do with his girlfriend right now is put her away somewhere safe and cozy for the next several months. Believe me, she's there. Just a question of getting to her, digging in, and waiting for Onbekend to come running. And then killing the motherfucker."

He slammed the next shot, rattled it in the jaws. It didn't go down.

He peeled off his coat, unslung the sharkpunch, and dumped it on the kitchenette bar. He checked himself for damage. The Marstech impact jacket, disguised through airport security as part of his scuba gear, had soaked up the slugs he'd collected and left him with no worse than bruising, maybe a couple of cracked ribs. He pressed on the tender areas, grimaced, shrugged. He'd gotten off lightly.

So far.

He stripped the dead men of their weapons, piling them up on the shot-splintered breakfast bar. He dragged the worst of the wreckage from the man he'd killed in the kitchenette out the door and left him with his companions. He'd get the rest with a mop and bucket if there was time.

In the upstairs gallery of the lodge, he found a room that extended back into the cliff the house was built against. There was a heavy-duty lock on the door but he shot it out with one of his several newly acquired handguns. The door swung weightily inward on a curved womb-like space lit by subdued orange LCLS paneling at knee height along the walls. He found a panel of switches next to the door

and flipped them until a harsher white light sprang up. Assumption confirmed—
he'd found Greta Jurgens.

She lay like some dead Viking noblewoman on a broad, carved wood platform
with lines that vaguely suggested a boat. Thick tangles of gray-green insulene
foam netting supported her and wrapped her over. Carl could smell the stuff as
he stepped toward her, the signature nanotech reek of tightly engineered carbon
plastics. He'd used the netting on Mars a lot, camping out on expeditions in the
Wells uplands.

—Flash recall of sitting out in the warm glow of a heating element while the
Martian night came on in all its thin-air glory, thick shingles of stars everywhere
and the tiny, on-and-off tracery of burn-up from the leftover seed particles as they
kept coming down, decades overdue for their date with atmospheric modifica-
tion. Sutherland, staring up there at it all, pleased smile on the scarred ebony features, as if all of it, the sky and everything in it, had been put there just for him.
Musing, nodding along with whatever it was the young Carl Marsalis had been
bitching about. Soaking it up, then turning it around so Carl'd have to look at it
from an angle that hadn't occurred to him before. *You ever wondered, soak, if that
doesn't just mean . . .*

Jurgens stirred just barely as the lights came up, but the down end of her cycle
had her buried too deep for any substantial reaction. She was naked in the foam,
skin taut and shiny with the adipose buildup, lidded eyes bruised and gummed
shut with the secretions of the hibernoid sleep. Carl stood looking down at her for
a long while, handgun at the end of his arm like a hammer. Images of the last
month flickered behind his eyes like flames, like something burning down.

South Florida State. The Perez nanorack. Sevgi Ertekin beside him on the
beach. New York, and the futon she made up for him. Gunfire in the street outside, the first warm crushing pressure as he flattened her under him.

Istanbul, the walk to Moda. The gleaming, glittering grins-in-darkness escaping feel to everything they did.

His mouth twitched upward in echo.

The wind across the stones at Sacsayhuamán. Sevgi leaned against the jeep at
his back, the tight feeling of cover, of safety.

The road to Arequipa, her face in the soft dashboard glow.

San Francisco and *Bulgakov's Cat,* the predawn view out of starboard loading.
Don't gloat, Marsalis. It's not attractive.

Sevgi dead.

The smile fell off his face. He stared down at the sleeping woman.

Greta Jurgens is Onbekend's?

So it would appear. A curious match, is it not? But then they do at least have in common that they are both objects for the hormonal hatred the rest of humanity seems constantly to need a target for.

The mesh surged a little in the pit of his stomach, maybe aftermath of the fire-fight, maybe something else. He thought of Sevgi's eyes closing in the hospital. He stared at Jurgens like she was a problem he had to solve.

Only live with what you've done, and try in the future to do only what you're happy to live with. That's the whole game, soak, that's all there is.

He reached out left-handed. Spread the foam netting a little thicker over the hibernoid's body, pulled it up where one pale shoulder was exposed.

Then he went rapidly back to the door and killed the bright white LCLS, because something was happening to his vision that felt like blindness. He stood a moment in the warm orange gloom, looked twitchily around as if someone were there next to him, then slipped quietly out and closed the door behind him.

He moved along the gallery, checked doors until he found a darkened, window-less chamber with the fragrant hygiene reek of a woman's bathroom. He stepped inside, touched the switch panel; more bright white light exploded across the pastel-tiled space. His own face mugged him from a big circular mirror in one wall—sweat-streaked whitener melting and smudging, the black coming up underneath, eyes ringed with the stuff like dark water at the bottom of a pair of pale psychedelic wells. *Fuck, no wonder the guys at the bridge freaked.* He supposed he owed Carmen Ren for the inspiration.

Wherever she was right now.

He wondered briefly if Ren would make it, if she'd stay ahead of the cudlips and the Agency the way she had before. He wondered if the child growing inside her would make it out into the world safely, and what would happen then. What Ren would have to do to protect it after that.

He remembered the level gaze, the way she'd backed him off with nothing more than a look and the way she stood, the reek of survivability that came off her as she faced him by the tower. Not a bad set of cards to play with. He thought she might be in with a better chance than most of her male counterparts.

Mostly, he was just glad he wouldn't be the one sent to bring her down.

In a drawer beside the basin, he found capsules he recognized—codeine married to a tweaked caffeine delivery kick. They'd do for his ribs. He ran water from infrared taps into the broad, shallow scoop of marble in front of the mirror, soaped up, and started washing the white shit off his face. It took awhile. When he'd gotten the worst off, he stuck his head under the tap and ran the water on his scalp and the back of his neck. He took one of Greta Jurgens's pastel towels off the rail beside the basin and scrubbed himself dry with it, stared into the mirror again and didn't scare himself so much this time.

Now let's see if you can scare Onbekend.

He crunched up the codeine in his mouth, dry-swallowed a couple of times, tongued the clogged residue off his teeth, and rinsed it down with a swallow of water from the tap. He looked at himself once more in the mirror, as if his reflection might have some useful advice for him, then shrugged and extinguished the light.

He went downstairs to wait.

"You don't have to do this," Norton told him.

Carl walked past him around the table, eyeing up the angles. "Yeah, I do."

"It isn't going to bring her back."

He settled to a long, narrow shot down the side cushion. "I think we've already had this argument."

"For Christ's sake, I'm not arguing with you, Marsalis. I'm trying to make you see sense, maybe stop you throwing your life away down there. Look, Saturday is Sevgi's funeral. I can get you cleared through Union immigration, and keep the police off your back for the time it'd take. Why don't you come?"

"Because, as far as I can see, that won't bring her back, either."

Norton sighed. "This isn't what she would have wanted, Marsalis."

"Norton, you don't have the faintest fucking idea what Sevgi would have wanted." He rolled the shot, shaved the angle too fine, and watched it knock the object ball into the cushion and away from the pocket. "And neither do I."

"Then why are you going down there?"

"Because someone once told me the key to living with what you've done is to only do those things you're happy to live with. And I can't live with Sevgi dead and Onbekend still walking around."

Carl braced his arms wide on the edge of the table and nodded at the messed-up tangle of balls on the table.

"Your shot," he said. "See what you can make of that."

CHAPTER 54

The painkillers came on fast, left him with slight nausea and then a vague sense of well-being he could probably have done without. He prowled the lodge's downstairs space, measuring angles of fire and thinking halfheartedly about defensibility. He toyed with the piled-up weaponry on the breakfast bar, couldn't work up much interest there, either. Something was in the way.

He found a place where he could sit and look along the canyon to the jumbled rise of mountains it lay among. Sunlight knifed down over the ridges, turned the air luminous and slightly unreal. As if it was what she'd been waiting for all along, Sevgi Ertekin stepped into his thoughts.

It was the same feeling, the way he'd felt her as he watched the light die away over the hills of Marin County, and again as he left the canyons of Manhattan by way of the Queensboro Bridge. He sat and let the sensation rinse through him, and with it he felt a creeping sense of comprehension, conscious thought catching up with the undefined the way he'd caught up with Gray. Maybe it was the codeine, tripping a synaptic switch somewhere, letting the understanding through. Sevgi was *gone*, his brain was wired to process that much successfully. But not that she was *dead*. For the ancient Central African ancestor genes, that one just wouldn't compute. People don't just cease to exist, they don't just vanish into thin fucking air. *When people are gone*, some deeply programmed part of his consciousness was insisting, *it's because they're somewhere else, right? So Sevgi's gone. Fine. So where's she gone, let's find that out, because then we can fucking go there and find her, be with her, and finally get rid of this fucking ache.*

So.

Those hills dying into darkness on the other side of the bay—think she might be over there? Or in among all that glass and steel over there on the other side of the bridge, maybe? Or, okay, up this fucking canyon maybe, and over the other side of

*those mountains there. Maybe she's there. Up past the luminous unreal light, up in
the thin air, waiting there for you.*

For the first time in his life, he saw why the cudlips might find it hard not to
believe in an afterlife, in some *other place* you go when you're gone from here.

And then, as he beat his own wiring, as the comprehension settled in, the feeling it had come to explain melted away, and left him nothing in its place but the
raw pain in his chest and the stinging salve of the hate.

And out of thin air, as if in answer, the helicopters came.

There were two of them, nondescript commercial machines, bumping
down through the brilliant canyon air with the ungainly caution of crane flies.
They quartered noisily back and forth, dipped about for a while, angled rotor blur
shimmering in the sun, and then they held position over the river opposite the
lodge. Carl watched bleakly from the shattered picture window. Enough carrying
capacity in the two aircraft for a dozen men at least. He stayed back out of view,
let the scattered corpses on the ground around the lodge door paint the picture
he wanted. The helicopters dithered and dipped. Finally, he picked up one of the
Steyr assault rifles and loosed a quick burst out the window in their general direction. The response was immediate—both machines reared up and fled down-
river, presumably in search of a safe place to land.

The path ran on that way, he knew, grooving back down toward the water,
building another rock wall on its landward side. They'd be able to come back that
way, upriver, and stay hidden right to the edge of the cleared ground outside the
lodge, mirror-imaging the approach he'd made a couple of hours ago from the
other side. He frowned a little, cuddled the folding frame stock of the Steyr into
his shoulder, squinted along the sight, and panned experimentally across the
cleared ground. He was pretty sure he could knock down anyone coming for the
house before they'd made a couple of meters in the open. They might try a rush
assault but it wasn't likely—they didn't know how many were in the house, or
what they might have done with Greta Jurgens, whether she was alive or dead,
safe in her womb or dragged downstairs ready to be held up ragdoll-limp as a
shield.

And the lodge was a tough nut to crack. Ferrer had been clear about that
much. *Bitch got a fucking fortress there, man. Right into the fucking rock, no way
you can come down from above, smooth sides so you can't sneak up. I mean.* He sat
back, hands in the pockets of his clean new chinos, smirking and confident now
he'd done his deal. *Who the fuck she expecting, man, the fucking army? And all so
she can fucking sleep? Man, I don't know what hold that bitch got on Manco's*

balls, but it's gotta be something pretty fucking major, get him doing all this. Gotta give the mother of all blow jobs or something.

Like Stefan Nevant before him, Suerte saw the results and jumped to the obvious wrong conclusion. Onbekend stayed in the shadows. If you didn't know he was there already, you looked for other, more visible explanations.

Like unhuman monsters, home from Mars.

It was the dynamic Ortiz had built his whole cover-up effort around. *A monster stalks us! All hands to the palisades and the torches!* Don't ask, don't ever ask who's really making all this happen.

A head poked up from down near the river. Carl let him have a good look around, then fired off another burst. Stone chips and dust leapt in the air; the head jerked back down.

Just so they're clear on the situation.

"Marsalis?"

Manco Bambarén's voice. Carl got his back to the side of the window space, stayed in the shadows, and edged an eye around. Steep early-afternoon sunlight flooded down into the canyon. If you crouched and peered upward, you could just see the rich angled fall of it past the rim, and a restful blue gloom beneath where the higher parts of the valley wall were cast in shadow. It was very quiet now that the helicopters were gone—the whirring scrape of crickets, and the buzzing of flies on the bodies outside.

"Black man, is that you?"

"Good guess," he shouted back, dumping Bambarén's Spanish for Quechua. "What do you want?"

Brief hesitation. Carl wondered if Onbekend maybe couldn't follow a conversation in Quechua—there was no guarantee he'd have learned it in his time living hidden up on the altiplano. He'd get by easily enough with Spanish and English. And as Bambarén's pet *pistaco*, he'd have no need to integrate with the locals. Standard thirteen isolation would work like a dream.

Sure enough, Bambarén stayed in Spanish. "It's really about what you want, Marsalis. Can we talk?"

"Sure. Come on in."

"You guarantee not to shoot me before you've heard what I have to say?"

Carl grinned. "I don't know, you going to take the word of a twist on that?"

"Yes. I will."

"Then come on across. No weapons, no body armor, hands where I can see them." Carl paused. "Oh yeah, and bring your brother with you."

Long, long silence. The crickets scraped in the heated air outside.

"What's the matter, Manco? You not been watching the feeds? It's all burned down now, didn't you know? Ortiz is gone, COLIN are cleaning house. We know all about Onbekend. So let's see both of you."

It took a couple of minutes, but then the two figures emerged from the cover down by the path and walked steadily up toward the lodge, hands clasped over their heads. Carl watched them over the Steyr's sight. Onbekend was holding one arm lopsided, as if it hurt to lift. Carl remembered Sevgi in the Bayview bar—*Hit him a couple of times, but not enough to put him down. Thirteens, huh.*

Yeah, we're tough motherfuckers.

He lined up on Onbekend's face, flexed his trigger finger a couple of times, took up the tension. Then let it go, put the gun aside impatiently. He picked up a handgun, another Glock, from the pile on the floor, checked the load, and snapped the slide. As Bambarén and Onbekend reached the doorway, he stepped back, mindful of sniping angles through the picture window, and wagged the pistol at them.

"Come on in."

Onbekend stared at him, spat out English. "Where is she, Marsalis?"

"Not so hasty. Back there to the table in the alcove, both of you. Hands on your head at all times. I'm not going to mess about patting you down, so if either of you do move a hand anywhere near your body without my permission, I'll just make the assumption and kill you. Got that?"

Bambarén pivoted back and forth slightly, eyes sweeping the open-plan space inside the lodge. Understanding widened his eyes.

"You came here alone?"

"Go to the table. Sit down in the two chairs I've pulled out. Keep your hands on your heads until you're seated, and then put them on the table in front of you. No sudden moves. Sudden movement will get you dead."

He tugged the door closed, pulled it until the latch whined over into lock.

"Marsalis, I have fifteen men out there." Bambarén's voice was low and conversational as he walked to the table. He'd shifted into English as well. "You're sealed in. Let's talk about this."

"We're going to talk about it. But you're going to be sitting down when we do. Hands where I can see them, and then flat on the table in front of you."

They seated themselves, awkward with the need to keep their hands lifted. Bambarén took the head of the table, Onbekend the seat adjacent. This far back in the open-plan space, the lodge made inroads into the cliff face and it was cool and dim, so the two men looked like part of some arcane spiritualist gathering, stiff-backed in the chairs, palms down on the wood, expressions taut. Carl pulled out a chair opposite Onbekend and sat in it, well back from the edge of the table. He floated the Glock on his knee.

"And now what?" the other thirteen asked evenly.

"Now we talk about why I shouldn't kill you both. Any ideas?"

"Are you so anxious to die, black man?" Bambarén asked.

Carl gave him a faint smile. "Well, fifteen-to-one is long odds, it's true. But then again, eight-to-one didn't look good, either, and there they all are, out there for the flies."

"Have you learned nothing?" Onbekend was looking at him with the same contempt he'd given off in the Bayview bar. "Are you still nothing better than a soldier for the cudlips?"

Bambarén stiffened. Carl put a small smile together.

"Want to be careful who you use that word around, brother. It's not Manco here's fault he didn't get an upgraded limbic system and a beefed-up area thirteen out of Isabela's raw materials."

Onbekend barely flickered a glance at Bambarén. "I'm not talking about Manco, and he knows it. I'm talking about the men at the UN you sold your soul to."

"I'm not here for them."

Onbekend's eyes narrowed. "Then why did you come?"

"Because you killed a friend of mine."

"If you have friends, hired man, then I don't know them. Who have I killed?"

"You shot a woman called Sevgi Ertekin, a police officer, when she chased you out into the street in Bayview. You shot her with a Haag pistol, and she died."

"Were you fucking her?"

"Yeah, we were fucking each other. Rather like you and Jurgens."

Onbekend's face whitened as he saw the corollary. He cleared his throat.

"It was a firefight," he said quietly. "Not personal. You would have done the same in my place."

Carl thought of Garrod Horkan camp and Gaby. The Haag shells knocking her down.

"That's not the issue."

"Then what is?"

Carl stared at the other thirteen. "Payment."

"Listen to me, Marsalis." Manco Bambarén, misunderstanding what he'd heard. "Whatever you think you're owed, we can come to an agreement."

"Manco, shut up." The *tayta* looked at Onbekend as if the thirteen had slapped him. Onbekend ignored him, maybe didn't even notice. His eyes had never left Carl's face. "You want me to buy Greta's life with my own?"

"Why not? It's the same deal you offered Toni Montes in the Freeport, isn't it? Her life for her children."

Onbekend looked down at his hands. "If you knew what Toni Montes had done with her life before she acquired that name, had done with other children before she acquired her own, you would perhaps not judge me so harshly."

"I don't judge you at all. I just want you dead."

"If you kill him, black man, you'll have to kill me as well." There was a quiet determination in Bambarén's voice. "And then my men will cut you down like a rabid dog."

Carl threw him a glance. He smiled, shook his head a little.

"You're really enjoying having a younger brother all over again, aren't you, Manco. Well, I don't suppose I can blame you. But do you want to know something about this brother of yours?" He nodded at Onbekend. "This brother of yours is a twin. You've actually got two younger brothers by way of your mother's rather desperate attempts to stay afloat in Peru's new corporate dream. The other one's called Allen Merrin. Unfortunately, he's dead. Do you want to know why?"

Bambarén looked back and forth between the two thirteens.

"He's dead because you killed him, Marsalis," Onbekend said casually. "That's what I heard."

"He's dead because his twin brother, Onbekend here, had him brought back from Mars as a sacrificial gene set. Sold him to the people he's been working for. Would have used him to explain away—"

"But you did kill him, didn't you?"

The *tayta* stared at Onbekend. "What is this? What's he talking about?"

"It's nothing."

"*Don't* tell me it's nothing, Onbee." There was a gathering tightness in Bambarén's voice now. The same thing Carl had seen on his face when Onbekend used the word *cudlip*. "*What is he talking about?*"

"I'm talking about Isabela's other modified son." Carl kept the pistol raised in Onbekend's direction. "The egg your mother sold to the gringos sub-divided a few days in, Manco, and Project Lawman ended up with two identical thirteens for the price of one. That's very handy when it comes to crime scene genetic trace. While your brother here went about slaughtering inconvenient colleagues from his past, he also arranged for his twin to take the fall for it."

"Don't listen to him, Manco. This is—"

"Is he lying?" The look on the *tayta*'s face marked it as rhetorical. His voice sank almost to a whisper. "You did this? You used your own blood to cover yourself?"

"Manco, there really wasn't much option. I told you the situation Ortiz put me in, I told you the danger it—"

"*You did not tell me this!*"

And now Bambarén was trembling, still staring at the thirteen whose genes he shared. His face twitched with suppressed rage.

"A brother?" he asked hoarsely. "A twin? You *sold* your twin brother? After you came to me and I gave you—"

"It's not *important*, Manco. I never knew him, we never even *met*—"

"*He was your blood!*" Bambarén started to get up. Carl wagged the Glock at him and he sank back, sat like something coiled. "He was your *mother's* blood! I told you when you came to me, *blood is everything.* The corporations have stolen our souls, they shatter the bonds that make us strong, turn us into uniform strangers living out our lives alone in polymered boxes. *Family is all we have.*"

"Not if you're a thirteen," Carl told him somberly.

There was a long pause.

"Manco, listen to me," Onbekend said. "I did this to protect—"

"Did you ever even tell our mother?" Bambarén's face had gone cold and hard as the stones out at Sacsayhuamán, and his voice had grown quiet as the wind. "Did you ever tell Isabela that she had another son somewhere?"

Onbekend's temper snapped across. "For *fuck's* sake, Manco, *there would have been no point!*"

"No?"

"No. *He was on Mars!*"

The quiet swept in after the words like a tide, like a breath snuffing candle flames out. They sat in silence in the dim light.

"I don't suppose you'd like to know how your other brother was persuaded to come home from Mars, would you, Manco?"

Onbekend tensed. His voice grated. "Marsalis, I'm warning you."

"Don't even think about it," Carl told him. "I'll put you down before your arse comes off the chair."

He shifted slightly toward Bambarén. Kept the Glock leveled on the thirteen. The *tayta* stared back at him.

"See, Manco, your unexpected brother here did a deal with Mars. I'm guessing you didn't know about that?"

"It was not a deal," Onbekend growled. "It was a strategy, a deception."

"Okay, he organized a deception, in your name. Your other brother was supposed to be coming back as an assassin for the Martian chapters. Some story about clearing out the Lima *familias* by way of reparation, laying the whole *afrenta Marciana* to rest so you could all do business with Mars again. That about right, Onbekend?"

"You did this?" Manco Bambarén whispered. "Even this?"

"Come on, Manco, we've talked about it often enough." Onbekend gestured impatiently. "It wasn't for real anyway, but—"

"You used my name?"

"By association, yeah. Marsalis, you fuck, listen to me—"

Bambarén lunged across the table at Onbekend. The thirteen jumped, blindsided, fended him off. Carl raised the Glock.

"Gentlemen," he said warningly.

Bambarén appeared not to hear. He braced his arms on the table, still staring down into the face of the man he'd made into his brother. Rage brought up his accent, bruised the English he used.

"You used my fucking name?"

"Sit down, Manco," Carl told him. "I won't tell you again."

But the *familia* chief did not sit. Instead he turned himself deliberately to face Carl and the Glock. He drew a deep breath.

"I wish to leave now," he said stiffly. "I have no further interest in this matter. I withdraw my protection from Greta Jurgens."

"Oh, Manco, you *can't* fucking—"

"Don't tell me what I can do, twist." Manco pushed himself off the table with his hands. He looked at Carl. "Well? Is our business concluded, black man?"

"Sure." Carl hadn't expected it to work nearly this well, but he wasn't about to miss the sudden bonus. "Walk to the door, hands on your head. Let yourself out and shut it behind you. And I'd better hear those helicopters leaving inside ten minutes."

Bambarén stood up and laced his hands together over his head. He and Onbekend looked at each other for a long moment.

"Don't do this," Onbekend said tightly. "I'm your brother, Manco. Fourteen years, I'm your fucking brother."

"No." Bambarén's voice was as cold now as the chill coming off the alcove rock. "You are not my brother, you are a mistake. My mistake, my mother's mistake, and the mistake of gringos without souls. You are a twisted fucking *thing*, a thing that crept into my family and used me, a thing that cut the living fat from my bones to feed itself. I should have listened to the others when you came."

"You used me, too, you fuck!"

"Yes. I used you for what you are." Bambarén spat on the table in front of the thirteen. *"Twist! Pistaco! You are nothing to me."*

Onbekend stared down at the spittle. Then, abruptly, he swayed to his feet.

"That's it, Onbekend." Carl rapped on the tabletop, gestured with the Glock. "Sit the fuck down."

There was a grim smile stamped onto Onbekend's mouth. "I don't think so."

Carl came to his feet like whiplash. The chair went over behind him, the Glock leveled on Onbekend's face.

"I said—"

And then Bambarén was on him like an opsdog.

Later, he never knew why the *tayta* jumped. Maybe the rage, rage at Onbekend but sloshing generally to include all thirteens, maybe all variants, maybe just anybody within reach. Maybe rage at the unaccustomed powerlessness of sitting at the table under another man's gun. Or maybe—he hated the thought—not rage at all, maybe the two of them, Bambarén and Onbekend, the two unlikely brothers, maybe in the end they just played Carl, improvised, used the angle, and it worked.

Bambarén slapped a hand into the Glock, swept it wide, and came around the edge of the table yelling. The gun went off, once, nowhere useful. Carl twisted, took the other man's momentum, and dumped it over his hip. Most of him was still trying to work out where Onbekend had gone. Bambarén clung on with street-fighter savagery, fingers digging for eyes, knee to groin. Carl dropped the gun. They both went down, thrashing to get the upper position.

Tanindo and the mesh won out. Bambarén had an antique street-honed savagery to call on, but it was blurred with age and years of rank. Carl broke his holds, took the punches through the padding of the weblar jacket, teeth gritted tight as pain flared across his cracked ribs and through the codeine veil. He vented a snarl, smothered a knee jab to his groin, and then smashed an elbow into the *tayta*'s face. The other man reeled off him. Carl stabbed stiffened fingers in under the chin. Bambarén gagged and—

Behind him, the recently familiar chatter of a Steyr assault rifle erupted across the living room space. Short, controlled burst.

He flailed loose of Bambarén, rolled for the cover of the table and the chairs around it. The *tayta* yelled something, and then another brief storm of automatic fire swept over them both and the shout choked off. The tabletop was ripped into splinters, the assault rifle slugs punching through as if it were cardboard. He heard impacts off the rock behind him. Something slammed into his back, *ricochet* he knew fleetingly. *The Glock, the fucking Glock—*

—was gone. From his position on the floor, he saw Onbekend's legs moving forward, cautious, bent-kneed stance, edging around for a clear shot. He did the only thing left, stormed to his feet, mesh-fed speed and raging strength, hurled the chewed-up table off two legs and forward like a shield. Onbekend snapped off more fire, the table toppled like a tossed playing card, impossibly slow, he dodged sideways. The Steyr chattered, impacts caught him, the impact jacket squeezed and warmed as it worked, the shots twisted and slammed him backward into the alcove wall . . .

And the firing stopped.

It was almost comical. Onbekend stood with the suddenly silent weapon in his hands. Faint ping of the load alert, into the quiet like a dripping tap. His gaze dropped from Carl's face to the Steyr, saw the blinking red light. He'd had no time to check the magazine, must have grabbed the first decent weapon he saw off the pile on the breakfast bar, and he'd come away with one almost fully discharged.

Carl came off the wall with a yell.

Onbekend threw the emptied Steyr at him. He batted it aside. The other thirteen tried to grapple, he punched and stamped the attempt apart, drove Onbekend back across the space in a flurry of *tanindo* technique. The thirteen blocked and covered, launched jabbing counters, but all the time Carl read out the damage Sevgi's slugs had done in the way the other man moved. He felt a snarl peel his lips, savage satisfaction, the heart-deep anticipation of damage. He closed, broke up a defense, lanced a high blow through, and caught Onbekend across the jaw. The other thirteen staggered, his back almost to the shattered picture window now. Blood and translucent light behind—Carl caught it out of the corner of his eye, dull red smears on the jagged lower line of the remaining glass, glint of the sun's rays on the sawtoothed edges. He closed with Onbekend again—

And there was a crouched figure beyond the glass.

Carl had time to register the shocked, frightened face, the raised shotgun. His attack momentum was already committed, all he could do was let it carry him stumbling across the living room, trying to get out of the way. The shotgun went off, fresh glass smashed off the ruined window, and Onbekend bellowed. Carl fetched up against the breakfast bar, clawed down a clatter of weapons, and hit the floor. He grabbed at random, found himself with another of the assault rifles, dragged it around—*safety off*—and triggered it just as the door blew inward.

There were a pair of Bambarén's men gathered there. They'd shot out the lock and burst in, one high, one low. Carl was sitting on the floor, back to the breakfast bar, nowhere near where they'd expected. He held down the trigger on the Steyr and sprayed. The hammering fire kicked both men backward, limbs waving as if they were trying to fend the bullets off. One of them flew back through the entryway and landed in a puffed cloud of dust outside; the other caught an ankle on the doorjamb and went down tangled where he was. Carl skidded back upright, got cover at the edge of the picture window, and then hooked around and hosed the shotgunner off his feet.

Sporadic fire from farther off. No more bodies. In the sudden quiet, the Steyr pinged insistently for more ammunition. The weapon's previous owner had doubled magazines, taped two back-to-back and inverted. Carl unlocked the gun, swapped the ends, and snicked the fresh magazine into place.

Somewhere on the floor, Onbekend groaned.

Carl peered out and saw crouched figures backing hastily off, slithering back to their cover by the path. He chased them with a quick burst from the Steyr, drew a deep breath, went back to the doorway, shoved the body on the threshold out of the way with his boot so he could get the door closed. Halfway through, he realized the man was still alive, breathing shallowly and rapidly, eyes closed. Carl shot him in the head with the Steyr, kicked him the rest of the way out, and shut the door. Then he dragged an armchair across the floor and pushed it hard up against the handle. Vague realization of pain as he worked—he stopped and looked down at the impact jacket, saw the shiny bulges where the gene-tweaked weblar had stopped the slugs and melted closed around them. But blood trickled down past the lower hem of the garment. He pulled it up and saw an ugly gouge in the flesh above his hip. Angled fire from someone as he jumped or twisted or fell sometime in the last minute and a half. Could have been Onbekend or the guys in the door, maybe even a stray long shot from outside.

With the sight, the pain rolled in. He sagged onto the arm of the wedging chair.

"That's fucking ironic," Onbekend coughed wetly from the floor. "I come that close to taking you down and one of Manco's fucking goons takes me out instead."

Carl shot him a tired look. "You were nowhere near."

"Yeah? Well, fuck you." Onbekend propped himself up. "Manco?"

No reply.

"*Manco?*"

Carl watched the other thirteen's face curiously from across the room. Onbekend's features contorted with effort as he tried to get himself into a sitting position. His chest was drenched with blood from the shotgun blast. He growled through gritted teeth, pushed with both hands, couldn't do it. He fell back.

"I'll go look," Carl told him.

Manco Bambarén was flat on his back in a pool of his own blood, gazing blankly up at the ceiling. It looked to have been instant—Onbekend's shots must have nailed him across the chest as he was trying to get up. Carl looked down at the *familia* chief for a moment, then headed back.

"He's dead," Onbekend said. Blood in his throat turned his voice deep and muddy. "Right?"

"Yeah, he's dead. Nice shooting."

A bubbling laugh. "I was trying for you."

"Yeah? Try harder next time." Carl felt spreading wet warmth, glanced down at his leg, saw blood soaking through the material of his trousers at the belt and thigh. Even through the painkillers, his chest ached as if he'd been crushed in a vise. He wondered if the weblar had failed, let something through somewhere else as well—it could happen with multiple impacts in the same region of the jacket, he'd seen it before. Or maybe someone out there, some fucking gun fetishist, had an armor-piercing load he liked to show off. Power enough to bring down a coked-up black man, just like in Rovayo's history books; power enough to bring down the thirteen. Power to stop the beast in its tracks.

"Ah. Not a complete waste, then."

Onbekend had seen the blood as well.

Carl sank onto the floor, put his back against the armchair he had blocking the door, and pulled his feet in so his knees went up. He propped the Steyr on his legs and checked the load. Filtering sunlight slanted in past him, missed his shoulder by half a meter, made him shiver unreasonably in the contrasting shade.

"How many are there out there really?" he asked Onbekend.

The other thirteen turned his head and grinned across the short expanse of stone-tiled floor that separated them. His teeth were bloody.

"More than you're in any state to deal with, I'd say." He swallowed liquidly. "Tell me something, Marsalis. Tell me the truth. You didn't hurt Greta, did you?"

Carl looked at him for a while. "No," he said finally. "She's fine, she's sleeping. I didn't come here for her."

"That's good." A spasm of pain passed across Onbekend's face. "Just came for me, huh? Sorry you got beaten to the draw, brother."

"I'm not your fucking brother."

Quiet, apart from the sound of Onbekend's wet rasping breath. Something had happened to the angle of the light outside. Carl and Onbekend were both in pools of shadow, but between them bright sunlight fell in on the dark tiles, seemed to burn back up off them in a blurry dust-moted haze. Carl reached over with a little jagged effort and dipped his hand in the glow, brushed the tips of his fingers over the warmth in the tiles.

Definitely blood trickling somewhere inside the strictures of the weblar jacket. He tipped back his head and sighed.

So.

He wondered, suddenly, what *Fat Men Are Harder to Kidnap* would sound like when they took the Mars Memorial Hall stage in Blythe next week. If they'd be any good.

"Fifteen."

He looked across at Onbekend. "What?"

"Fifteen men. Manco was telling you the truth. Plus two pilots, but they don't count as guns."

"Fifteen, huh?"

"Yeah. But you downed a couple just now in the doorway, right?"

"Three." Carl raised his eyebrows at the gallery rail. He thought for just a moment he saw Elena Aguirre leaning there, watching. "Including the guy that got you. Leaves an even dozen. How'd you rate them?"

Onbekend coughed up more laughter, and some blood with it. "Pretty fucking poor. I mean, they're good by gangster standards. But up against Osprey training? Against a thirteen? A dozen shit-scared cudlips? No contest."

Carl grimaced. "Just want me to get out there and leave you alone with Greta, right?"

"Nah, stay awhile. Gives us time to talk."

Carl shot the other thirteen a strange look. "We've got something to talk about?"

"Sure we do." Onbekend held his eye for a moment, then his head rolled back to face the ceiling. He sighed, blood burbling through it. "You still don't get it, do you. Even now, the two of us in here, all of them out there. You still don't see it."

"See what?"

"What we are." The other thirteen swallowed hard, and his voice lost some of its pipey hydraulic sound. "Look, the fucking cudlips, they talk such a great fight about equality, democratic accountability, freedom of expression. But what does it come down to in the end? Ortiz. Norton. Roth. Plausible, power-grubbing men and women with a smile for the electors, the common fucking touch, and the same old agenda they've had since they wiped us out the first time around. And every cudlip fucker just lines right up for that shit."

The words wiped out in throaty panting. Carl nodded and stared at the gray matte surface of the weapon in his hands.

"But not us, right?"

"Fucking right, not us." Onbekend spasmed with coughing. Carl saw flecks of blood in the slanting flood of sunlight just past where the other thirteen lay. He waited while the spasm passed and Onbekend got his breath back. "Fucking right, not us. You know how you breed contemporary humans from a thirteen? You fucking domesticate them. Same thing they did with wolves to make them into dogs. Same thing they did with fox farming in Siberia back in the 1900s. You select for fucking *tameness*, Marsalis. For lack of aggression, and for *compliance*. And you know how you get that?"

Carl said nothing. He'd read about this stuff, a long time ago. Back when there'd been that long gulf of time in the early nineties, while Osprey was mothballed and they all sat around waiting to see what Jacobsen would mean to them. He'd read but he'd let it wash over him at the time, didn't recall much now. But he remembered talking to Sutherland about the origin mythology, remembered the big man dismissing it with a grunt. *Got to live here and now, soak,* he rumbled. *You're on Mars now.*

But let Onbekend talk his way out.

"Tell you how you get that," the dying thirteen rasped. "How you get a modern human. You get it by taking immature individuals, individuals showing the characteristics of fucking puppies. Area thirteen, man. It's one of the last parts of the human brain to develop, the final stages of human maturity. The part they bred out twenty thousand years ago because it was too dangerous to their fucking crop-growing plans. We aren't the variant, Marsalis—we're the last true humans. It's the cudlips that are the fucking twists." More coughing, and now the voice was turning hollow and bubbling again. "Modern humans are fucking infantilized adolescent cutoffs. Is it any wonder they do what they're told?"

"Yeah, so did we," Carl said somberly. "Remember."

"They tried to contain us." Onbekend shifted over onto his side, looked desperately across at Carl. He spat out more blood in the gloom, cleared his throat for what seemed like forever. "But we'll beat that. We will, we're fucking *wired* to beat it. We're their last hope, Marsalis. We're what's going to rescue them from the Ortizes and the Nortons and the Roths. We're the only thing that scares those people, because we *won't comply,* we won't stay infantile and go out and play nice in their plastic fucking world."

"If you say so." Carl watched the creep of the sun across the tiles. It seemed to be moving toward Onbekend, like the walking edge of fire on a piece of paper burning up.

"Yeah, I do fucking say so." The other thirteen grinned weakly at him across the light, head drooping. He moved a hand, pressed it flat on the sun-touched tiles and tried to push down. The hand slid instead; the arm was limp behind it. "We're the long walk back to hunter-gatherer egalitarianism, Marsalis. We're going to show those fuckers what freedom *really* means."

"You aren't," Carl pointed out.

Twist of lips, bloodied teeth. "No, but you can."

"I'm injured, Onbekend. There are twelve of them out there."

"Hey, you're the lottery guy." Onbekend was gasping now. "Telling me you don't feel lucky?"

"I cheated the lottery. I fixed it."

Laughter, like tiny hands beating a slow rhythm on a thin tin oil drum a long, long way off. "There you go. That's pure thirteen, brother. Don't play their fucking games, find a way to fuck them all instead. Marsalis, you're it. You'll do fine out there."

He rolled over onto his back again. Stared up at the ceiling. The creeping edge of sunlight came and licked at his hand.

"You'll show them," he bubbled.

The sun crept on. It began to cover his body in the same burnishing, dusty glow. He didn't speak again.

Outside, Carl could hear Bambarén's men talking. Nerving each other up.

I'll see you all in the garden, I guess.

It was almost as if she were there, speaking in his ear. Or maybe that was Elena Aguirre again. He remembered squeezing her hand in the hospital, the dry weightlessness of it. Telling her *all that sunlight through the trees.*

He pulled the full magazine from the Steyr and looked at the soft gleam of the top shell. Snicked it back into the gun.

I'll be along, Sevgi. I'll catch you up.

We all will.

Onbekend's breathing had stopped. The sunlight covered him. Carl shivered in the gloom on his side of the window. He thought he could hear stealthy movement somewhere outside.

He sighed and pushed himself to his feet. It was harder than he'd expected. He edged across to the weapons that had fallen from the bar, took a Glock, and tucked it into his belt for later. Lifted another Steyr, checked the magazines, and then slung it around his neck, adjusting the strap carefully. He'd grab it when he threw away the one in his hands, when that was emptied. It was extra weight, but it couldn't be any worse than lugging the sharkpunch all the way down here had been.

A dozen shit-scared cudlips. Good odds for the lottery guy.

You'll show them.

"Yeah, right," he muttered.

Drag the armchair aside, crack the door, and peer out. He couldn't see anybody, hadn't expected to really. But they'd come in sooner or later, to check on the man who gave them their orders, told them what to do, kept them fed.

I'll see you in the garden.

The whisper ghosted past his ear again, behind him in the gloom. This time he heard it for sure. It lifted the hairs on the back of his neck. Carl nodded and reached back with his left hand, cupped the place on his neck where the voice had touched. He looked one more time at Onbekend's incandescent corpse, checked his weapons one more time, nodded to himself again.

Deep breath.

Then he went out into the sun.

RICHARD K. MORGAN is the acclaimed author of *Woken Furies, Market Forces, Broken Angels,* and *Altered Carbon,* a *New York Times* Notable Book that also won the Philip K. Dick Award. Morgan sold the movie rights for *Altered Carbon* to Joel Silver and Warner Bros. His third book, *Market Forces,* has also been sold to Warner Bros. and was winner of the John W. Campbell Award. He lives in Scotland.

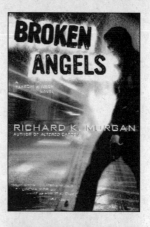